The Best Crime Stories

The Best Crime Stories

Introduction
by
Michael Stapleton

HAMLYN

Published 1977 by
Hamlyn Publishing,
a division of The Hamlyn Publishing
Group Limited,
Bridge House, London Road,
Twickenham, Middlesex

This collection, and Introduction,
© The Hamlyn Publishing Group 1977
Second impression 1984
Third impression 1985

ISBN 0 600 38241 9

Printed in Great Britain by
Hazell Watson & Viney Limited,
Member of the BPCC Group,
Aylesbury, Bucks

Contents

CONTENTS

CONTENTS

7

Introduction

The crime story, paradoxically, is a product of societies which maintain a considerable degree of law and order, and in which unlawful deeds are usually detected and punished. Crime was written about in earlier days but, probably until the time of Defoe, it was usually an element in tragedy and a part of the lives of those whose high place postulated an element of nobility. The poets never thought of examining the lives of ordinary people and the emotions which they, no less than the nobly born, were heir to. It was just as well, perhaps; common speech was no part of literature as yet and the dialogue of poetic tragedy would have sounded strange in the mouth of a ploughman or a seamstress, and such ordinary people were hardly likely, when apprehended in the commission of a crime, to find inspiration for lofty statements in the vicious punishments which were their usual fate.

It was not until the English novel began to flourish that crime, in the ordinary sense, was written about. Both Defoe and Fielding used the subject; Scott and the romantics ignored it in common terms but Dickens was soon to come, and much of his fiction deals with those ordinary people the poets ignored.

At this time – the first half of the 19th century – the law was growing stronger and order was beginning to be better maintained. Efforts were being made to define what was lawful and what was criminal, and speculation about the so-called criminal mind was bound to follow, though it was a long time coming. Meanwhile, crime remained for most people a matter of that which looked black *being* black – there was little room for humanity in an age which believed that everyone's place was ordained by God. One can only wonder what a well-bred Victorian miss – if she read a book like *Oliver Twist* – would have made of the character and terrible fate of poor Nancy. The Industrial Revolution notwithstanding, the lot of the underprivileged in England was, if possible, worse than ever before, and destitution was no farther away than the loss of a job. Those who had work were just able to pay their way and were usually regarded by their betters as commendable people who knew their station in life, and stayed there. Those who could not get work were in desperate straits indeed, and our well-bred Victorian miss would have probably believed that girls like Nancy had either been guilty of deserting their station – or of having failed to comprehend what that station was. Dickens' humanity and his powerful pleading seems to have made little difference, in spite of his enormous readership, to Victorian attitudes.

Oliver Twist was written before Edgar Allan Poe gave us the first exercises in detection, the three stories of the 1840s which featured the scholarly amateur, C. Auguste Dupin. His analytical powers solve the mysteries of *The Murders in the Rue Morgue* and *The Purloined Letter*, and of Marie Rogêt. These are the first examples of the now classic puzzle, resolved by an astute individual. The pattern is famous and it relies on the sequence of events being reversed. Thus the crime comes first; then the suspects usually make their appearance, and leave or have left clues – and red herrings – scattered about. Astute individual, who is almost never a police officer, discovers how the crime was committed. He examines the motive for it, checks the clues, artfully rejects the red herrings, asks searching questions of the suspects and, finally, discloses the identity of the guilty party. He takes care, of course, to have a police officer in attendance to whom the guilty one can be handed over – rather like a cardinal delivering a heretic to the secular arm.

This ratiocination was also the method of the French writer, Èmile Gaboriau, and of the renowned Arthur Conan Doyle, who seized the popular imagination as no one else and held it unchallenged from 1879 until 1905. In the meantime, in 1868, Dickens' friend and contemporary, Wilkie Collins, had written a full-length detective novel, *The Moonstone*, which is acknowledged as an English fiction classic. An American novelist, Anna Katharine Green, published *The Leavenworth Case* in 1878, which was a huge success and marked the beginning of the American detective novel. The pattern was set fair and looked like lasting forever. Sherlock Holmes was succeeded by Austin Freeman's Dr Thorndyke, Ernest Bramah's Max Carrados, G. K. Chesterton's Father Brown, A. E. W. Mason's Inspector Hanaud. Yet to come were Agatha Christie's Mr Quin, Hercule Poirot, and Miss Marples; Margery Allingham's Albert Campion and Dorothy L. Sayers' Lord Peter Wimsey.

It is strange that the convention, once established, was never questioned. Conan Doyle's is a world of such blandness and convenience as to be unbelievable to anyone who has some real idea of what London was like in the 1880s and 90s. The author was himself following a pattern by making his hero a private person and not a police officer; Dr Watson, as loyal as a retriever and rather less bright, was to be the forerunner of a multitude of thick-headed friends. Even the dubious Raffles had his Bunny.

Changes could be discerned, however, after the First World War. The Americans, S. S. Van Dine, Rex Stout and Ellery Queen introduced a sharper tone and gained a whole new readership, and real policemen were beginning to appear as the astute individual. But the old pattern more than held its own and still commands a faithful public. That this should be so is curious, the world having moved on; but the fact is unarguable and the world-that-never-was is obviously the preferred setting for many people.

No derogation of the readership just mentioned is intended but the observation prompts the reflection that many people have always seen right and wrong in terms of the law. But crime is many more things than what the law declares it to be, and the law is powerless against the vast incidence of mental and physical cruelty, mendacity and sexual bullying. The world had to move on much farther before crime, in the humanitarian sense, became a subject in the genre. Usually there is need for a wider canvas to give room for a more subtle exploration of motive and personality and it remains to be seen whether it will be developed and become as popular in fiction as the legal crime.

There have been great novels concerned with crime, like *Les Miserables* and *Crime and Punishment*: Dickens, in *Martin Chuzzlewit*, painted a chilling picture of a wretched girl nearly bullied to death by an evil husband. The years between the wars saw the production of fine crime films, like Fritz Lang's *You only live once* and the unforgettable *I am a Fugitive*. The thirties was also the decade of *Brighton Rock* and *On the Night of the Fire*; but it is unlikely that those who enjoyed reading about the improbable worlds of Sapper and E. Phillips Oppenheim would have much time for the novels of F. L. Green and Graham Greene, or the harsh reality of the better American films. The crime of the real world is uncomfortable and hardly a matter for entertainment; most writers of crime stories are superb entertainers, and that is their business. The possibility that the weak, the hungry and the frightened might become involved in crime no less than the vicious and the greedy is something which the 'straight' writer explores and which seems to interest most crime story writers very little.

I use the word 'most' advisedly. A different note was struck by some American writers before the Second World War, and the abrasive, laconic style has contributed much to a form which was in need of new ideas and a broader canvas. After the Second World War, however, familiar and undisturbing themes were doubly welcome – comfort was hard to find and life had been grim for four or five years. Most people did not perceive that something was going; law and order were as much the victims of war's necessity as any other value and post-war governments both here and in America were too busy with bright new worlds to realize that they would have desperate need of an efficient, stabilizing force – one that had served the old worlds well.

Crime is not only a matter of deliberate, wilful evil-doing; any law-breaking is crime in the strict sense. And more laws are broken now, I would venture, by more people over a broader social spectrum than ever before. It may seem foolish to describe for instance, the widespread flouting of traffic and noise-abatement laws, and the national pre-occupation with tax-dodging as law-breaking but that is what they are, in the strict sense, no less than drug and sex offences, and there is almost no hope of enforcing the laws which are meant to deal with them. It is common knowledge that a legitimate debt cannot, under English law, be collected from anyone who really has their wits about them. Dozens of landlords know only too well how a defaulter can fight a rearguard action for months and months, through Rent Tribunals and further appeals, without paying a penny of what he owes – and go on living free in the space he occupies. But the law can be seen to evict without a trace of compassion when weighty-enough authority supports it. Children go on being beaten to death, and desperate wives find no succour from brutal husbands if they go to the law. Vandalism is rife and school-children seem to have no trouble getting hold of drugs if they really want them. Teachers are exposed to assault and battery, and they have no hope of redress. The point being that the law can be seen to be not only ignored but actively flouted. The lesson is quickly learned that the law is ineffectual, and no time is lost in taking advantage of the fact.

These reflections arose from a period of musing on the possible development of the crime story. If the range is ever extended the impulse will have come, I believe, from America, where the inimitable style of the best writers has a between-the-eyes directness not found in England yet (though some promising talents have shown up in television plays), and an ability to enter the world of crime itself, a place where human values undergo considerable adjustment. They bring the matter of crime close enough to smell. Dashiell Hammett set a high standard with his lean prose and deft character-drawing. Cornell Woolrich, who deserves to be better known, was better at exploring the springs of impulse and motive than Hammett, or Raymond Chandler, though he was, perhaps, a lesser craftsman. Stanley Ellin's story, *You can't be a little girl all your life* is unique – a vivid example of a marital crime that rings uncomfortably true. And the highly-successful John D. MacDonald can, in the course of unfolding one of his sharp-edged thrillers, comment disturbingly on the debasement of life in over-crowded, ungovernable cities.

'It was just past noon and the offices were beginning to flood the streets with a warm hurrying flow of girls. A burly man, in more than a hurry than I was, bumped into me and thrust me into a tall girl. They both whirled and snarled at me.

'New York is where it is going to begin, I think. You can see it coming. The insect experts have learned how it works with locusts. Until locust population reaches a certain density, they all act like any grasshoppers. When the critical point is reached they turn savage and swarm, and try to eat the world. We're nearing a critical point. One day soon two strangers will bump into each other at high noon in the middle of New York. But this time they won't snarl and go on. They will stop and stare and then leap at each other's throats in a dreadful silence. Old ladies will crack skulls with their deadly handbags. Cars will plunge down the crowded sidewalks. Drivers will be torn out of their cars and stamped. It will spread to all the huge cities of the world, and by dawn of the next day there will be a horrid silence of sprawled bodies and tumbled vehicles, gutted buildings and a few wisps of smoke. And through that silence will prowl a few, a very few of the most powerful ones, ragged and bloody, slowly tracking each other down.

'I went back to my sterile cheerful miracle-plastic automated rectangle set high in the flank of a new hotel. I shucked my jacket and lay cradled on foam, breathing air made by careful machines, supine in a sub-audio hum that silenced all the city sounds.' (*Nightmare in Pink*. Robert Hale Ltd, 1966 and Pan Books, 1968).

But wherever the new direction comes from it is on the way, I feel sure, and it will be plain to the reader that I have read a great many crime stories which are meant, principally, to entertain. I have been very entertained, and look forward to more of the same, and I hope that my comments on crime and the relation to it of the crime story will be seen for what they are – a brief examination of the possibilities which lie in the form and which have not, so far, been fully realized. The reader will find nonetheless a great range of stories in this volume, from Poe himself to the careful, measured tale by Wilkie Collins and on to Arthur Conan Doyle before some favourite detectives – Father Brown, Mr Reeder, Lord Peter Wimsey – make their appearance. To season them there is W. W. Jacobs at his chilling best and striking contributions from Somerset Maugham, Aldous Huxley, John Steinbeck and Julian Symons. Both English and American writers, it will be seen, offer a formidable array of talents and the puzzle, as usual, was what one could possibly leave out. Two stories I am very glad to include are *Special Release* by the late Eric Parr and *Scandal at Sandkop* by James McClure, both of them out of the ordinary in tone and setting. Roald Dahl's *The Way up to Heaven* is a fine story of a woman who escapes from a lifetime of subtle bullying. It is a crime story of the first order; I will leave it to the reader to name the criminal. The same author's macabre sense of humour is on display in *Lamb to the Slaughter*, which describes the most original murder weapon

I've ever come across. Cornell Woolrich, in *Dusk to Dawn*, depicts a set of circumstances which make an apparently innocuous young man into a killer. The means have to exist, of course; but the means did, and do, and there is no comfort to be drawn from the reflection that Woolrich was writing in America in the thirties. Law and order are as tightly stretched in England, now.

One of the names which I mention in this Introduction does not, to my great regret, appear in this volume. Raymond Chandler was denied me by his executors; I respect their reasons but feel the omission keenly. I hope very much that the richness of what is here will compensate for the lack though one volume cannot, by any means, do full justice to the subject. But there is something for everyone here – stories to entertain, stories to chill, and stories to provoke.

Michael Stapleton
London, 1977

Edgar Allan Poe

The Purloined Letter

'Nil sapientiæ odiosius acumine nimio.' SENECA

At Paris, just after dark one gusty evening in the autumn of 18—, I was enjoying the twofold luxury of meditation and a meerschaum, in company with my friend, C. Auguste Dupin, in his little back library or book-closet, *au troisième*, No. 33 Rue Dunôt, Faubourg St. Germain. For one hour at least we had maintained a profound silence; while each, to any casual observer, might have seemed intently and exclusively occupied with the curling eddies of smoke that oppressed the atmosphere of the chamber. For myself, however, I was mentally discussing certain topics which had formed matter for conversation between us at an earlier period of the evening; I mean the affair of the Rue Morgue, and the mystery attending the murder of Marie Rogét. I looked upon it, therefore, as something of a coincidence, when the door of our apartment was thrown open and admitted our old acquaintance, Monsieur G—, the Prefect of the Parisian police.

We gave him a hearty welcome; for there was nearly half as much of the entertaining as of the contemptible about the man, and we had not seen him for several years. We had been sitting in the dark, and Dupin now arose for the purpose of lighting a lamp, but sat down again, without doing so, upon G.'s saying that he had called to consult us, or rather to ask the opinion of my friend, about some official business which had occasioned a great deal of trouble.

'If it is any point requiring reflection,' observed Dupin, as he forbore to enkindle the wick, 'we shall examine it to better purpose in the dark.'

'That is another of your odd notions,' said the Prefect, who had a fashion of calling everything 'odd' that was beyond his comprehension, and thus lived amid an absolute legion of 'oddities'.

'Very true,' said Dupin, as he supplied his visitor with a pipe, and rolled towards him a comfortable chair.

'And what is the difficulty now?' I asked. 'Nothing more in the assassination way, I hope?'

'Oh, no; nothing of that nature. The fact is, the business is *very* simple indeed, and I make no doubt that we can manage it sufficiently well ourselves; but then I thought Dupin would like to hear the details of it, because it is so excessively *odd*.'

'Simple and odd,' said Dupin.

'Why, yes; and not exactly that, either. The fact is, we have all been a good deal puzzled because the affair *is* so simple, and yet baffles us altogether.'

'Perhaps it is the very simplicity of the thing which puts you at fault,' said my friend.

'What nonsense you *do* talk!' replied the Prefect, laughing heartily.

'Perhaps the mystery is a little *too* plain,' said Dupin.

'Oh, good heavens! who ever heard of such an idea?'

'A little *too* self-evident.'

'Ha! ha! ha! – ha! ha! ha! – ho! ho! ho!' roared our visitor, profoundly amused; 'O Dupin, you will be the death of me yet!'

'And what, after all, *is* the matter on hand?' I asked.

'Why, I will tell you,' replied the Prefect, as he gave a long, steady, and contemplative puff, and settled himself in his chair. 'I will tell you in a few words; but, before I begin, let me caution you that this is an affair demanding the greatest secrecy, and that I should most probably lose the position I now hold, were it known that I confided it to any one.'

'Proceed,' said I.

'Or not,' said Dupin.

'Well, then; I have received personal information, from a very high quarter, that a certain document of the last importance has been purloined from the royal apartments. The individual who purloined it is known; this beyond a doubt; he was seen to take it. It is known, also, that it still remains in his possession.'

'How is this known?' asked Dupin.

'It is clearly inferred,' replied the Prefect, 'from the nature of the document, and from the non-appearance of certain results which would at once arise from its passing *out* of the robber's possession – that is to say, from his employing it as he must design in the end to employ it.'

'Be a little more explicit,' I said.

'Well, I may venture so far as to say that the paper gives its holder a certain power in a certain quarter where such power is immensely valuable.' The Prefect was fond of the cant of diplomacy.

'Still I do not quite understand,' said Dupin.

'No? Well; the disclosure of the document to a third person, who shall be nameless, would bring in question the honour of a personage of most exalted station; and this fact gives the holder of the document an ascendency over the illustrious personage whose honour and peace are so jeopardised.'

'But this ascendency,' I interposed, 'would depend upon the robber's knowledge of the loser's knowledge of the robber. Who would dare—'

'The thief,' said G., 'is the Minister D—, who dares all things, those unbecoming as well as those becoming a man. The method of the theft was not less ingenious than bold. The document in question – a letter, to be frank – had been received by the personage robbed while alone in the royal *boudoir*. During its perusal she was suddenly interrupted by the entrance of the other exalted personage from whom especially it was her wish to conceal it. After a hurried and vain endeavour to thrust it in a drawer, she was forced to place it, open as it was, upon a table. The address, however, was uppermost, and, the contents thus unexposed, the letter escaped notice. At this juncture enters the Minister D—. His lynx eye immediately perceives the paper, recognises the handwriting of the address, observes the confusion of the personage addressed, and fathoms her secret. After some business transactions, hurried through in his ordinary manner, he produces a letter somewhat similar to the one in question, opens it, pretends to read it, and then places it in close juxtaposition to the other. Again he converses, for some fifteen minutes, upon the public affairs. At length, in taking leave, he takes also from the table the letter to which he had no claim. Its rightful owner saw, but, of course, dared not call attention to the act, in the presence of the third personage who stood at her elbow. The Minister decamped, leaving his own letter – one of no importance – upon the table.'

'Here, then,' said Dupin to me, 'you have precisely what you demand to make the ascendency complete – the robber's knowledge of the loser's knowledge of the robber.'

'Yes,' replied the Prefect; 'and the power thus attained has, for some months past, been wielded, for political purposes, to a very dangerous extent. The personage robbed is more thoroughly convinced, every day, of the necessity of reclaiming her letter. But this, of course, cannot be done openly. In fine, driven to despair, she has committed the matter to me.'

'Than whom,' said Dupin, amid a perfect whirlwind of smoke, 'no more sagacious agent could, I suppose, be desired, or even imagined.'

'You flatter me,' replied the Prefect; 'but it is possible that some such opinion may have been entertained.'

'It is clear,' said I, 'as you observe, that the letter is still in the possession of the Minister; since it is this possession, and not any employment of the letter, which bestows the power. With the employment the power departs.'

'True,' said G.; 'and upon this conviction I proceeded. My first care was to make thorough search of the Minister's hotel; and here my chief embarrassment lay in the necessity of searching without his knowledge. Beyond all things, I have been warned of the danger which would result from giving him reason to suspect our design.'

'But,' said I, 'you are quite *au fait* in these investigations. The Parisian police have done this thing often before.'

'Oh yes; and for this reason I did not despair. The habits of the Minister gave me, too, a great advantage. He is frequently absent from home all night. His servants are by no means numerous. They sleep at a distance from their master's apartment, and, being chiefly Neapolitans, are readily made drunk. I have keys, as you know, with which I can open any chamber or cabinet in Paris. For three months a night has not passed, during the greater part of which I have not been engaged, personally, in ransacking the D— Hôtel. My honour is interested, and, to mention a great secret, the reward is enormous. So I did not abandon the search until I had become fully satisfied that the thief is a more astute man than myself. I fancy that I have investigated every nook and corner of the premises in which it is possible that the paper can be concealed.'

'But is it not possible,' I suggested, 'that although the letter may be in possession of the Minister, as it unquestionably is, he may have concealed it elsewhere than upon his own premises?'

'This is barely possible,' said Dupin. 'The present peculiar condition of affairs at court, and especially of those intrigues in which D— is known to be involved, would render the instant availability of the document – its susceptibility of being produced at a moment's notice – a point of nearly equal importance with its possession.'

'Its susceptibility of being produced?' said I.

'That is to say, of being *destroyed*,' said Dupin.

'True,' I observed; 'the paper is clearly then upon the premises. As for its being upon the person of the Minister, we may consider that as out of the question.'

'Entirely,' said the Prefect. 'He has been twice waylaid, as if by foot-pads, and his person rigorously searched under my own inspection.'

'You might have spared yourself this trouble,' said Dupin. 'D—, I presume, is not altogether a fool, and, if not, must have anticipated these waylayings, as a matter of course.'

'Not *altogether* a fool,' said G.; 'but then he's a poet, which I take to be only one remove from a fool.'

'True,' said Dupin, after a long and thoughtful whiff from his meer-schaum, 'although I have been guilty of certain doggerel myself.'

'Suppose you detail,' said I, 'the particulars of your search.'

'Why, the fact is we took our time, and we searched *everywhere*. I have had long experience in these affairs. I took the entire building, room by room; devoting the nights of a whole week to each. We examined, first, the furniture of each department. We opened every possible drawer; and I presume you know that, to a properly trained police agent, such a thing as a *secret* drawer is impossible. Any man is a dolt who permits a "secret" drawer to escape him in a search of this kind. The thing is *so* plain. There is a certain amount of bulk – of space – to be accounted for in every cabinet. Then we have accurate rules. The fiftieth part of a line could not escape us. After the cabinets we took the chairs. The cushions we probed with the fine long needles you have seen me employ. From the tables we removed the tops.'

'Why so?'

'Sometimes the top of a table, or other similarly arranged piece of furniture, is removed by the person wishing to conceal an article; then the leg is excavated, the article deposited within the cavity, and the top replaced. The bottoms and tops of bedposts are employed in the same way.'

'But could not the cavity be detected by sounding?' I asked.

'By no means, if, when the article is deposited, a sufficient wadding of cotton be placed around it. Besides, in our case, we were obliged to proceed without noise.'

'But you could not have removed – you could not have taken to pieces *all* articles of furniture in which it would have been possible to make a deposit in the manner you mention. A letter may be compressed into a thin spiral roll, not differing much in shape or bulk from a large knitting-needle, and in this form it might be inserted into the rung of a chair, for example. You did not take to pieces all the chairs?'

'Certainly not; but we did better – we examined the rungs of every chair in the hotel, and, indeed, the jointings of every description of furniture, by the aid of a most powerful microscope. Had there been any traces of recent disturbance we should not have failed to detect it instantly. A single grain of gimlet-dust, for example, would have been as obvious as an apple. Any disorder in the glueing – any unusual gaping in the joints – would have sufficed to ensure detection.'

'I presume you looked to the mirrors, between the boards and the plates, and you probed the beds and the bedclothes, as well as the curtains and carpets.'

'That of course; and when we had absolutely completed every article of the furniture in this way, then we examined the house itself. We divided its entire surface into compartments, which we numbered, so that none might be missed; then we scrutinised each individual square inch throughout the premises, including the two houses immediately adjoining, with the microscope, as before.'

'The two houses adjoining!' I exclaimed; 'you must have had a great deal of trouble.'

'We had; but the reward offered is prodigious.'

'You include the *grounds* about the houses?'

'All the grounds are paved with brick. They gave us comparatively little trouble. We examined the moss between the bricks, and found it undisturbed.'

'You looked among D—'s papers, of course, and into the books of the library?'

'Certainly; we opened every package and parcel; we not only opened every book, but we turned over every leaf in each volume, not contenting ourselves with a mere shake, according to the fashion of some of our police officers. We also measured the thickness of every book-*cover*, with the most accurate ad-measurement, and applied to each the most jealous scrutiny of the microscope. Had any of the bindings been recently meddled with, it would have been utterly impossible that the fact should have escaped observation. Some five or six volumes, just from the hands of the binder we carefully probed longitudinally, with the needles.'

'You explored the floors beneath the carpets?'

'Beyond doubt. We removed every carpet, and examined the boards with the microscope.'

'And the paper on the walls?'

'Yes.'

'You looked into the cellars?'

'We did.'

'Then,' I said, 'you have been making a miscalculation, and the letter is *not* upon the premises, as you suppose.'

'I fear you are right there,' said the Prefect. 'And now, Dupin, what would you advise me to do?'

'To make a thorough research of the premises.'

'That is absolutely needless,' replied G—. 'I am not more sure than I breathe than I am that the letter is not at the hotel.'

'I have no better advice to give you,' said Dupin. 'You have, of course, an accurate description of the letter?'

'Oh yes!' And here the Prefect, producing a memorandum-book, proceeded to read aloud a minute account of the internal, and especially of the external appearance of the missing document. Soon after finishing the perusal of this description, he took his departure more entirely depressed in spirits than I had ever known the good gentleman before.

In about a month afterwards he paid us another visit, and found us occupied very nearly as before. He took a pipe and a chair and entered into some ordinary conversation. At length I said—

'Well, but G—, what of the purloined letter? I presume you have at last made up your mind that there is no such thing as overreaching the Minister?'

'Confound him, say I – yes; I made the re-examination, however, as Dupin suggested – but it was all labour lost, as I knew it would be.'

'How much was the reward offered, did you say?' asked Dupin.

'Why, a very great deal – a *very* liberal reward – I don't like to say how much, precisely; but I *will* say, that I wouldn't mind giving my individual cheque for fifty thousand francs to any one who could obtain me that letter. The fact is, it is becoming of more and more importance every day; and the reward has been lately doubled. If it were trebled, however, I could do no more than I have done.'

'Why, yes,' said Dupin drawingly, between the whiffs of his meerschaum, 'I really – think, G—, you have not exerted yourself – to the utmost this matter. You might – do a little more, I think, eh?'

'How? – in what way?'

'Why – puff, puff – you might – puff, puff – employ counsel in the matter, eh? – puff, puff, puff. Do you remember the story they tell of Abernethy?'

'No; hang Abernethy!'

'To be sure! hang him and welcome. But once upon a time, a certain rich miser conceived the design of sponging upon this Abernethy for a medical opinion. Getting up, for this purpose, an ordinary conversation in a private company, he insinuated his case to the physician, as that of an imaginary individual.

' "We will suppose," said the miser, "that his symptoms are such and such; now, doctor, what would *you* have directed him to take?"

' "Take!" said Abernethy, "why, take *advice*, to be sure." '

'But,' said the Prefect, a little discomposed, 'I am *perfectly* willing to take advice, and to pay for it. I would *really* give fifty thousand francs to any one who would aid me in the matter.'

'In that case,' replied Dupin, opening a drawer, and producing a cheque-book, 'you may as well fill me up a cheque for the amount mentioned. When you have signed it, I will hand you the letter.'

I was astounded. The Prefect appeared absolutely thunderstricken. For some minutes he remained speechless and motionless, looking incredulously at my friend with open mouth, and eyes that seemed starting from their sockets; then, apparently recovering himself in some measure, he seized a pen, and after several pauses and vacant stares, finally filled up and signed a cheque for fifty thousand francs, and handed it across the table to Dupin. The latter examined it carefully and deposited it in his pocket-book; then, unlocking an *escritoire*, took thence a letter and gave it to the Prefect. This functionary grasped it in a perfect agony of joy, opened it with a trembling hand, cast a rapid glance at its contents, and then, scrambling and struggling to the door, rushed at length unceremoniously from the room and from the house, without having uttered a syllable since Dupin had requested him to fill up the cheque.

When he had gone, my friend entered into some explanations.

'The Parisian police,' he said, 'are exceedingly able in their way. They are persevering, ingenious, cunning, and thoroughly versed in the knowledge which their duties seem chiefly to demand. Thus, when G— detailed to us his mode of searching the premises at the Hôtel D—, I felt entire confidence in his having made a satisfactory investigation – so far as his labours extended.'

'So far as his labours extended?' said I.

'Yes,' said Dupin. 'The measures adopted were not only the best of their kind, but carried out to absolute perfection. Had the letter been deposited within the range of their search, these fellows would, beyond a question, have found it.'

I merely laughed – but he seemed quite serious in all that he said.

'The measures, then,' he continued, 'were good in their kind, and well executed; their defect lay in their being inapplicable to the case, and to the man. A certain set of highly ingenious resources are, with the Prefect, a sort of Procrustean bed, to which he forcibly adapts his designs. But he perpetually errs by being too deep or too shallow for the matter in hand; and many a schoolboy is a better reasoner than he. I knew one about eight years of age, whose success at guessing in the game of "even and odd" attracted universal admiration. This game is simple, and is played with marbles. One player holds in his hand a number of these toys, and demands of another whether that number is even or odd. If the guess is right, the guesser wins one; if wrong, he loses one. The boy to whom I allude won all the marbles of the school. Of course he had some principle of guessing; and this lay in mere observation and admeasurement of the astuteness of his opponents. For example, an arrant simpleton is his opponent, and, holding up his closed hand, asks, "Are they even or odd?" Our schoolboy replies "Odd," and loses; but upon the second trial he wins, for he then says to himself, "The simpleton had them even upon the first trial, and his amount of cunning is just sufficient to make him have them odd upon the second; I will therefore guess odd" – he guesses odd, and wins. Now, with a simpleton a degree above the first, he would have reasoned thus: "This fellow finds that in the first instance I guessed odd, and, in the second, he will propose to himself, upon the first impulse, a simple variation from even to odd, as did the first simpleton; but then a second thought will suggest that this is too simple a variation and finally he will decide upon putting it even as before. I will therefore guess even" – he guesses even, and wins. Now this mode of reasoning in the schoolboy, whom his fellows termed "lucky" – what, in its last analysis, is it?'

'It is merely,' I said, 'an identification of the reasoner's intellect with that of his opponent.'

'It is,' said Dupin; 'and upon inquiring of the boy by what means he effected the *thorough* identification in which his success consisted, I received answer as follows: "When I wish to find out how wise, or how stupid, or how good, or how wicked is any one, or what are his thoughts at the moment, I fashion the expression of my face, as accurately as possible, in accordance with the expression of his, and then wait to see what thoughts or sentiments arise in my mind or heart, as if to match or correspond with the expression." This response of the schoolboy lies at the bottom of all the spurious profundity which has been attributed to Rochefoucauld, to La Bougive, to Machiavelli, and to Campanella.'

'And the identification,' I said, 'of the reasoner's intellect with that of his opponent, depends, if I understand you aright, upon the accuracy with which the opponent's intellect is admeasured.'

'For its practical value it depends upon this,' replied Dupin; 'and the Prefect and his cohort fail so frequently, first, by default of his identification, and, secondly, by ill-admeasurement, or rather through non-admeasurement, of the intellect with which they are engaged. They consider only their *own* ideas of ingenuity; and, in searching for anything hidden, advert only to the modes in which *they* would have hidden it. They are right in this much – that their own ingenuity is a faithful representative of that of *the mass*; but when the cunning of the individual felon is diverse in character from their own, the felon foils them, of course. This always happens when it is above their own, and very usually when it is below. They have no variation of principle in their investigations; at best, when urged by some unusual emergency – by some extraordinary reward – they extend or exaggerate their old modes of *practice*, without touching their principles. What, for example, in this case of D—, has been done to vary the principle of action? What is all this boring, and probing, and sounding, and scrutinising with the microscope, and dividing the surface of the building into registered square inches – what is it all but an exaggeration *of the application* of the one principle or set of principles of search, which are based upon the one set of notions regarding human ingenuity, to which the Prefect, in the long routine of his duty, has been accustomed? Do you not see he has taken it for granted that *all* men proceed to conceal a letter – not exactly in a gimlet-hole bored in a chair-leg – but, at least, in *some* out-of-the-way hole or corner suggested by the same tenor of thought which would urge a man to secrete a letter in a gimlet-hole bored in a chair-leg? And do you not see also, that such *recherchés* nooks for concealment are adapted only for ordinary occasions, and would be adopted only by ordinary intellects; for, in all cases of concealment, a disposal of the article concealed – a disposal of it in this *recherché* manner – is, in the very first instance, presumable and presumed; and thus its discovery depends, not at all upon the acumen, but altogether upon the mere care, patience, and determination of the seekers; and where the case is of importance – or, what amounts to the same thing in the political eyes, when the reward is of magnitude – the qualities in question have *never* been known to fail. You will now understand what I meant in suggesting that, had the purloined letter been hidden anywhere within the limits of the Prefect's examination – in other words, had the principle of its concealment been comprehended within the principles of the Prefect – its discovery would have been a matter altogether beyond question. This functionary, however, has been thoroughly mystified; and the remote source of his defeat lies in the supposition that the Minister is a fool, because he has acquired renown as a poet. All fools are poets – this the Prefect *feels*; and he is merely guilty of a *non distributio medii* in thence inferring that all poets are fools.'

'But is this really the poet?' I asked. 'There are two brothers, I know; and both have attained reputation in letters. The Minister, I believe, has written learnedly on the Differential Calculus. He is a mathematician, and no poet.'

'You are mistaken; I know him well; he is both. As poet *and* mathematician, he would reason well; as mere mathematician, he could not have reasoned at all, and thus would have been at the mercy of the Prefect.'

'You surprise me,' I said, 'by these opinions, which have been contradicted by the voice of the world. You do not mean to set at naught the well-digested idea of centuries. The mathematical reason has long been regarded as *the* reason *par excellence*.'

' "*Il y a à parièr*," ' replied Dupin, quoting from Chamfort, ' "*que toute idée publique, toute convention reçue, est une sottise, car elle a convenue au plus grand nombre*." The mathematicians, I grant you, have done their best to promulgate the popular error to which you allude, and which is none the less an error for its promulgation as truth. With an art worthy a better cause, for example, they have insinuated the term "analysis" into application to algebra. The French are the originators of this particular deception; but if a term is of any importance – if words derive any value from applicability – then "analysis" conveys "algebra" about as much as, in Latin, "*ambitus*" implies "ambition," "*religio*" "religion", or "*homines honesti*" a set of *honourable* men.'

24

'You have a quarrel on hand, I see,' said I, 'with some of the algebraists of Paris; but proceed.'

'I dispute the availability, and thus the value, of that reason which is cultivated in any especial form other than the abstractly logical. I dispute, in particular, the reason educed by mathematical study. The mathematics are the science of form and quantity; mathematical reasoning is merely logic applied to observation upon form and quantity. The great error lies in supposing that even the truths of what is called *pure* algebra, are abstract or general truths. And this error is so egregious that I am confounded at the universality with which it has been received. Mathematical axioms are *not* axioms of general truth. What is true of *relation* – of form and quantity – is often grossly false in regard to morals, for example. In this latter science it is very usually *un*true that the aggregated parts are equal to the whole. In chemistry also the axiom fails. In the consideration of motive it fails; for two motives, each of a given value, have not, necessarily, a value when united, equal to the sum of their values apart. There are numerous other mathematical truths which are only truths within the limits of *relation*. But the mathematician argues, from his *finite truths*, through habit, as if they were of an absolutely general applicability – as the world indeed imagines them to be. Bryant, in his very learned "Mythology", mentions an analogous source of error, when he says that "although the Pagan fables are not believed, yet we forget ourselves continually, and make inferences from them as existing realities." With the algebraists, however, who are Pagans themselves, the "Pagan fables" *are* believed, and the inferences are made, not so much through lapse of memory, as through an unaccountable addling of the brains. In short, I never yet encountered the mere mathematician who could be trusted out of equal roots, or one who did not clandestinely hold it as a point of his faith that x^2+px was absolutely and unconditionally equal to q. Say to one of these gentlemen, by way of experiment, if you please, that you believe occasions may occur where x^2+px is *not* altogether equal to q, and, having made him understand what you mean, get out of his reach as speedily as convenient, for, beyond doubt, he will endeavour to knock you down.

'I mean to say,' continued Dupin, while I merely laughed at his last observations, 'that if the Minister had been no more than a mathematician, the Prefect would have been under no necessity of giving me this cheque. I knew him, however, as both mathematician and poet, and my measures were adapted to his capacity, with reference to the circumstances by which he was surrounded. I knew him as a courtier, too, and as a bold *intriguant*. Such a man, I considered, could not fail to be aware of the ordinary policial modes of action. He could not have failed to anticipate – and events have proved that he did not fail to anticipate –

the waylayings to which he was subjected. He must have foreseen, I reflected, the secret investigations of his premises. His frequent absences from home at night, which were hailed by the Prefect as certain aids to his success, I regarded only as ruses, to afford opportunity for thorough search to the police, and thus the sooner to impress them with the conviction to which G—, in fact, did finally arrive – the conviction that the letter was not upon the premises. I felt, also, that the whole train of thought, which I was at some pains in detailing to you just now, concerning the invariable principle of policial action in searches for articles concealed – I felt that this whole train of thought would necessarily pass through the mind of the Minister. It would imperatively lead him to despise all the ordinary *nooks* of concealment. *He* could not, I reflected, be so weak as not to see that the most intricate and remote recess of his hotel would be as open as his commonest closets to the eyes, to the probes, to the gimlets, and to the microscopes of the Prefect. I saw, in fine, that he would be driven, as a matter of course, to *simplicity*, if not deliberately induced to it as a matter of choice. You will remember, perhaps, how desperately the Prefect laughed when I suggested, upon our first interview, that it was just possible this mystery troubled him so much on account of its being so *very* self-evident.'

'Yes,' said I, 'I remember his merriment well. I really thought he would have fallen into convulsions.'

'The material world,' continued Dupin, 'abounds with very strict analogies to the immaterial; and thus some colour of truth has been given to the rhetorical dogma, that metaphor, or simile, may be made to strengthen an argument, as well as to embellish a description. The principle of the *vis inertiæ*, for example, seems to be identical in physics and metaphysics. It is not more true in the former, that a large body is with more difficulty set in motion than a smaller one, and that its subsequent momentum is commensurate with this difficulty, than it is, in the latter, that intellects of the vaster capacity, while more forcible, more constant, and more eventful in their movements than those of inferior grade, are yet the less readily moved, and more embarrassed and full of hesitation in the first few steps of their progress. Ag n, have you ever noticed which of the street signs over the shop-doors are the most attractive of attention?'

'I have never given the matter a thought,' I said.

'There is a game of puzzles,' he resumed, 'which is played upon a map. One party playing requires another to find a given word – the name of town, river, state or empire – any word, in short, upon the motley and perplexed surface of the chart. A novice in the game generally seeks to embarrass his opponents by giving them the most minutely lettered names; but the adept selects such words as stretch, in large characters, from one end of the chart to the other. These, like the over-largely lettered signs and placards of the street, escape observation by dint of being excessively obvious; and here the physical oversight is precisely analogous with the moral inapprehension by which the intellect suffers to pass unnoticed those considerations which are too obtrusively and too palpably self-evident. But this is a point, it appears, somewhat above or beneath the understanding of the Prefect. He never once thought it probable, or possible, that the Minister had deposited the letter immediately beneath the nose of the whole world, by way of best preventing any portion of that world from perceiving it.

'But the more I reflected upon the daring, dashing, and discriminating ingenuity of D—; upon the fact that the document must always have been *at hand*, if he intended to use it to good purpose; and upon the decisive evidence, obtained by the Prefect, that it was not hidden within the limits of that dignitary's ordinary search – the more satisfied I became that, to conceal this letter, the Minister had resorted to the comprehensive and sagacious expedient of not attempting to conceal it at all.

'Full of these ideas, I prepared myself with a pair of green spectacles, and called one fine morning, quite by accident, at the Ministerial hotel. I found D— at home, yawning, lounging, and dawdling, as usual, and pretending to be in the last extremity of *ennui*. He is, perhaps, the most really energetic human being now alive – but that is only when nobody sees him.

'To be even with him, I complained of my weak eyes, and lamented the necessity of the spectacles, under cover of which I cautiously and thoroughly surveyed the whole apartment, while seemingly intent only upon the conversation of my host.

'I paid especial attention to a large writing-table near which he sat, and upon which lay confusedly some miscellaneous letters and other papers, with one or two musical instruments and a few books. Here, however, after a long and very deliberate scrutiny, I saw nothing to excite particular suspicion.

'At length my eyes, in going the circuit of the room, fell upon a trumpery filigree card-rack of paste-board, that hung dangling by a dirty blue ribbon, from a little brass knob just beneath the middle of the mantelpiece. In this rack, which had three or four compartments, were five or six visiting cards and a solitary letter. This last was much soiled and crumpled. It was torn nearly in two, across the middle – as if a design, in the first instance, to tear it entirely up as worthless, had been altered, or stayed, in the second. It had a large black seal, bearing the D— cipher *very* conspicuously, and was addressed, in a diminutive female hand, to D—, the Minister, himself. It was thrust carelessly, and even, as it seemed, contemptuously, into one of the uppermost divisions of the rack.

'No sooner had I glanced at this letter, than I concluded it to be that of which I was in search. To be sure, it was, to all appearance, radically different from the one of which the Prefect had read us so minute a description. Here the seal was large and black, with the D— cipher; there it was small and red, with the ducal arms of the S— family. Here, the address, to the Minister, was diminutive and feminine; there the superscription, to a certain royal personage, was markedly bold and decided; the size alone formed a point of correspondence. But then the *radicalness* of these differences, which was excessive; the dirt; the soiled and torn condition of the paper, so inconsistent with the *true* methodical habits of D—, and so suggestive of a design to delude the beholder into an idea of the worthlessness of the document; these things, together with the hyper-obtrusive situation of this document, full in the view of every visitor, and thus exactly in accordance with the conclusions to which I had previously arrived; these things, I say, were strongly corroborative of suspicion, in one who came with the intention to suspect.

'I protracted my visit as long as possible, and, while I maintained a most animated discussion with the Minister, upon a topic which I knew well had never failed to interest and excite him. I kept my attention really riveted upon the letter. In this examination, I committed to memory its external appearance and arrangement in the rack; and also fell, at length, upon a discovery, which set at rest whatever trivial doubt I might have entertained. In scrutinising the edges of the paper, I observed them to be more *chafed* than seemed necessary. They presented the *broken* appearance which is manifested when a stiff paper, having been once folded and pressed with a folder, is refolded in a reversed direction, in the same creases or edges which had formed the original fold. This discovery was sufficient. It was clear to me that the letter had been turned, as a glove, inside out, redirected and resealed. I bade the Minister good-morning, and took my departure at once, leaving a gold snuff-box upon the table.

'The next morning I called for the snuff-box, when we resumed, quite eagerly, the conversation of the preceding day. While thus engaged, however, a loud report, as if of a pistol, was heard immediately beneath the windows of the hotel, and was succeeded by a series of fearful screams, and the shoutings of a terrified mob. D— rushed to a casement, threw it open, and looked out. In the meantime, I stepped to the card-rack, took the letter, put it in my pocket, and replaced it by a fac-simile (so far as regards externals) which I had carefully prepared at my lodgings – imitating the D— cipher, very readily, by means of a seal formed of bread.

'The disturbance in the street had been occasioned by the frantic behaviour of a man with a musket. He had fired it among a crowd of women and children. It proved, however, to have been without ball, and the fellow was suffered to go his way as a lunatic or a drunkard. When he had gone, D— came from the window, whither I had followed him immediately upon securing the object in view. Soon afterwards I bade him farewell. The pretended lunatic was a man in my own pay.'

'But what purpose had you,' I asked, 'in replacing the letter by a fac-simile? Would it not have been better, at the first visit, to have seized it openly, and departed?'

'D—,' replied Dupin, 'is a desperate man, and a man of nerve. His hotel, too, is not without attendants devoted to his interests. Had I made the wild attempt you suggest, I might never have left the Ministerial presence alive. The good people of Paris might have heard of me no more. But I had an object apart from these considerations. You know my political prepossessions. In this matter, I act as a partisan of the lady concerned. For eighteen months the Minister has had her in his power. She has now him in hers – since, being unaware that the letter is not in his possession, he will proceed with his exactions as if it was. Thus will he inevitably commit himself, at once, to his political destruction. His downfall, too, will not be more precipitate than awkward. It is all very well to talk about the *facilis descensus Averni*; but in all kinds of climbing, as Catalani said of singing, it is far more easy to get up than to come down. In the present instance I have no sympathy – at least no pity – for him who descends. He is that *monstrum horrendum*, an unprincipled man of genius. I confess, however, that I should like very well to know the precise character of his thoughts, when, being defied by her whom the Prefect terms "a certain personage", he is reduced to opening the letter which I left for him in the card-rack.'

'How? did you put anything particular in it?'

'Why – it did not seem altogether right to leave the interior blank – that would have been insulting. D—, at Vienna once, did me an evil turn, which I told him, quite good-humouredly, that I should remember. So, as I knew he would feel some curiosity in regard to the identity of the person who had outwitted him, I thought it a pity not to give him a clew. He is well acquainted with my MS., and I just copied into the middle of the blank sheet the words:—

' "– Un dessein si funeste,
S'il n'est digne d'Atrée, est digne de Thyeste."

They are to be found in Crébillon's "Atrée." '

29

Wilkie Collins

The Angler's Story of the
Lady of Glenwith Grange

I have known Miss Welwyn long enough to be able to bear personal testimony to the truth of many of the particulars which I am now about to relate. I knew her father, and her younger sister Rosamond; and I was acquainted with the Frenchman who became Rosamond's husband. These are the persons of whom it will be principally necessary for me to speak. They are the only prominent characters in my story.

Miss Welwyn's father died some years since. I remember him very well – though he never excited in me, or in any one else that I ever heard of, the slightest feeling of interest. When I have said that he inherited a very large fortune, amassed during his father's time, by speculations of a very daring, very fortunate, but not always very honourable kind, and that he bought this old house with the notion of raising his social position, by making himself a member of our landed aristocracy in these parts, I have told you as much about him, I suspect, as you would care to hear. He was a thoroughly commonplace man, with no great virtues and no great vices in him. He had a little heart, a feeble mind, an amiable temper, a tall figure, and a handsome face. More than this need not, and cannot, be said on the subject of Mr Welwyn's character.

I must have seen the late Mrs Welwyn very often as a child; but I cannot say that I remember anything more of her than that she was tall and handsome, and very generous and sweet-tempered towards me when I was in her company. She was her husband's superior in birth, as in everything else; was a great reader of books in all languages; and possessed such admirable talents as a musician, that her wonderful playing on the organ is remembered and talked of to this day among the old people in our country houses about here. All her friends, as I have heard, were disappointed when she married Mr Welwyn, rich as he was; and were afterwards astonished to find her preserving the appearance, at least, of being perfectly happy with a husband who, neither in mind nor heart, was worthy of her.

It was generally supposed (and I have no doubt correctly), that she found her great happiness and her great consolation in her little girl Ida – now the lady from whom we have just parted. The child took after her mother from the first – inheriting her mother's fondness for books, her mother's love of music, her mother's quick sensibilities, and, more than all, her mother's quiet firmness, patience, and loving kindness of disposition. From Ida's earliest years, Mrs Welwyn undertook the whole superintendence of her education. The two were hardly ever apart, within doors or without. Neighbours and friends said that the little girl was being brought up too fancifully, was not enough among other children, was sadly neglected as to all reasonable and practical teaching, and was perilously encouraged in those dreamy and imaginative tendencies of which she had naturally more than her due share. There was, perhaps, some truth in this; and there might have been still more, if Ida had possessed an ordinary character, or had been reserved for an ordinary destiny. But she was a strange child from the first, and a strange future was in store for her.

Little Ida reached her eleventh year without either brother or sister to be her playfellow and companion at home. Immediately after that period, however, her sister Rosamond was born. Though Mr Welwyn's own desire was to have had a son, there were, nevertheless, great rejoicings yonder in the old house on the birth of this second daughter. But they were all turned, only a few months afterwards, to the bitterest grief and despair: the Grange lost its mistress. While Rosamond was still an infant in arms, her mother died.

Mrs Welwyn had been afflicted with some disorder after the birth of her second child, the name of which I am not learned enough in medical science to be able to remember. I only know that she recovered from it, to all appearance, in an unexpectedly short time; that she suffered a fatal relapse, and that she died a lingering and a painful death. Mr Welwyn (who, in after years, had a habit of vain-gloriously describing his marriage as 'a love-match on both sides') was really fond of his wife in his own frivolous feeble way, and suffered as acutely as such a man could suffer, during the latter days of her illness, and at the terrible time when the doctors, one and all, confessed that her life was a thing to be despaired of. He burst into irrepressible passions of tears, and was always obliged to leave the sick-room whenever Mrs Welwyn spoke of her approaching end. The last solemn words of the dying woman, the tenderest messages that she could give, the dearest parting wishes that she could express, the most earnest commands that she could leave behind her, the gentlest reasons for consolation that she could suggest to the survivors among those who loved her, were not poured into her husband's ear, but into her child's. From the first period of her illness, Ida had persisted in remaining in the sick-room, rarely speaking, never showing outwardly any signs of terror or grief, except when she was removed from it; and then bursting into hysterical passions of weeping, which no expostulations, no arguments, no commands – nothing, in short, but bringing her back to the bedside – ever availed to calm. Her mother had been her playfellow, her companion, her dearest and most familiar friend; and there seemed something in the remembrance of this which, instead of overwhelming the child with despair, strengthened her to watch faithfully and bravely by her dying parent to the very last.

When the parting moment was over, and when Mr Welwyn, unable to bear the shock of being present in the house of death at the time of his wife's funeral, left home and went to stay with one of his relations in a distant part of England, Ida, whom it had been his wish to take away with him, petitioned earnestly to be left behind. 'I promised mamma before she died that I would be as good to my little sister Rosamond as she had been to me,' said the child, simply; 'and she told me in return that I might wait here and see her laid in her grave.' There happened to be an aunt of Mrs Welwyn, and an old servant of the family, in the house at this time, who understood Ida much better than her father did, and they persuaded him not to take her away. I have heard my mother say that the effect of the child's appearance at the funeral on her, and on all who went to see it, was something that she could never think of without the tears coming into her eyes, and could never forget to the last day of her life.

It must have been very shortly after this period that I saw Ida for the first time.

I remember accompanying my mother on a visit to the old house we have just left, in the summer, when I was at home for the holidays. It was a lovely, sunshiny morning. There was nobody indoors, and we walked out into the garden. As we approached that lawn yonder, on the other side of the shrubbery, I saw, first, a young woman in mourning (apparently a servant) sitting reading; then a little girl, dressed all in black, moving towards us slowly over the bright turf, and holding up before her a baby, whom she was trying to teach to walk. She looked, to my ideas, so very young to be engaged in such an occupation as this, and her gloomy black frock appeared to be such an unnaturally grave garment for a mere child of her age, and looked so doubly dismal by contrast with the brilliant sunny lawn on which she stood, that I quite started when I first saw her, and eagerly asked my mother who she was. The answer informed me of the sad family story, which I have been just relating to you. Mrs Welwyn had then been buried about three months; and Ida, in her childish way, was trying, as she had promised, to supply her mother's place to her infant sister Rosamond.

I only mention this simple incident, because it is necessary, before I proceed to the eventful part of my narrative, that you should know exactly in what relation the sisters stood towards one another from the first. Of all the last parting words that Mrs Welwyn had spoken to her child, none had been oftener repeated, none more solemnly urged, than those which had commended the little Rosamond to Ida's love and care. To other persons, the full, the all-trusting dependence which the dying mother was known to have placed in a child hardly eleven years old, seemed merely a proof of that helpless desire to cling even to the feeblest consolations, which the approach of death so often brings with it. But the event showed that the trust so strangely placed had not been ventured vainly when it was committed to young and tender hands. The whole future existence of the child was one noble proof that she had been worthy of her mother's dying confidence, when it was first reposed in her. In that simple incident which I have just mentioned, the new life of the two motherless sisters was all foreshadowed.

Time passed. I left school – went to college – travelled in Germany, and stayed there some time to learn the language. At every interval when I came home, and asked about the Welwyns, the answer was, in substance, almost always the same. Mr Welwyn was giving his regular dinners, performing his regular duties as a county magistrate, enjoying his regular recreations as an amateur farmer and an eager sportsman. His two daughters were never separate. Ida was the same strange, quiet, retiring girl, that she had always been; and was still (as the phrase went) 'spoiling' Rosamond in every way in which it was possible for an elder sister to spoil a younger by too much kindness.

I myself went to the Grange occasionally, when I was in this neighbourhood, in holiday and vacation time; and was able to test the correctness of the picture of life there which had been drawn for me. I remember the two sisters, when Rosamond was four or five years old; and when Ida seemed to me, even then, to be more like the child's mother than her sister. She bore with her little caprices as sisters do not bear with one another. She was so patient at lesson-time, so anxious to conceal any weariness that might overcome her in play-hours, so proud when Rosamond's beauty was noticed, so grateful for Rosamond's kisses when the child thought of bestowing them, so quick to notice all that Rosamond did, and to attend to all that Rosamond said, even when visitors were in the room; that she seemed, to my boyish observation, altogether different

33

from other elder sisters in other family circles into which I was then received.

I remember then, again, when Rosamond was just growing to womanhood, and was in high spirits at the prospect of spending a season in London, and being presented at Court. She was very beautiful at that time – much handsomer than Ida. Her 'accomplishments' were talked of far and near in our country circles. Few, if any, of the people, however, who applauded her playing and singing, who admired her water-colour drawings, who were delighted at her fluency when she spoke French, and amazed at her ready comprehension when she read German, knew how little of all this elegant mental cultivation and nimble manual dexterity she owed to her governesses and masters, and how much to her elder sister. It was Ida who really found out the means of stimulating her when she was idle; Ida who helped her through all her worst difficulties; Ida who gently conquered her defects of memory over her books, her inaccuracies of ear at the piano, her errors of taste when she took the brush or pencil in hand. It was Ida alone who worked these marvels, and whose all-sufficient reward for her hardest exertions was a chance word of kindness from her sister's lips. Rosamond was not unaffectionate, and not ungrateful; but she inherited much of her father's commonness and frivolity of character. She became so accustomed to owe everything to her sister – to resign all her most trifling difficulties to Ida's ever-ready care – to have all her tastes consulted by Ida's ever-watchful kindness – that she never appreciated, as it deserved, the deep devoted love of which she was the object. When Ida refused two good offers of marriage, Rosamond was as much astonished as the veriest strangers, who wondered why the elder Miss Welwyn seemed bent on remaining single all her life.

When the journey to London, to which I have already alluded, took place, Ida accompanied her father and sister. If she had consulted her own tastes, she would have remained in the country; but Rosamond declared that she should feel quite lost and helpless twenty times a day, in town, without her sister. It was in the nature of Ida to sacrifice herself to any one whom she loved, on the smallest occasions as well as the greatest. Her affection was as intuitively ready to sanctify Rosamond's slightest caprices as to excuse Rosamond's most thoughtless faults. So she went to London cheerfully, to witness with pride all the little triumphs won by her sister's beauty; to hear, and never tire of hearing, all that admiring friends could say in her sister's praise.

At the end of the season, Mr Welwyn and his daughters returned for a short time to the country; they left home again to spend the latter part of the autumn and the beginning of the winter in Paris.

They took with them excellent letters of introduction, and saw a great deal of the best society in Paris, foreign as well as English. At one of the first of the evening parties which they attended, the general topic of conversation was the conduct of a certain French nobleman, the Baron Franval, who had returned to his native country after a long absence, and who was spoken of in terms of high eulogy by the majority of the guests present. The history of who Franval was, and of what he had done, was readily communicated to Mr Welwyn and his daughters, and was briefly this:

The Baron inherited little from his ancestors besides his high rank and his ancient pedigree. On the death of his parents, he and his two un-married sisters (their only surviving children) found the small territorial property of the Franvals, in Normandy, barely productive enough to afford a comfortable subsistence for the three. The Baron, then a young man of three-and-twenty, endeavoured to obtain such military or civil employment as might become his rank; but, although the Bourbons were at that time restored to the throne of France, his efforts were ineffectual. Either his interest at Court was bad, or secret enemies were at work to oppose his advancement. He failed to obtain even the slightest favour; and, irritated by undeserved neglect, resolved to leave France, and seek occupation for his energies in foreign countries, where his rank would be no bar to his bettering his fortunes, if he pleased, by engaging in com-mercial pursuits.

An opportunity of the kind that he wanted unexpectedly offered itself. He left his sisters in care of an old male relative of the family at the château in Normandy, and sailed, in the first instance, to the West Indies; afterwards extending his wanderings to the continent of South America, and there engaging in mining transactions on a very large scale. After fifteen years of absence (during the latter part of which time false reports of his death had reached Normandy), he had just returned to France; having realised a handsome independence, with which he proposed to widen the limits of his ancestral property, and to give his sisters (who were still, like himself, unmarried) all the luxuries and advantages that affluence could bestow. The Baron's independent spirit, and generous devotion to the honour of his family and the happiness of his surviving relatives, were themes of general admiration in most of the social circles of Paris. He was expected to arrive in the capital every day; and it was naturally enough predicted that his reception in society there could not fail to be of the most flattering and most brilliant kind.

The Welwyns listened to this story with some little interest; Rosamond, who was very romantic, being especially attracted by it, and openly avowing to her father and sister, when they got back to their hotel, that she felt as ardent a curiosity as anybody to see the adventurous and generous Baron. The desire was soon gratified. Franval came to Paris, as had been anticipated – was introduced to the Welwyns – met them constantly in society – made no favourable impression on Ida, but won the good opinion of Rosamond from the first; and was regarded with such high approval by their father, that when he mentioned his intention of visiting England in the spring of the new year, he was cordially invited to spend the hunting season at Glenwith Grange.

I came back from Germany about the same time that the Welwyns returned from Paris, and at once set myself to improve my neighbourly intimacy with the family. I was very fond of Ida; more fond, perhaps, than my vanity will now allow me to – but that is of no consequence. It is much more to the purpose to tell you, that I heard the whole of the Baron's story enthusiastically related by Mr Welwyn and Rosamond; that he came to the Grange at the appointed time; that I was introduced to him; and that he produced as unfavourable an impression upon me as he had already produced upon Ida.

It was whimsical enough; but I really could not tell why I disliked him, though I could account very easily, according to my own notions, for his winning the favour and approval of Rosamond and her father. He was certainly a handsome man, as far as features went; he had a winning gentleness and graceful respect in his manner when he spoke to women; and he sang remarkably well, with one of the sweetest tenor voices I ever heard. These qualities alone were quite sufficient to attract any girl of Rosamond's disposition; and I certainly never wondered why he was a favourite of hers.

Then, as to her father, the Baron was not only fitted to win his sympathy and regard in the field, by proving himself an ardent sportsman and an excellent rider; but was also, in virtue of some of his minor personal peculiarities, just the man to gain the friendship of his host. Mr Welwyn was as ridiculously prejudiced as most weak-headed Englishmen are, on the subject of foreigners in general. In spite of his visit to Paris, the vulgar notion of a Frenchman continued to be *his* notion, both while he was in France and when he returned from it. Now, the Baron was as unlike the traditional 'Mounseer' of English songs, plays, and satires, as a man could well be; and it was on account of this very dissimilarity that Mr Welwyn first took a violent fancy to him, and then invited him to his house. Franval spoke English remarkably well; wore neither beard, moustachios nor whiskers; kept his hair cut almost unbecomingly short; dressed in the extreme of plainness and modest good taste; talked little in general society; uttered his words, when he did speak, with singular calmness and deliberation; and, to crown all, had the greater part of his acquired property invested in English securities. In Mr Welwyn's estimation, such a man as this was a perfect miracle of a Frenchman, and he admired and encouraged him accordingly.

I have said that I disliked him, yet could not assign a reason for my dislike; and I can only repeat it now. He was remarkably polite to me; we often rode together in hunting, and sat near each other at the Grange table; but I could never become familiar with him. He always gave me the idea of a man who had some mental reservation in saying the most trifling thing. There was a constant restraint, hardly perceptible to most people, but plainly visible, nevertheless, to me, which seemed to accompany his lightest words, and to hang about his most familiar manner. This, however, was no just reason for my secretly disliking and distrusting him as I did. Ida said as much to me, I remember, when I confessed to her what my feelings towards him were, and tried (but vainly) to induce her to be equally candid with me in return. She seemed to shrink from the tacit condemnation of Rosamond's opinion which such a confidence on her part would have implied. And yet she watched the growth of that opinion – or, in other words, the growth of her sister's liking for the Baron – with an apprehension and sorrow which she tried fruitlessly to conceal. Even her father began to notice that her spirits were not so good as usual, and to suspect the cause of her melancholy. I remember he jested, with all the dense insensibility of a stupid man, about Ida having invariably been jealous, from a child, if Rosamond looked kindly upon anybody except her elder sister.

The spring began to get far advanced towards summer. Franval paid a visit to London; came back in the middle of the season to Glenwith Grange; wrote to put off his departure for France; and, at last (not at all to the surprise of anybody who was intimate with the Welwyns) proposed to Rosamond, and was accepted. He was candour and generosity itself when the preliminaries of the marriage settlement were under discussion. He quite overpowered Mr Welwyn and the lawyers with references, papers, and statements of the distribution and extent of his property, which were found to be perfectly correct. His sisters were written to, and returned the most cordial answers: saying that the state of their health would not allow them to come to England for the marriage; but adding a warm invitation to Normandy for the bride and her family. Nothing, in short, could be more straightforward and satisfactory than the Baron's behaviour, and the testimonies to his worth and integrity which the news of the approaching marriage produced from his relatives and his friends.

The only joyless face at the Grange now was Ida's. At any time it would have been a hard trial to her to resign that first and foremost place which she had held since childhood in her sister's heart, as she knew she must resign it when Rosamond married. But, secretly disliking and distrusting Franval as she did, the thought that he was soon to become the husband of her beloved sister filled her with a vague sense of terror which she could not explain to herself; which it was imperatively necessary that she should conceal; and which, on those very accounts, became a daily and hourly torment to her that was almost more than she could bear.

One consolation alone supported her: Rosamond and she were not to be separated. She knew that the Baron secretly disliked her as much as she disliked him; she knew that she must bid farewell to the brighter and happier part of her life on the day when she went to live under the same roof with her sister's husband; but, true to the promise made years and years ago, by her dying mother's bed – true to the affection which was the ruling and beautiful feeling of her whole existence – she never hesitated about indulging Rosamond's wish, when the girl, in her bright light-hearted way, said that she could never get on comfortably in the marriage state unless she had Ida to live with her, and help her just the same as ever. The Baron was too polite a man even to *look* dissatisfied when he heard of the proposed arrangement; and it was therefore settled from the beginning that Ida was always to live with her sister.

The marriage took place in the summer, and the bride and bridegroom went to spend their honeymoon in Cumberland. On their return to Glenwith Grange, a visit to the Baron's sisters, in Normandy, was talked of; but the execution of this project was suddenly and disastrously suspended by the death of Mr Welwyn from an attack of pleurisy.

In consequence of this calamity, the projected journey was of course deferred; and when autumn and the shooting season came, the Baron was unwilling to leave the well-stocked preserves of the Grange. He seemed, indeed, to grow less and less inclined, as time advanced, for the trip to Normandy; and wrote excuse after excuse to his sisters, when letters arrived from them urging him to pay the promised visit. In the winter-time, he said he would not allow his wife to risk a long journey. In the spring, his health was pronounced to be delicate. In the genial summer-time, the accomplishment of the proposed visit would be impossible, for at that period the Baroness expected to become a mother. Such were the apologies which Franval seemed almost glad to be able to send to his sisters in France.

The marriage was, in the strictest sense of the term, a happy one. The Baron, though he never altogether lost the strange restraint and reserve of his manner, was, in his quiet, peculiar way, the fondest and kindest of husbands. He went to town occasionally on business, but always seemed glad to return to the Baroness; he never varied in the politeness of his bearing towards his wife's sister; he behaved with the most courteous hospitality towards all the friends of the Welwyns: in short, he thoroughly justified the good opinion which Rosamond and her father had formed of him when they first met at Paris. And yet no experience of his character thoroughly reassured Ida. Months passed on quietly and pleasantly; and still that secret sadness, that indefinable, unreasonable apprehension on

Rosamond's account, hung heavily on her sister's heart.

At the beginning of the first summer months, a little domestic inconvenience happened, which showed the Baroness, for the first time, that her husband's temper could be seriously ruffled – and that by the veriest trifle. He was in the habit of taking in two French provincial newspapers – one published at Bordeaux, and the other at Havre. He always opened these journals the moment they came, looked at one particular column of each with the deepest attention for a few minutes, then carelessly threw them aside into his waste-paper basket. His wife and her sister were at first rather surprised at the manner in which he read his two papers; but they thought no more of it when he explained that he only took them in to consult them about French commercial intelligence, which might be, occasionally, of importance to him.

These papers were published weekly. On the occasion to which I have just referred, the Bordeaux paper came on the proper day, as usual; but the Havre paper never made its appearance. This trifling circumstance seemed to make the Baron seriously uneasy. He wrote off directly to the country post office, and to the newspaper agent in London. His wife, astonished to see his tranquillity so completely overthrown by so slight a cause, tried to restore his good-humour by jesting with him about the missing newspaper. He replied by the first angry and unfeeling words that she had heard issue from his lips. She was then within about six weeks of her confinement, and very unfit to bear harsh answers from anybody – least of all from her husband.

On the second day no answer came. On the afternoon of the third, the Baron rode off to the post town to make inquiries. About an hour after he had gone, a strange gentleman came to the Grange, and asked to see the Baroness. On being informed that she was not well enough to receive visitors, he sent up a message that his business was of great importance, and that he would wait downstairs for a second answer.

On receiving this message, Rosamond turned, as usual, to her elder sister for advice. Ida went downstairs immediately to see the stranger. What I am now about to tell you of the extraordinary interview which took place between them, and of the shocking events that followed it, I have heard from Miss Welwyn's own lips.

She felt unaccountably nervous when she entered the room. The stranger bowed very politely, and asked, in a foreign accent, if she were the Baroness Franval. She set him right on this point, and told him she attended to all matters of business for the Baroness; adding, that, if his errand at all concerned her sister's husband, the Baron was not then at home.

The stranger answered that he was aware of it when he called, and that the unpleasant business on which he came could not be confided to the Baron – at least in the first instance.

She asked why. He said he was there to explain; and expressed himself as feeling greatly relieved at having to open his business to her, because she would, doubtless, be best able to prepare her sister for the bad news that he was, unfortunately, obliged to bring. The sudden faintness which overcame her, as he spoke those words, prevented her from addressing him in return. He poured out some water for her from a bottle which happened to be standing on the table, and asked if he might depend on her fortitude. She tried to say 'Yes'; but the violent throbbing of her heart seemed to choke her. He took a foreign newspaper from his pocket, saying that he was a secret agent of the French police – that the paper was the *Havre Journal* for the past week, and that it had been expressly kept from reaching the Baron, as usual, through his (the agent's) interference. He then opened the newspaper, and begged that she would nerve herself sufficiently (for her sister's sake) to read certain lines, which would give her some hint of the business that brought him there. He pointed to the passage as he spoke. It was among the 'Shipping Entries' and was thus expressed:

'Arrived, the *Berenice*, from San Francisco, with a valuable cargo of hides. She brings one passenger, the Baron Franval, of Château Franval, in Normandy.'

As Miss Welwyn read the entry, her heart, which had been throbbing violently but the moment before, seemed suddenly to cease from all action, and she began to shiver, though it was a warm June evening. The agent held the tumbler to her lips, and made her drink a little of the water, entreating her very earnestly to take courage and listen to him. He then sat down, and referred again to the entry; every word he uttered seeming to burn itself in for ever (as she expressed it) on her memory and her heart.

He said: 'It has been ascertained beyond the possibility of doubt that there is no mistake about the name in the lines you have just read. And it is as certain as that we are here, that there is only *one* Baron Franval now alive. The question, therefore, is, whether the passenger by the *Berenice* is the true Baron, or – I beg you most earnestly to bear with me and to compose yourself – or the husband of your sister. The person who arrived last week at Havre was scouted as an impostor by the ladies at the château, the moment he presented himself there as their brother, returning to them after sixteen years of absence. The authorities were communicated with, and I and my assistants were instantly sent for from Paris.

'We wasted no time in questioning the supposed impostor. He either was, or affected to be, in a perfect frenzy of grief and indignation. We just ascertained, from competent witnesses, that he bore an extraordinary resemblance to the real Baron, and that he was perfectly familiar with places and persons in and about the château: we just ascertained that, and then proceeded to confer with the local authorities, and to examine their private entries of suspected persons in their jurisdiction, ranging back over a past period of twenty years or more. One of the entries thus consulted contained these particulars: "Hector Auguste Monbrun, son of a respectable proprietor in Normandy. Well educated; gentlemanlike manners. On bad terms with his family. Character: bold, cunning, unscrupulous, self-possessed. Is a clever mimic. May be easily recognised by his striking likeness to the Baron Franval. Imprisoned at twenty for theft and assault." '

Miss Welwyn saw the agent look up at her after he had read this extract from the police-book, to ascertain if she was still able to listen to him. He asked, with some appearance of alarm, as their eyes met, if she would like some more water. She was just able to make a sign in the negative. He took a second extract from his pocket-book, and went on.

He said: 'The next entry under the same name was dated four years later, and ran thus: "H. A. Monbrun, condemned to the galleys for life, for assassination, and other crimes not officially necessary to be here specified. Escaped from custody at Toulon. Is known, since the expiration of his first term of imprisonment, to have allowed his beard to grow, and to have worn his hair long, with the intention of rendering it impossible for those acquainted with him in his native province to recognise him, as heretofore, by his likeness to the Baron Franval." There were more particulars added, not important enough for extract. We immediately examined the supposed impostor: for, if he was Monbrun, we knew that we should find on his shoulder the two letters of the convict brand, "T.F." standing for (*Traveaux Forcés*). After the minutest examination with the mechanical and chemical tests used on such occasions, not the slightest trace of the brand was to be found. The moment this astounding discovery was made, I started to lay an embargo on the forthcoming numbers of the *Havre Journal* for that week, which were about to be sent to the English agent in London. I arrived at Havre on Saturday (the morning of publication), in time to execute my design. I waited there long enough to communicate by telegraph with my superiors in Paris, then hastened to this place. What my errand here is, you may—'

He might have gone on speaking for some moments longer; but Miss Welwyn heard no more.

Her first sensation of returning consciousness was the feeling that water was being sprinkled on her face. Then she saw that all the windows in the room had been set wide open, to give her air; and that she and the agent were still alone. At first, she felt bewildered, and hardly knew who he was; but he soon recalled to her mind the horrible realities that had brought him there, by apologising for not having summoned assistance, when she fainted. He said it was of the last importance, in Franval's absence, that no one in the house should imagine that anything unusual was taking place in it. Then, after giving her an interval of a minute or two to collect what little strength she had left, he added that he would not increase her sufferings by saying anything more, just then, on the shocking subject of the investigation which it was his duty to make – that he would leave her to recover herself, and to consider what was the best course to be taken with the Baroness in the present terrible emergency – and that he would privately return to the house between eight and nine o'clock that evening, ready to act as Miss Welwyn wished, and to afford her and her sister any aid and protection of which they might stand in need. With these words he bowed, and noiselessly quitted the room.

For the first few awful minutes after she was left alone, Miss Welwyn sat helpless and speechless; utterly numbed in heart, and mind, and body – then a sort of instinct (she was incapable of thinking) seemed to urge her to conceal the fearful news from her sister as long as possible. She ran upstairs to Rosamond's sitting-room, and called through the door (for she dared not trust herself in her sister's presence) that the visitor had come on some troublesome business from their late father's lawyers, and that she was going to shut herself up, and write some long letters in connection with that business. After she had got into her own room, she was never sensible of how time was passing – never conscious of any feeling within her, except a baseless, helpless hope that the French police might yet be proved to have made some terrible mistake – until she heard a violent shower of rain come on a little after sunset. The noise of the rain, and the freshness it brought with it in the air, seemed to awaken her as if from a painful and a fearful sleep. The power of reflection returned to her; her heart heaved and bounded with an overwhelming terror, as the thought of Rosamond came back vividly to it; her memory recurred despairingly to the long-past day of her mother's death, and to the farewell promise she had made by her mother's bedside. She burst into an hysterical passion of weeping that seemed to be tearing her to pieces. In the midst of it she heard the clatter of a horse's hoofs in the courtyard, and knew that Rosamond's husband had come back.

Dipping her handkerchief in cold water, and passing it over her eyes as she left the room, she instantly hastened to her sister.

Fortunately the daylight was fading in the old-fashioned chamber that Rosamond occupied. Before they could say two words to each other, Franval was in the room. He seemed violently irritated; said that he had waited for the arrival of the mail – that the missing newspaper had not come by it – that he had got wet through – that he felt a shivering fit coming on – and that he believed he had caught a violent cold. His wife anxiously suggested some simple remedies. He roughly interrupted her, saying there was but one remedy, the remedy of going to bed; and so left them without another word. She just put her handkerchief to her eyes, and said softly to her sister, 'How he is changed!' – then spoke no more. They sat silent for half an hour or longer. After that, Rosamond went affectionately and forgivingly to see how her husband was. She returned, saying that he was in bed, and in a deep, heavy sleep; and predicting hopefully that he would wake up quite well the next morning. In a few minutes more the clock struck nine; and Ida heard the servant's step ascending the stairs. She suspected what his errand was, and went out to meet him. Her presentment had not deceived her, the police agent had arrived, and was waiting for her downstairs.

He asked her if she had said anything to her sister, or had thought of any plan of action, the moment she entered the room; and, on receiving a reply in the negative, inquired further if 'the Baron' had come home yet. She answered that he had; that he was ill and tired, and vexed, and that he had gone to bed. The agent asked in an eager whisper if she knew that he was asleep, and alone in bed? and, when he received her reply, said that he must go up into the bedroom directly.

She began to feel the faintness coming over her again, and with it sensations of loathing and terror that she could neither express to others nor define to herself. He said that if she hesitated to let him avail himself of this unexpected opportunity, her scruples might lead to fatal results. He reminded her that if 'the Baron' were really the convict Monbrun, the claims of society and of justice demanded that he should be discovered by the first available means; and that if he were not – if some inconceivable mistake had really been committed – then, such a plan for getting immediately at the truth as was now proposed, would ensure the delivery of an innocent man from suspicion, and at the same time spare him the knowledge that he had ever been suspected. This last argument had its effect on Miss Welwyn. The baseless, helpless hope that the French authorities might yet be proved to be in error, which she had already felt in her own room, returned to her now. She suffered the agent to lead her upstairs.

He took the candle from her hand when she pointed to the door; opened it softly; and, leaving it ajar, went into the room.

She looked through the gap, with a feverish, horror-struck curiosity. Franval was lying on his side in a profound sleep, with his back turned towards the door. The agent softly placed the candle upon a small reading-table between the door and the bedside, softly drew down the bed-clothes a little way from the sleeper's back, then took a pair of scissors from the toilet-table, and very gently and slowly began to cut away, first the loose folds, then the intervening strips of linen from the part of Franval's

43

nightgown, that was over his shoulders. When the upper part of his back had been bared in this way, the agent took the candle and held it near the flesh. Miss Welwyn heard him ejaculate some word under his breath, then saw him looking round to where she was standing, and beckoning to her to come in.

Mechanically she obeyed; mechanically she looked down where his finger was pointing. It was the convict Monbrun – there, just visible under the bright light of the candle, were the fatal letters 'T.F.' branded on the villain's shoulder!

Though she could neither move nor speak, the horror of this discovery did not deprive her of her consciousness. She saw the agent softly draw up the bed-clothes again into their proper position, replace the scissors on the toilet-table, and take from it a bottle of smelling-salts. She felt him removing her from the bedroom, and helping her quickly downstairs, giving her the salts to smell by the way. When they were alone again, he said, with the first appearance of agitation that he had yet exhibited, 'Now, madam, for God's sake, collect all your courage, and be guided by me. You and your sister had better leave the house immediately. Have you any relatives in the neighbourhood, with whom you could take refuge?' They had none. 'What is the name of the nearest town where you could get good accommodation for the night?' Harleybrook (he wrote the name down on his tablets). 'How far off is it?' Twelve miles. 'You had better have the carriage out at once, to go there with as little delay as possible: leaving me to pass the night here. I will communicate with you tomorrow at the principal hotel. Can you compose yourself sufficiently to be able to tell the head-servant, if I ring for him, that he is to obey my orders till further notice?'

The servant was summoned, and received his instructions, the agent going out with him to see that the carriage was got ready quietly and quickly. Miss Welwyn went upstairs to her sister.

How the fearful news was first broken to Rosamond, I cannot relate to you. Miss Welwyn has never confided to me, has never confided to anybody, what happened at the interview between her sister and herself that night. I can tell you nothing of the shock they both suffered, except that the younger and the weaker died under it; that the elder and the stronger has never recovered from it, and never will.

They went away the same night, with one attendant, to Harleybrook, as the agent had advised. Before daybreak Rosamond was seized with the pains of premature labour. She died three days after, unconscious of the horror of her situation: wandering in her mind about past times, and singing old tunes that Ida had taught her, as she lay in her sister's arms.

The child was born alive, and lives still. You saw her at the window as we came in at the back way to the Grange. I surprised you, I dare say, by asking you not to speak of her to Miss Welwyn. Perhaps you noticed something vacant in the little girl's expression. I am sorry to say that her mind is more vacant still. If 'idiot' did not sound like a mocking word, however tenderly and pityingly one may wish to utter it, I should tell you that the poor thing had been an idiot from her birth.

You will, doubtless, want to hear now what happened at Glenwith Grange, after Miss Welwyn and her sister had left it. I have seen the letter which the police agent sent the next morning to Harleybrook; and, speaking from my recollection of that, I shall be able to relate all you can desire to know.

First, as to the past history of the scoundrel Monbrun, I need only tell you that he was identical with an escaped convict, who, for a long term of years, had successfully eluded the vigilance of the authorities all over Europe, and in America as well. In conjunction with two accomplices, he had succeeded in possessing himself of large sums of money by the most criminal means. He also acted secretly as the 'banker' of his convict brethren, whose dishonest gains were all confided to his hands for safe keeping. He would have been certainly captured, on venturing back to France, along with his two associates, but for the daring imposture in which he took refuge; and which, if the true Baron Franval had really died abroad, as was reported, would, in all probability, never have been found out.

Besides his extraordinary likeness to the Baron, he had every other requisite for carrying on his deception successfully. Though his parents were not wealthy, he had received a good education. He was so notorious for his gentlemanlike manners among the villainous associates of his crimes and excesses, that they nicknamed him 'the Prince'. All his early life had been passed in the neighbourhood of the Château Franval. He knew what were the circumstances which had induced the Baron to leave it. He had been in the country to which the Baron had emigrated. He was able to refer familiarly to persons and localities, at home and abroad, with which the Baron was sure to be acquainted. And, lastly, he had an expatriation of fifteen years to plead for him as his all-sufficient excuse, if he made any slight mistakes before the Baron's sisters, in his assumed character of their long-absent brother. It will be, of course, hardly necessary for me to tell you, in relation to this part of the subject, that the true Franval was immediately and honourably reinstated in the family rights of which the impostor had succeeded for a time in depriving him.

According to Monbrun's own account, he had married poor Rosamond purely for love; and the probabilities certainly are, that the pretty, innocent English girl had really struck the villain's fancy for the time;

45

and that the easy, quiet life he was leading at the Grange pleased him, by contrast with his perilous and vagabond existence of former days. What might have happened if he had had time enough to grow wearied of his ill-fated wife and his English home, it is now useless to inquire. What really did happen on the morning when he awoke after the flight of Ida and her sister can be briefly told.

As soon as his eyes opened they rested on the police agent, sitting quietly by the bedside, with a loaded pistol in his hand. Monbrun knew immediately that he was discovered; but he never for an instant lost the self-possession for which he was famous. He said he wished to have five minutes allowed him to deliberate quietly in bed, whether he should resist the French authorities on English ground, and so gain time by obliging the one government to apply specially to have him delivered up by the other – or whether he should accept the terms officially offered to him by the agent, if he quietly allowed himself to be captured. He chose the latter course – it was suspected, because he wished to communicate personally with some of his convict associates in France, whose fraudulent gains were in his keeping, and because he felt boastfully confident of being able to escape again, whenever he pleased. Be his secret motives, however, what they might, he allowed the agent to conduct him peaceably from the Grange; first writing a farewell letter to poor Rosamond, full of heartless French sentiment and glib sophistries about Fate and Society. His own fate was not long in overtaking him. He attempted to escape again, as it had been expected he would, and was shot by the sentinel on duty at the time. I remember hearing that the bullet entered his head and killed him on the spot.

My story is done. It is ten years now since Rosamond was buried in the churchyard yonder; and it is ten years also since Miss Welwyn returned to be the lonely inhabitant of Glenwith Grange. She now lives but in the remembrances that it calls up before her of her happier existence of former days. There is hardly an object in the old house which does not tenderly and solemnly remind her of the mother, whose last wishes she lived to obey; of the sister, whose happiness was once her dearest earthly care. Those prints that you noticed on the library walls, Rosamond used to copy in the past time, when her pencil was often guided by Ida's hand. Those music-books that you were looking over, she and her mother have played from together, through many a long and quiet summer's evening. She has no ties now to bind her to the present but the poor child whose affliction it is her constant effort to lighten, and the little peasant population around her, whose humble cares and wants and sorrows she is always ready to relieve. Far and near her modest charities have penetrated among us; and far and near she is heartily beloved and blessed in many a labourer's household. There is no poor man's hearth, not in this village only, but for miles away from it as well, at which you would not be received with the welcome given to an old friend, if you only told the cottagers that you knew the Lady of Glenwith Grange!

Arthur Conan Doyle

The New Catacomb

'Look here, Burger,' said Kennedy, 'I do wish that you would confide in me.'

The two famous students of Roman remains sat together in Kennedy's comfortable room overlooking the Corso. The night was cold, and they had both pulled up their chairs to the unsatisfactory Italian stove which threw out a zone of stuffiness rather than of warmth. Outside under the bright winter stars lay the modern Rome, the long, double chain of the electric lamps, the brilliantly lighted cafés, the rushing carriages, and the dense throng upon the footpaths. But inside, in the sumptuous chamber of the rich young English archaeologist, there was only old Rome to be seen. Cracked and timeworn friezes hung upon the walls, grey old busts of senators and soldiers with their fighting heads and their hard, cruel faces peered out from the corners. On the centre table, amidst a litter of inscriptions, fragments, and ornaments, there stood the famous reconstruction by Kennedy of the Baths of Caracalla, which excited such interest and admiration when it was exhibited in Berlin. Amphorae hung from the ceiling, and a litter of curiosities strewed the rich red Turkey carpet. And of them all there was not one which was not of the most unimpeachable authenticity, and of the utmost rarity and value; for Kennedy, though little more than thirty, had a European reputation in this particular branch of research, and was, moreover, provided with that long purse which either proves to be a fatal handicap to the student's energies, or, if his mind is still true to its purpose, gives him an enormous advantage in the race for fame. Kennedy had often been seduced by whim and pleasure from his studies, but his mind was an incisive one, capable of long and concentrated efforts which ended in sharp reactions of sensuous languor. His handsome face, with its high, white forehead, its aggressive nose, and its somewhat loose and sensual mouth, was a fair index of the compromise between strength and weakness in his nature.

Of a very different type was his companion, Julius Burger. He came of a curious blend, a German father and an Italian mother, with the robust qualities of the North mingling strangely with the softer graces of the South. Blue Teutonic eyes lightened his sun-browned face, and above them rose a square, massive forehead, with a fringe of close yellow curls lying round it. His strong, firm jaw was clean-shaven, and his companion had frequently remarked how much it suggested those old Roman busts which peered out from the shadows in the corners of his chamber. Under its bluff German strength there lay always a suggestion of Italian subtlety, but the smile was so honest, and the eyes so frank, that one understood that this was only an indication of his ancestry, with no actual bearing upon his character. In age and in reputation, he was on the same level as his English companion, but his life and his work had both been far more arduous. Twelve years before, he had come as a poor student to Rome, and had lived ever since upon some small endowment for research which had been awarded to him by the University of Bonn. Painfully, slowly, and doggedly, with extraordinary tenacity and single-mindedness, he had climbed from rung to rung of the ladder of fame, until now he was a member of the Berlin Academy, and there was every reason to believe that he would shortly be promoted to the Chair of the greatest of German Universities. But the singleness of purpose which had brought him to the same high level as the rich and brilliant Englishman, had caused him in everything outside their work to stand infinitely below him. He had never found a pause in his studies in which to cultivate the social graces. It was only when he spoke of his own subject that his face was filled with life and soul. At other times he was silent and embarrassed, too conscious of his own limitations in larger subjects, and impatient of that small talk which is the conventional refuge of those who have no thoughts to express.

And yet for some years there had been an acquaintanceship which appeared to be slowly ripening into a friendship between these two very different rivals. The base and origin of this lay in the fact that in their own studies each was the only one of the younger men who had knowledge and enthusiasm enough to properly appreciate the other. Their common interests and pursuits had brought them together, and each had been attracted by the other's knowledge. And then gradually something had been added to this. Kennedy had been amused by the frankness and simplicity of his rival, while Burger in turn had been fascinated by the brilliancy and vivacity which had made Kennedy such a favourite in Roman society. I say 'had', because just at the moment the young Englishman was somewhat under a cloud. A love-affair, the details of which had never quite come out, had indicated a heartlessness and callousness upon his part which shocked many of his friends. But in the bachelor circles of students and artists in which he preferred to move there is no very rigid code of honour in such matters, and though a head might be shaken or a pair of shoulders shrugged over the flight of two and the return of one, the general sentiment was probably one of curiosity and perhaps of envy rather than of reprobation.

'Look here, Burger,' said Kennedy, looking hard at the placid face of his companion, 'I do wish that you would confide in me.'

As he spoke he waved his hand in the direction of a rug which lay upon the floor. On the rug stood a long, shallow fruit-basket of the light wicker-work which is used in the Campagna, and this was heaped with a litter of objects, inscribed tiles, broken inscriptions, cracked mosaics, torn papyri, rusty metal ornaments, which to the uninitiated might have seemed to have come straight from a dustman's bin, but which a specialist would have speedily recognised as unique of their kind. The pile of odds and ends in the flat wicker-work basket supplied exactly one of those missing links of social development which are of such interest to the student. It was the German who had brought them in, and the Englishman's eyes were hungry as he looked at them.

'I won't interfere with your treasure-trove, but I should very much like to hear about it,' he continued, while Burger very deliberately lit a cigar. 'It is evidently a discovery of the first importance. These inscriptions will make a sensation throughout Europe.'

'For every one here there are a million there!' said the German. 'There are so many that a dozen savants might spend a lifetime over them, and build up a reputation as solid as the Castle of St Angelo.'

Kennedy sat thinking with his fine forehead wrinkled and his fingers playing with his long, fair moustache.

'You have given yourself away, Burger!' said he at last. 'Your words can only apply to one thing. You have discovered a new catacomb.'

'I had no doubt that you had already come to that conclusion from an examination of these objects.'

'Well, they certainly appeared to indicate it, but your last remarks make it certain. There is no place except a catacomb which could contain so vast a store of relics as you describe.'

'Quite so. There is no mystery about that. I *have* discovered a new catacomb.'

'Where?'

'Ah, that is my secret, my dear Kennedy. Suffice it that it is so situated that there is not one chance in a million of anyone else coming upon it. Its date is different from that of any known catacomb, and it has been reserved for the burial of the highest Christians, so that the remains and the relics are quite different from anything which has ever been seen before. If I was not aware of your knowledge and of your energy, my friend, I would not hesitate, under the pledge of secrecy, to tell you everything about it. But as it is I think that I must certainly prepare my own report of the matter before I expose myself to such formidable competition.'

Kennedy loved his subject with a love which was almost a mania – a love which held him true to it, amidst all the distractions which come to a wealthy and dissipated young man. He had ambition, but his ambition was secondary to his mere abstract joy and interest in everything which concerned the old life and history of the city. He yearned to see this new underworld which his companion had discovered.

'Look here, Burger,' said he, earnestly, 'I assure you that you can trust me most implicitly in the matter. Nothing would induce me to put pen to paper about anything which I see until I have your express permission. I quite understand your feeling and I think it is most natural, but you have really nothing whatever to fear from me. On the other hand, if you don't tell me I shall make a systematic search, and I shall most certainly discover it. In that case, of course, I should make what use I liked of it, since I should be under no obligation to you.'

Burger smiled thoughtfully over his cigar.

'I have noticed, friend Kennedy,' said he, 'that when I want information over any point you are not always so ready to supply it.'

'When did you ever ask me anything that I did not tell you? You remember, for example, my giving you the material for your paper about the temple of the Vestals.'

'Ah, well, that was not a matter of much importance. If I were to question you upon some intimate thing would you give me an answer, I wonder! This new catacomb is a very intimate thing to me, and I should certainly expect some sign of confidence in return.'

'What you are driving at I cannot imagine,' said the Englishman, 'but if you mean that you will answer my question about the catacomb if I answer any question which you may put to me I can assure you that I will certainly do so.'

'Well, then,' said Burger, leaning luxuriously back in his settee, and puffing a blue tree of cigar-smoke into the air, 'tell me all about your relations with Miss Mary Saunderson.'

Kennedy sprang up in his chair and glared angrily at his impassive companion.

'What the devil do you mean?' he cried. 'What sort of a question is this? You may mean it as a joke, but you never made a worse one.'

'No, I don't mean it as a joke,' said Burger, simply. 'I am really rather interested in the details of the matter. I don't know much about the world and women and social life and that sort of thing, and such an incident has the fascination of the unknown for me. I know you, and I knew her by sight – I had even spoken to her once or twice. I should very much like to hear from your own lips exactly what it was which occurred between you.'

'I won't tell you a word.'

'That's all right. It was only my whim to see if you would give up a secret as easily as you expected me to give up my secret of the new catacomb. You wouldn't, and I didn't expect you to. But why should you expect otherwise of me? There's Saint John's clock striking ten. It is quite time that I was going home.'

'No; wait a bit, Burger,' said Kennedy; 'this is really a ridiculous caprice of yours to wish to know about an old love-affair which has burned out months ago. You know we look upon a man who kisses and tells as the greatest coward and villain possible.'

'Certainly,' said the German, gathering up his basket of curiosities, 'when he tells anything about a girl which is previously unknown he must be so. But in this case, as you must be aware, it was a public matter which was the common talk of Rome, so that you are not really doing Miss Mary Saunderson any injury by discussing her case with me. But still, I respect your scruples, and so good night!'

'Wait a bit, Burger,' said Kennedy, laying his hand upon the other's arm; 'I am very keen upon this catacomb business, and I can't let it drop quite so easily. Would you mind asking me something else in return – something not quite so eccentric this time?'

'No, no; you have refused, and there is an end of it,' said Burger, with his basket on his arm. 'No doubt you are quite right not to answer, and no doubt I am quite right also – and so again, my dear Kennedy, good night!'

The Englishman watched Burger cross the room, and he had his hand on the handle of the door before his host sprang up with the air of a man who is making the best of that which cannot be helped.

'Hold on, old fellow,' said he; 'I think you are behaving in a most ridiculous fashion; but still, if this is your condition, I suppose that I must submit to it. I hate saying anything about a girl, but, as you say, it is all over Rome, and I don't suppose I can tell you anything which you do not know already. What was it you wanted to know?'

The German came back to the stove, and, laying down his basket, he sank into his chair once more.

'May I have another cigar?' said he. 'Thank you very much! I never smoke when I work, but I enjoy a chat much more when I am under the influence of tobacco. Now, as regards this young lady, with whom you had this little adventure. What in the world has become of her?'

'She is at home with her own people.'

'Oh, really – in England?'

'Yes.'

'What part of England – London?'

'No, Twickenham.'

'You must excuse my curiosity, my dear Kennedy, and you must put it down to my ignorance of the world. No doubt it is quite a simple thing to persuade a young lady to go off with you for three weeks or so, and then to hand her over to her own family at – what did you call the place?'

'Twickenham.'

'Quite so – at Twickenham. But it is something so entirely outside my own experience that I cannot even imagine how you set about it. For example, if you had loved this girl your love could hardly disappear in three weeks, so I presume that you could not have loved her at all. But if you did not love her why should you make this great scandal which has damaged you and ruined her?'

Kennedy looked moodily into the red eye of the stove.

'That's a logical way of looking at it, certainly,' said he. 'Love is a big word, and it represents a good many different shades of feeling. I liked her, and – well, you say you've seen her – you know how charming she could look. But still I am willing to admit, looking back, that I could never have really loved her.'

'Then, my dear Kennedy, why did you do it?'

'The adventure of the thing had a great deal to do with it.'

'What! You are so fond of adventures!'

'Where would the variety of life be without them? It was for an adventure that I first began to pay my attentions to her. I've chased a good deal of game in my time, but there's no chase like that of a pretty woman. There was the piquant difficulty of it also, for, as she was the companion of Lady Emily Rood, it was almost impossible to see her alone. On the top of all the other obstacles which attracted me, I learned from her own lips very early in the proceedings that she was engaged.'

'Mein Gott! To whom?'

'She mentioned no names.'

'I do not think that anyone knows that. So that made the adventure more alluring, did it?'

'Well, it did certainly give a spice to it. Don't you think so?'

'I tell you that I am very ignorant about these things.'

'My dear fellow, you can remember that the apple you stole from your neighbour's tree was always sweeter than that which fell from your own. And then I found that she cared for me.'

'What – at once?'

'Oh, no, it took about three months of sapping and mining. But at last I won her over. She understood that my judicial separation from my wife made it impossible for me to do the right thing by her – but she came all the same, and we had a delightful time, as long as it lasted.'

'But how about the other man?'

Kennedy shrugged his shoulders.

'I suppose it is the survival of the fittest,' said he. 'If he had been the better man she would not have deserted him. Let's drop the subject, for I have had enough of it!'

'Only one other thing. How did you get rid of her in three weeks?'

'Well, we had both cooled down a bit, you understand. She absolutely refused, under any circumstances, to come back to face the people she had known in Rome. Now, of course, Rome is necessary to me, and I was already pining to be back at my work – so there was one obvious cause of separation. Then, again, her old father turned up at the hotel in London, and there was a scene, and the whole thing became so unpleasant that really – though I missed her dreadfully at first – I was very glad to slip out of it. Now, I rely upon you not to repeat anything of what I have said.'

'My dear Kennedy, I should not dream of repeating it. But all that you say interests me very much, for it gives me an insight into your way of looking at things, which is entirely different from mine, for I have seen so little of life. And now you want to know about my new catacomb. There's no use my trying to describe it, for you would never find it by that. There is only one thing, and that is for me to take you there.'

'That would be splendid.'

'When would you like to come?'

'The sooner the better. I am all impatience to see it.'

'Well, it is a beautiful night – though a trifle cold. Suppose we start in an hour. We must be very careful to keep the matter to ourselves. If anyone saw us hunting in couples they would suspect that there was something going on.'

'We can't be too cautious,' said Kennedy. 'Is it far?'

'Some miles.'

'Not too far to walk?'

'Oh no, we could walk there easily.'

'We had better do so, then. A cabman's suspicions would be aroused if he dropped us both at some lonely spot in the dead of the night.'

'Quite so. I think it would be best for us to meet at the Gate of the Appian Way at midnight. I must go back to my lodgings for the matches and candles and things.'

'All right, Burger! I think it is very kind of you to let me into this secret, and I promise you that I will write nothing about it until you have published your report. Good-bye for the present! You will find me at the Gate at twelve.'

The cold, clear air was filled with the musical chimes from that city of clocks as Burger, wrapped in an Italian overcoat, with a lantern hanging from his hand, walked up to the rendezvous. Kennedy stepped out of the shadow to meet him.

'You are ardent in work as well as in love!' said the German, laughing.

'Yes; I have been waiting here for nearly half an hour.'

'I hope you left no clue as to where we were going.'

'Not such a fool! By Jove, I am chilled to the bone! Come on, Burger, let us warm ourselves by a spurt of hard walking.'

Their footsteps sounded loud and crisp upon the rough stone paving of the disappointing road which is all that is left of the most famous highway of the world. A peasant or two going home from the wine-shop, and a few carts of country produce coming up to Rome, were the only things which they met. They swung along, with the huge tombs looming up through the darkness upon each side of them, until they had come as far as the Catacombs of St Calixtus, and saw against a rising moon the great circular bastion of Cecilia Metella in front of them. Then Burger stopped with his hand to his side.

'Your legs are longer than mine, and you are more accustomed to walking,' said he, laughing. 'I think that the place where we turn off is somewhere here. Yes, this is it, round the corner of the trattoria. Now, it is a very narrow path, so perhaps I had better go in front and you can follow.'

He had lit his lantern, and by its light they were enabled to follow a narrow and devious track which wound across the marshes of the Campagna. The great Aqueduct of old Rome lay like a monstrous caterpillar across the moonlit landscape, and their road led them under one of its huge arches, and past the circle of crumbling bricks which marks the old arena. At last Burger stopped at a solitary wooden cow-house, and he drew a key from his pocket.

'Surely your catacomb is not inside a house!' cried Kennedy.

'The entrance to it is. That is just the safeguard which we have against anyone else discovering it.'

'Does the proprietor know of it?'

'Not he. He had found one or two objects which made me almost certain that his house was built on the entrance to such a place. So I rented it from him, and did my excavations for myself. Come in, and shut the door behind you.'

It was a long, empty building, with the mangers of the cows along one wall. Burger put his lantern down on the ground, and shaded its light in all directions save one by draping his overcoat round it.

'It might excite remark if anyone saw a light in this lonely place,' said he. 'Just help me to move this boarding.'

The flooring was loose in the corner, and plank by plank the two savants raised it and leaned it against the wall. Below there was a square aperture and a stair of old stone steps which led away down into the bowels of the earth.

'Be careful!' cried Burger, as Kennedy, in his impatience, hurried down them. 'It is a perfect rabbits'-warren below, and if you were once to lose your way there the chances would be a hundred to one against your ever coming out again. Wait until I bring the light.'

'How do you find your own way if it is so complicated?'

'I had some very narrow escapes at first, but I have gradually learned to go about. There is a certain system to it, but it is one which a lost man, if he were in the dark, could not possibly find out. Even now I always spin out a ball of string behind me when I am going far into the catacomb. You can see for yourself that it is difficult, but every one of these passages divides and subdivides a dozen times before you go a hundred yards.'

They had descended some twenty feet from the level of the byre, and they were standing now in a square chamber cut out of the soft tufa. The lantern cast a flickering light, bright below and dim above, over the cracked brown walls. In every direction were the black openings of passages which radiated from this common centre.

'I want you to follow me closely, my friend,' said Burger. 'Do not loiter to look at anything upon the way, for the place to which I will take you contains all that you can see, and more. It will save time for us to go there direct.'

He led the way down one of the corridors, and the Englishman followed closely at his heels. Every now and then the passage bifurcated, but Burger was evidently following some secret marks of his own, for he neither stopped nor hesitated. Everywhere along the walls, packed like the berths upon an emigrant ship, lay the Christians of old Rome. The yellow light flickered over the shrivelled features of the mummies, and gleamed upon rounded skulls and long, white armbones crossed over fleshless chests. And everywhere as he passed Kennedy looked with wistful eyes upon inscriptions, funeral vessels, pictures, vestments, utensils, all lying as pious hands had placed them so many centuries ago. It was apparent to him, even in those hurried, passing glances, that this was the earliest and finest of the catacombs, containing such a storehouse of Roman remains as had never before come at one time under the observation of the student.

'What would happen if the light went out?' he asked, as they hurried onwards.

'I have a spare candle and a box of matches in my pocket. By the way, Kennedy, have you any matches?'

'No; you had better give me some.'

'Oh, that is all right. There is no chance of our separating.'

'How far are we going? It seems to me that we have walked at least a quarter of a mile.'

'More than that, I think. There is really no limit to the tombs – at least, I have never been able to find any. This is a very difficult place, so I think that I will use our ball of string.'

He fastened one end of it to a projecting stone and he carried the coil in the breast of his coat, paying it out as he advanced. Kennedy saw that it was no unnecessary precaution, for the passages had become more complex and tortuous than ever, with a perfect network of intersecting corridors. But these all ended in one large circular hall with a square pedestal of tufa topped with a slab of marble at one end of it.

'By Jove!' cried Kennedy in an ecstasy, as Burger swung his lantern over the marble. 'It is a Christian altar – probably the first one in existence. Here is the little consecration cross cut upon the corner of it. No doubt this circular space was used as a church.'

'Precisely,' said Burger. 'If I had more time I should like to show you all the bodies which are buried in these niches upon the walls, for they are the early popes and bishops of the Church, with their mitres, their croziers, and full canonicals. Go over to that one and look at it!'

Kennedy went across, and stared at the ghastly head which lay loosely on the shredded and mouldering mitre.

'This is most interesting,' said he, and his voice seemed to boom against the concave vault. 'As far as my experience goes, it is unique. Bring the lantern over, Burger, for I want to see them all.'

But the German had strolled away, and was standing in the middle of a yellow circle of light at the other side of the hall.

'Do you know how many wrong turnings there are between this and the stairs?' he asked. 'There are over two thousand. No doubt it was one of the means of protection which the Christians adopted. The odds are two thousand to one against a man getting out, even if he had a light; but if he were in the dark it would, of course, be far more difficult.'

'So I should think.'

'And the darkness is something dreadful. I tried it once for an experiment. Let us try it again!' He stooped to the lantern, and in an instant it was as if an invisible hand was squeezed tightly over each of Kennedy's eyes. Never had he known what such darkness was. It seemed to press upon him and to smother him. It was a solid obstacle against which the body shrank from advancing. He put his hands out to push it back from him.

'That will do, Burger,' said he, 'let's have the light again.'

But his companion began to laugh, and in that circular room the sound seemed to come from every side at once.

'You seem uneasy, friend Kennedy,' said he.

'Go on, man, light the candle!' said Kennedy impatiently.

'It's very strange. Kennedy, but I could not in the least tell by the sound in which direction you stand. Could you tell where I am?'

'No; you seem to be on every side of me.'

'If it were not for this string which I hold in my hand I should not have a notion which way to go.'

'I dare say not. Strike a light, man, and have an end of this nonsense.'

'Well, Kennedy, there are two things which I understand that you are very fond of. The one is an adventure, and the other is an obstacle to surmount. The adventure must be the finding of your way out of this catacomb. The obstacle will be the darkness and the two thousand wrong turns which make the way a little difficult to find. But you need not hurry, for you have plenty of time, and when you halt for a rest now and then, I should like you just to think of Miss Mary Saunderson, and whether you treated her quite fairly.'

'You devil, what do you mean?' roared Kennedy. He was running about in little circles and clasping at the solid blackness with both hands.

'Good-bye,' said the mocking voice, and it was already at some distance. 'I really do not think, Kennedy, even by your own showing that you did the right thing by that girl. There was only one little thing which you appeared not to know, and I can supply it. Miss Saunderson was engaged to a poor ungainly devil of a student, and his name was Julius Burger.'

There was a rustle somewhere, the vague sound of a foot striking a stone, and then there fell silence upon that old Christian church – a stagnant, heavy silence which closed round Kennedy and shut him in like water round a drowning man.

* * *

Some two months afterwards the following paragraph made the round of the European Press:—

'One of the most interesting discoveries of recent years is that of the new catacomb in Rome, which lies some distance to the east of the well-known vaults of St Calixtus. The finding of this important burial-place, which is exceeding rich in most interesting early Christian remains, is due to the energy and sagacity of Dr Julius Burger, the young German specialist, who is rapidly taking the first place as an authority upon ancient Rome. Although the first to publish his discovery, it appears that a less fortunate adventurer had anticipated Dr Burger. Some months ago, Mr Kennedy, the well-known English student, disappeared suddenly from his rooms in the Corso, and it was conjectured that his association with a recent scandal had driven him to leave Rome. It appears now that he had in reality fallen a victim to that fervid love of archaeology which had raised him to a distinguished place among living scholars. His body was discovered in the heart of the new catacomb, and it was evident from the condition of his feet and boots that he had tramped for days through the tortuous corridors which make these subterranean tombs so dangerous to explorers. The deceased gentleman had, with inexplicable rashness, made his way into this labyrinth without, as far as can be discovered, taking with him either candles or matches, so that his sad fate was the natural result of his own temerity. What makes the matter more painful is that Dr Julius Burger was an intimate friend of the deceased. His joy at the extraordinary find which he has been so fortunate as to make has been greatly marred by the terrible fate of his comrade and fellow-worker.'

G. K. Chesterton

The Hammer of God

The little village of Bohun Beacon was perched on a hill so steep that the tall spire of its church seemed only like the peak of a small mountain. At the foot of the church stood a smithy, generally red with fires and always littered with hammers and scraps of iron; opposite to this, over a rude cross of cobbled paths, was 'The Blue Boar', the only inn of the place. It was upon this crossway, in the lifting of a leaden and silver daybreak, that two brothers met in the street and spoke; though one was beginning the day and the other finishing it. The Rev. and Hon. Wilfred Bohun was very devout, and was making his way to some austere exercises of prayer or contemplation at dawn. Colonel the Hon. Norman Bohun, his elder brother, was by no means devout, and was sitting in evening dress on the bench outside 'The Blue Boar', drinking what the philosophic observer was free to regard either as his last glass on Tuesday or his first on Wednesday. The colonel was not particular.

The Bohuns were one of the very few aristocratic families really dating from the Middle Ages, and their pennon had actually seen Palestine. But it is a great mistake to suppose that such houses stand high in chivalric tradition. Few except the poor preserve traditions. Aristocrats live not in traditions but in fashions. The Bohuns had been Mohocks under Queen Anne and Mashers under Queen Victoria. But like more than one of the really ancient houses, they had rotted in the last two centuries into mere drunkards and dandy degenerates, till there had even come a whisper of insanity. Certainly there was something hardly human about the colonel's wolfish pursuit of pleasure, and his chronic resolution not to go home till morning had a touch of the hideous clarity of insomnia. He was a tall, fine animal, elderly, but with hair still startlingly yellow. He would have looked merely blond and leonine, but his blue eyes were sunk so deep in his face that they looked black. They were a little too close together. He had very long yellow moustaches; on each side of them a fold or furrow from nostril to jaw, so that a sneer seemed cut into his face. Over his evening clothes he wore a curious pale yellow coat that looked more like a very light dressing-gown than an overcoat, and on the back of his head was stuck an extraordinary broad-brimmed hat of a bright green colour, evidently some oriental curiosity caught up at random. He was proud of appearing in such incongruous attires – proud of the fact that he always made them look congruous.

His brother the curate had also the yellow hair and the elegance, but he was buttoned up to the chin in black, and his face was clean-shaven, cultivated, and a little nervous. He seemed to live for nothing but his religion; but there were some who said (notably the blacksmith, who was a Presbyterian) that it was a love of Gothic architecture rather than of God, and that his haunting of the church like a ghost was only another and purer turn of the almost morbid thirst for beauty which sent his brother raging after women and wine. This charge was doubtful, while the man's practical piety was indubitable. Indeed, the charge was mostly an ignorant misunderstanding of the love of solitude and secret prayer, and was founded on his being often found kneeling, not before the altar, but in peculiar places, in the crypts or gallery, or even in the belfry. He was at the moment about to enter the church through the yard of the smithy, but stopped and frowned a little as he saw his brother's cavernous eyes staring in the same direction. On the hypothesis that the colonel was interested in the church he did not waste any speculations. There only remained the blacksmith's shop, and though the blacksmith was a Puritan and none of his people, Wilfred Bohun had heard some scandals about a beautiful and rather celebrated wife. He flung a suspicious look across the shed, and the colonel stood up laughing to speak to him.

'Good morning, Wilfred,' he said. 'Like a good landlord I am watching sleeplessly over my people. I am going to call on the blacksmith.'

Wilfred looked at the ground, and said: 'The blacksmith is out. He is over at Greenford.'

'I know,' answered the other with silent laughter; 'that is why I am calling on him.'

'Norman,' said the cleric, with his eye on a pebble in the road, 'are you ever afraid of thunderbolts?'

'What do you mean?' asked the colonel. 'Is your hobby meteorology?'

'I mean,' said Wilfred, without looking up, 'do you ever think that God might strike you in the street?'

'I beg your pardon,' said the colonel; 'I see your hobby is folk-lore.'

'I know your hobby is blasphemy,' retorted the religious man, stung in the one live place of his nature. 'But if you do not fear God, you have good reason to fear man.'

The elder raised his eyebrows politely. 'Fear man?' he said.

'Barnes the blacksmith is the biggest and strongest man for forty miles round,' said the clergyman sternly. 'I know you are no coward or weakling, but he could throw you over the wall.'

This struck home, being true, and the lowering line by mouth and nostril darkened and deepened. For a moment he stood with the heavy sneer on his face. But in an instant Colonel Bohun had recovered his own cruel good humour and laughed, showing two dog-like front teeth under his yellow moustache. 'In that case, my dear Wilfred,' he said quite carelessly, 'it was wise for the last of the Bohuns to come out partially in armour.'

And he took off the queer round hat covered with green, showing that it was lined within with steel. Wilfred recognised it indeed as a light Japanese or Chinese helmet torn down from a trophy that hung in the old family hall. 'It was the first hat to hand,' explained his brother airily; 'always the nearest hat – and the nearest woman.'

'The blacksmith is away at Greenford,' said Wilfred quietly; 'the time of his return is unsettled.'

And with that he turned and went into the church with bowed head, crossing himself like one who wishes to be quit of an unclean spirit. He was anxious to forget such grossness in the cool twilight of his tall Gothic cloisters; but on that morning it was fated that his still round of religious exercises should be everywhere arrested by small shocks. As he entered the church, hitherto always empty at that hour, a kneeling figure rose hastily to its feet and came towards the full daylight of the doorway. When the curate saw it he stood still with surprise. For the early worshipper was none other than the village idiot, a nephew of the blacksmith, one who neither would nor could care for the church or for anything else. He was always called, 'Mad Joe', and seemed to have no other name; he was a dark, strong, slouching lad, with a heavy white face, dark straight hair, and a mouth always open. As he passed the priest, his moon-calf countenance gave no hint of what he had been doing or thinking of. He had never been known to pray before. What sort of prayers was he saying now? Extraordinary prayers surely.

Wilfred Bohun stood rooted to the spot long enough to see the idiot go out into the sunshine, and even to see his dissolute brother hail him with a sort of avuncular jocularity. The last thing he saw was the colonel throwing pennies at the open mouth of Joe, with the serious appearance of trying to hit it.

This ugly sunlight picture of the stupidity and cruelty of the earth sent the ascetic finally to his prayers for purification and new thoughts.

He went up to a pew in the gallery, which brought him under a coloured window which he loved and always quieted his spirit; a blue window with an angel carrying lilies. There he began to think less about the half-wit, with his livid face and mouth like a fish. He began to think less of his evil brother, pacing like a lean lion, in his terrible hunger. He sank deeper and deeper into those cold and sweet colours of silver blossoms and sapphire sky.

In this place half an hour afterwards he was found by Gibbs, the village cobbler, who had been sent for him in some haste. He got to his feet with promptitude, for he knew that no small matter would have brought Gibbs into such a place at all. The cobbler was, as in many villages, an atheist, and his appearance in church was a shade more extraordinary than Mad Joe's. It was a morning of theological enigmas.

'What is it?' asked Wilfred Bohun rather stiffly, but putting out a trembling hand for his hat.

The atheist spoke in a tone that, coming from him, was quite startlingly respectful, and even, as it were, huskily sympathetic.

'You must excuse me, sir,' he said in a hoarse whisper, 'but we didn't think it right not to let you know at once. I'm afraid a rather dreadful thing has happened, sir. I'm afraid your brother—'

Wilfred clenched his frail hands. 'What devilry has he done now?' he cried in involuntary passion.

'Why, sir,' said the cobbler, coughing, 'I'm afraid he's done nothing, and won't do anything. I'm afraid he's done for. You had really better come down, sir.'

The curate followed the cobbler down a short winding stair, which brought them out at an entrance rather higher than the street. Bohun saw the tragedy in one glance, flat underneath him like a plan. In the yard of the smithy were standing five or six men mostly in black, one in an inspector's uniform. They included the doctor, the Presbyterian minister, and the priest from the Roman Catholic chapel, to which the blacksmith's wife belonged. The latter was speaking to her, indeed, very rapidly, in an undertone, as she, a magnificent woman with red-gold hair, was sobbing blindly on a bench. Between these two groups, and just clear of the main heap of hammers, lay a man in evening dress, spread-eagled and flat on his face. From the height above Wilfred could have sworn to every item of his costume and appearance, down to the Bohun rings upon his fingers; but the skull was only a hideous splash, like a star of blackness and blood.

Wilfred Bohun gave but one glance, and ran down the steps into the yard. The doctor, who was the family physician, saluted him, but he scarcely took any notice. He could only stammer out: 'My brother is dead. What does it mean? What is this horrible mystery?' There was an unhappy silence; and then the cobbler, the most outspoken man present, answered: 'Plenty of horror, sir,' he said, 'but not much mystery.'

'What do you mean?' asked Wilfred, with a white face.

'It's plain enough,' answered Gibbs. 'There is only one man for forty miles round that could have struck such a blow as that, and he's the man that had most reason to.'

'We must not prejudge anything,' put in the doctor, a tall, black-bearded man, rather nervously; 'but it is competent for me to corroborate what Mr Gibbs says about the nature of the blow, sir; it is an incredible blow. Mr Gibbs says that only one man in this district could have done it. I should have said myself that nobody could have done it.'

A shudder of superstition went through the slight figure of the curate. 'I can hardly understand,' he said.

'Mr Bohun,' said the doctor in a low voice, 'metaphors literally fail me. It is inadequate to say that the skull was smashed to bits like an egg-shell. Fragments of bone were driven into the body and the ground like bullets into a mud wall. It was the hand of a giant.'

He was silent a moment, looking grimly through his glasses; then he added: 'The thing has one advantage – that it clears most people of suspicion at one stroke. If you or I or any normally made man in the country were accused of this crime, we should be acquitted as an infant would be acquitted of stealing the Nelson Column.'

'That's what I say,' repeated the cobbler obstinately; 'there's only one man that could have done it, and he's the man that would have done it. Where's Simeon Barnes, the blacksmith?'

'He's over at Greenford,' faltered the curate.

'More likely over in France,' muttered the cobbler.

'No; he is in neither of those places,' said a small and colourless voice, which came from the little Roman priest who had joined the group. 'As a matter of fact, he is coming up the road at this moment.'

The little priest was not an interesting man to look at, having stubbly brown hair and a round and stolid face. But if he had been as splendid as Apollo no one would have looked at him at that moment. Everyone turned round and peered at the pathway which wound across the plain below, along which was indeed walking, at his own huge stride and with a hammer on his shoulder, Simeon the smith. He was a bony and gigantic man, with deep, dark, sinister eyes and a dark chin beard. He was walking and talking quietly with two other men; and though he was never specially cheerful, he seemed quite at his ease.

'My God!' cried the atheistic cobbler, 'and there's the hammer he did it with.'

'No,' said the inspector, a sensible-looking man with a sandy moustache, speaking for the first time. 'There's the hammer he did it with over there by the church wall. We have left it and the body exactly as they are.'

All glanced round, and the short priest went across and looked down in silence at the tool where it lay. It was one of the smallest and the lightest of the hammers, and would not have caught the eye among the rest; but on the iron edge of it were blood and yellow hair.

After a silence the short priest spoke without looking up, and there was a new note in his dull voice. 'Mr Gibbs was hardly right,' he said, 'in saying that there is no mystery. There is at least the mystery of why so big a man should attempt so big a blow with so little a hammer.'

'Oh, never mind that,' cried Gibbs, in a fever. 'What are we to do with Simeon Barnes?'

'Leave him alone,' said the priest quietly. 'He is coming here of himself. I know those two men with him. They are very good fellows from Greenford, and they have come over about the Presbyterian chapel.'

Even as he spoke the tall smith swung round the corner of the church, and strode into his own yard. Then he stood there quite still, and the hammer fell from his hand. The inspector, who had preserved impenetrable propriety, immediately went up to him.

'I won't ask you, Mr Barnes,' he said, 'whether you know anything about what has happened here. You are not bound to say. I hope you don't know, and that you will be able to prove it. But I must go through the form of arresting you in the King's name for the murder of Colonel Norman Bohun.'

'You are not bound to say anything,' said the cobbler in officious excitement. 'They've got to prove everything. They haven't proved yet that it is Colonel Bohun, with the head all smashed up like that.'

'That won't wash,' said the doctor aside to the priest. 'That's out of the detective stories. I was the colonel's medical man, and I knew his body better than he did. He had very fine hands, but quite peculiar ones. The second and third fingers were the same in length. Oh, that's the colonel right enough.'

As he glanced at the brained corpse upon the ground the iron eyes of the motionless blacksmith followed them, and rested there also.

'Is Colonel Bohun dead?' said the smith quite calmly. 'Then he's damned.'

'Don't say anything! Oh, don't say anything,' cried the atheist cobbler, dancing about in an ecstasy of admiration of the English legal system. For no man is such a legalist as the good Secularist.

The blacksmith turned on him over his shoulder the august face of a fanatic.

'It's well for you infidels to dodge like foxes because the world's law favours you,' he said; 'but God guards His own in His pocket, as you shall see this day.'

Then he pointed to the colonel and said: 'When did this dog die in his sins?'

'Moderate your language,' said the doctor.

'Moderate the Bible's language, and I'll moderate mine. When did he die?'

'I saw him alive at six o'clock this morning,' stammered Wilfred Bohun.

'God is good,' said the smith. 'Mr Inspector, I have not the slightest objection to being arrested. It is you who may object to arresting me. I don't mind leaving the court without a stain on my character. You do mind, perhaps, leaving the court with a bad set-back in your career.'

The solid inspector for the first time looked at the blacksmith with a lively eye; as did everybody else, except the short, strange priest, who was still looking down at the little hammer that had dealt the dreadful blow.

'There are two men standing outside this shop,' went on the blacksmith with ponderous lucidity, 'good tradesmen in Greenford whom you all know, who will swear that they saw me from before midnight till daybreak and long after in the committee-room of our Revival Mission, which sits all night, we save souls so fast. In Greenford itself twenty people could swear to me for all that time. If I were a heathen, Mr Inspector, I would let you walk on to your downfall. But as a Christian man I feel bound to give you your chance, and ask you whether you will hear my alibi now or in court.'

The inspector seemed for the first time disturbed, and said, 'Of course I should be glad to clear you altogether now.'

The smith walked out of his yard with the same long and easy stride, and returned to his two friends from Greenford, who were indeed friends of nearly everyone present. Each of them said a few words which no one ever thought of disbelieving. When they had spoken, the innocence of Simeon stood up as solid as the great church above them.

One of those silences struck the group which are more strange and insufferable than any speech. Madly, in order to make conversation, the curate said to the Catholic priest:

'You seem very much interested in that hammer, Father Brown.'

'Yes, I am,' said Father Brown; 'why is it such a small hammer?'

The doctor swung round on him.

'By George, that's true,' he cried; 'who would use a little hammer with ten larger hammers lying about?'

Then he lowered his voice in the curate's ear and said: 'Only the kind of person that can't lift a large hammer. It is not a question of force or courage between the sexes. It's a question of lifting power in the shoulders. A bold woman could commit ten murders with a light hammer and never turn a hair. She could not kill a beetle with a heavy one.'

Wilfred Bohun was staring at him with a sort of hypnotised horror, while Father Brown listened with his head a little on one side, really interested and attentive. The doctor went on with more hissing emphasis:

'Why do these idiots always assume that the only person who hates the wife's lover is the wife's husband? Nine times out of ten the person who most hates the wife's lover is the wife. Who knows what insolence or treachery he had shown her – look there?'

He made a momentary gesture towards the red-haired woman on the bench. She had lifted her head at last and the tears were drying on her splendid face. But the eyes were fixed on the corpse with an electric glare that had in it something of idiocy.

The Rev. Wilfred Bohun made a limp gesture as if waving away all desire to know; but Father Brown, dusting off his sleeve some ashes blown from the furnace, spoke in his indifferent way.

'You are like so many doctors,' he said; 'your mental science is really suggestive. It is your physical science that is utterly impossible. I agreed that the woman wants to kill the co-respondent much more than the petitioner does. And I agree that a woman will always pick up a small hammer instead of a big one. But the difficulty is one of physical impossibility. No woman ever born could have smashed a man's skull out flat like that.' Then he added reflectively, after a pause: 'These people haven't grasped the whole of it. The man was actually wearing an iron helmet, and the blow scattered it like broken glass. Look at that woman. Look at her arms.'

Silence held them all up again, and then the doctor said rather sulkily: 'Well, I may be wrong; there are objections to everything. But I stick to the main point. No man but an idiot would pick up that little hammer if he could use a big hammer.'

With that the lean and quivering hands of Wilfred Bohun went up to his head and seemed to clutch his scanty yellow hair. After an instant they dropped, and he cried: 'That was the word I wanted; you have said the word.'

Then he continued, mastering his discomposure: 'The words you said were, "No man but an idiot would pick up the small hammer".'

'Yes,' said the doctor. 'Well?'

'Well,' said the curate, 'no man but an idiot did.' The rest stared at him with eyes arrested and riveted, and he went on in a febrile and feminine agitation.

'I am a priest,' he cried unsteadily, 'and a priest should be no shedder of blood. I – I mean that he should bring no one to the gallows. And I thank God that I see the criminal clearly now – because he is a criminal who cannot be brought to the gallows.'

'You will not denounce him?' enquired the doctor.

'He would not be hanged if I did denounce him,' answered Wilfred with a wild but curiously happy smile. 'When I went into the church this morning I found a madman praying there – that poor Joe, who has been wrong all his life. God knows what he prayed; but with such strange folk it is not incredible to suppose that their prayers are all upside down. Very likely a lunatic would pray before killing a man. When I last saw poor Joe he was with my brother. My brother was mocking him.'

'By Jove!' cried the doctor, 'this is talking at last. But how do you explain—'

The Rev. Wilfred was almost trembling with the excitement of his own glimpse of the truth. 'Don't you see; don't you see,' he cried feverishly; 'that is the only theory that covers both the queer things, that answers both the riddles. The two riddles are the little hammer and the big blow. The smith might have struck the big blow, but would not have chosen the little hammer. His wife would have chosen the little hammer, but she could not have struck the big blow. But the madman might have done both. As for the little hammer – why, he was mad and might have picked up anything. And for the big blow, have you never heard, doctor, that a maniac in his paroxysm may have the strength of ten men?'

The doctor drew a deep breath and then said, 'By golly, I believe you've got it.'

Father Brown had fixed his eyes on the speaker so long and steadily as to prove that his large grey, ox-like eyes were not quite so insignificant as the rest of his face. When silence had fallen he said with marked respect: 'Mr Bohun, yours is the only theory yet propounded which holds water every way and is essentially unassailable, I think, therefore, that you deserve to be told, on my positive knowledge, that it is not the true one.' And with that the old little man walked away and stared again at the hammer.

'That fellow seems to know more than he ought to,' whispered the doctor peevishly to Wilfred. 'Those popish priests are deucedly sly.'

'No, no,' said Bohun, with a sort of wild fatigue. 'It was the lunatic. It was the lunatic.'

The group of the two clerics and the doctor had fallen away from the more official group containing the inspector and the man he had arrested. Now, however, that their own party had broken up, they heard voices from the others. The priest looked up quietly and then looked down again as he heard the blacksmith say in a loud voice:

'I hope I've convinced you, Mr Inspector. I'm a strong man, as you say, but I couldn't have flung my hammer bang here from Greenford. My hammer hasn't any wings that it should come flying half a mile over hedges and fields.'

The inspector laughed amicably and said: 'No, I think you can be considered out of it, though it's one of the rummiest coincidences I ever saw. I can only ask you to give us all the assistance you can in finding a man as big and strong as yourself. By George! you might be useful, if only to hold him! I suppose you yourself have no guess at the man?'

'I may have a guess,' said the pale smith, 'but it is not at a man.' Then, seeing the scared eyes turn towards his wife on the bench, he put his huge hand on her shoulder and said: 'Nor a woman either.'

'What do you mean?' asked the inspector jocularly. 'You don't think cows use hammers, do you?'

'I think no thing of flesh held that hammer,' said the blacksmith in a stifled voice; 'mortally speaking, I think the man died alone.'

Wilfred made a sudden forward movement and peered at him with burning eyes.

'Do you mean to say, Barnes,' came the sharp voice of the cobbler, 'that the hammer jumped up of itself and knocked the man down?'

'Oh, you gentlemen may stare and snigger,' cried Simeon; 'you clergymen who tell us on Sunday in what a stillness the Lord smote Sennacherib. I believe that One who walks invisible in every house defended the honour of mine, and laid the defiler dead before the door of it. I believe the force in that blow was just the force there is in earthquakes, and no force less.'

Wilfred said, with a voice utterly undescribable: 'I told Norman myself to beware of the thunderbolt.'

'That agent is outside my jurisdiction,' said the inspector with a slight smile.

'You are not outside His,' answered the smith; 'see you to it,' and, turning his broad back, he went into the house.

The shaken Wilfred was led away by Father Brown, who had an easy and friendly way with him. 'Let us get out of this horrid place, Mr Bohun,' he said. 'May I look inside your church? I hear it's one of the oldest in England. We take some interest, you know,' he added with a comical grimace, 'in old English churches.'

Wilfred Bohun did not smile, for humour was never his strong point. But he nodded rather eagerly, being only too ready to explain the Gothic splendours to someone more likely to be sympathetic than the Presbyterian blacksmith or the atheist cobbler.

'By all means,' he said; 'let us go in at this side.' And he led the way into the high side entrance at the top of the flight of steps. Father Brown was mounting the first step to follow him when he felt a hand on his shoulder, and turned to behold the dark, thin figure of the doctor, his face darker yet with suspicion.

'Sir,' said the physician harshly, 'you appear to know some secrets in this black business. May I ask if you are going to keep them to yourself?'

'Why, doctor,' answered the priest, smiling quite pleasantly, 'there is one very good reason why a man of my trade should keep things to himself when he is not sure of them, and that is that it is so constantly his duty to keep them to himself when he is sure of them. But if you think I have been discourteously reticent with you or anyone, I will go to the extreme limit of my custom. I will give you two very large hints.'

'Well, sir?' said the doctor gloomily.

'First,' said Father Brown quietly, 'the thing is quite in your own province. It is a matter of physical science. The blacksmith is mistaken, not perhaps in saying that the blow was divine, but certainly in saying that it came by a miracle. It was no miracle, doctor, except in so far as a man is himself a miracle, with his strange and wicked and yet half-heroic heart. The force that smashed that skull was a force well known to scientists – one of the most frequently debated of the laws of nature.'

The doctor, who was looking at him with frowning intentness, only said: 'And the other hint!'

'The other hint is this,' said the priest. 'Do you remember the black-smith, though he believes in miracles, talking scornfully of the impossible fairy tale that his hammer had wings and flew half a mile across country?'

'Yes,' said the doctor, 'I remember that.'

'Well,' added Father Brown, with a broad smile, 'that fairy tale was the nearest thing to the real truth that has been said to-day.' And with that he turned his back and stumped up the steps after the curate.

The Reverend Wilfred, who had been waiting for him, pale and impatient, as if this little delay were the last straw for his nerves, led him immediately to his favourite corner of the church, that part of the gallery closest to the carved roof and lit by the wonderful window with the angel. The little Latin priest explored and admired everything exhaustively, talking cheerfully but in a low voice all the time. When in the course of his investigation he found the side exit and the winding stair down which Wilfred had rushed to find his brother dead, Father Brown ran not down but up, with the agility of a monkey, and his clear voice came from an outer platform above.

'Come up here, Mr Bohun,' he called. 'The air will do you good.'

Bohun followed him, and came out on a kind of stone gallery or balcony outside the building, from which one could see the illimitable plain in which their small hill stood, wooded away to the purple horizon and dotted with villages and farms. Clear and square, but quite small beneath them, was the blacksmith's yard, where the inspector still stood taking notes and the corpse still lay like a smashed fly.

'Might be the map of the world, mightn't it?' said Father Brown.

'Yes,' said Bohun very gravely, and nodded his head.

Immediately beneath and about them the lines of the Gothic building plunged outwards into the void with a sickening swiftness akin to suicide. There is that element of Titan energy in the architecture of the Middle Ages that, from whatever aspect it be seen, it always seems to be rushing away, like the strong back of some maddened horse. This church was hewn out of ancient and silent stone, bearded with old fungoids and stained with the nests of birds. And yet, when they saw it from below, it sprang like a fountain at the stars; and when they saw it, as now, from above, it poured like a cataract into a voiceless pit. For these two men on the tower were left alone with the most terrible aspect of the Gothic; the monstrous foreshortening and disproportion, the dizzy perspectives, the glimpses of great things small and small things great; a topsy-turvydom of stone in the mid-air. Details of stone, enormous by their proximity, were relieved against a pattern of fields and farms, pygmy in their distance. A carved bird or beast at a corner seemed like some vast walking or flying dragon wasting the pastures and villages below. The whole atmosphere was dizzy and dangerous, as if men were upheld in air amid the gyrating wings of colossal genii; and the whole of that old church, as tall and rich as a cathedral, seemed to sit upon the sunlit country like a cloud-burst.

'I think there is something rather dangerous about standing on these high places even to pray,' said Father Brown. 'Heights were made to be looked at, not to be looked from.'

'Do you mean that one may fall over?' asked Wilfred.

'I mean that one's soul may fall if one's body doesn't,' said the other priest.

'I scarcely understand you,' remarked Bohun indistinctly.

'Look at that blacksmith, for instance,' went on Father Brown calmly; 'a good man, but not a Christian – hard, imperious, unforgiving. Well, his Scotch religion was made up by men who prayed on hills and high crags, and learnt to look down on the world more than to look up at heaven. Humility is the mother of giants. One sees great things from the valley; only small things from the peak.'

'But he – he didn't do it,' said Bohun tremulously.

'No,' said the other in an odd voice; 'we know he didn't do it.'

After a moment he resumed, looking tranquilly out over the plain with his pale grey eyes. 'I knew a man,' he said, 'who began by worshipping with others before the altar, but who grew fond of high and lonely places to pray from, corners or niches in the belfry or the spire. And once in one of those dizzy places, where the whole world seemed to turn under him like a wheel, his brain turned also, and he fancied he was God. So that though he was a good man, he committed a great crime.'

Wilfred's face was turned away, but his bony hands turned blue and white as they tightened on the parapet of stone.

'He thought it was given to *him* to judge the world and strike down the sinner. He would never have had such a thought if he had been kneeling with other men upon a floor. But he saw all men walking about like insects. He saw one especially strutting just below him, insolent and evident by the bright green hat – a poisonous insect.'

Rooks cawed round the corners of the belfry; but there was no other sound till Father Brown went on.

'This also tempted him, that he had in his hand one of the most awful engines of nature; I mean gravitation, that mad and quickening rush by which all earth's creatures fly back to her heart when released. See, the inspector is strutting just below us in the smithy. If I were to toss a pebble over this parapet it would be something like a bullet by the time it struck him. If I were to drop a hammer – even a small hammer—'

Wilfred Bohun threw one leg over the parapet, and Father Brown had him in a minute by the collar.

'Not by that door,' he said quite gently; 'that door leads to hell.'

Bohun staggered back against the wall, and stared at him with frightful eyes.

'How do you know all this?' he cried. 'Are you a devil?'

'I am a man,' answered Father Brown gravely; 'and therefore have all devils in my heart. Listen to me,' he said after a short pause. 'I know what you did – at least, I can guess the great part of it. When you left your brother you were racked with no unrighteous rage to the extent even that you snatched up a small hammer, half inclined to kill him with his foulness on his mouth. Recoiling, you thrust it under your buttoned coat instead, and rushed into the church. You pray wildly in many places, under the angel window, upon the platform above, and on a higher platform still, from which you could see the colonel's Eastern hat like the back of a green beetle crawling about. Then something snapped in your soul, and you let God's thunderbolt fall.'

Wilfred put a weak hand to his head, and asked in a low voice: 'How did you know that his hat looked like a green beetle?'

'Oh, that,' said the other with the shadow of a smile, 'that was common sense. But hear me further. I say I know all this; but no one else shall know it. The next step is for you; I shall take no more steps; I will seal this with the seal of confession. If you ask me why, there are many reasons, and only one that concerns you. I leave things to you because you have not yet gone very far wrong, as assassins go. You did not help to fix the crime on the smith when it was easy; or on his wife, when that was easy. You tried to fix it on the imbecile because you knew that he could not suffer. That was one of the gleams that it is my business to find in assassins. And now come down into the village, and go your own way as free as the wind; for I have said my last word.'

They went down the winding stairs in utter silence, and came out into the sunlight by the smithy. Wilfred Bohun carefully unlatched the wooden gate of the yard, and going up to the inspector, said: 'I wish to give myself up; I have killed my brother.'

W. W. Jacobs

The Interruption

I

The last of the funeral guests had gone and Spencer Goddard, in decent black, sat alone in his small, well-furnished study. There was a queer sense of freedom in the house since the coffin had left it; the coffin which was now hidden in its solitary grave beneath the yellow earth. The air, which for the last three days had seemed stale and contaminated, now smelt fresh and clean. He went to the open window and, looking into the fading light of the autumn day, took a deep breath.

He closed the window, and, stooping down, put a match to the fire, and, dropping into his easy chair, sat listening to the cheery crackle of the wood. At the age of thirty-eight he had turned over a fresh page. Life, free and unencumbered, was before him. His dead wife's money was at last his, to spend as he pleased instead of being doled out in reluctant driblets.

He turned at a step at the door and his face assumed the appearance of gravity and sadness it had worn for the last four days. The cook, with the same air of decorous grief, entered the room quietly and, crossing to the mantelpiece, placed upon it a photograph.

'I thought you'd like to have it, sir,' she said, in a low voice, 'to remind you.'

Goddard thanked her, and, rising, took it in his hand and stood regarding it. He noticed with satisfaction that his hand was absolutely steady.

'It is a very good likeness – till she was taken ill,' continued the woman. 'I never saw anybody change so sudden.'

'The nature of her disease, Hannah,' said her master.

The woman nodded, and, dabbing at her eyes with her handkerchief, stood regarding him.

'Is there anything you want?' he inquired, after a time.

She shook her head. 'I can't believe she's gone,' she said, in a low voice. 'Every now and then I have a queer feeling that she's still here—'

'It's your nerves,' said her master sharply.

'—and wanting to tell me something.'

By a great effort Goddard refrained from looking at her.

'Nerves,' he said again. 'Perhaps you ought to have a little holiday. It has been a great strain upon you.'

'You, too, sir,' said the woman respectfully. 'Waiting on her hand and foot as you have done, I can't think how you stood it. If you'd only had a nurse—'

'I preferred to do it myself, Hannah,' said her master. 'If I had had a nurse it would have alarmed her.'

The woman assented. 'And they are always peeking and prying into what doesn't concern them,' she added. 'Always think they know more than the doctors do.'

Goddard turned a slow look upon her. The tall, angular figure was standing in an attitude of respectful attention; the cold slatey-brown eyes were cast down, the sullen face expressionless.

'She couldn't have had a better doctor,' he said, looking at the fire again. 'No man could have done more for her.'

'And nobody could have done more for her than you did, sir,' was the reply. 'There's few husbands that would have done what you did.'

Goddard stiffened in his chair. 'That will do, Hannah,' he said curtly.

'Or done it so well,' said the woman, with measured slowness.

With a strange, sinking sensation, her master paused to regain his control. Then he turned and eyed her steadily. 'Thank you,' he said slowly; 'you mean well, but at present I cannot discuss it.'

For some time after the door had closed behind her he sat in deep thought. The feeling of well-being of a few minutes before had banished, leaving in its place an apprehension which he refused to consider, but which would not be allayed. He thought over his actions of the last few weeks, carefully, and could remember no flaw. His wife's illness, the doctor's diagnosis, his own solicitous care, were all in keeping with the ordinary. He tried to remember the woman's exact words – her manner. Something had shown him Fear. What?

He could have laughed at his fears next morning. The dining-room was full of sunshine and the fragrance of coffee and bacon was in the air. Better still, a worried and commonplace Hannah. Worried over two eggs with false birth-certificates, over the vendor of which she became almost lyrical.

'The bacon is excellent,' said her smiling master, 'so is the coffee; but your coffee always is.'

Hannah smiled in return, and, taking fresh eggs from a rosy-cheeked maid, put them before him.

A pipe, followed by a brisk walk, cheered him still further. He came home glowing with exercise and again possessed with that sense of freedom and freshness. He went into the garden – now his own – and planned alterations.

After lunch he went over the house. The windows of his wife's bedroom were open and the room neat and airy. His glance wandered from the made-up bed to the brightly polished furniture. Then he went to the dressing-table and opened the drawers, searching each in turn. With the exception of a few odds and ends they were empty. He went out on to the landing and called for Hannah.

'Do you know whether your mistress locked up any of her things?' he inquired.

'What things?' said the woman.

'Well, her jewellery mostly.'

'Oh!' Hannah smiled. 'She gave it all to me,' she said, quietly.

Goddard checked an exclamation. His heart was beating nervously, but he spoke sternly.

'When?'

'Just before she died – of gastro-enteritis,' said the woman.

There was a long silence. He turned and with great care mechanically closed the drawers of the dressing-table. The tilted glass showed him the pallor of his face, and he spoke without turning round.

'That is all right, then,' he said, huskily. 'I only wanted to know what had become of it. I thought, perhaps Milly—'

Hannah shook her head. 'Milly's all right,' she said, with a strange smile. 'She's as honest as we are. Is there anything more you want, sir?'

She closed the door behind her with the quietness of the well-trained servant; Goddard, steadying himself with his hand on the rail of the bed, stood looking into the future.

II

The days passed monotonously, as they pass with a man in prison. Gone was the sense of freedom and the idea of a wider life. Instead of a cell, a house with ten rooms – but Hannah, the jailer, guarding each one. Respectful and attentive, the model servant, he saw in every word a threat against his liberty – his life. In the sullen face and cold eyes he saw her knowledge of power; in her solicitude for his comfort and approval, a sardonic jest. It was the master playing at being the servant. The years of unwilling servitude were over, but she felt her way carefully with infinite zest in the game. Warped and bitter, with a cleverness which had never before had scope, she had entered into her kingdom. She took it little by little, savouring every morsel.

'I hope I've done right, sir,' she said one morning. 'I have given Milly notice.'

Goddard looked up from his paper. 'Isn't she satisfactory?' he inquired.

'Not to my thinking, sir,' said the woman. 'And she says she is coming to see you about it. I told her that would be no good.'

'I had better see her and hear what she has to say,' said her master.

'Of course, if you wish to,' said Hannah; 'only, after giving her notice, if she doesn't go, I shall. I should be sorry to go – I've been very comfortable here – but it's either her or me.'

'I should be sorry to lose you,' said Goddard in a hopeless voice.

'Thank you, sir,' said Hannah. 'I'm sure I've tried to do my best. I've been with you some time now – and I know all your little ways. I expect I understand you better than anybody else would. I do all I can to make you comfortable.'

'Very well, I will leave it to you,' said Goddard in a voice which strove to be brisk and commanding. 'You have my permission to dismiss her.'

'There's another thing I wanted to see you about,' said Hannah; 'my wages. I was going to ask for a rise, seeing that I'm really housekeeper here now.'

'Certainly,' said her master, considering, 'that only seems fair. Let me see – what are you getting?'

'Thirty-six.'

Goddard reflected for a moment and then turned with a benevolent smile. 'Very well,' he said cordially, 'I'll make it forty-two. That's ten shillings a month more.'

'I was thinking of a hundred,' said Hannah dryly.

The significance of the demand appalled him. 'Rather a big jump,' he said at last. 'I really don't know that I—'

'It doesn't matter,' said Hannah. 'I thought I was worth it – to you – that's all. You know best. Some people might think I was worth *two* hundred. That's a bigger jump, but after all a big jump is better than—'

She broke off and tittered. Goddard eyed her.

'—than a big drop,' she concluded.

Her master's face set. The lips almost disappeared and something came into the pale eyes that was revolting. Still eyeing her, he rose and approached her. She stood her ground and met him eye to eye.

'You are jocular,' he said at last.

'Short life and a merry one,' said the woman.

'Mine or yours?'

77

'Both, perhaps,' was the reply.

'If – if I give you a hundred,' said Goddard, moistening his lips, 'that ought to make your life merrier, at any rate.'

Hannah nodded. 'Merry and long, perhaps,' she said slowly. 'I'm careful, you know – very careful.'

'I am sure you are,' said Goddard, his face relaxing.

'Careful what I eat and drink, I mean,' said the woman, eyeing him steadily.

'That is wise,' he said slowly. 'I am myself – that is why I am paying a good cook a large salary. But don't overdo things, Hannah; don't kill the goose that lays the golden eggs.'

'I am not likely to do that,' she said coldly. 'Live and let live; that is my motto. Some people have different ones. But I'm careful; nobody won't catch me napping. I've left a letter with my sister, in case.'

Goddard turned slowly and in a casual fashion put the flowers straight in a bowl on the table, and, wandering to the window, looked out. His face white again and his hands trembled.

'To be opened after my death,' continued Hannah. 'I don't believe in doctors – not after what I've seen of them – I don't think they know enough; so if I die I shall be examined. I've given good reasons.'

'And suppose,' said Goddard, coming from the window, 'suppose she is curious, and opens it before you die?'

'We must chance that,' said Hannah, shrugging her shoulders; 'but I don't think she will. I sealed it up with sealing-wax, with a mark on it.'

'She might open it and say nothing about it,' persisted her master.

An unwholesome grin spread slowly over Hannah's features. 'I should know it soon enough,' she declared boisterously, 'and so would other people. Lord, there would be an upset! Chidham would have something to talk about for once. We should be in the papers – both of us.'

Goddard forced a smile. 'Dear me!' he said gently. 'Your pen seems to be a dangerous weapon, Hannah, but I hope that the need to open it will not happen for another fifty years. You look well and strong.'

The woman nodded. 'I don't take up my troubles before they come,' she said, with a satisfied air; 'but there's no harm in trying to prevent them coming. Prevention is better than cure.'

'Exactly,' said her master; 'and, by the way, there's no need for this little financial arrangement to be known by anybody else. I might become unpopular with my neighbours for setting a bad example. Of course, I am giving you this sum because I really think you are worth it.'

'I'm sure you do,' said Hannah. 'I'm not sure I ain't worth more, but this'll do to go on with. I shall get a girl for less than we are paying Milly, and that'll be another little bit extra for me.'

'Certainly,' said Goddard, and smiled again.

'Come to think of it,' said Hannah, pausing at the door, 'I ain't sure I shall get anybody else; then there'll be more than ever for me. If I do the work I might as well have the money.'

Her master nodded, and, left to himself, sat down to think out a position which was as intolerable as it was dangerous. At a great risk he had escaped from the dominion of one woman only to fall, bound and helpless, into the hands of another. However vague and unconvincing the suspicions of Hannah might be, they would be sufficient. Evidence could be unearthed. Cold with fear one moment, and hot with fury the next, he sought in vain for some avenue of escape. It was his brain against that of a cunning, illiterate fool; a fool whose malicious stupidity only added to his danger. And she drank. With largely increased wages she would drink more and his very life might depend upon a hiccuped boast. It was clear that she was enjoying her supremacy; later on her vanity would urge her to display it before others. He might have to obey the crack of her whip before witnesses, and that would cut off all possibility of escape.

He sat with his head in his hands. There must be a way out and he must find it. Soon. He must find it before gossip began; before the changed position of master and servant lent colour to her story when that story became known. Shaking with fury, he thought of her lean, ugly throat and the joy of choking her life out with his fingers. He started suddenly, and took a quick breath. No, not fingers – a rope.

III

Bright and cheerful outside and with his friends, in the house he was quiet and submissive. Milly had gone, and, if the service was poorer and the rooms neglected, he gave no sign. If a bell remained unanswered he made no complaint, and to studied insolence turned the other cheek of politeness. When at this tribute to her power the woman smiled, he smiled in return. A smile which, for all its disarming softness, left her vaguely uneasy.

'I'm not afraid of you,' she said once, with a menacing air.

'I hope not,' said Goddard in a slightly surprised voice.

'Some people might be, but I'm not,' she declared. 'If anything happened to me—'

'Nothing could happen to such a careful woman as you are,' he said, smiling again. 'You ought to live to ninety – with luck.'

It was clear to him that the situation was getting on his nerves. Unremembered but terrible dreams haunted his sleep. Dreams in which some great, inevitable disaster was always pressing upon him, although he could never discover what it was. Each morning he awoke unrefreshed to face another day of torment. He could not meet the woman's eyes for fear of revealing the threat that was in his own.

Delay was dangerous and foolish. He had thought out every move in that contest of wits which was to remove the shadow of the rope from his own neck and place it about that of the woman. There was a little risk, but the stake was a big one. He had but to set the ball rolling and others would keep it on its course. It was time to act.

He came in a little jaded from his afternoon walk, and left his tea untouched. He ate but little dinner, and, sitting hunched up over the fire, told the woman that he had taken a slight chill. Her concern, he felt grimly, might have been greater if she had known the cause.

He was no better next day, and after lunch called into consult his doctor. He left with a clean bill of health except for a slight digestive derangement, the remedy for which he took away with him in a bottle. For two days he swallowed one tablespoonful three times a day in water, without result, then he took to his bed.

'A day or two in bed won't hurt you,' said the doctor. 'Show me that tongue of yours again.'

'But what is the matter with me, Roberts?' inquired the patient.

The doctor pondered. 'Nothing to trouble about – nerves a bit wrong – digestion a little bit impaired. You'll be all right in a day or two.'

Goddard nodded. So far, so good; Roberts had not outlived his usefulness. He smiled grimly after the doctor had left at the surprise he was preparing for him. A little rough on Roberts and his professional reputation, perhaps, but these things could not be avoided.

He lay back and visualised the programme. A day or two longer, getting gradually worse, then a little sickness. After that a nervous, somewhat shamefaced patient hinting at things. His food has a queer taste – he felt worse after taking it; he knew it was ridiculous, still – there was some of his beef-tea he had put aside, perhaps the doctor would like to examine it? and the medicine? Secretions, too; perhaps he would like to see those?

Propped on his elbow, he stared fixedly at the wall. There would be a trace – a faint trace – of arsenic in the secretions. There would be more than a trace in the other things. An attempt to poison him would be clearly indicated, and – his wife's symptoms had resembled his own – let Hannah get out of the web he was spinning if she could. As for the letter she had threatened him with, let her produce it; it could only recoil upon herself. Fifty letters could not save her from the doom he was preparing for her. It was her life or his, and he would show no mercy. For three days he doctored himself with sedulous care, watching himself anxiously the while. His nerve was going and he knew it. Before him was the strain of the discovery, the arrest, and the trial. The gruesome business of his wife's death. A long business. He would wait no longer, and he would open the proceedings with dramatic suddenness.

It was between nine and ten o'clock at night when he rang his bell, and it was not until he had rung four times that he heard the heavy steps of Hannah mounting the stairs.

'What d'you want?' she demanded, standing in the doorway.

'I'm very ill,' he said, gasping. 'Run for the doctor. Quick!'

The woman stared at him in genuine amazement. 'What, at this time o' night?' she exclaimed. 'Not likely.'

'I'm dying!' said Goddard in a broken voice.

'Not you,' she said, roughly. 'You'll be better in the morning.'

'I'm dying,' he repeated. 'Go – for – the – doctor.'

The woman hesitated. The rain beat in heavy squalls against the window, and the doctor's house was a mile distant on the lonely road. She glanced at the figure on the bed.

'I should catch my death o' cold,' she grumbled.

She stood sullenly regarding him. He certainly looked very ill, and his death would by no means benefit her. She listened, scowling, to the wind and the rain.

'All right,' she said at last, and went noisily from the room.

His face set in a mirthless smile, he heard her bustling about below. The front-door slammed violently and he was alone.

He waited for a few moments and then, getting out of bed, put on his dressing-gown and set about his preparations. With a steady hand he added a little white powder to the remains of his beef-tea and to the contents of his bottle of medicine. He stood listening a moment at some faint sound from below, and, having satisfied himself, lit a candle and made his way to Hannah's room. For a space he stood irresolute, looking about him. Then he opened one of the drawers and, placing the broken packet of powder under a pile of clothing at the back, made his way back to bed.

He was disturbed to find that he was trembling with excitement and nervousness. He longed for tobacco, but that was impossible. To reassure himself he began to rehearse his conversation with the doctor, and again he thought over every possible complication. The scene with the woman would be terrible; he would have to be too ill to take any part in it. The less he said the better. Others would do all that was necessary.

He lay for a long time listening to the sound of the wind and the rain. Inside, the house seemed unusually quiet, and with an odd sensation he suddenly realised that it was the first time he had been alone in it since his wife's death. He remembered that she would have to be disturbed. The thought was unwelcome. He did not want her to be disturbed. Let the dead sleep.

He sat up in bed and drew his watch from beneath the pillow.

Hannah ought to have been back before; in any case she could not be long now. At any moment he might hear her key in the lock. He lay down again and reminded himself that things were shaping well. He had shaped them, and some of the satisfaction of the artist was his.

The silence was oppressive. The house seemed to be listening, waiting. He looked at his watch again and wondered, with a curse, what had happened to the woman. It was clear that the doctor must be out, but that was no reason for her delay. It was close on midnight, and the atmosphere of the house seemed in some strange fashion to be brooding and hostile.

In a lull in the wind he thought he heard footsteps outside, and his face cleared as he sat up listening for the sound of the key in the door below. In another moment the woman would be in the house and the fears engendered by a disordered fancy would have flown. The sound of the steps had ceased, but he could hear no sound of entrance. Until all hope had gone, he sat listening. He was certain he had heard footsteps. Whose?

Trembling and haggard he sat waiting, assailed by a crowd of murmuring fears. One whispered that he had failed and would have to pay the penalty of failing; that he had gambled with Death and lost.

By a strong effort he fought down these fancies and, closing his eyes, tried to compose himself to rest. It was evident now that the doctor was out and that Hannah was waiting to return with him in his car. He was frightening himself for nothing. At any moment he might hear the sound of their arrival.

He heard something else, and, sitting up, suddenly, tried to think what it was and what had caused it. It was a very faint sound – stealthy. Holding his breath he waited for it to be repeated. He heard it again, the mere ghost of a sound – a whisper of a sound, but significant as most whispers are.

He wiped his brow with his sleeve and told himself firmly that it was nerves, and nothing but nerves; but, against his will, he still listened. He fancied now that the sound came from his wife's room, the other side of the landing. It increased in loudness and became more insistent, but with his eyes fixed on the door of his room he still kept himself in hand, and tried to listen to the wind and the rain.

For a time he heard nothing but that. Then there came a scraping, scurrying noise from his wife's room, and a sudden, terrific crash.

With a loud scream his nerve broke, and springing from the bed he sped downstairs and, flinging open the front-door, dashed into the night. The door, caught by the wind, slammed behind him.

With his hand holding the garden gate open ready for further flight, he stood sobbing for breath. His bare feet were bruised and the rain was very cold, but he took no heed. Then he ran a little way along the road and stood for some time, hoping and listening.

He came back slowly. The wind was bitter and he was soaked to the skin. The garden was black and forbidding, and unspeakable horror might be lurking in the bushes. He went up the road again, trembling with cold. Then, in desperation, he passed through the terrors of the garden to the house, only to find the door closed. The porch gave a little protection from the icy rain, but none from the wind, and, shaking in every limb, he leaned in abject misery against the door. He pulled himself together after a time and stumbled round to the back-door. Locked! And all the lower windows were shuttered. He made his way back to the porch and, crouching there in hopeless misery, waited for the woman to return.

IV

He had a dim memory when he awoke of somebody questioning him, and then of being half-pushed, half-carried upstairs to bed. There was something wrong with his head and his chest and he was trembling violently, and very cold. Somebody was speaking.

'You must have taken leave of your senses,' said the voice of Hannah. 'I thought you were dead.'

He forced his eyes to open. 'Doctor,' he muttered, 'doctor.'

'Out on a bad case,' said Hannah. 'I waited till I was tired of waiting, and then came along. Good thing for you I did. He'll be round first thing this morning. He ought to be here now.'

She bustled about, tidying up the room, his leaden eyes following her as she collected the beef-tea and other things on a tray and carried them out.

'Nice thing I did yesterday,' she remarked, as she came back. 'Left the missus's bedroom window open. When I opened the door this morning I found that beautiful Chippendale glass of hers had blown off the table and smashed to pieces. Did you hear it?'

Goddard made no reply. In a confused fashion he was trying to think. Accident or not, the fall of the glass had served its purpose. Were there such things as accidents? Or was Life a puzzle – a puzzle into which every piece was made to fit? Fear and the wind . . . no: conscience and the wind . . . had saved the woman. He must get the powder back from her drawer . . . before she discovered it and denounced him. The medicine . . . he must remember not to take it . . .

He was very ill, seriously ill. He must have taken a chill owing to that panic flight into the garden. Why didn't the doctor come? He had come . . . at last . . . he was doing something to his chest . . . it was cold. Again . . . the doctor . . . there was something he wanted to tell him. . . .

Hannah and a powder . . . what was it?

Later on he remembered, together with other things that he had hoped to forget. He lay watching an endless procession of memories, broken at times by a glance at the doctor, the nurse, and Hannah, who were all standing near the bed regarding him. They had been there a long time and they were all very quiet. The last time he looked at Hannah was the first time for months that he had looked at her without loathing and hatred. Then he knew that he was dying.

Aldous Huxley

The Gioconda Smile

'Miss Spence will be down directly, sir.'

'Thank you,' said Mr Hutton, without turning round. Janet Spence's parlourmaid was so ugly – ugly on purpose, it always seemed to him, malignantly, criminally ugly – that he could not bear to look at her more than was necessary. The door closed. Left to himself, Mr Hutton got up and began to wander round the room, looking with meditative eyes at the familiar objects it contained.

Photographs of Greek statuary, photographs of the Roman Forum, coloured prints of Italian masterpieces, all very safe and well known. Poor, dear Janet, what a prig – what an intellectual snob! Her real taste was illustrated in that water-colour by the pavement artist, the one she had paid half a crown for (and thirty-five shillings for the frame). How often he had heard her tell the story, how often expatiate on the beauties of that skilful imitation of an oleograph! 'A real Artist in the streets,' and you could hear the capital A in Artist as she spoke the words. She made you feel that part of his glory had entered into Janet Spence when she tendered him that half-crown for the copy of the oleograph. She was implying a compliment to her own taste and penetration. A genuine Old Master for half a crown. Poor, dear Janet!

Mr Hutton came to a pause in front of a small oblong mirror. Stooping a little to get a full view of his face, he passed a white, well-manicured finger over his moustache. It was as curly, as freshly auburn as it had been twenty years ago. His hair still retained its colour, and there was no sign of baldness yet – only a certain elevation of the brow. 'Shakespearean,' thought Mr Hutton, with a smile, as he surveyed the smooth and polished expanse of his forehead.

Others abide our question, thou art free. . . . Footsteps in the sea . . .

Majesty . . . Shakespeare, thou shouldst be living at this hour. No, that was Milton, wasn't it? Milton, the Lady of Christ's. There was no lady about him. He was what the women would call a manly man. That was why they liked him – for the curly auburn moustache and the discreet redolence of tobacco. Mr Hutton smiled again; he enjoyed making fun of himself. Lady of Christ's? No, no. He was the Christ of Ladies. Very pretty, very pretty. The Christ of Ladies. Mr Hutton wished there were somebody he could tell the joke to. Poor, dear Janet wouldn't appreciate it, alas!

He straightened himself up, patted his hair, and resumed his peregrination. Damn the Roman Forum; he hated those dreary photographs.

Suddenly he became aware that Janet Spence was in the room, standing near the door. Mr Hutton started, as though he had been taken in some felonious act. To make these silent and spectral appearances was one of Janet Spence's peculiar talents. Perhaps she had been there all the time, had seen him looking at himself in the mirror. Impossible! But, still, it was disquieting.

'Oh, you gave me such a surprise,' said Mr Hutton, recovering his smile and advancing with outstretched hand to meet her.

Miss Spence was smiling too: her Gioconda smile, he had once called it in a moment of half-ironical flattery. Miss Spence had taken the compliment seriously, and had always tried to live up to the Leonardo standard. She smiled on his silence while Mr Hutton shook hands; that was part of the Gioconda business.

'I hope you're well,' said Mr Hutton. 'You look it.'

What a queer face she had! That small mouth pursed forward by the Gioconda expression into a little snout with a round hole in the middle as though for whistling – it was like a penholder seen from the front. Above the mouth a well-shaped nose, finely aquiline. Eyes large, lustrous, and dark, with the largeness, lustre, and darkness that seems to invite sties and an occasional bloodshot suffusion. They were fine eyes, but unchangingly grave. The penholder might do its Gioconda trick, but the eyes never altered in their earnestness. Above them, a pair of boldly arched, heavily pencilled black eyebrows lent a surprising air of power, as of a Roman matron, to the upper portion of the face. Her hair was dark and equally Roman; Agrippina from the brows upward.

'I thought I'd just look in on my way home,' Mr Hutton went on. 'Ah, it's good to be back here' – he indicated with a wave of his hand the flowers in the vases, the sunshine and greenery beyond the windows – 'it's good to be back in the country after a stuffy day of business in town.'

Miss Spence, who had sat down, pointed to a chair at her side.

'No, really, I can't sit down,' Mr Hutton protested. 'I must get back to see how poor Emily is. She was rather seedy this morning.' He sat down, nevertheless. 'It's these wretched liver chills. She's always getting them. Women—' He broke off and coughed, so as to hide the fact that he had uttered. He was about to say that women with weak digestions ought not to marry; but the remark was too cruel, and he didn't really believe it. Janet Spence, moreover, was a believer in eternal flames and spiritual attachments. 'She hopes to be well enough,' he added, 'to see you at luncheon tomorrow. Can you come? Do!' He smiled persuasively. 'It's my invitation too, you know.'

She dropped her eyes, and Mr Hutton almost thought that he detected a certain reddening of the cheek. It was a tribute; he stroked his moustache.

'I should like to come if you think Emily's really well enough to have a visitor.'

'Of course. You'll do her good. You'll do us both good. In married life three is often better company than two.'

'Oh, you're cynical.'

Mr Hutton always had a desire to say 'Bow-wow-wow' whenever that last word was spoken. It irritated him more than any other word in the language. But instead of barking he made haste to protest.

'No, no. I'm only speaking a melancholy truth. Reality doesn't always come up to the ideal, you know. But that doesn't make me believe any the less in the ideal. Indeed, I believe in it passionately – the ideal of a matrimony between two people in perfect accord. I think it's realisable. I'm sure it is.'

He paused significantly and looked at her with an arch expression. A virgin of thirty-six, but still unwithered; she had her charms. And there was something really rather enigmatic about her. Miss Spence made no reply but continued to smile. There were times when Mr Hutton got rather bored with the Gioconda. He stood up.

'I must really be going now. Farewell, mysterious Gioconda.' The smile grew intenser, focused itself, as it were, in a narrower snout. Mr Hutton made a cinquecento gesture, and kissed her extended hand. It was the first time he had done such a thing; the action seemed not to be resented. 'I look forward to tomorrow.'

'Do you?'

For answer Mr Hutton once more kissed her hand, than turned to go. Miss Spence accompanied him to the porch.

'Where's your car?' she asked.

'I left it at the gate of the drive.'

'I'll come and see you off.'

'No, no.' Mr Hutton was playful, but determined. 'You must do no such thing. I simply forbid you.'

'But I should like to come,' Miss Spence protested, throwing a rapid

Gioconda at him.

Mr Hutton held up his hand. 'No,' he repeated, and then, with a gesture that was almost the blowing of a kiss, he started to run down the drive, lightly on his toes, with long, bounding strides like a boy's. He was proud of that run; it was quite marvellously youthful. Still, he was glad the drive was no longer. At the last bend, before passing out of sight of the house, he halted and turned round. Miss Spence was still standing on the steps, smiling her smile. He waved his hand, and this time quite definitely and overtly wafted a kiss in her direction. Then, breaking once more into his magnificent canter, he rounded the last dark promontory of trees. Once out of sight of the house he let his high paces decline to a trot, and finally to a walk. He took out his handkerchief and began wiping his neck inside his collar. What fools, what fools! Had there ever been such an ass as poor, dear Janet Spence? Never, unless it was himself. Decidedly he was the more malignant fool, since he, at least, was aware of his folly and still persisted in it. Why did he persist? Ah, the problem that was himself, the problem that was other people.

He had reached the gate. A large, prosperous-looking motor was standing at the side of the road.

'Home, M'Nab.' The chauffeur touched his cap. 'And stop at the crossroads on the way, as usual,' Mr Hutton added, as he opened the door of the car. 'Well?' he said, speaking into the obscurity that lurked within.

'Oh, Teddy Bear, what an age you've been!' It was a fresh and childish voice that spoke the words. There was the faintest hint of Cockney impurity about the vowel sounds.

Mr Hutton bent his large form and darted into the car with the agility of an animal regaining its burrow.

'Have I?' he said, as he shut the door. The machine began to move. 'You must have missed me a lot if you found the time so long.' He sat back in the low seat; a cherishing warmth enveloped him.

'Teddy bear . . .' and with a sigh of contentment a charming little head declined on to Mr Hutton's shoulder. Ravished, he looked down sideways at the round, babyish face.

'Do you know, Doris, you look like the picture of Louise de Kerouaille.' He passed his fingers through a mass of curly hair.

'Who's Louise de Kera-whatever-it-is?' Doris spoke from remote distances.

'She was, alas! *Fuit*. We shall all be "was" one of these days. Meanwhile . . .'

Mr Hutton covered the babyish face with kisses. The car rushed smoothly along. M'Nab's back, through the front window was stonily impassive, the back of a statue.

'Your hands,' Doris whispered. 'Oh, you mustn't touch me. They give me electric shocks.'

Mr Hutton adored her for the virgin imbecility of the words. How late in one's existence one makes the discovery of one's body!

'The electricity isn't in me, it's in you.' He kissed her again, whispering her name several times: Doris, Doris, Doris. The scientific appellation of the sea mouse, he was thinking as he kissed the throat she offered him, white and extended like the throat of a victim awaiting the sacrificial knife. The sea mouse was a sausage with iridescent fur: very peculiar. Or was Doris the sea cucumber, which turns itself inside out in moments of alarm? He would really have to go to Naples again, just to see the aquarium. These sea creatures were fabulous, unbelievably fantastic.

'Oh, Teddy Bear!' (More zoology; but he was only a land animal. His poor little jokes!) 'Teddy Bear, I'm so happy.'

'So am I,' said Mr Hutton. Was it true?

'But I wish I knew if it were right. Tell me, Teddy Bear, is it right or wrong?'

'Ah, my dear, that's just what I've been wondering for the last thirty years.'

'Be serious, Teddy Bear. I want to know if this is right; if it's right that I should be here with you and that we should love one another, and that it should give me electric shocks when you touch me.'

'Right? Well, it's certainly good that you should have electric shocks rather than sexual repressions. Read Freud; repressions are the devil.'

'Oh, you don't help me. Why aren't you ever serious? If only you knew how miserable I am sometimes, thinking it's not right. Perhaps, you know, there is a hell, and all that. I don't know what to do. Sometimes I think I ought to stop loving you.'

'But could you?' asked Mr Hutton, confident in the powers of his seduction and his moustache.

'No, Teddy Bear, you know I couldn't. But I could run away, I could hide from you, I could lock myself up and force myself not to come to you.'

'Silly little thing!' He tightened his embrace.

'Oh, dear, I hope it isn't wrong. And there are times when I don't care if it is.'

Mr Hutton was touched. He had a certain protective affection for this little creature. He laid his cheek against her hair and so, interlaced, they sat in silence, while the car, swaying and pitching a little as it hastened along, seemed to draw in the white road and the dusty hedges toward it devouringly.

'Good-bye, good-bye.'

The car moved on, gathered speed, vanished round a curve, and Doris was left standing by the signpost at the crossroads, still dizzy and weak with the languor born of those kisses and the electrical touch of those gentle hands. She had to take a deep breath, to draw herself up deliberately, before she was strong enough to start her homeward walk. She had half a mile in which to invent the necessary lies.

Alone, Mr Hutton suddenly found himself the prey of an appalling boredom.

Mrs Hutton was lying on the sofa in her boudoir, playing Patience. In spite of the warmth of the July evening a wood fire was burning on the hearth. A black Pomeranian, extenuated by the heat and the fatigues of digestion, slept before the blaze.

'Phew! Isn't it rather hot in here?' Mr Hutton asked as he entered the room.

'You know I have to keep warm, dear.' The voice seemed breaking on the verge of tears. 'I get so shivery.'

'I hope you're better this evening.'

'Not much, I'm afraid.'

The conversation stagnated. Mr Hutton stood leaning his back against the mantelpiece. He looked down at the Pomeranian lying at his feet, and with the toe of his right boot he rolled the little dog over and rubbed its white-flecked chest and belly. The creature lay in an inert ecstasy. Mrs Hutton continued to play Patience. Arrived at an impasse, she altered the position of one card, took back another, and went on playing. Her Patiences always came out.

'Dr Libbard thinks I ought to go to Llandrindod Wells this summer.'

'Well – go, my dear – go, most certainly.'

Mr Hutton was thinking of the events of the afternoon: how they had driven, Doris and he, up to the hanging wood, had left the car to wait for them under the shade of the trees, and walked together out into the windless sunshine of the chalk down.

'I'm to drink the waters for my liver, and he thinks I ought to have massage and electric treatment, too.'

Hat in hand, Doris had stalked four blue butterflies that were dancing round a scabious flower with a motion that was like the flickering of blue fire. The blue fire burst and scattered into whirling sparks; she had given chase, laughing and shouting like a child.

'I'm sure it will do you good, my dear.'

'I was wondering if you'd come with me, dear.'

'But you know I'm going to Scotland at the end of the month.'

Mrs Hutton looked up at him entreatingly. 'It's the journey,' she said. 'The thought of it is such a nightmare. I don't know if I can manage it. And you know I can't sleep in hotels. And then there's the luggage and all the worries. I can't go alone.'

'But you won't be alone. You'll have your maid with you.' He spoke impatiently. The sick woman was usurping the place of the healthy one. He was being dragged back from the memory of the sunlit down and the quick, laughing girl, back to this unhealthy, overheated room and its complaining occupant.

'I don't think I shall be able to go.'

'But you must, my dear, if the doctor tells you to. And, besides, a change will do you good.'

'I don't think so.'

'But Libbard thinks so, and he knows what he's talking about.'

'No, I can't face it. I'm too weak. I can't go alone.' Mrs Hutton pulled a handkerchief out of her black silk bag, and put it to her eyes.

'Nonsense, my dear, you must make the effort.'

'I had rather be left in peace to die here.' She was crying in earnest now.

'O Lord! Now do be reasonable. Listen now, please.' Mrs Hutton only sobbed more violently. 'Oh, what is one to do?' He shrugged his shoulders and walked out of the room.

Mr Hutton was aware that he had not behaved with proper patience; but he could not help it. Very early in his manhood he had discovered that not only did he not feel sympathy for the poor, the weak, the diseased, and deformed; he actually hated them. Once, as an undergraduate, he spent three days at a mission in the East End. He had returned, filled with a profound and ineradicable disgust. Instead of pitying, he loathed the unfortunate. It was not, he knew, a very comely emotion; and he had been ashamed of it at first. In the end he had decided that it was temperamental, inevitable, and had felt no further qualms. Emily had been healthy and beautiful when he married her. He had loved her then. But now – was it his fault that she was like this?

Mr Hutton dined alone. Food and drink left him more benevolent than he had been before dinner. To make amends for his show of exasperation he went up to his wife's room and offered to read to her. She was touched, gratefully accepted the offer, and Mr Hutton, who was particularly proud of his accent, suggested a little light reading in French.

'French? I am so fond of French.' Mrs Hutton spoke of the language of Racine as though it were a dish of green peas.

Mr Hutton ran down to the library and returned with a yellow volume. He began reading. The effort of pronouncing perfectly absorbed his whole attention. But how good his accent was! The fact of its goodness seemed to improve the quality of the novel he was reading.

At the end of fifteen pages an unmistakable sound aroused him. He looked up; Mrs Hutton had gone to sleep. He sat still for a little while, looking with a dispassionate curiosity at the sleeping face. Once it had been beautiful; once, long ago, the sight of it, the recollection of it, had moved him with an emotion profounder, perhaps, than any he had felt before or since. Now it was lined and cadaverous. The skin was stretched tightly over the cheekbones, across the bridge of the sharp, birdlike nose. The closed eyes were set in profound bone-rimmed sockets. The lamplight striking on the face from the side emphasised with light and shade its cavities and projections. It was the face of a dead Christ by Morales.

Le squelette était invisible
Au temps heureux de l'art païn.

He shivered a little, and tiptoed out of the room.

On the following day Mrs Hutton came down to luncheon. She had had some unpleasant palpitations during the night, but she was feeling better now. Besides, she wanted to do honour to her guest. Miss Spence listened to her complaints about Llandrindod Wells, and was loud in sympathy, lavish with advice. Whatever she said was always said with intensity. She leaned forward, aimed, so to speak, like a gun, and fired her words. Bang! the charge in her soul was ignited, the words whizzed forth at the narrow barrel of her mouth. She was a machine-gun riddling her hostess with sympathy. Mr Hutton had undergone similar bombardments, mostly of a literary or philosophic character – bombardments of Maeterlinck, of Mrs Besant, of Bergson, of William James. Today the missiles were medical. She talked about insomnia, she expatiated on the virtues of harmless drugs and beneficent specialists. Under the bombardment Mrs Hutton opened out, like a flower in the sun.

Mr Hutton looked on in silence. The spectacle of Janet Spence evoked in him an unfailing curiosity. He was not romantic enough to imagine that every face masked an interior physiognomy of beauty or strangeness, that every woman's small talk was like a vapour hanging over mysterious gulfs. His wife, for example, and Doris; they were nothing more than what they seemed to be. But with Janet Spence it was somehow different. Here one could be sure that there was some kind of queer face behind the Gioconda smile and the Roman eyebrows. The only question was: What exactly was there? Mr Hutton could never quite make out.

'But perhaps you won't have to go to Llandrindod after all,' Miss Spence was saying. 'If you get well quickly Dr Libbard will let you off.'

'I only hope so. Indeed. I do really feel rather better today.'

Mr Hutton felt ashamed. How much was it his own lack of sympathy that prevented her from feeling well every day? But he comforted himself by reflecting that it was only a case of feeling, not of being better.

Sympathy does not mend a diseased liver or a weak heart.

'My dear, I wouldn't eat those red currants if I were you,' he said, suddenly solicitous. 'You know that Libbard has banned everything with skins and pips.'

'But I am so fond of them,' Mrs Hutton protested, 'and I feel so well today.'

'Don't be a tyrant,' said Miss Spence, looking first at him and then at his wife. 'Let the poor invalid have what she fancies; it will do her good.' She laid her hand on Mrs Hutton's arm and patted it affectionately two or three times.

'Thank you, my dear.' Mrs Hutton helped herself to the stewed currants.

'Well, don't blame me if they make you ill again.'

'Do I ever blame you, dear?'

'You have nothing to blame me for,' Mr Hutton answered playfully. 'I am the perfect husband.'

They sat in the garden after luncheon. From the island of shade under the old cypress tree they looked out across a flat expanse of lawn, in which the parterres of flowers shone with a metallic brilliance.

Mr Hutton took a deep breath of the warm and fragrant air. 'It's good to be alive,' he said.

'Just to be alive,' he wife echoed, stretching one pale, knot-jointed hand into the sunlight.

A maid brought the coffee; the silver pots and the little blue cups were set on a folding table near the group of chairs.

'Oh, my medicine!' exclaimed Mrs Hutton. 'Run in and fetch it, Clara, will you? The white bottle on the sideboard.'

'I'll go,' said Mr Hutton. 'I've got to go and fetch a cigar in any case.'

He ran in towards the house. On the threshold he turned round for an instant. The maid was walking back across the lawn. His wife was sitting up in her deck-chair, engaged in opening her white parasol. Miss Spence was bending over the table, pouring out the coffee. He passed into the cool obscurity of the house.

'Do you like sugar in your coffee?' Miss Spence inquired.

'Yes, please. Give me rather a lot. I'll drink it after my medicine to take the taste away.'

Mrs Hutton leaned back in her chair, lowering the sunshade over her eyes, so as to shut out from her vision the burning sky.

Behind her, Miss Spence was making a delicate clinking among the coffee cups.

'I've given you three large spoonfuls. That ought to take the taste away. And here comes the medicine.'

Mr Hutton had reappeared, carrying a wineglass, half full of a pale liquid.

'It smells delicious,' he said, as he handed it to his wife.

'That's only the flavouring.' She drank it off at a gulp, shuddered and made a grimace. 'Ugh, it's so nasty. Give me my coffee.'

Miss Spence gave her the cup; she sipped at it. 'You've made it like syrup. But it's very nice, after that atrocious medicine.'

At half-past three Mrs Hutton complained that she did not feel as well as she had done, and went indoors to lie down. Her husband would have said something about the red currants, but checked himself; the triumph of an 'I told you so' was too cheaply won. Instead, he was sympathetic, and gave her his arm to the house.

'A rest will do you good,' he said. 'By the way, I shan't be back till after dinner.'

'But why? Where are you going?'

'I promised to go to Johnson's this evening. We have to discuss the war memorial you know.'

'Oh, I wish you weren't going.' Mrs Hutton was almost in tears. 'Can't you stay? I don't like being alone in the house.'

'But, my dear, I promised – weeks ago.' It was a bother having to lie like this. 'And now I must get back and look after Miss Spence.'

He kissed her on the forehead and went out again into the garden. Miss Spence received him aimed and intense.

'Your wife is dreadfully ill,' she fired at him.

'I thought she cheered up so much when you came.'

'That was purely nervous, purely nervous, I was watching her closely. With a heart in that condition and her digestion wrecked – yes, wrecked – anything might happen.'

'Libbard doesn't take so gloomy a view of poor Emily's health.' Mr Hutton held open the gate that led from the garden into the drive; Miss Spence's car was standing by the front door.

'Libbard is only a country doctor. You ought to see a specialist.'

He could not refrain from laughing. 'You have a macabre passion for specialists.'

Miss Spence held up her hand in protest. 'I am serious. I think poor Emily is in a very bad state. Anything might happen – at any moment.'

He handed her into the car and shut the door. The chauffeur started the engine and climbed into his place, ready to drive off.

'Shall I tell him to start?' He had no desire to continue the conversation.

Miss Spence leaned forward and shot a Gioconda in his direction. 'Remember, I expect you to come and see me again soon.'

Mechanically he grinned, made a polite noise, and, as the car moved forward, waved his hand. He was happy to be alone.

A few minutes afterwards Mr Hutton himself drove away. Doris was waiting at the crossroads. They dined together twenty miles from home, at a roadside hotel. It was one of these bad, expensive meals which are only cooked in country hotels frequented by motorists. It revolted Mr Hutton, but Doris enjoyed it. She always enjoyed things. Mr Hutton ordered a not very good brand of champagne. He was wishing he had spent the evening in his library.

When they started homewards Doris was a little tipsy and extremely affectionate. It was very dark inside the car, but looking forward, past the motionless form of M'Nab, they could see a bright and narrow universe of forms and colours scooped out of the night by the electric headlamps.

It was after eleven when Mr Hutton reached home. Dr Libbard met him in the hall. He was a small man with delicate hands and well-formed features that were almost feminine. His brown eyes were large and melancholy. He used to waste a great deal of time sitting at the bedside of his patients, looking sadness through those eyes and talking in a sad, low voice about nothing in particular. His person exhaled a pleasing odour, decidedly antiseptic but at the same time suave and discreetly delicious.

'Libbard?' said Mr Hutton in surprise. 'You here? Is my wife ill?'

'We tried to fetch you earlier,' the soft, melancholy voice replied. 'It was thought you were at Mr Johnson's, but they had no news of you there.'

'No, I was detained. I had a breakdown,' Mr Hutton answered irritably. It was tiresome to be caught out in a lie.

'Your wife wanted to see you urgently.'

'Well, I can go now.' Mr Hutton moved toward the stairs.

Dr Libbard laid a hand on his arm. 'I am afraid it's too late.'

'Too late?' He began fumbling with his watch; it wouldn't come out of the pocket.

'Mrs Hutton passed away half an hour ago.'

The voice remained even in its softness, the melancholy of the eyes did not deepen. Dr Libbard spoke of death as he would speak of a local cricket match. All things were equally vain and equally deplorable.

Mr Hutton found himself thinking of Janet Spence's words. At any moment – at any moment. She had been extraordinary right.

'What happened?' he asked. 'What was the cause?'

Dr Libbard explained. It was heart failure brought on by a violent attack of nausea, caused in its turn by the eating of something of an irritant nature. Red currants? Mr Hutton suggested. Very likely. It had been too much for the heart. There was chronic valvular disease: something had collapsed under the strain. It was all over; she could not have suffered much.

'It's a pity they should have chosen the day of the Eton and Harrow match for the funeral,' old General Grego was saying as he stood, his top hat in his hand, under the shadow of the lych gate, wiping his face with his handkerchief.

Mr Hutton overheard the remark and with difficulty restrained a desire to inflict grievous bodily pain on the General. He would have liked to hit the old brute in the middle of his big red face. Monstrous great mulberry, spotted with meal! Was there no respect for the dead? Did nobody care? In theory he didn't much care; let the dead bury their dead. But here, at the graveside, he had found himself actually sobbing. Poor Emily, they had been pretty happy once. Now she was lying at the bottom of a seven-foot hole. And here was Grego complaining that he couldn't go to the Eton and Harrow match.

Mr Hutton looked round at the groups of black figures that were drifting slowly out of the churchyard toward the fleet of cabs and motors assembled in the road outside. Against the brilliant background of the July grass and flowers and foliage, they had a horribly alien and unnatural appearance. It pleased him to think that all these people would soon be dead, too.

That evening Mr Hutton sat up late in his library reading the life of Milton. There was no particular reason why he should have chosen Milton; it was the book that first came to hand, that was all. It was after midnight when he had finished. He got up from his armchair, unbolted the French windows, and stepped out on to the little paved terrace. The night was quiet and clear. Mr Hutton looked at the stars and at the holes between them, dropped his eyes to the dim lawns and hueless flowers of the garden, and let them wander over the farther landscape, black and grey under the moon.

He began to think with a kind of confused violence. There were the stars, there was Milton. A man can be somehow the peer of stars and night. Greatness, nobility. But is there seriously a difference between the noble and the ignoble? Milton, the stars, death, and himself – himself. The soul, the body; the higher and the lower nature. Perhaps there was something in it, after all. Milton had a god on his side and righteousness. What had he? Nothing, nothing whatever. There were only Doris's little breasts. What was the point of it all? Milton, the stars, death, and Emily in her grave, Doris and himself – always himself . . .

Oh, he was a futile and disgusting being. Everything convinced him of it. It was a solemn moment. He spoke aloud: 'I will, I will.' The sound of his own voice in the darkness was appalling; it seemed to him that he had sworn that infernal oath which binds even the gods; 'I will, I will.' There had been New Year's days and solemn anniversaries in the past, when he had felt the same contritions and recorded similar resolutions.

They had all thinned away, these resolutions, like smoke, into nothingness. But this was a greater moment and he had pronounced a more fearful oath. In the future it was to be different. Yes, he would live by reason, he would be industrious, he would curb his appetites, he would devote his life to some good purpose. It was resolved and it would be so.

In practice he saw himself spending his mornings in agricultural pursuits, riding round with the bailiff, seeing that his land was farmed in the best modern way – silos and artificial manures and continuous cropping and all that. The remainder of the day should be devoted to serious study. There was that book he had been intending to write for so long – *The Effect of Diseases on Civilisation*.

Mr Hutton went to bed humble and contrite, but with a sense that grace had entered into him. He slept for seven and a half hours, and woke to find the sun brilliantly shining. The emotions of the evening had been transformed by a good night's rest into his customary cheerfulness. It was not until a good many seconds after his return to conscious life that he remembered his resolutions, his Stygian oath. Milton and death seemed somehow different in the sunlight. As for the stars, they were not there. But the resolutions were good; even in the daytime he could see that. He had his horse saddled after breakfast, and rode round the farm with the bailiff. After luncheon he read Thucydides on the plague at Athens. In the evening he made a few notes on malaria in Southern Italy. While he was undressing he remembered that there was a good anecdote in Skelton's jest-book about the Sweating Sickness. He would have made a note of it if only he could have found a pencil.

On the sixth morning of his new life Mr Hutton found among his correspondence an envelope addressed in that peculiarly vulgar handwriting which he knew to be Doris's. He opened it, and began to read. She didn't know what to say; words were so inadequate. His wife dying like that, and so suddenly – it was too terrible. Mr Hutton sighed, but his interest revived somewhat as he read on:

Death is so frightening, I never think of it when I can help it. But when something like this happens, or when I am feeling ill or depressed, then I can't help remembering it is there so close, and I think about all the wicked things I have done and about you and me, and I wonder what will happen. And I am so frightened. I am so lonely, Teddy Bear, and so unhappy, and I don't know what to do. I can't get rid of the idea of dying, I am so wretched and helpless without you. I didn't mean to write to you; I meant to wait till you were out of mourning and could come and see me again, but I was so lonely and miserable, Teddy Bear, I had to write. I couldn't help it. Forgive me, I want you so much; I have nobody in the world but you. You are so good and gentle and understanding; there is nobody like you. I shall never forget how good and kind you have been to me, and you are so clever and know so much. I can't understand how you ever came to pay any attention to me, I am so dull and stupid, much less like me and love me, because you do love me a little, don't you, Teddy Bear?

Mr Hutton was touched with shame and remorse. To be thanked like this, worshipped for having seduced the girl – it was too much. It had just been a piece of imbecile wantonness. Imbecile, idiotic: there was no other way to describe it. For, when all was said, he had derived very little pleasure from it. Taking all things together, he had probably been more bored than amused. Once upon a time he had believed himself to be a hedonist. But to be a hedonist implies a certain process of reasoning, a deliberate choice of known pleasures, a rejection of known pains. This had been done without reason, against it. For he knew beforehand – so well, so well – that there was no interest or pleasure to be derived from these wretched affairs. And yet each time the vague itch came upon him he succumbed, involving himself once more in the old stupidity. There had been Maggie, his wife's maid, and Edith, the girl on the farm, and Mrs Pringle, and the waitress in London, and others – there seemed to be dozens of them. It had all been so stale and boring. He knew it would be; he always knew. And yet, and yet . . . Experience doesn't teach.

Poor little Doris! He would write to her kindly, comfortingly, but he wouldn't see her again. A servant came to tell him that his horse was saddled and waiting. He mounted and rode off. That morning the old bailiff was more irritating than usual.

Five days later Doris and Mr Hutton were sitting together on the pier at Southend; Doris, in white muslin with pink garnishings, radiated happiness; Mr Hutton, legs outstretched and chair tilted, had pushed the panama back from his forehead, and was trying to feel like a tripper. That night, when Doris was asleep, breathing and warm by his side, he recaptured, in this moment of darkness and physical fatigue, the rather cosmic emotion which had possessed him that evening, not a fortnight ago, when he had made his great resolution. And so his solemn oath had already gone the way of so many other resolutions. Unreason had triumphed; at the first itch of desire he had given way. He was hopeless, hopeless.

For a long time he lay with closed eyes, ruminating his humiliation. The girl stirred in her sleep. Mr Hutton turned over and looked in her direction. Enough vague light crept in between the half-drawn curtains to show her bare arm and shoulder, her neck, and the dark tangle of hair on the pillow. She was beautiful, desirable. Why did he lie there moaning over his sins? What did it matter? If he were hopeless, then so be it; he would make the best of his hopelessness. A glorious sense of irresponsibility suddenly filled him. He was free, magnificently free. In a kind of exaltation he drew the girl towards him. She woke, bewildered almost frightened under his rough kisses.

The storm of his desire subsided into a kind of serene merriment. The whole atmosphere seemed to be quivering with enormous silent laughter.

'Could anyone love you as much as I do, Teddy Bear?' The question came faintly from distant worlds of love.

'I think I know somebody who does,' Mr Hutton replied. The submarine laughter was swelling, rising, ready to break the surface o' silence and resound.

'Who? Tell me. Who do you mean?' The voice had come very close charged with suspicion, anguish, indignation, it belonged to this immediate world.

'A – ah!'

'Who?'

'You'll never guess.' Mr Hutton kept up the joke until it began to grow tedious, and then pronounced the name 'Janet Spence.'

Doris was incredulous. 'Miss Spence of the Manor? That old woman?' It was too ridiculous. Mr Hutton laughed too.

'But it's quite true,' he said. 'She adores me.' Oh, the vast joke. He would go and see her as soon as he returned – see and conquer. 'I believe she wants to marry me,' he added.

'But you wouldn't . . . you don't intend . . .'

The air was fairly crepitating with humour. Mr Hutton laughed aloud. 'I intend to marry you,' he said. It seemed to him the best joke he had ever made in his life.

When Mr Hutton left Southend he was once more a married man. It was agreed that, for the time being, the fact should be kept secret. In the autumn they would go abroad together, and the world should be informed. Meanwhile he was to go back to his own house and Doris to hers.

The day after his return he walked over in the afternoon to see Miss Spence. She received him with the old Gioconda.

'I was expecting you to come.'

'I couldn't keep away,' Mr Hutton gallantly replied.

They sat in the summerhouse. It was a pleasant place – a little old stucco temple bowered among dense bushes of evergreen. Miss Spence had left her mark on it by hanging up over the seat a blue-and-white Della Robbia plaque.

'I am thinking of going to Italy this autumn,' said Mr Hutton. He felt like a ginger-beer bottle, ready to pop with bubbling humorous excitement.

'Italy . . .' Miss Spence closed her eyes ecstatically. 'I feel drawn there too.'

'Why not let yourself be drawn?'

'I don't know. One somehow hasn't the energy and initiative to set out alone.'

'Alone . . .' Ah, sound of guitars and throaty singing! 'Yes, travelling alone isn't much fun.'

Miss Spence lay back in her chair without speaking. Her eyes were still closed. Mr Hutton stroked his moustache. The silence prolonged itself for what seemed a very long time.

Pressed to stay to dinner, Mr Hutton did not refuse. The fun had hardly started. The table was laid in the loggia. Through its arches they looked out on to the sloping garden, to the valley below and the farther hills. Light ebbed away; the heat and silence were oppressive. A huge cloud was mounting up the sky, and there were distant breathings of thunder. The thunder drew nearer, a wind began to blow, and the first drops of rain fell. The table was cleared. Miss Spence and Mr Hutton sat on in the growing darkness.

Miss Spence broke a long silence by saying meditatively:

'I think everyone has a right to a certain amount of happiness, don't you?'

'Most certainly.' But what was she leading up to? Nobody makes generalisations about life unless they mean to talk about themselves. Happiness: he looked back on his own life, and saw a cheerful, placid existence disturbed by no great griefs or discomforts or alarms. He had always had money and freedom; he had been able to do very much as he wanted. Yes, he supposed he had been happy – happier than most men. And now he was not merely happy; he had discovered in irresponsibility the secret of gaiety. He was about to say something about his happiness when Miss Spence went on speaking.

'People like you and me have a right to be happy some time in our lives.'

'Me?' said Mr Hutton surprised.

'Poor Henry! Fate hasn't treated either of us very well.'

'Oh, well, it might have treated me worse.'

'You're being cheerful. That's brave of you. But don't think I can't see behind the mask.'

Miss Spence spoke louder and louder as the rain came down more and more heavily. Periodically the thunder cut across her utterances. She talked on, shouting against the noise.

'I have understood you so well and for so long.'

A flash revealed her, aimed and intent, leaning towards him. Her eyes were two profound and menacing gun barrels. The darkness re-engulfed her.

'You were a lonely soul seeking a companion soul. I could sympathise with you in your solitude. Your marriage . . .'

The thunder cut short the sentence. Miss Spence's voice became audible once more with the words:

'. . . could offer no companionship to a man of your stamp. You needed a soul mate.'

A soul mate – he! A soul mate. It was incredibly fantastic. 'Georgette Leblanc, the ex-soul mate of Maurice Maeterlinck.' He had seen that in the paper a few days ago. So it was thus that Janet Spence had painted him in her imagination – a soul-mater. And for Doris he was a picture of goodness and the cleverest man in the world. And actually, really, he was what? Who knows?

'My heart went out to you. I could understand. I was lonely, too.' Miss Spence laid her hand on his knee. 'You were so patient.' Another flash. She was still aimed, dangerously. 'You never complained. But I could guess – I could guess.'

'How wonderful of you!' So he was an *âme imcomprise*. 'Only a woman's intuition . . .'

The thunder crashed and rumbled, died away, and only the sound of the rain was left. The thunder was his laughter, magnified, externalised. Flash and crash, there is was again, right on top of them.

'Don't you feel that you have within you something that is akin to this storm?' He could imagine her leaning forward as she uttered the words. 'Passion makes one the equal of the elements.'

What was his gambit now? Why obviously, he should have said 'Yes,' and ventured on some unequivocal gesture. But Mr Hutton suddenly took fright. The ginger beer in him had gone flat. The woman was serious – terribly serious. He was appalled.

Passion? 'No,' he desperately answered. 'I am without passion.'

But his remark was either unheard or unheeded, for Miss Spence went on with a growing exaltation, speaking so rapidly, however, and in such a burningly intimate whisper that Mr Hutton found it very difficult to distinguish what she was saying. She was telling him, as far as he could make out, the story of her life. The lightning was less frequent now, and there were long intervals of darkness. But at each flash he saw her still aiming towards him, still yearning forward with a terrifying intensity. Darkness, the rain, and then flash! her face was there, close at hand. A pale mask, greenish white; the large eyes, the narrow barrel of the mouth, the heavy eyebrows. Agrippina, or wasn't it rather – yes, wasn't it rather George Robey?

He began devising absurd plans for escaping. He might suddenly jump up, pretending he had seen a burglar – Stop thief! stop thief! – and dash off into the night in pursuit. Or should he say that he felt faint, a heart attack? or that he had seen a ghost – Emily's ghost – in the garden? Absorbed in his childish plotting, he had ceased to pay any attention to Miss Spence's words. The spasmodic clutching of her hand recalled his thoughts.

'I honoured you for that, Henry,' she was saying.

Honoured him for what?

'Marriage is a sacred tie, and your respect for it, even when the marriage was, as it was in your case, an unhappy one, made me respect you and admire you, and – shall I dare say the word?'

Oh, the burglar, the ghost in the garden! But it was too late.

'. . . yes, love you, Henry, all the more. But we're free now, Henry.'

Free? There was a movement in the dark, and she was kneeling on the floor by his chair.

'Oh, Henry, Henry, I have been unhappy too.'

Her arms embraced him, and by the shaking of her body he could feel that she was sobbing. She might have been a suppliant crying for mercy.

'You mustn't, Janet,' he protested. Those tears were terrible, terrible. 'Not now, not now! You must be calm; you must go to bed.' He patted her shoulder, then got up, disengaging himself from her embrace. He left her still crouching on the floor beside the chair on which he had been sitting.

Groping his way into the hall, and without waiting to look for his hat, he went out of the house, taking infinite pains to close the front door noiselessly behind him. The clouds had blown over, and the moon was shining from a clear sky. There were puddles all along the road, and a noise of running water rose from the gutters and ditches. Mr Hutton splashed along, not caring if he got wet.

How heart-rendingly she had sobbed! With the emotions of pity and remorse that the recollection evoked in him there was a certain resentment: why couldn't she have played the game that he was playing – the heartless, amusing game? Yes, but he had known all the time that she wouldn't, she couldn't play that game; he had known and persisted.

What had she said about passion and the elements. Something absurdly stale, but true, true. There she was, a cloud black-bosomed and charged with thunder, and he, like some absurd little Benjamin Franklin, had sent up a kite into the heart of the menace. Now he was complaining that his toy had drawn the lightning.

She was probably still kneeling by that chair in the loggia, crying.

But why hadn't he been able to keep up the game? Why had his irresponsibility deserted him, leaving him suddenly sober in a cold world? There were no answers to any of his questions. One idea burned steady and luminous in his mind – the idea of flight. He must get away at once.

'What are you thinking about, Teddy Bear?'

'Nothing.'

There was a silence. Mr Hutton remained motionless, his elbows on the parapet of the terrace, his chin in his hands, looking down over Florence. He had taken a villa on one of the hilltops to the south of the city. From a little raised terrace at the end of the garden one looked down a long fertile valley on to the town and beyond it to the bleak mass of Monte Morello and, eastwards of it, to the peopled hill of Fiesole, dotted with white houses. Everything was clear and luminous in the September sunshine.

'Are you worried about anything?'

'No, thank you.'

'Tell me, Teddy Bear.'

'But, my dear, there's nothing to tell.' Mr Hutton turned round, smiled, and patted the girl's hand. 'I think you'd better go in and have your siesta. It's too hot for you here.'

'Very well, Teddy Bear. Are you coming too?'

'When I've finished my cigar.'

'All right. But do hurry up and finish it, Teddy Bear.' Slowly, reluctantly, she descended the steps of the terrace and walked toward the house.

Mr Hutton continued his contemplation of Florence. He had need to be alone. It was good sometimes to escape from Doris and the restless solicitude of her passion. He had never known the pains of loving hopelessly, but he was experiencing now the pains of being loved. These last weeks had been a period of growing discomfort. Doris was always with him, like an obsession, like a guilty conscience. Yes, it was good to be alone.

He pulled an envelope out of his pocket and opened it; not without reluctance. He hated letters; they always contained something unpleasant – nowadays, since his second marriage. This was from his sister. He began skimming through the insulting home truths of which it was composed.

The words 'indecent haste', 'social suicide', 'scarcely cold in her grave', 'person of the lower classes', all occurred. They were inevitable now in any communication from a well-meaning and right-thinking relative. Impatient, he was about to tear the stupid letter to pieces when his eyes fell on a sentence at the bottom of the third page. His heart beat with uncomfortable violence as he read it. It was too monstrous! Janet Spence was going about telling everyone that he had poisoned his wife in order to marry Doris. What damnable malice! Ordinarily a man of the suavest temper, Mr Hutton found himself trembling with rage. He took the childish satisfaction of calling names – he cursed the woman.

Then suddenly he saw the ridiculous side of the situation. The notion that he should have murdered anyone in order to marry Doris! If they only knew how miserably bored he was. Poor, dear Janet! She had tried to be malicious; she had only succeeded in being stupid.

A sound of footsteps aroused him; he looked round. In the garden below the little terrace the servant girl of the house was picking fruit. A Neapolitan, strayed somehow as far north as Florence, she was a specimen of the classical type – a little debased. Her profile might have been taken from a Sicilian coin of a bad period. Her features, carved floridly in the grand tradition, expressed an almost perfect stupidity. Her mouth was the most beautiful thing about her; the calligraphic hand of nature had richly curved it into an expression of mulish bad temper. . . . Under her hideous black clothes, Mr Hutton divined a powerful body, firm and massive. He had looked at her before with a vague interest and curiosity. Today the curiosity defined and focused itself into a desire. An idyll of Theocritus. Here was the woman; he, alas, was not precisely like a goatherd on the volcanic hills. He called to her.

'Armida!'

The smile with which she answered him was so provocative, attested so easy a virtue, that Mr Hutton took fright. He was on the brink once more – on the brink. He must draw back, oh! quickly, quickly, before it was too late. The girl continued to look up at him.

'*Ha chiamato?*' she asked at last.

Stupidity or reason? Oh, there was no choice now. It was imbecility every time.

'*Scendo,*' he called back to her. Twelve steps led from the garden to the terrace. Mr Hutton counted them. Down, down, down, down. . . . He saw a vision of himself descending from one circle of the inferno to the next – from a darkness full of wind and hail to an abyss of stinking mud.

For a good many days the Hutton case had a place on the front page of every newspaper. There had been no more popular murder trial since George Smith had temporarily eclipsed the European War by drowning in a warm bath his seventh bride. The public imagination was stirred by this tale of murder brought to light months after the date of the crime. Here, it was felt, was one of those incidents in human life, so notable because they are so rare, which do definitely justify the ways of God to man. A wicked man had been moved by an illicit passion to kill his wife. For months he had lived in sin and fancied security – only to be dashed at last more horribly into the pit he had prepared for himself. Murder will out, and here was a case of it. The readers of the newspapers were in a position to follow every movement of the hand of God. There had been vague, but persistent, rumours in the neighbourhood; the police had taken action at last. Then came the exhumation order, the post-mortem examination, the inquest, the evidence of the experts, the verdict of the coroner's jury, the trial, the condemnation. For once Providence had done its duty, obviously, grossly, didactically, as in a melodrama. The newspapers were right in making of the case the staple intellectual food of a whole season.

Mr Hutton's first emotion when he was summoned from Italy to give evidence at the inquest was one of indignation. It was a monstrous, a scandalous thing that the police should take such idle, malicious gossip seriously. When the inquest was over he would bring an action for malicious prosecution against the Chief Constable; he would sue the Spence woman for slander.

The inquest was opened; the astonishing evidence unrolled itself. The experts had examined the body, and had found traces of arsenic; they were of the opinion that the late Mrs Hutton had died of arsenic poisoning.

Arsenic poisioning . . . Emily died of arsenic poisoning? After that, Hutton learned with surprise that there was enough arsenicated insecticide in his greenhouse to poison an army.

It was now, quite suddenly, that he saw it: there was a case against him. Fascinated, he watched it growing, growing, like some monstrous tropical plant. It was enveloping him, surrounding him; he was lost in a tangled forest.

When was the poison administered? The experts agreed that it must have been swallowed eight or nine hours before death. About lunchtime? Yes, about lunchtime. Clara, the parlourmaid, was called. Mrs Hutton, she remembered, had asked her to go and fetch her medicine. Mr Hutton had volunteered to go instead; he had gone alone. Miss Spence – ah, the memory of the storm, the white, aimed face! the horror of it all! – Miss Spence confirmed Clara's statement, and added that Mr Hutton had come back with the medicine already poured out in a wineglass, not in the bottle.

Mr Hutton's indignation evaporated. He was dismayed, frightened. It was all too fantastic to be taken seriously, and yet this nightmare was a fact – it was actually happening.

M'Nab had seen them kissing, often. He had taken them for a drive on the day of Mrs Hutton's death. He could see them reflected in the windscreen, sometimes out of the tail of his eye.

The inquest was adjourned. That evening Doris went to bed with a headache. When he went to her room after dinner, Mr Hutton found her crying.

'What's the matter?' He sat down on the edge of her bed and began to stroke her hair. For a long time she did not answer, and he went on stroking her hair mechanically, almost unconsciously; sometimes, even, he bent down and kissed her bare shoulder. He had his own affairs, however, to think about. What had happened? How was it that the stupid gossip had actually come true? Emily had died of arsenic poisoning. It was absurd, impossible. The order of things had been broken, and he was at the mercy of an irresponsibility. What had happened, what was going to happen? He was interrupted in the midst of his thoughts.

'It's my fault – it's my fault!' Doris suddenly sobbed out. 'I shouldn't have loved you; I oughtn't to have let you love me. Why was I ever born?'

Mr Hutton didn't say anything, but looked down in silence at the abject figure of misery lying on the bed.

'If they do anything to you I shall kill myself.'

She sat up, held him for a moment at arm's length, and looked at him with a kind of violence, as though she were never to see him again.

'I love you, I love you, I love you.' She drew him, inert and passive, towards her, clasped him, and pressed herself against him. 'I didn't know you loved me as much as that, Teddy Bear. But why did you do it – why did you do it?'

Mr Hutton undid her clasping arms and got up. His face became very red. 'You seem to take it for granted that I murdered my wife,' he said. 'It's really too grotesque. What do you all take me for? A cinema hero?' He had begun to lose his temper. All the exasperation, all the fear and bewilderment of the day, was transformed into a violent anger against her. 'It's all such damned stupidity. Haven't you any conception of a civilised man's mentality? Do I look the sort of man who'd go about slaughtering people? I suppose you imagined I was so insanely in love with you that I could commit any folly. When will you women understand that one isn't insanely in love? All one asks for is a quiet life, which you won't allow one to have. I don't know what the devil ever induced me to marry you. It was all a damned stupid, practical joke. And now you go about saying I'm a murderer. I won't stand it.'

Mr Hutton stamped toward the door. He had said horrible things, he knew – odious things that he ought speedily to unsay. But he wouldn't. He closed the door behind him.

'Teddy Bear!' He turned the handle; the latch clicked into place. 'Teddy Bear!' The voice that came to him through the closed door was agonised. Should he go back? He ought to go back. He touched the handle, then withdrew his fingers and quickly walked away. When he was half-way down the stairs he halted. She might try to do something silly – throw herself out of the window or God knows what! He listened attentively; there was no sound. But he pictured her very clearly, tiptoeing across the room, lifting the sash as high as it would go, leaning out into the cold night air. It was raining a little. Under the window lay the paved terrace. How far below? Twenty-five or thirty feet? Once, when he was walking along Piccadilly, a dog had jumped out of a third-storey window of the Ritz. He had seen it fall; he had heard it strike the pavement. Should he go back? He was damned if he would; he hated her.

He sat for a long time in the library. What had happened? What was happening? He turned the question over and over in his mind and could find no answer. Suppose the nightmare dreamed itself out to its horrible conclusion. Death was waiting for him. His eyes filled with tears; he wanted so passionately to live. 'Just to be alive.' Poor Emily had wished it too, he remembered: 'Just to be alive.' There were still so many places in this astonishing world unvisited, so many queer delightful people still unknown, so many lovely women never so much as seen. The huge white oxen would still be dragging their wains along the Tuscan roads, the cypresses would still go up, straight as pillars, to the blue heaven; but he would not be there to see them. And the sweet southern wines – Tear of Christ and Blood of Judas – others would drink them, not he. Others would walk down the obscure and narrow lanes between the bookshelves in the London Library, sniffing the dusty perfume of good literature, peering at strange titles, discovering unknown names, exploring the fringes of vast domains of knowledge. He would be lying in a hole in the ground. And why, why? Confusedly he felt that some extraordinary kind of justice was being done. In the past he had been wanton and imbecile and irresponsible. Now Fate was playing as wantonly, as irresponsibly, with him. It was tit for tat, and God existed after all.

He felt that he would like to pray. Forty years ago he used to kneel by his bed every evening. The nightly formula of his childhood came to him almost unsought from some long unopened chamber of the memory. 'God bless Father and Mother, Tom and Cissie and the Baby, Mademoiselle and Nurse, and everybody that I love, and make me a good boy. Amen.' They were all dead now – all except Cissie.

His mind seemed to soften and dissolve; a great calm descended upon his spirit. He went upstairs to ask Doris's forgiveness. He found her lying on the couch at the foot of the bed. On the floor beside her stood a blue bottle of liniment, marked 'Not to be taken'; she seemed to have drunk about half of it.

'You didn't love me,' was all she said when she opened her eyes to find him bending over her.

Dr Libbard arrived in time to prevent any very serious consequences. 'You mustn't do this again,' he said while Mr Hutton was out of the room.

'What's to prevent me?' she asked defiantly.

Dr Libbard looked at her with his large, sad eyes. 'There's nothing to prevent you,' he said. 'Only yourself and your baby. Isn't it rather bad luck on your baby, not allowing it to come into the world because you want to go out of it?'

Doris was silent for a time. 'All right,' she whispered. 'I won't.'

Mr Hutton sat by her bedside for the rest of the night. He felt himself now to be indeed a murderer. For a time he persuaded himself that he loved this pitiable child. Dozing in his chair, he woke up, stiff and cold, to find himself drained dry, as it were, of every emotion. He had become nothing but a tired and suffering carcass. At six o'clock he undressed and went to bed for a couple of hours' sleep. In the course of the same afternoon the coroner's jury brought in a verdict of 'Wilful Murder,' and Mr Hutton was committed for trial.

Miss Spence was not at all well. She had found her public appearances in the witness box very trying, and when it was all over she had something that was very nearly a breakdown. She slept badly, and suffered from nervous indigestion. Dr Libbard used to call every other day. She talked to him a great deal – mostly about the Hutton case. . . . Her moral indignation was always on the boil. Wasn't it appalling to think that one had had a murderer in one's house? Wasn't it extraordinary that one could have been for so long mistaken about the man's character? (But she had had an inkling from the first.) And then the girl he had gone off with – so low class, so little better than a prostitute. The news that the second Mrs Hutton was expecting a baby – the posthumous child of a condemned and executed criminal – revolted her; the thing was shocking – an obscenity. Dr Libbard answered her gently and vaguely, and prescribed bromide.

One morning he interrupted her in the midst of her customary tirade. 'By the way,' he said in his soft, melancholy voice, 'I suppose it was really you who poisoned Mrs Hutton.'

Miss Spence stared at him for two or three seconds with enormous eyes, and then quietly said, 'Yes.' After that she started to cry.

'In the coffee, I suppose.'

She seemed to nod assent. Dr Libbard took out his fountain pen, and in his neat, meticulous calligraphy wrote out a prescription for a sleeping draught.

Henry Holt

The Almost Perfect Crime

At his club, Mr David Porlock leaned back in a comfortable chair and lighted a well-seasoned cigar, content with the good things of this world. He had dined, as he did everything, deliberately and artistically.

After watching the first fragrant wisps of smoke go upward, he turned his attention to the golden-hued contents of a liqueur glass, and was on the point of raising it to his lips when a waiter approached with a card on a silver salver.

'Detective-Inspector Silver, of New Scotland Yard,' Mr Porlock read aloud, with an impassive face. 'What does he want?'

'He didn't say, sir.'

'Show him into the visitors' room. I will be there in a few minutes.'

Mr Porlock finished the liqueur and, in his own good time, strolled away to see what Scotland Yard could want of him.

'I'm sorry to trouble you, sir,' said Inspector Silver. 'It's about Mr Charles Cavendish, the bank manager.'

'Cavendish? What's wrong with him?' asked Mr Porlock with quick interest.

'Well, to tell you the truth, I don't know. He seems to have disappeared in some mysterious way.'

Porlock's expression, which had become serious, suddenly relaxed.

'Oh, nonsense!' he said. 'Men like Cavendish don't disappear. He dined with me last night. There can't be very much wrong.'

'That's what everybody hopes, but he never got home last night, and he hasn't been seen since.'

Porlock's eyes held a puzzled look as they rested on those of the C.I.D. man.

'I can't understand it,' he said. 'Mr Cavendish seemed all right when he left here.'

'What time was that, sir?'

'Oh, I should say about eleven or soon after. I didn't particularly notice.'

'Did he say where he was going?'

'No. But naturally I assumed he was heading straight home, and I had every reason to suppose that was so.'

Silver touched his iron-grey moustache with his fingers.

'Did he seem quite normal then, sir?'

'Perfectly. As a matter of fact he was in excellent spirits. We had arranged to do a little fishing together next Saturday.'

'You and Mr Cavendish are old friends, I believe?'

'That is so. We were at school together twenty-five years ago. I shouldn't take this too seriously, inspector. He's sure to turn up very soon. Unless, of course, he had met with some accident.'

'We've made enquiries at the hospitals, but they've seen nothing of him.'

'Wait a moment, didn't he say – yes, I think he told me his wife was away. In Eastbourne, or somewhere like that.'

'Mrs Cavendish came home last night unexpectedly, sir, and was very worried. She rang us up at four this morning. We have made exhaustive enquiries without success. It was only this evening that the chief cashier remembered he'd overheard Mr Cavendish say something about going to dine with you last night.'

'Well, it certainly does sound rather odd,' commented Porlock.

'Would you mind telling me just what happened last night, sir?'

'With pleasure. I met him at my club at eight o'clock. We dined and had a game of billiards. Then we took a taxi to my flat.'

'What time did you get to your flat, sir?'

'It must have been about ten.'

'Had you any special reason for going there?'

'Yes. I have some very fine old Napoleon brandy, and I wanted him to taste it.'

'So he stayed at your home for just over an hour?'

'Something like that.'

'Where were you when you said "good-night" to him?'

'At the door of my flat.'

'Then he went down in the lift alone?'

'No. Actually, he didn't use the lift. He said he couldn't be bothered to wait for it.'

'Did you leave the flat again, sir?'

'No. I read for a while, and went to bed at about midnight.'

The inspector's fingers strayed to his moustache again.

'That all seems very clear,' he said. 'You must have been the last person to see him.'

'Apparently. That is, with the exception of the night porter, who generally sits in his little office in the hall. I don't know whether he noticed Mr Cavendish go out, though.'

'Thank you, sir. We've got to make enquiries in a case like this. Let's hope the gentleman will turn up, as you say, pretty soon.'

'It certainly is queer. Bank managers are such stolid, dependable people. Perhaps he's lost his memory and wandered away. One can't help feeling a little anxious.'

II

Another day passed. The newspapers printed a few cautious paragraphs, but did not display any violent interest in the matter because people vanish every day. True, this was a bank manager, which made the thing more noteworthy. Some publicity was obtained by means of a wireless S.O.S. By the end of the week, however, other things had claimed the attention of the public, and the bank continued to function perfectly with the assistant manager temporarily at the helm.

At the end of a month everybody, excepting those who knew Mr Cavendish personally, had forgotten all about his disappearance, and Mrs Cavendish began to assume that she had, in some inexplicable fashion, become a widow.

Mr David Porlock, who was a gentleman of leisure, decided to spend a few weeks in Paris, this being the month of June when the gay city was at its best. All his luggage was deposited in the cloakroom at Victoria station. Then he did one or two little errands, and called in at the club for luncheon, but before he had tasted the delicate sole that was set before him, a waiter presented him with a card bearing the name of Detective Inspector Silver.

Glancing at his luncheon, Mr Porlock frowned slightly.

'Tell him I'll be down presently,' he told the waiter, and picked up his knife and fork. When, in due course, he descended, the detective was waiting patiently.

'What is it now, inspector?' asked the clubman with superficial amiability. 'I can't stay very long as I'm leaving for Paris to-day.'

'It's about that business of Mr Cavendish again, sir. We've still got it on our books.'

'Oh yes, of course. Once you fellows get your teeth into a thing you never let go, do you?'

'Not if we can help it. And this case has never been explained to our satisfaction.'

'I'm afraid he must have lost his memory.'

'You might think so, in a way, sir,' said Silver, 'but his doctor can't see it in that light. Says he'd have thought the last man in the world to suffer from amnesia was Mr Cavendish.'

'Then I give it up,' mused the clubman, in a slightly perplexed fashion.'

'But that's what we never do.'

'Well, what did you wish to see me about? I can only give you a few minutes.'

The stolid inspector fingered his iron-grey moustache.

'I'm sorry, sir, but we can't hurry a thing like this. There are one or two points I should like to take up with you again, if you don't mind. I've got my notes here of what you said on the day after Mr Cavendish disappeared.'

'There is obviously nothing I can add to what I said then.'

'Maybe not, sir. But all the same, even if it's only a matter of routine, I've got to carry on. Now, I see you said that you arrived at your flat with Mr Cavendish at ten o'clock at night, and you did not go out again?'

Porlock gave a little laugh.

'Yes, but this is all ancient history. I assure you—'

'How long are you going away for, sir?'

'Oh, a month or possibly six weeks. It depends what I find to do in Paris.'

'May I ask what luggage you're taking?'

Mr Porlock, a man of some dignity, looked faintly surprised.

'I don't quite see how that can possibly concern Scotland Yard, but if you really wish to know, I have no objection to explaining.'

'I'd like you to, sir,' replied Silver, stolid as ever.

'Let me see, there's a trunk, a suit-case and an attache-case. Now, *why* on earth did you want to know?'

'No special reason, sir, excepting that, as you put it, once we get our teeth into a job, we keep them there. Some day we may find out what happened to Mr Cavendish, but until then we can't afford to leave any stone unturned.'

'Highly commendable, but I'm afraid I can't help you any more. If you'll excuse me, inspector—'

'Excuse *me*, sir. There are one or two stones that we haven't quite finished turning over yet. If you'll give me your help for a little while, I'll soon mop this up, and then you'll be able to go away and forget all about the matter. Just as a formality, would you be so kind as to tell me where your luggage is?'

'Certainly. In the cloakroom at Victoria Station. But isn't all this rather ridiculous?'

'Where the question of a man's life is at stake, sir, we have to do all kinds of things, whether they look ridiculous to other people or not. There's no reason why you shouldn't answer my question, I suppose?'

'None at all, excepting that it seems a waste of time.'

'And you wouldn't mind accompanying me to Victoria Station?'

'Not if you wish,' said Mr Porlock. 'But I still don't see your point.'

'Just routine, sir,' murmured the inspector. 'There's a lot of that in police work. Some folks get their backs up when we have to ask questions, but it doesn't make any difference to us, though we try not to irritate people more than we can help. Shall we go, sir?'

Porlock's shoulders moved slightly. Then he agreed.

'Now, sir,' said the inspector when they reached Victoria, 'I'd like to see your things, please. You've got a cloakroom ticket?'

With a weary smile, Porlock handed it to the inspector.

'There you are,' he said, 'and if you would like to see inside the baggage, here are the keys. I don't know what you expect to find, but don't disarrange my clothes more than you can help.'

Almost apologetically, Silver unfastened the lock of the trunk and, after a cursory glance within, closed it again.

'That's all right, sir,' he said. 'No ill feeling, I hope.'

'Not the slightest,' replied Mr Porlock, quite amiably. 'Now tell me why you wanted to look inside my trunk?'

'Just to see what there was in it, sir,' was the bland reply.

'Well, are you satisfied?'

'Naturally I can believe the evidence of my own eyes.' Silver gave a gentle tug at his moustache. 'By the way, sir, you haven't any more luggage?'

'Heavens, man! How much do you think one wants to take to Paris for a month?'

'But are these the only things that were taken from your flat this morning?'

'What are you getting at, inspector?'

'I should just like an answer to my question, sir, if it's all the same to you.'

'These are the only things that I'm taking to Paris.'

'I asked if these are the only things that were taken from your flat this morning.'

'Of course.'

For a fraction of a second there was an ominous glitter in Silver's eyes.

'You are quite sure of that?'

'Quite.'

'Only one trunk and these two cases?'

'That is so.'

'I should like you to think again and be certain about your answer,

Mr Porlock.'

'I am not in the habit of making mis-statements, inspector,' was the steady reply.

'I see. Then in this case it must be that you have forgotten.'

'Forgotten what?'

'I am told that you brought two trunks from your flat to this cloak-room.'

Mr Porlock's eyes narrowed thoughtfully for a moment.

'You're quite right, inspector,' he said. 'I'm terribly sorry, but you're getting me quite confused with all this cross-examination. There *was* another case. It contains a number of somewhat valuable articles – trophies and so on, which I never care to leave in the flat when I go away. Until you mentioned it I had absolutely forgotten.'

'I understand, sir. Very natural, too, just when you're in the middle of going away. Where did you leave that other case?'

'In the strong room at my bank. They always keep it there for me.'

'I suppose you wouldn't mind me having a peep inside that too, would you?'

'Not at all. Here, take the key. I shan't want it until I come back. Good-bye, inspector. Scotland Yard certainly is persistent. However, I suppose you have to be. I must go now.'

There was a slightly more alert air about Silver.

'I'm afraid that doesn't quite finish the routine, sir. I'd like you to accompany me to the bank.'

'What on earth for? I should miss my train.'

'Just the same, sir, I must ask you to go to the bank with me.'

Porlock's dignity peeped out again.

'Aren't you rather exceeding your duty, inspector? I don't mind fall-ing in with your wishes up to a point, but I have made definite plans about going away and—'

'I can't help that, sir. I'm only doing my duty, and I can't allow any one's plans to interfere.'

Porlock appeared to waver for a few seconds.

'Oh, well,' he said at last. 'It's a damned nuisance, but if you insist I suppose I must.'

'That's the spirit, sir,' replied Silver. 'It won't take long in a taxi.'

They walked out into the station yard and engaged a cab.

'One moment,' said Porlock before stepping into it. 'I want some cigarettes.'

'Funny thing, so do I,' said Silver.

Ten seconds later Porlock thrust out his leg to trip the detective up, and darted away like a trout, but Silver, recovering his balance quickly, was after him. The chase was brief, and after a short struggle a band of metal was securely placed round the clubman's wrist.

'Just to make quite sure, you know,' said Silver. 'Now, if you don't mind, we'll be moving on to the bank.'

Mr Porlock sighed as their taxi slid through the traffic.

'The boulevards of Paris are beautiful in June,' he said.

'So I've always heard,' remarked the C.I.D. man. 'I was thinking of taking my wife over there when I go on my holidays shortly.'

The cab was held up at traffic lights.

'I suppose there really is no chance of my seeing Paris again,' mused Mr Porlock.

'Not if that case at the bank contains what I think it does.'

'I wonder if you could oblige me with a cigarette?'

'Sorry. I never carry them. I don't smoke.'

Mr Porlock looked at him oddly.

'Then you knew all the time?'

'I had a pretty good idea.'

'You intrigue me, inspector. I didn't see how anybody on earth could find out. I was flattering myself that I had committed a perfect crime. How did you get on to it?'

'Just routine,' remarked Silver.

'You're very modest. You must have a touch of genius.'

'Genius? Well, we don't go in much for that at the Yard, sir. We've no time for fancy tricks. We generally get there though, by plodding on.'

'I must have made a mistake somewhere. Won't you satisfy my curiosity?'

'If it's any satisfaction to you, sir, I'll say you did a pretty neat job of work. Why did you kill Cavendish? We like to find a motive and then work backwards, but in this case—'

'The motive was my secret, inspector. Cavendish was the only man alive who might have stumbled on something which would have ended in my being sentenced to a long term of imprisonment. He never really suspected how near he was to the truth, but there was danger. With him out of the way, I was safe, and, but for your persistence, he would have remained hermetically sealed up in that case in the strong room of his own bank for an indefinite period. Banks never interfere with anything stowed away in their strong room. It was Mr Cavendish himself who put me on to the neat idea. In six months or so, when the whole thing had been more or less forgotten, I intended to remove the case and dispose of it at leisure. The situation seemed fool-proof to me. Where did I make a slip?'

'To be quite fair,' said Silver in matter-of-fact tones, 'I don't think you made a slip at all – that is not one which you could have anticipated.'

'My manner was quite natural when you first questioned me?'

'Very convincing. It's a miracle you didn't get away with the whole thing, only, as I say, we keep plodding on, and, sooner or later, run up against some queer little thing. It may lead nowhere, but we track it down, just in case.'

'And what was the queer little thing that led to my Waterloo?'

'Well, first of all, you got Mr Cavendish up into your flat and gave him a glass of old Napoleon brandy. And while he was tasting it – mind you, this is only my surmise – you knocked him on the head.'

'That happens to be perfectly correct.'

'It seemed probable, anyway. Then you finished him off and put him into the case which had been stored many times already in the strong room of the bank. The clerks, therefore, would accept it again as a matter of habit.'

'Why not?'

'Quite so. But you knew there was a night porter on duty at the flats where you lived. He had seen you and Mr Cavendish go in. You felt you would be doubly safe if Milligan, the night porter, could see him walk out again.'

'Please go on.'

'You and Mr Cavendish were somewhat alike. You were about the same height and there was a certain facial resemblance, excepting that he wore a moustache and you were clean shaven. Finally he wore gold-rimmed spectacles and you don't. You put on his spectacles and a false moustache which you had carefully prepared beforehand, and you made your eyebrows bushy like his. You thought it would be too risky to descend in the lift with Milligan, so you walked down the steps and passed out into the street, disguised as Mr Cavendish, wearing his hat and overcoat.'

'That is perfectly true,' remarked Mr Porlock, 'and, as far as I am aware, it worked. Afterwards, I put the hat and a few stones into the pockets of the overcoat, and threw it into the Thames, thinking that it would sink.'

'You were probably right,' agreed Silver.

'And I returned to the flat again at about four o'clock in the morning, knowing that the night porter would, as usual, be dozing in his chair then. I'm certain he didn't see me, and, anyhow, I often return to the flat very late.'

'Milligan didn't see you come in again, Mr Porlock.'

'Then I fail to see where I tripped up.'

'I'm not surprised,' remarked the C.I.D. man. 'I didn't get on to it myself until long afterwards. As far as we knew, the night porter was the last man to have seen Mr Cavendish alive. For that reason I talked to him on several occasions. In the end he mentioned a curious thing which he didn't think important. He is not a particularly observant person, but he has a trick of noticing people's hands. Personally I glance at their feet: we're all different in that respect. Milligan said that as "Mr Cavendish" walked out he caught sight of the man's hands, and observed that they were like yours. Long, slender fingers and so forth – quite the artistic type. This provided me with the one more stone to overturn. I found that Mr Cavendish had broad, stumpy hands, and then I knew I'd struck something.'

'When was that.'

'Yesterday afternoon. From then on I had you kept under close observation. We had no means of knowing what you might have done with the body. I hardly thought you still had it in the flat, though I was going to make a search there. If you'd removed the trunks a few days earlier we might never have got at the truth. But our man saw them go out this morning, and after that – well, it was just a matter of routine.'

W. Somerset Maugham

The Letter

Outside on the quay the sun beat fiercely. A stream of motors, lorries and buses, private cars and hirelings, sped up and down the crowded thoroughfare, and every chauffeur blew his horn; rickshaws threaded their nimble path amid the throng, and the panting coolies found breath to yell at one another; coolies, carrying heavy bales, sidled along with their quick jog-trot and shouted to the passer-by to make way; itinerant vendors proclaimed their wares. Singapore is the meeting-place of a hundred peoples; and men of all colours, black Tamils, yellow Chinks, brown Malays, Armenians, Jews and Bengalis, called to one another in raucous tones. But inside the office of Messrs. Ripley, Joyce and Naylor it was pleasantly cool; it was dark after the dusty glitter of the street and agreeably quiet after its unceasing din. Mr Joyce sat in his private room, at the table, with an electric fan turned full on him. He was leaning back, his elbows on the arms of the chair, with the tips of the outstretched fingers of one hand resting neatly against the tips of the outstretched fingers of the other. His gaze rested on the battered volumes of the Law Reports which stood on a long shelf in front of him. On the top of a cupboard were square boxes of japanned tin, on which were painted the names of various clients.

There was a knock at the door.

'Come in.'

A Chinese clerk, very neat in his white ducks, opened it.

'Mr Crosbie is here, sir.'

He spoke beautiful English, accenting each word with precision, and Mr Joyce had often wondered at the extent of his vocabulary. Ong Chi Seng was a Cantonese, and he had studied law at Gray's Inn. He was spending a year or two with Messrs Ripley, Joyce and Naylor in order to prepare himself for practice on his own account. He was industrious, obliging, and of exemplary character.

'Show him in,' said Mr Joyce.

He rose to shake hands with his visitor and asked him to sit down. The light fell on him as he did so. The face of Mr Joyce remained in shadow. He was by nature a silent man, and now he looked at Robert Crosbie for quite a minute without speaking. Crosbie was a big fellow, well over six feet high, with broad shoulders, and muscular. He was a rubber-planter, hard with the constant exercise of walking over the estate, and with the tennis which was his relaxation when the day's work was over. He was deeply sunburned. His hairy hands, his feet in clumsy boots were enormous, and Mr Joyce found himself thinking that a blow of that great fist would easily kill the fragile Tamil. But there was no fierceness in his blue eyes; they were confiding and gentle; and his face, with its big, undistinguished features, was open, frank and honest. But at this moment it bore a look of deep distress. It was drawn and haggard.

'You look as though you hadn't had much sleep the last night or two,' said Mr Joyce.

'I haven't.'

Mr Joyce noticed now the old felt hat, with its broad double brim, which Crosbie had placed on the table; and then his eyes travelled to the khaki shorts he wore, showing his red hairy thighs, the tennis shirt open at the neck, without a tie, and the dirty khaki jacket with the ends of the sleeves turned up. He looked as though he had just come in from a long tramp among the rubber trees. Mr Joyce gave a slight frown.

'You must pull yourself together, you know. You must keep your head.'

'Oh, I'm all right.'

'Have you seen your wife to-day?'

'No, I'm to see her this afternoon. You know, it is a damned shame that they should have arrested her.'

'I think they had to do that,' Mr Joyce answered in his level, soft tone.

'I should have thought they'd have let her out on bail.'

'It's a very serious charge.'

'It is damnable. She did what any decent woman would do in her place. Only, nine women out of ten wouldn't have the pluck. Leslie's the best woman in the world. She wouldn't hurt a fly. Why, hang it all, man, I've been married to her for twelve years, do you think I don't know her? God, if I'd got hold of the man I'd have wrung his neck, I'd have killed him without a moment's hesitation. So would you.'

'My dear fellow, everybody's on your side. No one has a good word to say for Hammond. We're going to get her off. I don't suppose either the assessors or the judge will go into court without having already made up their minds to bring in a verdict of not guilty.'

'The whole thing's a farce,' said Crosbie violently. 'She ought never to have been arrested in the first place, and then it's terrible, after all the poor girl's gone through, to subject her to the ordeal of a trial. There's not a soul I've met since I've been in Singapore, man or woman, who hasn't told me that Leslie was absolutely justified. I think it's awful to keep her in prison all these weeks.'

'The law is the law. After all, she confesses that she killed the man. It is terrible, and I'm dreadfully sorry for both you and for her.'

'I don't matter a hang,' interrupted Crosbie.

'But the fact remains that murder has been committed, and in a civilised community a trial is inevitable.'

'Is it murder to exterminate noxious vermin? She shot him as she would have shot a mad dog.'

Mr Joyce leaned back again in his chair and once more placed the tips of his ten fingers together. The little construction he formed looked like the skeleton of a roof. He was silent for a moment.

'I should be wanting in my duty as your legal adviser,' he said at last, in an even voice, looking at his client with his cool, brown eyes, 'if I did not tell you that there is one point which causes me just a little anxiety. If your wife had only shot Hammond once, the whole thing would be absolutely plain sailing. Unfortunately she fired six times.'

'Her explanation is perfectly simple. In the circumstances anyone would have done the same.'

'I dare say,' said Mr Joyce, 'and of course I think the explanation is very reasonable. But it's no good closing our eyes to the facts. It's always a good plan to put yourself in another man's place, and I can't deny that if I were prosecuting for the Crown that is the point on which I should centre my enquiry.'

'My dear fellow, that's perfectly idiotic.'

Mr Joyce shot a sharp glance at Robert Crosbie. The shadow of a smile hovered over his shapely lips. Crosbie was a good fellow, but he could hardly be described as intelligent.

'I dare say it's of no importance,' answered the lawyer, 'I just thought it was a point worth mentioning. You haven't got very long to wait now, and when it's all over I recommend you to go off somewhere with your wife on a trip, and forget all about it. Even though we are almost dead certain to get an acquittal, a trial of that sort is anxious work, and you'll both want a rest.'

For the first time Crosbie smiled, and his smile strangely changed his face. You forgot the uncouthness and saw only the goodness of his soul.

'I think I shall want it more than Leslie. She's borne up wonderfully. By God, there's a plucky little woman for you.'

'Yes, I've been very much struck by her self-control,' said the lawyer. 'I should never have guessed that she was capable of such determination.'

His duties as her counsel had made it necessary for him to have a good many interviews with Mrs Crosbie since her arrest. Though things had been made as easy as could be for her, the fact remained that she was in gaol, awaiting her trial for murder, and it would not have been surprising if her nerves had failed her. She appeared to bear her ordeal with composure. She read a great deal, took such exercise as was possible, and by favour of the authorities worked at the pillow lace which had always formed the entertainment of her long hours of leisure. When Mr Joyce saw her, she was neatly dressed in cool, fresh, simple frocks, her hair was carefully arranged, and her nails were manicured. Her manner was collected. She was able even to jest upon the little inconveniences of her position. There was something casual about the way in which she spoke of the tragedy, which suggested to Mr Joyce that only her good breeding prevented her from finding something a trifle ludicrous in a situation which was eminently serious. It surprised him, for he had never thought that she had a sense of humour.

He had known her off and on for a good many years. When she paid visits to Singapore she generally came to dine with his wife and himself, and once or twice she had passed a week-end with them at their bungalow by the sea. His wife had spent a fortnight with her on the estate, and had met Geoffrey Hammond several times. The two couples had been on friendly, if not on intimate, terms, and it was on this account that Robert Crosbie had rushed over to Singapore immediately after the catastrophe and begged Mr Joyce to take charge personally of his unhappy wife's defence.

The story she told him the first time he saw her she had never varied in the smallest detail. She told it as coolly then, a few hours after the tragedy, as she told it now. She told it connectedly, in a level, even voice, and her only sign of confusion was when a slight colour came into her cheeks as she described one or two of its incidents. She was the last woman to whom one would have expected such a thing to happen. She was in the early thirties, a fragile creature, neither short nor tall, and graceful rather than pretty. Her wrists and ankles were very delicate, but she was extremely thin, and you could see the bones of her hands through the white skin, and the veins were large and blue. Her face was colourless, slightly sallow, and her lips were pale. You did not notice the colour of her eyes. She had a great deal of light brown hair, and it had a slight natural wave; it was the sort of hair that with a little touching-up would have been very pretty, but you could not imagine that Mrs Crosbie would think of resorting to any such device. She was a quiet, pleasant, unassuming woman. Her manner was engaging, and if she was not very popular it was because she suffered from a certain shyness. This was comprehensible enough, for the planter's life is lonely, and in her own house, with people she knew, she was in her quiet way charming. Mrs Joyce, after her fortnight's stay, had told her husband that Leslie was a very agreeable hostess. There was more in her, she said, than people thought; and when you came to know her you were surprised how much she had read and how entertaining she could be.

She was the last woman in the world to commit murder.

Mr Joyce dismissed Robert Crosbie with such reassuring words as he could find and, once more alone in his office, turned over the pages of the brief. But it was a mechanical action, for all its details were familiar to him. The case was the sensation of the day, and it was discussed in all the clubs, at all the dinner tables, up and down the Peninsula, from Singapore to Penang. The facts that Mrs Crosbie gave were simple. Her husband had gone to Singapore on business, and she was alone for the night. She dined by herself, late, at a quarter to nine, and after dinner sat in the sitting-room working at her lace. It opened on the verandah. There was no one in the bungalow, for the servants had retired to their own quarters at the back of the compound. She was surprised to hear a step on the gravel path in the garden, a booted step, which suggested a white man rather than a native, for she had not heard a motor drive up, and she could not imagine who could be coming to see her at that time of night. Someone ascended the few stairs that led up to the bungalow, walked across the verandah, and appeared at the door of the room in which she sat. At the first moment she did not recognise the visitor. She sat with a shaded lamp, and he stood with his back to the darkness.

'May I come in?' he said.

She did not even recognise the voice.

'Who is it?' she asked.

She worked with spectacles, and she took them off as she spoke.

'Geoff Hammond.'

'Of course. Come in and have a drink.'

She rose and shook hands with him cordially. She was a little surprised to see him, for though he was a neighbour neither she nor Robert had been lately on very intimate terms with him, and she had not seen him for some weeks. He was the manager of a rubber estate nearly eight miles from theirs, and she wondered why he had chosen this late hour to come and see them.

'Robert's away,' she said. 'He had to go to Singapore for the night.'

Perhaps he thought his visit called for some explanation, for he said:

'I'm sorry. I felt rather lonely to-night, so I thought I'd just come along and see how you were getting on.'

'How on earth did you come? I never heard a car.'

'I left it down the road. I thought you might both be in bed and asleep.'

This was natural enough. The planter gets up at dawn in order to take the roll-call of the workers, and soon after dinner he is glad to go to bed. Hammond's car was in point of fact found next day a quarter of a mile from the bungalow.

Since Robert was away there was no whisky and soda in the room. Leslie did not call the boy, who was probably asleep, but fetched it herself. Her guest mixed himself a drink and filled his pipe.

Geoff Hammond had a host of friends in the colony. He was at this time in the late thirties, but he had come out as a lad. He had been one of the first to volunteer on the outbreak of war, and had done very well. A wound in the knee caused him to be invalided out of the army after two years, but he returned to the Federated Malay States with a D.S.O. and an M.C. He was one of the best billiard-players in the colony. He had been a beautiful dancer and a fine tennis-player, but though able no longer to dance, and his tennis, with a stiff knee, was not so good as it had been, he had the gift of popularity and was universally liked. He was a tall, good-looking fellow, with attractive blue eyes and a fine head of black, curling hair. Old stagers said his only fault was that he was too fond of the girls, and after the catastrophe they shook their heads and vowed that they had always known this would get him into trouble.

He began now to talk to Leslie about the local affairs, the forth-coming races in Singapore, the price of rubber, and his chances of killing a tiger which had been lately seen in the neighbourhood. She was anxious to finish by a certain date the piece of lace on which she was working, for she wanted to send it home for her mother's birthday, and so put on her spectacles again, and drew towards her chair the little table on which stood the pillow.

'I wish you wouldn't wear those great horn-spectacles,' he said. 'I don't know why a pretty woman should do her best to look plain.'

She was a trifle taken aback at this remark. He had never used that tone with her before. She thought the best thing was to make light of it.

'I have no pretensions to being a raving beauty, you know, and if you ask me point-blank, I'm bound to tell you that I don't care two pins if you think me plain or not.'

'I don't think you're plain. I think you're awfully pretty.'

'Sweet of you,' she answered, ironically. 'But in that case I can only think you half-witted.'

He chuckled. But he rose from his chair and sat down in another by her side.

'You're not going to have the face to deny that you have the prettiest hands in the world,' he said.

He made a gesture as though to take one of them. She gave him a little tap.

'Don't be an idiot. Sit down where you were before and talk sensibly, or else I shall send you home.'

He did not move.

'Don't you know that I'm awfully in love with you?' he said.

She remained quite cool.

'I don't. I don't believe it for a minute, and even if it were true I don't want you to say it.'

She was the more surprised at what he was saying, since during the seven years she had known him he had never paid her any particular attention. When he came back from the war they had seen a good deal of one another, and once when he was ill Robert had gone over and brought him back to their bungalow in his car. He had stayed with them for a fortnight. But their interests were dissimilar, and the acquaintance had never ripened into friendship. For the last two or three years they had seen little of him. Now and then he came over to play tennis, now and then they met him at some planter's who was giving a party, but it often happened that they did not set eyes on him for a month at a time.

Now he took another whisky and soda. Leslie wondered if he had been drinking before. There was something odd about him, and it made her a trifle uneasy. She watched him help himself with disapproval.

'I wouldn't drink any more if I were you,' she said, good-humouredly still.

He emptied his glass and put it down.

'Do you think I'm talking to you like this because I'm drunk?' he asked abruptly.

'That is the most obvious explanation, isn't it?'

'Well, it's a lie. I've loved you ever since I first knew you. I've held my tongue as long as I could, and now it's got to come out. I love you, I love you, I love you.'

She rose and carefully put aside the pillow.

'Good-night,' she said.

'I'm not going now.'

At last she began to lose her temper.

'But, you poor fool, don't you know that I've never loved anyone but Robert, and even if I didn't love Robert you're the last man I should care for.'

'What do I care? Robert's away.'

'If you don't go away this minute I shall call the boys, and have you thrown out.'

'They're out of earshot.'

She was very angry now. She made a movement as though to go on to the verandah, from which the house-boy would certainly hear her, but he seized her arm.

'Let me go,' she cried furiously.

'Not much. I've got you now.'

She opened her mouth and called 'Boy, boy,' but with a quick gesture he put his hand over it. Then before she knew what he was about he had taken her in his arms and was kissing her passionately. She struggled, turning her lips away from his burning mouth.

'No, no, no,' she cried. 'Leave me alone. I won't.'

She grew confused about what happened then. All that had been said before she remembered accurately, but now his words assailed her ears through a mist of horror and fear. He seemed to plead for her love. He broke into violent protestations of passion. And all the time he held her in his tempestuous embrace. She was helpless, for he was a strong, powerful man, and her arms were pinioned to her sides; her struggles were unavailing, and she felt herself grow weaker; she was afraid she would faint, and his hot breath on her face made her feel desperately sick. He kissed her mouth, her eyes, her cheeks, her hair. The pressure of his arms was killing her. He lifted her off her feet. She tried to kick him, but he only held her more closely. He was carrying her now. He wasn't speaking any more, but she knew that his face was pale and his eyes hot with desire. He was taking her into the bedroom. He was no longer a civilised man, but a savage. And as he ran he stumbled against a table which was in the way. His stiff knee made him a little awkward on his feet, and with the burden of the woman in his arms he fell. In a moment she had snatched herself away from him. She ran round the sofa. He was up in a flash, and flung himself towards her. There was a revolver on the desk. She was not a nervous woman, but Robert was to be away for the night, and she had meant to take it into her room when she went to bed. That was why it happened to be there. She was frantic with terror now. She did not know what she was doing. She heard a report. She saw Hammond stagger. He gave a cry. He said something, she didn't know what. He lurched out of the room on to the verandah. She was in a frenzy now, she was beside herself, she followed him out, yes, that was it, she must have followed him out, though she remembered nothing of it, she followed firing automatically, shot after shot, till the six chambers were empty. Hammond fell down on the floor of the verandah. He crumpled up into a bloody heap.

When the boys, startled by the reports, rushed up, they found her standing over Hammond with the revolver still in her hand and Hammond lifeless. She looked at them for a moment without speaking. They stood in a frightened, huddled bunch. She let the revolver fall from her hand, and without a word turned and went into the sitting-room. They watched her go into her bedroom and turn the key in the lock. They dared not touch the dead body, but looked at it with terrified eyes, talking excitedly to one another in undertones. Then the head-boy collected himself; he had been with them for many years, he was Chinese and a level-headed fellow. Robert had gone into Singapore on his motor-cycle, and the car stood in the garage. He told the seis to get it out; they must go at once to the Assistant District Officer and tell him what had happened. He picked up the revolver and put it in his pocket. The A.D.O., a man called Withers, lived on the outskirts of the nearest town, which was about thirty-five miles away. It took them an hour and a half to reach him. Everyone was asleep, and they had to rouse the boys. Presently Withers came out and they told him their errand. The head-boy showed him the revolver in proof of what he said. The A.D.O. went into his room to dress, sent for his car, and in a little while was following them back along the deserted road. The dawn was just breaking as he reached the Crosbies' bungalow. He ran up the steps of the verandah, and stopped short as he saw Hammond's body lying where he fell. He touched the face. It was quite cold.

'Where's mem?' he asked the house-boy.

The Chinese pointed to the bedroom. Withers went to the door and knocked. There was no answer. He knocked again.

'Mrs Crosbie,' he called.

'Who is it?'

'Withers.'

There was another pause. Then the door was unlocked and slowly opened. Leslie stood before him. She had not been to bed, and wore the tea-gown in which she had dined. She stood and looked silently at the A.D.O.

'Your house-boy fetched me,' he said. 'Hammond. What have you done?'

'He tried to rape me, and I shot him.'

'My God. I say, you'd better come out here. You must tell me exactly what happened.'

'Not now. I can't. You must give me time. Send for my husband.'

Withers was a young man, and he did not know exactly what to do in an emergency which was so out of the run of his duties. Leslie refused to say anything till at last Robert arrived. Then she told the two men the story, from which since then, though she had repeated it over and over again, she had never in the slightest degree diverged.

The point to which Mr Joyce recurred was the shooting. As a lawyer he was bothered that Leslie had fired not once, but six times, and the examination of the dead man showed that four of the shots had been fired close to the body. One might almost have thought that when the man fell she stood over him and emptied the contents of the revolver into him. She confessed that her memory, so accurate for all that had preceded, failed her here. Her mind was blank. It pointed to an uncontrollable fury; but uncontrollable fury was the last thing you would have expected from this quiet and demure woman. Mr Joyce had known her a good many years, and had always thought her an unemotional person; during the weeks that had passed since the tragedy her composure had been amazing.

Mr Joyce shrugged his shoulders.

'The fact is, I suppose,' he reflected, 'that you can never tell what hidden possibilities of savagery there are in the most respectable of women.'

There was a knock at the door.

'Come in.'

The Chinese clerk entered and closed the door behind him. He closed it gently, with deliberation, but decidedly, and advanced to the table at which Mr Joyce was sitting.

'May I trouble you, sir, for a few words private conversation?' he said.

The elaborate accuracy with which the clerk expressed himself always faintly amused Mr Joyce, and now he smiled.

'It's no trouble, Chi Seng,' he replied.

'The matter on which I desire to speak to you, sir, is delicate and confidential.'

'Fire away.'

Mr Joyce met his clerk's shrewd eyes. As usual Ong Chi Seng was dressed in the height of local fashion. He wore very shiny patent-leather shoes and gay silk socks. In his black tie was a pearl and ruby pin, and on the fourth finger of his left hand a diamond ring. From the pocket of his neat white coat protruded a gold fountain pen and a gold pencil. He wore a gold wrist-watch, and on the bridge of his nose invisible pince-nez. He gave a little cough.

'The matter has to do with the case R. *v.* Crosbie, sir.'

'Yes?'

'A circumstance has come to my knowledge, sir, which seems to me to put a different complexion on it.'

'What circumstance?'

'It has come to my knowledge, sir, that there is a letter in existence from the defendant to the unfortunate victim of the tragedy.'

'I shouldn't be at all surprised. In the course of the last seven years I have no doubt that Mrs Crosbie often had occasion to write to Mr Hammond.'

Mr Joyce had a high opinion of his clerk's intelligence and his words were designed to conceal his thoughts.

'That is very probable, sir. Mrs Crosbie must have communicated with the deceased frequently, to invite him to dine with her for example, or to propose a tennis game. That was my first thought when the matter was brought to my notice. This letter, however, was written on the day of the late Mr Hammond's death.'

Mr Joyce did not flicker an eyelash. He continued to look at Ong Chi Seng with the smile of faint amusement with which he generally talked to him.

'Who has told you this?'

'The circumstances were brought to my knowledge, sir, by a friend of mine.'

Mr Joyce knew better than to insist.

'You will no doubt recall, sir, that Mrs Crosbie has stated that until the fatal night she had had no communication with the deceased for several weeks.'

'Have you got the letter?'

'No, sir.'

'What are its contents?'

'My friend gave me a copy. Would you like to peruse it, sir?'

'I should.'

Ong Chi Seng took from an inside pocket a bulky wallet. It was filled with papers, Singapore dollar notes and cigarette cards. From the confusion he presently extracted a half-sheet of thin notepaper and placed it before Mr Joyce. The letter read as follows:—

R. will be away for the night. I absolutely must see you. I shall expect you at eleven. I am desperate, and if you don't come I won't answer for the consequences. Don't drive up. – L.

It was written in the flowing hand which the Chinese were taught at the foreign schools. The writing, so lacking in character, was oddly incongruous with the ominous words.

'What makes you think that this note was written by Mrs Crosbie?'

'I have every confidence in the veracity of my informant, sir,' replied Ong Chi Seng. 'And the matter can very easily be put to the proof. Mrs Crosbie will, no doubt, be able to tell you at once whether she wrote such a letter or not.'

Since the beginning of the conversation Mr Joyce had not taken his eyes off the respectable countenance of his clerk. He wondered now if he discerned in it a faint expression of mockery.

'It is inconceivable that Mrs Crosbie should have written such a letter,' said Mr Joyce.

'If that is your opinion, sir, the matter is of course ended. My friend spoke to me on the subject only because he thought, as I was in your office, you might like to know of the existence of this letter before a communication was made to the Deputy Public Prosecutor.'

'Who has the original?' asked Mr Joyce sharply.

Ong Chi Seng made no sign that he perceived in this question and its manner a change of attitude.

'You will remember, sir, no doubt, that after the death of Mr Hammond it was discovered that he had had relations with a Chinese woman. The letter is at present in her possession.'

That was one of the things which had turned public opinion most vehemently against Hammond. It came to be known that for several months he had had a Chinese woman living in his house.

For a moment neither of them spoke. Indeed everything had been said and each understood the other perfectly.

'I'm obliged to you, Chi Seng. I will give the matter my consideration.'

'Very good, sir. Do you wish me to make a communication to that effect to my friend?'

'I dare say it would be as well if you kept in touch with him,' Mr Joyce answered with gravity.

'Yes, sir.'

The clerk noiselessly left the room, shutting the door again with deliberation, and left Mr Joyce to his reflections. He stared at the copy, in its neat, impersonal writing, of Leslie's letter. Vague suspicions troubled him. They were so disconcerting that he made an effort to put them out of his mind. There must be a simple explanation of the letter, and Leslie without doubt could give it at once, but, by heaven, an explanation was needed. He rose from his chair, put the letter in his pocket, and took his topee. When he went out Ong Chi Seng was busily writing at his desk.

'I'm going out for a few minutes, Chi Seng,' he said.

'Mr George Reed is coming by appointment at twelve o'clock, sir. Where shall I say you've gone?'

Mr Joyce gave him a thin smile.

'You can say that you haven't the least idea.'

But he knew perfectly well that Ong Chi Seng was aware that he was going to the gaol. Though the crime had been committed in Belanda and the trial was to take place at Belanda Bharu, since there was in the gaol no convenience for the detention of a white woman, Mrs Crosbie had been brought to Singapore.

When she was led into the room in which he waited she held out her thin, distinguished hand, and gave him a pleasant smile. She was as ever neatly and simply dressed, and her abundant, pale hair was arranged with care.

'I wasn't expecting to see you this morning,' she said, graciously.

She might have been in her own house, and Mr Joyce almost expected to hear her call the boy and tell him to bring the visitor a gin pahit.

'How are you?' he asked.

'I'm in the best of health, thank you.' A flicker of amusement flashed across her eyes. 'This is a wonderful place for a rest cure.'

The attendant withdrew and they were left alone.

'Do sit down,' said Leslie.

He took a chair. He did not quite know how to begin. She was so cool that it seemed almost impossible to say to her the thing he had come to say. Though she was not pretty there was something agreeable in her appearance. She had elegance, but it was the elegance of good breeding in which there was nothing of the artifice of society. You had only to look at her to know what sort of people she had and what kind of surroundings she had lived in. Her fragility gave her a singular refinement. It was impossible to associate her with the vaguest idea of grossness.

'I'm looking forward to seeing Robert this afternoon,' she said, in her good-humoured, easy voice. (It was a pleasure to hear her speak, her voice and her accent were so distinctive of her class.) 'Poor dear, it's been a great trial to his nerves. I'm thankful it'll all be over in a few days.'

'It's only five days now.'

'I know. Each morning when I awake I say to myself, "one less."' She smiled then. 'Just as I used to do at school and the holidays were coming.'

'By the way, am I right in thinking that you had no communication whatever with Hammond for several weeks before the catastrophe?'

'I'm quite positive of that. The last time we met was at a tennis-party at the MacFarrens. I don't think I said more than two words to him. They have two courts, you know, and we didn't happen to be in the same sets.'

'And you haven't written to him?'

'Oh, no.'

'Are you quite sure of that?'

'Oh, quite,' she answered, with a little smile. 'There was nothing I should write to him for except to ask him to dine or to play tennis, and I hadn't done either for months.'

'At one time you'd been on fairly intimate terms with him. How did it happen that you had stopped asking him to anything?'

Mrs Crosbie shrugged her thin shoulders.

'One gets tired of people. We hadn't anything very much in common. Of course, when he was ill Robert and I did everything we could for him, but the last year or two he'd been quite well, and he was very popular. He had a good many calls on his time, and there didn't seem to be any need to shower invitations upon him.'

'Are you quite certain that was all?'

Mrs Crosbie hesitated for a moment.

'Well, I may just as well tell you. It had come to our ears that he was living with a Chinese woman, and Robert said he wouldn't have him in the house. I had seen her myself.'

Mr Joyce was sitting in a straight-backed arm-chair, resting his chin on his hand, and his eyes were fixed on Leslie. Was it his fancy that, as she made this remark, her black pupils were filled on a sudden, for the fraction of a second, with a dull red light? The effect was startling. Mr Joyce shifted in his chair. He placed the tips of his ten fingers together. He spoke very slowly, choosing his words.

'I think I should tell you that there is in existence a letter in your handwriting to Geoff Hammond.'

He watched her closely. She made no movement, nor did her face change colour, but she took a noticeable time to reply.

'In the past I've often sent him little notes to ask him to something or other, or to get me something when I knew he was going to Singapore.'

'This letter asks him to come and see you because Robert was going to Singapore.'

'That's impossible. I never did anything of the kind.'

'You'd better read it for yourself.'

He took it out of his pocket and handed it to her. She gave it a glance and with a smile of scorn handed it back to him.

'That's not my handwriting.'

'I know, it's said to be an exact copy of the original.'

She read the words now, and as she read a horrible change came over her. Her colourless face grew dreadful to look at. It turned green. The flesh seemed on a sudden to fall away and her skin was tightly stretched over the bones. Her lips receded, showing her teeth, so that she had the appearance of making a grimace. She stared at Mr Joyce with eyes that started from their sockets. He was looking now at a gibbering death's head.

'What does it mean?' she whispered.

Her mouth was so dry that she could utter no more than a hoarse sound. It was no longer a human voice.

'That is for you to say,' he answered.

'I didn't write it. I swear I didn't write it.'

'Be very careful what you say. If the original is in your handwriting it would be useless to deny it.'

'It would be a forgery.'

'It would be difficult to prove that. It would be easy to prove that it was genuine.'

A shiver passed through her lean body. But great beads of sweat stood on her forehead. She took a handkerchief from her bag and wiped the palms of her hands. She glanced at the letter again and gave Mr Joyce a sidelong look.

'It's not dated. If I had written it and forgotten all about it, it might have been written years ago. If you'll give me time, I'll try and remember the circumstances.'

'I noticed there was no date. If this letter were in the hands of the prosecution they would cross-examine the boys. They would soon find out whether someone took a letter to Hammond on the day of his death.'

Mrs Crosbie clasped her hands violently and swayed in her chair so that he thought she would faint.

'I swear to you that I didn't write that letter.'

Mr Joyce was silent for a little while. He took his eyes from her distraught face, and looked down on the floor. He was reflecting.

'In these circumstances we need not go into the matter further,' he said slowly, at last breaking the silence. 'If the possessor of this letter sees fit to place it in the hands of the prosecution you will be prepared.'

His words suggested that he had nothing more to say to her, but he made no movement of departure. He waited. To himself he seemed to wait a very long time. He did not look at Leslie, but he was conscious that she sat very still. She made no sound. At last it was he who spoke.

'If you have nothing more to say to me I think I'll be getting back to my office.'

'What would anyone who read the letter be inclined to think that it meant?' she asked then.

'He'd know that you had told a deliberate lie,' answered Mr Joyce sharply.

'When?'

'You have stated definitely that you had had no communication with Hammond for at least three months.'

'The whole thing has been a terrible shock to me. The events of that dreadful night have been a nightmare. It's not very strange if one detail has escaped my memory.'

'It would be unfortunate, when your memory has reproduced so exactly every particular of your interview with Hammond, that you should have forgotten so important a point as that he came to see you in the bungalow on the night of his death at your express desire.'

'I hadn't forgotten. After what happened I was afraid to mention it. I thought you'd none of you believe my story if I admitted that he'd come at my invitation. I dare say it was stupid of me; but I lost my head, and after I'd said once that I'd had no communication with Hammond I was obliged to stick to it.'

By now Leslie had recovered her admirable composure, and she met Mr Joyce's appraising glance with candour. Her gentleness was very disarming.

'You will be required to explain, then, *why* you asked Hammond to come and see you when Robert was away for the night.'

She turned her eyes full on the lawyer. He had been mistaken in thinking them insignificant, they were rather fine eyes, and unless he was mistaken they were bright now with tears. Her voice had a little break in it.

'It was a surprise I was preparing for Robert. His birthday is next month. I knew he wanted a new gun and you know I'm dreadfully stupid about sporting things. I wanted to talk to Geoff about it. I thought I'd get him to order it for me.'

'Perhaps the terms of the letter are not very clear to your recollection. Will you have another look at it?'

'No, I don't want to,' she said quickly.

'Does it seem to you the sort of letter a woman would write to a somewhat distant acquaintance because she wanted to consult him about buying a gun?'

'I dare say it's rather extravagant and emotional. I do express myself like that, you know. I'm quite prepared to admit it's very silly.' She smiled. 'And after all, Geoff Hammond wasn't quite a distant acquaintance. When he was ill I'd nursed him like a mother. I asked him to come when Robert was away, because Robert wouldn't have him in the house.'

Mr Joyce was tired of sitting so long in the same position. He rose and walked once or twice up and down the room, choosing the words he proposed to say; then he leaned over the back of the chair in which he had been sitting. He spoke slowly in a tone of deep gravity.

'Mrs Crosbie, I want to talk to you very, very seriously. This case was comparatively plain sailing. There was only one point which seemed to me to require explanation: as far as I could judge, you had fired no less than four shots into Hammond when he was lying on the ground. It was hard to accept the possibility that a delicate, frightened, and habitually self-controlled woman, of gentle nature and refined instincts, should have surrendered to an absolutely uncontrolled frenzy. But of course it was admissible. Although Geoffrey Hammond was much liked and on the whole thought highly of, I was prepared to prove that he was the sort of man who might be guilty of the crime which in justification of your act you accused him of. The fact, which was discovered after his death, that he had been living with a Chinese woman gave us something very definite to go upon. That robbed him of any sympathy which might have been felt for him. We made up our minds to make use of the odium which such a connection cast upon him in the minds of all respectable people. I told your husband this morning that I was certain of an acquittal, and I wasn't just telling him that to give him heart. I do not believe the assessors would have left the court.'

They looked into one another's eyes. Mrs Crosbie was strangely still. She was like a little bird paralysed by the fascination of a snake. He went on in the same quiet tones.

'But this letter has thrown an entirely different complexion on the case. I am your legal adviser, I shall represent you in court. I take your story as you tell it me, and I shall conduct your defence according to its terms. It may be that I believe your statements, and it may be that I doubt them. The duty of counsel is to persuade the court that the evidence placed before it is not such as to justify it in bringing in a verdict of guilty, and any private opinion he may have of the guilt or innocence of his client is entirely beside the point.'

He was astonished to see in Leslie's eyes the flicker of a smile. Piqued, he went on somewhat dryly:

'You're not going to deny that Hammond came to your house at your urgent, and I may even say, hysterical invitation?'

Mrs Crosbie, hesitating for an instant, seemed to consider.

'They can prove that the letter was taken to his bungalow by one of the house-boys. He rode over on his bicycle.

'You mustn't expect other people to be stupider than you. The letter will put them on the track of suspicions which have entered nobody's head. I will not tell you what I personally thought when I saw the copy. I do not wish you to tell me anything but what is needed to save your neck.'

Mrs Crosbie give a shrill cry. She sprang to her feet, white with terror.

'You don't think they'd hang me?'

'If they came to the conclusion that you hadn't killed Hammond in self-defence, it would be the duty of the assessors to bring in a verdict of guilty. The charge is murder. It would be the duty of the judge to sentence you to death.'

'But what can they prove?' she gasped.

'I don't know what they can prove. You know. I don't want to know. But if their suspicions are aroused, if they begin to make inquiries, if the natives are questioned – what is it that can be discovered?'

She crumpled up suddenly. She fell on the floor before he could catch her. She had fainted. He looked round the room for water, but there was none there, and he did not want to be disturbed. He stretched her out on the floor, and kneeling beside her waited for her to recover. When she opened her eyes he was disconcerted by the ghastly fear that he saw in them.

'Keep quite still,' he said. 'You'll be better in a moment.'

'You won't let them hang me,' she whispered.

She began to cry, hysterically, while in undertones he sought to quieten her.

'For goodness sake pull yourself together,' he said.

'Give me a minute.'

Her courage was amazing. He could see the effort she made to regain her self-control, and soon she was once more calm.

'Let me get up now.'

He gave her his hand and helped her to her feet. Taking her arm, he led her to the chair. She sat down wearily.

'Don't talk to me for a minute or two,' she said.

'Very well.'

When at last she spoke it was to say something which he did not expect. She gave a little sigh.

'I'm afraid I've made rather a mess of things,' she said.

He did not answer, and once more there was a silence.

'Isn't it possible to get hold of the letter?' she said at last.

'I do not think anything would have been said to me about it if the person in whose possession it is was not prepared to sell it.'

'Who's got it?'

'The Chinese woman who was living in Hammond's house.'

A spot of colour flickered for an instant on Leslie's cheek-bones.

'Does she want an awful lot for it?'

'I imagine that she has a very shrewd idea of its value. I doubt if it would be possible to get hold of it except for a very large sum.'

'Are you going to let me be hanged?'

'Do you think it's so simple as all that to secure possession of an unwelcome piece of evidence? It's no different from suborning a witness. You have no right to make any such suggestion to me.'

'Then what is going to happen to me?'

'Justice must take its course.'

She grew very pale. A little shudder passed through her body.

'I put myself in your hands. Of course I have no right to ask you to do anything that isn't proper.'

Mr Joyce had not bargained for the little break in her voice which her habitual self-restraint made quite intolerably moving. She looked at him with humble eyes, and he thought that if he rejected their appeal they would haunt him for the rest of his life. After all, nothing could bring poor Hammond back to life again. He wondered what really was the explanation of that letter. It was not fair to conclude from it that she had killed Hammond without provocation. He had lived in the East a long time and his sense of professional honour was not perhaps so acute as it had been twenty years before. He stared at the floor. He made up his mind to do something which he knew was unjustifiable, but it stuck in his throat and he felt dully resentful towards Leslie. It embarrassed him a little to speak.

'I don't know exactly what your husband's circumstances are?'

Flushing a rosy red, she shot a swift glance at him.

'He has a good many tin shares and a small share in two or three rubber estates. I suppose he could raise money.'

'He would have to be told what it was for.'

She was silent for a moment. She seemed to think.

'He's in love with me still. He would make any sacrifice to save me. Is there any need for him to see the letter?'

Mr Joyce frowned a little, and, quick to notice, she went on.

'Robert is an old friend of yours. I'm not asking you to do anything for me, I'm asking you to save a rather simple, kind man who never did you any harm from all the pain that's possible.'

Mr Joyce did not reply. He rose to go and Mrs Crosbie, with the grace that was natural to her, held out her hand. She was shaken by the scene, and her look was haggard, but she made a brave attempt to speed him with courtesy.

'It's so good of you to take all this trouble for me. I can't begin to tell you how grateful I am.'

Mr Joyce returned to his office. He sat in his own room, quite still, attempting to do no work, and pondered. His imagination brought him many strange ideas. He shuddered a little. At last there was the discreet knock on the door which he was expecting. Ong Chi Seng came in.

'I was just going out to have my tiffin, sir,' he said.

'All right.'

'I didn't know if there was anything you wanted before I went, sir.'

'I don't think so. Did you make another appointment for Mr Reed?'

'Yes, sir. He will come at three o'clock.'

'Good.'

Ong Chi Seng turned away, walked to the door, and put his long slim fingers on the handle. Then, as though on an afterthought, he turned back.

'Is there anything you wish me to say to my friend, sir?'

Although Ong Chi Seng spoke English so admirably he had still a difficulty with the letter R, and he pronounced it "fliend.'

'What friend?'

'About the letter Mrs Crosbie wrote to Hammond deceased, sir.'

'Oh! I'd forgotten about that. I mentioned it to Mrs Crosbie and she denies having written anything of the sort. It's evidently a forgery.'

Mr Joyce took the copy from his pocket and handed it to Ong Chi Seng. Ong Chi Seng ignored the gesture.

'In that case, sir, I suppose there would be no objection if my fliend delivered the letter to the Deputy Public Prosecutor.'

'None. But I don't quite see what good that would do your friend.'

'My fliend, sir, thought it was his duty in the interests of justice.'

'I am the last man in the world to interfere with anyone who wishes to do his duty, Chi Seng.'

The eyes of the lawyer and of the Chinese clerk met. Not the shadow of a smile hovered on the lips of either, but they understood each other perfectly.

'I quite understand, sir,' said Ong Chi Seng, 'but from my study of the case R. *v.* Crosbie I am of opinion that the production of such a letter would be damaging to our client.'

'I have always had a very high opinion of your legal acumen, Chi Seng.'

'It has occurred to me, sir, that if I could persuade my fliend to induce the Chinese woman who has the letter to deliver it into our hands it would save a great deal of trouble.'

Mr Joyce idly drew faces on his blotting-paper.

'I suppose your friend is a business man. In what circumstances do you think he would be induced to part with the letter?'

'He has not got the letter. The Chinese woman has the letter. He is only a relation of the Chinese woman. She is an ignorant woman; she did not know the value of that letter till my fliend told her.'

'What value did he put on it?'

'Ten thousand dollars, sir.'

'Good God! Where on earth do you suppose Mrs Crosbie can get ten thousand dollars! I tell you the letter's a forgery.'

He looked up at Ong Chi Seng as he spoke. The clerk was unmoved by the outburst. He stood at the side of the desk, civil, cool and observant.

'Mr Crosbie owns an eighth share of the Betong Rubber Estate and a sixth share of the Selantan River Rubber Estate. I have a fliend who will lend him the money on the security of his property.'

'You have a large circle of acquaintance, Chi Seng.'

'Yes sir.'

'Well, you can tell them all to go to hell. I would never advise Mr Crosbie to give a penny more than five thousand for a letter that can be very easily explained.'

'The Chinese woman does not want to sell the letter, sir. My fliend took a long time to persuade her. It is useless to offer her less than the sum mentioned.'

Mr Joyce looked at Ong Chi Seng for at least three minutes. The clerk bore the searching scrutiny without embarrassment. He stood in a respectful attitude with downcast eyes. Mr Joyce knew his man. Clever fellow, Chi Seng, he thought, I wonder how much he's going to get out of it.

'Ten thousand dollars is a very large sum.'

'Mr Crosbie will certainly pay it rather than see his wife hanged, sir.'

Again Mr Joyce paused. What more did Chi Seng know than he had said? He must be pretty sure of his ground if he was obviously so unwilling to bargain. That sum had been fixed because whoever it was that was managing the affair knew it was the largest amount that Robert Crosbie could raise.

'Where is the Chinese woman now?' asked Mr Joyce.

'She is staying at the house of my fliend, sir.'

'Will she come here?'

'I think it more better if you go to her, sir. I can take you to the house to-night and she will give you the letter. She is a very ignorant woman, sir, and she does not understand cheques.'

'I wasn't thinking of giving her a cheque. I will bring bank-notes with me.'

'It would only be waste of valuable time to bring less than ten thousand dollars, sir.'

'I quite understand.'

'I will go and tell my fliend after I have had my tiffin, sir.'

'Very good. You'd better meet me outside the club at ten o'clock to-night.'

'With pleasure, sir,' said Ong Chi Seng.

He gave Mr Joyce a little bow and left the room. Mr Joyce went out to luncheon, too. He went to the club and here, as he had expected, he saw Robert Crosbie. He was sitting at a crowded table, and as he passed him, looking for a place, Mr Joyce touched him on the shoulder.

'I'd like a word or two with you before you go,' he said.

'Right you are. Let me know when you're ready.'

Mr Joyce had made up his mind how to tackle him. He played a rubber of bridge after luncheon in order to allow time for the club to empty itself. He did not want on this particular matter to see Crosbie in his office. Presently Crosbie came into the card-room and looked on till the game was finished. The other players went on their various affairs, and the two were left alone.

'A rather unfortunate thing has happened, old man,' said Mr Joyce, in a tone which he sought to render as casual as possible. 'It appears that your wife sent a letter to Hammond asking him to come to the bungalow on the night he was killed.'

'But that's impossible,' cried Crosbie. 'She's always stated that she had had no communication with Hammond. I know from my own knowledge that she hadn't set eyes on him for a couple of months.'

'The fact remains that the letter exists. It's in the possession of the Chinese woman Hammond was living with. Your wife meant to give you a present on your birthday, and she wanted Hammond to help her to get it. In the emotional excitement that she suffered from after the tragedy, she forgot all about it, and having once denied having any communication with Hammond she was afraid to say that she had made a mistake. It was, of course, very unfortunate, but I dare say it was not unnatural.'

Crosbie did not speak. His large, red face bore an expression of complete bewilderment, and Mr Joyce was at once relieved and exasperated by his lack of comprehension. He was a stupid man, and Mr Joyce had no patience with stupidity. But his distress since the catastrophe had touched a soft spot in the lawyer's heart; and Mrs Crosbie had struck the right note when she asked him to help her, not for her sake, but for her husband's.

'I need not tell you that it would be very awkward if this letter found its way into the hands of the prosecution. Your wife has lied, and she would be asked to explain the lie. It alters things a little if Hammond did not intrude, an unwanted guest, but came to your house by invitation. It would be easy to arouse in the assessors a certain indecision of mind.'

Mr Joyce hesitated. He was face to face now with his decision. If it had been a time for humour, he could have smiled at the reflection that he was taking so grave a step, and that the man for whom he was taking it had not the smallest conception of its gravity. If he gave the matter a thought, he probably imagined that what Mr Joyce was doing was what any lawyer did in the ordinary run of business.

'My dear Robert, you are not only my client, but my friend. I think we must get hold of that letter. It'll cost a good deal of money. Except for that I should have preferred to say nothing to you about it.'

'How much?'

'Ten thousand dollars.'

'That's a devil of a lot. With the slump and one thing and another it'll take just about all I've got.'

'Can you get it at once?'

'I suppose so. Old Charlie Meadows will let me have it on my tin shares and on those two estates I'm interested in.'

'Then will you?'

'Is it absolutely necessary?'

'If you want your wife to be acquitted.'

Crosbie grew very red. His mouth sagged strangely.

'But . . .' he could not find words, his face now was purple. 'But I don't understand. She can explain. You don't mean to say they'd find her guilty? They couldn't hang her for putting a noxious vermin out of the way.'

'Of course they wouldn't hang her. They might only find her guilty of manslaughter. She'd probably get off with two or three years.'

Crosbie started to his feet and his red face was distraught with horror.

'Three years.'

Then something seemed to dawn in that slow intelligence of his. His mind was darkness across which shot suddenly a flash of lightning, and though the succeeding darkness was as profound, there remained the memory of something not seen but perhaps just descried. Mr Joyce saw that Crosbie's big red hands, coarse and hard with all the odd jobs he had set them to, trembled.

'What was the present she wanted to make me?'

'She says she wanted to give you a new gun.'

Once more that great red face flushed a deeper red.

'When have you got to have the money ready?'

There was something odd in his voice now. It sounded as though he spoke with invisible hands clutching at his throat.

'At ten o'clock to-night. I thought you could bring it to my office at about six.'

'Is the woman coming to you?'

'No, I'm going to her.'

'I'll bring the money. I'll come with you.'

Mr Joyce looked at him sharply.

'Do you think there's any need for you to do that? I think it would be better if you left me to deal with this matter by myself.'

'It's my money, isn't it? I'm going to come.'

Mr Joyce shrugged his shoulders. They rose and shook hands. Mr Joyce looked at him curiously.

At ten o'clock they met in the empty club.

'Everything all right?' asked Mr Joyce.

'Yes. I've got the money in my pocket.'

'Let's go then.'

They walked down the steps. Mr Joyce's car was waiting for them in the square, silent at that hour, and as they came to it Ong Chi Seng stepped out of the shadow of a house. He took his seat beside the driver and gave him a direction. They drove past the Hotel de l'Europe and turned up by the Sailor's Home to get into Victoria Street. Here the Chinese shops were still open, idlers lounged about, and in the roadway rickshaws and motor-cars and gharries gave a busy air to the scene. Suddenly their car stopped and Chi Seng turned round.

'I think it more better if we walk here, sir,' he said.

They got out and he went on. They followed a step or two behind. Then he asked them to stop.

'You wait here, sir. I go in and speak to my fliend.'

He went into a shop, open to the street, where three or four Chinese were standing behind the counter. It was one of those strange shops where nothing was on view, and you wondered what it was they sold there. They saw him address a stout man in a duck suit with a large gold chain across his breast, and the man shot a quick glance out into the night. He gave Chi Seng a key and Chi Seng came out. He beckoned to the two men waiting and slid into a doorway at the side of the shop. They followed him and found themselves at the foot of a flight of stairs.

'If you wait a minute I will light a match,' he said, always resourceful. 'You come upstairs, please.'

He held a Japanese match in front of them, but it scarcely dispelled the darkness and they groped their way up behind him. On the first floor he unlocked a door and going in lit a gas-jet.

'Come in, please,' he said.

It was a small square room, with one window, and the only furniture consisted of two low Chinese beds covered with matting. In one corner was a large chest, with an elaborate lock, and on this stood a shabby tray with an opium pipe on it and a lamp. There was in the room the faint, acrid scent of the drug. They sat down and Ong Chi Seng offered them cigarettes. In a moment the door was opened by the fat Chinaman whom they had seen behind the counter. He bade them good-evening in very good English, and sat down by the side of his fellow-countryman.

'The Chinese woman is just coming,' said Chi Seng.

A boy from the shop brought in a tray with a teapot and cups and the Chinaman offered them a cup of tea. Crosbie refused. The Chinese talked to one another in undertones, but Crosbie and Mr Joyce were silent. At last there was the sound of a voice outside; someone was calling in a low tone; and the Chinaman went to the door. He opened it, spoke a few words, and ushered a woman in. Mr Joyce looked at her. He had heard much about her since Hammond's death, but he had never seen her. She was a stoutish person, not very young, with a broad, phlegmatic face, she was powdered and rouged and her eyebrows were a thin black line, but she gave you the impression of a woman of character. She wore a pale blue jacket and a white shirt, her costume was not quite European nor quite Chinese, but on her feet were little Chinese silk slippers. She wore heavy gold chains round her neck, gold bangles on her wrists, gold ear-rings and elaborate gold pins in her black hair. She walked in slowly, with the air of a woman sure of herself, but with a certain heaviness of tread, and sat down on the bed beside Ong Chi Seng. He said something to her and nodding she gave an incurious glance at the two white men.

'Has she got the letter?' asked Mr Joyce.

'Yes, sir.'

Crosbie said nothing, but produced a roll of five-hundred-dollar notes. He counted out twenty and handed them to Chi Seng.

'Will you see if that is correct?'

The clerk counted them and gave them to the fat Chinaman.

'Quite correct, sir.'

The Chinaman counted them once more and put them in his pocket. He spoke again to the woman and she drew from her bosom a letter. She gave it to Chi Seng who cast his eyes over it.

'This is the right document, sir,' he said, and was about to give it to Mr Joyce when Crosbie took it from him.

'Let me look at it,' he said.

Mr Joyce watched him read and then held out his hand for it.

'You'd better let me have it.'

Crosbie folded it up deliberately and put it in his pocket.

'No, I'm going to keep it myself. It's cost me enough money.'

Mr Joyce made no rejoinder. The three Chinese watched the little passage, but what they thought about it, or whether they thought, it was impossible to tell from their impassive countenances. Mr Joyce rose to his feet.

'Do you want me any more to-night, sir?' said Ong Chi Seng.

'No.' He knew that the clerk wished to stay behind in order to get his agreed share of the money, and he turned to Crosbie. 'Are you ready?'

Crosbie did not answer, but stood up. The Chinaman went to the door and opened it for them. Chi Seng found a bit of candle and lit it in order to light them down, and the two Chinese accompanied them to the street. They left the woman sitting quietly on the bed smoking a cigarette. When they reached the street the Chinese left them and went once more upstairs.

'What are you going to do with that letter?' asked Mr Joyce.

'Keep it.'

They walked to where the car was waiting for them and here Mr Joyce offered his friend a lift. Crosbie shook his head.

'I'm going to walk.' He hesitated a little and shuffled his feet. 'I went to Singapore on the night of Hammond's death partly to buy a new gun that a man I knew wanted to dispose of. Good-night.'

He disappeared quickly into the darkness.

Mr Joyce was quite right about the trial. The assessors went into court fully determined to acquit Mrs Crosbie. She gave evidence on her own behalf. She told her story simply and with straightforwardness. The D.P.P. was a kindly man and it was plain that he took no great pleasure in his task. He asked the necessary questions in a deprecating manner. His speech for the prosecution might really have been a speech for the defence, and the assessors took less than five minutes to consider their popular verdict. It was impossible to prevent the great outburst of applause with which it was received by the crowd that packed the court-house. The judge congratulated Mrs Crosbie and she was a free woman.

No one had expressed a more violent disapprobation of Hammond's behaviour than Mrs Joyce; she was a woman loyal to her friends and she had insisted on the Crosbies staying with her after the trial, for she in common with everyone else had no doubt of the result, till they could make arrangements to go away. It was out of the question for poor, dear, brave Leslie to return to the bungalow at which the horrible catastrophe had taken place. The trial was over by half-past twelve and when they reached the Joyces' house a grand luncheon was awaiting them. Cocktails were ready, Mrs Joyce's million-dollar cocktail was celebrated through all the Malay States, and Mrs Joyce drank Leslie's health. She was a talkative, vivacious woman, and now she was in the highest spirits. It was fortunate, for the rest of them were silent. She did not wonder; her husband never had much to say, and the other two were naturally exhausted from the long strain to which they had been subjected. During luncheon she carried on a bright and spirited mono-logue. Then coffee was served.

'Now, children,' she said in her gay, bustling fashion, 'you must have a rest and after tea I shall take you both for a drive to the sea.'

Mr Joyce, who lunched at home only by exception, had of course to go back to his office.

'I'm afraid I can't do that, Mrs Joyce,' said Crosbie. 'I've got to get back to the estate at once.'

'Not to-day?' she cried.

'Yes, now. I've neglected it for too long and I have urgent business. But I shall be very grateful if you will keep Leslie until we have decided what to do.'

Mrs Joyce was about to expostulate, but her husband prevented her.

'If he must go, he must, and there's an end of it.'

There was something in the lawyer's tone which made her look at him quickly. She held her tongue and there was a moment's silence. Then Crosbie spoke again.

'If you'll forgive me, I'll start at once so that I can get there before dark.' He rose from the table. 'Will you come and see me off, Leslie?'

'Of course.'

They went out of the dining-room together.

'I think that's rather inconsiderate of him,' said Mrs Joyce. 'He must know that Leslie wants to be with him just now.'

'I'm sure he wouldn't go if it wasn't absolutely necessary.'

'Well, I'll just see that Leslie's room is ready for her. She wants a complete rest, of course, and then amusement.'

Mrs Joyce left the room and Joyce sat down again. In a short time he heard Crosbie start the engine of his motor-cycle and then noisily scrunch over the gravel of the garden path. He got up and went into the drawing-room. Mrs Crosbie was standing in the middle of it, looking into space, and in her hand was an open letter. He recognised it. She gave him a glance as he came in and he saw that she was deathly pale.

'He knows,' she whispered.

Mr Joyce went up to her and took the letter from her hand. He lit a match and set the paper afire. She watched it burn. When he could hold it no longer he dropped it on the tiled floor and they both looked at the paper curl and blacken. Then he trod it into ashes with his foot.

'What does he know?'

She gave him a long, long stare and into her eyes came a strange look. Was it contempt or despair? Mr Joyce could not tell.

'He knows that Geoff was my lover.'

Mr Joyce made no movement and uttered no sound.

'He'd been my lover for years. He became my lover almost immediately after he came back from the war. We knew how careful we must be. When we became lovers I pretended I was tired of him, and he seldom came to the house when Robert was there. I used to drive out to a place we knew and he met me, two or three times a week, and when Robert went to Singapore he used to come to the bungalow late, when the boys had gone for the night. We saw one another constantly, all the time, and not a soul had the smallest suspicion of it. And then lately, a year ago, he began to change. I didn't know what was the matter. I couldn't believe that he didn't care for me any more. He always denied it. I was frantic. I made him scenes. Sometimes I thought he hated me. Oh, if you knew what agonies I endured. I passed through hell. I knew he didn't want me any more and I wouldn't let him go. Misery! Misery! I loved him. I'd given him everything. He was my life. And then I heard he was living with a Chinese woman. I couldn't believe it. I wouldn't believe it. At last I saw her, I saw her with my own eyes, walking in the village, with her gold bracelets and her necklaces, an old, fat, Chinese woman. She was older than I was. Horrible! They all knew in the kampong that she was his mistress. And when I passed her, she looked at me and I knew that she knew I was his mistress too. I sent for him. I told him I must see him. You've read the letter. I was mad to write it. I didn't know what I was doing. I didn't care. I hadn't seen him for ten days. It was a lifetime. And when last we'd parted he took me in his arms and kissed me, and told me not to worry. And he went straight from my arms to hers.'

She had been speaking in a low voice, vehemently, and now she stopped and wrung her hands.

'That damned letter. We'd always been so careful. He always tore up any word I wrote to him the moment he'd read it. How was I to know he'd leave that one? He came, and I told him I knew about the Chinawoman. He denied it. He said it was only scandal. I was beside myself. I don't know what I said to him. Oh, I hated him then. I tore him limb from limb. I said everything I could to wound him. I insulted him. I could have spat in his face. And at last he turned on me. He told me he was sick and tired of me and never wanted to see me again. He said I bored him to death. And then he acknowledged that it was true about the Chinawoman. He said he'd known her for years, before the war, and she was the only woman who really meant anything to him, and the rest was just pastime. And he said he was glad I knew and now at last I'd leave him alone. And then I don't know what happened, I was beside myself, I saw red. I seized the revolver and I fired. He gave a cry and I saw I'd hit him. He staggered and rushed for the verandah. I ran after him and fired again. He fell and then I stood over him and I fired and fired till the revolver went click, click, and I knew there were no more cartridges.'

At last she stopped, panting. Her face was no longer human, it was distorted with cruelty, and rage and pain. You would never have thought that this quiet, refined woman was capable of such fiendish passion. Mr Joyce took a step backwards. He was absolutely aghast at the sight of her. It was not a face, it was a gibbering, hideous mask. Then they heard a voice calling from another room, a loud, friendly, cheerful voice. It was Mrs Joyce.

'Come along, Leslie darling, your room's ready. You must be dropping with sleep.'

Mrs Crosbie's features gradually composed themselves. Those passions, so clearly delineated, were smoothed away as with your hand you would smooth a crumpled paper, and in a minute the face was cool and calm and unlined. She was a trifle pale, but her lips broke into a pleasant, affable smile. She was once more the well-bred and even distinguished woman.

'I'm coming, Dorothy dear. I'm sorry to give you so much trouble.'

Dashiell Hammett

The Farewell Murder

I

I was the only one who left the train at Farewell.

A man came through the rain from the passenger shed. He was a small man. His face was dark and flat. He wore a grey waterproof cap and a grey coat cut in military style.

He didn't look at me. He looked at the valise and gladstone bag in my hands. He came forward quickly, walking with short, choppy steps.

He didn't say anything when he took the bags from me. I asked: 'Kavalov's?'

He had already turned his back to me and was carrying my bags towards a tan Stutz coach that stood in the roadway beside the gravel station platform. In answer to my question he bowed twice at the Stutz without looking around or checking his jerky half-trot.

I followed him to the car.

Three minutes of riding carried us through the village. We took a road that climbed westward into the hills. The road looked like a seal's back in the rain.

The flat-faced man was in a hurry. We purred over the road at a speed that soon carried us past the last of the cottages sprinkled up the hillside.

Presently we left the shiny black road for a paler one curving south to run along a hill's wooded crest. Now and then this road, for a hundred feet or more at a stretch, was turned into a tunnel by tall trees' heavily leafed boughs interlocking overhead.

Rain accumulated in fat drops on the boughs and came down to thump the Stutz's roof. The dullness of rainy early evening became almost the blackness of night inside these tunnels.

The flat-faced man switched on the lights, and increased our speed.

He sat rigidly erect at the wheel. I sat behind him. Above his military collar, among the hairs that were clipped short on the nape of his neck, globules of moisture made tiny shining points. The moisture could have been rain. It could have been sweat.

We were in the middle of one of the tunnels.

The flat-faced man's head jerked to the left, and he screamed:
'A-a-a-a-a-a!'

It was a long, quivering, high-pitched bleat, thin with terror.

I jumped up, bending forward to see what was the matter with him.

The car swerved and plunged ahead, throwing me back on the seat again.

Through the side window I caught a one-eyed glimpse of something dark lying in the road.

I twisted around to try the back window, less rain-bleared.

I saw a black man lying on his back in the road, near the left edge. His body was arched, as if its weight rested on his heels and the back of his head. A knife handle that couldn't have been less than six inches long stood straight up in the air from the left side of his chest.

By the time I had seen this much we had taken a curve and were out of the tunnel.

'Stop,' I called to the flat-faced man.

He pretended he didn't hear me. The Stutz was a tan streak under us. I put a hand on the driver's shoulder.

His shoulder squirmed under my hand, and he screamed 'A-a-a-a-a!' again as if the dead black man had him.

I reached past him and shut off the engine.

He took his hands from the wheel and clawed up at me. Noises came from his mouth, but they didn't make any words that I knew.

I got a hand on the wheel. I got my other forearm under his chin. I leaned over the back of his seat so that the weight of my upper body was on his head, mashing it down against the wheel.

Between this and that and the help of God, the Stutz hadn't left the road when it stopped moving.

I got up off the flat-faced man's head and asked:

'What the hell's the matter with you?'

He looked at me with white eyes, shivered, and didn't say anything.

'Turn it around,' I said. 'We'll go back there.'

He shook his head from side to side, desperately, and made some more of the mouth-noises that might have been words if I could have understood them.

'You know who that was?' I asked.

He shook his head.

'You do,' I growled.

He shook his head.

By then I was beginning to suspect that no matter what I said to this fellow I'd get only headshakes out of him.

I said:

'Get away from the wheel, then. I'm going to drive back there.'

He opened the door and scrambled out.

'Come back here,' I called.

He backed away, shaking his head.

I cursed him, slid in behind the wheel, said, 'All right, wait here for me,' and slammed the door.

He retreated backwards slowly, watching me with scared, whitish eyes while I backed and turned the coach.

I had to drive back farther than I had expected, something like a mile. I didn't find the black man. The tunnel was empty.

If I had known the exact spot in which he had been lying, I might have been able to find something to show how he had been removed. But I hadn't had time to pick out a landmark, and now any one of four or five places looked like the spot.

With the help of the coach's lamps I went over the left side of the road from one end of the tunnel to the other.

I didn't find any blood. I didn't find any footprints. I didn't find anything to show that anybody had been lying in the road. I didn't find anything.

It was too dark by now for me to try searching the woods.

I returned to where I had left the flat-faced man.

He was gone.

It looked, I thought, as if Mr Kavalov might be right in thinking he needed a detective.

II

Half a mile beyond the place where the flat-faced man had deserted me, I stopped the Stutz in front of a grilled steel gate that blocked the road. The gate was padlocked on the inside. From either side of it tall hedging ran off into the woods. The upper part of a brown-roofed small house was visible over the hedge-top to the left.

I worked the Stutz's horn.

The racket brought a gawky boy of fifteen or sixteen to the other side of the gate. He had on bleached whipcord pants and a wildly striped sweater. He didn't come out to the middle of the road, but stood at one side, with one arm out of sight as if holding something that was hidden from me by the hedge.

'This Kavalov's?' I asked.

'Yes, sir,' he said uneasily.

I waited for him to unlock the gate. He didn't unlock it. He stood there looking uneasily at the car and at me.

'Please, mister,' I said, 'can I come in?'

'What – who are you?'

'I'm the guy that Kavalov sent for. If I'm not going to be let in, tell me, so I can catch the six-fifty back to San Francisco.'

The boy chewed his lip, said, 'Wait till I see if I can find the key,' and went out of sight behind the hedge.

He was gone long enough to have had a talk with somebody.

When he came back he unlocked the gate, swung it open, and said: 'It's all right, sir. They're expecting you.'

When I had driven through the gate I could see lights on a hilltop a mile or so ahead and to the left.

'Is that the house?' I asked.

'Yes, sir. They're expecting you.'

Close to where the boy had stood while talking to me through the gate, a double-barrel shotgun was propped up against the hedge.

I thanked the boy and drove on. The road wound gently uphill through farmland. Tall, slim trees had been planted at regular intervals on both sides of the road.

The road brought me at last to the front of a building that looked like a cross between a fort and a factory in the dusk. It was built of concrete. Take a flock of squat cones of various sizes, round off the points bluntly, mash them together with the largest one somewhere near the centre, the others grouped around it in not too strict accordance with their sizes, adjust the whole collection to agree with the slopes of a hilltop, and you would have a model of the Kavalov house. The windows were steel-sashed. There weren't very many of them. No two were in line either vertically or horizontally. Some were lighted.

As I got out of the car, the narrow front door of this house opened.

A short, red-faced woman of fifty or so, with faded blonde hair wound around and around her head, came out. She wore a high-necked, tight-sleeved, grey woollen dress. When she smiled her mouth seemed wide as her lips.

She said:

'You're the gentleman from the city?'

'Yeah. I lost your chauffeur somewhere back on the road.'

'Lord bless you,' she said amiably, 'that's all right.'

A thin man with thin dark hair plastered down above a thin, worried face came past her to take my bags when I had lifted them out of the car. He carried them indoors.

The woman stood aside for me to enter, saying:

'Now I suppose you'll want to wash up a little bit before you go in to dinner, and they won't mind waiting for you the few minutes you'll take if you hurry.'

I said, 'Yeah, thanks,' waited for her to get ahead of me again, and followed her up a curving flight of stairs that climbed along the inside of one of the cones that made up the building.

She took me to a second-storey bedroom where the thin man was unpacking my bags.

'Martin will get you anything you need,' she assured me from the doorway, 'and when you're ready, just come on downstairs.'

I said I would, and she went away. The thin man had finished unpacking by the time I had got out of coat, vest, collar and shirt. I told him there wasn't anything else I needed, washed up in the adjoining bathroom, put on a fresh shirt and collar, my vest and coat, went downstairs.

The wide hall was empty. Voices came through an open doorway to the left.

One voice was a nasal whine. It complained:

'I will not have it. I will not put up with it. I am not a child, and I will not have it.'

This voice's t's were a little too thick for t's, but not thick enough to be d's.

Another voice was a lively, but slightly harsh, baritone. It said cheerfully:

'What's the good of saying we won't put up with it, when we are putting up with it?'

The third voice was feminine, a soft voice, but flat and spiritless. It said:

'But perhaps he did kill him.'

The whining voice said: 'I do not care. I will not have it.'

The baritone voice said, cheerfully as before: 'Oh, won't you?'

A doorknob turned farther down the hall. I didn't want to be caught standing there listening. I advanced to the open doorway.

III

I was in the doorway of a low-ceilinged oval room furnished and decorated in grey, white and silver. Two men and a woman were there.

The older man – he was somewhere in his fifties – got up from a deep grey chair and bowed ceremoniously at me. He was a plump man of medium height, completely bald, dark-skinned and pale-eyed. He wore a wax-pointed grey moustache and a straggly grey imperial.

'Mr Kavalov?' I asked.

'Yes, sir.' His was the whining voice.

I told him who I was. He shook my hand and then introduced me to the others.

The woman was his daughter. She was probably thirty. She had her father's narrow, full-lipped mouth, but her eyes were dark, her nose was short and straight, and her skin was almost colourless. Her face had Asia in it. It was pretty, passive, unintelligent.

The man with the baritone voice was her husband. His name was Ringgo. He was six or seven years older than his wife, neither tall nor heavy, but well set-up. His left arm was in splints and a sling. The knuckles of his right hand were darkly bruised. He had a lean, bony, quick-witted face, bright dark eyes with plenty of lines around them, and a good-natured hard mouth.

He gave me his bruised hand, wriggled his bandaged arm at me, grinned, and said:

'I'm sorry you missed this, but the future injuries are yours.'

'How did it happen?' I asked.

Kavalov raised a plump hand.

'Time enough it is to go into that when we have eaten,' he said. 'Let us have our dinner first.'

We went into a small green and brown dining-room where a small square table was set. I sat facing Ringgo across a silver basket of orchids that stood between tall silver candlesticks in the centre of the table. Mrs Ringgo sat to my right, Kavalov to my left. When Kavalov sat down I saw the shape of an automatic pistol in his hip pocket.

Two men servants waited on us. There was a lot of food and all of it was well turned out. We ate caviar, some sort of consommé, sand dabs, potatoes and cucumber jelly, roast lamb, corn and string beans, asparagus, wild duck and hominy cakes, artichoke-and-tomato salad, and orange ice. We drank white wine, claret, Burgundy, coffee and crème de menthe.

Kavalov ate and drank enormously. None of us skimped.

Kavalov was the first to disregard his own order that nothing be said about his troubles until after we had eaten. When he had finished his soup he put down his spoon and said:

'I am not a child. I will not be frightened.'

He blinked pale, worried eyes defiantly at me, his lips pouting between moustache and imperial.

Ringgo grinned pleasantly at him. Mrs Ringgo's face was as serene and unattentive as if nothing had been said.

'What is there to be frightened of?' I asked.

'Nothing,' Kavalov said. 'Nothing excepting a lot of idiotic and very pointless trickery and play-acting.'

'You can call it anything you want to call it,' a voice grumbled over my shoulder, 'but I seen what I seen.'

The voice belonged to one of the men who was waiting on the table, a sallow, youngish man with a narrow, slack-lipped face. He spoke with a subdued sort of stubbornness, and without looking up from the dish he was putting before me.

Since nobody else paid any attention to the servant's clearly audible remark, I turned my face to Kavalov again. He was trimming the edge of a sand dab with the side of his fork.

'What kind of trickery and play-acting?' I asked.

Kavalov put down his fork and rested his wrists on the edge of the table. He rubbed his lips together and leaned over his plate towards me.

'Supposing' – he wrinkled his forehead so that his bald scalp twitched forward – 'you have done injury to a man ten years ago.' He turned his wrists quickly, laying his hands palm-up on the white cloth. 'You have done this injury in the ordinary business manner – you understand? – for profit. There is not anything personal concerned. You do not hardly know him. And then supposing he came to you after all those ten years and said to you: "I have come to watch you die." ' He turned his hands over, palms down. 'Well, what would you think?'

'I wouldn't,' I replied, 'think I ought to hurry up my dying on his account.'

The earnestness went out of his face, leaving it blank. He blinked at me for a moment and then began eating his fish. When he had chewed and swallowed the last piece of sand dab he looked up at me again. He shook his head slowly, drawing down the corners of his mouth.

'That was not a good answer,' he said. He shrugged, and spread his fingers. 'However, you will have to deal with this Captain Cat-and-mouse. It is for that I engaged you.'

I nodded.

Ringgo smiled and patted his bandaged arm, saying:

'I wish you more luck with him than I had.'

Mrs Ringgo put out a hand and let the pointed fingertips touch her husband's wrist for a moment.

I asked Kavalov:

'This injury I was to suppose I had done: how serious was it?'

He pursed his lip, made little wavy motions with the fingers of his right hand, and said:

'Oh – ah – ruin.'

'We can take it for granted, then, that your captain's really up to something?'

'Good God!' said Ringgo, dropping his fork, 'I wouldn't like to think he'd broken my arm just in fun.'

Behind me the sallow servant spoke to his mate:

'He wants to know if we think the captain's really up to something.'

'I heard him,' the other said gloomily. 'A lot of help he's going to be to us.'

Kavalov tapped his plate with a fork and made angry faces at the servants.

'Shut up,' he said. 'Where is the roast?' He pointed the fork at Mrs Ringgo. 'Her glass is empty.' He looked at the fork. 'See what care they take of my silver,' he complained, holding it out to me. 'It has not been cleaned decently in a month.'

He put the fork down. He pushed back his plate to make room for his forearms on the table. He leaned over them, hunching his shoulders. He sighed. He frowned. He stared at me with pleading pale eyes.

'Listen,' he whined. 'Am I a fool? Would I send to San Francisco for a detective if I did not need a detective? Would I pay you what you are charging me, when I could get plenty of good enough detectives for half of that, if I did not require the best detective I could secure? Would I require so expensive a one if I did not know this captain for a completely dangerous fellow?'

I didn't say anything. I sat still and looked attentive.

'Listen,' he whined. 'This is not April-foolery. This captain means to murder me. He came here to murder me. He will certainly murder me if somebody does not stop him from it.'

'Just what has he done so far?' I asked.

'That is not it.' Kavalov shook his bald head impatiently. 'I do not ask you to undo anything that he has done. I ask you to keep him from killing me. What has he done so far? Well, he has terrorised my people most completely. He has broken Dolph's arm. He has done these things so far, if you must know.'

'How long has this been going on? How long has he been here?' I asked.

'A week and two days.'

'Did your chauffeur tell you about the black man we saw in the road?'

Kavalov pushed his lips together and nodded slowly.

'He wasn't there when I went back,' I said.

He blew out his lips with a little puff and cried excitedly:

'I do not care anything about your black men and your roads. I care about not being murdered.'

'Have you said anything to the sheriff's office?' I asked, trying to pretend I wasn't getting peevish.

'That I have done. But to what good? Has he threatened me? Well, he has told me he has come to watch me die. From him, the way he said it, that is a threat. But to your sheriff it is not a threat. He has terrorised my people. Have I proof that he has done that? The sheriff says I have not. What absurdity! Do I need proof? Don't I know? Must he leave fingerprints on the fright he causes? So it comes to this: the sheriff will keep an eye on him. "An eye," he said, mind you. Here I have twenty people, servants and farm hands, with forty eyes. And he comes and goes as he likes. An eye!'

'How about Ringgo's arm?' I asked.

Kavalov shook his head impatiently and began to cut up his lamb with short, quick strokes.

Ringgo said:

'There's nothing we can do about that. I hit him first.' He looked at his bruised knuckles. 'I didn't think he was that tough. Maybe I'm not as good as I used to be. Anyway, a dozen people saw me punch his jaw before he touched me. We performed at high noon in front of the post office.'

'Who is this captain?'

'It's not him,' the sallow servant said. 'It's that black devil.'

Ringgo said:

'Sherry's his name, Hugh Sherry. He was a captain in the British army when we knew him before – quartermaster's department in Cairo. That was in 1917, all of twelve years ago. The commodore' – he nodded his head at his father-in-law – 'was speculating in military supplies. Sherry should have been a line officer. He had no head for desk work. He wasn't timid enough. Somebody decided the commodore wouldn't have made so much money if Sherry hadn't been so careless. They knew Sherry hadn't made any money for himself. They cashiered Sherry at the same time they asked the commodore please to go away.'

Kavalov looked up from his plate to explain.

'Business is like that in wartime. They wouldn't let me go away if I had done anything they could keep me there for.'

'And now, twelve years after you had him kicked out of the army in disgrace,' I said, 'he comes here, threatens to kill you, so you believe, and sets out to spread panic among your people. Is that it?'

'That is not it,' Kavalov whined. 'That is not it at all. I did not have him kicked out of my armies. I am a man of business. I take my profits where I find them. If somebody let me take a profit that angers his employers, what is their anger to me? Second, I do not believe he means to kill me. I know that.'

I said:

'I'm trying to get it straight in my mind.'

'There is nothing to get straight. A man is going to murder me. I ask you not to let him do it. Is not that simple enough?'

'Simple enough,' I agreed, and I stopped trying to talk to him.

Kavalov and Ringgo were smoking cigars, Mrs Ringgo and I cigarettes over *crème de menthe* when the red-faced blonde woman in grey wool came in.

She came in hurriedly. Her eyes were wide open and dark.

She said:

'Anthony says there's a fire in the upper field.'

Kavalov crunched his cigar between his teeth and looked pointedly at me.

I stood up, asking:

'How do I get there?'

'I'll show you the way,' Ringgo said, leaving his chair.

'Dolph,' his wife protested, 'your arm.'

He smiled gently at her and said:

'I'm not going to interfere. I'm only going along to see how an expert handles these things.'

IV

I ran up to my room for hat, coat, flashlight and gun.

The Ringgos were standing at the front door when I started downstairs again.

He had put on a dark raincoat, buttoned tight over his injured arm, its left sleeve hanging empty. His right arm was around his wife. Both of her bare arms were around his neck. She was bent far back, he far forward over her. Their mouths were together.

Retreating a little, I made more noise with my feet when I came into sight again. They were standing apart at the door, waiting for me. Ringgo was breathing heavily, as if he had been running. He opened the door.

Mrs Ringgo addressed me:

'Please don't let my foolish husband be too reckless.'

I said I wouldn't, and asked him:

'Worth while taking any of the servants or farm hands along?'

He shook his head.

'Those that aren't hiding would be as useless as those that are,' he said. 'They've all had it taken out of them.'

He and I went out, leaving Mrs Ringgo looking after us from the doorway. The rain had stopped for the time, but a black muddle overhead promised more presently.

Ringgo led me around the side of the house, along a narrow path that went downhill, through shrubbery, past a group of small buildings in a shallow valley, and diagonally up another, lower, hill.

The path was soggy. At the top of the hill we left the path, going through a wire gate and across a stubby field that was both gummy and slimy under our feet. We moved along swiftly. The gumminess of the ground, the sultriness of the night air, and our coats, made the going warm work.

When we had crossed this field we could see the fire, a spot of flickering orange beyond intervening trees. We climbed a low wire fence and wound through the trees.

A violent rustling broke out among the leaves overhead, starting at the left, ending with a solid thud against a tree trunk just to our right. Then something *plopped* on the soft ground under the tree.

Off to the left a voice laughed, a savage, hooting laugh.

The laughing voice couldn't have been far away. I went after it.

The fire was too small and too far away to be of much use to me: blackness was nearly perfect among the trees.

I stumbled over roots, bumped into trees, and found nothing. The flashlight would have helped the laugher more than me, so I kept it idle in my hand.

When I got tired of playing peek-a-boo with myself, I cut through the woods to the field on the other side, and went down to the fire.

The fire had been built in one end of the field, a dozen feet or less from the nearest tree. It had been built of dead twigs and broken branches that the rain had missed, and had nearly burnt itself out by the time I reached it.

Two small forked branches were stuck in the ground on opposite sides of the fire. Their forks held the ends of a length of green sapling. Spitted on the sapling, hanging over the fire, was an eighteen-inch-long carcass, headless, tail-less, footless, skinless, and split down the front.

On the ground a few feet away lay an Airedale puppy's head, pelt, feet, tail, insides, and a lot of blood.

There were some dry sticks, broken in convenient lengths, beside the fire. I put them on as Ringgo came out of the woods to join me. He carried a stone the size of a grapefruit in his hand.

'Get a look at him?' he asked.

'No. He laughed and went.'

He held out the stone to me, saying:

'This is what was chucked at us.'

Drawn on the smooth grey stone, in red, were round blank eyes, a triangular nose, and a grinning, toothy mouth – a crude skull.

I scratched one of the red eyes with a fingernail, and said:

'Crayon.'

Ringgo was staring at the carcass sizzling over the fire and at the trimmings on the ground.

'What do you make of that?' I asked.

He swallowed and said:

'Mickey was damned good little dog.'

'Yours?'

He nodded.

I went around with my flashlight on the ground, I found some footprints, such as they were.

'Anything?' Ringgo asked.

'Yeah.' I showed him one of the prints. 'Made with rags tied around his shoes. They're no good.'

We turned to the fire again.

'This is another show,' I said. 'Whoever killed and cleaned the pup knew his stuff; knew it too well to think he could cook him decently like that. The outside will be burnt before the inside's even warm, and the way he's put on the spit he'd fall off if you tried to turn him.'

Ringgo's scowl lightened a bit.

'That's a little better,' he said. 'Having him killed is rotten enough, but I'd hate to think of anybody eating Mickey, or even meaning to.'

'They didn't,' I assured him. 'They were putting on a show. This the sort of thing that's been happening?'

'Yes.'

'What's the sense of it?'

He glumly quoted Kavalov:

'Captain Cat-and-mouse.'

I gave him a cigarette, took one myself, and lighted them with a stick from the fire.

He raised his face to the sky, said, 'Raining again; let's go back to the house,' but remained by the fire, staring at the cooking carcass. The stink of scorched meat hung thick around us.

'You don't take this very seriously yet, do you?' he asked presently, in a low, matter-of-fact voice.

'It's a funny layout.'

'He's cracked,' he said in the same low voice. 'Try to see this. Honour meant something to him. That's why we had to trick him instead of bribing him, back in Cairo. Less than ten years of dishonour can crack a man like that. He'd go off and hide and brood. It would be either shoot himself when the blow fell – or that. I was like you at first.' He kicked at the fire. 'This is silly. But I can't laugh at it now, except when I'm around Miriam and the commodore. When he first showed up I didn't have the slightest idea that I couldn't handle him. I had handled him all right in Cairo. When I discovered I couldn't handle him I lost my head a little. I went down and picked a row with him. Well, that was no good either. It's the silliness of this that makes it bad. In Cairo he was the kind of man who combs his hair before he shaves, so his mirror will show an orderly picture. Can you understand some of this?'

'I'll have to talk to him first,' I said. 'He's staying in the village?'

'He has a cottage on the hill above. It's the first one on the left after you turn into the main road.' Ringgo dropped his cigarette into the fire and looked thoughtfully at me, biting his lower lip. 'I don't know how you and the commodore are going to get along. You can't make jokes with him. He doesn't understand them, and he'll distrust you on that account.'

'I'll try to be careful,' I promised. 'No good offering this Sherry money?'

'Hell, no,' he said softly. 'He's too cracked for that.'

We took down the dog's carcass, kicked the fire apart, and trod it out in the mud before we returned to the house.

V

The country was fresh and bright under clear sunlight the next morning. A warm breeze was drying the ground and chasing raw-cotton clouds across the sky.

At ten o'clock I set out afoot for Captain Sherry's. I didn't have any trouble finding his house, a pinkish stuccoed bungalow with a terra cotta roof – reached from the road by a cobbled walk.

A white-clothed table with two places set stood on the tiled veranda that stretched across the front of the bungalow.

Before I could knock, the door was opened by a slim black man, not much more than a boy, in a white jacket. His features were thinner than most American Negroes', aquiline, pleasantly intelligent.

'You're going to catch colds lying around in wet roads,' I said, 'if you don't get run over.'

His mouth-ends ran towards his ears in a grin that showed me a lot of strong yellow teeth.

'Yes, sir,' he said, buzzing his s's, rolling the r, bowing. 'The *capitaine* have waited breakfast that you be with him. You do sit down, sir. I will call him.'

'Not dog meat?'

His mouth-ends ran back and up again and he shook his head vigorously.

'No, sir.' He held up his black hands and counted the fingers. 'There is orange and kippers and kidneys grilled and eggs and marmalade and toast and tea or coffee. There is not dog meat.'

'Fine,' I said, and sat down in one of the wicker armchairs on the veranda.

I had time to light a cigarette before Captain Sherry came out.

He was a gaunt tall man of forty. Sandy hair, parted in the middle, was brushed flat to his small head, above a sunburned face. His eyes were grey, with lower lids as straight as ruler-edges. His mouth was another hard straight line under a close-clipped sandy moustache. Grooves like gashes ran from his nostrils past his mouth-corners. Other grooves, just as deep, ran down his cheeks to the sharp ridge of his jaw. He wore a gaily striped flannel bathrobe over sand-coloured pajamas.

'Good morning,' he said pleasantly, and gave me a semi-salute. He didn't offer to shake hands. 'Don't get up. It will be some minutes before Marcus has breakfast ready. I slept late. I had a most abominable dream.' His voice was a deliberately languid drawl. 'I dreamed that Theodore Kavalov's throat had been cut from here to here.' He put bony fingers under his ears. 'It was an atrociously gory business. He bled and screamed horribly, the swine.'

I grinned up at him, asking:

'And you didn't like that?'

'Oh, getting his throat cut was all to the good, but he bled and screamed so filthily.' He raised his nose and sniffed. 'That's honeysuckle somewhere, isn't it?'

'Smells like it. Was it throat-cutting that you had in mind when you threatened him?'

'When I threatened him,' he drawled. 'My dear fellow, I did nothing of the sort. I was in Udja, a stinking Moroccan town close to the Algerian frontier, and one morning a voice spoke to me from an orange tree. It said: "Go to Farewell, in California, in the States, and there you will see Theodore Kavalov die." I thought that a capital idea. I thanked the voice, told Marcus to pack, and I came here. As soon as I arrived I told Kavalov about it, thinking perhaps he would die then and I wouldn't be hung up here waiting. He didn't, though, and too late, I regretted not having asked the voice for a definite date. I should hate having to waste months here.'

'That's why you've been trying to hurry it up?' I asked.

'I beg your pardon?'

'*Schrecklichkeit*,' I said, 'rocky skulls, dog barbecues, vanishing corpses.'

'I've been fifteen years in Africa,' he said. 'I've too much faith in voices that come from orange trees where no one is to try to give them a hand. You needn't fancy I've had anything to do with whatever has happened.'

'Marcus?'

Sherry stroked his freshly shaven cheeks and replied:

'That's possible. He has an incorrigible bent for the ruder sort of African horseplay. I'll gladly cane him for any misbehaviour of which you've reasonably definite proof.'

'Let me catch him at it,' I said, 'and I'll do my own caning.'

Sherry leaned forward and spoke in a cautious undertone:

'Be sure he suspects nothing till you've a firm grip on him. He's remarkably effective with either of his knives.'

'I'll try to remember that. The voice didn't say anything about Ringgo?'

'There was no need. When the body dies, the hand is dead.'

Black Marcus came out carrying food. We moved to the table and I started on my second breakfast.

Sherry wondered whether the voice that had spoken to him from the orange tree had also spoken to Kavalov. He had asked Kavalov, he said, but hadn't received a very satisfactory answer. He believed that voices which announced deaths of people's enemies usually also warned the one who was to die. 'That is,' he said, 'the conventional way of doing it, I believe.'

'I don't know,' I said. 'I'll try to find out for you. Maybe I ought to ask him what he dreamed last night, too.'

'Did he look nightmarish this morning?'

'I don't know. I left before he was up.'

Sherry's eyes became hot grey points.

'Do you mean,' he asked, 'that you've no idea what shape he's in this morning, whether he's alive or not, whether my dream was a true one or not?'

'Yeah.'

The hard line of his mouth loosened into a slow delighted smile.

'By Jove,' he said, 'that's capital! I thought – you gave me the impression of knowing positively that there was nothing to my dream, that it was only a meaningless dream.'

He clapped his hands sharply.

Black Marcus popped out of the door.

'Pack,' Sherry ordered. 'The bald one is finished. We're off.'

Marcus bowed and backed grinning into the house.

'Hadn't you better wait to make sure?' I asked.

'But I am sure,' he drawled, 'as sure as when the voice spoke from the orange tree. There is nothing to wait for now: I have seen him die.'

'In a dream.'

'Was it a dream?' he asked carelessly.

When I left, ten or fifteen minutes later, Marcus was making noises indoors that sounded as if he actually was packing.

Sherry shook hands with me, saying:

'Awfully glad to have had you for breakfast. Perhaps we'll meet again if your work ever brings you to northern Africa. Remember me to Miriam and Dolph. I can't sincerely send condolences.'

Out of sight of the bungalow, I left the road for a path along the hillside above, and explored the country for a higher spot from which

Sherry's place could be spied on. I found a pip, a vacant ramshackle house on a jutting ridge off to the northeast. The whole of the bungalow's front, part of one side, and a good stretch of the cobbled walk, including its juncture with the road, could be seen from the vacant house's front porch. It was a rather long shot for naked eyes, but with field glasses it would be just about perfect, even to a screen of over-grown bushes in front.

When I got back to the Kavalov house Ringgo was propped up on gay cushions in a reed chair under a tree, with a book in his hand.

'What do you think of him?' he asked. 'Is he cracked?'

'Not very. He wanted to be remembered to you and Mrs Ringgo. How's the arm this morning?'

'Rotten. I must have let it get too damp last night. It gave me hell all night.'

'Did you see Captain Cat-and-mouse?' Kavalov's whining voice came from behind me. 'And did you find any satisfaction in that?'

I turned around. He was coming down the walk from the house. His face was more grey than brown this morning, but what I could see of his throat, above the v of a wing collar, was uncut enough.

'He was packing when I left,' I said. 'Going back to Africa.'

VI

That day was Thursday. Nothing else happened that day.

Friday morning I was awakened by the noise of my bedroom door being opened violently.

Martin, the thin-faced valet, came dashing into my room and began shaking me by the shoulder, though I was sitting up by the time he reached by bedside.

His thin face was lemon-yellow and ugly with fear.

'It's happened,' he babbled. 'Oh, my God, it's happened!'

'What's happened?'

'It's happened. It's happened.'

I pushed him aside and got out of bed. He turned suddenly and ran into my bathroom. I could hear him vomiting as I pushed my feet into slippers.

Kavalov's bedroom was three doors below mine, on the same side of the building.

The house was full of noises, excited voices, doors opening and shutting, though I couldn't see anybody.

I ran down to Kavalov's door. It was open.

Kavalov was in there, lying on a low Spanish bed. The bed-clothes were thrown down across the foot.

Kavalov was lying on his back. His throat had been cut, a curving cut that paralleled the line of his jaw between points an inch under his ear lobes.

Where his blood had soaked into the blue pillow case and blue sheet it was purple as grape-juice. It was thick and sticky, already clotting.

Ringgo came in wearing a bathrobe like a cape.

'It's happened,' I growled, using the valet's words.

Ringgo looked dully, miserably, at the bed and began cursing in a choked, muffled voice.

The red-faced blonde woman – Louella Qually, the house-keeper – came in, screamed, pushed past us, and ran to the bed, still screaming. I caught her arm when she reached for the covers.

'Let things alone,' I said.

'Cover him up. Cover him up, the poor man!' she cried.

I took her away from the bed. Four or five servants were in the room by now. I gave the housekeeper to a couple of them, telling them to take her out and quiet her down. She went away laughing and crying.

Ringgo was still staring at the bed.

'Where's Mrs Ringgo?' I asked.

He didn't hear me. I tapped his good arm and repeated the question.

'She's in her room. She – she didn't have to see it to know what had happened.'

'Hadn't you better look after her?'

He nodded, turned slowly, and went out.

The valet, still lemon-yellow, came in.

'I want everybody on the place, servants, farm hands, everybody downstairs in the front room,' I told him. 'Get them all there right away, and they're to stay there till the sheriff comes.'

'Yes, sir,' he said and went downstairs, the others following him.

I closed Kavalov's door and went across to the library, where I phoned the sheriff's office in the county seat. I talked to a deputy named Hilden. When I had told him my story he said the sheriff would be at the house within half an hour.

I went to my room and dressed. By the time I had finished, the valet came up to tell me that everybody was assembled in the front room – everybody except the Ringgos and Mrs Ringgo's maid.

I was examining Kavalov's bedroom when the sheriff arrived. He was a white-haired man with mild blue eyes and a mild voice that came out indistinctly under a white moustache. He had brought three deputies, a doctor and a coroner with him.

'Ringgo and the valet can tell you more than I can,' I said when we had shaken hands all around. 'I'll be back as soon as I can make it. I'm going to Sherry's. Ringgo will tell you where he fits in.'

In the garage I selected a muddy Chevrolet and drove to the bungalow.

Its doors and windows were tight, and my knocking brought no answer.

I went back along the cobbled walk to the car, and rode down into Farewell. There I had no trouble learning that Sherry and Marcus had taken the two-ten train for Los Angeles, the afternoon before, with three trunks and half a dozen bags that the village expressman had checked for them.

After sending a telegram to the Agency's Los Angeles branch, I hunted up the man from whom Sherry had rented the bungalow.

He could tell me nothing about his tenants except that he was disappointed in their not staying even a full two weeks. Sherry had returned the keys with a brief note saying he had been called away unexpectedly.

I pocketed the note. Handwriting specimens are always convenient to have. Then I borrowed the keys to the bungalow and went back to it.

I didn't find anything of value there, except a lot of fingerprints that might possibly come in handy later. There was nothing there to tell me where my men had gone.

I returned to Kavalov's.

The sheriff had finished running the staff through the mill.

'Can't get a thing out of them,' he said. 'Nobody heard anything and nobody saw anything, from bedtime last night, till the valet opened the door to call him at eight o'clock this morning, and saw him dead like that. You know any more than that?'

'No. They tell you about Sherry?'

'Oh, yes. That's our meat, I guess, huh?'

'Yeah. He's supposed to have cleared out yesterday afternoon, with his man, for Los Angeles. We ought to be able to find the work in that. What does the doctor say?'

'Says he was killed between three and four this morning, with a heavyish knife – one clean slash from left to right, like a left-handed man would do it.'

'Maybe one clean cut,' I agreed, 'but not exactly a slash. Slower than that. A slash, if it curved, ought to curve up, away from the slasher, in the middle, and down towards him at the ends – just the opposite of what this does.'

'Oh, all right. Is this Sherry a southpaw?'

'I don't know.' I wondered if Marcus was. 'Find the knife?'

'Nary hide nor hair of it. And what's more, we didn't find anything else, inside or out. Funny a fellow as scared as Kavalov was, from all accounts, didn't keep himself locked up tighter. His windows were open. Anybody could of got in them with a ladder. His door wasn't locked.'

'There could be half a dozen reasons for that. He—'

One of the deputies, a big-shouldered blond man, came to the door and said:

'We found the knife.'

The sheriff and I followed the deputy out of the house, around to the side on which Kavalov's room was situated. The knife's blade was buried in the ground, among some shrubs that bordered a path leading down to the farm hands' quarters.

The knife's wooden handle – painted red – slanted a little toward the house. A little blood was smeared on the blade, but the soft earth had cleaned off most. There was no blood on the painted handle, and nothing like a fingerprint.

There were no footprints in the soft ground near the knife. Apparently it had been tossed into the shrubbery.

'I guess that's all there is here for us,' the sheriff said. 'There's nothing much to show that anybody here had anything to do with it, or didn't. Now we'll look after this here Captain Sherry.'

I went down to the village with him. At the post office we learned that Sherry had left a forwarding address: General Delivery, St Louis, Mo. The postmaster said Sherry had received no mail during his stay in Farewell.

We went to the telegraph office, and were told that Sherry had neither received nor sent any telegrams. I sent one to the Agency's St Louis branch.

The rest of our poking around in the village brought us nothing – except we learned that most of the idlers in Farewell had seen Sherry and Marcus board the southbound two-ten train.

Before we returned to the Kavalov house a telegram came from the Los Angeles branch for me:

Sherry's trunks and bags in baggage room here not yet called for are keeping them under surveillance.

When we got back to the house I met Ringgo in the hall, and asked him:

'Is Sherry left-handed?'

He thought, and then shook his head.

'I can't remember,' he said. 'He might be. I'll ask Miriam. Perhaps she'll know – women remember things like that.'

When he came downstairs again he was nodding:

'He's very nearly ambidextrous, but uses his left hand more than his right. Why?'

'The doctor thinks it was done with a left hand. How is Mrs Ringgo now?'

'I think the worst of the shock is over, thanks.'

VII

Sherry's baggage remained uncalled for in the Los Angeles passenger station all day Saturday. Late that afternoon the sheriff made public the news that Sherry and the Negro were wanted for murder, and that night the sheriff and I took a train south.

Sunday morning, with a couple of men from the Los Angeles police department, we opened the baggage. We didn't find anything except legitimate clothing and personal belongings that told us nothing.

That trip paid no dividends.

I returned to San Francisco and had bales of circulars printed and distributed.

Two weeks went by, two weeks in which the circulars brought us nothing but the usual lot of false alarms.

Then the Spokane police picked up Sherry and Marcus in a Stevens Street rooming house.

Some unknown person had phoned the police that one Fred Williams living there had a mysterious Negro visitor nearly every day, and that their actions were very suspicious. The Spokane police had copies of our circular. They hardly needed the H. S. monograms on Fred Williams' cuff links and handkerchiefs to assure tham that he was our man.

After a couple of hours of being grilled, Sherry admitted his identity, but denied having murdered Kavalov.

Two of the sheriff's men went north and brought the prisoners down to the county seat.

Sherry had shaved off his moustache. There was nothing in his face or voice to show that he was the least bit worried.

'I knew there was nothing more to wait for after my dream,' he drawled, 'so I went away. Then, when I heard the dream had come true, I knew you johnnies would be hot after me – as if one can help his dreams – and I – ah – sought seclusion.'

He solemnly repeated his orange-tree-voice story to the sheriff and district attorney. The newspapers liked it.

He refused to map his route for us, to tell us how he had spent his time.

'No, no,' he said. 'Sorry, but I shouldn't do it. It may be I shall have to do it again some time, and it wouldn't do to reveal my methods.'

He wouldn't tell us where he had spent the night of the murder. We were fairly certain that he had left the train before it reached Los Angeles, though the train crew had been able to tell us nothing.

'Sorry,' he drawled. 'But if you chaps don't know where I was, how do you know that I was where the murder was?'

We had even less luck with Marcus. His formula was:

'Not understand the English very good. Ask the *capitaine*. I don't know.'

The district attorney spent a lot of time walking his office floor, biting his fingernails, and telling us fiercely that the case was going to fall apart if we couldn't prove that either Sherry or Marcus was within reach of the Kavalov house at, or shortly before or after, the time of the murder.

The sheriff was the only one of us who hadn't a sneaky feeling that Sherry's sleeves were loaded with assorted aces. The sheriff saw him already hanged.

Sherry got a lawyer, a slick-looking pale man with hornrim glasses and a thin twitching mouth. His name was Schaeffer. He went around smiling to himself and at us.

When the district attorney had only thumb nails left and was starting to work on them, I borrowed a car from Ringgo and started following the railroad south, trying to learn where Sherry had left the train. We had mugged the pair, of course, so I carried their photographs with me.

I displayed those damned photographs at every railroad stop between Farewell and Los Angeles, at every village within twenty miles of the tracks on either side, and at most of the houses in between. And it got me nothing.

There was no evidence that Sherry and Marcus hadn't gone through to Los Angeles.

Their train would have put them there at ten-thirty that night. There was no train out of Los Angeles that would have carried them back to Farewell in time to kill Kavalov. There were two possibilities: an airplane could have carried them back in plenty of time, and an automobile might have been able to do it, though that didn't look reasonable.

I tried the airplane angle first, and couldn't find a flyer who had had a passenger that night. With the help of the Los Angeles police and some operatives from the Continental's Los Angeles branch, I had everybody who owned a plane – public or private – interviewed. All the answers were no.

We tried the less promising automobile angle. The larger taxicab and hire-car companies said, 'No.' Four privately owned cars had been reported stolen between ten and twelve o'clock that night. Two of them had been found in the city the next morning: they couldn't have made the trip to Farewell and back. One of the others had been picked up in San Diego the next day. That let that one out. The other was still loose, a Packard sedan. We got a printer working on post card descriptions of it.

To reach all the small-fry taxi and hire-car owners was quite a job, and then there were the private car owners who might have hired out for one night. We went into the newspapers to cover these fields.

We didn't get any automobile information, but this new line of inquiry – trying to find traces of our men here a few hours before the murder – brought results of another kind.

At San Pedro (Los Angeles's seaport, twenty-five miles away) a Negro had been arrested at one o'clock on the morning of the murder. The Negro spoke English poorly, but had papers to prove that he was Pierre Tisano, a French sailor. He had been arrested on a drunk and disorderly charge.

The San Pedro police said that the photograph and description of the man we knew as Marcus fitted the drunken sailor exactly.

That wasn't all the San Pedro police said.

Tisano had been arrested at one o'clock. At a little after two o'clock, a white man who gave his name as Henry Somerton had appeared and had tried to bail the Negro out. The desk sergeant had told Somerton that nothing could be done till morning, and that, anyway, it would be better to let Tisano sleep off his jag before removing him. Somerton had readily agreed to that, had remained talking to the desk sergeant for more than half an hour, and had left at about three. At ten o'clock that morning he had reappeared to pay the black man's fine. They had gone away together.

The San Pedro police said that Sherry's photograph – without the moustache – and description were Henry Somerton's.

Henry Somerton's signature on the register of the hotel to which he had gone between his two visits to the police matched the handwriting in Sherry's note to the bungalow's owner.

It was pretty clear that Sherry and Marcus had been in San Pedro – a nine-hour train ride from Farewell – at the time that Kavalov was murdered.

Pretty clear isn't quite clear enough in a murder job: I carried the San Pedro desk sergeant north with me for a look at the two men.

'Them's them, all righty,' he said.

VIII

The district attorney ate up the rest of his thumb nails.

The sheriff had the bewildered look of a child who had held a balloon in his hand, had heard a pop, and couldn't understand where the balloon had gone.

I pretended I was perfectly satisfied.

'Now we're back where we started,' the district attorney wailed disagreeably, as if it was everybody's fault but his, 'and with all those weeks wasted.'

The sheriff didn't look at the district attorney, and didn't say anything.

I said:

'Oh, I wouldn't say that. We've made some progress.'

'What?'

'We know that Sherry and the servant have alibis.'

The district attorney seemed to think I was trying to kid him. I didn't pay any attention to the faces he made at me, and asked:

'What are you going to do with them?'

'What can I do with them but turn them loose? This shoots the case to hell.'

'It doesn't cost the county much to feed them,' I suggested. 'Why not hang on to them as long as you can, while we think it over? Something new may turn up, and you can always drop the case if nothing does. You don't think they're innocent, do you?'

He gave me a look that was heavy and sour with pity for my stupidity.

'They're guilty as hell, but what good's that to me if I can't get a conviction? And what's the good of saying I'll hold them? Damn it, man, you know as well as I do that all they've got to do now is ask for their release and any judge will hand it to them.'

'Yeah,' I agreed. 'I'll bet you the best hat in San Francisco that they don't ask for it.'

'What do you mean?'

'They want to stand trial,' I said, 'or they'd have sprung that alibi before we dug it up. I've an idea that they tipped off the Spokane police themselves. And I'll bet you that hat that you get no *habeas corpus* motions out of Schaeffer.'

The district attorney peered suspiciously into my eyes.

'Do you know something that you're holding back?' he demanded.

'No, but you'll see I'm right.'

I was right. Schaeffer went around smiling to himself and making no attempt to get his clients out of the county prison.

Three days later something new turned up.

A man named Archibald Weeks, who had a small chicken farm some ten miles south of the Kavalov place, came to see the district attorney. Weeks said he had seen Sherry on his – Weeks's – place early on the morning of the murder.

Weeks had been leaving for Iowa that morning to visit his parents. He had got up early to see that everything was in order before driving twenty miles to catch an early morning train.

At somewhere between half-past five and six o'clock he had gone to the shed where he kept his car, to see if it held enough gasoline for the trip.

A man ran out of the shed, vaulted the fence, and dashed away down the road. Weeks chased him for a short distance, but the other was too speedy for him. The man was too well-dressed for a hobo: Weeks supposed he had been trying to steal the car.

Since Weeks's trip east was a necessary one, and during his absence his wife would have only their two sons – one seventeen, one fifteen – there with her, he had thought it wisest not to frighten her by saying anything about the man he had surprised in the shed.

He had returned from Iowa the day before his appearance in the district attorney's office, and after hearing the details of the Kavalov murder, and seeing Sherry's picture in the papers, had recognised him as the man he had chased.

We showed him Sherry in person. He said Sherry was the man. Sherry said nothing.

With Weeks's evidence to refute the San Pedro police's, the district attorney let the case against Sherry come to trial. Marcus was held as a material witness, but there was nothing to weaken his San Pedro alibi, so he was not tried.

Weeks told his story straight and simply on the witness stand, and then, under cross-examination, blew up with a loud bang. He went to pieces completely.

He wasn't, he admitted in answer to Schaeffer's questions, quite as sure that Sherry was the man as he had been before. The man had certainly, the little he had seen of him, looked something like Sherry, but perhaps he had been a little hasty in saying positively that it was Sherry. He wasn't, now that he had had time to think it over, really sure that he had actually got a good look at the man's face in the dim morning light. Finally, all that Weeks would swear to was that he had seen a man who had seemed to look a little bit like Sherry.

It was funny as hell.

The district attorney, having no nails left, nibbled his fingerbones.

The jury said, 'Not guilty.'

Sherry was freed, forever in the clear as far as the Kavalov murder was concerned, no matter what might come to light later.

Marcus was released.

The district attorney wouldn't say good-bye to me when I left for San Francisco.

IX

Four days after Sherry's aquittal, Mrs Ringgo was shown into my office.

She was in black. Her pretty, unintelligent, Oriental face was not placid.

'Please, you won't tell Dolph I have come here?' were the first words she spoke.

'Of course not, if you say not,' I promised.

She sat down and looked big-eyed at me.

'He's so reckless,' she said.

I nodded sympathetically, wondering what she was up to.

'And I'm so afraid,' she added, twisting her gloves. Her chin trembled. Her lips formed words jerkily: 'They've come back to the bungalow.'

'Yeah?' I sat up straight. I knew who *they* were.

'They can't,' she cried, 'have come back for any reason except that they mean to murder Dolph as they did Father. And he won't listen to me. He's so sure of himself. He laughs and calls me a foolish child, and tells me he can take care of himself. But he can't. Not, at least, with a broken arm. And they'll kill him as they killed Father. I know it. I know it.'

'Sherry hates your husband as much as he hated your father?'

'Yes, that's it. He does. Dolph was working for Father, but Dolph's part in the – the business that led up to Hugh's trouble was more – more active than father's. Will you – will you keep them from killing Dolph? Will you?'

'Surely.'

'And you mustn't let Dolph know,' she insisted, 'and if he does find out you're watching them, you mustn't tell him I got you to. He'd be angry with me. I asked him to send for you, but he—' She broke off, looking embarrassed: I supposed her husband had mentioned my lack of success in keeping Kavalov alive. 'But he wouldn't.'

'How long have they been back?'

'Since the day before yesterday.'

'I'll be down tomorrow,' I promised. 'If you'll take my advice you'll tell your husband that you've employed me, but I won't tell him if you don't.'

'And you won't let him harm Dolph?'

I promised to do my best, took some money away from her, gave her a receipt, and bowed her out.

Shortly after dark that evening I reached Farewell.

X

The bungalow's windows were lighted when I passed it on my way uphill. I was tempted to get out of my coupé and do some snooping, but was afraid that I couldn't out-Indian Marcus on his own grounds.

When I turned into the dirt road leading to the vacant house I had spotted on my first trip to Farewell, I switched off the coupé's lights and crept along by the light of a very white moon overhead.

Close to the vacant house I got the coupé off the path.

Then I went up on the rickety porch, located the bungalow, and began to adjust my field-glasses to it.

I had them partly adjusted when the bungalow's front door opened, letting out a slice of yellow light and two people.

One of the people was a woman.

Another least turn of the set-screw and her face came clear in my eyes – Mrs Ringgo.

She raised her coat collar around her face and hurried away down the cobbled walk. Sherry stood on the veranda looking after her.

When she reached the road she began running uphill, towards her house.

Sherry went indoors and shut the door.

Two hours and a half later a man turned into the cobbled walk from the road. He walked swiftly to the bungalow, with a cautious sort of swiftness, and he looked from side to side as he walked.

I suppose he knocked on the door.

The door opened, throwing a yellow glow on his face, Dolph Ringgo's face.

He went indoors. The door shut.

I put away the field-glasses, left the porch, and set out for the bungalow. I wasn't sure that I could find another good spot for the coupé, so I left it where it was and walked.

I was afraid to take a chance on the cobbled walk.

Twenty feet above it, I left the road and moved as silently as I could over sod and among trees, bushes and flowers. I knew the sort of folks I was playing with: I carried my gun in my hand.

All of the bungalow's windows on my side showed lights, but all the windows were closed and their blinds drawn. I didn't like the way the light that came through the blinds helped the moon illuminate the surrounding ground. That had been swell when I was up on the ridge getting cock-eyed squinting through glasses. It was sour now that I was trying to get close enough to do some profitable listening.

I stopped in the closest dark spot I could find – fifteen feet from the building – to think the situation over.

Crouching there, I heard something.

It wasn't in the right place. It wasn't what I wanted to hear. It was the sound of somebody coming down the walk towards the house.

I wasn't sure that I couldn't be seen from the path. I turned my head to make sure. And by turning my head I gave myself away.

Mrs Ringgo jumped, stopped dead still in the path, and then cried: 'Is Dolph in there? Is he? Is he?'

I was trying to tell her that he was by nodding, but she made so much noise with her *Is he's* that I had to say 'Yeah' out loud to make her hear.

I don't know whether the noise we made hurried things up indoors or not, but guns had started going off inside the bungalow.

You don't stop to count shots in circumstances like those, and anyway these were too blurred together for accurate score-keeping, but my impression was that at least fifty of them had been fired by the time I was bruising my shoulder on the front door.

Luckily, it was a California door. It went in the second time I hit it.

Inside was a reception hall opening through a wide arched doorway into a living-room. The air was hazy and the stink of burnt powder was sharp.

Sherry was on the polished floor by the arch, wriggling side-wise on one elbow and one knee, trying to reach a Luger that lay on an amber rug some four feet away.

At the other end of the room, Ringgo was upright on his knees, steadily working the trigger of a black revolver in his good hand. The pistol was empty. It went snap, snap, snap, snap foolishly, but he kept on working the trigger. His broken arm was still in the splints, but had fallen out of the sling and was hanging down. His face was puffy and florid with blood. His eyes were wide and dull. The white bone handle of a knife stuck out of his back, just over one hip, its blade all the way in. He was clicking the empty pistol at Marcus.

The black boy was on his feet, feet far apart under bent knees. His left hand was spread wide over his chest, and the black fingers were shiny with blood. In his right hand he held a white bone-handled knife – its blade a foot long – held it, knife-fighter fashion, as you'd hold a sword. He was moving toward Ringgo, not directly, but from side to side, obliquely, closing in with shuffling steps, crouching, his hand turning the knife restlessly, but holding the point always towards Ringgo.

He didn't see us. He didn't hear us. All of his world just then was the man on his knees, the man in whose back a knife – brother of the one in the black hand – was wedged.

Ringgo didn't see us. I don't suppose he even saw Marcus. He knelt there and persistently worked the trigger of his empty gun.

I jumped over Sherry and swung the barrel of my gun at the base of Marcus's skull. It hit. Marcus dropped.

Ringgo stopped working the gun and looked surprised at me.

'That's the idea; you've got to put bullets in them or they're no good,' I told him, pulled the knife out of Marcus's hand and went back to pick up the Luger that Sherry had stopped trying to get.

Sherry was lying on his back now. His eyes were closed.

He looked dead, and he had enough bullet holes in him to make death a good guess.

Hoping he wasn't dead, I knelt beside him – going around him so I could kneel facing Ringgo – and lifted his head up a little from the floor.

'Sherry,' I said sharply. 'Sherry.'

He didn't move. His eyelids didn't even twitch.

I raised the fingers of the hand that was holding up his head, making his head move just a trifle.

'Did Ringgo kill Kavalov?' I asked the dead or dying man.

Even if I hadn't known Ringgo was looking at me I could have felt his eyes on me.

'Did he, Sherry?' I barked into the still face.

The dead or drying man didn't move.

I cautiously moved my fingers again so that his dead or dying head nodded, twice.

Then I made his head jerk back, and let it gently down on the floor again.

'Well,' I said, standing up and facing Ringgo, 'I've got you at last.'

XI

I've never been able to decide whether I would actually have gone on the witness stand and sworn that Sherry was alive when he nodded, and nodded voluntarily, if it had been necessary for me to do so to convict Ringgo.

I don't like perjury, but I knew Ringgo was guilty, and there I had him.

Fortunately, I didn't have to decide.

Ringgo believed Sherry had nodded, and then, when Marcus gave the show away, there was nothing much for Ringgo to do but try his luck with a plea of guilty.

We didn't have much trouble getting the story out of Marcus. Ringgo had killed his beloved *capitaine*. The boy was easily persuaded that the law would give him his best revenge.

After Marcus had talked, Ringgo was willing to talk.

He stayed in the hospital until the day before his trial opened. The knife Marcus had planted in his back had permanently paralysed one of his legs, though aside from that he recovered from the stabbing.

Marcus had three of Ringgo's bullets in him. The doctors fished two of them out, but were afraid to touch the third. It didn't seem to worry him. By the time he was shipped north to begin an indeterminate sentence in San Quentin for his part in the Kavalov murder he was apparently as sound as ever.

Ringgo was never completely convinced that I had suspected him before the last minute when I had come charging into the bungalow.

'Of course I had, right along,' I defended my skill as a sleuth. That was while he was still in the hospital. 'I didn't believe Sherry was cracked. He was one hard, sane-looking scoundrel. And I didn't believe he was the sort of man who'd be worried much over any disgrace that came his way. I was willing enough to believe that he was out for Kavalov's scalp, but only if there was some profit in it. That's why I went to sleep and let the old man's throat get cut. I figured Sherry was scaring him up – nothing more – to get him in shape for a big-money shakedown. Well, when I found out I had been wrong there I began to look around.

'So far as I knew, your wife was Kavalov's heir. From what I had seen, I imagined your wife was enough in love with you to be completely in your hands. All right, you, as the husband of his heir, seemed the one to profit most directly by Kavalov's death. You were the one who'd have control of his fortune when he died. Sherry could only profit by the murder if he was working with you.'

'But didn't his breaking my arm puzzle you?'

'Sure. I could understand a phony injury, but that seemed carrying it a little too far. But you made a mistake there that helped me. You were too careful to imitate a left-hand cut on Kavalov's throat; did it by standing by his head, facing his body when you cut him, instead of by his body, facing his head, and the curve of the slash gave you away. Throwing the knife out the window wasn't so good, either. How'd he happen to break your arm? An accident?'

'You can call it that. We had that supposed fight arranged to fit in with the rest of the play, and I thought it would be fun to really sock him. So I did. And he was tougher than I thought, tough enough to even up by snapping my arm. I suppose that's why he killed Mickey too. That wasn't on the schedule. On the level, did you suspect us of being in cahoots?'

I nodded.

'Sherry had worked the game up for you, had done everything possible to draw suspicion on himself, and then, the day before the murder, had run off to build himself an alibi. There couldn't be any other answer to it: he had to be working with you. There it was, but I couldn't prove it. I couldn't prove it till you were trapped by the thing that made the whole game possible – your wife's love for you set her to hire me to protect you. Isn't that one of the things they call ironies of life?'

Ringgo smiled ruefully and said:

'They should call it that. You know what Sherry was trying on me, don't you?'

'I can guess. That's why he insisted on standing trial.'

'Exactly. The scheme was for him to dig out and keep going, with his alibi ready in case he was picked up, but staying uncaught as long as possible. The more time they wasted hunting him, the less likely they were to look elsewhere, and the colder the trail would be when they found he wasn't their man. He tricked me there. He had himself picked up, and his lawyer hired that Weeks fellow to egg the district attorney into not dropping the case. Sherry wanted to be tried and acquitted, so he'd be in the clear. Then he had me by the neck. He was legally cleared forever. I wasn't. He had me. He was supposed to get a hundred thousand dollars for his part. Kavalov had left Miriam something more than three million dollars. Sherry demanded one-half of it. Otherwise, he said, he'd go to the district attorney and make a complete confession. They couldn't do anything to him. He'd been acquitted. They'd hang me. That was sweet.'

'You'd have been wise at that to have given it to him,' I said.

'Maybe. Anyway I suppose I would have given it to him if Miriam hadn't upset things. There'd have been nothing else to do. But after she came back from hiring you she went to see Sherry, thinking she could talk him into going away. And he lets something drop that made her suspect I had a hand in her father's death, though she doesn't even now actually believe that I cut this throat.

'She said you were coming down the next day. There was nothing for me to do but go down to Sherry's for a showdown that night, and have the whole thing settled before you came poking around. Well, that's what I did, though I didn't tell Miriam I was going. The showdown wasn't going along very well, too much tension, and when Sherry heard you outside he thought I had brought friends, and – fireworks.'

'Whatever got you into a game like that in the first place?' I asked. 'You were sitting pretty enough as Kavalov's son-in-law, weren't you?'

'Yes, but it was tiresome being cooped up in that hole with him. He was young enough to live a long time. And he wasn't always easy to get along with. I'd no guarantee that he wouldn't get up on his ear and kick me out, or change his will, or anything of the sort.

'Then I ran across Sherry in San Francisco, and we got to talking it over, and this plan came out of it. Sherry had brains. On the deal back in Cairo that you know about, both he and I made plenty that Kavalov didn't know about. Well, I was a chump. But don't think I'm sorry that I killed Kavalov. I'm sorry I got caught. I'd done his dirty work since he picked me up as a kid of twenty, and all I'd got out of it was damned little except the hopes that since I'd married his daughter I'd probably get his money when he died – if he didn't do something else with it.'

They hanged him.

Margery Allingham

They Never Get Caught

'Millie dear, this does explain itself, doesn't it? Henry.'

Mr Henry Brownrigg signed his name on the back of the little blue bill with a flourish. Then he set the scrap of paper carefully in the exact centre of the imperfectly scoured developing bath, and, leaving the offending utensil on the kitchen table for his wife to find when she came in, he stalked back to the shop, feeling that he had administered the rebuke surely and at the same time gracefully.

In fifteen years Mr Brownrigg felt that he had mastered the art of teaching his wife her job. Not that he had taught her. That, Mr Brownrigg felt, with a woman of Millie's staggering obtuseness was past praying for. But now, after long practice, he could deliver the snub or administer the punishing word in a way which would penetrate her placid dullness.

Within half an hour after she had returned from shopping and before lunch was set upon the table, he knew the bath would be back in the dark-room, bright and pristine as when it was new, and nothing more would be said about it. Millie would be a little more ineffectually anxious to please at lunch, perhaps, but that was all.

Mr Brownrigg passed behind the counter and flicked a speck of dust off the dummy cartons of face-cream. It was twelve twenty-five and a half. In four and a half minutes Phyllis Bell would leave her office further down the High Street, and in seven and a half minutes she would come in through that narrow, sunlit doorway to the cool, drug-scented shop.

On that patch of floor where the sunlight lay blue and yellow, since it had found its way in through the enormous glass vases in the window which were the emblem of his trade, she would stand and look at him, her blue eyes limpid and her small mouth pursed and adorable.

176

The chemist took up one of the ebony-backed hand mirrors exposed on the counter for sale and glanced at himself in it. He was not altogether a prepossessing person. Never a tall man, at forty-two his wide, stocky figure showed a definite tendency to become fleshy, but there was strength and virility in his thick shoulders, while his clean-shaven face and broad neck were short and bull-like and his lips were full.

Phyllis liked his eyes. They held her, she said, and most of the other young women who bought their cosmetics at the corner shop and chatted with Mr Brownrigg across the counter might have been inclined to agree with her.

Over-dark, round, hot eyes had Mr Brownrigg; not at all the sort of eyes for a little, plump, middle-aged chemist with a placid wife like Millie.

But Mr Brownrigg did not contemplate his own eyes. He smoothed his hair, wiped his lips, and then, realising that Phyllis was almost due, he disappeared behind the dispensing desk. It was as well, he always thought, not to appear too eager.

He was watching the door, though, when she came in. He saw the flicker of her green skirt as she hesitated on the step and saw her half-eager, half apprehensive expression as she glanced towards the counter.

He was glad she had not come in when a customer was there. Phyllis was different from any of the others whose little histories stretched back through the past fourteen years. When Phyllis was in the shop Mr Brownrigg found he was liable to make mistakes, liable to drop things and fluff the change.

He came out from his obscurity eager in spite of himself, and drew the little golden-haired girl sharply towards him over that part of the counter which was lowest and which he purposely kept uncluttered.

He kissed her and the sudden hungry force of the movement betrayed him utterly. He heard her quick intake of breath before she released herself and stepped back.

'You – you shouldn't,' she said, nervously tugging her hat back into position.

She was barely twenty, small and young looking for her years, with yellow hair and a pleasant, quiet style. Her blue eyes were frightened and a little disgusted now, as though she found herself caught up in an emotion which her instincts considered not quite nice.

Henry Brownrigg recognised the expression. He had seen it before in other eyes, but whereas on past occasions he and been able to be tolerantly amused and therefore comforting and glibly reassuring, in Phyllis it irritated and almost frightened him.

'Why not?' he demanded sharply, too sharply he knew immediately, and the blood rushed into his face.

Phyllis took a deep breath.

'I came to tell you,' she said jerkily, like a child saying its piece. 'I've been thinking things over. I can't go on with all this. You're married. I want to be married some day. I – I shan't come in again.'

'You haven't been talking to someone?' he demanded, suddenly cold.

'About you? Good heavens, no!'

Her vehemence was convincing, and because of that he shut his mind to its uncomplimentary inference and experienced only relief.

'You love me,' said Henry Brownrigg. 'I love you and you love me. You know that.'

He spoke without intentional histrionics, but adopted a curious monotone which, some actors have discovered, is one of the most convincing methods of conveying deep sincerity.

Phyllis nodded miserably and then seemed oddly embarrassed. Wistfully her eyes wandered to the sunlit street and back again.

'Good-bye,' she said huskily and fled.

He saw her speeding past the window, almost running.

For some time Henry Brownrigg remained looking down at the patch of blue sunlight where she had stood. Finally he raised his eyes and smiled with conscious wryness. She would come back. To-morrow, or in a week, or in ten days perhaps, she would come back. But the obstacle, the unsurmountable obstacle would arise again, in time it would defeat him and he would lose her.

Phyllis was different from the others. He would lose her. Unless that obstacle were removed.

Henry Brownrigg frowned.

There were other considerations too. The old, mottled ledger told those only too clearly.

If the obstacle were removed it would automatically wipe away those difficulties also, for was there not the insurance and that small income Millie's father had left so securely tied, as though the old man had divined his daughter would grow up a fool?

Mr Brownrigg's eyes rested upon the little drawer under the counter marked: 'Prescriptions: private.' It was locked and not even young Perry, his errand boy and general assistant, who poked his nose into most things, guessed that under the pile of slips within was a packet of letters scrawled in Phyllis's childish hand.

He turned away abruptly. His breath was hard to draw and he was trembling. The time had come.

Some months previously Henry Brownrigg had decided that he must become a widower before the end of the year, but the interview of the morning had convinced him that he must hurry.

At this moment Millie, her face still pink with shame at the recollection of the affair of the ill-washed bath, put her head round the inner door.

'Lunch is on the table, Henry,' she said, and added with that stupidity which had annoyed him ever since it had ceased to please him by making him feel superior, 'Well, you do look serious. Oh, Henry, you haven't made a mistake and given somebody a wrong bottle?'

'No, my dear Millie,' said her husband, surveying her coldly and speaking with heavy sarcasm. 'That is the peculiar sort of idiot mistake I have yet to make. I haven't reached my wife's level yet.'

And as he followed her uncomplaining figure to the little room behind the shop a word echoed rhythmically in the back of his mind and kept time with the beating of his heart. 'Hurry! Hurry! Hurry!'

'Henry, dear,' said Millie Brownrigg, turning a troubled face towards her husband, 'why Doctor Crupiner? He's so expensive and so old.'

She was standing in front of the dressing-table in the big front bedroom above the shop, brushing her brown, grey streaked hair before she plaited it and coiled it round her head.

Henry Brownrigg, laying awake in his bed on the far side of the room, did not answer her.

Millie went on talking. She was used to Henry's silence. Henry was so clever. Most of his time was spent in thought.

'I've heard all sorts of odd things about Doctor Crupiner,' she remarked. 'They say he's so old he forgets. Why shouldn't we go to Mother's man? She swears by him.'

'Unfortunately for your mother she has your intelligence, without a man to look after her, poor woman,' said Henry Brownrigg.

Millie made no comment.

'Crupiner,' continued Henry Brownrigg, 'may not be much good as a general practitioner, but there is one subject on which he is a master. I want him to see you. I want to get you well, old dear.'

Millie's gentle, expressionless face flushed and her blue eyes looked moist and foolish in the mirror. Henry cold see her reflection in the glass and he turned away. There were moments when, by her obvious gratitude for a kind word from him, Millie made him feel a certain distaste for his project. He wished to God she would go away and leave him his last few moments in bed to think of Phyllis in peace.

'You know, Henry,' said Mrs Brownrigg suddenly, 'I don't feel ill. Those things you're giving me are doing me good, I'm sure. I don't feel nearly so tired at the end of the day now. Can't you treat me yourself?'

The man in the bed stiffened. Any compunction he may have felt vanished and he became wary.

'Of course they're doing you good,' he said with the satisfaction of knowing that he was telling the truth up to a point, or at least of knowing that he was doing nothing reprehensible – yet.

'I don't believe in patent medicines as a rule, but Fender's Pills are good. They're a well known formula, and they certainly do pick one up. But I just want to make sure that you're organically sound. I don't like you getting breathless when you hurry, and the colour of your lips isn't good, you know.'

Plump, foolish Millie looked in the mirror and nervously ran her forefinger over her mouth.

Like many women of her age she had lost much of her colour, and there certainly was a faint, very faint, blue streak round the edge of her lips.

The chemist was heavily reassuring.

'Nothing to worry about, I'm sure, but I think we'll go down and see Crupiner this evening,' he said, and added adroitly, 'we want to be on the safe side, don't we?'

Millie nodded, her mouth trembling.

'Yes, dear,' she said, and paused, adding afterwards in that insufferable way of hers, 'I suppose so.'

When she had gone downstairs to attend to breakfast Henry Brownrigg rose with his own last phrase still on his lips. He repeated it thoughtfully.

'The safe side.' That was right. The safe side. No ghastly hash of it for Henry Brownrigg.

Only fools made a hash of things. Only fools got caught. This was almost too easy. Millie was so simple-minded, so utterly unsuspecting.

By the end of the day Mr Brownrigg was nervy. The boy Perry had reported innocently enough that he had seen young Hill in his new car going down Acacia Road at something over sixty, and had added casually that he had had the Bell girl with him. The youngest one. Phyllis. Did Mr Brownrigg remember her? She was rather pretty.

For a moment Henry Brownrigg was in terror lest the boy had discovered his secret and was wounding him maliciously. But, having convinced himself that this was not so, the fact and the sting remained.

Young Hill was handsome and a bachelor. Phyllis was young and impressionable. The chemist imagined them pulling up in some shady copse outside the town, holding hands, perhaps even kissing, and the heart which could remain steady while Millie's stupid eyes met his anxiously as she spoke of her illness turned over painfully in Henry Brownrigg's side at the thought of that embrace.

'Hurry.' The word formed itself again in the back of his mind. Hurry . . . hurry.

Millie was breathless when they arrived at Doctor Crupiner's old-fashioned house. Henry had been self-absorbed and had walked very fast.

Doctor Crupiner saw them immediately. He was a vast, dusty old man. Privately Millie thought she would like to take a good stiff broom to him, and the picture the idea conjured in her mind was so ridiculous that she giggled nervously and Henry had to shake his head at her warningly.

She flushed painfully, and the old, stupid expression settled down over her face again.

Henry explained her symptoms to the doctor and Millie looked surprised and gratified at the anxiety he betrayed. Henry had evidently noticed her little wearinesses much more often than she had supposed.

When he had finished his recital of her small ills, none of them alarming in themselves but piling up in total to a rather terrifying sum of evidence, Doctor Crupiner turned his eyes, which were small and greasy, with red veins in their whites, on to Millie, and his old lips, which were mottled like Henry's ledger, moved for a fraction of a second before his voice came, wheezy and sepulchral.

'Well, madam,' he said, 'your husband here seems worried about you. Let's have a look at you.'

Millie trembled. She was getting breathless again from sheer apprehension. Once or twice lately it had occurred to her that the Fender's Pills made her feel breathless, even while they bucked her up in other ways, but she had not liked to mention this to Henry.

Doctor Crupiner came close to her, breathing heavily through his nose in an effort of concentration. He thrust a stubby, unsteady finger into her eye socket, dragging down the skin so that he could peer shortsightedly at her eyeball. He thumped her half-heartedly on the back and felt the palms of her hands.

Mr Brownrigg, who watched all this somewhat meaningless ritual, his round eyes thoughtful and uneasy, suddenly took the doctor on one side, and the two men had a muttered conversation at the far end of the long room.

Millie could not help overhearing some of it, because Doctor Crupiner was deaf these days and Henry was anxious to make himself understood.

'Twenty years ago,' she heard. 'Very sudden.' And then, after a pause, the awful word 'hereditary.'

Millie's trembling fit increased in intensity and her broad, stupid face looked frightened. They were talking about her poor papa. He had died very suddenly of heart disease.

Her own heart jumped painfully. So that was why Henry seemed so anxious.

Doctor Crupiner came back to her. She had to undo her dress and

Doctor Crupiner listened to her heart with an ancient stethoscope. Millie, already trembling, began to breathe with difficulty as her alarm became unbearable.

At last the old man finished with her. He stared at her unwinkingly for some seconds and finally turned to Henry, and together they went back to the far end of the room.

Millie strained her ears and heard the old man's rumbling voice.

'A certain irregularity. Nothing very alarming. Bring her to see me again.'

Then there was a question from Henry which she could not catch, but afterwards, as the doctor seemed to be fumbling in his mind for a reply, the chemist remarked in an ordinary tone: 'I've been giving her Fender's pills.'

'Fender's pills?' Doctor Crupiner echoed the words with relief. 'Excellent. Excellent. You chemists like patent medicines, I know, and I don't want to encourage you, but that's a well-known formula and will save you mixing up my prescription. Carry on with those for a while. Very good things; I often recommend them. Take them in moderation, of course.'

'Oh, of course,' said Henry. 'But do you think I'm doing right, Doctor?'

Millie looked pleased and startled at the earnestness of Henry's tone.

'Oh, without doubt, Mr Brownrigg, without doubt.' Doctor Crupiner repeated the words again as he came back to Millie. 'There, Mrs Brownrigg,' he said with spurious jollity, 'you take care of yourself and do what your husband says. Come to see me again in a week or so and you'll be as right as ninepence. Off you go. Oh, but Mrs Brownrigg, no shocks, mind. No excitements. No little upsets. And don't over-tire yourself.'

He shook hands perfunctorily, and, while Henry was helping Millie to collect her things with a solicitude quite unusual in him, the old man took down a large, dusty book from the shelves.

Just before they left he peered at Henry over his spectacles.

'Those Fender's pills are quite a good idea,' he remarked in a tone quite different from his professional rumble. 'Just the things. They contain a small percentage of digitalin.'

One of Mr Brownrigg's least attractive habits was his method of spending Saturday nights.

At half-past seven the patient but silently disapproving Millie would clear away the remains of the final meal of the day and place one glass and an unopened bottle of whisky and a siphon of soda on the green serge tablecloth.

This done, she would retire to the kitchen, wash up, and complete the week's ironing. She usually left this job until then, because it was a longish business, with frequent pauses for minor repairs to Henry's shirts and her own underclothing, and she knew she had plenty of undisturbed time on her hands.

She had, in fact, until midnight. When the kitchen clock wheezed twelve Millie folded her ironing board and turned up the irons on the stove to cool.

Then she went into the living-room and took away the glass and the empty bottle, so that the daily help should not see them in the morning. She also picked up the papers and straightened the room.

Finally, when the gas fire had been extinguished, she attended to Henry.

A fortnight and three days after her first visit to Doctor Crupiner – the doctor, at Henry's suggestion, had increased her dose of Fender's pills from three to five a day – she went through her Saturday ritual as usual.

For a man engaged in Mr Brownrigg's particular programme to get hopelessly and incapably drunk once, much less once a week, might well have been suicidal lunacy.

One small glass of whisky reduced him to taciturnity. Twelve large glasses of whisky, or one bottle, made of him a limp, silent sack of humanity, incapable of movement or speech, but, quite remarkably, not a senseless creature.

It might well have occurred to Millie to wonder why her husband should choose to transform himself into a Thérèse Raquin paralytic once every week in his life, but in spite of her awful stupidity she was a tolerant woman and honestly believed that men were odd, privileged creatures who took delight in strange perversions. So she humoured him and kept his weakness secret even from her mother.

Oddly enough, Henry Brownrigg enjoyed his periodical orgy. He did not drink during the week, and his Saturday experience was at once an adventure and a habit. At the outset of his present project he had thought of foregoing it until his plan was completed, but he realised the absolute necessity of adhering rigidly to his normal course of life, so that there could be no hook, however small, on which the garment of suspicion could catch and take hold.

On this particular evening Millie quite exhausted herself getting him upstairs and into bed. She was so tired when it was all over that she sat on the edge of her couch and breathed hard, quite unable to pull herself together sufficiently to undress.

So exhausted was she that she forgot to take the two Fender's pills that Henry had left on the dressing-table for her, and once in bed she could not persuade herself to get out again for them.

In the morning Henry found them still in the little box. He listened to her startled explanations in silence and then, as she added apology to apology, suddenly became himself again.

'Dear Millie,' he said in the old exasperated tone she knew so well, 'isn't it enough for me to do all I can to get you well without you hampering me at every turn?'

Millie bent low over the stove and, as if he felt she might be hiding sudden tears, his manner became more conciliatory.

'Don't you like them?' he inquired softly. 'Don't you like the taste of them? Perhaps they're too big? Look here, old dear, I'll put them up in an easier form. You shall have them in jelly cases. Leave it to me. There, there, don't worry. But you must take your medicine, you know.'

He patted her plump shoulder awkwardly and hurried upstairs to dress.

Millie became thoughtful. Henry was clearly very worried about her indeed, or he would never be so nice about her silly mistake.

Young Bill Perry, Brownrigg's errand boy assistant, was at the awkward stage, if indeed he would ever grow out of it.

He was scrawny, red headed, with a tendency to acne, and great raw, scarlet wrists. Mr Brownrigg he loathed as only the young can loathe the possessor of a sarcastic tongue, but Millie he liked, and his pale, sandy-fringed eyes twinkled kindly when she spoke to him.

Young Perry did not think Millie was half so daft as the Old Man made out.

If only because she was kind to him, young Perry was interested in the state of Millie's health.

On the Monday night young Perry saw Mr Brownrigg putting up the contents of the Fender's pills in jelly cases and he inquired about them.

Mr Brownrigg was unusually communicative. He told young Perry in strict confidence that Mrs Brownrigg was far from well and that Doctor Crupiner was worried about her.

Mr Brownrigg also intimated that he and Doctor Crupiner were, as professional men, agreed that if complete freedom from care and Fender's pills could not save Mrs Brownrigg, nothing could.

'Do you mean she might die?' said young Perry, aghast. 'Suddenly, I mean, sir?'

He was sorry as soon as he had spoken, because Mr Brownrigg's hand trembled so much that he dropped one of the jelly cases and young Perry realised that the Old Man was really wild about the Old Girl after all, and that his bullyragging her was all a sham to hide his feelings.

At that moment young Perry's sentimental, impressionable heart went out to Mr Brownrigg, and he generously forgave him for his observation that young Perry was patently cut out for the diplomatic service, since his tact and delicacy were so great.

The stores arrived. Bill Perry unpacked the two big cases; the smaller case he opened, but left the unpacking to his employer.

Mr Brownrigg finished his pill making, although he was keeping the boy waiting, rinsed his hands and got down to work with his usual deliberation.

There were not a great many packages in the case and young Perry, who had taken a peep at the mottled ledger some time before, thought he knew why. The Old Man was riding close to the edge. Bills and receipts had to be juggled very carefully these days.

The boy read the invoice from the wholesaler's, and Mr Brownrigg put the drugs away.

'Sodii Bicarbonas, Magnesia Levis,' he read, stumbling over the difficult words. 'Iodine, Quininæ Hydrochloridum, Tincture Digitalin ... that must be it, Mr Brownrigg. There, in the biggish packet.'

Bill Perry knew he read badly and was only trying to be helpful when he indicated the parcel, but Mr Brownrigg shot a truly terrifying glance in his direction as he literally snatched up the package and carried it off to the drug cabinet.

Young Perry was dismayed. He was late and he wanted to go. In his panic he floundered on, making matters worse.

'I'm sorry, sir,' he said. 'I was only trying to help. I thought you might be – er – thinking of something else and got a bit muddled.'

'Oh,' said Mr Brownrigg slowly, fixing him with those hot, round eyes in a way which was oddly disturbing. 'And of what should I be thinking when I am doing my work, boy?'

'Of – of Mrs Brownrigg, sir,' stammered the wretched Perry helplessly.

Henry Brownrigg froze. The blood congealed in his face and his eyes seemed to sink into his head.

Young Perry, who realised he had said the wrong thing, and who a had natural delicacy which revolted at prying into another's sorrow, mistook his employer's symptoms for acute embarrassment.

'I'm sorry,' he said again. 'I was really trying to help. I'm a bit – er – windy myself, sir. Mrs Brownrigg's been very kind to me. I'm sorry she's so ill.'

A great sigh escaped Henry Brownrigg.

'That's all right, my boy,' he said, with a gentleness his assistant had never before heard in his tone. 'I'm a bit rattled myself, too. You can go now. I'll see to these few things.'

Young Perry sped off, happy to be free on such a sunny evening, but also a little awe-stricken by the revelation of this tragedy of married love.

Phyllis hurried down Coe's Lane, which was a short cut between her own road and Priory Avenue. It was a narrow, paper-baggy little thoroughfare, with a dusty hedge on one side and high tarred fence on the other.

On this occasion Coe's Lane appeared to be deserted, but when Phyllis reached the stunted may tree half-way down the hedge a figure stepped out and came to meet her.

The girl stopped abruptly in the middle of the path. Her cheeks were patched with pink and white and she caught her breath sharply as though afraid of herself.

Henry Brownrigg himself was unprepared for the savagery of the sudden pain in his breast when he saw her, and the writhing, vicious, mindless passion which checked his breathing and made his eyelids feel sticky and his mouth dry, frightened him a little also.

They were alone in the lane and he kissed her, putting into his hunched shoulders and greedy lips all the insufferable, senseless longing of the past eighteen days.

When he released her she was crying. The big, bright tears which filled her eyes brimmed over on to her cheeks and made her mouth look hot and wet and feverish.

'Go away,' she said and her tone was husky and imploring. 'Oh, go away – please, please!'

After the kiss Henry Brownrigg was human again and no longer the fiend-possessed soul in torment he had been while waiting in the lane. Now he could behave normally, for a time at least.

'All right,' he said, and added so lightly that she was deceived, 'going out with Peter Hill again this afternoon?'

The girl's lips trembled and her eyes were pleading.

'I'm trying to get free,' she said. 'Don't you see I'm trying to get free from you? It's not easy.'

Henry Brownrigg stared at her inquisitively for a full minute. Then he laughed shortly and explosively and strode away back down the lane at a great pace.

Henry Brownrigg went home. He walked very fast, his round eyes introspective but his step light and purposeful. His thoughts were pleasant. So Phyllis was there when he wanted her, there for the taking when the obstacle was once removed. That had been his only doubt. Now he was certain of it. The practical part of his project alone remained.

Small, relatively unimportant things like the new story the mottled ledger would have to tell when the insurance money was in the bank and Millie's small income was realised and reinvested crowded into his mind, but he brushed them aside impatiently. This afternoon he must be grimly practical. There was delicate work to do.

When he reached home Millie had gone over to her mother's.

It was also early-closing day and young Perry was far away, bowling wides for the St Anne's parish cricket club.

Mr Brownrigg went round the house carefully and made sure that all the doors were locked. The shop shutters were up too, and he knew from careful observation that they permitted no light from within to escape.

He removed his jacket and donned his working overall, switched on the lights, locked the door between the shop and the living-room, and set to work.

He knew exactly what he had to do. Millie had been taking five Fender's pills regularly now for eight days. Each pill contained $\frac{1}{16}$ gr. Nativelle's Digitalin, and the stuff was cumulative. No wonder she had been complaining of biliousness and headaches lately! Millie was a hopeless fool.

He took out the bottle of Tincturæ Digitalin, which had come when young Perry had given him such a scare, and looked at it. He wished he had risked it and bought the Quevenne's, or the freshly powdered leaves. He wouldn't have had all this trouble now.

Still, he hadn't taken the chance, and on second thoughts he was glad. As it was, the wholesalers couldn't possibly notice anything unusual in his order. There could be no inquiry: it meant he need never worry – afterwards.

He worked feverishly as his thoughts raced on. He knew the dose. All that had been worked out months before when the idea had first occurred to him, and he had gone over his part of the proceedings again and again in his mind so that there could be no mistake, no slip.

Nine drachms of the tincture had killed a patient with no digitalin already in the system. But then the tincture was notoriously liable to deteriorate. Still, this stuff was fresh; barely six days old if the wholesalers could be trusted. He had thought of that.

He prepared his burner and the evaporator. It took a long time. Although he was so practised, his hands were unsteady and clumsy, and the irritant fumes got into his eyes.

Suddenly he discovered that it was nearly four o'clock. He was panic-stricken. Only two hours and Millie would come back, and there was a lot to be done.

As the burner did its work his mind moved rapidly. Digitalin was so difficult to trace afterwards; that was the beauty of it. Even the great Tardieu had been unable to state positively if it was digitalin that had been used in the Pommeraise case, and that after the most exhaustive PM and tests on frogs and all that sort of thing.

Henry Brownrigg's face split into the semblance of a smile. Old Crupiner was no Tardieu. Crupiner would not advise a PM if he could possibly avoid it. He'd give the certificate all right; his mind was prepared for it. Probably he wouldn't even come and look at the body.

Millie's stupid, placid body. Henry Brownrigg put the thought from him. No use getting nervy now.

A shattering peal on the back door startled him so much that he nearly upset his paraphernalia. For a moment he stood breathing wildly, like a trapped animal, but he pulled himself together in the end, and, changing into his coat, went down to answer the summons.

He locked the shop door behind him, smoothed his hair, and opened the back door confident that he looked normal, even ordinary.

But the small boy with the evening paper did not wait for his Saturday's sixpence but rushed away after a single glance at Mr Brownrigg's face. He was a timid twelve-year-old, however, who often imagined things, and his employer, an older boy, cuffed him for the story and made a mental note to call for the money himself on the Monday night.

The effect of the incident on Henry Brownrigg was considerable. He went back to his work like a man in a nightmare, and for the rest of the proceedings he kept his mind resolutely on the physical task.

At last it was done.

He turned out the burner, scoured the evaporator, measured the toxic dose carefully, adding to it considerably to be on the safe side. After all, one could hardly overdo it; that was the charm of this stuff.

Then he effectively disposed of the residue and felt much better.

He had locked the door and changed his coat again before he noticed the awful thing. A layer of fine dust on the top of one of the bottles first attracted his attention. He removed it with fastidious care. He hated a frowsy shop.

He had replaced his handkerchief before he saw the showcase ledger and the first glimmering of the dreadful truth percolated his startled mind.

From the ledge his eyes travelled to the counter top, to the dummy cartoons, to the bottles and jars, to the window shutters, to the very floor.

Great drops appeared on Henry Brownrigg's forehead. There was not an inch of surface in the whole shop that was innocent of the thinnest, faintest coat of yellowish dust.

Digitalin! Digitalin over the whole shop! Digitalin over the whole world! The evidence of his guilt everywhere, damning, unescapable, clear to the first intelligent observer.

Henry Brownrigg stood very still.

Gradually his brain, cool at the bidding of the instinct of self-preservation, began to work again. Delay. That was the all-important note. Millie must not take the capsule to-night as he had planned. Not to-night, nor to-morrow. Millie must not die until every trace of that yellow dust had been driven from the shop.

Swiftly he rearranged his plan. To-night he must behave as usual and to-morrow, when Millie went to church, he must clear off the worst of the stuff before young Perry noticed anything.

Then on Monday he would make an excuse and have the vacuum cleaning people in. They came with a great machine and put pipes in through the window. He had often said he would have it done.

They worked quickly; so on Tuesday . . .

Meanwhile, normality. That was the main thing. He must do nothing to alarm Millie or excite her curiosity.

It did not occur to him that there would be a grim irony in getting Millie to help him dust the shop that evening. But he dismissed the idea. They'd never do it thoroughly in the time.

He washed in the kitchen and went back into the hall. A step on the stairs above him brought a scream to his throat which he only just succeeded in stifling.

It was Millie. She had come in the back way without him hearing her, heaven knew how long before.

'I've borrowed a portière curtain from Mother for your bedroom door, Henry,' she said mildly. 'You won't be troubled by the draught up there any more. It's such a good thick one. I've just been fixing it up. It looks very nice.'

Henry Brownrigg made a noise which might have meant anything. His nerves had gone to pieces.

Her next remark was reassuring, however; so reassuring that he almost laughed aloud.

'Oh, Henry,' she said, 'you only gave me four of those pills to-day, dear. You won't forget the other one, will you?'

'Cold ham from the cooked meat shop, cold tinned peas, potato salad and Worcester sauce. What a cook! What a cook I've married, my dear Millie.'

Henry Brownrigg derived a vicious pleasure from the clumsy sarcasm, and when Millie's pale face became wooden he was gratified.

As he sat at the small table and looked at her he was aware of a curious phenomenon. The woman stood out from the rest of the room's contents as though she alone was in relief. He saw every line of her features, every fold of her dark cotton foulard dress, as though they were drawn with a thick black pencil.

Millie was silent. Even her usual flow of banality had dried up, and he was glad of it.

He found himself regarding her dispassionately, as though she had been a stranger. He did not hate her, he decided. On the contrary, he was prepared to believe that she was quite an estimable, practicable person in her own limited fashion. But she was in the way.

This plump, fatuous creature, not even different in her very obtuseness from many of the other matrons in the town, had committed the crowning impudence of getting in the way of Henry Brownrigg. She, this ridiculous, lowly woman, actually stood between Henry Brownrigg and the inmost desires of his heart.

It was an insight into the state of the chemist's mind that at that moment nothing impressed him so forcibly as her remarkable audacity.

Monday, he thought. Monday, and possibly Tuesday, and then . . .

Millie cleared away.

Mr Brownrigg drank his first glass of whisky and soda with a relish he did not often experience. For him the pleasure of his Saturday night libations lay in the odd sensation he experienced when really drunk.

When Henry Brownrigg was a sack of limp, uninviting humanity to his wife and the rest of the world, to himself he was a quiet, all-powerful ghost, seated, comfortable and protected, in the shell of his body, able to see and comprehend everything, but too mighty and too important to direct any of the drivelling little matters which made up his immediate world.

On these occasions Henry Brownrigg tasted godhead.

The evening began like all the others, and by the time there was but an inch of amber elixir in the square bottle, Millie and the dust in the shop and Doctor Crupiner had become in his mind as ants and ant burdens, while he towered above them, a colossus in mind and power.

When the final inch had dwindled to a yellow stain in the bottom of the white glass bottle Mr Brownrigg sat very still. In a few minutes now he would attain the peak of that ascendancy over his fellow mortals when the body, so important to them, was for him literally nothing; not even a dull encumbrance, not even a nerveless covering but a nothingness, an unimportant, unnoticed element.

When Millie came in at last a pin could have been thrust deep into Mr Brownrigg's flesh and he would not have noticed it.

It was when he was in bed, his useless body clad in clean pyjamas, that he noticed that Millie was not behaving quite as usual. She had folded his clothes neatly on the chair at the end of the bed when he saw her peering at something intently.

He followed her eyes and saw for the first time the new portière curtain. It certainly was a fine affair, a great, thick, heavy plush thing that looked as though it would stop any draught there ever had been.

He remembered clearly losing his temper with Millie in front of young Perry one day, and, searching in his mind for a suitable excuse, had invented this draught beneath his bedroom door. And there wasn't one, his ghost remembered; that was the beauty of it. The door fitted tightly in the jamb. But it gave Millie something to worry about.

Millie went out of the room without extinguishing the lights. He tried to call out to her and only then realised the disadvantages of being a disembodied spirit. He could not speak, of course.

He was lying puzzled at this obvious flaw in his omnipotence when he heard her go downstairs instead of crossing into her room. He was suddenly furious and would have risen, had it been possible. But in the midst of his anger he remembered something amusing and lay still, inwardly convulsed with secret laughter.

Soon Millie would be dead. Dead – dead – dead.

Millie would be stupid no longer. Millie would appal him by her awful mindlessness no more. Millie would be dead.

She came up again and stepped softly into the room.

The alcohol was beginning to take its full effect now and he could not move his head. Soon oblivion would come and he would leave his body and rush off into the exciting darkness, not to return until the dawn.

He saw only Millie's head and shoulders when she came into his line of vision. He was annoyed. She still had those thick black lines round her, and there was an absorbed expression upon her face which he remembered seeing before when she was engrossed in some particularly difficult household task.

She switched out the light and then went over to the far window. He was interested now, and saw her pull up the blinds.

Then to his astonishment he heard the crackle of paper; not an ordinary crackle, but something familiar, something he had heard hundreds of times before.

He placed it suddenly. Sticky paper. His own reel of sticky paper from the shop.

He was so cross with her for touching it that for some moments he did not wonder what she was doing with it, and it was not until he saw her silhouetted against the second row of panes that he guessed. She was sticking up the window cracks.

His ghost laughed again. The draught. Silly, stupid Millie trying to stop the draught.

She pulled down the blinds and turned on the light again. Her face was mild and expressionless as ever, her blue eyes vacant and foolish.

He saw her go to the dressing-table, still moving briskly, as she always did when working about the house.

Once again the phenomenon he had noticed at the evening meal became startlingly apparent. He saw her hand and its contents positively glowing because of its black outline, thrown up in high relief against the white table cover.

Millie was putting two pieces of paper there: one white with a deckle edge, one blue and familiar.

Henry Brownrigg's ghost yammered in its prison. His body ceased to be negligible: it became a coffin, a sealed, leaden coffin suffocating him in its senseless shell. He fought to free himself, to stir that mighty weight, to move.

Millie knew.

The white paper with the deckle edge was a letter from Phyllis out of the drawer in the shop, and the blue paper – he remembered it now – the blue paper he had left in the dirty developing bath.

He re-read his own pencilled words as clearly as if his eye had become possessed of telescopic sight:

'*Millie dear, this does explain itself, doesn't it?*'

And then his name, signed with a flourish. He had been so pleased with himself when he had written it.

He fought wildly. The coffin was made of glass now, thick, heavy glass which would not respond to his greatest effort.

Millie was hesitating. She had picked up Phyllis's letter. Now she was reading it again.

He saw her frown and tear the paper into shreds, thrusting the pieces into the pocket of her cardigan.

Henry Brownrigg, understood. Millie was sorry for Phyllis. For all her obtuseness she had guessed at some of the girl's piteous infatuation and had decided to keep her out of it.

What then? Henry Brownrigg writhed inside his inanimate body.

Millie was back at the table now. She was putting something else there. What was it? Oh, what was it?

The ledger! He saw it plainly, the old mottled ledger, whose story was plain for any fool coroner to read and misunderstand.

Millie had turned away now. He hardly noticed her pause before the fire-place. She did not stoop. Her felt-shod slipper flipped the gas tap over.

Then she passed out of the door, extinguishing the light as she went. He heard the rustle of the thick curtain as she drew the door shut. There was an infinitesimal pause and then the key turned in the lock.

She had behaved throughout the whole proceeding as though she had been getting dinner or tidying the spare room.

In his prison Henry Brownrigg's impotent ghost listened. There was a hissing from the far end of the room.

In the attic, although he could not possibly hear it, he knew the meter ticked every two or three seconds.

Henry Brownrigg saw in a vision the scene in the morning. Every room in the house had the same key, so Millie would have no difficulty explaining that on awakening she had noticed the smell of gas and, on finding her husband's door locked, had opened it with her own key.

The ghost stirred in its shell. Once again the earth and earthly incidents looked small and negligible. The oblivion was coming, the darkness was waiting; only now it was no longer exciting darkness.

The shell moved. He felt it writhe and choke. It was fighting – fighting – fighting.

The darkness drew him. He was no longer conscious of the shell now. It had been beaten. It had given up the fight.

The streak of light beneath the blind where the street lamp shone was fading. Fading. Now it was gone.

As Henry Brownrigg's ghost crept out into the cold a whisper came to it, ghastly in its conviction:

'They never get caught, that kind. They're too dull, too practical, too unimaginative. They never get caught.'

George Goodchild

The Siamese Cat

One of McLean's most interesting cases was brought to light by no more intelligent a creature than a Siamese cat. It was on a bitterly cold night towards the end of January when a Mr Andrew Goff was awakened from sleep by the plaintive mewing of a cat, and, believing it to be his own cat in trouble, he slipped on a dressing-gown, muttered a few curses, and went downstairs.

In the kitchen he found his own fat animal asleep before what was left of the fire, and apparently indifferent to the misery of any feline cousin. Goff was not so great a lover of cats as to feel like engaging in a hunt round his garden, and he was about to turn out the light and seek his comfortable bed when a plaintive wail came from the direction of the kitchen window. The curtain was partly drawn, and he plainly saw a cat on the window-sill pawing the window.

Possibly it was the snow on the animal's back which melted his heart, for he changed his mind, opened the kitchen door, and finally persuaded the cat to enter. Mr Goff had not seen a Siamese cat for many years, and was momentarily overwhelmed by the curious shape of the eyes, which looked frightfully crossed. Then he noticed that the creature was very emaciated and so weak, it could scarcely walk

'Well, well!' he muttered. 'I guess we can spare a drop of milk.'

The milk which he poured into a saucer was eagerly lapped up, and Mr Goff wondered whether he should put the cat outside again. But its condition aroused his deepest sympathy, and he finally decided to give it the freedom of the kitchen and to remove his own cat to slightly less comfortable quarters.

The following morning Mrs Goff heard of the new arrival, and immediately took an interest in it, but, like her husband, she had no idea to whom it belonged.

'The poor thing's half starved, Jim,' she said. 'It's a valuable cat, too. Don't you think his eyes are wonderful?'

'Uncanny,' said her husband. 'Ill omen, if you ask me.'

'It isn't only black cats that are lucky.'

'Well, we'll have to try and find the owner.'

Inquiries were made in the neighbouring houses, but no one appeared to know who owned the cat, and Mrs Goff was wondering whether she would be allowed to keep it, since it seemed to get on very well with her own animal. But her hopes were dashed to the ground a day later when a tradesman said he had seen the cat at a house called Southlands, where he had delivered a load of coal about a week before. It was situated about a mile from Mr Goff's cottage, and an old gentleman named Tollinger lived there.

Mrs Goff was a trifle disappointed, but her husband did not share her disappointment, feeling that one cat in a house was quite sufficient. He decided to walk over to Southlands during the afternoon, and with him he took the Siamese cat in a basket. He knew the house quite well, but to the best of his knowledge had never seen Mr Tollinger, although he had known the tenants who occupied it before Mr Tollinger came to the district.

It was not a very attractive house, for in the past various trees and heavy shrubs had been planted far too near it, and these had been allowed to get out of control, and shrouded the quite small building. Ivy, too, had grown over some of the windows, and the paths were full of grass and moss.

Mr Goff went first to the front door, and rang a number of times without getting any response. He then tried the back door, and finally came to the conclusion that no one was at home. So he took back the cat, much to his wife's delight, and made another call the following morning – with the same negative result as before.

A little disgruntled by his two fruitless visits, he made for home again, but happened to meet the village constable in a lane, to whom he told his trouble.

'I don't think Mr Tollinger can be away,' said the constable. 'Because he would have asked us to keep an eye on the house. He's done that on several occasions. I'll make some inquiries in the village.'

The result of the constable's inquiries was that the milkboy had found a slip of paper on the doorstep five days before marked, 'No milk until further notice,' which made it appear that Tollinger had gone away. But the grocer had not been informed of this, and was wondering why he had not received his weekly list, which usually reached him on Thursday – and it was now Friday. Then there was the curious absence of the maid. She could be accounted for if indeed Mr Tollinger had gone away for any long period. But had he? The maidservant had come from another district, and no one knew her address. But the cat was definitely proved to belong to Mr Tollinger.

Failing to arrive at any satisfactory solution, the constable got in touch with headquarters, and was instructed to enter the house. He did this through a downstairs window, and on entering the sitting-room he found a dead man lying on the couch. To his surprise it was not old Mr Tollinger, but a much younger man, and a bullet wound in his chest told its own story.

The constable at once got into communication with headquarters, and some police officers and a police surgeon were soon on the spot. In view of the extraordinary circumstances – the fact that Mr Tollinger was missing and that the dead man had nothing on his person to establish his identity – Scotland Yard was called in, and within an hour McLean and Sergeant Brook were at the house, which was situated about fifteen miles south of London, in a district which still contained some open spaces.

McLean was assured that no single thing had been touched, except the corpse, which the doctor had examined. The latter gave it as his opinion that the man had been dead five or six days, and that the wound he had received must have been instantly fatal. After McLean had examined the victim and taken everything from the pockets of the clothing, he was removed.

'Can I open the windows now?' asked Brook, who found the atmosphere insufferable.

'Yes – as many as you like.'

'Funny business,' said Brook, as he let in the fresh, cold air. 'Looks as if he was shot while sitting on the couch, for there isn't a sign of blood anywhere else.'

McLean nodded and examined a number of things for fingerprints. Being disappointed in this, he then gave his attention to the floor, and, with Brook's help, finally found two cartridge-cases.

'One shot must have missed,' he said. 'See if you can find where it went.'

Brook searched the room diligently, while McLean went over the rest of the house with a view to seeing if there were any sign of burglary. The front bedroom appeared to be the only one that had been used recently. The bed was rather roughly made, and some garments were lying about, but everywhere else things were tidy, as they were downstairs.

Attached to the kitchen was a scullery, in which was a large modern gas-stove. The place smelt of gas, and McLean found that one tap of the stove was turned on. It was a small burner, and on it was a large kettle – empty. An examination of the gas-meter showed it was a shilling-in-the-slot apparatus. and the last shilling's worth had undoubtedly been used up.

'That gas jet was turned on when the murder was committed,' he said. 'It was left on afterwards and boiled away all the water in the kettle. Have a look at those gas burners.'

Brook did this, and reported that they were all turned off. He then went into the hall, and found that all the taps there were in the 'off' position.

'Proves nothing,' said McLean. 'For the murderer might have turned off all the lights when he left the house – except the gas-stove, which he overlooked.'

'Can't find any sign of that bullet,' said Brook.

'H'm!' said McLean in his non-committal way.

II

There were a number of photographs in the house showing Mr Tollinger. The latest, which was dated two years back, presented a man of about sixty years of age, with a small moustache and beard, and rather hunched shoulders.

McLean had been informed that Tollinger had rented the house two years previously and that he was a retired tea planter from Ceylon. He had lived entirely by himself, with the exception of a maidservant, who had been with him ever since he took the house.

'We must find the servant,' said McLean. 'Also, if possible, the piece of paper which the milkboy said he found outside the kitchen door five days ago. He left it there, but it had doubtless been blown about. Have a look for that.'

Brook spent over an hour on his quest, but finally he succeeded, and brought in a strip of paper, on which was written: 'No milk until further notice.'

'Good!' said McLean. 'Here's a slate from the kitchen on which some-one – the maid presumably – wrote down certain household commodities. The writing is quite different. Now, did Tollinger himself write that? I've an old book of cheque counterfoils here. That may clear up the matter.'

A comparison of the writing on the counterfoils with that on the slip of paper showed there was no similarity at all.

'Well, then, who wrote it?' asked Brook. 'No, don't tell me, sir,' he added a little shamefacedly.

'Thank you, Brook. Yes, it was the murderer of the unknown man. He had the sense to realise that certain tradesmen would call regularly.

The milkman, for example, and the newsboy. He wrote the note to settle any questions in the milkman's mind.'

'And overlooked the newsboy?'

'Not at all. Here is the morning newspaper for the past five mornings. They were slipped through the large letter-box in the front door. There are also a few letters – all bills. That rather looks as if the clever person who wrote the note knew quite well that the newspapers were usually slipped through the letter-box.'

'You mean it was some one who knew Tollinger fairly well?'

'Yes.'

'But, admitting that – where is Tollinger?'

'Dead.'

'But why—?'

'Yes, why does the murderer take Tollinger away and leave the other man here? Possibly to make it appear that Tollinger is the murderer. The local police are already inclined to believe that. But there are too many arguments against it. The two shots that were fired – the message that was left for the milkman – the fact that Tollinger left the Siamese cat behind. Fortunately, the note and the date of the first newspaper enable us to fix the day of the crime. It was Monday, January the 28th.'

'Yes, that seems clear,' agreed Brook.

McLean was now endeavouring to find where the paper had come from on which the message was written. It was rather thin, and ruled with faint blue lines, and was not a complete sheet, but torn as if from a book, very irregularly at the side.

'Here's a writing block,' said Brook. 'It was in the drawer under the dresser.'

McLean shook his head.

'Nothing like,' he said. 'Wait a moment – let me look at that.'

He took the almost finished cheap writing block to the window and found something of very great importance. The last sheet which had been used had apparently been written with a hard pencil, and some of the impressions had come through. He read what he could make of them:

'. . . *fed up with him . . . told me . . . that did it. I let him have . . . not going to bother for a bit . . . first train . . . Fore Street, Hastings, until . . .*
'*Edith.*'

'That's going to expedite matters a lot,' said McLean. 'The postman will probably be able to tell us what her full name is. You'd better get on to that while I have another look round here.'

The postman, when found, remembered the maidservant quite well, although he had no idea where she hailed from. Her name was Edith

Tuckwell, and he described her as a cheeky kind of girl of about twenty years of age. The postman's feeling was that Tollinger was getting on her nerves, for she had once admitted that he was a 'holy terror,' and that if he 'thought she was a bloomin' slave he'd find himself mistaken.'

'We'd better get down to Hastings,' said McLean. 'The girl ought to be able to tell us something.'

They went down to the coast by road and made inquiries in Fore Street. A considerable time was wasted, because the street in question was given up to boarding-houses of the cheaper kind, and no one knew any young lady of the name of Tuckwell. But finally McLean was directed to a Mrs Rogers, whose sister recently came to stay with her. Mrs Rogers kept a small boarding-house called Spray House, although it was about a mile and a half from any spray. On inquiring there he learned that she was the married sister of Edith Tuckwell, and that Edith was staying with her. At that moment Edith was out shopping, but she returned some time later, and gasped when she was told that two police officers were waiting to see her. Very timidly she came to McLean and gave her name.

'You were in service with Mr Tollinger?' asked McLean.

'Yes, sir – for two years.'

'When did you leave him?'

'Last Monday morning.'

'That would be the twenty-eighth?'

'Yes.'

'Why did you leave him?'

'I quarrelled with him. He had a bad temper, and I stuck it for over two years. On the Sunday I broke a vegetable dish, and he raved at me, and called me names. I up and told him what I thought of him, and he said I could take a month's notice. I said I wasn't taking any month's notice – that I could get a job anywhere, servants being as rare as gold. I said I'd clear out next morning, and he could do what he liked about it. He said he would be glad to see the back of me.'

'And you went?'

'Yes. My sister, who lives here, had told me I could always spend a week or so with her in the off season, so I sent her a telegram telling her I was coming down.'

'You wrote to some one else?'

'Yes – on the Sunday – after the bust-up. A friend of mine who's in service in London. I told her all about the quarrel.'

'At what time did you leave the house?'

'Just after ten o'clock in the morning. Mr Tollinger told me not to be a fool, but I'd had enough.'

'Was he expecting any visitors that day?'

'He never said he was.'

'Did you tell any one that you were leaving him on the Monday morning.'

'No.'

'Are you sure about that?'

'Yes. Why, I never knew myself until the Sunday morning, when we had the quarrel – Mr Tollinger and me.'

McLean was a little puzzled by this, because, according to his theory, the person who had murdered Tollinger must have known that there was no one in the house but the old man. The alternative was a sheer coincidence.

'Well,' he said finally, 'I want you to come and attempt to identify a man.'

'What man?'

'I don't know – but it is possible you may.'

When she learned from Brook that the man in question was dead, she didn't want to accompany them.

'This is an important matter,' said McLean. 'Get your coat on – quickly!'

When she was ultimately confronted with the ghastly spectacle of the man who had been dead for five days, she fainted, but on being brought round she stated that she had seen the man before, but couldn't think where.

'Was it in Mr Tollinger's house?' asked McLean.

'I can't remember,' she wailed.

'Try. Where else could you have seen him?'

'It may have been in the house, but I'm not sure. Yes, I think it was – a long time ago. I think – yes, it was one evening. He called in a car, and Mr Tollinger said he would see him. He stayed about half an hour.'

'Can you remember what name he gave you?'

'No. It's too long ago. That's all I know – he came to the house. Can I go now, please?'

III

For some days McLean was in a dilemma. The clothing of the dead man had been carefully examined for laundry marks and so forth, and a full description of him was circulated and published. Then came Edith Tuckwell with a revived memory.

'I've just remembered,' she said. 'While that man was in the house he used the telephone. The instrument is in the hall, by the grandfather clock. He pencilled a number on the wall. I know, because I tried to get it off, and couldn't. I thought it was a rotten thing to do in some-one else's house. It's just by the side of the telephone in indelible pencil.'

McLean paid another visit to the house, and found the telephone number exactly as described. It was very faint, but he managed to read it. Some time later he was given the address of the person who worked at that number.

'John Lightley,' he said. 'Crandon Street, W.C.'

Before he could pay John Lightley a visit he heard that the dead man had been identified by a lady who said she was his sister. McLean saw the sister at the first opportunity.

'You have identified your brother – Harry Tangye?'

'Yes.'

'You have no doubt about it?'

'None at all.'

'When did you last see him alive?'

'It was about six months ago. He came to visit me and my husband.'

'What was his occupation?'

She didn't know. She and her brother had seen very little of each other during the past ten years. He had been abroad – to Paris, Berlin, and other big capitals, but she had never questioned him about his business.

'Do you know whether he was friendly with a man named Tollinger?'

'No. I have never heard that name before.'

'Have you ever heard the name – John Lightley?'

'Lightley? Yes, I have.'

'In what connection?'

'About two years ago my brother met me by accident in a London street. He had a man with him – very dark and good-looking. He said his name was John Lightley.'

'Can you be sure of that?'

'Quite sure, because I was very impressed by him.'

'Do you know anything about Lightley?'

'Yes,' she admitted, looking embarrassed. 'I saw him again – unbeknown to my brother – and we went out together once or twice. My brother got to know of it, and was very angry. He said I was a fool to "play about" with Lightley as I was doing.

'I told him I wasn't "playing about," but that I liked Lightley. He laughed and said I was a silly little fool, and that Lightley was a dangerous man. I didn't know what he meant by that, but I think he must have spoken to Lightley, for I never saw him again, and for over a year I never spoke to my brother.'

'You sound as if you had seen a great deal more of him than you led me to believe just now.'

'Oh no, not more than six times in the last ten years, and most of those occasions were during the past two years.'

'Do you know where Lightley lives?'

'No – not now.'

McLean let her go, and then decided to see Mr John Lightley as quickly as possible. After waiting for over an hour he saw Lightley enter his flat.

'We'll go in now,' he said to Sergeant Brook.

'Are you Mr John Lightley?' asked McLean.

'Yes.'

'I am a police officer, and want to ask you a few questions.'

'Come right in,' said Lightley cheerily.

He showed them into a cosy sitting-room, and threw off his coat as he remarked on the cold, bright weather. McLean could well understand Miss Tangye's reference to his looks, for he was as handsome as a Greek statue, but carried a cunning expression in his dark eyes.

'Do you know a Mr Tollinger?' asked McLean.

'Tollinger – Tollinger? You don't mean Toler?'

'I mean Tollinger.'

'No. That's a new one on me.'

'Do you know a Mr Harry Tangye?'

He hesitated, and McLean thought he was remembering Tangye's sister, and realised the need for caution.

'Yes, I do,' he said.

'When did you last see him?'

'Let me see – it would be Tuesday – no, last Monday week. He came here – about ten o'clock in the morning, to ask me if I cared to go to the coast with him. I said I couldn't spare the time. He had a drink, and then got into his car and drove away.'

'You haven't seen him since?'

'No.'

'Had you business connections with him?'

'Oh, no. I think he was independent.'

'And you?'

'I'm an engineer – out of a job at the moment, but I hope to go to South Africa soon.'

'I have a search warrant,' said McLean.

'What on earth for?'

McLean made no reply, but started to ransack the flat. He found nothing that would implicate Lightley. There was no sign of a fire-arm, and no correspondence. It looked as if Lightley had made a beautiful clear-up, if indeed he had anything to do with the murder – or murders.

'Satisfied, inspector?' asked Lightley, when McLean came in from the bedroom with empty hands.

'So far,' said McLean. 'But I must make a personal search.'

Lightley seemed not quite so pleased, and this was due to the presence of a very large packet of bank-notes in his inside pocket. They represented nearly five hundred pounds in all, and were quite good ones.

'Where did you get these?' asked McLean.

'Dog racing. I had some luck.'

'So I should imagine.'

In the inside pocket of the overcoat which he had taken off McLean found a priceless clue. It was a large note-book, with thin paper, on which was blue ruling. The entries in it were not of great interest, as they dealt with racing form, but on turning back a few pages McLean found that a page had been torn out clumsily, leaving a small portion still in the book.

'Got it!' he said.

He then produced the note which had been left at Tollinger's house for the milk-boy, and the torn edge of it fitted exactly into the piece that was still left in the book. In addition, the handwriting tallied.

'I arrest you for the murder of Harry Tangye,' he said, and Brook was quick with the handcuffs.

Two days later Tollinger's body was found strapped to the driving wheel of a two-seater car and sunk in a deep pond not far from Tollinger's house. There was a bullet wound in the chest, as with Tangye, and the pistol which had fired that shot was in the car, There was also a partly-used cheque-book in Tollinger's pocket, and on the last counterfoil was the sum of £500 made out to 'Self.' The bank-notes found on Lightley were traced to the bank which had cashed Mr Tollinger's cheque.

'A pretty clear case,' said McLean. 'I don't think he'll stand much chance.'

He was hopeful that in the end Lightley would confess, but he refused to do so, even after he knew he would hang.

'And what's the real solution?' asked Brook.

'Some dishonest game, in which Tollinger took a part. Those two men went there to collect money – £500. Tollinger had obviously drawn it to pay out to them. They may have quarrelled, but I think it's more likely that while they were there Lightley got to know that the maid-servant had left suddenly, and realised what a fine chance it was to take all the plunder.

'He then struck the idea of leaving the note, and of taking Tollinger away in Tangye's car and sinking it in that old quarry pond. Had we been longer in finding Tangye's body, Lightley might have gone to South Africa, but our little friend the Siamese cat – whom he overlooked – prevented that. I think I shall try to buy that cat,' he added reflectively.

Anthony Berkeley

The Avenging Chance

Roger Sheringham was inclined to think afterwards that the Poisoned Chocolates Case, as the papers called it, was perhaps the most perfectly planned murder he had ever encountered. The motive was so obvious, when you knew where to look for it – but you didn't know; the method was so significant when you had grasped its real essentials – but you didn't grasp them; the traces were so thinly covered, when you had realised what was covering them – but you didn't realise. But for a piece of the merest bad luck, which the murderer could not possibly have foreseen, the crime must have been added to the classical list of great mysteries.

This is the gist of the case, as Chief-Inspector Moresby told it one evening to Roger in the latter's rooms in the Albany a week or so after it happened:

On Friday morning, the fifteenth of November, at half-past ten in the morning, in accordance with his invariable custom, Sir William Anstruther walked into his club in Piccadilly, the very exclusive Rainbow Club, and asked for his letters. The porter handed him three and a small parcel. Sir William walked over to the fireplace in the big lounge hall to open them.

A few minutes later another member entered the club, a Mr Graham Beresford. There were a letter and a couple of circulars for him, and he also strolled over to the fireplace, nodding to Sir William, but not speaking to him. The two men only knew each other very slightly, and had probably never exchanged more than a dozen words in all.

Having glanced through his letters, Sir William opened the parcel and, after a moment, snorted with disgust. Beresford looked at him, and with a grunt Sir William thrust out a letter which had been enclosed in the parcel. Concealing a smile (Sir William's ways were a matter of some amusement to his fellow-members), Beresford read the letter. It was from a big firm of chocolate manufacturers, Mason & Sons, and set forth that they were putting on the market a new brand of liqueur chocolates designed especially to appeal to men; would Sir William do them the honour of accepting the enclosed two-pound box and letting the firm have his candid opinion of them?

'Do they think I'm a blank chorus-girl?' fumed Sir William. 'Write 'em testimonials about their blank chocolates, indeed! Blank 'em! I'll complain to the blank committee. That sort of blank thing can't blank well be allowed here.'

'Well, it's an ill wind so far as I'm concerned,' Beresford soothed him. 'It's reminded me of something. My wife and I had a box at the Imperial last night. I bet her a box of chocolates to a hundred cigarettes that she wouldn't spot the villain by the end of the second act. She won. I must remember to get them. Have you seen it – *The Creaking Skull*? Not a bad show.'

Sir William had not seen it, and said so with force.

'Want a box of chocolates, did you say?' he added, more mildly. 'Well, take this blank one. I don't want it.'

For a moment Beresford demurred politely and then, most unfortunately for himself, accepted. The money so saved meant nothing to him for he was a wealthy man; but trouble was always worth saving.

By an extraordinarily lucky chance neither the outer wrapper of the box nor its covering letter were thrown into the fire, and this was the more fortunate in that both men had tossed the envelopes of their letters into the flames. Sir William did, indeed, make a bundle of the wrapper, letter and string, but he handed it over to Beresford, and the latter simply dropped it inside the fender. This bundle the porter subsequently extracted and, being a man of orderly habits, put it tidily away in the waste-paper basket, whence it was retrieved later by the police.

Of the three unconscious protagonists in the impending tragedy, Sir William was without doubt the most remarkable. Still a year or two under fifty, he looked, with his flaming red face and thick-set figure, a typical country squire of the old school, and both his manners and his language were in accordance with tradition. His habits, especially as regards women, were also in accordance with tradition – the tradition of the bold, bad baronet which he undoubtedly was.

In comparison with him, Beresford was rather an ordinary man, a tall, dark, not unhandsome fellow of two-and-thirty, quiet and reserved. His father had left him a rich man, but idleness did not appeal to him, and he had a finger in a good many business pies.

Money attracts money. Graham Beresford had inherited it, he made it, and, inevitably, he had married it, too. The daughter of a late ship-owner in Liverpool, with not far off half a million in her own right. But the money was incidental, for he needed her and would have married her just as inevitably (said his friends) if she had not had a farthing. A tall, rather serious-minded, highly cultured girl, and not so young that her character had not had time to form (she was twenty-five when Beresford married her, three years ago), she was the ideal wife for him. A bit of a Puritan perhaps in some ways, but Beresford, whose wild oats, though duly sown, had been a sparse crop, was ready enough to be a Puritan himself by that time if she was. To make no bones about it, the Beresfords succeeded in achieving that eighth wonder of the modern world, a happy marriage.

And into the middle of it there dropped with irretrievable tragedy, the box of chocolates.

Beresford gave them to her after lunch as they sat over their coffee, with some jesting remark about paying his honourable debts, and she opened the box at once. The top layer, she noticed, seemed to consist only of kirsch and maraschino. Beresford, who did not believe in spoiling good coffee, refused when she offered him the box, and his wife ate the first one alone. As she did so she exclaimed in surprise that the filling seemed exceedingly strong and positively burnt her mouth.

Beresford explained that they were samples of a new brand and then, made curious by what his wife had said, took one too. A burning taste, not intolerable but much too strong to be pleasant, followed the release of the liquid, and the almond flavouring seemed quite excessive.

'By jove,' he said, 'they are strong. They must be filled with neat alcohol.'

'Oh, they wouldn't do that, surely,' said his wife, taking another. 'But they are very strong. I think I rather like them, though.'

Beresford ate another, and disliked it still more. 'I don't,' he said with decision. 'They make my tongue feel quite numb. I shouldn't eat any more of them if I were you. I think there's something wrong with them.'

'Well, they're only an experiment, I suppose,' she said. 'But they do burn. I'm not sure whether I like them or not.'

A few minutes later Beresford went out to keep a business appointment in the city. He left her still trying to make up her mind whether she liked them, and still eating them to decide. Beresford remembered that scrap of conversation afterwards very vividly, because it was the last time he saw his wife alive.

That was roughly half-past two. At a quarter to four Beresford arrived at his club from the city in a taxi, in a state of collapse. He was helped into the building by the driver and the porter, and both described him subsequently as pale to the point of ghastliness, with staring eyes and livid lips, and his skin damp and clammy. His mind seemed un-affected, however, and when they had got him up the steps he was able to walk, with the porter's help, into the lounge.

The porter, thoroughly alarmed, wanted to send for a doctor at once, but Beresford, who was the last man in the world to make a fuss, refused to let him, saying that it must be indigestion and he would be all right in a few minutes. To Sir William Anstruther, however, who was in the lounge at the time, he added, after the porter had gone:

'Yes, and I believe it was those infernal chocolates you gave me, now I come to think of it. I thought there was something funny about them at the time. I'd better go and find out if my wife—' He broke off abruptly. His body, which had been leaning back limply in his chair, suddenly heaved rigidly upright; his jaws locked together, the livid lips drawn back in a horrible grin, and his hands clenched on the arms of his chair. At the same time Sir William became aware of an unmistakable smell of bitter almonds.

Thoroughly alarmed, believing indeed that the man was dying under his eyes, Sir William raised a shout for the porter and a doctor. The other occupants of the lounge hurried up, and between them they got the convulsed body of the unconscious man into a more comfortable position. Before the doctor could arrive a telephone message was received at the club from an agitated butler asking if Mr Beresford was there, and if so would he come home at once as Mrs Beresford had been taken seriously ill. As a matter of fact she was already dead.

Beresford did not die. He had taken less of the poison than his wife, who after his departure must have eaten at least three more of the chocolates, so that its action was less rapid and the doctor had time to save him. As a matter of fact it turned out afterwards that he had not had a fatal dose. By about eight o'clock that night he was conscious; the next day he was practically convalescent.

As for the unfortunate Mrs Beresford, the doctor had arrived too late to save her, and she passed away very rapidly in a deep coma.

The police had taken the matter in hand as soon as Mrs Beresford's death was reported to them and the fact of poison established, and it was only a very short time before things had become narrowed down to the chocolates as the active agent.

Sir William was interrogated, the letter and wrapper were recovered from the waste-paper basket, and, even before the sick man was out of danger, a detective-inspector was asking for an interview with the managing-director of Mason & Sons. Scotland Yard moves quickly.

It was the police theory at this stage, based on what Sir William and the two doctors had been able to tell them, that by an act of criminal carelessness on the part of one of Mason's employees, an excessive amount of oil of bitter almonds had been included in the filling mixture of the chocolates, for that was what the doctors had decided must be the poisoning ingredient. However, the managing-director quashed this idea at once: oil of bitter almonds, he asserted, was never used by Mason's.

He had more interesting news still. Having read with undisguised astonishment the covering letter, he at once declared that it was a forgery. No such letter, no such samples had been sent out by the firm at all; a new variety of liqueur-chocolates had never even been mooted. The fatal chocolates were their ordinary brand.

Unwrapping and examining one more closely, he called the Inspector's attention to a mark on the underside, which he suggested was the remains of a small hole drilled in the case, through which the liquid could have been extracted and the fatal filling inserted, the hole afterwards being stopped up with softened chocolate, a perfectly simple operation.

He examined it under a magnifying-glass and the Inspector agreed. It was now clear to him that somebody had been trying deliberately to murder Sir William Anstruther.

Scotland Yard doubled its activities. The chocolates were sent for analysis, Sir William was interviewed again, and so was the now conscious Beresford. From the latter the doctor insisted that the news of his wife's death must be kept till the next day, as in his weakened condition the shock might be fatal, so that nothing very helpful was obtained from him.

Nor could Sir William throw any light on the mystery or produce a single person who might have any grounds for trying to kill him. He was living apart from his wife, who was the principal beneficiary in his will, but she was in the South of France, as the French police subsequently confirmed. His estate in Worcestershire, heavily mortgaged, was entailed and went to a nephew; but as the rent he got for it barely covered the interest on the mortgage, and the nephew was considerably better off than Sir William himself, there was no motive there. The police were at a dead end.

The analysis brought one or two interesting facts to light. Not oil of bitter almonds but nitrobenzine, a kindred substance, chiefly used in the manufacture of aniline dyes, was the somewhat surprising poison employed. Each chocolate in the upper layer contained exactly six minims of it, in a mixture of kirsch and maraschino. The chocolates in the other layers were harmless.

As to the other clues, they seemed equally useless. The sheet of Mason's notepaper was identified by Merton's, the printers, as of their work, but there was nothing to show how it had got into the murderer's possession. All that could be said was that, the edges being distinctly yellowed, it must be an old piece. The machine on which the letter had been typed, of course, could not be traced. From the wrapper, a piece of ordinary brown paper with Sir William's address hand-printed on it in large capitals, there was nothing to be learnt at all beyond that the parcel had been posted at the office in Southampton Street between the hours of 8.30 and 9.30 on the previous evening.

Only one thing was quite clear. Whoever had coveted Sir William's life had no intention of paying for it with his or her own.

'And now you know as much as we do, Mr Sheringham,' concluded Chief-Inspector Moresby; 'and if you can say who sent those chocolates to Sir William, you'll know a good deal more.'

Roger nodded thoughtfully.

'It's a brute of a case. I met a man only yesterday who was at school with Beresford. He didn't know him very well because Beresford was on the modern side and my friend was a classical bird, but they were in the same house. He says Beresford's absolutely knocked over by his wife's death. I wish you could find out who sent those chocolates, Moresby.'

'So do I, Mr Sheringham,' said Moresby gloomily.

'It might have been any one in the whole world,' Roger mused. 'What about feminine jealousy, for instance? Sir William's private life doesn't seem to be immaculate. I dare say there's a good deal of off with the old light-o'-love and on with the new.'

'Why, that's just what I've been looking into, Mr Sheringham, sir,' retorted Chief-Inspector Moresby reproachfully. 'That was the first thing that came to me. Because if anything does stand out about this business it is that it's a woman's crime. Nobody but a woman would send poisoned chocolates to a man. Another man would send a poisoned sample of whisky, or something like that.'

'That's a very sound point, Moresby,' Roger meditated. 'Very sound indeed. And Sir William couldn't help you?'

'Couldn't,' said Moresby, not without a trace of resentment, 'or wouldn't. I was inclined to believe at first that he might have his suspicions and was shielding some woman. But I don't think so now.'

'Humph!' Roger did not seem quite so sure. 'It's reminiscent, this case, isn't it? Didn't some lunatic once send poisoned chocolates to the Commissioner of Police himself? A good crime always gets imitated, as you know.'

Moresby brightened.

'It's funny you should say that, Mr Sheringham, because that's the very conclusion I've come to. I've tested every other theory, and so far as I know there's not a soul with an interest in Sir William's death, whether from motives of gain, revenge, or what you like, whom I haven't had to rule quite out of it. In fact, I've pretty well made up my mind that the person who sent those chocolates was some irresponsible lunatic of a woman, a social or religious fanatic who's probably never seen him. And if that's the case,' Moresby sighed, 'a fat chance I have of ever laying hands on her.'

'Unless Chance steps in, as it so often does,' said Roger brightly, 'and helps you. A tremendous lot of cases get solved by a stroke of sheer luck, don't they? *Chance the Avenger*. It would make an excellent film-title. But there's a lot of truth in it. If I were superstitious, which I'm not, I should say it wasn't chance at all, but Providence avenging the victim.'

'Well, Mr Sheringham,' said Moresby, who was not superstitious either, 'to tell the truth, I don't mind what it is, so long as it lets me get my hands on the right person.'

If Moresby had paid his visit to Roger Sheringham with any hope of tapping that gentleman's brains, he went away disappointed.

To tell the truth, Roger was inclined to agree with the Chief Inspector's conclusion, that the attempt on the life of Sir William Anstruther and the actual murder of the unfortunate Mrs Beresford must be the work of some unknown criminal lunatic. For this reason, although he thought about it a good deal during the next few days, he made no attempt to take the case in hand. It was the sort of affair, necessitating endless inquiries that a private person would have neither the time nor the authority to carry out, which can be handled only by the official police. Roger's interest in it was purely academic.

It was hazard, a chance encounter nearly a week later, which translated this interest from the academic into the personal.

Roger was in Bond Street, about to go through the distressing ordeal of buying a new hat. Along the pavement he suddenly saw bearing down on him Mrs Verreker-le-Flemming. Mrs Verreker-le-Flemming was small, exquisite, rich, and a widow, and she sat at Roger's feet whenever he gave her the opportunity. But she talked. She talked, in fact, and talked, and talked. And Roger, who rather liked talking himself, could not bear it. He tried to dart across the road, but there was no opening in the traffic stream. He was cornered.

Mrs Verreker-le-Flemming fastened on him gladly.

'Oh, Mr Sheringham! *Just* the person I wanted to see. Mr Sheringham, *do* tell me. In confidence. *Are* you taking up this dreadful business of poor Joan Beresford's death?'

Roger, the frozen and imbecile grin of civilised intercourse on his face, tried to get a word in; without result.

'I was horrified when I heard of it – simply horrified. You see, Joan and I were such *very* close friends. Quite intimate. And the awful thing, the truly *terrible* thing is that Joan brought the whole business on herself. Isn't that *appalling*?'

Roger no longer wanted to escape.

'What did you say?' he managed to insert incredulously.

'I suppose it's what they call tragic irony,' Mrs Verreker-le-Flemming chattered on. 'Certainly it was tragic enough, and I've never heard anything so terribly ironical. You know about that bet she made with her husband, of course, so that he had to get her a box of chocolates, and if he hadn't Sir William would never have given him the poisoned ones and he'd have eaten them and died himself and good riddance? Well, Mr Sheringham—' Mrs Verreker-le-Flemming lowered her voice to a conspirator's whisper and glanced about her in the approved manner. 'I've never told anybody else this, but I'm telling you because I know you'll appreciate it. *Joan wasn't playing fair!*'

'How do you mean?' Roger asked, bewildered.

Mrs Verreker-le-Flemming was artlessly pleased with her sensation.

'Why, she's seen the play before. We went together, the very first week it was on. She *knew* who the villain was all the time.'

'By jove!' Roger was as impressed as Mrs Verreker-le-Flemming could have wished. 'Chance the Avenger! We're none of us immune from it.'

'Poetic justice, you mean?' twittered Mrs Verreker-le-Flemming, to whom these remarks had been somewhat obscure. 'Yes, but Joan Beresford of all people! That's the extraordinary thing. I should never have thought Joan *would* do a thing like that. She was such a *nice* girl. A little close with money, of course, considering how well-off they are, but that isn't anything. Of course it was only fun, and pulling her husband's leg, but I always used to think Joan was such a *serious* girl, Mr Sheringham. I mean, ordinary people don't talk about honour, and truth, and playing the game, and all those things one takes for granted. But Joan did. She was always saying that this wasn't honourable, or that wouldn't be playing the game. Well, she paid herself for not playing the game, poor girl, didn't she? Still, it all goes to show the truth of the old saying, doesn't it?'

'What old saying?' said Roger, hypnotised by this flow.

'Why, that still waters run deep. Joan must have been deep, I'm afraid.' Mrs Verreker-le-Flemming sighed. It was evidently a social error to be deep. 'I mean, she certainly took me in. She can't have been quite so honourable and truthful as she was always pretending, can she? And I can't help wondering whether a girl who'd deceive her husband in a little thing like that might not – oh, well, I don't want to say anything against poor Joan now she's dead, poor darling, but she can't have been *quite* such a plaster saint after all, can she? I mean,' said Mrs Verreker-le-Flemming, in hasty extenuation of these suggestions, 'I do think psychology is so very interesting, don't you, Mr Sheringham?'

'Sometimes, very,' Roger agreed gravely. 'But you mentioned Sir William Anstruther just now. Do you know him, too?'

'I used to,' Mrs Verreker-le-Flemming replied, without particular interest. 'Horrible man! Always running after some woman or other. And when he's tired of her, just drops her – biff! – like that. At least,' added Mrs Verreker-le-Flemming somewhat hastily, 'so I've heard.'

'And what happens if she refuses to be dropped?'

'Oh, dear, I'm sure I don't know. I suppose you've heard the latest?'

Mrs Verreker-le-Flemming hurried on, perhaps a trifle more pink than the delicate aids to nature on her cheeks would have warranted.

'He's taken up with that Bryce woman now. You know, the wife of the oil man, or petrol, or whatever he made his money in. It began about three weeks ago. You'd have thought that dreadful business of being responsible, in a way, for poor Joan Beresford's death would have sobered him up a little, wouldn't you? But not a bit of it; he—'

Roger was following another line of thought.

'What a pity you weren't at the Imperial with the Beresfords that evening. She'd never have made that bet if you had been.' Roger looked extremely innocent. 'You weren't, I suppose?'

'I?' queried Mrs Verreker-le-Flemming in surprise. 'Good gracious, no. I was at the new revue at the Pavilion. Lady Gavelstoke had a box and asked me to join her party.'

'Oh, yes. Good show, isn't it? I thought that sketch *The Sempiternal Triangle* very clever. Didn't you?'

'*The Sempiternal Triangle*?' wavered Mrs Verreker-le-Flemming.

'Yes, in the first half.'

'Oh! Then I didn't see it. I got there disgracefully late, I'm afraid. But then,' said Mrs Verreker-le-Flemming with pathos. 'I always do seem to be late for simply everything.'

Roger kept the rest of the conversation resolutely upon theatres. But before he left her he had ascertained that she had photographs of both Mrs Beresford and Sir William Anstruther, and had obtained permission to borrow them some time. As soon as she was out of view he hailed a taxi and gave Mrs Verreker-le-Flemming's address. He thought it better to take advantage of her permission at a time when he would not have to pay for it a second time over.

The parlourmaid seemed to think there was nothing odd in his mission, and took him up to the drawing-room at once. A corner of the room was devoted to the silver-framed photographs of Mrs Verreker-le-Flemming's friends, and there were many of them. Roger examined them with interest, and finally took away with him not two photographs but six, those of Sir William, Mrs Beresford, Beresford, two strange males who appeared to belong to the Sir William period, and, lastly, a likeness of Mrs Verreker-le-Flemming herself. Roger liked confusing his trail.

For the rest of the day he was very busy.

His activities would have no doubt seemed to Mrs Verreker-le-Flemming not merely baffling but pointless. He paid a visit to a public library, for instance, and consulted a work of reference, after which he took a taxi and drove to the offices of the Anglo-Eastern Perfumery Company, where he inquired for a certain Mr Joseph Lea Hardwick and seemed much put out on hearing that no such gentleman was known to the firm and was certainly not employed in any of their branches. Many questions had to be put about the firm and its branches before he consented to abandon the quest.

After that he drove to Messrs Weall and Wilson, the well-known institution which protects the trade interests of individuals and advises its subscribers regarding investments. Here he entered his name as a subscriber, and explaining that he had a large sum of money to invest, filled in one of the special inquiry forms which are headed Strictly Confidential.

Then he went to the Rainbow Club, in Piccadilly.

Introducing himself to the porter without a blush as connected with Scotland Yard, he asked the man a number of questions, more or less trivial, concerning the tragedy.

'Sir William, I understand,' he said finally, as if by the way, 'did not dine here the evening before?'

There it appeared that Roger was wrong. Sir William had dined in the club, as he did about three times a week.

'But I quite understood he wasn't here that evening?' Roger said plaintively.

The porter was emphatic. He remembered quite well. So did a waiter, whom the porter summoned to corroborate him. Sir William had dined, rather late, and had not left the dining-room till about nine o'clock. He spent the evening there, too, the waiter knew, or at least some of it, for he himself had taken him a whisky-and-soda in the lounge not less than half an hour later.

Roger retired.

He retired to Merton's, in a taxi.

It seemed that he wanted some new notepaper printed, of a very special kind, and to the young woman behind the counter he specified at great length and in wearisome detail exactly what he did want. The young woman handed him the books of specimen pieces and asked him to see if there was any style there which would suit him. Roger glanced through them, remarking garrulously to the young woman that he had been recommended to Merton's by a very dear friend, whose photograph he happened to have on him at that moment. Wasn't that a curious coincidence? The young woman agreed that it was.

'About a fortnight ago, I think, my friend was in here last,' said Roger, producing the photograph. 'Recognise this?'

The young woman took the photograph, without apparent interest.

'Oh, yes, I remember. About some notepaper, too, wasn't it? So that's your friend. Well, it's a small world. Now this is a line we're selling a good deal of just now.'

Roger went back to his rooms to dine. Afterwards, feeling restless, he wandered out of the Albany and turned up Piccadilly. He wandered round the Circus, thinking hard, and paused for a moment out of habit to inspect the photographs of the new revue hung outside the Pavilion. The next thing he realised was that he had got as far as Jermyn Street and was standing outside the Imperial Theatre. Glancing at the advertisements of *The Creaking Skull*, he saw that it began at half-past eight. Glancing at his watch, he saw that the time was twenty-nine minutes past that hour. He had an evening to get through somehow. He went inside.

The next morning, very early for Roger, he called on Moresby at Scotland Yard.

'Moresby,' he said without preamble, 'I want you to do something for me. Can you find me a taximan who took a fare from Piccadilly Circus or its neighbourhood at about ten-past nine on the evening before the Beresford crime, to the Strand somewhere near the bottom of Southampton Street, and another who took a fare back between those points. I'm not sure about the first. Or one taxi might have been used for the double journey, but I doubt that. Anyhow, try to find out for me, will you?'

'What are you up to now, Mr Sheringham?' Moresby asked suspiciously.

'Breaking down an interesting alibi,' replied Roger serenely. 'By the way, I know who sent those chocolates to Sir William. I'm just building up a nice structure of evidence for you. Ring up my rooms when you've got those taximen.'

He strolled out, leaving Moresby positively gaping after him.

The rest of the day he spent apparently trying to buy a second-hand typewriter. He was very particular that it should be a Hamilton No. 4. When the shop-people tried to induce him to consider other makes he refused to look at them, saying that he had had the Hamilton No. 4 so strongly recommended to him by a friend, who had bought one about three weeks ago. Perhaps it was at this very shop? No? They hadn't sold a Hamilton No. 4 for the last three months? How odd.

But at one shop they had sold a Hamilton No. 4 within the last month, and that was odder still.

At half-past four Roger got back to his rooms to await the telephone message from Moresby. At half-past five it came.

'There are fourteen taxi-drivers here, littering up my office,' said Moresby offensively. 'What do you want me to do with 'em?'

'Keep them till I come, Chief Inspector,' returned Roger with dignity.

The interview with the fourteen was brief enough, however. To each man in turn Roger showed a photograph, holding it so that Moresby could not see it, and asked if he could recognize his fare. The ninth man did so, without hesitation.

At a nod from Roger, Moresby dismissed them, then sat at his table and tried to look official. Roger seated himself on the table, looking most unofficial, and swung his legs. As he did so, a photograph fell unnoticed out of his pocket and fluttered, face downwards, under the table. Moresby eyed it but did not pick it up.

'And now, Mr Sheringham, sir,' he said, 'perhaps you'll tell me what you've been doing?'

'Certainly, Moresby,' said Roger blandly. 'Your work for you. I really have solved the thing, you know. Here's your evidence.' He took from his note-case an old letter and handed it to the Chief Inspector. 'Was that typed on the same machine as the forged letter from Mason's, or was it not?'

Moresby studied it for a moment, then drew the forged letter from a drawer of his table and compared the two minutely.

'Mr Sheringham,' he said soberly, 'where did you get hold of this?'

'In a second-hand typewriter shop in St Martin's Lane. The machine was sold to an unknown customer about a month ago. They identified the customer from that same photograph. As it happened, this machine had been used for a time in the office after it was repaired, to see that it was O.K., and I easily got hold of that specimen of its work.'

'And where is the machine now?'

'Oh, at the bottom of the Thames, I expect,' Roger smiled. 'I tell you, this criminal takes no unnecessary chances. But that doesn't matter. There's your evidence.'

'Humph! It's all right so far as it goes,' conceded Moresby. 'But what about Mason's paper?'

'That,' said Roger calmly, 'was extracted from Merton's book of sample notepapers, as I'd guessed from the very yellowed edges might be the case. I can prove contact of the criminal with the book, and there is a gap which will certainly turn out to have been filled by that piece of paper.'

'That's fine,' Moresby said more heartily.

'As for that taximan, the criminal had an alibi. You've heard it broken down. Between ten-past nine and twenty-five past, in fact, during the time when the parcel must have been posted, the murderer took a hurried journey to that neighbourhood, going probably by bus or Underground, but returning, as I expected, by taxi, because time would be getting short.'

'And the murderer, Mr Sheringham?'

'The person whose photograph is in my pocket,' Roger said unkindly. 'By the way, do you remember what I was saying the other day about Chance the Avenger, my excellent film-title? Well, it's worked again. By a chance meeting in Bond Street with a silly woman I was put, by the merest accident, in possession of a piece of information which showed me then and there who had sent those chocolates addressed to Sir William. There were other possibilities, of course, and I tested them, but then and there on the pavement I saw the whole thing, from first to last.'

'Who was the murderer, then, Mr Sheringham?' repeated Moresby.

'It was so beautifully planned,' Roger went on dreamily. 'We never grasped for one moment that we were making the fundamental mistake that the murderer all along intended us to make.'

'And what was that?' asked Moresby.

'Why, that the plan had miscarried. That the wrong person had been killed. That was just the beauty of it. The plan had *not* miscarried. It had been brilliantly successful. The wrong person was *not* killed. Very much the right person was.'

Moresby gaped.

'Why, how on earth do you make that out, sir?'

'Mrs Beresford was the objective all the time. That's why the plot was so ingenious. Everything was anticipated. It was perfectly natural that Sir William should hand the chocolates over to Beresford. It was foreseen that we should look for the criminal among Sir William's associates and not the dead woman's. It was probably even foreseen that the crime would be considered the work of a woman!'

Moresby, unable to wait any longer, snatched up the photograph.

'Good heavens! But Mr Sheringham, you don't mean to tell me that ... Sir William himself!'

'He wanted to get rid of Mrs Beresford,' Roger continued. 'He had liked her well enough at the beginning, no doubt, though it was her money he was after all the time.

'But the real trouble was that she was too close with her money. He wanted it, or some of it, pretty badly; and she wouldn't part. There's no doubt above the motive. I made a list of the firms he's interested in and got a report on them. They're all rocky, every one. He'd got through all his own money, and he had to get more.

'As for the nitrobenzine which puzzled us so much, that was simple enough, I looked it up and found that beside the uses you told me, it's used largely in perfumery. And he's got a perfumery business. The Anglo-Eastern Perfumery Company. That's how he'd know about it being poisonous, of course. But I should not think he got his supply from there. He'd be cleverer than that. He probably made the stuff himself. Any schoolboy knows how to treat benzol with nitric acid to get nitro-benzine.'

'But,' stammered Moresby, 'but Sir William. . . . He was at Eton.'

'Sir William?' said Roger sharply. 'Who's talking about Sir William? I told you the photograph of the murderer was in my pocket.' He whipped out the photograph in question and confronted the astounded Chief Inspector with it. 'Beresford, man! Beresford's the murderer of his own wife.

'Beresford, who still had hankerings after a gay life,' he went on more mildly, 'didn't want his wife but did want her money. He contrived this plot, providing as he thought against every contingency that could possibly arise. He established a mild alibi, if suspicion ever should arise, by taking his wife to the Imperial, and slipped out of the theatre at the first interval. (I sat through the first act of the dreadful thing myself last night to see when the interval came.) Then he hurried down to the Strand, posted his parcel, and took a taxi back. He had ten minutes, but nobody would notice if he got back to the box a minute late.

'And the rest simply followed. He knew Sir William came to the club every morning at ten-thirty, as regularly as clockwork; he knew that for a psychological certainty he could get the chocolates handed over to him if he hinted for them; he knew that the police would go chasing after all sorts of false trails starting from Sir William. And as for the wrapper and the forged letter, he carefully didn't destroy them because they were calculated not only to divert suspicion but actually to point away from him to some anonymous lunatic.'

'Well, it's very smart of you, Mr Sheringham,' Moresby said, with a little sigh, but quite ungrudgingly. 'Very smart indeed. What was it the lady told you that showed you the whole thing in a flash?'

'Why, it wasn't so much what she actually told me as what I heard between her words, so to speak. What she told me was that Mrs Beresford knew the answer to that bet; what I deduced was that, being the sort of person she was, it was quite incredible that she should have made a bet to which she knew the answer. *Ergo*, she didn't. *Ergo*, there never was such a bet. *Ergo*, Beresford was lying. *Ergo*, Beresford wanted to get hold of those chocolates for some reason other than he stated. After all, we only had Beresford's word for the bet, hadn't we?

'Of course he wouldn't have left her that afternoon till he'd seen her take, or somehow made her take, at least six of the chocolates, more than a lethal dose. That's why the stuff was in those meticulous six-minim doses. And so that he could take a couple himself, of course. A clever stroke, that.'

Moresby rose to his feet.

'Well, Mr Sheringham, I'm much obliged to you, sir. And now I shall have to get busy myself.' He scratched his head. 'Chance the Avenger, eh? Well, I can tell you one pretty big thing Beresford left to Chance the Avenger, Mr Sheringham. Suppose Sir William hadn't handed over the chocolates after all? Supposing he'd kept 'em, to give to one of his own ladies?'

Roger positively snorted. He felt a personal pride in Beresford by this time.

'Really, Moresby! It wouldn't have had any serious results if Sir William had. Do give my man credit for being what he is. You don't imagine he sent the poisoned ones to Sir William, do you? Of course not! He'd send harmless ones, and exchange them for the others on his way home. Dash it all, he wouldn't go right out of his way to present opportunities to Chance.

'If,' added Roger, 'Chance really is the right word.'

Dorothy L. Sayers

The Necklace of Pearls

Sir Septimus Shale was accustomed to assert his authority once in the year and once only. He allowed his young and fashionable wife to fill his house with diagrammatic furniture made of steel; to collect advanced artists and anti-grammatical poets; to believe in cocktails and relativity and to dress as extravagantly as she pleased; but he did insist on an old-fashioned Christmas. He was a simple-hearted man, who really liked plum-pudding and cracker mottoes, and he could not get it out of his head that other people, 'at bottom,' enjoyed these things also. At Christmas, therefore, he firmly retired to his country house in Essex, called in the servants to hang holly and mistletoe upon the cubist electric fittings; loaded the steel sideboard with delicacies from Fortnum & Mason; hung up stockings at the heads of the polished walnut bedsteads; and even, on this occasion only, had the electric radiators removed from the modernist grates and installed wood fires and a Yule log. He then gathered his family and friends about him, filled them with as much Dickensian good fare as he could persuade them to swallow, and, after their Christmas dinner, set them down to play 'Charades' and 'Clumps' and 'Animal, Vegetable and Mineral' in the drawing-room, concluding these diversions by 'Hide-and-Seek' in the dark all over the house. Because Sir Septimus was a very rich man, his guests fell in with this invariable programme, and if they were bored, they did not tell him so.

Another charming and traditional custom which he followed was that of presenting to his daughter Margharita a pearl on each successive birthday – this anniversary happening to coincide with Christmas Eve. The pearls now numbered twenty, and the collection was beginning to enjoy a certain celebrity, and had been photographed in the Society papers. Though not sensationally large – each one being about the size of a marrowfat pea – the pearls were of very great value. They were of exquisite colour and perfect shape and matched to a hair's weight. On this particular Christmas Eve, the presentation of the twenty-first pearl had been the occasion of a very special ceremony. There was a dance and there were speeches. On the Christmas night following, the more restricted family party took place, with the turkey and the Victorian games. There were eleven guests, in addition to Sir Septimus and Lady Shale and their daughter, nearly all related or connected to them in some way: John Shale, a brother, with his wife and their son and daughter Henry and Betty; Betty's *fiancé*, Oswald Truegood, a young man with parliamentary ambitions; George Comphrey, a cousin of Lady Shale's, aged about thirty and known as a man about town; Lavinia Prescott, asked on George's account; Joyce Trivett, asked on Henry Shale's account; Richard and Beryl Dennison, distant relations of Lady Shale, who lived a gay and expensive life in town on nobody precisely knew what resources; and Lord Peter Wimsey, asked, in a touching spirit of unreasonable hope, on Margharita's account. There were also, of course, William Norgate, secretary to Sir Septimus, and Miss Tomkins, secretary to Lady Shale, who had to be there because, without their calm efficiency, the Christmas arrangements could not have been carried through.

Dinner was over – a seemingly endless succession of soup, fish, turkey, roast beef, plum-pudding, mince-pies, crystallised fruit, nuts and five kinds of wine, presided over by Sir Septimus, all smiles, by Lady Shale, all mocking depreciation, and by Margharita, pretty and bored, with the necklace of twenty-one pearls gleaming softly on her slender throat. Gorged and dyspeptic and longing only for the horizontal position, the company had been shepherded into the drawing-room and set to play 'Musical Chairs' (Miss Tomkins at the piano), 'Hunt the Slipper' (slipper provided by Miss Tomkins), and 'Dumb Crambo' (costumes by Miss Tomkins and Mr William Norgate). The back drawing-room (for Sir Septimus clung to these old-fashioned names) provided an admirable dressing-room, being screened by folding doors from the large drawing-room in which the audience sat on aluminium chairs, scrabbling uneasy toes on a floor of black glass under the tremendous illumination of electricity reflected from a brass ceiling.

It was William Norgate who, after taking the temperature of the meeting, suggested to Lady Shale that they should play at something less athletic. Lady Shale agreed and, as usual, suggested bridge. Sir Septimus, as usual, blew the suggestion aside.

'Bridge? Nonsense! Nonsense! Play bridge every day of your lives. This is Christmas time. Something we can all play together. How about

"Animal, Vegetable and Mineral"?'

This intellectual pastime was a favourite with Sir Septimus; he was rather good at putting pregnant questions. After a brief discussion, it became evident that this game was an inevitable part of the programme. The party settled down to it, Sir Septimus undertaking to 'go out' first and set the thing going.

Presently they had guessed among other things Miss Tomkin's mother's photograph, a gramophone record of 'I want to be happy' (much scientific research into the exact composition of records, settled by William Norgate out of the *Encyclopaedia Britannica*,) the smallest stickleback in the stream at the bottom of the garden, the new planet Pluto, the scarf worn by Mrs Dennison (very confusing, because it was not silk, which would be animal, or artificial silk, which would be vegetable, but made of spun glass – mineral, a very clever choice of subject), and had failed to guess the Prime Minister's wireless speech – which was voted not fair, since nobody could decide whether it was animal by nature or a kind of gas. It was decided that they should do one more word and then go on to 'Hide-and-Seek.' Oswald Truegood had retired into the back room and shut the door behind him while the party discussed the next subject of examination, when suddenly Sir Septimus broke in on the argument by calling to his daughter:

'Hullo, Margy! What have you done with your necklace?'

'I took it off, Dad, because I thought it might get broken in "Dumb Crambo." It's over here on this table. No, it isn't. Did you take it, mother?'

'No, I didn't. If I'd seen it, I should have. You are a careless child.'

'I believe you've got it yourself, Dad. You're teasing,'

Sir Septimus denied the accusation with some energy. Everybody got up and began to hunt about. There were not many places in that bare and polished room where a necklace could be hidden. After ten minutes' fruitless investigation, Richard Dennison, who had been seated next to the table where the pearls had been placed, began to look rather uncomfortable.

'Awkward, you know,' he remarked to Wimsey.

At this moment, Oswald Truegood put his head through the folding-doors and asked whether they hadn't settled on something by now, because he was getting the fidgets.

This directed the attention of the searchers to the inner room. Margharita must have been mistaken. She had taken it in there, and it had got mixed up with the dressing-up clothes somehow. The room was ransacked. Everything was lifted up and shaken. The thing began to look serious. After half an hour of desperate energy it became apparent that the pearls were nowhere to be found.

'They must be somewhere in these two rooms, you know,' said Wimsey. 'The back drawing-room has no door and nobody could have gone out of the front drawing-room without being seen. Unless the windows—'

No. The windows were all guarded on the outside by heavy shutters which it needed two footmen to take down and replace. The pearls had not gone out that way. In fact, the mere suggestion that they had left the drawing-room at all was disagreeable. Because – because—

It was William Norgate, efficient as ever, who coldly and boldly faced the issue.

'I think, Sir Septimus, it would be a relief to the minds of everybody present if we could all be searched.'

Sir Septimus was horrified, but the guests, having found a leader, backed up Norgate. The door was locked, and the search was conducted – the ladies in the inner room and the men in the outer.

Nothing resulted from it except some very interesting information about the belongings habitually carried about by the average man and woman. It was natural that Lord Peter Wimsey should possess a pair of forceps, a pocket lens and a small folding foot-rule – was he not a Sherlock Holmes in high life? But that Oswald Truegood should have two liver-pills in a screw of paper and Henry Shale a pocket edition of *The Odes of Horace* was unexpected. Why did John Shale distend the pockets of his dress-suit with a stump of red sealing-wax, an ugly little mascot and a five-shilling piece? George Comphrey had a pair of folding scissors, and three wrapped lumps of sugar, of the sort served in restaurants and dining-cars – evidence of a not uncommon form of kleptomania; but that the tidy and exact Norgate should burden himself with a reel of white cotton, three separate lengths of string and twelve safety-pins on a card seemed really remarkable till one remembered that he had superintended all the Christmas decorations. Richard Dennison, amid some confusion and laughter, was found to cherish a lady's garter, a powder-compact and half a potato; the last-named, he said, was a prophylactic against rheumatism (to which he was subject), while the other objects belonged to his wife. On the ladies' side, the more striking exhibits were a little book on palmistry, three invisible hair-pins and a baby's photograph (Miss Tomkins); a Chinese trick cigarette-case with a secret compartment (Beryl Dennison); a *very* private letter and an outfit for mending stocking-ladders (Lavinia Prescott); and a pair of eyebrow tweezers and a small packet of white powder, said to be for headaches (Betty Shale). An agitating moment followed the production from Joyce Trivett's handbag of a small string of pearls – but it was promptly remembered that these had come out of one of the crackers at dinner-time, and they were, in fact, synthetic. In short, the search was unproductive of anything beyond a general shamefacedness and the discomfort always produced by undressing and re-dressing in a hurry at the wrong time of the day.

It was then that somebody, very grudgingly and haltingly, mentioned the horrid word 'Police.' Sir Septimus, naturally, was appalled by the idea. It was disgusting. He would not allow it. The pearls must be somewhere. They must search the rooms again. Could not Lord Peter Wimsey, with his experience of – er – mysterious happenings, do something to assist them?

'Eh?' said his lordship. 'Oh, by Jove, yes – by all means, certainly. That is to say, provided nobody supposes – eh, what? I mean to say, you don't know that I'm not a suspicious character, do you, what?'

Lady Shale interposed with authority.

'We don't think *anybody* ought to be suspected,' she said, 'but, if we did, we'd know it couldn't be you. You know *far* too much about crimes to want to commit one.'

'All right,' said Wimsey. 'But after the way the place has been gone over—' He shrugged his shoulders.

'Yes, I'm afraid you won't be able to find any footprints,' said Margharita. 'But we may have overlooked something.'

Wimsey nodded.

'I'll try. Do you all mind sitting down on your chairs in the outer room and staying there. All except one of you – I'd better have a witness to anything I do or find. Sir Septimus – you'd be the best person, I think.'

He shepherded them to their places and began a slow circuit of the two rooms, exploring every surface, gazing up to the polished brazen ceiling, and crawling on hands and knees in the approved fashion across the black and shining desert of the floors. Sir Septimus followed, staring when Wimsey stared, bending with his hands upon his knees when Wimsey crawled, and puffing at intervals with astonishment and chagrin. Their progress rather resembled that of a man taking out a very inquisitive puppy for a very leisurely constitutional. Fortunately, Lady Shale's taste in furnishing made investigation easier; there were scarcely any nooks or corners where anything could be concealed.

They reached the inner drawing-room, and here the dressing-up clothes were again minutely examined, but without result. Finally, Wimsey lay down flat on his stomach to squint under a steel cabinet which was one of the very few pieces of furniture which possessed short legs. Something about it seemed to catch his attention. He rolled up his sleeve and plunged his arm into the cavity, kicked convulsively in the effort to reach farther than was humanly possible, pulled out from his pocket and extended his folding foot-rule, fished with it under the cabinet and eventually succeeded in extracting what he sought.

It was a very minute object – in fact, a pin. Not an ordinary pin, but one resembling those used by entomologists to impale extremely small moths on the setting-board. It was about three-quarters of an inch in length, as fine as a very fine needle, with a sharp point and a particularly small head.

'Bless my soul!' said Sir Septimus. 'What's that?'

'Does anybody here happen to collect moths or beetles or anything?' asked Wimsey, squatting on his haunches and examining the pin.

'I'm pretty sure they don't,' replied Sir Septimus. 'I'll ask them.'

'Don't do that.' Wimsey bent his head and stared at the floor, from which his own face stared meditatively back at him.

'I see,' said Wimsey presently. 'That's how it was done. All right, Sir Septimus. I know where the pearls are, but I don't know who took them. Perhaps it would be as well – for everybody's satisfaction – just to find out. In the meantime they are perfectly safe. Don't tell any one that we've found this pin or that we've discovered anything. Send all these people to bed. Lock the drawing-room door and keep the key, and we'll get our man – or woman – by breakfast-time.'

'God bless my soul,' said Sir Septimus, very much puzzled.

Lord Peter Wimsey kept careful watch that night upon the drawing-room door. Nobody, however, came near it. Either the thief suspected a trap or he felt confident that any time would do to recover the pearls. Wimsey, however, did not feel that he was wasting his time. He was making a list of people who had been left alone in the back drawing-room during the playing of 'Animal, Vegetable or Mineral.' The list ran as follows.

Sir Septimus Shale
Lavinia Prescott
William Norgate
Joyce Trivett and Henry Shale (together, because they had claimed to be incapable of guessing anything unaided)
Mrs Dennison
Betty Shale
George Comphrey
Richard Dennison
Miss Tomkins
Oswald Truegood.

He also made out a list of the persons to whom pearls might be useful or desirable. Unfortunately, this list agreed in almost all respects with the first (always excepting Sir Septimus) and so was not very helpful. The two secretaries had both come well recommended, but that was exactly what they would have done had they come with ulterior designs; the Dennisons were notorious livers from hand to mouth; Betty Shale carried mysterious white powders in her handbag, and was known to be in with a rather rapid set in town; Henry was a harmless dilettante, but Joyce Trivett could twist him round her little finger and was what Jane Austen liked to call 'expensive and dissipated'; Comphrey speculated; Oswald Truegood was rather frequently present at Epsom and Newmarket – the search for motives was only too fatally easy.

When the second housemaid and the under-footman appeared in the passage with household implements, Wimsey abandoned his vigil, but he was down early to breakfast. Sir Septimus with his wife and daughter were down before him, and a certain air of tension made itself felt. Wimsey, standing on the hearth before the fire, made conversation about the weather and politics.

The party assembled gradually, but, as though by common consent, nothing was said about pearls until after breakfast, when Oswald Truegood took the bull by the horns.

'Well now!' said he. 'How's the detective getting along? Got your man, Wimsey?'

'Not yet,' said Wimsey easily.

Sir Septimus, looking at Wimsey as though for his cue, cleared his throat and dashed into speech.

'All very tiresome,' he said, 'all very unpleasant. Hr'rm. Nothing for it but the police, I'm afraid. Just at Christmas, too. Hr'rm. Spoilt the party. Can't stand seeing all this stuff about the place.' He waved his hand towards the festoons of evergreens and coloured paper that adorned the walls. 'Take it all down, eh, what? No heart in it. Hr'rm. Burn the lot.'

'What a pity, when we worked so hard over it,' said Joyce.

'Oh, leave it, Uncle,' said Henry Shale. 'You're bothering too much about the pearls. They're sure to turn up.'

'Shall I ring for James?' suggested William Norgate.

'No,' interrupted Comphrey, 'let's do it ourselves. It'll give us something to do and take our minds off our troubles.'

'That's right,' said Sir Septimus. 'Start right away. Hate the sight of it.'

He savagely hauled a great branch of holly down from the mantelpiece and flung it, crackling, into the fire.

'That's the stuff,' said Richard Dennison. 'Make a good old blaze!' He leapt up from the table and snatched the mistletoe from the chandelier. 'Here goes! One more kiss for somebody before it's too late.'

'Isn't it unlucky to take it down before the New Year?' suggested Miss Tomkins.

'Unlucky be hanged. We'll have it all down. Off the stairs and out of the drawing-room too. Somebody go and collect it.'

'Isn't the drawing-room locked?' asked Oswald.

'No. Lord Peter says the pearls aren't there, wherever else they are, so it's unlocked. That's right, isn't it, Wimsey?'

'Quite right. The pearls were taken out of these rooms. I can't yet tell you how, but I'm positive of it. In fact, I'll pledge my reputation that wherever they are, they're not up there.'

'Oh, well,' said Comphrey, 'in that case, have at it! Come along, Lavinia – you and Dennison do the drawing-room and I'll do the back room. We'll have a race.'

'But if the police are coming in,' said Dennison, 'oughtn't everything to be left just as it is?'

'Damn the police!' shouted Sir Septimus. 'They don't want ever-greens.'

Oswald and Margharita were already pulling the holly and ivy from the staircase, amid peals of laughter. The party dispersed. Wimsey went quietly upstairs and into the drawing-room, where the work of demolition was taking place at a great rate, George having bet the other two ten shillings to a tanner that they would not finish their part of the job before his finished his.

'You mustn't help,' said Lavinia, laughing, to Wimsey. 'It wouldn't be fair.'

Wimsey said nothing, but waited till the room was clear. Then he followed them down again to the hall, where the fire was sending up a great roaring and spluttering, suggestive of Guy Fawkes night. He whispered to Sir Septimus, who went forward and touched George Comphrey on the shoulder.

'Lord Peter wants to say something to you, my boy,' he said.

Comphrey started and went with him a little reluctantly, as it seemed. He was not looking very well.

'Mr Comphrey,' said Wimsey, 'I fancy these are some of your property.' He held out the palm of his hand, in which rested twenty-two fine, small-headed pins.

'Ingenious,' said Wimsey, 'but something less ingenious would have served his turn better. It was very unlucky, Sir Septimus, that you should have mentioned the pearls when you did. Of course, he hoped that the loss wouldn't be discovered till we'd chucked guessing games and taken to "Hide-and-Seek." Then the pearls might have been anywhere in the house, we shouldn't have locked the drawing-room door, and he could have recovered them at his leisure. He had had this possibility in his mind when he came here, obviously, and that was why he brought the pins, and Miss Shale's taking off the necklace to play "Dumb Crambo" gave him his opportunity.

'He had spent Christmas here before, and knew perfectly well that "Animal, Vegetable and Mineral" would form part of the entertainment. He had only to gather up the necklace from the table when it came to his turn to retire, and he knew he could count on at least five minutes by himself while we were all arguing about the choice of a word. He had only to snip the pearls from the string with his pocket-scissors, burn the string in the grate and fasten the pearls to the mistletoe with the fine pins. The mistletoe was hung on the chandelier, pretty high – it's a lofty room – but he could easily reach it by standing on the glass table, which wouldn't show footmarks, and it was almost certain that nobody would think of examining the mistletoe for extra berries. I shouldn't have thought of it myself if I hadn't found that pin which he had dropped. That gave me the idea that the pearls had been separated and the rest was easy. I took the pearls off the mistletoe last night – the clasp was there, too, pinned among the holly leaves. Here they are. Comphrey must have got a nasty shock this morning. I knew he was our man when he suggested that the guests should tackle the decorations themselves and that he should do the back drawing-room – but I wish I had seen his face when he came to the mistletoe and found the pearls gone.'

'And you worked it all out when you found the pin?' said Sir Septimus.

'Yes; I knew then where the pearls had gone to.'

'But you never even looked at the mistletoe.'

'I saw it reflected in the black glass floor, and it struck me then how much the mistletoe berries looked like pearls.'

Dorothy L. Sayers

The Man Who Knew How

For the twentieth time since the train had left Carlisle, Pender glanced up from *Murder at the Manse* and caught the eye of the man opposite.

He frowned a little. It was irritating to be watched so closely, and always with that faint, sardonic smile. It was still more irritating to allow oneself to be so much disturbed by the smile and the scrutiny. Pender wrenched himself back to his book with a determination to concentrate upon the problem of the minister murdered in the library.

But the story was of the academic kind that crowds all its exciting incidents into the first chapter, and proceeds thereafter by a long series of deductions to a scientific solution in the last. Twice Pender had to turn back to verify points that he had missed in reading. Then he became aware that he was not thinking about the murdered minister at all – he was becoming more and more actively conscious of the other man's face. A queer face, Pender thought.

There was nothing especially remarkable about the features in themselves; it was their expression that daunted Pender. It was a secret face, the face of one who knew a great deal to other people's disadvantage. The mouth was a little crooked and tightly tucked in at the corners, as though savouring a hidden amusement. The eyes, behind a pair of rimless pince-nez, glittered curiously; but that was possibly due to the light reflected in the glasses. Pender wondered what the man's profession might be. He was dressed in a dark lounge suit, a raincoat and a shabby soft hat; his age was perhaps about forty.

Pender coughed unnecessarily and settled back into his corner, raising the detective story high before his face, barrier-fashion. This was worse than useless. He gained the impression that the man saw through the manoeuvre and was secretly entertained by it. He wanted to fidget, but felt obscurely that his doing so would in some way constitute a victory for the other man. In his self-consciousness he held himself so rigid that attention to his book became a sheer physical impossibility.

There was no stop now before Rugby, and it was unlikely that any passenger would enter from the corridor to break up this disagreeable *solitude à deux*. Pender could, of course, go out into the corridor and not return, but that would be an acknowledgement of defeat. Pender lowered *Murder at the Manse* and caught the man's eye again.

'Getting tired of it?' asked the man.

'Night journeys are always a bit tedious,' replied Pender, half relieved and half reluctant. 'Would you like a book?'

He took *The Paper-Clip Clue* from his briefcase and held it out hopefully. The other man glanced at the title and shook his head.

'Thanks very much,' he said, 'but I never read detective stories. They're so – inadequate, don't you think so?'

'They are rather lacking in characterisation and human interest, certainly,' said Pender, 'but on a railway journey—'

'I don't mean that,' said the other man. 'I am not concerned with humanity. But all these murderers are so incompetent – they bore me.'

'Oh, I don't know,' replied Pender. 'At any rate they are usually a good deal more imaginative and ingenious than murderers in real life.'

'Than the murderers who are found out in real life, yes,' admitted the other man.

'Even some of those did pretty well before they got pinched,' objected Pender. 'Crippen, for instance; he need never have been caught if he hadn't lost his head and run off to America. George Joseph Smith did away with at least two brides quite successfully before fate and the *News of the World* intervened.'

'Yes,' said the other man, 'but look at the clumsiness of it all; the elaboration, the lies, the paraphernalia. Absolutely unnecessary.'

'Oh come!' said Pender. 'You can't expect committing a murder and getting away with it to be as simple as shelling peas.'

'Ah!' said the other man. 'You think that, do you?'

Pender waited for him to elaborate this remark, but nothing came of it. The man leaned back and smiled in his secret way at the roof of the carriage; he appeared to think the conversation not worth going on with. Pender found himself noticing his companion's hands. They were white and surprisingly long in the fingers. He watched them gently tapping upon their owner's knee – then resolutely turned a page – then put the book down once more and said:

'Well, if it's so easy, how would *you* set about committing a murder?'

'I?' repeated the man. The light on his glasses made his eyes quite blank to Pender, but his voice sounded gently amused. 'That's different; *I* should not have to think twice about it.'

'Why not?'

'Because I happen to know how to do it.'

'Do you indeed?' muttered Pender, rebelliously.

'Oh yes; there's nothing to it.'

'How can you be sure? You haven't tried, I suppose?'

'It isn't a case of trying,' said the man. 'There's nothing uncertain about my method. That's just the beauty of it.'

'It's easy to say that,' retorted Pender, 'but what *is* this wonderful method?'

'You can't expect me to tell you that, can you?' said the other man, bringing his eyes back to rest on Pender's. 'It might not be safe. You look harmless enough, but who could look more harmless than Crippen? Nobody is fit to be trusted with *absolute* control over other people's lives.'

'Bosh!' exclaimed Pender. 'I shouldn't think of murdering anybody.'

'Oh yes you would,' said the other man, 'if you really believed it was safe. So would anybody. Why are all these tremendous artificial barriers built up around murder by the Church and the law? Just because it's everybody's crime and just as natural as breathing.'

'But that's ridiculous!' cried Pender, warmly.

'You think so, do you? That's what most people would say. But I wouldn't trust 'em. Not with sulphate of thanatol to be bought for two pence at any chemist's.'

'Sulphate of what?' asked Pender sharply.

'Ah! you think I'm giving something away. Well, it's a mixture of that and one or two other things – all equally ordinary and cheap. For nine pence you could make up enough to poison the entire Cabinet. Though of course one wouldn't polish off the whole lot at once; it might look funny if they all died simultaneously in their baths.'

'Why in their baths?'

'That's the way it would take them. It's the action of the hot water that brings on the effect of the stuff, you see. Any time from a few hours to a few days after administration. It's quite a simple chemical reaction and it couldn't possibly be detected by analysis. It would just look like heart failure.'

Pender eyed him uneasily. He did not like the smile; it was not only derisive, it was smug, it was almost gloating, triumphant! He could not quite put the right name to it.

'You know,' pursued the man, pulling a pipe from his pocket and beginning to fill it, 'it is very odd how often one seems to read of people being found dead in their baths. It must be a very common accident. Quite temptingly so. After all, there is a fascination about murder. The thing grows upon one – that is, I imagine it would, you know.'

'Very likely,' said Pender.

'I'm sure of it. No, I wouldn't trust anybody with that formula – not even a virtuous young man like yourself.'

The long white fingers tamped the tobacco firmly into the bowl and struck a match.

'But how about you?' said Pender, irritated. (Nobody cares to be called a virtuous young man.) 'If nobody is fit to be trusted—'

'I'm not, eh?' replied the man. 'Well, that's true, but it can't be helped now, can it? I know the thing and I can't unknow it again. It's unfortunate, but there it is. At any rate you have the comfort of knowing that nothing disagreeable is likely to happen to *me*. Dear me! Rugby already. I get out here. I have a little bit of business to do at Rugby.'

He rose and shook himself, buttoned his raincoat about him, and pulled the shabby hat more firmly down about his enigmatic glasses. The train slowed down and stopped. With a brief good night and a crooked smile the man stepped on to the platform. Pender watched him stride quickly away into the drizzle beyond the radius of the gas light.

'Dotty or something,' said Pender, oddly relieved. 'Thank goodness, I seem to be going to have the compartment to myself.'

He returned to *Murder at the Manse*, but his attention still kept wandering from the book he held in his hand.

'What was the name of that stuff the fellow talked about? Sulphate of what?'

For the life of him he could not remember.

It was on the following afternoon that Pender saw the news item. He had bought the *Standard* to read at lunch, and the word 'Bath' caught his eye; otherwise he would probably have missed the paragraph altogether, for it was only a short one.

WEALTHY MANUFACTURER DIES IN BATH

WIFE'S TRAGIC DISCOVERY

A distressing discovery was made early this morning by Mrs John Brittlesea, wife of the well-known head of Brittlesea's Engineering Works at Rugby. Finding that her husband, whom she had seen alive and well less than an hour previously, did not come down in time for his breakfast, she searched for him in the bathroom, where the engineer was found lying dead in his bath, life having been extinct, according to the medical men, for half an hour. The cause of the death is pronounced to be heart failure. The deceased manufacturer . . .

'That's an odd coincidence,' said Pender. 'At Rugby. I should think my unknown friend would be interested – if he is still there, doing his bit of business. I wonder what his business is, by the way.'

It is a very curious thing how, when once your attention is attracted to any particular set of circumstances, that set of circumstances seems to haunt you. You get appendicitis: immediately the newspapers are filled with paragraphs about statesmen suffering from appendicitis and victims dying of it; you learn that all your acquaintances have had it, or know friends who have had it and either died of it, or recovered from it with more surprising and spectacular rapidity than yourself; you cannot open a popular magazine without seeing its cure mentioned as one of the triumphs of modern surgery, or dip into a scientific treatise without coming across a comparison of the vermiform appendix in men and monkeys. Probably these references to appendicitis are equally frequent at all times, but you only notice them when your mind is attuned to the subject. At any rate, it was in this way that Pender accounted to himself for the extraordinary frequency with which people seemed to die in their baths at this period.

The thing pursued him at every turn. Always the same sequence of events: the hot bath, the discovery of the corpse, the inquest. Always the same medical opinion: heart failure following immersion in too hot water. It began to seem to Pender that it was scarcely safe to enter a hot bath at all. He took to making his own bath cooler and cooler every day, until it almost ceased to be enjoyable.

He skimmed his paper each morning for headlines about baths before settling down to read the news; and was at once relieved and vaguely disappointed if a week passed without a hot-bath tragedy.

One of the sudden deaths that occurred in this way was that of a young and beautiful woman whose husband, an analytical chemist, had tried without success to divorce her a few months previously. The coroner displayed a tendency to suspect foul play, and put the husband through a severe cross-examination. There seemed, however, to be no getting behind the doctor's evidence. Pender, brooding over the improbable possible, wished, as he did every day of the week, that he could remember the name of that drug the man in the train had mentioned.

Then came the excitement in Pender's own neighbourhood. An old Mr Skimmings, who lived alone with a housekeeper in a street just around the corner, was found dead in his bathroom. His heart had never been strong. The housekeeper told the milkman that she had always expected something of the sort to happen, for the old gentlemen would always take his bath so hot. Pender went to the inquest.

The housekeeper gave her evidence. Mr Skimmings had been the kindest of employers, and she was heartbroken at losing him. No, she had not been aware that Mr Skimmings had left her a large sum of money, but it was just like this goodness of heart. The verdict of course was accidental death.

Pender, that evening, went out for his usual stroll with the dog. Some feeling of curiosity moved him to go around past the late Mr Skimmings' house. As he loitered by, glancing up at the blank windows, the garden gate opened and a man came out. In the light of a street lamp, Pender recognised him at once.

'Hullo!' he said.

'Oh, it's you, is it?' said the man. 'Viewing the site of the tragedy, eh? What do *you* think about it all?'

'Oh, nothing very much,' said Pender. 'I didn't know him. Odd, our meeting again like this.'

'Yes, isn't it? You live near here, I suppose.'

'Yes,' said Pender; and then wished he hadn't. 'Do you live in these parts too?'

'Me?' said the man. 'Oh no. I was only here on a little matter of business.'

'Last time we met,' said Pender, 'you had business at Rugby.' They had fallen into step together, and were walking slowly down to the turning Pender had to take in order to reach his house.

'So I had,' agreed the other man. 'My business takes me all over the country. I never know where I may be wanted next, you see.'

'It was while you were at Rugby that old Brittlesea was found dead in his bath, wasn't it?' remarked Pender carelessly.

'Yes. Funny thing, coincidence.' The man glanced up at him sideways through his glittering glasses. 'Left all his money to his wife, didn't he? She's a rich woman now. Good-looking girl – a lot younger than he was.'

They were passing Pender's gate. 'Come in and have a drink,' said Pender, and again immediately regretted the impulse.

The man accepted, and they went into Pender's bachelor study.

'Remarkable lot of these bath deaths lately,' observed Pender as he squirted soda into the tumblers.

'You think it's remarkable?' said the man, with his irritating trick of querying everything that was said to him. 'Well, I don't know. Perhaps it is. But it's always a fairly common accident.'

'I suppose I've been taking more notice on account of that conversation we had in the train.' Pender laughed, a little self-consciously. 'It just makes me wonder – you know how one does – whether anybody else had happened to hit on that drug you mentioned – what was its name?'

The man ignored the question.

'Oh, I shouldn't think so,' he said. 'I fancy I'm the only person who knows about that. I only stumbled on the thing by accident myself when I was looking for something else. I don't imagine it could have been discovered simultaneously in so many parts of the country. But all these verdicts just show, don't they, what a safe way it would be of getting rid of a person.'

'You're a chemist, then?' asked Pender, catching at the one phrase which seemed to promise information.

'Oh, I'm a bit of everything. Sort of general utility man. I do a good bit of studying on my own, too. You've got one or two interesting books here, I see.'

Pender was flattered. For a man in his position – he had been in a bank until he came into that little bit of money – he felt that he had improved his mind to some purpose, and he knew that his collection of modern first editions would be worth money some day. He went over to the glass-fronted bookcase and pulled out a volume or two to show his visitor.

The man displayed intelligence, and presently joined him in front of the shelves.

'These, I take it, represent your personal tastes?' He took down a volume of Henry James and glanced at the fly-leaf. 'That your name? E. Pender?'

Pender admitted that it was. 'You have the advantage of me,' he added.

'Oh! I am one of the great Smith clan,' said the other with a laugh, 'and work for my bread. You seem to be very nicely fixed here.'

Pender explained about the clerkship and the legacy.

'Very nice, isn't it?' said Smith. 'Not married? No. You're one of the lucky ones. Not likely to be needing any sulphate of . . . any useful drugs in the near future. And you never will, if you stick to what you've got and keep off women and speculation.'

He smiled up sideways at Pender. Now that his hat was off, Pender saw that he had a quantity of closely curled grey hair, which made him look older than he had appeared in the railway carriage.

'No, I shan't be coming to you for assistance yet a while,' said Pender, laughing. 'Besides, how should I find you if I wanted you?'

'You wouldn't have to,' said Smith. '*I* should find *you*. There's never any difficulty about that.' He grinned, oddly. 'Well, I'd better be getting on. Thank you for your hospitality. I don't expect we shall meet again – but we may, of course. Things work out so queerly, don't they?'

When he had gone, Pender returned to his own armchair. He took up his glass of whisky, which stood there nearly full.

'Funny!' he said to himself. 'I don't remember pouring that out. I suppose I got interested and did it mechanically.' He emptied his glass slowly, thinking about Smith.

What in the world was Smith doing at Skimmings' house?

An odd business altogether. If Skimmings' housekeeper had known about that money . . . But she had not known, and if she had, how could she have found out about Smith and his sulphate of . . . the word had been on the tip of his tongue, then.

'You would not need to find me. *I* should find *you*.' What had the man meant by that? But this was ridiculous. Smith was not the devil, presumably. But if he really had this secret – if he liked to put a price upon it – nonsense.

'Business at Rugby – a little bit of business at Skimmings' house.' Oh, absurd!

'Nobody is fit to be trusted. *Absolute* power over another man's life . . . it grows on you. That is, I imagine it would.'

Lunacy! And, if there was anything in it, the man was mad to tell Pender about it. If Pender chose to speak he could get the fellow hanged. The very existence of Pender would be dangerous.

That whisky!

More and more, thinking it over, Pender became persuaded that he had never poured it out. Smith must have done it while his back was turned. Why that sudden display of interest in the bookshelves? It had had no connection with anything that had gone before. Now Pender came to think of it, it had been a very stiff whisky. Was it imagination, or had there been something about the flavour of it?

A cold sweat broke out on Pender's forehead.

A quarter of an hour later, after a powerful dose of mustard and water, Pender was downstairs again, very cold and shivering, huddling over the fire. He had had a narrow escape – if he had escaped. He did not know how the stuff worked, but he would not take a hot bath again for some days. One never knew.

Whether the mustard and water had done the trick in time, or whether the hot bath was an essential part of the treatment, at any rate Pender's life was saved for the time being. But he was still uneasy. He kept the front door on the chain and warned his servant to let no strangers into the house.

He ordered two more morning papers and the *News of the World* on Sundays, and kept a careful watch upon their columns. Deaths in baths became an obsession with him. He neglected his first editions and took to attending inquests.

Three weeks later he found himself at Lincoln. A man had died of heart failure in a Turkish bath – a fat man, of sedentary habits. They jury added a rider to their verdict of accidental death to the effect that the management should exercise a stricter supervision over the bathers and should never permit them to be left unattended in the hot room.

As Pender emerged from the hall he saw ahead of him a shabby hat that seemed familiar. He plunged after it, and caught Mr Smith about to step into a taxi.

'Smith,' he cried, gasping a little. He clutched him fiercely by the shoulder.

'What, you again?' said Smith. 'Taking notes of the case, eh? *Can I do anything for you?*'

'You devil!' said Pender. 'You're mixed up in this! You tried to kill me the other day.'

'Did I? Why should I do that?'

'You'll swing for this,' shouted Pender menacingly.

A policeman pushed his way through the gathering crowd.

'Here!' said he. 'What's all this about?'

Smith touched his forehead significantly.

'It's all right, Officer,' said he. 'The gentleman seems to think I'm here for no good. Here's my card. The coroner knows me. But he attacked me. You'd better keep an eye on him.'

'That's right,' said a bystander.

'This man tried to kill me,' said Pender.

The policeman nodded.

'Don't you worry about that, sir,' he said. 'You think better of it. The 'eat in there has upset you a bit. All right, *all* right.'

'But I want to charge him,' said Pender.

'I wouldn't do that if I was you,' said the policeman.

'I tell you,' said Pender, 'that this man Smith has been trying to poison me. He's a murderer. He's poisoned scores of people.'

The policeman winked at Smith.

'Best be off, sir,' he said. 'I'll settle this. Now, my lad' – he held Pender firmly by the arms – 'just you keep cool and take it quiet. That gentleman's name ain't Smith nor nothing like it. You've got a bit mixed up like.'

'Well, what is his name?' demanded Pender.

'Never mind,' replied the constable. 'You leave him alone, or you'll be getting yourself into trouble.'

The taxi had driven away. Pender glanced around at the circle of amused faces and gave in.

'All right, Officer,' he said. 'I won't give you any trouble. I'll come round with you to the police station and tell you about it.'

'What do you think o' that one?' asked the inspector of the sergeant when Pender had stumbled out of the station.

'Up the pole an' 'alfway round the flag, if you ask me,' replied his subordinate. 'Got one o' them ideez fix what they talk about.'

'H'm!' replied the inspector. 'Well, we've got his name and address. Better make a note of 'em. He might turn up again. Poisoning people so as they die in their baths, eh? That's a pretty good 'un. Wonderful how these barmy ones thinks it all out, isn't it?'

The spring that year was a bad one – cold and foggy. It was March when Pender went down to an inquest at Deptford, but a thick blanket of mist was hanging over the river as though it were November. The cold ate into your bones. As he sat in the dingy little court, peering through the yellow twilight of gas and fog, he could scarcely see the witnesses as they came to the table. Everybody in the place seemed to be coughing. Pender was coughing too. His bones ached, and he felt as though he were about due for a bout of influenza.

Straining his eyes, he thought he recognised a face on the other side of the room, but the smarting fog which penetrated every crack stung and blinded him. He felt in his overcoat pocket, and his hand closed comfortably on something thick and heavy. Ever since that day in Lincoln he had gone about armed for protection. Not a revolver – he was no hand with firearms. A sandbag was much better. He had bought one from an old man wheeling a pushcart. It was meant for keeping out drafts from the door – a good, old-fashioned affair.

The inevitable verdict was returned. The spectators began to push their way out. Pender had to hurry now, not to lose sight of his man. He elbowed his way along, muttering apologies. At the door he almost touched the man, but a stout woman intervened. He plunged past her, and she gave a little squeak of indignation. The man in front turned his head, and the light over the door glinted on his glasses.

Pender pulled his hat over his eyes and followed. His shoes had crêpe rubber soles and made no sound on the pavement. The man went on, jogging quietly up one street and down another, and never looking back. The fog was so thick that Pender was forced to keep within a few yards of him. Where was he going? Into the lighted streets? Home by bus or tram? No. He turned off to the left, down a narrow street.

The fog was thicker here. Pender could no longer see his quarry, but he heard the footsteps going on before him at the same even pace. It seemed to him that they were two alone in the world – pursued and pursuer, slayer and avenger. The street began to slope more rapidly. They must be coming out somewhere near the river.

Suddenly the dim shapes of the houses fell away on either side. There was an open space, with a lamp vaguely visible in the middle. The footsteps paused. Pender, silently hurrying after, saw the man standing close beneath the lamp, apparently consulting something in a notebook.

Four steps, and Pender was upon him. He drew the sandbag from his pocket.

The man looked up.

'I've got you this time,' said Pender, and struck with all his force.

Pender was quite right. He did get influenza. It was a week before he was out and about again. The weather had changed, and the air was fresh and sweet. In spite of the weakness left by the malady he felt as though a heavy weight had been lifted from his shoulders. He tottered down to a favourite bookshop of his in the Strand, and picked up a D. H. Lawrence 'first' at a price which he knew to be a bargain. Encouraged by this, he turned into a small chophouse chiefly frequently by newspaper men, and ordered a grilled cutlet and a half-tankard of bitter.

Two journalists were seated by the next table.

'Going to poor old Buckley's funeral?' asked one.

'Yes,' said the other. 'Poor devil! Fancy his getting bashed on the head like that. He must have been on his way down to interview the widow of that fellow who died in a bath. It's a rough district. Probably one of Jimmy the Card's crowd had it in for him. He was a great crime-reporter – they won't get another like Bill Buckley in a hurry.'

'He was a decent sort, too. Great old sport. No end of a practical joker. Remember his great stunt sulphate of thanatol?'

Pender started. *That* was the word that had eluded him for so many months. A curious dizziness came over him.

'. . . looking at you as sober as a judge,' the journalist was saying. 'No such stuff, of course, but he used to work off that wheeze on poor boobs in railway carriages to see how they'd take it. Would you believe that one chap actually offered him—'

'Hullo!' interrupted his friend. 'That bloke over there has fainted. I thought he was looking a bit white.'

Edgar Wallace

The Poetical Policeman

The day Mr Reeder arrived at the Public Prosecutor's office was indeed a day of fate for Mr Lambton Green, Branch Manager of the London Scottish and Midland Bank.

That branch of the bank which Mr Green controlled was situated at the corner of Pell Street and Firling Avenue on the 'country side' of Ealing. It is a fairly large building and, unlike most suburban branch offices, the whole of the premises were devoted to banking business, for the bank carried very heavy deposits, the Lunar Traction Company, with three thousand people on its pay-roll, the Associated Novelties Corporation, with its enormous turnover, and the Laraphone Company being only three of the L.S.M.'s customers.

On Wednesday afternoons, in preparation for the pay days of these corporations, large sums in currency were brought from the head office and deposited in the steel and concrete strong-room, which was immediately beneath Mr Green's private office, but admission to which was gained through a steel door in the general office. This door was observable from the street, and to assist observation there was a shaded lamp fixed to the wall immediately above, which threw a powerful beam of light upon the door. Further security was ensured by the employment of a night watchman, Arthur Malling, an army pensioner.

The bank lay on a restricted police beat which had been so arranged that the constable on patrol passed the bank every forty minutes. It was his practice to look through the window and exchange signals with the night watchman, his orders being to wait until Malling appeared.

On the night of October 17th Police-Constable Burnett stopped as usual before the wide peep-hole and glanced into the bank. The first thing he noticed was that the lamp above the strong-room door had been extinguished. The night watchman was not visible, and, his suspicions aroused, the officer did not wait for the man to put in an appearance as he would ordinarily have done, but passed the window to the door, which, to his alarm, he found ajar. Pushing it open, he entered the bank, calling Malling by name. There was no answer.

Permeating the air was a faint, sweet scent which he could not locate. The general offices were empty and, entering the manager's room in which a light burnt, he saw a figure stretched upon the ground. It was the night watchman. His wrists were handcuffed, two straps had been tightly buckled about his knees and ankles.

The explanation for the strange and sickly aroma was now clear. Above the head of the prostrate man was suspended, by a wire hooked to the picture-rail, an old tin can, the bottom of which was perforated so that there fell an incessant trickle of some volatile liquid upon the thick cotton pad which covered Malling's face.

Burnett, who had been wounded in the war, had instantly recognised the smell of chloroform and, dragging the unconscious man into the outer office, snatched the pad from his face and, leaving him only long enough to telephone to the police station, sought vainly to bring him to consciousness.

The police reserves arrived within a few minutes, and with them the divisional surgeon who, fortunately, had been at the station when the alarm came through. Every effort to restore the unfortunate man to life proved unavailing.

'He was probably dead when he was found,' was the police doctor's verdict. 'What those scratches are on his right palm is a mystery.'

He pulled open the clenched fist and showed half a dozen little scratches. They were recent, for there was a smear of blood on the palm.

Burnett was sent at once to arouse Mr Green, the manager, who lived in Firling Avenue, at the corner of which the bank stood; a street of semi-detached villas of a pattern familiar enough to the Londoner. As the officer walked through the little front garden to the door he saw a light through the panels, and he had hardly knocked before the door was opened and Mr Lambton Green appeared, fully dressed and, to the officer's discerning eye, in a state of considerable agitation. Constable Burnett saw on a hall chair a big bag, a travelling rug and an umbrella.

The little manager listened, pale as death, whilst Burnett told him of his discovery.

'The bank robbed? Impossible!' he almost shrieked. 'My God! this is awful!'

He was so near the point of collapse that Burnett had to assist him into the street.

'I – I was going away on a holiday,' he said incoherently, as he walked up the dark thoroughfare towards the bank premises. 'The fact is – I was leaving the bank. I left a note – explaining to the directors.'

Into a circle of suspicious men the manager tottered. He unlocked the drawer of his desk, looked and crumbled up.

'They're not here!' he said wildly. 'I left them here – my keys – with the note!'

And then he swooned. When the dazed man recovered he found himself in a police cell and, later in the day, he drooped before a police magistrate, supported by two constables and listened, like a man in a dream, to a charge of causing the death of Arthur Malling, and further, of converting to his own use the sum of £100,000.

It was on the morning of the first remand that Mr John G. Reeder, with some reluctance for he was suspicious of all Government departments, transferred himself from his own office on Lower Regent Street to a somewhat gloomy bureau on the top floor of the building which housed the Public Prosecutor. In making this change he advanced only one stipulation: that he should be connected by private telephone wire with his old bureau.

He did not demand this – he never demanded anything. He asked, nervously and apologetically. There was a certain wistful helplessness about John G. Reeder that made people feel sorry for him, that caused even the Public Prosecutor a few uneasy moments of doubt as to whether he had been quite wise in substituting this weak-appearing man of middle age for Inspector Holford – bluff, capable and heavily mysterious.

Mr Reeder was something over fifty, a long-faced gentleman with sandy-grey hair and a slither of side whiskers that mercifully distracted attention from his large outstanding ears. He wore half-way down his nose a pair of steel-rimmed pince-nez, through which nobody had ever seen him look – they were invariably removed when he was reading. A high and flat-crowned bowler hat matched and yet did not match a frock-coat tightly buttoned across his sparse chest. His boots were square-toed, his cravat – of the broad, chest-protector pattern – was ready-made and buckled into place behind a Gladstonian collar. The neatest appendage to Mr Reeder was an umbrella rolled so tightly that it might be mistaken for a frivolous walking cane. Rain or shine, he carried this article hooked to his arm, and within living memory it had never been unfurled.

Inspector Holford (promoted now to the responsibilities of Superintendent) met him in the office to hand over his duties, and a more tangible quantity in the shape of old furniture and fixings.

'Glad to know you, Mr. Reeder. I haven't had the pleasure of meeting you before, but I've heard a lot about you. You've been doing Bank of England work, haven't you?'

Mr Reeder whispered that he had had that honour, and sighed as though he regretted the drastic sweep of fate that had torn him from the obscurity of his labours. Mr Holford's scrutiny was full of misgivings.

'Well,' he said awkwardly, 'this job is different, though I'm told that you are one of the best informed men in London, and if that is the case this will be easy work. Still, we've never had an outsider – I mean, so to speak, a private detective – in this office before, and naturally the Yard is a bit—'

'I quite understand,' murmured Mr Reeder, hanging up his immaculate umbrella. 'It is very natural. Mr Boland expected the appointment. His wife is annoyed – very properly. But she has no reason to be. She is an ambitious woman. She has a third interest in a West End dancing club that might be raided one of these days.'

Holford was staggered. Here was news that was little more than a whispered rumour at Scotland Yard.

'How the devil do you know that?' he blurted.

Mr Reeder's smile was one of self-depreciation.

'One picks up odd scraps of information,' he said apologetically. 'I – I see wrong in everything. That is my curious perversion – I have a criminal mind!'

Holford drew a long breath.

'Well – there is nothing much doing. That Ealing case is pretty clear. Green is an ex-convict, who got a job at the bank during the war and worked up to manager. He has done seven years for conversion.'

'Embezzlement and conversion,' murmured Mr Reeder. 'I – er – I'm afraid I was the principal witness against him: bank crimes were rather – er – a hobby of mine. Yes, he got into difficulties with money-lenders. Very foolish – extremely foolish. And he doesn't admit his error.' Mr Reeder sighed heavily. 'Poor fellow! With his life at stake one may forgive and indeed condone his pitiful prevarications.'

The inspector stared at the new man in amazement.

'I don't know that there is much "poor fellow" about him. He has cached £100,000 and told the weakest yarn that I've ever read – you'll find copies of the police reports here, if you'd like to read them. The scratches on Malling's hand are curious – they've found several on the other hand. They are not deep enough to suggest a struggle. As to the yarn that Green tells—'

Mr J. G. Reeder nodded sadly.

'It was not an ingenious story,' he said, almost with regret. 'If I remember rightly, his story was something like this: he had been recognised by a man who served in Dartmoor with him, and this fellow wrote a blackmailing letter telling him to pay or clear out. Sooner than return to a life of crime, Green wrote out all the facts to his directors, put the letter in the drawer of his desk with his keys, and left a note for his head cashier on the desk itself, intending to leave London and try to make a fresh start where he was unknown.'

'There were no letters in or on the desk, and no keys,' said the inspector decisively. 'The only true part of the yarn was that he had done time.'

'Imprisonment,' suggested Mr Reeder plaintively. He had a horror of slang. 'Yes, that was true.'

Left alone in his office, he spent a very considerable time at his private telephone, communing with the young person who was still a young person, although the passage of time had dealt unkindly with her. For the rest of the morning he was reading the depositions which his predecessor had put on the desk.

It was late in the afternoon when the Public Prosecutor strolled into his room and glanced at the big pile of manuscript through which his subordinate was wading.

'What are you reading – the Green business?' he asked, with a note of satisfaction in his voice. 'I'm glad that is interesting you – though it seems a fairly straightforward case. I have had a letter from the president of the man's bank, who for some reason seems to think Green was telling the truth.'

Mr Reeder looked up with that pained expression of his which he invariably wore when he was puzzled.

'Here is the evidence of Policeman Burnett,' he said. 'Perhaps you can enlighten me, sir. Policeman Burnett stated in his evidence – let me read it:

' "Some time before I reached the bank premises I saw a man standing at the corner of the street, immediately outside the bank. I saw him distinctly in the light of a passing mail van. I did not attach any importance to his presence, and I did not see him again. It was possible for this man to have gone round the block and come to 120, Firling Avenue without being seen by me. Immediately after I saw him, my foot struck against a piece of iron on the sidewalk. I put my lamp on the object and found it was an old horse-shoe; I had seen children playing with this particular shoe earlier in the evening. When I looked again towards the corner, the man had disappeared. He would have seen the light of my lamp. I saw no other person, and so far as I can remember, there was no light showing in Green's house when I passed it." '

Mr Reeder looked up.

'Well?' said the Prosecutor. 'There's nothing remarkable about that. It was probably Green who dodged round the block and came in at the back of the constable.'

Mr Reeder scratched his chin.

'Yes,' he said thoughtfully, 'ye-es.' He shifted uncomfortably in his chair. 'Would it be considered indecorous if I made a few inquiries, independent of the police?' he asked nervously. 'I should not like them to think that a mere dilettante was interfering with their lawful functions.'

'By all means,' said the Prosecutor heartily. 'Go down and see the officer in charge of the case: I'll give you a note to him – it is by no means unusual for my officer to conduct a separate investigation, though I am afraid you will discover very little. The ground has been well covered by Scotland Yard.'

'It would be permissible to see the man?' hesitated Reeder.

'Green? Why, of course! I will send you up the necessary order.'

The light was fading from a grey, blustering sky, and rain was falling fitfully, when Mr Reeder, with his furled umbrella hooked to his arm, his coat collar turned up, stepped through the dark gateway of Brixton Prison and was led to the cell where a distracted man sat, his head upon his hands, his pale eyes gazing into vacancy.

'It's true; it's true! Every word.' Green almost sobbed the words.

A pallid man, inclined to be bald, with a limp yellow moustache, going grey. Reeder, with his extraordinary memory for faces, recognised him the moment he saw him, though it was some time before the recognition was mutual.

'Yes, Mr Reeder, I remember you now. You were the gentleman who caught me before. But I've been as straight as a die. I've never taken a farthing that didn't belong to me. What my poor girl will think—'

'Are you married?' asked Mr Reeder sympathetically.

'No, but I was going to be – rather late in life. She's nearly thirty years younger than me, and the best girl that ever—'

Reeder listened to the rhapsody that followed, the melancholy deepening in his face.

'She hasn't been into the court, thank God, but she knows the truth. A friend of mine told me that she has been absolutely knocked out.'

'Poor soul!' Mr Reeder shook his head.

'It happened on her birthday, too,' the man went on bitterly.

'Did she know you were going away?'

'Yes, I told her the night before. I'm not going to bring her into the case. If we'd been properly engaged it would be different; but she's married and is divorcing her husband, but the decree hasn't been made absolute yet. That's why I never went about with her or saw much of her. And of course, nobody knew about our engagement, although we lived in the same street.'

'Firling Avenue?' asked Reeder, and the bank manager nodded despondently.

'She was married when she was seventeen to a brute. It was pretty galling for me, having to keep quiet about it – I mean, for nobody to know about our engagement. All sorts of rotten people were making up to her, and I had just to grind my teeth and say nothing. Impossible people! Why, that fool Burnett, who arrested me, he was sweet on her; used to write her poetry – you wouldn't think it possible in a policeman, would you?'

The outrageous incongruity of a poetical policeman did not seem to shock the detective.

'There is poetry in every soul, Mr Green,' he said gently, 'and a policeman is a man.'

Though he dismissed the eccentricity of the constable so lightly, the poetical policeman filled his mind all the way home to his house in the Brockley Road, and occupied his thoughts for the rest of his waking time.

It was a quarter to eight o'clock in the morning, and the world seemed entirely populated by milkmen and whistling newspaper boys, when Mr J. G. Reeder came into Firling Avenue.

He stopped only for a second outside the bank, which had long since ceased to be an object of local awe and fearfulness, and pursued his way down the broad avenue. On either side of the thoroughfare ran a row of pretty villas – pretty although they bore a strong family resemblance to one another; each house with its little forecourt, sometimes laid out simply as a grass plot, sometimes decorated with flower-beds. Green's house was the eighteenth in the road on the right-hand side. Here he had lived with a cook-housekeeper, and apparently gardening was not his hobby, for the forecourt was covered with grass that had been allowed to grow at its will.

Before the twenty-sixth house in the road Mr Reeder paused and gazed with mild interest at the blue blinds which covered every window. Evidently Miss Magda Grayne was a lover of flowers, for geraniums filled the window-boxes and were set at intervals along the tiny border under the bow window. In the centre of the grass plot was a circular flower-bed with one flowerless rose tree, the leaves of which were drooping and brown.

As he raised his eyes to the upper window, the blind went up slowly, and he was dimly conscious that there was a figure behind the white lace curtains. Mr Reeder walked hurriedly away, as one caught in an immodest act, and resumed his peregrinations until he came to the big nursery gardener's which formed the corner lot at the far end of the road.

Here he stood for some time in contemplation, his arm resting on the iron railings, his eyes staring blankly at the vista of greenhouses. He remained in this attitude so long that one of the nurserymen, not un-naturally thinking that a stranger was seeking a way into the gardens, came over with the laborious gait of the man who wrings his living from the soil, and asked if he was wanting anybody.

'Several people,' sighed Mr Reeder; 'several people!'

Leaving the resentful man to puzzle out his impertinence, he slowly retraced his steps. At No. 412 he stopped again, opened the little iron gate and passed up the path to the front door. A small girl answered his knock and ushered him into the parlour.

The room was not well furnished; it was scarcely furnished at all. A strip of almost new linoleum covered the passage; the furniture of the parlour itself was made up of wicker chairs, a square of art carpet and a table. He heard the sound of feet above his head, feet on bare boards, and then presently the door opened and a girl came in.

She was pretty in a heavy way, but on her face he saw the marks of sorrow. It was pale and haggard; the eyes looked as though she had been recently weeping.

'Miss Magda Grayne?' he asked, rising as she came in.

She nodded.

'Are you from the police?' she asked quickly.

'Not exactly the police,' he corrected carefully. 'I hold an – er – an appointment in the office of the Public Prosecutor, which is analogous to, but distinct from, a position in the Metropolitan Police Force.'

She frowned, and then:

'I wondered if anybody would come to see me,' she said. 'Mr Green sent you?'

'Mr Green told me of your existence: he did not send me.'

There came to her face in that second a look which almost startled him. Only for a fleeting space of time, the expression had dawned and passed almost before the untrained eye could detect its passage.

'I was expecting somebody to come,' she said. Then: 'What made him do it?' she asked.

'You think he is guilty?'

'The police think so.' She drew a long sigh. 'I wish to God I had never seen – this place!'

He did not answer; his eyes were roving round the apartment. On a bamboo table was an old vase which had been clumsily filled with golden chrysanthemums, of a peculiarly beautiful variety. Not all, for amidst them flowered a large Michaelmas daisy that had the forlorn appearance of a parvenu that had strayed by mistake into noble company.

'You're fond of flowers?' he murmured.

She looked at the vase indifferently.

'Yes, I like flowers,' she said. 'The girl put them in there.' Then: 'Do you think they will hang him?'

The brutality of the question, put without hesitation, pained Reeder.

'It is a very serious charge,' he said. And then: 'Have you a photograph of Mr Green?'

She frowned.

'Yes; do you want it?'

He nodded.

She had hardly left the room before he was at the bamboo table and had lifted out the flowers. As he had seen through the glass, they were roughly tied with a piece of string. He examined the ends, and here again his first observation had been correct: none of these flowers had been cut; they had been plucked bodily from their stalks. Beneath the string was the paper which had been first wrapped about the stalks. It was a page torn from a notebook; he could see the red lines, but the pencilled writing was indecipherable.

As her foot sounded on the stairs, he replaced the flowers in the vase, and when she came in he was looking through the window into the street.

'Thank you,' he said, as he took the photograph from her.

It bore an affectionate inscription on the back.

'You're married, he tells me, madam?'

'Yes, I am married, and practically divorced,' she said shortly.

'Have you been living here long?'

'About three months,' she answered. 'It was his wish that I should live here.'

He looked at the photograph again.

'Do you know Constable Burnett?'

He saw a dull flush come to her face and die away again.

'Yes, I know the sloppy fool!' she said viciously. And then, realising that she had been surprised into an expression which was not altogether ladylike, she went on, in a softer tone: 'Mr Burnett is rather sentimental, and I don't like sentimental people, especially – well, you understand, Mr—'

'Reeder,' murmured that gentleman.

'You understand, Mr Reeder, that when a girl is engaged and in my position, those kind of attentions are not very welcome.'

Reeder was looking at her keenly. Of her sorrow and distress there could be no doubt. On the subject of the human emotions, and the ravages they make upon the human countenance, Mr Reeder was almost as great an authority as Mantegazza.

'On your birthday,' he said. 'How very sad! You were born on the seventeenth of October. You are English, of course?'

'Yes, I'm English,' she said shortly. 'I was born in Walworth – in Wallington. I once lived in Walworth.'

'How old are you?'

247

'Twenty-three,' she answered.

Mr Reeder took off his glasses and polished them on a large silk handkerchief.

'The whole thing is inexpressibly sad,' he said. 'I am glad to have had the opportunity of speaking with you, young lady. I sympathise with you very deeply.'

And in this unsatisfactory way he took his departure.

She closed the door on him, saw him stop in the middle of the path and pick up something from a border bed, and wondered, frowning, why this middle-aged man had picked up the horseshoe she had thrown through the window the night before. Into Mr Reeder's tail pocket went this piece of rusted steel and then he continued his thoughtful way to the nursery gardens, for he had a few questions to ask.

The men of Section 10 were parading for duty when Mr Reeder came timidly into the charge room and produced his credentials to the inspector in charge.

'Oh, yes, Mr Reeder,' said that officer affably. 'We have had a note from the P.P.'s office, and I think I had the pleasure of working with you on that big slush* case a few years ago. Now what can I do for you? . . . Burnett? Yes, he's here.'

He called the man's name and a young and good-looking officer stepped from the ranks.

'He's the man who discovered the murder – he's marked for promotion,' said the inspector. 'Burnett, this gentleman is from the Public Prosecutor's office and he wants a little talk with you. Better use my office, Mr Reeder.'

The young policeman saluted and followed the shuffling figure into the privacy of the inspector's office. He was a confident young man: already his name and portrait had appeared in the newspapers, the hint of promotion had become almost an accomplished fact, and before his eyes was the prospect of a supreme achievement.

'They tell me that you are something of a poet, officer,' said Mr Reeder.

Burnett blushed.

'Why, yes, sir. I write a bit,' he confessed.

'Love poems, yes?' asked the other gently. 'One finds time in the night – er – for such fancies. And there is no inspiration like – er – love, officer.'

Burnett's face was crimson.

'I've done a bit of writing in the night, sir,' he said, 'though I've never neglected my duty.'

*Slush = forged Bank of England Notes

'Naturally,' murmured Mr Reeder. 'You have a poetical mind. It was a poetical thought to pluck flowers in the middle of the night—'

'The nurseryman told me I could take any flowers I wanted,' Burnett interrupted hastily. 'I did nothing wrong.'

Reeder inclined his head in agreement.

'That I know. You picked the flowers in the dark – by the way, you inadvertently included a Michaelmas daisy with your chrysanthemums – tied up your little poem to them and left them on the doorstep with – er – a horseshoe. I wondered what had become of that horseshoe.'

'I threw them up on to her – to the lady's window-sill,' corrected the uncomfortable young man. 'As a matter of fact, the idea didn't occur to me until I had passed the house—'

Mr Reeder's face was thrust forward.

'This is what I want to confirm,' he said softly. 'The idea of leaving the flowers did not occur to you until you had passed her house? The horseshoe suggested the thought? Then you went back, picked the flowers, tied them up with the little poem you had already written, and tossed them up to her window – we need not mention the lady's name.'

Constable Burnett's face was a study.

'I don't know how you guessed that, but it is a fact. If I've done anything wrong—'

'It is never wrong to be in love,' said Mr J. G. Reeder soberly. 'Love is a very beautiful experience – I have frequently read about it.'

Miss Magda Grayne had dressed to go out for the afternoon and was putting on her hat, when saw saw the queer man who had called so early that morning, walking up the tessellated path. Behind him she recognised a detective engaged in the case. The servant was out; nobody could be admitted except by herself. She walked quickly behind the dressing-table into the bay of the window and glanced up and down the road. Yes, there was a taxicab which usually accompanies such visitations, and, standing by the driver, another man, obviously a 'busy.'

She pulled up the overlay of her bed, took out the flat pad of bank-notes that she found, and thrust them into her handbag, then, stepping on tiptoe, she went out to the landing, into the unfurnished back room, and, opening the window, dropped to the flat roof of the kitchen. In another minute she was in the garden and through the back gate. A narrow passage divided the two lines of villas that backed on one another. She was in High Street and had boarded a car before Mr Reeder grew tired of knocking. To the best of his knowledge Mr Reeder never saw her again.

II

At the Public Prosecutor's request, he called at his chief's house after dinner and told his surprising story.

'Green, who had the unusual experience of being promoted to his position over the heads of his seniors, for special services he rendered during the war, was undoubtedly an ex-convict, and he spoke the truth when he said that he had received a letter from a man who had served a period of imprisonment with him. The name of his blackmailer is, or rather was, Arthur George Crater, whose other name was Malling!'

'Not the night watchman?' said the Public Prosecutor, in amazement. Mr Reeder nodded.

'Yes, sir, it was Arthur Malling. His daughter, Miss Magda Crater, was, as she very truly said, born at Walworth on the 17th of October, 1900. She said Wallington after, but Walworth first. One observes that when people adopt false family names, they seldom change their given names, and the "Magda" was easy to identify.

'Evidently Malling had planned this robbery of the bank very carefully. He had brought his daughter, in a false name, to Ealing, and had managed to get her introduced to Mr Green. Magda's job was to worm her way into Green's confidence and learn all that she could. Possibly it was part of her duty to secure casts of the keys. Whether Malling recognised in the manager an old prison acquaintance, or whether he obtained the facts from the girl, we shall never know. But when the information came to him, he saw, in all probability, an opportunity of robbing the bank and of throwing suspicion upon the manager.

'The girl's rôle was that of a woman who was to be divorced, and I must confess this puzzled me until I realised that in no circumstances would Malling wish his daughter's name to be associated with the bank manager.

'The night of the seventeenth was chosen for the raid. Malling's plan to get rid of the manager had succeeded. He saw the letter on the table in Green's private office, read it, secured the keys – although he had in all probability a duplicate set – and at a favourable moment cleared as much portable money from the bank vaults as he could carry, hurried them round to the house in Firling Avenue, where they were buried in the central bed of the front garden, under a rose bush – I rather imagined there was something interfering with the nutrition of that unfortunate bush the first time I saw it. I can only hope that the tree is not altogether dead, and I have given instructions that it shall be replanted and well fertilised.'

'Yes, yes,' said the Prosecutor, who was not at all interested in horticulture.

'In planting the tree, as he did in some haste, Malling scratched his hand. Roses have thorns – I went to Ealing to find the rose bush that had scratched his hand. Hurrying back to the bank, he waited, knowing that Constable Burnett was due at a certain time. He had prepared the can of chloroform, the handcuffs and straps were waiting for him, and he stood at the corner of the street until he saw the flash of Burnett's lamp; then, running into the bank and leaving the door ajar, he strapped himself, fastened the handcuffs and lay down, expecting that the policeman would arrive, find the open door and rescue him before much harm was done.

'But Constable Burnett had had some pleasant exchanges with the daughter. Doubtless she had received instructions from her father to be as pleasant to him as possible. Burnett was a poetical young man, knew it was her birthday, and as he walked along the street his foot struck an old horseshoe and the idea occurred to him that he should return, attach the horseshoe to some flowers, which the nurseryman had given him permission to pick, and leave his little bouquet, so to speak, at his lady's feet – a poetical idea, and one worthy of the finest traditions of the Metropolitan Police Force. This he did, but it took some time; and all the while this young man was philandering – Arthur Crater was dying!

'In a few seconds after lying down he must have passed from consciousness . . . the chloroform still dripped, and when the policeman eventually reached the bank, ten minutes after he was due, the man was dead!'

The Public Prosecutor sat back in his padded chair and frowned at his new subordinate.

'How on earth did you piece together all this?' he asked in wonder.

Mr Reeder shook his head sadly.

'I have that perversion,' he said. 'It is a terrible misfortune, but it is true. I see evil in everything . . . in dying rose bushes, in horseshoes – in poetry even. I have the mind of a criminal. It is deplorable!'

Agatha Christie

S.O.S.

I

'Ah!' said Mr Dinsmead appreciatively.

He stepped back and surveyed the round table with approval. The firelight gleamed on the coarse white tablecloth, the knives and forks, and the other table appointments.

'Is – is everything ready?' asked Mrs Dinsmead hesitatingly. She was a little faded woman, with a colourless face, meagre hair scraped back from her forehead, and a perpetually nervous manner.

'Everything's ready,' said her husband with a kind of ferocious geniality.

He was a big man, with stooping shoulders, and a broad red face. He had little pig's eyes that twinkled under his bushy brows, and a big jowl devoid of hair.

'Lemonade?' suggested Mrs Dinsmead, almost in a whisper.

Her husband shook his head.

'Tea. Much better in every way. Look at the weather, streaming and blowing. A nice cup of hot tea is what's needed for supper on an evening like this.'

He winked facetiously, then fell to surveying the table again.

'A good dish of eggs, cold corned beef, and bread and cheese. That's my order for supper. So come along and get it ready, mother. Charlotte's in the kitchen waiting to give you a hand.'

Mrs Dinsmead rose, carefully winding up the ball of her knitting.

'She's grown a very good-looking girl,' she murmured. 'Sweetly pretty, I say.'

'Ah!' said Mr Dinsmead. 'The mortal image of her Ma! So go along with you, and don't let's waste any more time.'

He strolled about the room humming to himself for a minute or two. Once he approached the window and looked out.

'Wild weather,' he murmured to himself. 'Not much likelihood of our having visitors to-night.'

Then he too left the room.

About ten minutes later Mrs Dinsmead entered bearing a dish of fried eggs. Her two daughters followed, bringing in the rest of the provisions. Mr Dinsmead and his son Johnnie brought up the rear. The former seated himself at the head of the table.

'And for what we are to receive, etcetera,' he remarked humorously. 'And blessings on the man who first thought of tinned foods. What would we do, I should like to know, miles from anywhere, if we hadn't a tin now and then to fall back upon when the butcher forgets his weekly call?'

He proceeded to carve corned beef dexterously.

'I wonder who ever thought of building a house like this, miles from anywhere,' said his daughter Magdalen pettishly. 'We never see a soul.'

'No,' said her father. 'Never a soul.'

'I can't think what made you take it, father,' said Charlotte.

'Can't you, my girl? Well, I had my reasons – I had my reasons.'

His eyes sought his wife's furtively, but she frowned.

'And haunted too,' said Charlotte. 'I wouldn't sleep alone here for anything.'

'Pack of nonsense,' said her father. 'Never seen anything, have you? Come now.'

'Not *seen* anything perhaps, but—'

'But what?'

Charlotte did not reply, but she shivered a little. A great surge of rain came driving against the window-pane, and Mrs Dinsmead dropped a spoon with a tinkle on the tray.

'Not nervous, are you, mother?' said Mr Dinsmead. 'It's a wild night, that's all. Don't you worry, we're safe here by our fireside, and not a soul from outside likely to disturb us. Why, it would be a miracle if anyone did. And miracles don't happen. No,' he added as though to himself, with a kind of peculiar satisfaction. 'Miracles don't happen.'

As the words left his lips there came a sudden knocking at the door. Mr Dinsmead stayed as though petrified.

'Whatever's that?' he muttered. His jaw fell.

Mrs Dinsmead gave a little whimpering cry and pulled her shawl up round her. The colour came into Magdalen's face and she leant forward and spoke to her father.

'The miracle has happened,' she said. 'You'd better go and let whoever it is in.'

II

Twenty minutes earlier Mortimer Cleveland had stood in the driving rain and mist surveying his car. It was really cursed bad luck. Two punctures within ten minutes of each other, and here he was, stranded, miles from anywhere, in the midst of these bare Wiltshire downs with night coming on, and no prospect of shelter. Serve him right for trying to take a short-cut. If only he had stuck to the main road! Now he was lost on what seemed a mere cart-track on the hillside, with no possibility of getting the car further, and with no idea if there were even a village anywhere near.

He looked round him perplexedly, and his eye was caught by a gleam of light on the hillside above him. A second later the mist obscured it once more, but, waiting patiently, he presently got a second glimpse of it. After a moment's cogitation, he left the car and struck up the side of the hill.

Soon he was out of the mist, and he recognised the light as shining from the lighted window of a small cottage. Here, at any rate, was shelter. Mortimer Cleveland quickened his pace, bending his head to meet the furious onslaught of wind and rain which seemed to be trying its best to drive him back.

Cleveland was in his own way something of a celebrity though doubtless the majority of folks would have displayed complete ignorance of his name and achievements. He was an authority on mental science and had written two excellent text books on the subconscious. He was also a member of the Psychical Research Society and a student of the occult in so far as it affected his own conclusions and line of research.

He was by nature peculiarly susceptible to atmosphere, and by deliberate training he had increased his own natural gift. When he had at last reached the cottage and rapped at the door, he was conscious of an excitement, a quickening of interest, as though all his faculties had suddenly been sharpened.

The murmur of voices within had been plainly audible to him. Upon his knock there came a sudden silence, then the sound of a chair being pushed back along the floor. In another minute the door was flung open by a boy of about fifteen. Cleveland could look straight over his shoulder upon the scene within.

It reminded him of an interior by some Dutch Master. A round table spread for a meal, a family party sitting round it, one or two flickering candles and the firelight's glow over all. The father, a big man, sat one side of the table, a little grey woman with a frightened face sat opposite him. Facing the door, looking straight at Cleveland, was a girl. Her startled eyes looked straight into his, her hand with a cup in it was arrested half-way to her lips.

She was, Cleveland saw at once, a beautiful girl of an extremely uncommon type. Her hair, red gold, stood out round her face like a mist, her eyes, very far apart, were a pure grey. She had the mouth and chin of an early Italian Madonna.

There was a moment's dead silence. Then Cleveland stepped into the room and explained his predicament. He brought his trite story to a close, and there was another pause harder to understand. At last, as though with an effort, the father rose.

'Come in, sir – Mr Cleveland, did you say?'

'That is my name,' said Mortimer, smiling.

'Ah! yes. Come in, Mr Cleveland. Not weather for a dog outside, is it? Come in by the fire. Shut the door, can't you, Johnnie? Don't stand there half the night.'

Cleveland came forward and sat on a wooden stool by the fire. The boy Johnnie shut the door.

'Dinsmead, that's my name,' said the other man. He was all geniality now. 'This is the Missus, and these are my two daughters, Charlotte and Magdalen.'

For the first time, Cleveland saw the face of the girl who had been sitting with her back to him, and saw that, in a totally different way, she was quite as beautiful as her sister. Very dark, with a face of marble pallor, a delicate aquiline nose, and a grave mouth. It was a kind of frozen beauty, austere and almost forbidding. She acknowledged her father's introduction by bending her head, and she looked at him with an intent gaze that was searching in character. It was as though she were summing him up, weighing him in the balance of her clear young judgment.

'A drop of something to drink, eh, Mr Cleveland?'

'Thank you,' said Mortimer. 'A cup of tea will meet the case admirably.'

Mr Dinsmead hesitated a minute, then he picked up the five cups, one after another, from the table and emptied them into the slop bowl.

'This tea's cold,' he said brusquely. 'Make us some more, will you, Mother?'

Mrs Dinsmead got up quickly and hurried off with the teapot. Mortimer had an idea that she was glad to get out of the room.

The fresh tea soon came, and the unexpected guest was plied with viands.

Mr Dinsmead talked and talked. He was expansive, genial, loquacious. He told the stranger all about himself. He'd lately retired from the building trade – yes, made quite a good thing out of it. He and the Missus thought they'd like a bit of country air – never lived in the country before. Wrong time of year to choose, of course, October and November, but they didn't want to wait. 'Life's uncertain, you know, sir.' So they had taken this cottage. Eight miles from anywhere, and nineteen miles from anything you could call a town. No, they didn't complain. The girls found it a bit dull, but he and mother enjoyed the quiet.

So he talked on, leaving Mortimer almost hypnotised by the easy flow. Nothing here, surely, but rather commonplace domesticity. And yet, at that first glimpse of the interior, he had diagnosed something else, some tension, some strain, emanating from one of those four people – he didn't know which. Mere foolishness, his nerves were all awry! They were startled by his sudden appearance – that was all.

He broached the question of a night's lodging, and was met with a ready response.

'You'll have to stop with us, Mr Cleveland. Nothing else for miles round. We can give you a bedroom, and though my pyjamas may be a bit roomy, why, they're better than nothing, and your own clothes will be dry by morning.'

'It's very good of you.'

'Not at all,' said the other genially. 'As I said just now, one couldn't turn away a dog on a night like this. Magdalen, Charlotte, go up and see to the room.'

The two girls left the room. Presently Mortimer heard them moving about overhead.

'I can quite understand that two attractive young ladies like your daughters might find it dull here,' said Cleveland.

'Good lookers, aren't they?' said Mr Dinsmead with fatherly pride, 'Not much like their mother or myself. We're a homely pair, but much attached to each other, I'll tell you that, Mr Cleveland. Eh, Maggie, isn't that so?'

Mrs Dinsmead smiled primly. She had started knitting again. The needles clicked busily. She was a fast knitter.

Presently the room was announced ready, and Mortimer, expressing thanks once more, declared his intention of turning in.

'Did you put a hot water-bottle in the bed?' demanded Mrs Dinsmead, suddenly mindful of her house pride.

'Yes, Mother, two.'

'That's right,' said Dinsmead. 'Go up with him, girls, and see that there's nothing else he wants.'

Magdalen preceded him up the staircase, her candle held aloft. Charlotte came behind.

The room was quite a pleasant one, small and with a sloping roof, but the bed looked comfortable, and the few pieces of somewhat dusty furniture were of old mahogany. A large can of hot water stood in the basin, a pair of pink pyjamas of ample proportions were laid over a chair, and the bed was made and turned down.

Magdalen went over to the window and saw that the fastenings were secure. Charlotte cast a final eye over the washstand appointments. Then they both lingered by the door.

'Good-night, Mr Cleveland. You are sure there is everything?'

'Yes, thank you, Miss Magdalen. I am ashamed to have given you both so much trouble. Good-night.'

'Good-night.'

They went out, shutting the door behind them. Mortimer Cleveland was alone. He undressed slowly and thoughtfully. When he had donned Mr Dinsmead's pink pyjamas, he gathered up his own wet clothes and put them outside the door as his host had bade him. From downstairs he could hear the rumble of Dinsmead's voice.

What a talker the man was! Altogether an odd personality – but indeed there was something odd about the whole family, or was it his imagination?

He went slowly back into his room and shut the door. He stood by the bed lost in thought. And then he started—

The mahogany table by the bed was smothered in dust. Written in the dust were three letters, clearly visible. *S.O.S.*

Mortimer stared as if he could hardly believe his eyes. It was a confirmation of all his vague surmises and forebodings. He was right, then. Something was wrong in this house.

S.O.S. A call for help. But whose finger had written it in the dust? Magdalen's or Charlotte's? They had both stood there, he remembered, for a moment or two, before going out of the room. Whose hand had secretly dropped to the table and traced out those three letters?

The faces of the two girls came up before him. Magdalen's, dark and aloof, and Charlotte's, as he had seen it first, wide-eyed, startled, with an unfathomable something in her glance. . . .

He went again to the door and opened it. The boom of Mr Dinsmead's voice was no longer to be heard. The house was silent.

He thought to himself.

'I can do nothing to-night. To-morrow – well, we shall see.'

III

Cleveland woke early. He went down through the living-room, and out into the garden. The morning was fresh and beautiful after the rain. Someone else was up early, too. At the bottom of the garden, Charlotte was leaning on the fence staring out over the Downs. His pulses quickened a little as he went down to join her. All along he had been secretly convinced that it was Charlotte who had written the message. As he came up to her, she turned and wished him 'Good-morning.' Her eyes were direct and childlike, with no hint of a secret understanding in them.

'A very good morning,' said Mortimer, smiling. 'The weather this morning is a contrast to last night.'

'It is indeed.'

Mortimer broke off a twig from a tree near by. With it he began idly to draw on the smooth, sandy patch at his feet. He traced an S, then an O, then an S, watching the girl narrowly as he did so. But again he could detect no gleam of comprehension.

'Do you know what these letters represent?' he said abruptly.

Charlotte frowned a little. 'Aren't they what boats – liners, send out when they are in distress?' she asked.

Mortimer nodded. 'Someone wrote that on the table by my bed last night,' he said quietly. 'I thought perhaps *you* might have done so.'

She looked at him in wide-eyed astonishment.

'I? Oh, no.'

He was wrong then. A sharp pang of disappointment shot through him. He had been so sure – so sure. It was not often that his intuitions led him astray.

'You are quite certain?' he persisted.

'Oh, yes.'

They turned and went slowly together toward the house. Charlotte seemed preoccupied about something. She replied at random to the few observations he made. Suddenly she burst out in a low, hurried voice:

'It – it's odd your asking that about those letters, S.O.S. I didn't write them, of course, but – I so easily might have done.'

He stopped and looked at her, and she went on quickly:

'It sounds silly, I know, but I have been so frightened, so dreadfully frightened, and when you came in last night, it seemed like an – an answer to something.'

'What are you frightened of?' he asked quickly.

'I don't know.'

'You don't know.'

'I think – it's the house. Ever since we came here it has been growing and growing. Everyone seems different somehow. Father, Mother, and Magdalen, they all seem different.'

Mortimer did not speak at once, and before he could do so, Charlotte went on again.

'You know this house is supposed to be haunted?'

'What?' All his interest was quickened.

'Yes, a man murdered his wife in it, oh, some years ago now. We only found out about it after we got here. Father says ghosts are all nonsense, but I – don't know.'

Mortimer was thinking rapidly.

'Tell me,' he said in a businesslike tone, 'was this murder committed in the room I had last night?'

'I don't know anything about that,' said Charlotte.

'I wonder now,' said Mortimer half to himself, 'yes, that may be it.'

Charlotte looked at him uncomprehendingly.

'Miss Dinsmead,' said Mortimer, gently, 'have you ever had any reason to believe that you are mediumistic?'

She stared at him.

'I think you know that you *did* write S.O.S. last night,' he said quietly. 'Oh! quite unconsciously, of course. A crime stains the atmosphere, so to speak. A sensitive mind such as yours might be acted upon in such a manner. You have been reproducing the sensations and impressions of the victim. Many years ago *she* may have written S.O.S. on that table and you unconsciously reproduced her act last night.'

Charlotte's face brightened.

'I see,' she said. 'You think that is the explanation?'

A voice called her from the house, and she went in, leaving Mortimer to pace up and down the garden paths. Was he satisfied with his own explanation? Did it cover the facts as he knew them? Did it account for the tension he had felt on entering the house last night?

Perhaps, and yet he still had the odd feeling that his sudden appearance had produced something very like consternation, he thought to himself:

'I must not be carried away by the psychic explanation, it might account for Charlotte – but not for the others. My coming as I did upset them horribly, all except Johnnie. Whatever it is that's the matter, Johnnie is out of it.'

He was quite sure of that, strange that he should be so positive, but there it was.

At that minute, Johnnie himself came out of the cottage and approached the guest.

'Breakfast's ready,' he said awkwardly. 'Will you come in?'

Mortimer noticed that the lad's fingers were much stained. Johnnie felt his glance and laughed ruefully.

'I'm always messing about with chemicals, you know,' he said. 'It makes Dad awfully wild sometimes. He wants me to go into the building, but I want to do chemistry and research work.'

Mr Dinsmead appeared at the window ahead of them, broad, jovial, smiling, and at sight of him all Mortimer's distrust and antagonism re-awakened. Mrs Dinsmead was already seated at the table. She wished him 'Good-morning' in her colourless voice, and he had again the impression that for some reason or other, she was afraid of him.

Magdalen came in last. She gave him a brief nod and took her seat opposite him.

'Did you sleep well?' she asked abruptly. 'Was your bed comfortable?'

She looked at him very earnestly, and when he replied courteously in the affirmative he noticed something very like a flicker of disappointment pass over her face. What had she expected him to say, he wondered?

He turned to his host.

'This lad of yours is interested in chemistry, it seems!' he said pleasantly.

There was a crash. Mrs Dinsmead had dropped her tea cup.

'Now then, Maggie, now then,' said her husband.

It seemed to Mortimer that there was admonition, warning, in his voice. He turned to his guest and spoke fluently of the advantages of the building trade, and of not letting young boys get above themselves.

After breakfast, he went out in the garden by himself, and smoked. The time was clearly at hand when he must leave the cottage. A night's shelter was one thing, to prolong it was difficult without an excuse, and what possible excuse could he offer? And yet he was singularly loath to depart.

Turning the thing over and over in his mind, he took a path that led round the other side of the house. His shoes were soled with crêpe rubber, and made little or no noise. He was passing the kitchen window, when he heard Dinsmead's words from within, and the words attracted his attention immediately.

'It's a fair lump of money, it is.'

Mrs Dinsmead's voice answered. It was too faint in tone for Mortimer to hear the words, but Dinsmead replied:

'Nigh on £60,000, the lawyer said.'

Mortimer had no intention of eavesdropping, but he retraced his steps very thoughtfully. The mention of money seemed to crystallise the situation. Somewhere or other there was a question of £60,000 – it made the thing clearer – and uglier.

Magdalen came out of the house, but her father's voice called her almost immediately, and she went in again. Presently Dinsmead himself joined his guest.

'Rare good morning,' he said genially.

'I hope your car will be none the worse.'

'Wants to find out when I'm going,' thought Mortimer to himself. Aloud he thanked Mr Dinsmead once more for his timely hospitality.

'Not at all, not at all,' said the other.

Magdalen and Charlotte came together out of the house, and strolled arm in arm to a rustic seat some little distance away. The dark head and the golden one made a pleasant contrast together, and on an impulse Mortimer said:

'Your daughters are very unlike, Mr Dinsmead.'

The other who was just lighting his pipe gave a sharp jerk of the wrist, and dropped the match.

'Do you think so?' he asked. 'Yes, well, I suppose they are.'

Mortimer had a flash of intuition.

'But of course they are not both your daughters,' he said smoothly.

He saw Dinsmead look at him, hesitate for a moment, and then make up his mind.

'That's very clever of you, sir,' he said. 'No, one of them is a foundling, we took her in as a baby and we have brought her up as our own. She herself has not the least idea of the truth, but she'll have to know soon.' He sighed.

'A question of inheritance?' suggested Mortimer quietly.

The other flashed a suspicious look at him.

Then he seemed to decide that frankness was best; his manner became almost aggressively frank and open.

'It's odd that you should say that, sir.'

'A case of telepathy, eh?' said Mortimer, and smiled.

'It is like this, sir. We took her in to oblige the mother – for a consideration, as at the time I was just starting in the building trade. A few months ago I noticed an advertisement in the papers, and it seemed to me that the child in question must be our Magdalen. I went to see the lawyers, and there has been a lot of talk one way and another. They were suspicious – naturally, as you might say, but everything is cleared up now. I am taking the girl herself to London next week; she doesn't know anything about it so far. Her father, it seems, was one of these rich Jewish gentlemen. He only learnt of the child's existence a few months before his death. He set agents on to try and trace her, and left all his money to her when she should be found.'

Mortimer listened with close attention. He had no reason to doubt Mr Dinsmead's story. It explained Magdalen's dark beauty; explained too, perhaps, her aloof manner. Nevertheless, though the story itself might be true, something lay behind it undivulged.

But Mortimer had no intention of rousing the other's suspicions. Instead, he must go out of his way to allay them.

'A very interesting story, Mr Dinsmead,' he said. 'I congratulate Miss Magdalen. An heiress and a beauty, she has a great time ahead of her.'

'She has that,' agreed her father warmly, 'and she's a rare good girl too, Mr Cleveland.'

There was every evidence of hearty warmth in his manner.

'Well,' said Mortimer, 'I must be pushing along now, I suppose. I have got to thank you once more, Mr Dinsmead, for your singularly well-timed hospitality.'

Accompanied by his host, he went into the house to bid farewell to Mrs Dinsmead. She was standing by the window with her back to them, and did not hear them enter. At her husband's jovial: 'Here's Mr Cleveland come to say good-bye,' she started nervously and swung round, dropping something which she held in her hand. Mortimer picked it up for her. It was a miniature of Charlotte done in the style of some twenty-five years ago. Mortimer repeated to her the thanks he had already proffered to her husband. He noticed again her look of fear and the furtive glances that she shot at him from beneath her eyelids.

The two girls were not in evidence, but it was not part of Mortimer's policy to seem anxious to see them; also he had his own idea, which was shortly to prove correct.

He had gone about half a mile from the house on his way down to where he had left the car the night before, when the bushes on one side of the path were thrust aside, and Magdalen came out on the track ahead of him.

'I had to see you,' she said.

'I expected you,' said Mortimer. 'It was you who wrote S.O.S. on the table in my room last night, wasn't it?'

Magdalen nodded.

'Why?' asked Mortimer gently.

The girl turned aside and began pulling off leaves from a bush.

'I don't know,' she said, 'honestly, I don't know.'

'Tell me,' said Mortimer.

Magdalen drew a deep breath.

'I am a practical person,' she said, 'not the kind of person who imagines things or fancies them. You, I know, believe in ghosts and spirits. I don't, and when I tell you that there is something very wrong in that house,' she pointed up the hill, 'I mean that there is something tangibly wrong; it's not just an echo of the past. It has been coming on ever since we've been there. Every day it grows worse, father is different, mother is different, Charlotte is different.'

Mortimer interposed. 'Is Johnnie different?' he asked.

Magdalen looked at him, a dawning appreciation in her eyes. 'No,' she said, 'now I come to think of it, Johnnie is not different. He is the only one who's – who's untouched by it all. He was untouched last night at tea.'

'And you?' asked Mortimer.

'I was afraid – horribly afraid, just like a child – without knowing what it was I was afraid of. And father was – queer, there's no other word for it, queer. He talked about miracles and then I prayed – actually prayed for a miracle, and *you* knocked on the door.'

She stopped abruptly, staring at him.

'I seem mad to you, I suppose,' she said defiantly.

'No,' said Mortimer, 'on the contrary you seem extremely sane. All sane people have a premonition of danger if it is near them.'

'You don't understand,' said Magdalen. 'I was not afraid – for myself.'

'For whom, then?'

But again Magdalen shook her head in a puzzled fashion. 'I don't know.'

She went on:

'I wrote S.O.S. on an impulse. I had an idea – absurd, no doubt, that they would not let me speak to you – the rest of them, I mean. I don't know what it was I meant to ask you to do. I don't know now.'

'Never mind,' said Mortimer. 'I shall do it.'

'What can you do?'

Mortimer smiled a little.

'I can think.'

She looked at him doubtfully.

'Yes,' said Mortimer, 'a lot can be done that way, more than you would ever believe. Tell me, was there any chance word or phrase that attracted your attention just before that meal last evening?'

Magdalen frowned. 'I don't think so,' she said. 'At least I heard father say something to mother about Charlotte being the living image of her, and he laughed in a very queer way, but – there's nothing odd in that, is there?'

'No,' said Mortimer slowly, 'except that Charlotte is not like your mother.'

He remained lost in thought for a minute or two, then looked up to find Magdalen watching him uncertainly.

'Go home, child,' he said, 'and don't worry; leave it in my hands.'

She went obediently up the path towards the cottage. Mortimer strolled on a little further, then threw himself down on the green turf. He closed his eyes, detached himself from conscious thought or effort, and let a series of pictures flit at will across the surface of his mind.

Johnnie! He always came back to Johnnie. Johnnie, completely innocent, utterly free from all the network of suspicion and intrigue, but nevertheless the pivot round which everything turned. He remembered the crash of Mrs Dinsmead's cup on her saucer at breakfast that morning. What had caused her agitation? A chance reference on his part to the lad's fondness for chemicals? At the moment he had not been conscious of Mr Dinsmead, but he saw him now clearly, as he sat, his teacup poised half-way to his lips.

That took him back to Charlotte, as he had seen her when the door opened last night. She had sat so staring at him over the rim of her teacup. And swiftly on that followed another memory. Mr Dinsmead emptying teacups one after the other, and saying 'this tea is cold.'

He remembered the steam that went up. Surely the tea had not been so very cold after all?

Something began to stir in his brain. A memory of something read not so very long ago, within a month perhaps. Some account of a whole family poisoned by a lad's carelessness. A packet of arsenic left in the larder had all dripped through on the bread below. He had read it in the paper. Probably Mr Dinsmead had read it too.

Things began to grow clearer. . . .

Half an hour later, Mortimer Cleveland rose briskly to his feet.

IV

It was evening once more in the cottage. The eggs were poached to-night and there was a tin of brawn. Presently Mrs Dinsmead came in from the kitchen bearing the big teapot. The family took their places round the table.

'A contrast to last night's weather,' said Mrs Dinsmead, glancing towards the window.

'Yes,' said Mr Dinsmead, 'it's so still to-night that you could hear a pin drop. Now then, Mother, pour out, will you?'

Mrs Dinsmead filled the cups and handed them round the table. Then, as she put the teapot down, she gave a sudden little cry and pressed her hand to her heart. Mr Dinsmead swung round in his chair, following the direction of her terrified eyes. Mortimer Cleveland was standing in the doorway.

He came forward. His manner was pleasant and apologetic.

'I'm afraid I startled you,' he said. 'I had to come back for something.'

'Back for something,' cried Mr Dinsmead. His face was purple, his veins swelling. 'Back for what, I should like to know?'

'Some tea,' said Mortimer.

With a swift gesture he took something from his pocket, and, taking up one of the teacups from the table, emptied some of its contents into a little test-tube he held in his left hand.

'What – what are you doing?' gasped Mr Dinsmead. His face had gone chalky-white, the purple dying out as if by magic. Mrs Dinsmead gave a thin, high, frightened cry.

'You read the papers, I think, Mr Dinsmead? I am sure you do. Sometimes one reads accounts of a whole family being poisoned, some of them recover, some do not. In this case, *one would not*. The first explanation would be the tinned brawn you were eating, but supposing the doctor to be a suspicious man, not easily taken in by the tinned food theory? There is a packet of arsenic in your larder. On the shelf below it is a packet of tea. There is a convenient hole in the top shelf, what more natural to suppose then that the arsenic found its way into the tea by accident? Your son Johnnie might be blamed for carelessness, nothing more.'

'I – I don't know what you mean,' gasped Dinsmead.

'I think you do.' Mortimer took up a second teacup and filled a second test-tube. He fixed a red label to one and a blue label to the other.

'The red-labelled one,' he said, 'contains tea from your daughter Charlotte's cup, the other from your daughter Magdalen's. I am prepared to swear that in the first I shall find four or five times the amount of arsenic than in the latter.'

'You are mad,' said Dinsmead.

'Oh! dear me, no. I am nothing of the kind. You told me to-day, Mr Dinsmead, that Magdalen was not your own daughter. You lied to me. Magdalen *is* your daughter. Charlotte was the child you adopted, the child who was so like her mother that when I held a miniature of that mother in my hand to-day I mistook it for one of Charlotte herself. Your own daughter was to inherit the fortune, and since it might be impossible to keep your supposed own daughter Charlotte out of sight, and someone who knew the mother might have realised the truth of the resemblance, you decided on, well – a pinch of white arsenic at the bottom of a tea-cup.'

Mrs Dinsmead gave a sudden high cackle, rocking herself to and fro in violent hysterics.

'Tea,' she squeaked, 'that's what he said, tea, not lemonade.'

'Hold your tongue, can't you?' roared her husband wrathfully.

Mortimer saw Charlotte looking at him, wide-eyed, wondering, across the table. Then he felt a hand on his arm, and Magdalen dragged him out of earshot.

'Those,' she pointed at the phials – 'Daddy. You won't—'

Mortimer laid his hand on her shoulder. 'My child,' he said, 'you don't believe in the past. I do. I believe in the atmosphere of this house. If he had not come to it, perhaps – I say *perhaps* – your father might not have conceived the plan he did. I keep these two test-tubes to safeguard Charlotte now and in the future. Apart from that, I shall do nothing, in gratitude, if you will, to that hand that wrote S.O.S.'

Agatha Christie

Wireless

'Above all, avoid worry and excitement,' said Dr Meynell, in the comfortable fashion affected by doctors.

Mrs Harter, as is often the case with people hearing these soothing but meaningless words, seemed more doubtful than relieved.

'There is a certain cardiac weakness,' continued the doctor fluently, 'but nothing to be alarmed about. I can assure you of that.'

'All the same,' he added, 'it might be as well to have a lift installed. Eh? What about it?'

Mrs Harter looked worried.

Dr Meynell, on the contrary, looked pleased with himself. The reason he liked attending rich patients rather than poor ones was that he could exercise his active imagination in prescribing for their ailments.

'Yes, a lift,' said Dr Meynell, trying to think of something else even more dashing – and failing. 'Then we shall avoid all undue exertion. Daily exercise on the level on a fine day, but avoid walking up hills. And above all,' he added happily, 'plenty of distraction for the mind. Don't dwell on your health.'

To the old lady's nephew, Charles Ridgeway, the doctor was slightly more explicit.

'Do not misunderstand me,' he said. 'Your aunt may live for years, probably will. At the same time, shock or over over-exertion might carry her off like that!' He snapped his fingers. 'She must lead a very quiet life. No exertion. No fatigue. But, of course, she must not be allowed to brood. She must be kept cheerful and the mind well distracted.'

'Distracted,' said Charles Ridgeway thoughtfully.

Charles was a thoughtful young man. He was also a young man who believed in furthering his own inclinations whenever possible.

That evening he suggested the installation of a wireless set.

Mrs Harter, already seriously upset at the thought of the lift, was disturbed and unwilling. Charles was fluent and persuasive.

'I do not know that I care for these new-fangled things,' said Mrs Harter piteously. 'The waves, you know – the electric waves. They might affect me.'

Charles in a superior and kindly fashion pointed out the futility of this idea.

Mrs Harter, whose knowledge of the subject was of the vaguest, but who was tenacious of her own opinion, remained unconvinced.

'All that electricity,' she murmured timorously. 'You may say what you like, Charles, but some people *are* affected by electricity. I always have a terrible headache before a thunderstorm. I know that.'

She nodded her head triumphantly.

Charles was a patient young man. He was also persistent.

'My dear Aunt Mary,' he said, 'let me make the thing clear to you.'

He was something of an authority on the subject. He delivered now quite a lecture on the theme; warming to his task, he spoke of bright-emitter valves, of dull-emitter valves, of high frequency and low frequency, of amplification and on condensers.

Mrs Harter, submerged in a sea of words that she did not understand, surrendered.

'Of course, Charles,' she murmured, 'if you really think—'

'My dear Aunt Mary,' said Charles enthusiastically. 'It is the very thing for you, to keep you from moping and all that.'

The lift prescribed by Dr Meynell was installed shortly afterwards and was very nearly the death of Mrs Harter since, like many other old ladies, she had a rooted objection to strange men in the house. She suspected them one and all of having designs on her old silver.

After the lift the wireless set arrived. Mrs Harter was left to contemplate the, to her, repellant object – a large ungainly-looking box, studded with knobs.

It took all Charles' enthusiasm to reconcile her to it.

Charles was in his element, he turned knobs, discoursing eloquently the while.

Mrs Harter sat in her high-backed chair, patient and polite, with a rooted conviction in her own mind that these new-fangled notions were neither more nor less than unmitigated nuisances.

'Listen, Aunt Mary, we are on to Berlin, isn't that splendid? Can you hear the fellow?'

'I can't hear anything except a good deal of buzzing and clicking,' said Mrs Harter.

Charles continued to twirl knobs. 'Brussels,' he announced with enthusiasm.

'It is really?' said Mrs Harter with no more than a trace of interest.

Charles again turned knobs and an unearthly howl echoed forth into the room.

'Now we seem to be on to the Dogs' Home,' said Mrs Harter, who was an old lady with a certain amount of spirit.

'Ha, ha!' said Charles, 'you will have your joke, won't you, Aunt Mary? Very good that!'

Mrs Harter could not help smiling at him. She was very fond of Charles. For some years a niece, Miriam Harter, had lived with her. She had intended to make the girl her heiress, but Miriam had not been a success. She was impatient and obviously bored by her aunt's society. She was always out, 'gadding about' as Mrs Harter called it. In the end, she had entangled herself with a young man of whom her aunt thoroughly disapproved. Miriam had been returned to her mother with a curt note much as if she had been goods on approval. She had married the young man in question and Mrs Harter usually sent her a handkerchief case or a table-centre at Christmas.

Having found nieces disappointing, Mrs Harter turned her attention to nephews. Charles, from the first, had been an unqualified success. He was always pleasantly deferential to his aunt, and listened with an appearance of intense interest to the reminiscences of her youth. In this he was a great contrast to Miriam, who had been frankly bored and showed it. Charles was never bored, he was always good-tempered, always gay. He told his aunt many times a day that she was a perfectly marvellous old lady.

Highly satisfied with her new acquisition, Mrs Harter had written to her lawyer with instructions as to the making of a new will. This was sent to her, duly approved by her and signed.

And now, in the matter of the wireless, Charles was soon proved to have won fresh laurels.

Mrs Harter, at first antagonistic, became tolerant and finally fascinated. She enjoyed it very much better when Charles was out. The trouble with Charles was that he could not leave the thing alone. Mrs Harter would be seated in her chair comfortably listening to a symphony concert or a lecture on Lucrezia Borgia or Pond Life, quite happy and at peace with the world. Not so Charles. The harmony would be shattered by discordant shrieks while he enthusiastically attempted to get foreign stations. But on those evenings when Charles was dining out with friends Mrs Harter enjoyed the wireless very much indeed. She would turn on two switches, sit in her high-backed chair and enjoy the programme of the evening.

It was about three months after the wireless had been installed that the first eerie happening occurred. Charles was absent at a bridge party.

The programme for that evening was a ballad concert. A well-known soprano was singing 'Annie Laurie,' and in the middle of 'Annie Laurie' a strange thing happened. There was a sudden break, the music ceased for a moment, the buzzing, clicking noise continued and then that too died away. There was dead silence, and then very faintly a low buzzing sound was heard.

Mrs Harter got the impression, why she did not know, that the machine was tuned in to somewhere very far away, and then clearly and distinctly a voice spoke, a man's voice with a faint Irish accent.

'*Mary – can you hear me, Mary? It is Patrick speaking. . . . I am coming for you soon. You will be ready, won't you, Mary?*'

Then, almost immediately, the strains of 'Annie Laurie' once more filled the room.

Mrs Harter sat rigid in her chair, her hands clenched on each arm in it. Had she been dreaming? Patrick! Patrick's voice! Patrick's voice, this very room, speaking to her. No, it must be a dream, a hallucination perhaps. She must just have dropped off to sleep for a minute or two. A curious thing to have dreamed – that her dead husband's voice should speak to her over the ether. It frightened her just a little. What were the words he had said?

'*I am coming for you soon, Mary. You will be ready, won't you?*'

Was it, could it be a premonition? Cardiac weakness. Her heart. After all, she was getting on in years.

'It's a warning – that's what it is,' said Mrs Harter, rising slowly and painfully from her chair, and added characteristically:

'All that money wasted on putting in a lift!'

She said nothing of her experience to anyone, but for the next day or two she was thoughtful and a little preoccupied.

And then came the second occasion. Again she was alone in the room. The wireless, which had been playing an orchestral selection, died away with the same suddenness as before. Again there was silence, the sense of distance, and finally Patrick's voice, not as it had been in life – but a voice rarefied, far away, with a strange unearthly quality.

'*Patrick speaking to you, Mary. I will be coming for you very soon now. . . .*'

Then click, buzz, and the orchestral selection was in full swing again.

Mrs Harter glanced at the clock. No, she had not been asleep this time. Awake and in full possession of her faculties, she had heard Patrick's voice speaking. It was no hallucination, she was sure of that. In a confused way she tried to think over all that Charles had explained to her of the theory of ether waves.

Could it be that Patrick had *really* spoken to her? That his actual voice had been wafted through space? There were missing wave lengths or something of that kind. She remembered Charles speaking of 'gaps in the scale.' Perhaps the missing waves explained all the so-called psychological phenomena? No, there was nothing inherently impossible in the idea. Patrick had spoken to her. He had availed himself of modern science to prepare her for what must soon be coming.

Mrs Harter rang the bell for her maid, Elizabeth.

Elizabeth was a tall gaunt woman of sixty. Beneath an unbending exterior she concealed a wealth of affection and tenderness for her mistress.

'Elizabeth,' said Mrs Harter when her faithful retainer had appeared, 'you remember what I told you? The top left-hand drawer of my bureau. It is locked, the long key with the white label. Everything is there ready.'

'Ready, ma'am?'

'For my burial,' snorted Mrs Harter. 'You know perfectly well what I mean, Elizabeth. You helped me to put the things there yourself.'

Elizabeth's face began to work strangely.

'Oh, ma'am,' she wailed, 'don't dwell on such things. I thought you was a sight better.'

'We have all got to go sometime or another,' said Mrs Harter practically. 'I am over my three score years and ten, Elizabeth. There, there, don't make a fool of yourself. If you must cry, go and cry somewhere else.'

Elizabeth retired, still sniffing.

Mrs Harter looked after her with a good deal of affection.

'Silly old fool, but faithful,' she said, 'very faithful. Let me see, was it a hundred pounds, or only fifty I left her? It ought to be a hundred. She has been with me a long time.'

The point worried the old lady and the next day she sat down and wrote to her lawyer asking if he would send her her will so that she might look over it. It was that same day that Charles startled her by something he said at lunch.

'By the way, Aunt Mary,' he said, 'who is that funny old josser up in the spare room? The picture over the mantelpiece, I mean. The old johnny with the beaver and side whiskers?'

Mrs Harter looked at him austerely.

'That is your Uncle Patrick as a young man,' she said.

'Oh, I say, Aunt Mary, I am awfully sorry. I didn't mean to be rude.'

Mrs Harter accepted the apology with a dignified bend of the head. Charles went on rather uncertainly:

'I just wondered. You see—'

He stopped undecidedly and Mrs Harter said sharply:

'Well? What were you going to say?'

'Nothing,' said Charles hastily. 'Nothing that makes sense, I mean.'

For the moment the old lady said nothing more, but later that day, when they were alone together, she returned to the subject.

'I wish you would tell me, Charles, what it was made you ask me about that picture of your uncle.'

Charles looked embarrassed.

'I told you, Aunt Mary. It was nothing but a silly fancy of mine – quite absurd.'

'Charles,' said Mrs Harter in her most autocratic voice, 'I insist upon knowing.'

'Well, my dear aunt, if you will have it, I fancied I saw him – the man in the picture, I mean – looking out of the end window when I was coming up the drive last night. Some effect of the light, I suppose. I wondered who on earth he could be, the face was so – early Victorian, if you know what I mean. And then Elizabeth said there was no one, no visitor or stranger in the house, and later in the evening I happened to drift into the spare room, and there was the picture over the mantelpiece. My man to the life! It is quite easily explained, really, I expect. Subconscious and all that. Must have noticed the picture before without realising that I had noticed it, and then just fancied the face at the window.'

'The end window?' said Mrs Harter sharply.

'Yes, why?'

'Nothing,' said Mrs Harter.

But she was startled all the same. That room had been her husband's dressing-room.

That same evening, Charles again being absent, Mrs Harter sat listening to the wireless with feverish impatience. If for the third time she heard the mysterious voice, it would prove to her finally and without a shadow of doubt that she was really in communication with some other world.

Although her heart beat faster, she was not surprised when the same break occurred, and after the usual interval of deathly silence the faint far-away Irish voice spoke once more.

'*Mary – you are prepared now. . . . On Friday I shall come for you. . . . Friday at half-past nine. . . . Do not be afraid – there will be no pain. . . . Be ready. . . .*'

Then, almost cutting short the last word, the music of the orchestra broke out again, clamourous and discordant.

Mrs Harter sat very still for a minute or two. Her face had gone white and she looked blue and pinched round the lips.

Presently she got up and sat down at her writing-desk. In a somewhat shaky hand she wrote the following lines:

'To-night, at 9.15, I have distinctly heard the voice of my dead husband. He told me that he would come for me on Friday night at 9.30. If I should die on that day and at that hour I should like the facts made known so as to prove beyond question the possibility of communicating with the spirit world. – MARY HARTER.*'*

Mrs Harter read over what she had written, enclosed it in an envelope and addressed the envelope. Then she rang the bell which was promptly answered by Elizabeth. Mrs Harter got up from her desk and gave the note she had just written to the old woman.

'Elizabeth,' she said, 'if I should die on Friday night I should like that note given to Dr Meynell. No' – as Elizabeth appeared to be about to protest – 'do not argue with me. You have often told me you believe in premonitions. I have a premonition now. There is one thing more. I have left you in my will £50. I should like you to have £100. If I am not able to go to the bank myself before I die Mr Charles will see to it.'

As before, Mrs Harter cut short Elizabeth's tearful protests. In pursuance of her determination, the old lady spoke to her nephew on the subject the following morning.

'Remember, Charles, that if anything should happen to me, Elizabeth is to have an extra £50.'

'You are very gloomy these days, Aunt Mary,' said Charles cheerfully. 'What is going to happen to you? According to Dr Meynell, we shall be celebrating your hundredth birthday in twenty years or so!'

Mrs Harter smiled affectionately at him but did not answer. After a minute or two she said:

'What are you doing on Friday evening, Charles?'

Charles looked a trifle surprised.

'As a matter of fact, the Ewings asked me to go in and play bridge, but if you would rather I stayed at home—'

'No,' said Mrs Harter with determination. 'Certainly not. I mean it, Charles. On that night of all nights I should much rather be alone.'

Charles looked at her curiously, but Mrs Harter vouchsafed no further information. She was an old lady of courage and determination. She felt that she must go through with her strange experience single-handed.

Friday evening found the house very silent. Mrs Harter sat as usual in her straight-backed chair drawn up to the fireplace. All her preparations were made. That morning she had been to the bank, had drawn out £50 in notes and had handed them over to Elizabeth despite the latter's tearful protests. She had sorted and arranged all her personal belongings and had labelled one or two pieces of jewellery with the names of friends or relations. She had also written out a list of instructions for Charles. The Worcester tea service was to go to Cousin Emma. The Sèvres jars to young William, and so on.

Now she looked at the long envelope she held in her hand and drew from it a folded document. This was her will sent to her by Mr Hopkinson in accordance with her instructions. She had already read it carefully, but now she looked over it once more to refresh her memory. It was a short, concise document. A bequest of £50 to Elizabeth Marshall in consideration of faithful service; two bequests of £500 to a sister and a first cousin, and the remainder to her beloved nephew Charles Ridgeway.

Mrs Harter nodded her head several times. Charles would be a very rich man when she was dead. Well, he had been a dear good boy to her. Always kind, always affectionate, and with a merry tongue which never failed to please her.

She looked at the clock. Three minutes to the half-hour. Well, she was ready. And she was calm – quite calm. Although she repeated these last words to herself several times, her heart beat strangely and unevenly. She hardly realised it herself, but she was strung up to a fine point of overwrought nerves.

Half-past nine. The wireless was switched on. What would she hear? A familiar voice announcing the weather forecast or that far-away voice belonging to a man who had died twenty-five years before?

But she heard neither. Instead there came a familiar sound, a sound she knew well but which to-night made her feel as though an icy hand were laid on her heart. A fumbling at the front door. . . .

It came again. And then a cold blast seemed to sweep through the room. Mrs Harter had now no doubt what her sensations were. She was afraid. . . . She was more than afraid – she was terrified. . . .

And suddenly there came to her the thought: '*Twenty-five years is a long time. Patrick is a stranger to me now.*'

Terror! That was what was invading her.

A soft step outside the door – a soft halting footstep. Then the door swung silently open. . . .

Mrs Harter staggered to her feet, swaying slightly from side to side, her eyes fixed on the open doorway, something slipped from her fingers into the grate.

She gave a strangled cry which died in her throat. In the dim light of the doorway stood a familiar figure with chestnut beard and whiskers and an old-fashioned Victorian coat.

Patrick had come for her!

Her heart gave one terrified leap and stood still. She slipped to the ground in a huddled heap.

There Elizabeth found her, an hour later.

Dr Meynell was called at once and Charles Ridgeway was hastily recalled from his bridge party. But nothing could be done. Mrs Harter had gone beyond human aid.

It was not until two days later that Elizabeth remembered the note given to her by her mistress. Dr Meynell read it with great interest and showed it to Charles Ridgeway.

'A very curious coincidence,' he said. 'It seems clear that your aunt had been having hallucinations about her dead husband's voice. She must have strung herself up to such a point that the excitement was fatal and when the time actually came she died of the shock.'

'Auto-suggestion?' said Charles.

'Something of the sort. I will let you know the result of the autopsy as soon as possible, though I have no doubt of it myself.' In the circumstances, an autopsy was desirable, though purely as a matter of form.

Charles nodded comprehendingly.

On the preceding night, when the household was in bed, he had removed a certain wire which ran from the back of the wireless cabinet to his bedroom on the floor above. Also, since the evening had been a chilly one, he had asked Elizabeth to light a fire in his room, and in that fire he had burned a chestnut beard and whiskers. Some Victorian clothing belonging to his late uncle he replaced in the camphor-scented chest in the attic.

As far as he could see, he was perfectly safe. His plan, the shadowy outline of which had first formed in his brain when Doctor Meynell had told him that his aunt might with due care live for many years, had succeeded admirably. A sudden shock, Dr Meynell had said. Charles, that affectionate young man, beloved of old ladies, smiled to himself.

When the doctor had departed, Charles went about his duties mechanically. Certain funeral arrangements had to be finally settled. Relatives coming from a distance had to have trains looked out for them. In one or two cases they would have to stay the night. Charles went about it all efficiently and methodically, to the accompaniment of an undercurrent of his own thoughts.

A very good stroke of business! That was the burden of them. Nobody, least of all his dead aunt, had known in what perilous straits Charles stood. His activities, carefully concealed from the world, had landed him where the shadow of a prison loomed ahead.

Exposure and ruin had stared him in the face unless he could in a few short months raise a considerable sum of money. Well – that was all right now. Charles smiled to himself. Thanks to – yes, call it a practical joke – nothing criminal about *that* – he was saved. He was now a very rich man. He had no anxieties on the subject, for Mrs Harter had never made any secret of her intentions.

Chiming in very appositely with these thoughts, Elizabeth put her head round the door and informed him that Mr Hopkinson was here and would like to see him.

About time, too, Charles thought, Repressing a tendency to whistle, he composed his face to one of suitable gravity and repaired to the library. There he greeted the precise old gentleman who had been for over a quarter of a century the late Mrs Harter's legal adviser.

The lawyer seated himself at Charles' invitation and with a dry little cough entered upon business matters.

'I did not quite understand your letter to me, Mr Ridgeway. You seemed to be under the impression that the late Mrs Harter's will was in our keeping?'

Charles stared at him.

'But surely – I've heard my aunt say as much.'

'Oh! quite so, quite so. It *was* in our keeping.'

'*Was?*'

'That is what I said. Mrs Harter wrote to us, asking that it might be forwarded to her on Tuesday last.'

An uneasy feeling crept over Charles. He felt a far-off premonition of unpleasantness.

'Doubtless it will come to light amongst her papers,' continued the lawyer smoothly.

Charles said nothing. He was afraid to trust his tongue. He had already been through Mrs Harter's papers pretty thoroughly, well enough to be quite certain that no will was amongst them. In a minute or two, when he had regained control of himself, he said so. His voice sounded unreal to himself, and he had a sensation as of cold water trickling down his back.

'Has anyone been through her personal effects?' asked the lawyer.

Charles replied that her own maid, Elizabeth, had done so. At Mr Hopkinson's suggestion, Elizabeth was sent for. She came promptly, grim and upright, and answered the questions put to her.

She had been through all her mistress's clothes and personal belongings. She was quite sure that there had been no legal document such as a will amongst them. She knew what the will looked like – her poor mistress had had it in her hand only the morning of her death.

'You are sure of that?' asked the lawyer sharply.

'Yes, sir. She told me so. And she made me take fifty pounds in notes. The will was in a long blue envelope.'

'Quite right,' said Mr Hopkinson.

'Now I come to think of it,' continued Elizabeth, 'that same blue envelope was lying on this table the morning after – but empty. I laid it on the desk.'

'I remember seeing it there,' said Charles.

He got up and went over to the desk. In a minute or two he turned round with an envelope in his hand which he handed to Mr Hopkinson. The latter examined it and nodded his head.

'That is the envelope in which I despatched the will on Tuesday last.' Both men looked hard at Elizabeth.

'Is there anything more, sir?' she inquired respectfully.

'Not at present, thank you.'

Elizabeth went towards the door.

'One minute,' said the lawyer. 'Was there a fire in the grate that evening?'

'Yes, sir, there was always a fire.'

'Thank you, that will do.'

Elizabeth went out. Charles leaned forward, resting a shaking hand on the table.

'What do you think? What are you driving at?'

Mr Hopkinson shook his head.

'We must still hope the will may turn up. If it does not—'

'Well, if it does not?'

'I am afraid there is only one conclusion possible. Your aunt sent for that will in order to destroy it. Not wishing Elizabeth to lose by that, she gave her the amount of her legacy in cash.'

'But why?' cried Charles wildly. 'Why?'

Mr Hopkinson coughed. A dry cough.

'You have had no – er – disagreement with your aunt, Mr Ridgeway?' he murmured.

Charles gasped.

'No, indeed,' he cried warmly. 'We were on the kindliest, most affectionate terms, right up to the end.'

'Ah!' said Mr Hopkinson, not looking at him.

It came to Charles with a shock that the lawyer did not believe him. Who knew what this dry old stick might not have heard? Rumours of Charles' doings might have come round to him. What more natural than that he should suppose that these same rumours had come to Mrs Harter, and that aunt and nephew should have had an altercation on the subject?

But it wasn't so! Charles knew one of the bitterest moments of his career. His lies had been believed. Now that he spoke the truth, belief was withheld. The irony of it!

Of course his aunt had never burnt the will! Of course—

His thoughts came to a sudden check. What was that picture rising before his eyes? An old lady with one hand clasped to her heart . . . something slipping . . . a paper . . . falling on the red-hot embers. . . .

Charles' face grew livid. He heard a hoarse voice – his own – asking: 'If that will's never found—?'

'There is a former will of Mrs Harter's still extant. Dated September, 1920. By it Mrs Harter leaves everything to her niece, Miriam Harter, now Miriam Robinson.'

What was the old fool saying? Miriam? Miriam with her nondescript husband, and her four whining brats. All his cleverness – for Miriam!

The telephone rang sharply at his elbow. He took up the receiver. It was the doctor's voice, hearty and kindly.

'That you, Ridgeway? Thought you'd like to know. The autopsy's just concluded. Cause of death as I surmised. But as a matter of fact the cardiac trouble was much more serious than I suspected when she was alive. With the utmost care, she couldn't have lived longer than two months at the outside. Thought you'd like to know. Might console you more or less.'

'Excuse me,' said Charles, 'would you mind saying that again?'

'She couldn't have lived longer than two months,' said the doctor in a slightly louder tone. 'All things work out for the best, you know, my dear fellow—'

But Charles had slammed back the receiver on its hook. He was conscious of the lawyer's voice speaking from a long way off.

'Dear me, Mr Ridgeway, are you ill?'

Damn them all! The smug-faced lawyer. That poisonous old ass Meynell. No hope in front of him – only the shadow of the prison wall....

He felt that Somebody had been playing with him – playing with him like a cat with a mouse. Somebody must be laughing....

James Hilton

The Mallet

'Feel the revivifying forces of youth coursing through your veins – see the pink flush of health in your cheeks when you catch sight of yourself in the bedroom mirror first thing in the morning – no more aches and pains – no more vague feelings of depression – no more hard-earned money thrown away on doctors and quack medicines! For this, ladies and gentlemen, is *not* a quack medicine, nor is it a drug – it is Nature's Peerless Herbal Remedy, discovered by myself and prepared after a life-time of trial and experiment! No other man in the world has the secret of it – no other man in the world can offer you the key of this wonderful gateway to Health, Strength, and Life! One shilling a box I ask you – no, I'll be even more generous that that – ninepence a box! Ninepence, ladies and gentlemen. . . . Is there any private doctor in this town who would charge you less than half a crown for a bottle of his worthless coloured water? . . . See – I'll tell you what I'll do – it's a special offer and I'll never make it again as long as I live – sixpence! *Sixpence!* . . . Who's going to be the first? . . . Thank you, sir. Two shillings? Thank you – here's your box and here's your one-and-six change. Are you satisfied? . . . That's right. You're quite sure you're satisfied? . . . Good. Then permit me to give you your sixpence back as well. Take this little box of Concentrated Health, my dear sir, as a gift from me to the most sensible person in this crowd . . . now, ladies and gentlemen, who's going to be the next? . . . Thank you, madam. . . .'

The loud, far-carrying voice of the cheap-jack echoed across the market square of the little northern town of Finchingfold. The parish clock showed ten minutes to nine; at nine, by order of the municipal authorities, he would have to pack up. Six times already he had gone through his well-worn patter about the marvellous Life-Giving Herb he had discovered years before on the banks of the Orinoco River, in South America. Captured by a fierce tribe of Indians and left by them to die of malaria, he had managed to crawl a few hundred yards into the trackless forest and there had caught sight of a curious unknown plant. Its pleasant aroma had tempted him to taste it, and lo! – within a quarter of an hour the fever had left him and he was a New Man! Prudently gathering an armful of the precious herb, he had escaped with great difficulty to civilisation, there to complete his life work by manufacturing the herb in pill form and selling it in the market places of England.

The story went well as a rule; nor had it ever gone better than in Finchingfold on that warm Saturday in July. Was it that the folk of Finchingfold were more than usually 'run down' after a broiling week in workshop and factory; or was it that he himself had been particularly eloquent? He could not make up his mind, but the fact remained – and an exceedingly pleasant one – that he had already sold no fewer than ninety-seven boxes that afternoon and evening. Ninety-seven sixpences – two pounds eight-and-six. Cost of boxes, wrappings and pills – say five shillings. Market fee – one shilling. Net profit – two pounds two-and-six. Not bad at all – oh, decidedly not bad.

Doctor Parker Potterson was therefore in a thundering good humour after his day's labour. His face beamed with joviality as he exchanged his last dozen boxes for the sixpences of the crowd. They were just the sort of people he liked best – quiet, respectable working men and their wives, a few farm labourers from the neighbouring countryside, perhaps a sprinkling, too, of better-class artisans. Sometimes in the bigger towns there were hooligans who tried to make trouble, or even that far greater nuisance – the 'superior' person, often a doctor, who asked awkward questions. But Finchingfold seemed full of exactly the right kind. And that quiet little fellow in the front row who had been the first to buy in the final round – he was just the kind to whom it paid to be generous. Most likely he would find that the pills did him a world of good, and for the next few months would be busily advertising Doctor Parker Potterson's Peerless Herbal Remedy at home, at the workshop, and amongst his friends. Yes, undoubtedly, he was well worth his free box.

By the time that the church clock began the chiming of the hour, Potterson had actually sold out – an event that had happened only once or twice before in his entire experience. He hummed cheerfully to himself as he packed his various *impedimenta* into the small bag. A stethoscope, a highly coloured chart of the human body, a fragment of the Life-Giving Herb in its natural state – it was all quite easy to transport. Feeling about in his pocket he abstracted another herb, which perhaps in his heart he felt even to be more life-giving; he lit it and puffed with satisfaction. Ah, Life was good. A pocketful of sixpences, a fine cigar, the cool twilight of a summer's day – what could add to the sweetness of such a mixture? Only one thing, and as he thought of it, he licked his lips in anticipation.

Doctor Parker Potterson was a conspicuous figure as he threaded his way amongst the market crowds towards the 'Crown and Woolpack'. To begin with, he was attired in a top-hat and a frock-coat – a costume that is not greatly in favour with Finchingfold on market day. But, apart from that, he was (and well he knew it) a man who would always command attention wherever he went. He was six foot three in height, and correspondingly broad; he really made a splendid advertisement for his Peerless Herbal Pills, which he consumed in public at the rate of a dozen or so a day. Fortunately they were quite harmless. His eyes were a bright and scintillating blue – the kind that rarely failed to fascinate a woman – and his complexion, tanned by years of open-air life, was all that a health vendor could desire.

The private bar of the 'Crown and Woolpack' seemed smaller and more thronged than ever when Potterson's huge figure entered in at the swing doors. Instinctively people made way for him as he approached the counter – instinctively people always had made way for him. He was well-known, of course; George, the bar-tender, knew what he liked and had it ready for him without waiting for an order. 'Warm night, George,' he said, enjoying the first exquisite sip of the long-anticipated 'double'. His deep baritone carried perfectly across the room full of loud conversation. ' 'Evening, boys,' he added, nodding to the room in general, and a confused murmur of salutations returned to him. Everybody was staring at him, thinking about him, admiring him – and suddenly, as he glanced over the top of his glass, he perceived that among the admirers was an extraordinarily pretty young woman.

Now Potterson was extremely susceptible to pretty young women, and to exercise his charm over them was the keenest of all his vanities. Wherefore, with a deliberation and a confidence born of long practice, he smiled at her.

Faintly, yet with undeniable encouragement, she smiled back. His spirits rose even higher. She found him irresistible, of course, as all women did. But, by Jove, she *was* a good-looker – red-lipped, dark-eyed, oval-faced – an absolute beauty. From her dress and manner and the hand that rested on the edge of the counter, he reckoned to size her up unerringly . . . working-class woman – not been married long – husband in a poor job – consequently kept short of money – consequently discontented, rebellious, eager to snatch at what life had denied her. . . . Ay, how well he knew the type, and how well he had profited by its existence!

'Thirsty weather,' he remarked, looking down at her.

'Too thirsty for me,' she answered, perhaps a shade crossly. Her voice, he noted, was pleasantly musical.

'Too thirsty, eh? Well, you're in the right place for that, anyway.'

'Yes, if my old man would only buy me another drink.'

'And won't he?'

'Not 'im. He's scared of me getting drunk. Now, I ask you, *do* I look like a woman who would get drunk?'

He wondered if she were slightly drunk already. But he replied, rather hoping she were: 'Of course you don't. And have another drink with me if your fellow's too mean to give you one.'

He had spoken loudly, and the crowd, as he had intended, overheard and began to titter. He liked them to be spectators of his prowess with a woman. In less than a minute he had reached that stage of jeering with her about her husband! Smart work, that!

' 'Ssh,' she whispered, mockingly. 'He might hear you, and then he'd knock you down for sayin' that! Better take care, young man!' Across the counter she snapped, 'Mine's a gin, George.'

The crowd's titter became a gathering roar of laughter, and suddenly Potterson glimpsed the reason for it. The woman's husband was actually standing beside her! Oh, this was really rich – something he would think of and enjoy in retrospect many a time afterwards! A little under-sized hollow-chested man, pale and careworn, shabbily dressed – the sort that is born to say 'Sir' to everybody. Then it occurred to him that he had seen the face somewhere before – why – heavens, yes – he was the man to whom he had given the pills that very night, not a quarter of an hour before! What a joke! And how on earth had he managed to net such a splendid creature as that woman? Ah, but life – and especially life as he knew it – was full of such mysteries. . . .

The situation, however, added full spice to his enjoyment. He always took a keen pleasure in emphasizing his own power in front of others who lacked it, and nothing gratified him more than to flirt with a pretty woman before the very eyes of a husband who had not the nerve to object. It made him feel 'big'.

To the little man he said, with patronising condescension: 'Too bad, my good man, to make myself known to your wife without your permission – but then, that's your fault for having such a darned pretty wife! Somebody'll steal her from you some day, you bet – especially if you don't give her what she asks for. Anyhow you'll join us both in a drink, won't you?'

The man smiled sheepishly (how well Potterson knew *his* type also), and said he would have a bitter.

Potterson went on, taking care that all the bar should hear: 'Your wife was warning me about you just now – told me I'd better be careful or you'd knock me down. Glad to see you don't intend to, after all. I should hate to be knocked down.'

Again the man smiled sheepishly. The crowd laughed in derision, and even the woman could not forbear a titter at her husband's expense. 'I won't let him,' she said, with mock pity in her voice. 'He's a real tiger when he's roused – you'd never believe. . . . Ain't you, Bert?' she added, sipping her gin.

'Don't give in to him,' said Potterson, keeping up the banter. 'He's a terrible fighter, I can see, but you'll win in the end, if you tackle him the right way. Fight and win is my motto in this world.' He relapsed a little into his market-place manner. 'If you want health, get it – it's there for you to have. If you want wealth – same thing – fight and win it! If you want to talk to a pretty woman in a pub – well, there's no reason why you shouldn't, is there?'

The woman giggled delightfully.

'Have another drink with me, my dear,' resumed Potterson, well pleased with his rate of progress. 'George, another gin for the lady and another double for me. And this gentleman will take another bitter, I daresay. . . . Yes, after a fairly adventurous life all over the world I think I can claim that I've won pretty nearly all I ever wanted to win. I'm not grumbling. Life's a grand thing when you can say that.'

'But a rotten thing when you can't,' put in a man's voice from the crowd.

Potterson heard and welcomed the interruption, it made him more the centre of attention than ever. 'But you *can*, sir!' he thundered, fixing the crowd in general with his carefully practised Napoleonic stare. 'To a man who has red blood in his veins, life is bursting with prizes ripe for capture!' (One of his stock phrases, that was.) 'You want something – very well, if you're a man – a *Man* in the fullest sense of the word – you get it! Fight for it, if need be – but get it – that's the main thing! Why, if I were to tell you half the things that have happened in my own life . . .' He drained his tumbler at a gulp, and through the glass he saw the little man looking up at him eagerly, evidently contemplating some remark. 'Yes?' he said encouragingly, as a schoolmaster might interrogate a small child.

'Mister,' began the man, with obvious shyness and embarrassment. His voice lacked even the semblance of refinement that his wife's had. 'Mister, you'll excuse me makin' bold to ask you a question – but what you says interests me a great deal. Now, I'm a bit of a readin' man – in my spare time, o' course – and I've heard about the philosophy of that German fellow Nitsky – or whatever 'is name is—'

Potterson's lip curled. Again he recognised the type – one of those down-at-heel fellows you found in public libraries poring over queer books. 'Nitsky my foot!' he cried, winking boldly at the woman. 'Never heard of the chap and don't want to. *I* have my own philosophy – my own rules of life – just as I have my own rules of health. And my own are quite good enough for me.'

'But Nitsky say—'

'To hell with what Nitsky says. Look here, my good man, it's not a bit of use your stuffing me with the damfool nonsense of some damned foreigner. What *I* want – and what I'll listen to with pleasure – are your own ideas, if you've got any.'

The man flushed under the brutality of the sarcasm. 'Well, sir,' he resumed, respectfully, 'if you'll let me put it in my own way, mabbe I can explain. It seems to me – not being an eddicated man, o' course – but it seems to me that it ain't much use expectin' to get everythin' in this world.'

'And why not?'

'Because there ain't enough of everythin' to go round.'

'There's enough for you, my man, if you go in and get it!'

'But some other fellow may get it first.'

'Then take it off him.'

'Fight 'im, you mean, mister?'

Potterson roared as he might have done across a market-place. The *naïveté* of the little fellow went to his brain as intoxicatingly as the whisky; never had he met a more perfect foil to his own self-conceit. 'Yes, my good fellow, *fight* him! Most things worth having have to be fought for! Lord, when I look back and think of the fights I've had—'

'You, mister?'

'Well, do you think I've never had to put up my fists to a man? *Look!*' With a sweeping gesture he rolled up his sleeve and bared his arm above the elbow. 'Look at that muscle, sir! *Feel* it! Hard as iron, eh? It's years since my real fighting days, but I'll wager tonight I could kill a man with one blow of this arm of mine if I was driven to it!'

He could feel the woman's admiration on him like a warm glow; how she must contrast his splendid strength and virility with the spongy weakness of her little whelp of a husband! With her eyes so eagerly looking upwards to him, and the whisky fumes pleasantly simmering in his head, he felt a veritable Superman. Was he not a Superman? Could he not dominate a whole multitude by the magic of his voice and personality? Was not this very ordinary little public-house crowd hanging upon his every word? His heart swelled with pride, he would show them all what sort of a fellow he was. 'Drinks all round on me, George,' he cried, loudly, and gloried in the respectful murmur of thanks that followed. How easy it was to handle these people! A loud voice and a free drink – or a free box of pills, for that matter – and they were his entirely. . . .

'*Kill?*' he heard the woman whisper, and the awe with which she spoke the word gave him the most rapturous sensation of power. 'Guess I wouldn't like to quarrel with you then, young feller.'

He liked the way she called him 'young feller'; he was fifty-seven and his hair beneath the dye was an already silvering grey. He laughed loudly and put his huge hand on her shoulder – it always marked a stage when you first touched a woman. And she winced, too – how delightful that was! 'My dear, you never need have any fear of me. Never in my life have I raised my hand to a woman. But, my God, if it was a man I was up against—'

'What would you do?' she breathed in an eager whisper, her dark eyes smouldering.

'*Do?*' He took a gulp of whisky to gain inspiration. 'What would I do? I think I'd better not tell you, m'dear. Not nice for a lady to know about.'

Suddenly her attitude changed. She began to laugh at him – mockingly – as formerly she had laughed at her husband. She was drunk, of course – quite drunk. 'Go on, young feller – but I don't believe you! You can brag about all you *would* do all right – so can anybody. But I'll bet you never *have* done anything!'

'Haven't I?' He leered down at her with a sharp half-angry light in his eyes. He could not endure to be jeered at – but she looked damnably pretty over it, he had to admit. God – she was a fine little creature. If only . . . But he had to nerve himself for the mental effort of answering her. 'That shows how little you know of me,' he said. 'I'm not a boaster. I don't go round telling everybody what I've done. I've done things, as a matter of fact, that nobody *would* believe.'

'An' I'm not surprised, either. We ain't all fools, even if we do buy your sugar-and-soap pills!'

He was angry then – furiously angry, and the crowd's laugh, for the first time directed against himself, stung him in his weakest spot. 'My good woman,' he said, carefully controlling himself. 'Like all women, you're damned unreasonable. You want to know too much. Nevertheless, I'll tell you – if you want to know, and if you don't believe it, I can't help it – it's the truth, anyway. I've not lived the life of a lounge-lizard. I've seen the world. I've lived with the raw, naked elementals of life.' (Another of his stock phrases.) 'I've had to fight. I've had to kill. Up the Orinoco River, when I was attacked by Indians with poisoned darts, I put three of them to sleep with my bare fists and nothing else!'

'Oh, out there – that don't count. Anythin' can happen in them sort o' places. It's over here that matters to most of us. An' if you was to kill a man in England with nothin' but your bare fists, you'd be copped by the police the next day and sent to swing within three months.'

'Perhaps,' he answered cautiously. 'Perhaps not.' He was glad that the little man was preparing for another of his plaintive interventions. He heard him say: 'She's right, mister – if you don't mind me sayin' so. A feller with your strength might easily kill a chap, but the trouble begins arterwards when the cops are out agin you.'

So the little man was turning on him too? Ah, well, he knew how to deal with *him*. A little heavy sarcasm. 'Cops, eh? So you're afraid of *them*, are you?'

'I daresay, I might be, mister, if I'd done a murder.'

'Murder! *Murder?* Who in the name of ten thousand devils was talking about murder?' For the moment his heart stopped beating – then raced on faster than ever as his brain came to the rescue. Murder? Very well, if they wanted to talk about it, *he'd* show them. He said, with studied insolence in voice and manner: 'Oh, you *would* be afraid, naturally, whether you'd done a murder or not. You were born that way.'

He waited for the general laugh and then continued, gathering impetus: 'But let me tell you, sir, that the Man who is sure of Himself – the Man, that is, who is a Man in the fullest sense of the word' – (he had used that phrase before, but no matter) – 'that Man, I say, is not afraid of the police or of anything or anybody in the whole world!' He paused impressively, enjoying the echoes of his voice.

'You mean, mister, that a man oughter be able to do a murder an' not be found out?'

'I mean, sir, that a man ought to be Successful. That's my creed – my rule of life. If he commits murder, it ought to be a successful murder. And the successful murder isn't found out.'

'You think it possible then, mister?'

'Possible? Of course it's possible. Everything in this world is possible to the Man who knows his job. What do you suppose happens when a fellow pulls off a really well-planned affair?'

'You think the police don't get him?'

'My good man, the police aren't even called in. Nobody dreams of 'em. The verdict is Accident, maybe, or perhaps even Suicide. I tell you, sir, the battle is half lost when the word murder is first mentioned.'

' 'Alf *lost*? You mean 'alf *won*, mister?'

'*Won?* No – lost, of course. Oh, well, looking at it from the police point of view, naturally. . . .' He signalled for another drink. 'Bah – the police – what are they? They ain't got an idea in their heads, most of 'em.'

'Ah, but mister, they gets 'old of ideas, some'ow. It's a queer thing, the way they gets 'old of clues an' things. Now my cousin's brother-in-law's at Scotland Yard, and '*e* tells me some o' the things that goes on.'

'And you believe him, of course. You *would*. Naturally what a police-man says about himself is very pleasant to hear. But all the time they know – they all know from experience – that the well-planned crime is *never* found out!'

He stopped, rather wondering what he had been talking about. He was being pretty eloquent, anyhow – he could see how closely he had seized on the attention of the whole room. Ah, yes, the question of crime and being found out – funny sort of argument to have, but taproom conversations did lead up to queer things. He took a gulp of neat whisky and added: 'Yes, sir, there are men walking the streets of this country today, respected and worthy citizens, who, if the truth were known, would be queuing up for the scaffold. If the truth were known, mark you. But it isn't. And it never will be. The affair was well planned.'

'Though they say, mister, that somethin' always gives you away.'

'Not if you've a ha'porth of brains,' he snapped, contemptuously. 'Of course, if you haven't, you'd better lead a respectable life.' He laughed loudly and finished his glass. Strange how he had been driven to lecture a bar-parlour on such a topic! 'Same again, George,' he muttered.

The woman was smiling at him provokingly. 'Seems to me, then, young fellow, that if I ever want to kill anybody I'd better come to you for advice?'

She was still half-mocking him, but he could see the light of admira-tion winning through again. It exhilarated him, made him want to renew his conquest to the full. 'Well, m'dear, it's not for me to say – but I guess I can give most people good advice about most things.'

'Still,' continued the little man, with naïve seriousness, 'I don't think I'd ever kill anybody, even if I knew 'ow. Not that there ain't some folks as deserve to be put out. My brother f'r instance. Lives up at Millport in a swell 'ouse – servants, motor-cars – all that. Rollin' in money – did me out o' my share when my father died. Made 'is fortune doing other people since – wouldn't gimme a penny not if I was starvin', 'e wouldn't. Sometimes I sees 'im at the station of an evenin' – 'e 'as a factory 'ere – I sees 'im steppin' into 'is first-class kerridge on the Millport train – and I could kill 'im with my own 'ands, straight, I could.'

Potterson stared at him with a certain interest; it was extraordinary that such a mild little fellow should nourish such a hatred. Hardly what one would expect – hardly even what he, Potterson, the student of human nature, would have expected. 'Well, why don't you kill him?' he said, with a wink at the crowd.

'I ain't got the courage, that I 'aven't,' replied the other. His frankness was so amusing. Potterson began to struggle with whiskified laughter. 'Besides, mister, come to think of it, I dunno as there'd be any way. 'E's so scared of burglars nobody'd ever get in 'is 'ouse.'

'Better kill him in the street, then,' said Potterson, almost hysterically. Really, the fellow was as good as a music-hall.

'No, mister – that wouldn't do, either, with everybody lookin' on.'

'Oh, don't – don't,' Potterson cried, holding his sides with merriment. 'Oh, Lord – you make me laugh more than I've laughed for months! I think I know now why your wife married you – she thought you were the damn funniest thing she'd ever seen!' He laughed till the tears streamed from his eyes and mingled with the perspiration on his nose and cheeks. 'Besides,' he added, pulling himself together, 'you're wrong. There *is* a way. There always is.'

'No, mister. Not with 'im. Even you couldn't find one.'

'Couldn't I?' Reaction, after the hysteria of laughing so much, gave him a tone that was curt and almost angry. 'Couldn't I, my little fellow? Don't you be too sure what I could do and couldn't do!'

He felt the woman's hand on his arm like a bar of fire – another stage, when the woman first did the touching. 'I suppose you think you could, eh?' she whispered.

'M'dear' – he began, thickly; he wondered if he might dare to put an encircling arm round her waist. He was almost doing so when she turned on him fiercely, 'None of that!' What a little spitfire she was! Hopelessly drunk, of course. . . . He heard her continuing, 'All talk – brag – boast – no proof – that's the sort he is!'

One or two of the crowd tittered and chuckled; he felt a dull angry flush mounting to his cheeks and stabbing his eyes from the inside. Making fun of him, was she? He's show her – and the rest, too. 'Look here!' he shouted, moving as if to take off his coat. 'If there's any man here who thinks I'm nothing but a boaster, let him come up and tell me so – man to man! And if there's any woman thinks so, let her keep her damned mouth shut!'

'Rot!' retorted the woman. 'I dare you to prove what you say. You say there was always a way of killin' a chap if you wanted to. Well, to prove that, you gotter take a test case. Take my 'usband's brother – 'e'll do as good as any. 'Ow would you work the trick with 'im?'

He felt the crowd veering away from him in sympathy – a thing he could never endure. 'Aye, that's a fair question,' he heard someone say. Other voices came to his ears – eager, critical, derisive voices. And at the same time, looking down at the woman's face so close to his own, he was filled with an over-mastering, intolerable longing to subdue her, to justify himself before her, to make himself for ever memorable in her life. She was the most beautiful thing he had ever seen. That woman at Portsmouth – nothing to her. Nor the little French girl. Nor even Maudie Raines – Maudie who years before had driven him to such madness that . . .

'Same again, George,' he muttered. Then he gritted his teeth and fortified himself for a new struggle. 'You're a fine pack of fools,' he cried irritably at last. 'How the hell can I tell what the best plan would be when I don't know the man or his ways or anything about him?'

'I'll tell you,' whispered the woman. 'I'll answer anything you want to know about 'im.'

Her eyes, lustrous and burning, seemed to swim into his seething brain. *She* would tell him. Could it be that she *wanted* him to succeed before her husband, before the crowd? Was she on his side? Extraordinary – there was something in her eyes – in the way she looked at him – that reminded him of Maudie Raines. . . . He began to speak loudly, in something of his market-place manner, yet with greater emphasis than he usually employed. 'Ladies and gentlemen,' he cried, 'I accept the challenge. I'm a man of my word and I mean every single word that I say. No nonsense about Parker Potterson. He's straight – he delivers the goods. Mind you – in my opinion, this is an entirely abshurd – absurd argument – discussing how to kill a man who is living a few miles away at this preshent moment – and who, despite our friend here, is probably a very decent and respectable member of the community. It is, I repeat, an absurd business altogether – and, if I may say so, in very bad taste. It was that, and that alone, that made me reluctant at first to enter into it. But' – and here his voice acquired a rich cathedral tone – 'but having had my word doubted, ladish – ladies and gentlemen – having had foul ashpershions cast upon my good faith – what can I do but take up the challenge, good tashte or bad tashte?'

'Get to the point, mister,' cried a voice in the crowd, and Potterson turned upon it savagely. 'I'll get to the point in *my* time, shir, and not in yours! And if you dare to interrupt me again I'll knock your damned head off!'

He paused to appreciate the silence; but, by God, he was getting them – calming them – thrilling them with his words – how marvellous it was to be able to do that! The old sense of power was on him again, but more than ever before – more than ever before in his life; a Berserker fierceness hammered at his temples. *He* would show them – never in Finchingfold would that night at the 'Crown and Woolpack' be forgotten. 'Ladies and gentlemen – where wash I? Ah, I remember. . . . Thish gentleman – unknown to me – who lives at Millport. . . . Very well, I accept the challenge. But' – and he leered down at the woman – 'but you must always bear in mind that because *I* could do a thing, it doesn't follow that anybody else could!'

'Never mind. Tell us how *you* would do it.'

'I'm going to. I'm going to make you realise that Parker Potterson is a

THE MALLET

man of his word. If Parker Potterson saysh he can do a thing, then he
can do it. Now then . . .' He turned to the little man. 'Did I, shir, or did
I not – hear you remark a moment or so ago that you often saw your
brother at Finchingfold Shtation – shtepping into a firsht-class carriage
on the train for Millport?'

'That's right, mister. 'E travels every day back'ards and for'ards.'

'Good. That givesh me an idea. He musht be killed on the train.'

'But 'ow, mister?'

'Ah, that'sh jusht where the brains comesh in. But it'sh ver' simple.
Get into the next carriage when hish train leavesh in an evening. Make
sure hish carriage and yoursh are empty – mosht likely they are, ash he
travelsh firsht. Then . . .' He stopped, caught his breath rather wildly,
and added, 'Ishn't there a long tunnel between Finchingfold and
Millport?'

'That's right, mister. You know the line, then?'

'Never you mind what I know – it'sh a deal more'n you ever will,
anyway. . . . Ver' good – the tunnel, then. All you gotter do is to wait
till the train entersh the tunnel, slip out of your compartment along the
footboard and get in *hish* compartment, then kill your man—'

'*Kill* 'im?'

'Yesh – *kill* him – you can't get out of that!'

'But 'ow?'

'How th'hell d'you think? Heapsh of waysh. . . . Throttle him if
y'like. Or a hammer. Know how t'ushe a hammer?'

'Tidy-sized mallet might do,' said the man, with fatuous simplicity.
'I'm a carpenter by trade, I am, an' I'm pretty well used to a mallet.'

Potterson's eyes lit up with a hectic gleam. 'Shplendid! Glad to hear
y'can do shomething. An' a mallet'sh all right – jusht as good as a hammer – perhapsh better.'

'But what abart after that, mister? My cousin's brother-in-law, what
I was tellin' you of, 'e ses to me that the real trouble abart these things
is gettin' rid o' the body arterwards.'

'Cousin'sh brother-in-lawsh's a fool. Dishpose of the body – eashy to
any man of brainsh!'

'Well, 'ow abart it?'

'Eashy, I tell you.'

'But – in this 'ere case, mister – on a train?'

'Eashy. Ain't there a river to crosh – an' a big bridge – jusht before
the train getsh to Millport?'

'That's right, mister. Three-arch bridge over the River Fayle.'

'Dammit, then – can't y'shee? Eashy to any man of brainsh. Ash
train croshes bridge, open door an' throw body over par – parapet into
river! Heh? Ain't that a good plan? Now would you – would you have

289

thought of that, hey? Or you, m'dear?' He turned to the woman, eager to taste the reward of his triumph.

She laughed. 'Somebody's see you from the towpath, most likely.'

'Ah! . . . that'sh clever of you, m'dear. Thish li'l plan o' mine worksh beshtin winter. Nobody on towpath in winter – choosh nice rainy night in December – November – Chrishmash. . . . An' lishen to me – it'sh a damn good plan, I tell you – becosh – becosh when the body comesh ashore – they'll shay – poor feller – shad accshident – fell backwardsh – mark on hish head where he hit par – parapet. An' thoshe who don't believe that'll shay – 'coursh it'sh shuicide really, on'y relativesh tryin' t'hush thingsh up. . . .' God – what was he talking about – what had he been saying? Who, anyway, had began this fool argument? He was mad; the room was whirling round and round; his brain was on fire.

The woman was still laughing. 'Yes, it's a plan all right, I'll grant that. Only I'd 'ike to see my Bert throwin' the body out, that's all! Why, 'e couldn't 'ardly throw a dead cat over a fence!'

For the second time that night Potterson laughed till the tears ran down from his whisky-sodden eyes. *Triumph!* He had scored over them all. She was laughing *with* him now, not at him; he could feel her yielding to him – realising his power and strength as he had willed her to. Lord – what a grand world it was for those who were born to be natural lords over their fellows!

'Mebbe he couldn't!' he cried hoarsely. 'But I never guar-guaranteed he could, did I? It'sh a job for a man of shtrength, not for a weakling! All th' world ish open to th' man of shtrength – shtrength and brainsh – both t'gether – an' the weakesht goesh to th'wall!' It was the eternal saga of his dreams.

'Well, mister,' said the little man, 'you've give me a fair answer, I'll say that. An' now p'rhaps you'll 'ave just a last drink with me?'

'Dummind. 'Nother one, Georhsh.'

He knew he was perfectly drunk – too drunk to know what he was doing or saying. Yet a blind insensate pride in himself made him believe that never, never had he triumphed so mightily. And all because of the woman. But for her a little idle boasting, might have been – but nothing else. It was she who had driven him to claim this strange and utmost triumph. She was the sort he would do anything for – just as he had done for Maudie Raines so many years ago. Always women had been his weakness – his weakness by making him feel so strong. There was nothing he would not have done for a woman he fancied. And there was nothing still that he would not do. At fifty-seven the same fire was in him – the same as at twenty-seven. . . .

While he was drinking he made to put his arm round the woman's waist and this time she did not repulse him. His head throbbed and sang with exhilaration. He was winning her! His arm closed round her, and again he felt that entrancing delicate shrinking of her body away from him. She shrank, but somehow diffidently, almost invitingly.

'Satishfied I'm a man of my word, m'dear?' he hiccupped, and she replied:

'I'll certainly say you are if you'll answer me just one more question You know, they always do say that it's the little things as gets a man down, as often as not. Not take that mallet, f'rinstance. What'd you do with it afterwards? If you was to throw it into the river with the body it'd float and be washed ashore somewhere, and then, mebbe, with the bloodstains on it, it'd give you away – quite likely, anyhow. So you see, young feller, that looks to me the weak spot in your plan – that mallet. Couldn't you get rid of it some way or another?'

'Yes, mister,' the little man echoed in his plaintive whine. 'I 'adn't thought o' that, I admit – but my old gel – she's a regl'lar smart 'un – trust 'er for not missin' anythin'.'

A murmur went round the bystanders. 'Yes, I reckon 'e's got you there, mister! Tell us what you'd do with the mallet!'

The mallet. . . . What *would* he do with it? Potterson fought for coherence – for coherence to think as well as to speak. *The Mallet* . . . extraordinary that anyone should be asking him questions about a mallet!

He glanced down and saw the woman's eyes fixed on him. His brain reeled with joy; he began to tremble. She was *his*; she no longer shrank away from his touch or even tried to – he could feel her breath rising and falling like a livid ache in his own body. It was his moment – the moment for which he had always lived.

'The mallet – the mallet – tell me!' she whispered, and he knew then that he would answer even that last question – that last question and answer that would remove the final barrier between himself and her! '*Mallet?*' he roared, in a voice that made passers-by in the market-place outside stop to wonder what was happening. 'Yesh – 'course you oughter deshtroy th'mallet! Think Parker Pottershon'sh fool enough t'forget important thin' li' that? Yesh . . . gotter deshtroy mallet – altogether – shomehow. . . .'

'But 'ow, that's the question, mister?' queried the little man, with that strange, half-pathetic, half-exasperating patience.

Potterson smiled then – a wide, uncanny smile from which all the light had gone out except the hideous light of evil. 'That'sh right. Lemme think. How deshtroy mallet? Ah . . . Idea. Idea o' mine – brainsh full o' good ideash – heh? Ain't there a slag-heap jusht outside Millport Shtation – one o' them burnin' shlag-heapsh near gashworksh?'

'That's right, mister.'

'Then, by God, ain't it eashy – eashy as kishin' a pretty women like yo' wife – throw mallet on shlag-heap – an' in a minute – two minitsh – all burned to shinder!'

And with a strange weakness in all his limbs he reeled towards the face that at that final moment sharply eluded his.

'So that's how you did it?' said the little man suddenly, speaking in a different voice, and, as it were, from a different world. 'I'd always had my suspicions, ever since they found that half-burned mallet on the edge of the slag-heap. You aimed badly, I'm afraid . . .' And in a more level voice he added: 'Parker Potterson, *alias* Richard Morley, I arrest you for the wilful murder of Thomas Raines on the night of December the twelfth, Eighteen-Ninety-Eight. . . .'

Two of the bystanders seized his arms and led him away, the little man and the woman following. . . .

'What puzzles me,' remarked the latter some hours later as she discussed the whole affair with her famous, though somewhat diminutive husband, 'is why he troubled to throw the mallet on the slag-heap at all? Why not simply have put it in a bag and carried it through the station barrier in the ordinary way? He could easily have destroyed it afterwards.'

'True,' answered Detective-Inspector Howard, of Scotland Yard, 'but then that wouldn't have been Morley. Some criminals are not clever enough, but Morley was *too* clever. That mallet on the slag-heap was the one quite unnecessary touch of genius that let him down. And he was so proud of it that years afterwards he couldn't resist the temptation to brag about it to a pretty woman . . .' He gave his wife an affectionate glance as he added: 'Well, Maud, it was *your* triumph, chiefly – you played a dashed unpleasant part remarkably well. But it was the mallet that finished him – as surely as it finished your poor father thirty years ago.'

Cornell Woolrich

Dusk to Dawn

It was just beginning to grow dark when Lew Stahl went in to the Odeon picture theatre where his roommate Tom Lee worked as an usher. It was exactly 6:15.

Lew Stahl was twenty-five, out of work, dead broke and dead honest. He'd never killed anyone. He'd never held a deadly weapon in his hand. He'd never even seen anyone lying dead. All he wanted to do was see a show, and he didn't have the necessary thirty cents on him.

The man on door duty gave him a disapproving look while Lew was standing out there in the lobby waiting for Tom to slip him in free. Up and down, and up again the doorman walked like 'You gotta nerve!' But Stahl stayed pat. What's the use having a pal as an usher in a movie house if you can't cadge an admission now and then?

Tom stuck his head through the doors and flagged him in. 'Friend of mine, Duke,' he pacified the doorman.

'Are you liable to get called down for this?' Stahl asked as he followed him in.

Tom said, 'It's O.K. as long as the manager don't see me. It's between shows anyway; everyone's home at supper. The place is so empty you could stalk deer up in the balcony. Come on up, you can smoke up there.'

Stahl trailed him upstairs, across a mezzanine, and out into the darkness of the sloping balcony. Tom gave the aisle his torch so his guest could see. On the screen below a woman's head was wavering, two or three times larger than life. A metallic voice clanged out, echoing sepulchrally all over the house, like a modern Delphic Oracle. 'Go back, go back!' she said. 'This is no place for you!'

Her big luminous eyes seemed to be looking right at Lew Stahl as she

293

spoke. Her finger came out and pointed, and it seemed to aim straight at him and him alone. It was weird; he almost stopped in his tracks, then went on again. He hadn't eaten all day; he figured he must be woozy, to think things like that.

Tom had been right; there was only one other guy in the whole balcony. Kids went up there, mostly, during the matinees, and they'd all gone home by now, and the evening crowd hadn't come in yet.

Stahl picked the second row, sat down in the exact middle of it. Tom left him, saying, 'I'll be back when my five-minute relief comes up.'

Stahl had thought the show would take his mind off his troubles. Later, thinking back over this part of the evening, he was willing to admit he hadn't known what real trouble was yet. But all he could think of was he hadn't eaten all day, and how hungry he was; his empty stomach kept his mind off the canned story going on on the screen.

He was beginning to feel weak and chilly, and he didn't even have a nickel for a cup of hot coffee. He couldn't ask Tom for any more money, not even that nickel. Tom had been tiding him over for weeks now, carrying his share of the room rent, and all he earned himself was a pittance. Lew Stahl was too decent, too fair-minded a young fellow, to ask him for another penny, not even if he dropped in his tracks from malnutrition. He couldn't get work. He couldn't beg on the street corner; he hadn't reached that point yet. He'd rather starve first. Well, he was starving already.

He pulled his belt over a notch to make his stomach seem tighter, and shaded his hand to his eyes for a minute.

That lone man sitting back there taking in the show had looked prosperous, well fed. Stahl wondered if he'd turn him down, if he went back to him and confidentially asked him for a dime. He'd probably think it was strange that Stahl should be in a movie house if he were down and out, but that couldn't be helped. Two factors emboldened him in his maiden attempt at panhandling. One was it was easier to do in here in the dark than out on the open street. The second was there was no one around to be a witness to his humiliation if the man bawled him out. If he was going to tackle him at all, he'd better not sit thinking about it any longer, he'd better do it before the house started to fill up, or he knew he'd never have the nerve. You'd be surprised how difficult it is to ask alms of a stranger when you've never done it before, what a psychological barrier separates the honest man from the panhandler.

Lew Stahl turned his head and glanced back at the man, to try and measure his chances ahead of time. Then he saw to his surprise that the man had dozed off in his seat; his eyes were closed. And suddenly it was no longer a matter of asking him for money, it was a matter of taking it, helping himself while the man slept. Tom had gone back to the main floor, and there was no one else up there but the two of them. Before he knew it he had changed seats, was in the one next to the sleeper.

'A dollar,' he kept thinking, 'that's all I'll take, just a dollar, if he has a wallet. Just enough to buy a big thick steak and . . .'

His stomach contracted into a painful knot at the very thought, and salt water came up into his mouth, and his hunger was so great that his hand spaded out almost of its own accord and was groping toward the inner pocket of the man's coat.

The coat was loosely buttoned and bulged conveniently open the way the man was sitting, and Stahl's downward dipping fingers found the stiff grained edge of a billfold without much trouble. It came up between his two fingers, those were all he'd dared insert in the pocket, and it was promisingly fat and heavy.

A second later the billfold was down between Lew's own legs and he was slitting it edgewise. The man must have been sweating, the leather was sort of sticky and damp on one side only, the side that had been next to his body. Some of the stickiness adhered to Stahl's own fingertips.

It was crammed with bills, the man must have been carrying between seventy and eighty dollars around with him. Stahl didn't count them, or even take the whole batch out. True to his word, he peeled off only the top one, a single, tucked it into the palm of his hand, started the wallet back where he'd found it.

It was done now; he'd been guilty of his first criminal offence.

He slipped it in past the mouth of the pocket, released it, started to draw his arm carefully back. The whole revere on that side of the man's coat started to come with Lew's arm, as though the two had become glued together. He froze, held his arm where it was, stiffly motionless across the man's chest. The slightest move, and the sleeper might awake. The outside button on Lew's cuff had freakishly caught in the man's lapel button hole, twisted around in some way. And it was a defective, jagged-edged button, he remember that now well; it had teeth to hang on by.

He tried to slip his other hand in between the lapel and his arm and free them. There wasn't enough room for leverage. He tried to hold the man's lapel down and pull his own sleeve free, insulating the tug so it wouldn't penetrate the sleeper's consciousness. The button held on, the thread was too strong to break that way.

It was the most excruciating form of mental agony. Any minute he expected the sleeper's eyes to pop open and fasten on him accusingly. Lew had a disreputable penknife in his pocket. He fumbled desperately for it with one hand, to cut the damnable button free. He was as in a strait-jacket; he got it out of his right-hand pocket with his left hand, crossing one arm over the other to do so. At the same time he had to hold his prisoned arm rigid, and the circulation was already leaving it.

He got the tarnished blade open with his thumbnail, jockeyed the knife around in his hand. He was sweating profusely. He started sawing away at the triple-ply button-thread that had fastened them together. The knife blade was none too keen, but it finally severed. Then something happened; not the thing he'd dreaded, not the accusation of suddenly opened eyes. Something worse. The sleeper started sagging slowly forward in his seat. The slight vibration of the hacking knife must have been transmitted to him, dislodged him. He was beginning to slop over like a sandbag. And people don't sleep like that, bending over at the floor.

Stahl threw a panicky glance behind him. And now accusing eyes did meet him, from four or five rows back. A woman had come in and taken a seat some time during the past minute or two. She must have seen the jockeying of a knife blade down there, she must have wondered what was going on. She was definitely not looking at the screen, but at the two of them.

All presence of mind gone, Lew tried to edge his crumpled seat-mate back upright, for appearances' sake. Pretend to her they were friends sitting side by side; anything, as long as she didn't suspect he had just picked his pocket. But there was something wrong – the flabbiness of muscle, the lack of heavy breathing to go with a sleep so deep it didn't break no matter how the sleeper's body fell. That told him all he needed to know; he'd been sitting quietly for the past five minutes next to a man who was either comatose or already a corpse. Someone who must have dropped dead during the show, without even falling out of his seat.

He jumped out into the aisle past the dead man, gave him a startled look, then started excitedly toward the back to tip off Tom or whomever he could find. But he couldn't resist looking back a second time as he went chasing off. The woman's eyes strayed accusingly after him as he flashed by.

Tom was imitating a statue against the wall of the lounge, beside the stairs.

'Come back there where I was sitting!' Lew panted. 'There's a guy next to me out cold, slopping all over!'

'Don't start any disturbance,' Tom warned in an undertone.

He went back with Lew and flashed his torch quickly on and off, and the face it high-lighted wasn't the colour of anything living; it was like putty.

'Help me carry him back to the rest-room,' Tom said under his breath, and picked him up by the shoulders. Lew took him by the legs, and they stumbled back up the dark aisle with the corpse.

The woman who had watched all this was feverishly gathering up innumerable belongings, with a determination that almost approached hysteria, as if about to depart forthwith on a mission of vital importance.

Lew and Tom didn't really see it until they got him in the rest-room and stretched him out on a divan up against the wall – the knife-hilt jammed into his back. It didn't stick out much, was in at an angle, nearly flat up against him. Sidewise from right to left, but evidently deep enough to touch the heart; they could tell by looking at him he was gone.

Tom babbled, 'I'll get the manager! Stay here with him a second. Don't let anyone in!' He grabbed up a 'No Admittance' sign on his way out, slapped it over the outside door-knob, then beat it.

Lew had never seen a dead man before. He just stood there, and looked and looked. Then he went a step closer, and looked some more. 'So that's what it's like!' he murmured inaudibly. Finally Lew reached out slowly and touched him on the face, and cringed as he met the clammy feel of it, pulled his hand back and whipped it down, as though to get something off it. The flesh was still warm and Lew knew suddenly he had no time alibi.

He threw something over that face and that got rid of the awful feeling of being watched by something from the other world. After that Lew wasn't afraid to go near him; he just looked like a bundle of old clothes. The dead man was on his side, and Lew fiddled with the knife-hilt, trying to get it out. It was caught fast, so he let it alone after grabbing it with his fingers from a couple of different directions.

Next he went through his pockets, thinking he'd be helping to identify him.

The man was Luther Kemp, forty-two, and he lived on 79th Street. But none of that was really true any more, Lew thought, mystified; he'd left it all behind. His clothes and his home and his name and his body and the show he'd paid to see were here. But where the hell had he gone to, anyway? Again that weird feeling came over Lew momentarily, but he brushed it aside. It was just that one of the commonest things in life – death – was still strange to him. But after strangeness comes familiarity, after familiarity, contempt.

The door flew open, and Tom bolted in again, still by himself and panting as though he'd run all the way up from the floor below. His face looked white, too.

'C'mere!' he said in a funny, jerky way. 'Get outside, hurry up!'

Before Lew knew what it was all about, they were both outside, and Tom had propelled him all the way across the dimly lighted lounge to the other side of the house, where there was another branch of the staircase going down. His grip on Lew's arm was as if something were skewered through the middle of it.

'What's the idea?' Lew managed to get out.

Tom jerked his head backward. 'You didn't really do that, did you? To that guy.'

Lew nearly dropped through the floor. His answer was just a welter of words.

Tom telescoped it into 'No,' rushed on breathlessly, 'Well, then all the more reason for you to get out of here quick! Come on down on this side, before they get up here! I'll tell you about it down below.'

Half-way down, on the landing, Tom stopped a second time, motioned Lew to listen. Outside in the street some place the faint, eerie wail of a patrol-car siren sounded, rushed to a crescendo as it drew nearer, then stopped abruptly, right in front of the theatre itself.

'Get that? Here they are now!' Tom said ominously, and rushed Lew down the remaining half-flight, around a turn to the back, and through a door stenciled 'Employees Only.'

A flight of steps led down to a sub-basement. He pushed Lew ahead of him the rest of the way down, but Tom stayed where he was. He pitched something that flashed, and Lew caught it adroitly before he even knew what it was. A key.

'Open twelve, and switch to my blue suit,' Tom said. 'Leave that grey of yours in the locker.'

Lew took a step back toward him, swung his arm back. 'I haven't done anything! What's the matter with you? You trying to get me in a jam?'

'You're in one already, I'm trying to get you out of it!' Tom snapped. 'There's a dame out there hanging onto the manager's neck with both arms, swears she saw you do it. Hallucinations, you know the kind! Says he started falling asleep on you, and you gave him a shove, one word led to another, then you knifed him. Robbed him, too. She's just hysterical enough to believe what she's saying herself.'

Lew's knees gave a dip. 'But holy smoke! Can't you tell 'em I was the first one told you about it myself? I even helped you carry him back to the rest-room! Does that look like I—'

'It took me long enough to get this job,' Tom said sourly. 'If the manager finds out I passed you in free – what with this giving his house a bad name and all – I can kiss my job good-bye! Think of my end of it, too. Why do they have to know anything about you? You didn't do it, so all right. Then why be a chump and spend the night in a station-house basement? By tomorrow they'll probably have the right guy and it'll be all over with.'

Lew thought of that dollar he had in his pocket. If he went back and let them question him, they'd want to know why he hadn't paid his way in, if he had a buck on him. That would tell them where the buck came from. He hated to pony up that buck now that he had it. And he remembered how he'd tampered with the knife-hilt, and vaguely knew there was something called fingerprints by which they had a way of telling who had handled it. And then the thought of bucking that woman – from what he remembered of the look on her face – took more nerve than he had. Tom was right, why not light out and steer clear of the whole mess, as long as he had the chance? And finally this argument presented itself: if they once got hold of him and believed he'd done it, that might satisfy them, they mightn't even try to look any further, and then where would he be? A clear conscience doesn't always make for courage, sometimes it's just the other way around. The mystic words 'circumstantial evidence' danced in front of his eyes, paralysing him.

'Peel!' Tom said. 'The show breaks in another couple minutes. When you hear the bugles bringing on the newsreel, slip out of here and mingle with the rest of them going out. She's tagged you wearing a grey suit, so it ought to be easy enough to make it in my blue. They won't think of busting open the lockers to look. Wait for me at our place.' Then Tom ducked out and the passageway-door closed noiselessly after him.

Lew didn't give himself time to think. He jumped into the blue suit as Tom had told him to, put on his hat and bent the brim down over his eyes with fingers that were shaking like ribbons in a breeze. He was afraid any minute that someone, one of the other ushers, would walk in and catch him. What was he going to say he was doing in there?

He banged the locker closed on his own clothes, just as a muffled *ta-da* came from the screen outside. In another minutes there were feet shuffling by outside the door and the hum of subdued voices. He edged the door open, and pressed it shut behind him with his elbow. The few movie goers who were leaving were all around him, and he let them carry him along with them. They didn't seem to be aware, down below here, of what had happened up above so short a time ago. Lew didn't hear any mention of it.

It was like running the gauntlet. There were two sets of doors and a brightly lighted lobby in between. One of the detectives was standing beside the doorman at the first set of doors. The watchful way he scanned all faces told Lew what he was. There was a second one outside the street doors. He kept looking so long at each person coming out – that told what he was.

Lew saw them both before he got up to them, through the clear glass of the inner doors. The lights were on their side, Lew was in the dark, with the show still going on in back of him. His courage froze, he wanted to stay in there where he was. But if he was going to get out at all, now was the time, with the majority of the crowd, not later on when he'd be more conspicuous.

One thing in his favour was the colour of his suit. He saw the detectives stopping all the men in grey and motioning them aside; he counted six being sidetracked before he even got out into the lobby. They weren't interfering with anyone else.

But that ticket-taker was a bigger risk than either of the plainclothes-men. So was the doorman. Before he'd gone in he'd been standing right under both their eyes a full five minutes waiting for Tom to come down. He'd gone in without paying, and that had burned the ticket-taker up. But going past them, Lew had to walk slow, as slowly as everyone else was walking, or he'd give himself away twice as quick. He couldn't turn around now and go back any more, either; he was too close to the detectives and they'd notice the manoeuvre.

A clod-hopper in front of him came to his rescue just when he thought he was a goner. The clod-hopper stepped backward unexpectedly to take a look at something, and his whole hoof landed like a stone-cutter's mallet across Lew's toes. Lew's face screwed up uncontrollably with pain, and before he straightened it out again, the deadly doorman's gaze had swept harmlessly over it without recognition, and Lew was past him and all he could see was the back of Lew's head.

Lew held his breath. Nothing happened. Right foot forward, left foot forward, right foot forward. . . . The lobby seemed to go on for miles. Someone's hand touched him, and the mercury went all the way down his spine to the bottom, but it was only a woman close behind him putting on her gloves.

After what seemed like an eternity of slow motion, he was flush with the street-doors at last. Only that second detective out there to buck now, and he didn't worry him much. He drifted through with all the others, passed close enough to the detective to touch him, and he wasn't even looking at Lew. His eyes were on the slap-slap of the doors as they kept swinging to and fro with each new egress.

Lew moved from under the revealing glare of the marquee lights into the sheltering darkness. He didn't look back, and presently the hellish place was just a blob of light far behind him. Then it wasn't even that any more.

He kept dabbing his face, and he felt limp in the legs for a long time afterwards. He's made it, but whew! what an experience; he said to himself that he'd undergone all the emotions of a hunted criminal, without having committed a crime.

Tom and Lew had a cheap furnished room in a tenement about half an hour's walk away. Lew walked there unhesitatingly now, in a straight line from the theatre. As far as he could see, it was all over, there wasn't anything to worry about now any more. He was out of the place, and that was all that mattered. They'd have the right guy in custody, maybe before the night was over, anyway by tomorrow at the latest.

He let himself into the front hallway with the key, climbed the stairs without meeting anyone, and closed the room door behind him. He snapped on the fly-blown bulb hanging from the ceiling, and sat down to wait for Tom.

Finally the clock rotated to 11 P.M. The last show broke at 11:30, and when Tom got here it would be about twelve.

About the time Tom should have been showing up, a newspaper delivery truck came rumbling by, distributing the midnight edition. Lew saw it stop by a stand down at the corner and dump out a bale of papers. On an impulse he got up and went down there to get one, wondering if it would have the story in it yet, and whether they'd caught the guy yet. He didn't open it until he'd got back.

It hadn't made a scare-head, but it had made a column on the front page. 'Man stabbed in movie house; woman sees crime committed.' Lew got sort of a vicarious thrill out of it for a minute, until he read further along. They were *still* looking for a guy just his height and build, wearing a grey suit, who had bummed his way in free. The motive – probably caught by the victim in the act of picking his pocket while he slept. In panic, Lew doused the light.

From then on it was a case of standing watching from behind the drawn shade and standing listening behind the door, and wearing down the flooring in between the two places like a caged bear. He knew he was crazy to stay there, and yet he didn't know where else to go. It would be even crazier, he thought, to roam around in the streets, he'd be sure to be picked up before morning. The sweat came out of every pore hot, and then froze cold. And yet never once did the idea of walking back there of his own accord, and saying to them, 'Well, here I am; I didn't do it,' occur to him. It looked too bad now, the way he'd changed clothes and run out. He cursed Tom for putting him up to it, and himself for losing his head and listening to him. It was too late now. There's a finality about print, especially to a novice; because that paper said they were looking for him, it seemed to kill Lew's last chance of clearing himself once and for all.

He didn't see Tom coming, although he was glancing out through a corner of the window the whole time; Tom must have slunk along close to the building line below. There was a sudden scurry of quick steps on the stairs, and Tom was trying the door-knob like fury. Lew had locked it on the inside when he'd put the light out.

'Hurry up, lemme in!' Tom panted. And then when Lew had unlocked the door: 'Leave that light out, you fool!'

'I thought you'd never get here!' Lew groaned. 'What'd they do, give
a midnight matinee?'

'Down at Headquarters, they did!' Tom said resentfully. 'Hauled
me down there and been holding me there ever since! I'm surprised
they let me go when they did. I didn't think they were gonna.' He
threw the door open. 'You gotta get out of here!'

'Where'm I gonna go?' Lew wailed. 'You're a fine louse of a friend!'

'Suppose a cop shows up here all of a sudden and finds you here, how's
that gonna make it look for me? How do I know I wasn't followed
coming back here? Maybe that's why they let me go!'

Tom kept trying to shoulder Lew out in the hall, and Lew kept trying
to hang onto the door-frame and stay in; in a minute more they would
have been at it hot and heavy, but suddenly there was a pounding at the
street-door three floors below. They both froze.

'I knew it!' Tom hissed. 'Right at my heels!'

The pounding kept up. 'Coming! Wait a minute, can't you?' a
woman's voice said from the back, and bedroom-slippers went slapping
across the oilcloth. Lew was out on the landing now of his own accord,
scuttling around it like a mouse trying to find a hole.

Tom jerked his thumb at the stairs going up. 'The roof!' he whispered.
'Maybe you can get down through the house next door.' But Lew could
see all he cared about was that he was out of the room.

Tom closed the door silently but definitely. The one below opened at
the same instant, to the accompaniment of loud beefs from the landlady,
that effectively covered the creaking of the stairs under Lew's flying feet.

'The idea, getting people out of their beds at this hour! Don't you
tell me to pipe down, detective or no detective! This is a respectable
hou—'

Lew was up past the top floor by that time. The last section was not
inclined stairs any more but a vertical iron ladder, ending just under a
flat, lead skylight, latched on the underside. He flicked the latch open,
climbed up a rung further and lowered his head out of the way, with
the thing pressing across his shoulders like Atlas supporting the world.
He had to stay there like that till he got in out of the stair-well; he
figured the cop would hear the thing creak and groan otherwise. It
didn't have hinges, had to be displaced bodily.

There was a sudden commanding knock at Tom's door on the third,
and an 'Open up here!' that left no room for argument. Tom opened it
instantly, with a whining, 'What do you want this time?' Then it
closed again, luckily for Lew, and the detective was in there with Tom.

Lew heaved upward with all his might, and felt as if he were lifting the roof bodily off the house. His head and shoulders pushed through into the open night. He caught the two lower corners of the thing back-handed so it wouldn't slam down again as he slipped out from under it, and eased it down gently on its frame. Before the opening had quite closed, though, he had a view down through it all the way to the bottom of the stair-well, and half-way along this, at the third floor, a face was sticking out over the bannister, staring up at him. The landlady, who had stayed out there eavesdropping. She had the same bird's-eye view of him that he had of her.

He let go the skylight cover and pounded across the gravelled tar toward the next roof for all he was worth. The detective would be up here after him in a minute now.

The dividing line between the two roofs was only a knee-high brick parapet easy enough to clear, but after that there was only one other roof, instead of a whole block-length of them. Beyond the next house was a drop of six stories to a vacant lot. The line of roofs, of varying but accessible heights, lay behind him in the other direction; he'd turned the wrong way in the dark. But it didn't matter, he thought, as long as he could get in through the twin to the skylight he'd come out of.

He couldn't. He found it by stabbing his toe against it and falling across it, rather than with the help of his eyes. Then when he knelt there clawing and tugging at it, it wouldn't come up. Latched underneath like the first one had been!

There wasn't any time to go back the other way now. Yellow light showed on the roof behind him as the detective lifted the trap. First a warning thread of it, then a big gash, and the dick was scrambling out on the roof-top. Lew thought he saw a gun in his hand, but he didn't wait to find out. There was a three-foot brick chimney a little ways behind Lew. He darted behind it while his pursuer's head was still turned up the other way. But the gravel under him gave a treacherous little rattle as he carried out the manoeuvre.

There was silence for a long time. He was afraid to stick his head out and look. Then there was another of those little give-away rustles, not his this time, coming from this same roof, from the other side of the chimney.

Then with a suddenness that made him jump, a new kind of planet joined the stars just over his head, blazed out and spotted him from head to foot. A pocket-torch. Lew just pressed his body inward, helpless against the brick work.

'Come on, get up,' the detective's voice said without any emotion, somewhere just behind the glare. To Lew it was like the headlight of a locomotive; he couldn't see a thing for a minute. He straightened up, blinking; even thought he was going to be calm and resigned for a minute. 'I didn't do it,' he said. 'Honest, I didn't do it! Gimme a break, will you?'

The detective said mockingly that he would, sure he would, using an expression that doesn't bear repetition. He collared Lew with one hand, by both sides of his coat at once, pulling the reveres together close up under Lew's chin. Then he balanced the lighted torch on the lip of the chimney-stack, so that it stayed pointed at Lew and drenched him all over. Then he frisked him with that hand.

'I tell you I was just sitting next to him! I didn't touch him, I didn't put a finger on him!'

'And that's why you're hiding out on the roof, is it? Changed your suit, too, didn't you? I'll beat the truth out of you, when I get you where we're going!'

It was that, and the sudden sight of the handcuffs twinkling in the rays of the torch, that made Lew lose his head. He jerked backwards in the detective's grip, trying to get away from him. His back brushed the brick work. The flashlight went out suddenly, and went rattling all the way down inside the chimney. Lew was wedged in there between the detective and the stack. He raised the point of his knee suddenly, jabbed it upward between them like a piston. The detective let go Lew's collar, the manacles fell with a clink, and he collapsed at Lew's feet, writhing and groaning. Agonised as he was, his hand sort of flailed helplessly around, groping for something; Lew saw that even in the dark. Lew beat him to it, tore the gun out of his pocket, and pitched it overhand and backwards. It landed way off somewhere behind Lew, but stayed on the roof.

The detective had sort of doubled up in the meantime, like a helpless beetle on its back, drawing his legs up toward his body. They offered a handle to grab him by. Lew was too frightened to run away and leave him, too frightened that he'd come after him and the whole thing would start over. It was really an excess of fright that made him do it; there is such a thing. He grabbed the man around the ankles with both hands, started dragging him on his back across the gravel toward the edge of the roof, puffing, 'You're not gonna get *me*! You're not gonna get *me*! You're not taking *me* with ya while I know it!'

Toward the side edge of the building he dragged the detective. He didn't bother looking to see what was below; just let go the legs, spun the detective around on his behind, so that the loose gravel shot out from under him in all directions, grabbed him by the shoulders, and pushed him over head-first. The dick didn't make a sound. Lew didn't know if he was still conscious or had fainted by now from the blow in the groin Lew had given him. Then he was snatched from sight as if a powerful magnet had suddenly pulled him down.

Then Lew did a funny thing. The instant after the detective was gone, Lew stretched out his arms involuntarily toward where he'd been, as if to grab him, catch him in time to save him. As though he hadn't really realised until then the actual meaning of what he was doing. Or maybe it was his last inhibition showing itself, before it left him altogether. A brake that would no longer work was trying to stop him after it was too late. The next minute he was feeling strangely light-headed, dizzy. But not dizzy from remorse, dizzy like someone who's been bound fast and is suddenly free.

Lew didn't look down toward where the man had gone, he looked up instead – at the stars that must have seen many another sight like the one just now, without blinking.

'Gosh, it's easy!' he marvelled, openmouthed. 'I never knew before how easy it is to kill anyone! Twenty years to grow 'em, and all it takes is one little push!'

He was suddenly drunk with some new kind of power, undiscovered until this minute. The power of life and death over his fellowmen! Everyone had it, everyone strong enough to raise a violent arm, but they were afraid to use it. Well, he wasn't! And here he'd been going around for weeks living from hand to mouth, without any money, without enough food, when everything he wanted lay within his reach all the while! He *had* been green all right, and no mistake about it!

Death had become familiar. At seven it had been the most mysterious thing in the world to him, by midnight it was already an old story.

'Now let 'em come after me!' he thought vindictively, as he swayed back across the roof toward the skylight of the other house. 'Now I've given 'em a real reason for trying to nab me!' And he added grimly, 'If they can!'

Something flat kicked away from under his foot, and he stopped and picked up the gun that he'd tossed out of reach. He looked it over after he was through the skylight and there was light to examine it by. He'd never held one in his hand before. He knew enough not to squint down the bore, and that was about all he knew.

The stair-well was empty; the landlady must have retreated temporarily to her quarters below to rouse her husband, so he wouldn't miss the excitement of the capture and towing away. Lew passed Tom's closed door and was going by it without stopping, going straight down to the street and the new career that awaited him in the slumbering city, when Tom opened it himself and looked out. He must have heard a creak and thought it was the detective returning, thought Lew, and figured a little bootlicking wouldn't hurt any.

'Did you get him – ?' Tom started to say. Then he saw who it was, and saw what Lew was holding in his hand.

Lew turned around and went back to him. 'No, he didn't get me,' he said, ominously quiet, 'I got him.' He went in and closed the door of the room after him. He kept looking at Tom, who backed away a little.

'Now you've finished yourself!' Tom breathed, appalled.

'You mean I'm just beginning,' Lew said.

'I'm going to get out of here!' Tom said, in a sudden flurry of panic, and tried to circle around Lew and get to the door.

Lew waved him back with the gun. 'No, you're not, you're going to stay right where you are! What'd you double-cross me for?'

Tom got behind a chair and hung onto it with both hands – as though that was any good! Then almost hysterically, as he read Lew's face: 'What's the matter, ya gone crazy? Not *me*, Lew! Not *me!*'

'Yes, you!' Lew said. 'You got me into it. You knew they'd follow you. You led 'em to me. But they still don't know what I look like – but you do! That one went up there after me can't tell now what I look like, but you still can! They can get me on sight, while you're still around.'

Tom was holding both palms flat out toward Lew, as though Lew thought they could stop or turn aside a bullet! Tom had time to get just one more thing out: 'You're not human at all!'

Then Lew pulled the trigger and the whole room seemed to lift with a roar, as though blasting were going on under it. The gun bucked Lew back half a step; he hadn't known those things had a kick to them. When he looked through the smoke, Tom's face and shoulders were gone from behind the chair, but his forearms were still hanging across the top of it, palms turned downward now, and all the fingers wiggling at once. Then they fell off it, went down to join the rest of him on the floor.

Lew watched him for a second, what he could see of him. Tom didn't move any more. Lew shook his head slowly from side to side. 'It sure is easy all right!' he said to himself. And this had been even less dramatic than the one up above on the roof.

Familiarity with death had already bred contempt for it.

He turned, pitched the door open, and went jogging down the stairs double-quick. Doors were opening on every landing as he whisked by, but not a move was made to stop him – which was just as well for them. He kept the gun out on his hand the whole time and cleared the bottom steps with a short jump at the bottom of each flight. Bang! and then around to the next.

The landlady had got herself into a bad position. She was caught between him and the closed street-door as he cleared the last flight and came down into the front hall. If she'd stayed where she belonged, Lew said to himself, she could have ducked back into her own quarters at the rear when he came down. But now her escape was cut off. When she saw it was Lew, and not the detective, she tried to get out the front way. She couldn't get the door open in time, so then she tried to turn back again. She dodged to one side to get out of Lew's way, and he went to that side too. Then they both went to the other side together and blocked each other again. It was like a game of puss-in-the-corner, with appalled faces peering tensely down the stair-well at them.

She was heaving like a sick cat in a sand-box, and Lew decided she was too ludicrous to shoot. New as he was at the game of killing, he had to have dignity in his murders. He walloped her back-handed aside like a gnat, and stepped over her suddenly upthrust legs. She could only give a garbled description of him any way.

The door wasn't really hard to open, if you weren't frightened, like Lew wasn't now. Just a twist of the knob and a wrench. A voice shrieked down inanely from one of the upper floors, 'Get the cops! He's killed a fellow up here!' Then Lew was out in the street, and looking both ways at once.

A passerby who must have heard the shot out there had stopped dead in his tracks, directly opposite the doorway on the other side of the street, and was gawking over. He saw Lew and called over nosily: 'What happened? Something wrong in there?'

It would have been easy enough to hand him some stall or other, pretend Lew was himself looking for a cop. But Lew had this new contempt of death hot all over him.

'Yeah!' he snarled viciously. 'I just shot a guy! And if you stand there looking at me like that, you're gonna be the next!'

He didn't know if the passerby saw the gun or not in the dark, probably not. The man didn't wait to make sure, took him at his word. He bolted for the nearest corner. *Scrunch*, and he was gone!

'There,' Lew said to himself tersely, 'is a sensible guy!'

Black window squares here and there were turning orange as the neighbourhood began belatedly to wake up. A lot of interior yelling and tramping was coming from the house Tom and Lew had lived in. He made for the corner opposite from the one his late questioner had fled around, turned it, and slowed to a quick walk. He put the gun away; it stuck too far out of the shallow side-pocket of Tom's suit, so he changed it to the inner breast-pocket, which was deeper. A cop's whistle sounded thinly behind him, at the upper end of the street he'd just left.

A taxi was coming toward him, and he jumped off the sidewalk and ran toward it diagonally. The driver tried to swerve without stopping, so he jumped up on the running-board and wrenched the wheel with his free hand. He had the other spaded into his pocket over the gun again. 'Turn around, you're going downtown with me!' he said. A girl's voice bleated in the back. 'I've got two passengers in there already!' the driver said, but he was turning with a lurch that nearly threw Lew off.

'I'll take care of that for you!' he yanked the back door open and got in with them. 'Out you go, that side!' he ordered. The fellow jumped first, as etiquette prescribed, but the girl clung to the door-strap, too terrified to move, so Lew gave her a push to help her make up her mind. 'Be a shame to separate the two of you!' he called after her. She turned her ankle, and went down kerplunk and lay there, with her escort bending over her in the middle of the street.

'Wh-where you want me to g-go with you, buddy?' chattered the driver.

'Out of this neighbourhood fast,' Lew said grimly.

He sped along for a while, then whined: 'I got a wife and kids, buddy—'

'You're a very careless guy,' Lew said to that.

He knew they'd pick up his trail any minute, what with those two left stranded in the middle of the street to direct them, so he made for the concealing labyrinth of the park, the least policed part of the city.

'Step it down a little,' he ordered, once they were in the park. 'Take off your shoes and throw them back here.' The driver's presence was a handicap, and Lew had decided to get rid of him, too. Driving zig-zag along the lane with one hand, the cabbie threw back his shoes. One of them hit Lew on the knee as it was pitched through the open slide, and for a minute Lew nearly changed his mind and shot him instead, as the easiest way out after all. The cabbie was half dead with fright by this time, anyway. Lew made him take off his pants, too, and then told him to brake and get out.

Lew got in at the wheel. The driver stood there on the asphalt in his socks and shirt-tails, pleading, 'Gee, don't leave me in the middle of the park like this, buddy, without my pants and shoes, it'll take me all night to get out!'

'That's the main idea,' Lew agreed vindictively, and added: 'You don't know how lucky you are! You're up against Death's right-hand man. Scram, before I change my mind!'

The cabbie went loping away into the dark, like a bow-legged scarecrow and Lew sat at the wheel belly-laughing after him. Then he took the cab away at top speed, and came out the other end about quarter of an hour later.

He was hungry, and decided the best time to eat was right then, before daylight added to the risk and a general alarm had time to circulate. The ability to pay, of course, was no longer a problem in this exciting new existence that had begun for him tonight. He picked the most expensive place open at that hour, an all-night delicatessen, where they charged a dollar for a sandwich and named it after a celebrity. A few high-hats were sitting around having bacon and eggs in the dim, artificial blue light that made them look like ghosts.

He left the cab right at the door and sat down where he could watch it. A waiter came over who didn't think much of him because he didn't have a boiled shirt. He ran his finger down the list and picked a five-dollar one.

'What's a Jimmy Cagney? Gimme one of them.'

'Hard-boiled egg with lots of paprika.' The waiter started away.

Lew picked up a glass of water and sloshed it across the back of his neck. 'You come back here! Do that over, and say sir!' he snarled.

'Hard-boiled egg with lots of paprika, sir,' the waiter stuttered, squirming to get the water off his backbone.

When he was through, Lew leaned back in his chair and thumbed him over. 'How much do you take in here a night?'

'Oh, around five hundred when it's slow like this.' He took out a pad and scribbed '5.00' at the bottom, tore it off and handed it to Lew.

'Lend me your pencil,' Lew said. He wrote 'Pay me' in front of it, and rubbed out the decimal point. 'I'll take this over to the cashier myself,' he told the waiter.

Then as he saw the waiter's glance sweep the bare table-top disappointedly, 'Don't worry, you'll get your tip; I'm not forgetting you.'

Lew found the tricky blue lighting was a big help. It made everyone's face look ghastly to begin with and you couldn't tell when anyone suddenly got paler. Like the cashier, when he looked up from reading the bill Lew presented and found the bore of the gun peering out from Lew's shirt at him like some kind of a bulky tie pin.

He opened the drawer and started counting bills out. 'Quit making your hands shake so,' Lew warned him out of the corner of his mouth, 'and keep your eyes down on what you're doing, or you're liable to short-change me!'

Lew liked doing it that way, adding to the risk by standing there letting the cashier count out the exact amount, instead of just cleaning the till and lamming. What was so hectic about a hold-up, he asked himself. Every crime seemed so simple, once you got the hang of it. He was beginning to like this life, it was swell!

There were thirty or so bucks left in the drawer when the cashier got through. But meanwhile the manager had got curious about the length of time Lew had been standing up there and started over toward them. Lew could tell by his face he didn't suspect even yet, only wanted to see if there was some difficulty. At the same line Lew caught sight of the waiter slinking along the far side of the room, toward the door in back of him. He hadn't been able to get over to the manager in time, and was going to be a hero on his own, and go out and get a cop.

So Lew took him first. The waiter was too close to the door already for there to be any choice in the matter. Lew didn't even aim, just fired what he'd heard called a snap-shot. The waiter went right down across the doorsill, like some new kind of a lumpy mat. Lew didn't even feel the thing buck as much as when he'd shot Tom. The cashier dropped too, as though the same shot had felled him. His voice came up from the bottom of the enclosure, 'There's your money, don't shoot me, don't shoot me!' Too much night-work isn't good for a guy's guts, Lew mused.

There was a doorman outside on the sidewalk. Lew got him through the open doorway just as he got to the curb, in the act of raising his whistle to his lips. He stumbled, grabbed one of the chromium stanchions supporting the entrance canopy, and went slipping down like a fireman sliding down a pole. The manager ducked behind a table, and everyone else in the place went down to floor-level with him, as suddenly as though they were all puppets jerked by strings. Lew couldn't see a face left in the room; just a lot of screaming coming from behind empty chairs.

Lew grabbed up the five hundred and sprinted for the door. He had to hurdle the waiter's body and he moved a little as Lew did so, so he wasn't dead. Then Lew stopped just long enough to peel off a ten and drop it down to him. 'There's your tip, chiseler!' Lew hollered at him, and beat it.

Lew couldn't get to the cab in time, so he had to let it go, and take it on foot. There was a car parked a few yards in back of it, and another a length ahead, that might have blocked his getting it out at the first try, and this was no time for lengthy extrications. A shot came his way from the corner, about half a block up, and he dashed around the next one. Two more came from that, just as he got to the corner ahead, and he fired back at the sound of them, just on general principle. He had no aim to speak of, had never held one of the things in his hand until that night.

He turned and sprinted down the side street, leaving the smoke of his shot hanging there disembodiedly behind him like a baby cloud above the sidewalk. There were two cops by now, but the original one was in the lead and he was a good runner. He quit shooting and concentrated on taking Lew the hard way, at arms' length. Lew turned his head in time to see him tear through the smoke up there at the corner and knock it invisible. He was a tall limber guy, must have been good in the heats at police games, and he came hurtling straight toward Death. Tick, tick, tick, his feet went, like a very quick clock.

A fifth shot boomed out in that instant, from ahead of Lew this time, down at the lower corner. Somebody had joined in from that direction, right where Lew was going toward. They had him sewn up now between them, on this narrow sidestreet. One in front, two behind him – and to duck in anywhere was curtains.

Something happened, with that shot, that happens once in a million years. The three of them were in a straight line – Lew in the middle, the sprinter behind him, the one who had just fired coming up the other way. Something spit past Lew's ear, and the tick, tick behind him scattered into a scraping, thumping fall – *plump!* – and stopped. The runner had been hit by his own man, up front.

He didn't look, his ears had seen the thing for him. He dove into a doorway between the two of them. Only a miracle could save him, and it had no more than sixty seconds in which to happen, to be any good.

His star, beaming overtime, made it an open street door, indicative of poverty. The street was between Second and Third Avenues, and poverty was rampant along it, the same kind of poverty that had turned Lew into a ghoul, snatching a dollar from a dead man's pocket, at six-thirty this night. He punched three bell-buttons as he flashed by.

'If they come in here after me,' he sobbed hotly, 'there's going to be shooting like there never was before!' And they would, of course. The header-offer down at Second, who had shot his own man, must have seen which entrance he'd dived for. Even if he hadn't, they'd dragnet all of them.

Lew reached in his pocket as he took the stairs, brought out a fistful of the money and not the gun for once. At least a hundred's worth came up in his paw. One of the bills escaped, fluttered down the steps behind him like a green leaf. What's ten, or even twenty, when you've got sixty seconds to buy your life?

'In there!' One of the winded, surviving cops' voices rang out clearly, penetrated the hall from the sidewalk. The screech of a prowl car chimed in.

He was holding the handful of green dough up in front of him, like the olive branch of the ancients, when the first of the three doors opened before him, second-floor front. A man with a curleycue moustache was blinking out as he raced at him.

'A hundred bucks!' Lew hissed. 'They're after me! Here, hundred bucks if you lemme get in your door!'

'Whassa mat?' he wanted to know, startled wide awake.

'Cops! Hundred bucks!' The space between them had been used up, Lew's whole body hit the door like a projectile. The man was holding onto it on the inside, so it wouldn't give. The impact swung Lew around sideways, he clawed at it with one hand, shoved the bouquet of money into the man's face with the other. 'Two hundred bucks!'

'Go 'way!' the man cried, tried to close Lew out. Lew had decided to shoot him out of the way if he couldn't buy his way in.

A deep bass voice came rumbling up behind him. '*Che cosa, Mario?*'

'Two hundred bucks,' Lew strangled, reaching for the gun with his left hand.

'*Due cento dollari!*' The door was torn away from him, opened wide. An enormous, moustached, garlicky Italian woman stood there. "Issa good? Issa rill?" Lew jammed them down her huge bosom as the quickest way of proving their authenticity. Maybe Mario Jr had had a run-in with cops about breaking a window or swiping fruit from a pushcart; maybe it was just the poverty. She slapped one hand on her chest to hold the money there, grabbed Lew's arm with the other. '*Si! Vene presto!*' and spat a warning '*Silenzio! La porta!*' at her reluctant old man.

She pounded down the long inner hall, towing Lew after her. The door closed behind them as the stairway outside was started vibrating with ascending feet – flat feet.

The bedroom was pitch black. She let go of him, gave him a push sideways and down, and he went sprawling across an enormous room-filling bed. A cat snatched itself out of the way and jumped down. He hoisted his legs up after him, clawed, pulled a garlicky quilt up to his chin. He began to undress hectically under it, lying on his side. She snapped a light on and was standing there counting the money. '*Falta cento—*' she growled aggressively.

'You get the other hundred after they go 'way.' He stuck his hand out under the cover, showed it to her. He took the gun out and showed her that too. 'If you or your old man give me away – !'

Pounding had already begun at their door. Her husband was standing there by it, not making a sound. She shoved the money down under the same mattress Lew was on. He got rid of his coat, trousers and shoes, pitched them out on the other side of him, just as she snapped out the light once more. He kept the gun and money with him, under his body.

The next thing he knew, the whole bed structure quivered under him, wobbled, all but sank flat. She'd got in alongside of him! The clothes billowed like sails in a storm, subsided. She went, 'Ssst!' like a steam radiator, and the sound carried out into the hall. Lew heard the man pick up his feet two or three times, plank them down again, right where he was standing, to simulate trudging toward the door. Then he opened it, and they were in. Lew closed his eyes, spaded one hand under him and kept it on the gun.

'Took you long enough!' a voice said at the end of the hall. 'Anyone come in here?'

'Nome-body.'

'Well, we'll take a look for ourselves! Give it the lights!'

The lining of Lew's eyelids turned vermilion, but he kept them down. The mountain next to him stirred, gyrated. '*Che cosa, Mario?*'

'*Polizia, non capisco.*'

Kids were waking up all over the place, in adjoining rooms, adding to the anvil chorus. It would have looked phony to go on sleeping any longer in that racket. Lew squirmed, stretched, blinked, yawned, popped his eyes in innocent surprise. There were two cops in the room, one of them standing still, looking at him, the other sticking his head into a closet.

Lew had black hair and was sallow from undernourishment, but he didn't know a word of Italian.

'Who's this guy?' the cop asked.

'*Il mio fratello.*' Her brother. The volume of noise she and Mario and the kids were making covered him.

The first cop went out. The second one came closer, pulled the corner of the covers off Lew. All he saw was a skinny torso in an undershirt. Lew's outside shirt was rolled in a ball down by his feet. His thumb found and went into the hollow before the trigger underneath him. If he said 'Get up outa there,' those would be the last words he ever said.

He said, 'Three in a bed?' disgustedly. 'Sure y'ain't got your grandfather in there, too? These guineas!' He threw the covers back at Lew and went stalking out.

Lew could hear him through the open door tramp up the stairs after the others to the floor above. A minute later their heavy footsteps sounded on the ceiling right above his head.

A little runty ten-year-old girl peered in at him from the doorway. He said, 'Put that light out! Keep them kids outa here! Leave the door open until they go! Tell your old man to stand there rubber-necking out, like all the others are doing!'

They quit searching in about fifteen minutes, and Lew heard them all go trooping down again, out into the street, and then he could hear their voices from the sidewalk right under the windows.

'Anything doing?' somebody asked.

'Naw, he musta got out through the back yard, and the next street over.'

'O'Keefe hurt bad?'

'Nicked him in the dome, stunned him, that was all.' So the cop wasn't dead.

When Mario came out the front door at eight-thirty on his way to the barber shop where he worked, his 'brother-in-law' was with him, as close to him as sticking plaster. Lew had on an old felt hat of Mario's and a baggy red sweater that hid the coat of Tom's blue suit. It would have looked too good to come walking out of a building like that on the way to work. That red sweater had cost Lew another fifty. The street looked normal, one wouldn't have known it for the shooting gallery it had been at four that morning. They walked side by side up toward Second, past the place where O'Keefe had led with his chin, past the corner where the smoke of Lew's shot had hung so ghostly in the lamplight. There was a newsstand open there now, and Lew bought a paper. Then he and Mario stood waiting for the bus.

It drew up and Lew pushed Mario on alone, and jerked his thumb at the driver. It went sailing off again, before Mario had time to say or do anything, if he'd wanted to. It had sounded to Lew, without knowing Italian, as though the old lady had been coaching Mario to get a stranglehold on the rest of Lew's money. Lew snickered aloud, ran his hand lightly over the pocket where the original five-hundred was intact once more. It had been too good to miss, the chance she'd given him of sneaking it out of the mattress she'd cached it under and putting it back in his pocket again, while her back was turned. They'd had all their trouble and risk for nothing.

Lew made tracks away from there, went west as far as Third and then started down that. He stayed with the sweater and hat, because they didn't look out of character on Third. The cops had seen him in the blue suit when they chased him from Rubin's; they hadn't seen him in this outfit. And no matter how the *signora* would blaze when she found out how Lew had gypped them, she couldn't exactly report it to the police, and tell them what he was wearing, without implicating herself and her old man.

But there was one thing had to be attended to right off, and that was the matter of ammunition. To the best of Lew's calculations (and so much had happened, that they were already pretty hazy) he had fired four shots out of the gun from the time he had taken it over from the dick on the roof. One at Tom, two in Rubin's, and one on the street when they'd been after him. There ought to be two left in it, and if the immediate future was going to be like the immediate past, he was going to need a lot more than that. He not only didn't know where any could be bought, he didn't even know how to break the thing and find out how many it packed.

He decided a pawnshop would be about the best bet, not up here in the mid-town district, but down around the lower East Side or on the Bowery somewhere. And if they didn't want to sell him any, he'd just blast and help himself.

He took a streetcar down as far as Chatham Square. He had a feeling that he'd be safer on one of them than on the El or the subway; he could jump off in a hurry without waiting for it to stop, if he had to. Also, he could see where he was going through the windows and not have to do too much roaming around on foot once he alighted. He was a little dubious about hailing a cab, dressed the way he now was. Besides, he couldn't exactly tell a hackman, 'Take me to a pawnshop.' You may ride in a taxi coming out of one, you hardly ride in a taxi going to one.

He went all the way to the rear end and opened the newspaper. He didn't have to hunt it up. This time it *had* made a scare-head. 'One-Man Crime Wave!' And then underneath, 'Mad dog gunman still at large somewhere in city.' Lew looked up at the oblivious backs of the heads up forward, riding on the same car with Lew. Not one of them had given him a second glance when he'd walked down the aisle in the middle of all of them just now. And yet more than one must be reading that very thing he was at the moment; he could see the papers in their hands. That was he, right in the same trolley they were, and they didn't even know it! His contempt for death was beginning to expand dangerously toward the living as well, and the logical step beyond that would be well past the confines of sanity – a superman complex.

Fortunately, he never quite got to it. Something within this same paper itself checked it, before it got well started. Two things that threw cold water over it, as it were. They occurred within a paragraph of each other, and had the effect of deflating his ego almost to the point at which it had been last night, before he'd touched that dead man's face in the theatre rest-room. The first paragraph read: 'The police, hoping that young Tom Lee might unknowingly provide a clue to the suspect's whereabouts, arranged to have him released at Headquarters shortly after midnight. Detective Walter Daly was detailed to follow him. Daly trapped Stahl on the roof of a tenement, only to lose his balance and fall six stories during the scuffle that ensued. He was discovered unconscious but still alive sometime after the young desperado had made good his second escape, lying with both legs broken on an ash-heap in a vacant lot adjoining the building.'

That was the first shock. Still alive, eh? And he'd lost his balance huh? A line or two farther on came the second jolt:

'Stahl, with the detective's gun in his possession, had meanwhile made his way down the stairs and brutally shot Lee in his room. The latter was rushed to the hospital with a bullet wound in his neck; although his condition is critical, he has a good chance to survive. . . .'

Lew let the thing fall to the floor and just sat there, stunned. Tom wasn't dead either! He wasn't quite as deadly as he'd thought he was; death wasn't so easy to dish out, not with the aim he seemed to have. A little of his former respect for death came back. Step one on the road to recovery. He remembered that waiter at Rubin's, flopping flat across the doorway; when he'd jumped over him, he's definitely cringed – so he hadn't finished him either. About all he'd really managed to accomplish, he said to himself, was successfully hold up a restaurant, separate a cab driver from his pants and his machine, and out-smart the cops three times – at the theatre, on the roof, and in the Italians' flat. Plenty for one guy, but not enough to turn him into a Manhattan Dillinger by a long shot.

A lot of his self-confidence had evaporated and he couldn't seem to get it back. There was a sudden, sharp increase of nervousness that had been almost totally lacking the night before.

He said to himself, 'I need some bullets to put into this gun! Once I get them, I'll be all right, that'll take away the chills, turn on the heat again!'

He spotted a likely looking hockshop, and hopped off the car.

He hurried in through the swinging doors of the pawnshop and got a lungful of camphor balls. The proprietor came up to him on the other side of the counter. He leaned sideways on his elbow, tried to stop the shaking that had set in, and said: 'Can you gimme something to fit this?' He reached for the pocket he'd put the gun in.

The proprietor's face was like a mirror. Expectancy, waiting to see what it was; then surprise, at how white his customer was getting; then astonishment, at why Lew should grip the counter like that, to keep from falling.

It was gone, it wasn't there any more. The frisking of the rest of his pockets was just reflex action; the emptiness of the first one told the whole story. He thought he'd outsmarted that Italian she-devil; well, she'd outsmarted him instead! Lifted the gun from him while she was busy seeming to straighten this old red sweater of her husband's on him, And the motive was easy to guess: so that Mario wouldn't be running any risk when he tried to blackmail Lew out on the street for the rest of the five hundred, like she'd told him to. Lew had walked a whole block with him, ridden all the way down here, and never even missed it until now! A fine killer he was!

He could feel what was left of his confidence crumbling away inside him, as though this had been the finishing touch it needed. Panic was coming on. He got a grip on himself; after all, he had five hundred in his pocket. It was just a matter of buying another gun and ammunition, now.

'I wanna buy a revolver. Show me what you've got.'

'Show me your license,' the man countered.

'Now, listen,' he was breathing hard, 'just skip that part of it. I'll pay you double.' He brought out the money.

'Yeah, skip it,' the proprietor scoffed. 'And then what happens to me, when they find out where you got it? I got myself to think of.'

Lew knew he had some guns; the very way he spoke showed he did. He sort of broke. 'For the love of Gawd, lemme have a gun!' he wailed.

'You're snowed up, mac,' he said. 'G'wan, get out of here.'

Lew clenched his teeth. 'You lemme have a gun, or else—' And he made a threatening gesture toward the inside of his coat. But he had nothing to threaten with; his hand dropped limply back again. He felt trapped, helpless. The crumbling away kept on inside him. He whined, pleaded, begged.

The proprietor took a step in the direction of the door. 'Get out of here now, or I'll call the police! You think I want my license taken away?' And then with sudden rage, 'Where's a cop?'

Police. Cops. Lew turned and powdered out like a streak.

And Lew knew then what makes a killer; not the man himself, just the piece of metal in his hand, fashioned by men far cleverer than he. Without that, just a snarling cur, no match even for a paunchy hockshop owner.

Lew lost track of what happened immediately after that. Headlong, incessant flight – from nothing, to nothing. He didn't actually run, but kept going, going, like a car without a driver, a ship without a rudder.

It was not long after that he saw the newspaper. Its headline screamed across the top of the stand where it was being peddled. 'Movie Murderer Confesses.' Lew picked it up, shaking all over.

The manager of Tom's theatre. Weeks, his name was. Somebody'd noticed that he'd been wearing a different suit during this afternoon show than the one he'd had on earlier. The seat behind Kemp's, the dead man's, had had chewing gum on it. They'd got hold of the suit Weeks had left at the dry-cleaner's, and that had chewing gum on the seat of the trousers, too. He'd come in in a hurry around six, changed from one to the other right in the shop, the tailor told them. He'd had one there, waiting to be called for. He admitted it now, claimed the man had been breaking up his home.

Lew dropped the paper and the sheets separated, fell across his shoes.

It stuck to his shoe and Lew was like someone trudging through snow. 'Movie Murderer Confesses – Murderer Confesses – Confesses. . . .'

Subconsciously he must have known where he was going, but he wasn't aware of it, was in a sort of fog in the broad daylight. The little blue and white plaque on the lamp-post said 'Centre Street.' He went slowly down it. He walked inside between the two green lamps at the police station entrance and went up to the guy at the desk and said, 'I guess you people are looking for me. I'm Lew Stahl.'

Somehow, Lew knew it would be better if they put him away for a long while, the longer the better. He had learned too much that one night, got too used to death. Murder might be a habit that, once formed, would be awfully hard to break. Lew didn't want to be a murderer.

John Steinbeck

The Murder

This happened a number of years ago in Monterey County, in central California. The Cañon del Castillo is one of those valleys in the Santa Lucia range which lie between its many spurs and ridges. From the main Cañon del Castillo a number of little arroyos cut back into the mountains, oak-wooded canyons, heavily brushed with poison oak and sage. At the head of the canyon there stands a tremendous stone castle, buttressed and towered like those strongholds the Crusaders put up in the path of their conquests. Only a close visit to the castle shows it to be a strange accident of time and water and erosion working on soft, stratified sandstone. In the distance the ruined battlements, the gates, the towers, even the arrow slits require little imagination to make out.

Below the castle, on the nearly level floor of the canyon, stands an old ranch house, a weathered and mossy barn and a warped feeding shed for cattle. The house is empty and deserted; the doors, swinging on rusted hinges, squeal and bang on nights when the wind courses down from the castle. Not many people visit the house. Sometimes a crowd of boys tramp through the rooms, peering into empty closets and loudly defying the ghosts they deny.

Jim Moore, who owns the land, does not like to have people about the house. He rides up from his new house, farther down the valley and chases the boys away. He has put NO TRESPASSING signs on his fences to keep curious and morbid people out. Sometimes he thinks of burning the old house down, but then a strange and powerful relation with the swinging doors, the blind and desolate windows forbids the destruction. If he should burn the house he would destroy a great and important piece of his life. He knows that when he goes to town with his plump and still pretty wife, people turn and look at his retreating back with awe and some admiration.

Jim Moore was born in the old house and grew up in it. He knew every grained and weathered board of the barn, every smooth, worn manger rack. His mother and father were both dead when he was thirty. He celebrated his majority by raising a beard. He sold the pigs and decided never to have any more. At last he bought a fine Guernsey bull to improve his stock, and he began to go to Monterey on Saturday nights, to get drunk and to talk with the noisy girls of the Three Star.

Within a year Jim Moore married Jelka Sepić, a Jugoslav girl, daughter of a heavy and patient farmer of Pine Canyon. Jim was not proud of her foreign family, of her many brothers and sisters and cousins, but he delighted in her beauty. Jelka had eyes as large and questioning as a doe's eyes. Her nose was thin and sharply faceted, and her lips were deep and soft. Jelka's skin always startled Jim, for between night and night he forgot how beautiful it was. She was so smooth and quiet and gentle, such a good house-keeper, that Jim often thought with disgust of her father's advice on the wedding day. The old man, bleary and bloated with festival beer, elbowed Jim in the ribs and grinned suggestively, so that his little dark eyes almost disappeared behind puffed and wrinkled lids.

'Don't be big fool now,' he said. 'Jelka is Slav girl. He's not like American girl. If he is bad, beat him. If he's good too long, beat him too. I beat his mama. Papa beat my mama. Slav girl! He's not like a man that don't beat hell out of him.'

'I wouldn't beat Jelka,' Jim said.

The father giggled and nudged him again with his elbow. 'Don't be big fool,' he warned. 'Sometimes you see.' He rolled back to the beer barrel.

Jim found soon enough that Jelka was not like American girls. She was very quiet. She never spoke first, but only answered his questions, and then with soft short replies. She learned her husband as she learned passages of Scripture. After they had been married a while, Jim never wanted for any habitual thing in the house but Jelka had it ready for him before he could ask. She was a fine wife, but there was no companionship in her. She never talked. Her great eyes followed him, and when he smiled, sometimes she smiled too, a distant and covered smile. Her knitting and mending and sewing were interminable. There she sat, watching her wise hands, and she seemed to regard with wonder and pride the little white hands that could do such nice and useful things. She was so much like an animal that sometimes Jim patted her head and neck under the same impulse that made him stroke a horse.

In the house Jelka was remarkable. No matter what time Jim came in from the hot dry range or from the bottom farm land, his dinner was exactly, steamingly ready for him. She watched while he ate, and pushed the dishes close when he needed them, and filled his cup when it was empty.

Early in the marriage he told her things that happened on the farm, but she smiled at him as a foreigner does who wishes to be agreeable even though he doesn't understand.

'The stallion cut himself on the barbed wire,' he said.

And she replied, 'Yes,' with a downward inflection that held neither question nor interest.

He realised before long that he could not get in touch with her in any way. If she had a life apart, it was so remote as to be beyond his reach. The barrier in her eyes was not one that could be removed, for it was neither hostile nor intentional.

At night he stroked her straight black hair and her unbelievably smooth golden shoulders, and she whimpered a little with pleasure. Only in the climax of his embrace did she seem to have a life apart and fierce and passionate. And then immediately she lapsed into the alert and painfully dutiful wife.

'Why don't you ever talk to me?' he demanded. 'Don't you want to talk to me?'

'Yes,' she said. 'What do you want me to say?' She spoke the language of his race out of a mind that was foreign to his race.

When a year had passed, Jim began to crave the company of women, the chattery exchange of small talk, the shrill pleasant insults, the shame-sharpened vulgarity. He began to go again to town, to drink and to play with the noisy girls of the Three Star. They liked him there for his firm, controlled face and for his readiness to laugh.

'Where's your wife?' they demanded.

'Home in the barn,' he responded. It was a never failing joke.

Saturday afternoons he saddled a horse and put a rifle in the scabbard in case he should see a deer. Always he asked. 'You don't mind staying alone?'

'No. I don't mind.'

And once he asked, 'Suppose someone should come?'

Her eyes sharpened for a moment, and then she smiled. 'I would send them away,' she said.

'I'll be back about noon tomorrow. It's too far to ride in the night.' He felt that she knew where he was going, but she never protested nor gave any sign of disapproval. 'You should have a baby,' he said.

Her face lighted up. 'Sometime God will be good,' she said eagerly.

He was sorry for her loneliness. If only she visited with the other women of the canyon she would be less lonely, but she had no gift for visiting. Once every month or so she put horses to the buckboard and went to spend an afternoon with her mother, and with the brood of brothers and sisters and cousins who lived in her father's house.

'A fine time you'll have,' Jim said to her. 'You'll gabble your crazy language like ducks for a whole afternoon. You'll giggle with that big grown cousin of yours with the embarrassed face. If I could find any fault with you, I'd call you a damn foreigner.' He remembered how she blessed the bread with the sign of the cross before she put it in the oven, how she knelt at the bedside every night, how she had a holy picture tacked to the wall in the closet.

On Saturday of a hot dusty June, Jim mowed the farm flat. The day was long. It was after six o'clock when the mower tumbled the last band of oats. He drove the clanking machine up into the barnyard and backed it into the implement shed, and there he unhitched the horses and turned them out to graze on the hills over Sunday. When he entered the kitchen Jelka was just putting his dinner on the table. He washed his hands and face, and sat down to eat.

'I'm tired,' he said, 'but I think I'll go to Monterey anyway. There'll be a full moon.'

Her soft eyes smiled.

'I'll tell you what I'll do,' he said. 'If you would like to go, I'll hitch up a rig and take you with me.'

She smiled again and shook her head. 'No, the stores would be closed. I would rather stay here.'

'Well all right, I'll saddle a horse then. I didn't think I was going. The stock's all turned out. Maybe I can catch a horse easy. Sure you don't want to go?'

'If it was early, and I could go to the stores – but it will be ten o'clock when you get there.'

'Oh, no – well, anyway, on horseback I'll make it a little after nine.'

Her mouth smiled to itself, but her eyes watched him for the development of a wish. Perhaps because he was tired from the long day's work, he demanded, 'What are you thinking about?'

'Thinking about? I remember, you used to ask that nearly every day when we were first married.'

'But what are you?' he insisted irritably.

'Oh – I'm thinking about the eggs under the black hen.' She got up and went to the big calendar on the wall. 'They will hatch tomorrow or maybe Monday.'

It was almost dusk when he had finished shaving and putting on his blue serge suit and his new boots. Jelka had the dishes washed and put away. As Jim went through the kitchen he saw that she had taken the lamp to the table near the window, and that she sat beside it knitting a brown wool sock.

'Why do you sit there tonight?' he asked. 'You always sit over here. You do funny things sometimes.'

Her eyes arose slowly from her flying hands. 'The moon,' she said quietly. 'You said it would be full tonight. I want to see the moon rise.'

'But you're silly. You can't see it from that window. I thought you knew direction better than that.'

She smiled remotely. 'I will look out of the bedroom window then.'

Jim put on his black hat and went out. Walking through the dark empty barn, he took a halter from the rack. On the grassy sidehill he whistled high and shrill. The horses stopped feeding and moved slowly in toward him, and stopped twenty feet away. Carefully he approached his bay gelding and moved his hand from its rump along its side and up and over its neck. The halterstrap clicked in its buckle. Jim turned and led the horse back to the barn. He threw his saddle on and cinched it tight, put his silver-bound bridle over the stiff ears, buckled the throat latch, knotted the tie-rope about the gelding's neck and fastened the neat coil-end to the saddle string. Then he slipped the halter and led the horse to the house. A radiant crown of soft red light lay over the eastern hills. The full moon would rise before the valley had completely lost the daylight.

In the kitchen Jelka still knitted by the window. Jim strode to the corner of the room and took up his 30-30 carbine. As he rammed shells into the magazine, he said, 'The moon glow is on the hills. If you are going to see it rise, you better go outside now. It's going to be a good red one at rising.'

'In a moment,' she replied, 'when I come to the end here.' He went to her and patted her sleek head.

'Good night. I'll probably be back by noon tomorrow.' Her dusty black eyes followed him out of the door.

Jim thrust the rifle into his saddle-scabbard, and mounted and swung his horse down the canyon. On his right, from behind the blackening hills, the great red moon slid rapidly up. The double light of the day's last afterglow and the rising moon thickened the outlines of the trees and gave a mysterious new perspective to the hills. The dusty oaks shimmered and glowed, and the shade under them was black as velvet. A huge, long-legged shadow of a horse and half a man rode to the left and slightly ahead of Jim. From the ranches near and distant came the sound of dogs tuning up for a night of song. And the roosters crowed, thinking a new dawn had come too quickly. Jim lifted the gelding to a trot. The spattering hoofsteps echoed back from the castle behind him. He thought of blonde May at the Three Star in Monterey. 'I'll be late. Maybe some-one else'll have her,' he thought. The moon was clear of the hills now.

Jim had gone a mile when he heard the hoofbeats of a horse coming toward him. A horseman cantered up and pulled to a stop. 'That you, Jim?'

'Yes. Oh, hello, George.'

'I was just riding up to your place. I want to tell you – you know the springhead at the upper end of my land?'

'Yes, I know.'

'Well, I was up there this afternoon. I found a dead campfire and a calf's head and feet. The skin was in the fire, half burned, but I pulled it out and it had your brand.'

'The hell,' said Jim. 'How old was the fire?'

'The ground was still warm in the ashes. Last night, I guess. Look, Jim, I can't go up with you. I've got to go to town, but I thought I'd tell you, so you could take a look around.'

Jim asked quietly, 'Any idea how many men?'

'No. I didn't look close.'

'Well, I guess I better go up and look. I was going to town too. But if there are thieves working, I don't want to lose any more stock. I'll cut up through your land if you don't mind, George.'

'I'd go with you, but I've got to go to town. You got a gun with you?'

'Oh yes, sure. Here under my leg. Thanks for telling me.'

'That's all right. Cut through any place you want. Good night.' The neighbour turned his horse and cantered back in the direction from which he had come.

For a few moments Jim sat in the moonlight, looking down at his stilted shadow. He pulled his rifle from its scabbard, levered a shell into the chamber, and held the gun across the pommel of his saddle. He turned left from the road, went up the little ridge, through the oak grove, over the grassy hog-back and down the other side into the next canyon.

In half an hour he had found the deserted camp. He turned over the heavy, leathery calf's head and felt its dusty tongue to judge by the dryness how long it had been dead. He lighted a match and looked at his brand on the half-burned hide. At last he mounted his horse again, rode over the bald grassy hills and crossed into his own land.

A warm summer wind was blowing on the hilltops. The moon, as it quartered up the sky, lost its redness and turned the colour of strong tea. Among the hills the coyotes were singing, and the dogs at the ranch houses joined them with broken-hearted howling. The dark green oaks below and the yellow summer grass showed their colours in the moon-light.

Jim followed the sound of the cowbells to his herd, and found them eating quietly, and a few deer feeding with them. He listened long for the sound of hoofbeats or the voices of men on the wind.

It was after eleven when he turned his horse toward home. He rounded the west tower of the sandstone castle, rode through the shadow and out into the moonlight again. Below, the roofs of his barn and house shone dully. The bedroom window cast back a streak of reflection.

The feeding horses lifted their heads as Jim came down through the pasture. Their eyes glinted redly when they turned their heads.

Jim had almost reached the corral fence – he heard a horse stamping in the barn. His hand jerked the gelding down. He listened. It came again, the stamping from the barn. Jim lifted his rifle and dismounted silently. He turned his horse loose and crept towards the barn.

In the blackness he could hear the grinding of the horse's teeth as it chewed hay. He moved along the barn until he came to the occupied stall. After a moment of listening he scratched a match on the butt of his rifle. A saddled and bridled horse was tied in the stall. The bit was slipped under the chin and the cinch loosened. The horse stopped eating and turned its head towards the light.

Jim blew out the match and walked quickly out of the barn. He sat on the edge of the horse trough and looked into the water. His thoughts came so slowly that he put them into words and said them under his breath.

'Shall I look through the window? No. My head would throw a shadow in the room.'

He regarded the rifle in his hand. Where it had been rubbed and handled, the black gun-finish had worn off, leaving the metal silvery.

At last he stood up with decision and moved toward the house. At the steps, an extended foot tried each board tenderly before he put his weight on it. The three ranch dogs came out from under the house and shook themselves, stretched and sniffed, wagged their tails and went back to bed.

The kitchen was dark, but Jim knew where every piece of furniture was. He put out his hand and touched the corner of the table, a chair-back, the towel hanger, as he went along. He crossed the room so silently that even he could hear only his breath and the whisper of his trousers legs together, and the beating of his watch in his pocket. The bedroom door stood open and spilled a patch of moonlight on the kitchen floor. Jim reached the door at last and peered through.

The moonlight lay on the white bed. Jim saw Jelka lying on her back, one soft bare arm flung across her forehead and eyes. He could not see who the man was, for his head was turned away. Jim watched, holding his breath. Then Jelka twitched in her sleep and the man rolled his head and sighed – Jelka's cousin, her grown, embarrassed cousin.

Jim turned and quickly stole back across the kitchen and down the back steps. He walked up the yard to the water trough again, and sat down on the edge of it. The moon was white as chalk, and it swam in the water, and lighted the straws and barley dropped by the horses' mouths. Jim could see the mosquito wigglers, tumbling up and down, end over end, in the water, and he could see a newt lying in the sun moss in the bottom of the trough.

He cried a few, dry, hard, smothered sobs, and wondered why, for his thought was of the grassed hilltops and of the lonely summer wind whisking along.

His thought turned to the way his mother used to hold a bucket to catch the throat blood when his father killed a pig. She stood as far away as possible and held the bucket at arm's length to keep her clothes from getting spattered.

Jim dipped his hand into the trough and stirred the moon to broken, swirling streams of light. He wetted his forehead with his damp hands and stood up. This time he did not move so quickly, but he crossed the kitchen on tiptoe and stood in the bedroom door. Jelka moved her arm and opened her eyes a little. Then the eyes sprang wide, then they glistened with moisture. Jim looked into her eyes; her face was blank of expression. A little drop ran out of Jelka's nose and lodged in the hollow of her upper lip. She stared back at him.

Jim cocked the rifle. The steel click sounded through the house. The man on the bed stirred uneasily in his sleep, Jim's hands were quivering. He raised the gun to his shoulder and held it tightly to keep from shaking. Over the sights he saw the little white square between the man's brows and hair. The front sight wavered a moment and then came to rest.

The gun crash tore the air. Jim, still looking down the barrel, saw the whole bed jolt under the blow. A small, black, bloodless hole was in the man's forehead. But behind, the hollow-point bullet took brain and bone and splashed them on the pillow.

Jelka's cousin gurgled in his throat. His hands came crawling out from under the covers like big white spiders, and they walked for a moment, then shuddered and fell quiet.

Jim looked slowly back at Jelka. Her nose was running. Her eyes had moved from him to the end of the rifle. She whined softly, like a cold puppy.

Jim turned in panic. His boot-heels beat on the kitchen floor, but outside he moved slowly towards the watering trough again. There was a taste of salt in his throat, and his heart heaved painfully. He pulled his hat off and dipped his head into the water, then he leaned over and vomited on the ground. In the house he could hear Jelka moving about. She whimpered like a puppy. Jim straightened up, weak and dizzy.

He walked tiredly through the corral and into the pasture. His saddled horse came at his whistle. Automatically he tightened the cinch, mounted and rode away, down the road to the valley. The squat black shadow travelled under him. The moon sailed high and white. The uneasy dogs barked monotonously.

At daybreak a buckboard and pair trotted up to the ranch yard, scattering the chickens. A deputy sheriff and a coroner sat in the seat. Jim Moore half reclined against his saddle in the wagon-box. His tired gelding followed behind. The deputy sheriff set the brake and wrapped the lines around it. The men dismounted.

Jim asked, 'Do I have to go in? I'm too tired and wrought up to see it now.'

The coroner pulled his lip and studied. 'Oh, I guess not. We'll tend to things and look around.'

Jim sauntered away towards the watering trough. 'Say,' he called, 'kind of clean up a little, will you? You know.'

The men went on into the house.

In a few minutes they emerged, carrying the stiffened body between them. It was wrapped up in a comforter. They eased it up into the wagon-box. Jim walked back towards them. 'Do I have to go in with you now?'

'Where's your wife, Mr Moore?' the deputy sheriff demanded.

'I don't know,' he said wearily. 'She's somewhere around.'

'You're sure you didn't kill her too?'

'No. I didn't touch her. I'll find her and bring her in this afternoon. That is, if you don't want me to go in with you now.'

'We've got your statement,' the coroner said. 'And by God, we've got eyes, haven't we, Will? Of course there's a technical charge of murder against you, but it'll be dismissed. Always is in this part of the country. Go kind of light on your wife, Mr Moore.'

'I won't hurt her,' said Jim.

He stood and watched the buckboard jolt away. He kicked his feet reluctantly in the dust. The hot June sun showed its face over the hills and flashed viciously on the bedroom window.

Jim went slowly into the house, and brought out a nine-foot, loaded bull whip. He crossed the yard and walked into the barn. And as he climbed the ladder to the hayloft, he heard the high, puppy whimpering start.

When Jim came out of the barn again, he carried Jelka over his shoulder. By the watering trough he set her tenderly on the ground.

Her hair was littered with bits of hay. The back of her shirtwaist was streaked with blood.

Jim wetted his bandana at the pipe and washed her bitten lips, and washed her face and brushed back her hair. Her dusty black eyes followed every move he made.

'You hurt me,' she said. 'You hurt me bad.'

He nodded gravely. 'Bad as I could without killing you.'

The sun shone hotly on the ground. A few blowflies buzzed about, looking for the blood.

Jelka's thickened lips tried to smile. 'Did you have any breakfast at all?'

'No,' he said. 'None at all.'

'Well, then I'll fry you up some eggs.' She struggled painfully to her feet.

'Let me help you,' he said. 'I'll help you get your waist off. It's drying stuck to your back. It'll hurt.'

'No. I'll do it myself.' Her voice had a peculiar resonance in it. Her dark eyes dwelt warmly on him for a moment, and then she turned and limped into the house.

Jim waited, sitting on the edge of the watering trough. He saw the smoke start up out of the chimney and sail straight up into the air. In a very few moments Jelka called him from the kitchen door.

'Come, Jim. Your breakfast.'

Four fried eggs and four thick slices of bacon lay on a warmed plate for him. 'The coffee will be ready in a minute,' she said.

'Won't you eat?'

'No. Not now. My mouth's too sore.'

He ate his eggs hungrily and then looked up at her. Her black hair was combed smooth. She had on a fresh white shirtwaist. 'We're going to town this afternoon,' he said. 'I'm going to order lumber. We'll build a new house farther down the canyon.'

Her eyes darted to the closed bedroom door and then back to him. 'Yes,' she said. 'That will be good.' And then, after a moment, 'Will you whip me any more – for this?'

'No, not any more, for this.'

Her eyes smiled. She sat down on a chair beside him, and Jim put out his hand and stroked her hair, and the back of her neck.

Robert Arthur

Eyewitness

Los Angeles, 1940

Outside it was raining – raining in hard black lines of water that slanted down out of the sky the way they had the night the girl vanished.

She was out there now, out there somewhere in the black wet night, just as she had been every night now for the last four weeks. Out there where her husband had left her, cold, crumpled, dead, all the warmth and love gone out of her, all the colour gone from her cheeks, all the light from her eyes. Out there in the night that had hidden her murder under a pall of blackness, and the rain that had been pouring down from the heavens when her husband hid her body.

Davis knew she had been murdered – knew it as well as he knew the alphabet, or his name, or the day of the week, all those things so familiar a man never has to think of them. Davis knew it, but he couldn't prove it; and desperately, doggedly, he wanted to prove it, as he had never wanted to prove anything before in fourteen years on the Force.

He parked his car and trudged through the acute angle of the falling rain, water dripping down his shapeless felt hat, down his square rugged face, down his old ulster, down his legs, over his shoes. Trudged through the alley and turned in the stage door of the theatre, where he slapped the rain from his hat and from his ulster before he asked to speak to Master.

With his hat off, his forehead gleamed where the hair was going back, and grey showed up in the hair that was left. He wasn't old, not even middle-aged, but his face looked old and tired tonight, like the face of a man who has been too long trying to do something he desperately wants to do and cannot.

The doorman showed Davis into the little dressing-room where Master sat, quietly smoking, while his Negro dresser bustled about. Master was a big man, broad-shouldered, with a mane of blond hair and bright blue eyes that stared unwinkingly – stared as if they never blinked, so that a man might become nervous merely from the impact of their moveless gaze.

It was almost an hour before the evening curtain rose on Master's act. Davis took a gingerly seat on the edge of a chair, the water running across the floor below him from his shoes, and began, choosing his words with great care, like a man anxious to hew exactly to the line of fact and err not a hair on either side.

'There's a lot of talk about perfect murders going around,' Davis said harshly. 'And if such a thing is possible, this may be it.'

Master nodded, as if he understood all that had not been said – understood, that Davis had heard of him somehow, somewhere, had heard of some murder he had brought his efforts to bear upon in the past, had come to him now for help and was trying desperately to interest him in the case he had brought; understood that Davis desperately, fiercely wanted help, but would not ask for it.

'We think she's dead, but we don't know,' Davis went on. 'We think he killed her; but we don't know that either. If she's dead, we can't find the body. If we could find the body, we might not be able to prove it was murder. If we could prove it was murder, still we might have trouble proving *he* did it. And yet we're sure she's dead, it's murder, and he did it. That's the only explanation that fits the facts.'

Master nodded again, understanding that it was Davis who was sure it was murder, and Davis was sure *he*, whoever *he* might be, had done it.

Master helped himself to a cigar from a box at hand, and passed one to the detective. Davis took it, but forgot to light it; merely put it in his mouth and chewed on it as he spoke.

'She died in the darkness,' Davis went on, still speaking carefully. 'Died in the complete blackness of a city without lights. It was the night of the big flood – Wednesday, the second of March – and all the lights went out for more than half an hour. There were no lights at all, except candles indoors and automobile headlights out, and the headlights cut only thin, pale paths of light through the rain and the darkness.'

He paused, as if suddenly feeling the words coming out too fast, too expressively for a Headquarters detective ten years in plainclothes.

But Master still nodded, still understanding the emotion behind what Davis was telling him, and after a moment of sucking hard on the unlighted cigar to collect his thoughts, Davis continued:

'She was young, sne was pretty, she was loving. She was always laughing, always gay. She had been married three years, and her husband was an actor – a young leading man in pictures. But he had been only a car-hop at a drive-and-eat before the movies, and she had been the same, making twelve dollars a week and living on it. They met, they got married – and then the movies found him and he began to make money and still more money.

'Began to see a big future ahead of him.'

Davis paused long enough to light the cigar with a hand that trembled a bit.

'You see, he's tall and smooth – that's the only word to describe him. Inside he's yellow, rotten; but outside he's big, tanned, with even white teeth and eyes that seem to promise something to every woman he meets. And he's been rising in pictures because of women – stars who have taken an interest in him. Lately there's been one in particular. She's getting old, but she's still powerful and can do a lot for him. But won't as long as he's married.

'So you see, he wants to get rid of his wife. He can't get a divorce. He has no grounds. But he feels that she's holding him back, keeping him from rising to the top, keeping him from becoming a big star; she's dead weight around his neck. He does not love her; he's too selfish to love anyone but himself. Now all he thinks of is getting rid of her. He even thinks of murder; or if somehow she would only disappear.

'Well, a month ago the lights went out, and she disappeared.'

The detective stopped again; his voice was becoming hoarse.

'They lived in Hollywood, off Beachwood Drive, in the hills above Hollywood Boulevard. Not as fashionable a place as he wanted, but the best he could afford yet. Besides, it kept her and her mother, who stayed with them, out of sight, behind the scenes.

'She kept house while he worked; she stayed at home while he was out, sometimes all night, making "contacts" and being "seen in fashionable places". Many of his associates didn't know he was married.

'She never complained, never chided him. She never even guessed he was sorry he had ever married her. She was loyal – loyal all the way through.'

Davis stopped, then went on more calmly.

'To amuse herself, she went for long walks in the hills or went to the movies alone. On this night, this Wednesday night, she went to an early show at the Pantages Theatre. Her mother was out playing bridge, and he was working.

'He came home around eight, just after her mother. A few minutes later she phoned him. It was raining. It had been raining for days.

There were floods all through the San Fernando Valley. A bridge in Long Beach washed out, drowning a dozen or more. But Hollywood saw only the rain. The floods scarcely touched Hollywood.

'So she phoned him that because of the rain she couldn't get a taxi. Would he come for her and pick her up in front of the theatre?

'He said he would. His mind was full of hot, bright, ambitious schemes that night. She – the movie star – had been talking to him that day, we've learned. She'd promised him the lead in her next picture. If – well, you know what that *if* was.

'No doubt he'd often thought of killing her before that night. But that night the opportunity came. Ten minutes after he left the house, every light in the city went out.'

Davis let his words sink in. He leaned forward and tapped the big blond man on the knee for extra emphasis.

'Every light in the city went out. It's a strange feeling when that happens, when the power fails, when the lights go off and the radios go silent, and all the street corners are as dark as the inside of a grave. A candle flickers here, a match there, and they only make the darkness darker. Well, that's what happened that night.

'He wasn't gone long. He came back to the house within forty-five minutes, before the lights came on again. And she wasn't with him.

'He said he couldn't find her. That he had parked the car and searched for her in front of the Pantages. He thought she must have gotten panicky when the lights went out, and found a taxi, or started walking, or something. He thought she'd be home ahead of him. But she wasn't. She never came home. So presently he called us. Called us and told us his story. That he had missed her in the darkness, and now she had vanished.

'Well, we took down his story and promised to broadcast an alarm. A lot of people vanished that night, in the flood, and we had our hands full. Some of them are still missing too. Possibly he figured on that.

'After taking down his story, we left; of course our investigation that night was only the sketchiest. It was several days before we got around to making any thorough investigation. And then it was too late.

'So there it was. She had vanished. Where? God knows. What can happen on the streets of a darkened city? Anything.

'Around midnight her husband went out in the car again. He was gone for hours, until almost morning, in the pouring rain. The lights were on again, but because of the weather the streets were deserted. No one could be found who had seen him or his car. Where had he gone? What had he done? He said he had been driving around in a half-crazy condition, hunting for her, calling her name, driving aimlessly, hoping to find her wandering in a daze, perhaps, but unhurt.

'Well, perhaps. But you know what we think?'

Davis tapped Master's knee again.

'We think that he found her in the darkness in front of the Pantages and she got in the car with him. In the darkness, no one would notice what car stopped, or who got in. No one saw her get in. He drove part way home, and still the lights didn't come on. He was burning with resentment of her.

'And suddenly, impulsively, there on a side street, unseen in the night, the windows of the car fogged by the driving rain, he throttled her. Throttled her and hid her body in the baggage trunk of the car, where it was when he returned home and called us.

'Where it was until he went out on that long drive, in which he claimed he was searching for her. But when he was really hiding her body – hiding it so well we've never found it.'

There was bitterness in the detective's voice, and Master understood that this case meant something personal to him; not just a routine assignment.

'Do you know Los Angeles?' the detective asked, and Master shook his head. 'Well,' Davis told him, 'Los Angeles is a big place. There are arroyos and caves in the hills, old quarries, parks, lakes, rivers, abandoned mine workings – places a man might hide a body, right inside the county limits.

'Suppose he had previously picked a place, had had it in mind all along. Suppose he had done that, you can see how difficult it would be for us to find her. In the end, we might never find her, unless chance stepped in.'

Davis sagged suddenly, like a tired man.

'If we could only find her,' he said quietly. 'That's all I hope to do. There's almost no chance to prove guilt against him under the circumstances. Though I'd like to. God knows how I'd like to!'

For the first time, though the fact had escaped the detective's attention, Master spoke.

'I think we will find her,' he said.

'But he'll go free!' Davis said harshly.

Master shook his head slowly.

'Perhaps not,' he said sombrely. 'You forget the eyewitness.'

'The eyewitness!' the detective exclaimed. 'There was no eyewitness!'

'To every murder there is an eyewitness,' the big blond man rumbled.

'Poppycock!' the detective snapped irritably. 'It would be a big help if there were. Don't you suppose more murderers would go to the chair if such a thing were true? Unless you mean God, who can't help us any.'

'There is always an eyewitness,' Master said quietly, but his words carried force and conviction. 'Sometimes it is hard to make him speak.'

He seemed to withdraw from the room for a moment into some inward meditation. Then:

'But tonight, I think, from what you have told me, we will be able to make him speak. We will find the body. And I think the one who saw the murder will give you the evidence needed to convict.'

Davis opened his mouth, to protest, to argue; then he shut it again. He did not know what the big man meant, but he was at the end of his own rope. And somehow Master's words carried conviction.

'First,' Master instructed, 'call the husband and tell him you are going to come tonight to take him to his wife's body. Say that an eye-witness to her disappearance knows where she is. Say that she was murdered, and her murder was seen, her murderer followed when he hid the body. Tell him nothing more. Let him think over your words until we come. Now I have a show to do. I will be with you later.'

Davis did as the big man told him. Then, with a growing sense of awe and wonder, he watched Master's performance. After that, just before midnight, when Master had changed into rough tweeds and an ulster, they took Davis's car and drove out towards Hollywood.

His name was Harold Murney, and at midnight they found him waiting for them, alone in a small house in the Hollywood hills, where from his living-room window the blue and red neons of Hollywood gleamed faintly through the pouring rain.

He was tall and broad-shouldered, as Davis had described him, and hard. Amazingly hard. It was in his voice, in his eyes. Hard and evil.

But Davis was hard too. His square face, dripping water from the rain blown into their faces as he and Master came up the long footpath from the drive to the house, glistened in the light. His eyes gleamed too, a peculiar blue gleam of hope and hatred. Murney was the man he wanted to convict, and Murney knew it. But he knew, the detective did, that there was no shadow of evidence against the younger man, and so did the actor.

So, whether guilty or innocent, Murney could easily stare back insolently at Davis without flinching, without showing any alarm.

'You said you'd found my wife?' Murney asked suspiciously, glancing from Master to Davis and back to the big blond man, whose presence the detective had not bothered to explain.

'I said we'd take you to her,' Davis replied dully.

Murney stared at him suspiciously, his eyes green beneath half-lowered lids.

'Where?' he asked.

'Where her murderer hid her,' Davis told him evenly.

'Murderer?'

Murney's voice indicated only what it should have – shock and surprise. If he was guilty, as a murderer he was a good actor too.

'Are you sure you're not mistaken?' the young man asked then, coolly, and Davis shook his head. 'No,' the actor answered himself, after a moment, 'I suppose it's your business to be sure. All right, you say you've found her and she was murdered. Have you got her murderer?'

Davis shook his head again, his eyes fixed unwinkingly on Murney.

'We'll have him shortly after we've taken you to the body,' he answered. 'The murder, as well as the concealment of the body, was seen by an eyewitness, fortunately.'

This time Murney's breath did suck in perceptibly.

'It seems incredible,' he said, and now he let amusement creep into his voice. 'Frankly, I don't believe you've found my wife, that she was murdered or that there is any such eyewitness. If there is, why didn't he speak up sooner?'

'He had his reasons,' Davis said, and his voice was suddenly harsh. 'But he will speak now. I suppose, Murney, you've no objection to coming with us to identify your wife and help us nab her killer?'

Murney hesitated for an instant. Some of the ruddy colour had gone from his cheeks. But when he spoke his voice was still easy, still confident.

'Of course not,' he said loudly. 'You know how much I want to help you.'

All this time Master had not spoken, had only stood there, his face wet with rain because he had worn no hat, his bright blue eyes staring unwinkingly at Murney. The actor took his eyes off Master now with an effort.

'I'll get my coat and be right with you,' he said roughly. 'Though I'm convinced it's a wild-goose chase.'

He got dressed for the weather, and Davis led the way down the footpath.

'We'll take my car,' he said. 'Too bad it's a coupé. We'll be a bit crowded.'

His words were regretful, but his voice was not. He slid in behind the wheel and Harold Murney, after a moment's hesitation, got in beside him. Last of all Master squeezed himself in and closed the car door.

Davis started the motor and let in the clutch. They were jammed tightly together, but none of the men commented on the fact. Davis and Master stared straight ahead, the detective seeming intent on his driving. Murney glanced quickly from one face to the other, but could read nothing in them. Jammed between the two, he sat stiffly, as if he found the space too small in which to relax.

'We are going to retrace the murderer's path,' Davis said quietly, as the car rolled silently downhill and into Beachwood Drive, the only direction in which it could go.

Murney started to speak, and then thought better of it. But he shifted a little uneasily as they coasted downward towards Franklin Avenue, and he almost jumped when Master, for the first time, spoke.

'Turn here,' he said suddenly. 'Right.'

Davis braked and turned into Scenic Drive, after almost over-running the narrow entrance of the street. Momentary surprise showed on Harold Murney's face; then his lips tightened, and he said nothing as they crossed Gower and came to Vista Del Mar, a crooked, hilly street lined with houses almost European in their picturesqueness.

'Left,' Master said abruptly.

They turned left, drifted down Vista Del Mar, and came out on Franklin. At Master's order they turned right on Franklin, crossed Argyle, Vine and Ivar, climbed the hill, dropped down a steep slope and pulled up at broad Cahuenga Boulevard.

'Right,' Master said here, as Harold Murney stirred again, and an instant later ordered them sharply left at the traffic light on to Wilcox, and then quickly right again on the continuation of Franklin.

From time to time Murney had shifted uneasily, wedged between the two men, at all this manoeuvring. When presently they pulled up for the stop light at Highland Avenue, and Master ordered them left, he burst out in a voice gone a little shrill:

'Where are we going with all this nonsensical driving?' he demanded. 'What kind of a game are you playing? There's no police station in this direction, no hospital, no morgue. I demand to know where you are taking me!'

'Along the path of a murderer,' Master told him, deeply, 'and that route is always twisted.'

They swung left, then right at the next light, and straight ahead until they came to a dead end. Then left, and drifted downward a hundred yards or so to stop where La Brea and Hollywood crossed, having reached the point by a devious and twisting route for whose choosing there seemed little reason.

Harold Murney seemed to be losing his self-control.

'I demand you let me out!' he said shrilly, his voice higher still. 'This is fantastic. This is some sort of plot. You haven't found my wife and you don't know where she is. I think you're trying to shake me down!'

'We are showing you the route a murderer took,' Master told him quietly. 'The devious, back-street route he took in the rainy night that was like this night, the winding route he took to obviate every possible chance of being seen and noticed.'

Murney gulped and swallowed hard.

'That's nonsense!' he cried. 'That's ridiculous! How do you know my wife's murderer came this way – if she was murdered? You don't. You couldn't.'

But his voice held a note that seemed to indicate he was trying to convince himself, not them. Davis did not even turn to look at him, merely guided the car straight ahead down La Brea Boulevard, past Sunset and past Santa Monica.

But as they swung right on Melrose at Master's orders, Murney tried to reach across the big blond man and open the car door.

'I demand that you let me out!' he gasped, almost sobbingly. 'You've no legal right to keep me if I want to get out.'

Master stretched out an arm and pinned him into his seat. Biting his lips and seeming to shake a little, as if from rage, Murney sat back.

Then they were turning northward again, the windshield wiper clicking busily, sweeping aside the water that filmed the glass between each downward swing of the arm. The rain beat down on the steel top of the coupé, and the motor purred with a soft, even beat.

They rolled along for block after block and then, in response to a quiet word from Master, their course changed. They turned, and presently they were climbing a long slope that led them away from Hollywood and its rain-haloed lights, towards the darkness of the valley beyond.

Murney was sitting rigidly between the two men. But he jumped when Master's voice rang out, almost accusingly.

'Right!'

Davis swung them into a side street, dark, deserted. They idled along, and no house lights showed, only dim street lights at long intervals. Presently their lights reflected from the rain-wet boards of a high fence. Master turned his head a little, from right to left. Between them Murney sat in wire-tight tenseness.

'Stop!' The word was like a pistol shot. Even Davis jumped a bit. Then he pulled to the kerb and cut the motor. It expired with a little cough, and for a moment they sat there in complete silence, broken only by the persistent beating of the rain.

'Apex Pictures' storage lot,' Davis said aloud, though as if to himself. 'Where they store all their old scenery and sets, stuff that hasn't any value.'

Master nodded.

'Let us get out here,' he suggested, and, opening the car door, descended.

He stood on the pavement until Murney reluctantly, it seemed, descended, though only a few minutes before he had been anxious to get out of the car. The actor tried to light a cigarette, cupping the match in his hand and bending over; but the flame wavered and shook and went out. With a curse he flung the wet cigarette into the gutter.

'I don't know why you've brought me here,' he said wildly. 'But I'm going home, do you hear? You can't keep me! You can't!'

Master linked an arm through his and held him.

'What are you afraid of?' Davis sneered. 'You haven't done anything, have you? You didn't murder her, did you?'

'No, no, you know well enough I didn't!' Harold Murney cried.

'Then come on,' Davis said, 'before you make us think different.'

'I think we will go inside,' Master said evenly, and beaten, shaking, the actor fell into step with him.

With Davis on the other side, they walked slowly along the high fence. The rain still fell, wetly and insistently, and there was no one to see them. They could have been taking the actor to murder him, and no one would have noticed.

After fifty yards they came to a high gate, and Master stopped.

'Gate,' Davis said. 'It's locked. I'll get tools.'

He went back to the car, returned with a flashlight and a tyre iron. A twist of the tyre iron burst the staples that held the padlock; that gate creaked open.

'Now we will go in,' Master said.

'No!' Murney cried, squirming but unable to break free. 'I won't go in with you! You have no right to bring me here! What do you want, anyway, what do you want?'

'Only for you to identify your wife,' Davis said. 'Come along. We're almost there.'

With the flashlight cutting a wedge out of the darkness in front of them they entered, their feet crunching loud on gravelled paths. Davis fanned the flashlight about, and the rays glinted off the peeling surface of a plaster mosque, off a Norman castle made of wood and paper, off the squat shape of an Egyptian pyramid.

Master led them down one of the dark paths, moving slowly, slowly, as if on the verge of stopping at any moment. They passed mouldering scenery flats, and the wreck of an entire Western town that consisted only of false building fronts, ragged and tattered. The path curved; they came back towards the Egyptian pyramid. Abruptly Master halted.

'Shine your light about,' he said to Davis. The detective did so.

'A pyramid made out of wood and plaster,' he said aloud. 'A model of the Sphynx with the head fallen off. A big, imitation Egyptian sarcophagus. Some artificial rocks. A—'

'The sarcophagus,' Master interrupted. 'Yes, the sarcophagus – an imitation of an ancient burial place; a fitting spot to find the body of a murder victim. Open it, and let us see if our eyewitness spoke the truth.'

'No!' Murney screamed now, and his lunge to break free was maddened, desperate. 'She's not here! You must be crazy, thinking she is. How could she be here? This is a trick, a trick!'

The two men held him until his struggles ceased and he stood, shaken by dry, gasping sobs. They did not speak. When the actor was quiet again, Davis released his arm. He strode forward, played his flashlight briefly over the scaling paint of the wooden sarcophagus. Then he thrust in the tyre iron. A push, and the lid of the sarcophagus lifted. Davis let it crash to the ground. He turned his flashlight into the interior.

She was there. She lay stretched out, one arm flung up across her face as if to shut out the light. But no light would trouble her eyes again. She had been there for a month, and she was no longer beautiful.

'She's here,' Davis said, and the words would hardly be heard above the soft sound of the rain.

'I know,' Master answered. 'I know. Our eyewitness told us the truth. Look at her, Murney. Look at her and identify her.'

'No!' the actor cried. 'No! You knew! You knew all along! You had to know. You couldn't have brought me here, couldn't have retraced the exact route I drove to get here that night, if you didn't know. Someone told you. Someone saw me and told you. Oh God, why did they have to see me?'

Davis had a pair of handcuffs. As the actor fell to his knees in the gravel path, breathing heavily, his mouth and eyes and face all loose, slack, twisted, Davis used them.

He pulled and Harold Murney rose shudderingly to his feet.

'But I couldn't have been followed!' he screamed. 'Couldn't have! I'd have known if I had been. Nobody could have followed me through all those twists and turns without my seeing them. Tell me! Tell me! How did you bring me here over the same route I used? How? How?'

He beat with his handcuffed wrists on the detective's chest, and Davis caught his arms and held them. Master moved over and fastened his bright gaze on the actor's face.

'You brought us here,' he said. 'Your guilty conscience brought us here. It was a trick, if you will. Nevertheless, it was you who guided us every inch of the way to this spot.'

'No! I didn't! I didn't!'

'You brought us here just as anyone who has hidden something, and has that hidden thing much on his mind, will inevitably lead one who knows the secret to the hiding-place.

'I said it was your conscience. Call it, if you want to be more technical, your involuntary muscular responses to mental commands that were not quite given. We passed a corner where you had turned that night. You did not want us to know you had turned there. Your brain thought of the turn, thought that we must not know of it. So you twitched. You jerked slightly in that direction. As your mind thought, your body moved – not much, but enough for me.

'For I was wedged tightly beside you, remember, and I knew how to read these little movements your body could not keep from making. I learned the trick from Harry Houdini, who was the master of us all. At your leisure you can learn more about it, for it is written in one of his books.

'It is always easy when the subject is nervous, and you were nervous. That is why we called you earlier in the evening, told you we would lead you to her body. To make you nervous.'

'Who – who are you?' Harold Murney whispered. 'You're not a detective. Who—'

'His name is Master.' Davis answered the question. 'He is a professional stage magician and prestidigitator. Too bad you'll never see him work. His act is a sensation. Especially when he has a member of the audience take something and hide it, and then, walking beside the hider, finds the hidden object without fail, every time.'

'Then who're you?' Murney screamed at Davis. 'You're not a detective either! No detective would have hounded me like this. No detective would have thought of it. Who're you?'

'I'm a detective,' Davis told him, 'but I'm also the fellow she was going to marry until you came along. That's who I am.'

'Oh – you – then you – you—'

The breath gasped and bubbled in Harold Murney's throat.

'Then you lied!' he choked out. 'You lied. There was no eyewitness. There was no one to give evidence. There was no witness and you couldn't have convicted me!'

Davis shook his head.

'No,' he said, 'I didn't lie. There was an eyewitness. He led us here and he gave us the evidence we needed. The eyewitness who is always present at every murder. The one who always sees the crime – the one who commits it. In this case you, Murney, you – you were the eyewitness we meant!'

Patrick Quentin

Puzzle for Poppy

'Yes, Miss Crump,' snapped Iris into the phone. 'No, Miss Crump. Oh nuts, Miss Crump.'

My wife flung down the receiver.

'Well?' I asked.

'She won't let us use the patio. It's that dog, that great fat St Bernard. It mustn't be disturbed.'

'Why?'

'It has to be alone with its beautiful thoughts. It's going to become a mother. Peter, it's revolting. There must be something in the lease.'

'There isn't,' I said.

When I'd rented our half of this La Jolla hacienda for my shore leave, the lease specified that all rights to the enclosed patio belonged to our eccentric co-tenant. It oughtn't to have mattered, but it did because Iris had recently skyrocketed to fame as a movie star and it was impossible for us to appear on the streets without being mobbed. For the last couple of days we have been virtually beleaguered in our apartment. We were crazy about being beleaguered together, but even Héloise and Abelard needed a little fresh air once in a while.

That's why the patio was so important.

Iris was staring through the locked French windows at the forbidden delights of the patio. Suddenly she turned.

'Peter, I'll die if I don't get things into my lungs – ozone and things. We'll just have to go to the beach.'

'And be torn limb from limb by your public again?'

'I'm sorry, darling. I'm terrible sorry.' Iris unzipped herself from her housecoat and scrambled into slacks and a shirtwaist. She tossed me my naval hat. 'Come, Lieutenant – to the slaughter.'

When we emerged on the street, we collided head-on with a man carrying groceries into the house. As we disentangled ourselves from celery stalks, there was a click and a squeal of delight followed by a powerful whistle. I turned to see a small girl who had been lying in wait with a camera. She was an unsightly little girl with sandy pigtails and a brace on her teeth.

'Gee,' she announced. 'I can get two buckth for thith thnap from Barney Thtone. He'th thappy about you, Mith Duluth.'

Other children, materialising in response to her whistle, were galloping towards us. The grocery man came out of the house. Passers-by stopped, stared and closed in – a woman in scarlet slacks, two sailors, a flurry of bobby-soxers, a policeman.

'This,' said Iris grimly, 'is the end.'

She escaped from her fans and marched back to the two front doors of our hacienda. She rang the buzzer on the door that wasn't ours. She rang persistently. At length there was the clatter of a chain sliding into place and the door opened wide enough to reveal the face of Miss Crump. It was a small, faded face with a most uncordial expression.

'Yes?' asked Miss Crump.

'We're the Duluths,' said Iris. 'I just called you. I know about your dog, but . . .'

'Not *my* dog,' corrected Miss Crump. 'Mrs Wilberframe's dog. The late Mrs Wilberframe of Glendale who has a nephew and a niece-in-law of whom I know a great deal in Ogden Bluffs, Utah. At least, they *ought* to be in Ogden Bluffs.'

This unnecessary information was flung at us like a challenge. Then Miss Crump's face flushed into sudden dimpled pleasure.

'Duluth! Iris Duluth. You're *the* Iris Duluth of the movies?'

'Yes,' said Iris.

'Oh, why didn't you tell me over the phone? My favourite actress! How exciting! Poor thing – mobbed by your fans. Of course you may use the patio. I will give you the key to open your French windows. Any time.'

Miraculously the chain was off the door. It opened halfway and then stopped. Miss Crump was staring at me with a return of suspicion.

'You *are* Miss Duluth's husband?'

'Mrs Duluth's husband,' I corrected her. 'Lieutenant Duluth.'

She still peered. 'I mean, you have proof?'

I was beyond being surprised by Miss Crump. I fumbled from my wallet a dog-eared snapshot of Iris and me in full wedding regalia outside the church. Miss Crump studied it carefully and then returned it.

'You must please excuse me. What a sweet bride! It's just that I can't be too careful – for Poppy.'

'Poppy?' queried Iris. 'The St Bernard?'

Miss Crump nodded. 'It is Poppy's house, you see. Poppy pays the rent.'

'The dog,' said Iris faintly, 'pays the rent?'

'Yes, my dear. Poppy is very well-to-do. She is hardly more than a puppy, but she is one of the richest dogs, I suppose, in the whole world.'

Although we entertained grave doubts as to Miss Crump's sanity, we were soon in swimming suits and stepping through our open French windows into the sunshine of the patio. Miss Crump introduced us to Poppy.

In spite of our former prejudices, Poppy disarmed us immediately. She was just a big, bouncing, natural girl unspoiled by wealth. She greeted us with great thumps of her tail. She leaped up at Iris, dabbing at her cheek with a long, pink tongue. Later, when we had settled on striped mattresses under orange trees, she curled into a big clumsy ball at my side and laid her vast muzzle on my stomach.

'Look, she likes you.' Miss Crump was glowing. 'Oh, I knew she would!'

Iris, luxuriating in the sunshine, asked the polite question. 'Tell us about Poppy. How did she make her money?'

'Oh, she did not make it. She inherited it.' Miss Crump sat down on a white iron chair. 'Mrs Wilberframe was a very wealthy woman. She was devoted to Poppy.'

'And left her all her money?' I asked.

'Not quite all. There was a little nest egg for me. I was her companion, you see, for many years. But I am to look after Poppy. That is why I received the nest egg. Poppy pays me a generous salary too.' She fingered nondescript beads at her throat. 'Mrs Wilberframe was anxious for Poppy to have only the best and I am sure I try to do the right thing. Poppy has the master bedroom, of course. I take the little one in front. And then if Poppy has steak for dinner, I have hamburger.' She stared intensely. 'I would not have an easy moment if I felt that Poppy did not get the best.'

Poppy, her head on my stomach, coughed. She banged her tail against the flagstones apologetically.

Iris reached across me to pat her. 'Has she been rich for long?'

'Oh no, Mrs Wilberframe passed on only a few weeks ago.' Miss Crump paused. 'And it has been a great responsibility for me.' She paused again and then blurted: 'You're my friends, aren't you? Oh, I am sure you are. Please, please, won't you help me? I am all alone and I am so frightened.'

'Frightened?' I looked up and, sure enough, her little bird face was peaked with fear.

'For Poppy.' Miss Crump leaned forward. 'Oh, Lieutenant, it is like a nightmare. Because I know. I just know they are trying to murder her!'

'They?' Iris sat up straight.

'Mrs Wilberframe's nephew and his wife. From Ogden Bluffs, Utah.'

'You mentioned them when you opened the door.'

'I mention them to everyone who comes to the house. You see, I do not know what they look like and I do not want them to think I am not on my guard.'

I watched her. She might have looked like a silly spinster with a bee in her bonnet. She didn't. She looked nice and quite sane, only scared.

'Oh, they are not good people. Not at all. There is nothing they would not stoop to. Back in Glendale, I found pieces of meat in the front yard. Poisoned meat, I know. And on a lonely road, they shot at Poppy. Oh, the police laughed at me. A car back-firing, they said. But I know differently. I know they won't stop till Poppy is dead.' She threw her little hands up to her face. 'I ran away from them in Glendale. That is why I came to La Jolla. But they have caught up with us. I know. Oh, dear, poor Poppy who is so sweet without a nasty thought in her head.'

Poppy, hearing her name mentioned, smiled and panted.

'But this nephew and his wife from Ogden Bluffs, why should they want to murder her?' My wife's eyes were gleaming with a detective enthusiasm I knew of old. 'Are they after her money?'

'Of course,' said Miss Crump passionately. 'It's the will. The nephew is Mrs Wilberframe's only living relative, but she deliberately cut him off and I am sure I do not blame her. All the money goes to Poppy and – er – Poppy's little ones.'

'Isn't the nephew contesting a screwy will like that?' I asked.

'Not yet. To contest a will takes a great deal of money – lawyer fees and things. It would be much, much cheaper for him to kill Poppy. You see, one thing is not covered by the will. If Poppy were to die before she became a mother, the nephew would inherit the whole estate. Oh, I have done everything in my power. The moment the – er – suitable season arrived, I found a husband for Poppy. In a few weeks now – the little ones are expected. But these next few weeks . . .'

Miss Crump dabbed at her eyes with a small handkerchief. 'Oh, the Glendale police were most unsympathetic. They even mentioned the fact that the sentence for shooting or killing a dog in this state is shockingly light – a small fine at most. I called the police here and asked for protection. They said they'd send a man around sometimes but they were hardly civil. So you see, there is no protection from the law and no redress. There is no one to help me.'

'You've got us,' said Iris in a burst of sympathy.

'Oh . . . oh . . .' The handkerchief fluttered from Miss Crump's face.

'I knew you were my friends. You dear, dear things. Oh Poppy, they are going to help us.'

Poppy, busy licking my stomach, did not reply. Somewhat appalled by Iris' hasty promise but ready to stand by her, I said:

'Sure, we'll help, Miss Crump. First, what's the nephew's name?'

'Henry. Henry Blodgett. But he won't use that name. Oh no, he will be too clever for that.'

'And you don't know what he looks like?'

'Mrs Wilberframe destroyed his photograph many years ago when he bit her as a small boy. With yellow curls, I understand. That is when the trouble between them started.'

'At least you know what age he is?'

'He should be about thirty.'

'And the wife?' asked Iris.

'I know nothing about her,' said Miss Crump coldly, 'except that she is supposed to be a red-headed person, a former actress.'

'And what makes you so sure one or both of them have come to La Jolla?'

Miss Crump folder her arms in her lap. 'Last night. A telephone call.'

'A telephone call?'

'A voice asking if I was Miss Crump, and then – silence.' Miss Crump leaned towards me. 'Oh, now they know I am here. They know I never let Poppy out. They know every morning I search the patio for meat, traps. They must realise that the only possible way to reach her is to enter the house.'

'Break in?'

Miss Crump shook her tight curls. 'It is possible. But I believe they will rely on guile rather than violence. It is against that we must be on our guard. You are the only people who have come to the door since that telephone call. Now anyone else that comes to your apartment or mine, whatever their excuse . . .' She lowered her voice. 'Anyone may be Henry Blodgett or his wife and we will have to outwit them.'

A fly settled on one of Poppy's valuable ears. She did not seem to notice it. Miss Crump watched us earnestly and then gave a self-scolding cluck.

'Dear me, here I have been burdening you with Poppy's problems and you must be hungry. How about a little salad for luncheon? I always feel guilty about eating in the middle of the day when Poppy has her one meal at night. But with guests – yes, and allies – I am sure Mrs Wilberframe would not have grudged the expense.'

With a smile that was half-shy, half-conspiratorial, she fluttered away.

I looked at Iris. 'Well,' I said, 'is she a nut or do we believe her?'

'I rather think,' said my wife, 'that we believe her.'

'Why?'

345

'Just because.' Iris' face wore the entranced expression which had won her so many fans in her last picture. 'Oh, Peter, don't you see what fun it will be? A beautiful St Bernard in peril. A wicked villain with golden curls who bit his aunt.'

'He won't have golden curls any more,' I said. 'He's a big boy now.'

Iris, her body warm from the sun, leaned over me and put both arms around Poppy's massive neck.

'Poor Poppy,' she said. 'Really, this shouldn't happen to a dog!'

The first thing happened some hours after Miss Crump's little salad luncheon while Iris and I were sunning ourselves. Miss Crump, who, had been preparing Poppy's dinner and her own in her apartment, came running to announce:

'There is a man at the door! He claims he is from the electric light company to read the meter. Oh dear, if he is legitimate and we do not let him in, there will be trouble with the electric light company and if . . .' She wrung her hands. 'Oh, what shall we do?'

I reached for a bathrobe. 'You and Iris stay here. And for Mrs Wilberframe's sake, hang on to Poppy.'

I found the man outside the locked front door. He was about thirty with thinning hair and wore an army discharge button. He showed me his credentials. They seemed in perfect order. There was nothing for it but to let him in. I took him into the kitchen where Poppy's luscious steak and Miss Crump's modest hamburger were lying where Miss Crump had left them on the table. I hovered over the man while he located the meter. I never let out him of my sight until he had departed. In answer to Miss Crump's anxious questioning, I could only say that if the man had been Henry Blodgett he knew how much electricity she'd used in the past month – but that was all.

The next caller showed up a few minutes later. Leaving Iris, indignant at being out of things, to stand by Poppy, Miss Crump and I handled the visitor. This time it was a slim, brash girl with bright auburn hair and a navy-blue slack suit. She was, she said, the sister of the woman who owned the hacienda. She wanted a photograph for the newspapers – a photograph of her Uncle William who had just been promoted to Rear Admiral in the Pacific. The photograph was in a trunk in the attic.

Miss Crump, reacting to the unlikeliness of the request, refused entry. The red-head wasn't the type that wilted. When she started talking darkly of eviction, I overrode Miss Crump and offered to conduct her to the attic. The girl gave me one quick experienced look and flounced into the hall.

The attic was reached by the back stairs through the kitchen. I conducted the red-head directly to her claimed destination. There were trunks. She searched through them. At length she produced a photograph of a limp young man in a raccoon coat.

'My Uncle William,' she snapped, 'as a youth.'

'Pretty,' I said.

I took her back to the front door and she left. If she had been Mrs Blodgett, she knew how to take care of herself, she knew how many trunks there were in the attic – and that was all.

Iris and I dressed and were drinking Daiquiris under a green-and-white-striped umbrella when Miss Crump appeared followed by a young policeman. She was very pleased about the policeman. He had come, she said, in answer to her complaint. She showed him Poppy; she babbled out her story of the Blodgetts. He obviously thought she was a harmless lunatic, but she didn't seem to realise it. After she had let him out, she settled beamingly down with us.

'I suppose,' said Iris, 'you asked him for his credentials?'

'I . . .' Miss Crump's face clouded. 'My dear, you don't think that perhaps he wasn't a real police . . .?'

'To me,' said Iris, 'everyone's a Blodgett until proved to the contrary.'

'Oh dear,' said Miss Crump.

Nothing else happened. By evening Iris and I were back in our part of the house. Poppy had hated to see us go. We had hated to leave her. A mutual crush had developed between us.

But now that we were alone again, the sinister Blodgetts did not seem very substantial. Iris made a creditable *Boeuf Stroganov* from yesterday's leftovers and changed into a lime-green negligée. I was busy being a sailor on leave with his girl when the phone rang. I reached over Iris for the receiver, said 'Hello,' and then sat rigid listening.

It was Miss Crump's voice. But something was horribly wrong with it. It came across hoarse and gasping.

'Come,' it said. 'Oh, come. The French windows. Oh, please . . .'

The voice faded. I heard the clatter of a dropped receiver.

'It must be Poppy,' I said to Iris. 'Quick.'

We ran out into the dark patio. Across it, I could see the French windows of Miss Crump's apartment. They were half open, and as I looked Poppy squirmed through to the patio. She bounded towards us, whining.

'Poppy's all right,' said Iris. 'Quick!'

We ran to Miss Crump's windows. Poppy barged past us into the living-room. We followed. All the lights were on. Poppy had galloped around a high-backed davenport. We went to it and looked over it.

Poppy was crouched on the carpet, her huge muzzle dropped on her paws. She was howling and staring straight at Miss Crump.

Poppy's paid companion was on the floor too. She lay motionless on her back, her legs twisted under her, her small, grey face distorted, her lips stretched in a dreadful smile.

I knelt down by Poppy. I picked up Miss Crump's thin wrist and felt for the pulse. Poppy was still howling. Iris stood, straight and white.

'Peter, tell me. Is she dead?'

'Not quite. But only just not quite. Poison. It looks like strychnine . . .'

We called a doctor. We called the police. The doctor came, muttered a shocked diagnosis of strychnine poisoning and rushed Miss Crump to the hospital. I asked if she had a chance. He didn't answer. I knew what that meant. Soon the police came and there was so much to say and do and think that I hadn't time to brood about poor Miss Crump.

We told Inspector Green the Blodgett story. It was obvious to us that somehow Miss Crump had been poisoned by them in mistake for Poppy. Since no one had entered the house that day except three callers, one of them, we said, must have been a Blodgett. All the Inspector had to do, we said, was to locate those three people and find out which was a Blodgett.

Inspector Green watched us pokerfaced and made no comment. After he'd left, we took the companionless Poppy back to our part of the house. She climbed on the bed and stretched out between us, her tail thumping, her head flopped on the pillows. We didn't have the heart to evict her. It was not one of our better nights.

Early next morning, a policeman took us to Miss Crump's apartment. Inspector Green was waiting in the living-room. I didn't like his stare.

'We've analysed the hamburger she was eating last night,' he said. 'There was enough strychnine in it to kill an elephant.'

'Hamburger!' exclaimed Iris. 'Then that proves she was poisoned by the Blodgetts!'

'Why?' asked Inspector Green.

'They didn't know how conscientious Miss Crump was. They didn't know she always bought steak for Poppy and hamburger for herself. They saw the steak and the hamburger and they naturally assumed the hamburger was for Poppy, so they poisoned that.'

'That's right,' I cut in. 'The steak and the hamburger were lying right on the kitchen table when all three of those people came in yesterday.'

'I see,' said the Inspector.

He nodded to a policeman who left the room and returned with three people – the balding young man from the electric light company, the red-headed vixen and the young policeman. None of them looked happy.

'You're willing to swear,' the Inspector asked us, 'that these were the only three people who entered this house yesterday.'

'Yes,' said Iris.

'And you think one of them is either Blodgett or his wife?'

'They've got to be.'

Inspector Green smiled faintly. 'Mr Burns here has been with the electric light company for five years except for a year when he was in the army. The electric light company is willing to vouch for that. Miss Curtis has been identified as the sister of the lady who owns this house and the niece of Rear Admiral Moss. She has no connection with any Blodgetts and has never been in Utah.' He paused. 'As for Officer Patterson, he has been a member of the police force here for eight years. I personally sent him around yesterday to follow up Miss Crump's complaint.'

The Inspector produced an envelope from his pocket and tossed it to me. 'I've had these photographs of Mr and Mrs Henry Blodgett flown from the files of the Ogden Bluffs *Tribune*.'

I pulled the photographs out of the envelope. We stared at them. Neither Mr or Mrs Blodgett looked at all the sort of person you would like to know. But neither of them bore the slightest resemblance to any of the three suspects in front of us.

'It might also interest you,' said the Inspector quietly, 'that I've checked with the Ogden Bluffs police. Mr Blodgett has been sick in bed for over a week and his wife has been nursing him. There is a doctor's certificate to that effect.'

Inspector Green gazed down at his hands. They were competent hands. 'It looks to me that the whole Blodgett story was built up in Miss Crump's mind – or yours.' His grey eyes stared right through us. 'If we have to eliminate the Blodgetts and these three people from suspicion, that leaves only two others who had the slightest chance of poisoning the hamburger.'

Iris blinked. 'Us?'

'You,' said Inspector Green almost sadly.

They didn't arrest us, of course. We had no conceivable motive. But Inspector Green questioned us minutely and when he left there was a policeman lounging outside the door.

We spent a harried afternoon racking our brains and getting nowhere. Iris was the one who had the inspiration. Suddenly, just after she had fed Poppy the remains of the *Stroganov*, she exclaimed:

'Good heavens above, of course!'

'Of course what?'

She spun to me, her eyes shining. 'Barney Thtone,' she lisped. 'Why didn't we realise? Come on!'

She ran out of the house into the street. She grabbed the lounging policeman by the arm.

'You live here,' she said. 'Who's Barney Stone?'

349

'Barney Stone?' The policeman stared. 'He's the son of the druggist on the corner.'

Iris raced me to the drugstore. She was attracting quite a crowd. The policeman followed, too.

In the drugstore, a thin young man with spectacles stood behind the prescription counter.

'Mr Stone?' asked Iris.

His mouth dropped open. 'Gee, Miss Duluth. I never dreamed . . . Gee, Miss Duluth, what can I do for you? Cigarettes? An alarm clock?'

'A little girl,' said Iris. 'A little girl with sandy pigtails and a brace on her teeth. What's her name? Where does she live?'

Barney Stone said promptly: 'You mean Daisy Kornfeld. Kind of homely. Just down the block. 712. Miss Duluth, I certainly . . .'

'Thanks,' cut in Iris and we were off again with our ever growing escort.

Daisy was sitting in the Kornfeld parlour, glumly thumping the piano. Ushered in by an excited, cooing Mrs Kornfeld, Iris interrupted Daisy's rendition of *The Jolly Farmer*.

'Daisy, that picture you took of me yesterday to sell to Mr Stone, is it developed yet?'

'Gee, no, Mith Duluth. I ain't got the developing money yet. Theventy-five thenth. Ma don't give me but a nickel an hour for practithing thith piano.'

'Here.' Iris thrust a ten-dollar bill into her hand. 'I'll buy the whole roll. Run get the camera. We'll have it developed right away.'

'Gee.' The mercenary Daisy stared with blank incredulity at the ten-dollar bill.

I stared just as blankly myself. I wasn't being bright at all.

I wasn't much brighter an hour later. We were back in our apartment, waiting for Inspector Green. Poppy, all for love, was trying to climb into my lap. Iris, who had charmed Barney Stone into developing Daisy's films, clutched the yellow envelope of snaps in her hand. She had sent our policeman away on a secret mission, but an infuriating passion for the dramatic had kept her from telling or showing me anything. I had to wait for Inspector Green.

Eventually Iris' policeman returned and whispered with her in the hall. Then Inspector Green came. He looked cold and hostile. Poppy didn't like him. She growled. Sometimes Poppy was smart.

Inspector Green said, 'You've been running all over town. I told you to stay here.'

'I know.' Iris' voice was meek. 'It's just that I wanted to solve poor Miss Crump's poisoning.'

'Solve it?' Inspector Green's query was sceptical.

'Yes. It's awfully simple really. I can't imagine why we didn't think of it from the start.'

'You mean you know who poisoned her?'

'Of course.' Iris smiled, a maddening smile. 'Henry Blodgett.'

'But . . .'

'Check with the airlines. I think you'll find that Blodgett flew in from Ogden Bluffs a few days ago and flew back today. As for his being sick in bed under his wife's care, I guess that'll make Mrs Blodgett an accessory before the fact, won't it?'

Inspector Green was pop-eyed.

'Oh, it's my fault really,' continued Iris. 'I said no one came to the house yesterday except those three people. There was someone else, but he was so ordinary, so run-of-the-mill, that I forgot him completely.'

I was beginning to see then. Inspector Green snapped, 'And this run-of-the-mill character?'

'The man,' said Iris sweetly, 'who had the best chance of all to poison the hamburger, *the man who delivered it* – the man from the Super-market.

'We don't have to guess. We have proof.' Iris fumbled in the yellow envelope. 'Yesterday morning as we were going out, we bumped into the man delivering Miss Crump's groceries. Just at that moment, a sweet little girl took a snap of us. This snap.'

She selected a print and handed it to Inspector Green. I moved to look at it over his shoulder.

'I'm afraid Daisy is an impressionistic photographer,' murmured Iris. 'That hip on the right is me. The buttocks are my husband. But the figure in the middle – quite a masterly likeness of Henry Blodgett, isn't it? Of course, there's the grocery apron, the unshaven chin . . .'

She was right. Daisy had only winged Iris and me but with the grocery man she had scored a direct hit. And the grocery man was unquestion-ably Henry Blodgett.

Iris nodded to her policeman. 'Sergeant Blair took a copy of the snap around the neighbourhood groceries. They recognised Blodgett at the Supermarket. They hired him day before yesterday. He made a few deliveries this morning, including Miss Crump's, and took a powder without his pay.'

'Well . . .' stammered Inspector Green. 'Well . . .'

'Just how many charges can you get him on?' asked my wife hopefully. 'Attempted homicide, conspiracy to defraud, illegal possession of poisonous drugs . . . I hope you give him the works when you get him.'

'We'll get him, all right,' said Inspector Green.

Iris leaned over and patted Poppy's head affectionately.

'Don't worry, darling. I'm sure Miss Crump will get well and we'll throw a lovely christening party for your little strangers . . .'

Iris was right about the Blodgetts. Henry got the works. And his wife was held as an accessory. Iris was right about Miss Crump too. She is still in the hospital but improving steadily and will almost certainly be well enough to attend the christening party.

Meanwhile, at her request, Poppy is staying with us, awaiting maternity with rollicking unconcern.

It's nice having a dog who pays the rent.

John D. MacDonald

The Homesick Buick

To get to Leeman, Texas, you go southwest from Beaumont on Route 90 for approximately thirty miles and then turn right on a two-lane concrete farm road. Five minutes from the time you turn, you will reach Leeman. The main part of town is six lanes wide and five blocks long. If the hand of a careless giant should remove the six gas stations, the two theatres, Willow's hardware store, the Leeman National Bank, the two big air-conditioned five-and-dimes, the Sears' store, four cafés, Rightsinger's dress shop, and The Leeman House, a twenty-room hotel, there would be very little left except the supermarket and four assorted drug-stores.

On October 3, 1949, a Mr Stanley Woods arrived by bus and carried his suitcase over to The Leeman House. In Leeman there is no social distinction of bus, train, or plane, since Leeman has neither airport facilities nor railroad station.

On all those who were questioned later, Mr Stanley Woods seemed to have made very little impression. They all spoke of kind of a medium-size fella in this thirties, or it might be his forties. No, he wasn't fat, but he wasn't thin either. Blue eyes? Could be brown. Wore a grey suit, I think. Can't remember whether his glasses had rims or not. If they did have, they were probably gold.

But all were agreed that Mr Stanley Woods radiated quiet confidence and the smell of money. According to the cards that were collected here and there, Mr Woods represented the Groston Precision Tool Company of Atlanta, Georgia. He had deposited in the Leeman National a certified cheque for twelve hundred dollars and the bank had made the routine check of looking up the credit standing of Groston. It was Dun and Bradstreet double-A, but, of course, the company explained later that they had never heard of Mr Stanley Woods. Nor could the fake calling cards be traced. They were of a type of paper and type face which could be duplicated sixty or a hundred times in every big city in the country.

Mr Woods' story, which all agreed on, was that he was 'nosing around to find a good location for a small plant. Decentralisation, you know. No, we don't want it right in town.'

He rented Tod Bishner's car during the day. Tod works at the Shell station on the corner of Beaumont and Lone Star Streets and doesn't have any use for his Plymouth sedan during the day. Mr Woods drove around all the roads leading out of town and, of course, real estate prices were jacked to a considerable degree during his stay.

Mr Stanley Woods left Leeman rather suddenly on the morning of October 17th under unusual circumstances.

The first person to note a certain oddness was Miss Trilla Price on the switchboard at the phone company. Her local calls were all right but she couldn't place Charley Anderson's call to Houston, nor, when she tried, could she raise Beaumont. Charley was upset because he wanted to wangle an invitation to go visit his sister over the coming weekend.

That was at five minutes to nine. It was probably at the same time that a car with two men in it parked on Beaumont Street, diagonally across from the bank, and one of the two men lifted the hood and began to fiddle with the electrical system.

Nobody agrees from what direction the Buick came into town. There were a man and a girl in it and they parked near the drug-store. No one seems to know where the third car parked, or even what kind of car it was.

The girl and the man got out of the Buick slowly, just as Stanley Woods came down the street from the hotel.

In Leeman the bank is open on weekdays from nine until two. And so, at nine o'clock, C. F. Hethridge, who is, or was, the chief teller, raised the green shades on the inside of the bank doors and unlocked the doors. He greeted Mr Woods, who went on over to the high counter at the east wall and began to ponder over his cheque book.

At this point, out on the street, a very peculiar thing happened. One of the two men in the first car strolled casually over and stood beside the Buick. The other man started the motor of the first car, drove down the street, and made a wide U-turn to swing in and park behind the Buick.

The girl and the man had gone over to Bob Kimball's window. Bob is second teller, and the only thing he can remember about the girl is that she was blonde and a little hard-looking around the mouth, and that she wore a great big alligator shoulder-bag. The man with her made no impression on Bob at all, except that Bob thinks the man was on the heavy side.

Old Rod Harrigan, the bank guard, was standing beside the front door, yawning, and picking his teeth with a broken match.

At this point C. F. Hethridge heard the buzzer on the big time-vault and went over and swung the door wide and went in to get the money for the cages. He was out almost immediately, carrying Bob's tray over to him. The girl was saying something about cashing a cheque and Bob had asked her for identification. She had opened the big shoulder-bag as her escort strolled over to the guard. At the same moment the girl pulled out a small vicious-looking revolver and aimed it between Bob's eyes, her escort sapped Old Rod Harrigan with such gusto that it was four that same afternoon before he came out of it enough to talk. And then, of course, he knew nothing.

C. F. Hethridge bolted for the vault, and Bob, wondering whether he should step on the alarm, looked over the girl's shoulder just in time to see Stanley Woods aim carefully and bring Hethridge down with a slug through the head, catching him on the fly, so to speak.

Bob says that things were pretty confusing and that the sight of Hethridge dying so suddenly sort of took the heart out of him. Anyway, there was a third car and it contained three men, two of them equipped with empty black-leather suitcases. They went into the vault, acting as though they had been all through the bank fifty times. They stepped over Hethridge on the way in, and on the way out again.

About the only cash they overlooked was the cash right in front of Bob, in his teller's drawer.

As they all broke for the door, Bob dropped and pressed the alarm button. He said later that he held his hands over his eyes, though what good that would do him, he couldn't say.

Henry Willows is the real hero. He was fuddying around in his hardware store when he heard the alarm. With a reaction-time remarkable in a man close to seventy, he took a little .22 rifle, slapped a clip into it, trotted to his store door, and quickly analysed the situation. He saw Mr Woods, whom he recognised, plus three strangers and a blonde woman coming out of the bank pretty fast. Three cars were lined up, each one with a driver. Two of the men coming out of the bank carried heavy suitcases. Henry levelled on the driver of the lead car, the Buick, and shot him in the left temple, killing him outright. The man slumped over the wheel, his body resting against the horn ring, which, of course, added its blare to the clanging of the bank alarm.

At that point a slug, later identified as having come from a Smith & Wesson Police Positive, smashed a neat hole in Henry's plate-glass store window, radiating cracks in all directions. Henry ducked, and by the time he got ready to take a second shot, the two other cars were gone. The Buick was still there. He saw Bob run out of the bank, and later on he told his wife that he had his finger on the trigger and his sights lines up before it come to him that it was Bob Kimball.

It was agreed that the two cars headed out towards Route 90 and, within two minutes, Hod Abrams and Lefty Quinn had roared out of town in the same direction in the only police car. They were followed by belligerent amateurs, to whom Henry Willows had doled out firearms. But on the edge of town all cars ran into an odd obstacle. The road was liberally sprinkled with metal objects shaped exactly like the jacks that little girls pick up when they bounce a ball, except they were four times normal size and all the points were sharpened. No matter how a tyre hit one, it was certain to be punctured.

The police car swerved to a screaming stop, nearly tipping over. The Stein twins, boys of nineteen, managed to avoid the jacks in their souped-up heap until they were hitting eighty. When they finally hit one, the heap rolled over an estimated ten times, killing the twins outright.

So that made four dead. Hethridge, the Stein twins, and one un-identified bank robber.

Nobody wanted to touch the robber, and he stayed right where he was until the battery almost ran down and the horn squawked into silence. Hod Abrams commandeered a car, and he and Lefty rode back into town and took charge. They couldn't get word out by phone and within a very short time they found that some sharpshooter with a high-powered rifle had gone to work on the towers of local station WLEE and had put the station out of business.

Thus, by the time the Texas Rangers were alerted and ready to set up road blocks, indecision and confusion had permitted an entire hour to pass.

The Houston office of the FBI assigned a detail of men to the case, and from the Washington headquarters two bank-robbery experts were dispatched by plane to Beaumont. Reporters came from Houston and Beaumont and the two national press services, and Leeman found itself on the front pages all over the country because the planning behind the job seemed to fascinate the average Joe. The FBI from Houston was there by noon on the particular Thursday, and the Washington con-tingent arrived late Friday. Everyone was very confident. There was a corpse and a car to work on. These would certainly provide the necessary clues to indicate which outfit had pulled the job, even though the method of the robbery did not point to any particular group whose habits were known.

Investigation headquarters were set up in the local police station, and

Hod and Lefty, very important in the beginning, had to stand around outside trying to look as though they knew what was going on.

Hethridge, who had been a cold, reserved, unpopular man, had, within twenty-four hours, fifty stories invented about his human kindness and generosity. The Stein twins, heretofore considered to be trash who would be better off in prison, suddenly became proper sons of old Texas.

Special Agent Randolph A. Sternweister who, fifteen years before, had found a law office to be a dull place, was in charge of the case, being the senior of the two experts who had flown down from Washington. He was forty-one years old, a chain smoker, a chubby man with incongruous hollow cheeks and hair of a shade of grey which his wife, Claire, tells him is distinguished.

The corpse was the first clue. Age between thirty and thirty-two. Brown hair, thinning on top. Good teeth, with only four small cavities, two of them filled. Height, five foot eight and a quarter, weight a hundred and forty-eight. No distinguishing scars or tattoos. X-ray plates showed that the right arm had been fractured years before. His clothes were neither new nor old. The suit had been purchased in Chicago. The shirt, underwear, socks, and shoes were all national brands, in the medium-price range. In his pockets they found an almost full pack of cigarettes, a battered Zippo lighter, three fives and a one in a cheap, trick billclip, eighty-five cents in change, a book of matches advertising a nationally known laxative, a white bone button, two wooden kitchen matches with blue and white heads, and a pencilled map, on cheap notebook paper, of the main drag of Leeman – with no indication as to escape routes. His fingerprint classification was teletyped to the Central Bureau files, and the answer came back that there was no record of him. It was at this point that fellow workers noted that Mr Sternweister became a shade irritable.

The next search of the corpse was more minute. No specific occupational calluses were found on his hands. The absence of laundry marks indicated that his linen, if it had been sent out, had been cleaned by a neighbourhood laundress. Since Willows had used a .22 hollow-point, the hydraulic pressure on the brain fluids had caused the eyes of Mr X to bulge in a disconcerting fashion. A local undertaker, experienced in the damage caused by the average Texas automobile accident, replaced the bulging eyeballs and smoothed out the expression for a series of pictures which were sent to many points. The Chicago office reported that the clothing store which had sold the suit was large and that the daily traffic was such that no clerk could identify the customer from the picture; nor was the youngish man known to the Chicago police.

Fingernail scrapings were put in a labelled glassine envelope, as well as the dust vacuumed from pants cuffs and other portions of the clothing likely to collect dust. The excellent lab in Houston reported back that the dust and scrapings were negative to the extent that the man could not be tied down to any particular locality.

In the meantime the Buick had been the object of equal scrutiny. The outside was a mass of prints from the citizens of Leeman who had peered morbidly in at the man leaning against the horn ring. The plates were Mississippi licence plates, and in checking with the Bureau of Motor Vehicle Registration, it was found that the plates had been issued for a 1949 Mercury convertible which had been totally destroyed in a head-on collision in June 1949. The motor number and serial number of the Buick were checked against central records and it was discovered that the Buick was one which had disappeared from Chapel Hill, North Carolina, on the 5th of July, 1949. The insurance company, having already replaced the vehicle, was anxious to take possession of the stolen car.

Pictures of Mr X, relayed to Chapel Hill, North Carolina, and to myriad points in Mississippi, drew a large blank. In the meantime a careful dusting of the car had brought out six prints, all different. Two of them turned out to be on record. The first was on record through the cross-classification of Army prints. The man in question was found working in a gas station in Lake Charles, Louisiana. He had a very difficult two hours until a bright police officer had him demonstrate his procedure for brushing out the front of a car. Ex-Sergeant Golden braced his left hand against the dashboard in almost the precise place where the print had been found. He was given a picture of Mr X to study. By that time he was so thoroughly annoyed at the forces of law and order that it was impossible to ascertain whether or not he had ever seen the man in question. But due to the apparent freshness of the paint, it was established – a reasonable assumption – that the gangsters had driven into Texas from the East.

The second print on record was an old print, visible when dust was carefully blown off the braces under the dismantled front seat. It belonged to a garage mechanic in Chapel Hill who once had a small misunderstanding with the forces of law and order and who was able to prove, through the garage work orders, that he had repaired the front-seat mechanism when it had jammed in April 1949.

The samples of road dirt and dust taken from the fender wells and the frame members proved nothing. The dust was proved, spectroscopically, to be from deep in the heart of Texas, and the valid assumption, after checking old weather reports, was that the car had come through some brisk thunderstorms en route.

Butts in the ashtray of the car showed that either two women, or one woman with two brands of lipstick, had ridden recently as a passenger.

Both brands of lipstick were of shades which would go with a fair-complexioned blonde, and both brands were available in Woolworth's, Kress's, Kresge's, Walgreen's – in fact, in every chain outfit of any importance.

One large crumb of stale whole-wheat bread was found on the floor mat, and even Sternweister could make little of that, despite the fact that the lab was able to report that the bread had been eaten in conjunction with liverwurst.

Attention was given to the oversized jacks which had so neatly punctured the tyres. An ex-OSS officer reported that similar items had been scattered on enemy roads in Burma during the late war, and after examining the samples, he stated confidently that the OSS merchandise had been better made. A competent machinist looked them over and stated with assurance that they had been made by cutting eighth-inch rods into short lengths, grinding them on a wheel, putting them in a jig, and spot-welding them. He said that the maker did not do much of a job on either the grinding or the welding, and that the jig itself was a little out of line. An analysis of the steel showed that it was a Jones & Laughlin product that could be bought in quantity in any wholesaler and in a great many hardware stores.

The auditors, after a careful examination of the situation at the bank, reported that the sum of exactly $94,725 had disappeared. They recommended that the balance remaining in Stanley Woods' account of $982.80 be considered as forfeited, thus reducing the loss to $93,742.20. The good citizens of Leeman preferred to think that Stanley had withdrawn his account.

Every person who had a glimpse of the gang was cross-examined. Sternweister was appalled at the difficulty involved in even establishing how many there had been. Woods, the blonde, and the stocky citizen were definite. And then there were two with suitcases – generally agreed upon. Total, so far – five. The big question was whether each car had a driver waiting. Some said no – that the last car in line had been empty. Willows insisted angrily that there had been a driver behind each wheel. Sternweister at last settled for a total of eight, seven of whom escaped.

No one had taken down a single licence number. But it was positively established that the other two cars had been either two- or four-door sedans in dark blue, black, green, or maroon, and that they had been either Buicks, Nashes, Oldsmobiles, Chryslers, Pontiacs, or Packards – or maybe Hudsons. And one lone woman held out for convertible Cadillacs. For each person that insisted that they had Mississippi registration, there was one equally insistent on Louisiana, Texas, Alabama, New Mexico, and Oklahoma. And one old lady said that she guessed she knew a

California plate when she saw one.

On Saturday morning, nine days after the robbery, Randolph Stern-weister paced back and forth in his suite at the hotel which he shared with the number two man from the Washington end, one Buckley Weed. Weed was reading through the transcripts of the testimony of the witnesses, in the vain hope of finding something to which insufficient importance had been given. Weed, though lean, a bit stooped and only thirty-one, had, through osmosis, acquired most of the personal manner-isms of his superior. Sternweister had noticed this and for the past year had been on the verge of mentioning it. As Weed had acquired Stern-weister's habit of lighting a cigarette off the last half-inch of the preceding one, any room in which the two of them remained for more than an hour took on the look and smell of any hotel room after a Legion convention.

'Nothing,' Sternweister said. 'Not one censored, unmentionable, unprintable, unspeakable thing! My God, if I ever want to kill anybody, I'll do it in the Pennsy Station at five-fifteen.'

'Yes, at five-fifteen,' said Weed.

'The Bureau has cracked cases when the only thing it had to go on was a human hair or a milligram of dust. My God, we've got a whole automobile that weighs nearly two tons, and a whole corpse! They'll think we're down here learning to rope calves. You know what?'

'What, Ran?'

'I think this was done by a bunch of amateurs. There ought to be a law restricting the practice of crime to professionals. A bunch of wise amateurs. And you can bet your loudest argyles, my boy, that they established identity, hideout, the works, before they knocked off that vault. Right now, blast their souls, they're being seven average citizens in some average community, making no splash with that ninety-four grand. People didn't used to move around so much. Since the war they've been migrating all over the place. Strangers don't stick out like sore thumbs any more. See anything in those transcripts?'

'Nothing.'

'Then stop rattling paper. I can't think. Since a week ago Thursday fifty-one stolen cars have been recovered in the South and Southwest. And we don't know which two, if any, belonged to this mob. We don't even know which route they took away from here. Believe it or not – nobody saw 'em!'

As the two specialists stared bleakly at each other, a young man of fourteen named Pink Dee was sidling inconspicuously through the shadows in the rear of Louie's Garage (Tow car service – open 24 hrs.). Pink was considered to have been the least beautiful baby, the most unprepossessing child, in Leeman, and he gave frank promise of growing up to be a rather coarse joke on the entire human race. Born with a milk-blue skin, dead-white hair, little reddish weak eyes, pipe-cleaner bones, narrow forehead, no chin, beaver teeth, a voice like an unoiled hinge, nature had made the usual compensation. His reaction-time was exceptional. Plenty of more rugged and more normal children had found out that Pink Dee could hit you by the time you had the word out of your mouth. The blow came from an outsize, knobbly fist at the end of a long thin arm, and he swung it with all the abandon of a bag of rocks on the end of a rope. The second important item about Pink Dee came to light when the Leeman School System started giving IQs. Pink's was higher than they were willing to admit the first time, as it did not seem proper that the only genius in Leeman should be old Homer Dee's only son. Pink caught on, and the second time he was rated he got it down into the cretin class. The third rating was nine-nine and everybody seemed happy with that.

At fourteen Pink was six feet tall and weighed a hundred and twenty pounds. He peered at the world through heavy lenses and maintained, in the back room of his home on Fountain Street, myriad items of apparatus, some made, some purchased. There he investigated certain electrical and magnetic phenomena, having tired of building radios, and carried on a fairly virulent correspondence on the quantum theory with a Cal Tech professor who was under the impression that he was arguing with someone of more mature years.

Dressed in his khakis, the uniform of Texas, Pink moved through the shadows, inserted the key he had filched into the Buick door, and then into the ignition lock. He turned it to the left to activate the electrical gimmicks, and then turned on the car radio. As soon as it warmed up he pushed the selector buttons, carefully noting the dial. When he had the readings he turned it to WLEE to check the accuracy of the dial. When WLEE roared in to a farm report, Louie of Louie's Garage (Tow car service – open 24 hrs.) appeared and dragged Pink out by the thin scruff of his neck.

'What the hell?' Louie said.

Being unable to think of any adequate explanation, Pink wriggled away and loped out.

Pink's next stop was WLEE, where he was well known. He found the manual he wanted and spent the next twenty minutes leafing through it.

Having been subjected to a certain amount of sarcasm from both Sternweister and Weed, Hod Adams and Lefty Quinn were in no mood for the approach Pink Dee used.

'I demand to see the FBI,' Pink said firmly, the effect spoiled a bit by the fact that his voice change was so recent that the final syllable was a reversion to his childhood squeaky-hinge voice.

'He demands,' Hod said to Lefty.

'Go away, Pink,' Lefty growled, 'before I stomp on your glasses.'

'I am a citizen who wishes to speak to a member of a federal agency,' Pink said with dignity.

'A citizen, maybe. A taxpayer, no. You give me trouble, kid, and I'm going to warm your pants right here in this lobby.'

Maybe the potential indignity did it. Pink darted for the stairs leading up from the lobby. Hod went roaring up the stairs after him and Lefty grabbed the elevator. They both snared him outside Sternweister's suite and found that they had a job on their hands. Pink bucked and contorted like a picnic on which a hornet's nest had just fallen.

The door to the suite opened and both Sternweister and Weed glared out, their mouths open.

'Just . . . just a fresh . . . kid!' Hod Abrams panted.

'I know where the crooks are!' Pink screamed.

'He's nuts,' Lefty yelled.

'Wait a minute,' Randolph Sternweister ordered sharply. They stopped dragging Pink but still clung to him. 'I admit he doesn't look as though he knew his way home, but you can't tell. You two wait outside. Come in here, young man.'

Pink marched erectly into the suite, selected the most comfortable chair, and sank into it, looking very smug.

'Where are they?'

'Well, I don't exactly—'

'Outside!' Weed said with a thumb motion.

'But I know how to find out.'

'Oh, you know how to find out, eh? Keep talking. I haven't laughed in nine days,' Sternweister said.

'Oh, I had to do a little checking first,' Pink said in a lofty manner. 'I stole the key to the Buick and got into it to test something.'

'Kid, experts have been over that car, half-inch by half-inch.'

'Please don't interrupt me, sir. And don't take that attitude. Because, if it turns out I have something, and I know I have, you're going to look as silly as anything.'

Sternweister flushed and then turned pale. He held hard to the edge of a table. 'Go ahead,' he said thickly.

'I am making an assumption that the people who robbed our bank started out from one hideout and then went back to the same one. I am further assuming that they were in their hideout some time – that is, while they were planning the robbery.'

Weed and Sternweister exchanged glances. 'Go on.'

'So my plan has certain possible flaws based on these assumptions, but at least it uncovers one possible pattern of investigation. I know that the car was stolen from Chapel Hill. That was in the paper. And I know the dead man was in Chicago. So I checked Chicago and Chapel Hill a little while ago.'

'Checked them?'

'At the radio station, of course. Modern car radios are easy to set to new stations by altering the push buttons. The current settings of the push buttons do not conform either to the Chicago or the Chapel Hill areas. There are six stations that the radio in the Buick is set for and . . .'

Sternweister sat down on the couch as though somebody had clubbed him behind the knees. 'Agh!' he said.

'So all you have to do,' Pink said calmly, 'is to check areas against the push-button settings until you find an area *where all six frequencies are represented by radio stations in the immediate geographical vicinity*. It will take a bit of statistical work, of course, and a map of the country, and a supply of push pins should simplify things, I would imagine. Then, after the area is located, I would take the Buick there, and due to variations in individual sets and receiving conditions, you might be able to narrow it down to within a mile or two. Then by showing the photograph of the dead gangster around at bars and such places . . .'

And that was why, on the following Wednesday, a repainted Buick with new plates and containing two agents of the Bureau roamed through the small towns near Tampa on the West Florida coast, and how they found that the car radio in the repainted Buick brought in Tampa, Clearwater, St Petersburg, Orlando, Winter Haven, and Dunedin on the push buttons with remarkable clarity the closer they came to a little resort town called Tarpon Springs. On Thursday morning at four, the portable floodlights bathed three beach cottages in a white glare, and the metallic voice of the P.A. system said, 'You are surrounded. Come out with your hands high. You are surrounded.'

The shots, a few moments later, cracked with a thin bitterness against the heavier sighing of the Gulf of Mexico. Mr Stanley Woods, or, as the blonde later stated, Mr Grebbs Fainstock, was shot, with poetic justice, through the head, and that was the end of resistance.

To Pink Dee in Leeman, the president of the Leeman National Bank turned over the envelope containing the reward. It came to a bit less than 6 per cent of the recovered funds, and it was ample to guarantee, at some later date, a Cal Tech degree.

In December the Sternweisters bought a new car. When Claire demanded to know why Randolph insisted on delivery *sans* car radio, his only answer was a hollow laugh.

She feels that he has probably been working too hard.

Charlotte Armstrong

The Enemy

They sat at the lunch table and afterward moved through the dim, cool, high-ceilinged rooms to the judge's library where, in their quiet talk, the old man's past and the young man's future seemed to telescope and touch. But at twenty minutes after three, on that hot, bright June Saturday afternoon, the present tense erupted. Out in the quiet street arose the sound of trouble.

Judge Kittinger adjusted his pince-nez, rose, and led the way to his old-fashioned veranda from which they could overlook the tree-roofed intersection of Greenwood Lane and Hannibal Street. Near the steps to the corner house, opposite, there was a surging knot of children and one man. Now, from the house on the judge's left, a woman in a blue house dress ran diagonally toward the excitement. And a police car slipped up Hannibal Street, gliding to the curb. One tall officer plunged into the group and threw restraining arms around a screaming boy.

Mike Russell, saying to his host, 'Excuse me, sir,' went rapidly across the street. Trouble's centre was the boy, ten or eleven years old, a towheaded boy, with tawny-lashed blue eyes, a straight nose, a fine brow. He was beside himself, writhing in the policeman's grasp. The woman in the blue dress was yammering at him. 'Freddy! Freddy! Freddy!' Her voice simply did not reach his ears.

'You ole stinker! You rotten ole stinker! You ole nut!' All the boy's heart was in the epithets.

'Now, listen . . .' The cop shook the boy who, helpless in those powerful hands, yet blazed. His fury had stung to crimson the face of the grown man at whom it was directed.

This man, who stood with his back to the house as one besieged, was plump, half-bald, with eyes much magnified by glasses. 'Attacked me!' he cried in a high whine. 'Rang my bell and absolutely leaped on me!'

Out of the seven or eight small boys clustered around them came overlapping fragments of shrill sentences. It was clear only that they opposed the man. A small woman in a print dress, a man in shorts, whose bare chest was winter-white, stood a little apart, hesitant and distressed. Up on the veranda of the house the screen door was half open, and a woman seated in a wheelchair peered forth anxiously.

On the green grass, in the shade, perhaps thirty feet away, there lay in death a small brown-and-white dog.

The judge's luncheon guest observed all this. When the judge drew near, there was a lessening of the noise. Judge Kittinger said, 'This is Freddy Titus, isn't it? Mr Matlin? What's happened?'

The man's head jerked. 'I,' he said, 'did nothing to the dog. Why would I trouble to hurt the boy's dog? I try – you know this, Judge – I try to live in peace here. But these kids are terrors! They've made this block a perfect hell for me and my family.' The man's voice shook. 'My wife, who is not strong . . . My step-daughter, who is a cripple . . . These kids are no better than a slum gang. They are vicious! That boy rang my bell and *attacked* . . . ! I'll have him up for assault! I . . .'

The judge's face was old ivory and he was aloof behind it.

On the porch a girl pushed past the woman in the wheelchair, a girl who walked with a lurching gait.

Mike Russell asked quietly, 'Why do the boys say it was you, Mr Matlin, who hurt the dog?'

The kids chorused. 'He's an ole mean . . .' 'He's a nut . . .' 'Just because . . .' 'Took Clive's bat and . . .' '. . . chases us . . .' 'Tries to put everything on us . . .' 'Told my mother lies . . .' 'Just because . . .'

He is our enemy, they were saying; *he is our enemy*.

'They . . .' began Matlin, his throat thick with anger.

'Hold it a minute.' The second cop, the thin one, walked toward where the dog was lying.

'Somebody,' said Mike Russell in a low voice, 'must do something for the boy.'

The judge looked down at the frantic child. He said gently, 'I am as sorry as I can be, Freddy . . .' But in his old heart there was too much known, and too many little dogs he remembered that had already died, and even if he were as sorry as he could be, he couldn't be sorry enough. The boy's eyes turned, rejected, returned. To the enemy.

Russell moved near the woman in blue, who pertained to this boy somehow. 'His mother?'

'His folks are away. I'm there to take care of him,' she snapped, as if she felt herself put upon by a crisis she had not contracted to face.

'Can they be reached?'

'No,' she said decisively.

The young man put his stranger's hand on the boy's rigid little shoulder. But he too was rejected. Freddy's eyes, brilliant with hatred, clung to the enemy. Hatred doesn't cry.

'Listen,' said the tall cop, 'if you could hang on to him for a minute—'

'Not I,' said Russell.

The thin cop came back. 'Looks like the dog got poison. When was he found?'

'Just now,' the kids said.

'Where? There?'

'Up Hannibal Street. Right on the edge of ole Matlin's back lot.'

'Edge of *my* lot!' Matlin's colour freshened again. 'On the sidewalk, why don't you say? Why don't you tell the truth?'

'We are! *We* don't tell lies!'

'Quiet, you guys,' the cop said. 'Pipe down, now.'

'Heaven's my witness, I wasn't even here!' cried Matlin. 'I played nine holes of golf today. I didn't get home until . . . May?' he called over his shoulder. 'What time did I come in?'

The girl on the porch came slowly down, moving awkwardly on her uneven legs. She was in her twenties, no child. Nor was she a woman. She said in a blurting manner, 'About three o'clock, Daddy Earl. But the dog was dead.'

'What's that, miss?'

'This is my stepdaughter—'

'The dog was dead,' the girl said, 'before he came home. I saw it from upstairs, before three o'clock. Lying by the sidewalk.'

'You drove in from Hannibal Street, Mr Matlin? Looks like you'd have seen the dog.'

Matlin said with nervous thoughtfulness, 'I don't know. My mind . . . Yes, I . . .'

'He's telling a lie!'

'Freddy!'

'Listen to that,' said May Matlin, 'will you?'

'She's a liar, too!'

The cop shook Freddy. Mr Matlin made a sound of helpless exasperation. He said to the girl, 'Go keep your mother inside, May.' He raised his arm as if to wave. 'It's all right, honey,' he called to the woman in the chair, with a false cheeriness that grated on the ear. 'There's nothing to worry about, now.'

Freddy's jaw shifted and young Russell's watching eyes winced. The girl began to lurch back to the house.

'It was my wife who put in the call,' Matlin said. 'After all, they were on me like a pack of wolves. Now, I . . . I *understand* that the boy's upset. But all the same, he cannot . . . He must learn . . . I will not have . . . I have enough to contend with, without this malice, this unwarranted antagonism, this persecution.'

Freddy's eyes were unwinking.

'It has got to stop!' said Matlin almost hysterically.

'Yes,' murmured Mick Russell, 'I should think so.' Judge Kittinger's white head, nodding, agreed.

'We've heard about quite a few dog-poisoning cases over the line in Redfern,' said the thin cop with professional calm. 'None here.'

The man in the shorts hitched them up, looking shocked. 'Who'd do a thing like that?'

A boy said boldly, 'Ole Matlin would.' He had an underslung jaw and wore spectacles on his snub nose. 'I'm Phil Bourchard,' he said to the cop. He had courage.

'We just know,' said another. 'I'm Ernie Allen.' Partisanship radiated from his whole thin body. 'Ole Matlin doesn't want anybody on his ole property.'

'Sure.' 'He doesn't want anybody on his ole property.' 'It was ole Matlin; all right.'

'It was. It was,' said Freddy Titus.

'Freddy,' said the housekeeper in blue, 'now you better be still. I'll tell your dad.' It was a meaningless fumble for control. The boy didn't even hear her.

Judge Kittinger tried, patiently. 'You can't accuse without cause, Freddy.'

'Bones didn't hurt his ole property. Bones wouldn't hurt anything. Ole Matlin did it.'

'You lying little devil!'

'*He's* a liar!'

The cop gave Freddy another shake. 'You kids found him, eh?'

'We were up at Bourchard's and were going down to the Titus house.'

'And he was dead,' said Freddy.

'*I* know nothing about it,' said Matlin icily. 'Nothing at all.'

The cop, standing between, said wearily, 'Any of you people see what coulda happened?'

'I was sitting in my back yard,' said the man in shorts. 'I'm Daugherty, next door, up Hannibal Street. Didn't see a thing.'

The small woman in a print dress spoke up. 'I am Mrs Page. I live across on the corner, Officer. I believe I did see a strange man go into Mr Matlin's driveway this morning.'

'When was this, ma'am?'

'About eleven o'clock. He was poorly dressed. He walked up the drive and around the garage.'

'Didn't go to the house?'

'No. He was only there a minute. I believe he was carrying something. He was rather furtive. And very poorly dressed, almost like a tramp.'

There was a certain relaxing, among the elders. 'Ah, the tramp,' said Mike Russell. 'The good old reliable tramp. Are you sure, Mrs Page? It's very unlikely that—'

But she bristled. 'Do you think I'm lying?'

Russell's lips parted, but he felt the judge's hand on his arm. 'This is my guest, Mr Russell . . . Freddy.' The judge's voice was gentle. 'Let him go, Officer. I'm sure he understands, now. Mr Matlin was not even at home, Freddy. It's possible that this . . . er . . . stranger . . . Or it may have been an accident.'

'Wasn't a tramp. Wasn't an accident.'

'You can't *know* that, boy,' said the judge, somewhat sharply. Freddy said nothing. As the officer slowly released his grasp, the boy took a free step, backward, and the other boys surged to surround him. There stood the enemy, the monster who killed and lied, and the grownups with their reasonable doubts were on the monster's side. But the boys knew what Freddy knew. They stood together.

'Somebody,' murmured the judge's guest, 'somebody's got to help the boy.' And the judge sighed.

The cops went up Hannibal Street, toward Matlin's back lot, with Mr Daugherty. Matlin lingered at the corner talking to Mrs Page. In the front window of Matlin's house the curtain fell across the glass.

Mike Russell sidled up to the housekeeper. 'Any uncles or aunts here in town? A grandmother?'

'No,' she said shortly.

'Brothers or sisters, Mrs . . . ?'

'Miz Somers. No, he's the only one. Only reason they didn't take him along was it's the last week of school and he didn't want to miss.'

Mike Russell's brown eyes suggested the soft texture of velvet, and they were deeply distressed. She slid away from their appeal. 'He'll just have to take it, I guess, like everybody else,' Mrs Somers said. 'These things happen.'

He was listening intently. 'Don't you care for dogs?'

'I don't mind a dog,' she said. She arched her neck. She was going to call to the boy.

'Wait. Tell me, does the family go to church? Is there a pastor or a priest who knows the boy?'

'They don't go, far as I ever saw.' She looked at him as if he were an eccentric.

'Then school. He has a teacher. What grade?'

'Sixth grade,' she said. 'Miss Dana. Oh, he'll be okay.' Her voice grew loud, to reach the boy and hint to him. 'He's a big boy.'

Russell said desperately, 'Is there no way to telephone his parents?'

'They're on the road. They'll be in some time tomorrow. That's all I know.' She was annoyed. 'I'll take care of him. That's why I'm here.' She raised her voice and this time it was arch and seductive. 'Freddy, better come wash your face. I know where there's some chocolate cookies.'

The velvet left the young man's eyes. Hard as buttons, they gazed for a moment at the woman. Then he whipped around and left her. He walked over to where the kids had drifted, near the little dead creature on the grass. He said softly, 'Bones had his own doctor, Freddy? Tell me his name?' The boy's eyes flickered. 'We must know what it was that he took. A doctor can tell. I think his own doctor would be best, don't you?'

The boy nodded, mumbled a name, an address. That Russell mastered the name and the number, asking for no repetition, was a sign of his concern. Besides, it was this young man's quality – that he listened. 'May I take him, Freddy? I have a car. We ought to have a blanket,' he added gently, 'a soft, clean blanket.'

'I got one, Freddy . . .' 'My mother'd let me . . .'

'I can get one,' Freddy said brusquely. They wheeled, almost in formation.

Mrs Somers frowned.

'You must let them take a blanket,' Russell warned her, and his eyes were cold.

'I will explain to Mrs Titus,' said the judge quickly.

'Quite a fuss,' she said, and tossed her head and crossed the road.

Russell gave the judge a quick nervous grin. He walked to the returning cops. 'You'll want to run tests, I suppose? Can the dog's own vet do it?'

'Certainly. Humane officer will have to be in charge. But that's what the vet'll want.'

'I'll take the dog, then. Any traces up there?'

'Not a thing.'

'Will you explain to the boy that you are investigating?'

'Well, you know how these things go.' The cop's feet shuffled. 'Humane officer does what he can. Probably, Monday, after we identify the poison, he'll check the drugstores. Usually, if it *is* a cranky neighbour, he has already put in a complaint about the dog. This Matlin says he never did. The humane officer will get on it, Monday. He's out of town today. The devil of these cases, we can't prove a thing, usually. You get an idea who it was, maybe you can scare him. It's a misdemeanor, all right. Never heard of a conviction, myself.'

'But will you explain to the boy?' Russell stopped, chewed his lip, and the judge sighed.

'Yeah, it's tough on a kid,' the cop said.

When the judge's guest came back it was nearly five o'clock. He said, 'I came to say goodbye, sir, and to thank you for the . . .' But his mind wasn't on the sentence and he lost it and looked up.

The judge's eyes were affectionate. 'Worried?'

'Judge, sir,' the young man said, '*must* they feed him? Where, sir, in this classy neighbourhood is there an understanding woman's heart? I herded them to that Mrs Allen. But she winced, sir, and she diverted them. She didn't want to think about it. She offered cakes and cokes and games.'

'But my dear boy—'

'What do they teach the kids these days, Judge? To turn away? Put something in your stomach. Take a drink. Play a game. Don't weep for your dead. Just skip it, think about something else.'

'I'm afraid the boy's alone,' the judge said, 'but it's only for the night.' His voice was melodious. 'Can't be sheltered from grief when it comes. None of us can.'

'Excuse me, sir, but I wish he *would* grieve. I wish he would bawl his heart out. Wash out that black hate. I ought to go home. None of my concern. It's a woman's job.' He moved and his hand went toward the phone. 'He has a teacher. I can't help feeling concerned, sir. May I try?'

The judge said, 'Of course, Mike,' and he put his brittle old bones into a chair.

Mike Russell pried the number out of the Board of Education. 'Miss Lillian Dana? My name is Russell. You know a boy named Freddy Titus?'

'Oh, yes. He's in my class.' The voice was pleasing.

'Miss Dana, there is trouble. You know Judge Kittinger's house? Could you come there?'

'What is the trouble?'

'Freddy's little dog is dead of poison. I'm afraid Freddy is in a bad state. There is no one to help him. His folks are away. The woman taking care of him,' Mike's careful explanatory sentences burst into indignation, 'has no more sympathetic imagination than a broken clothes pole.' He heard a little gasp. 'I'd like to help him, Miss Dana, but I'm a man and a stranger, and the judge—' He paused.

'—is old,' said the judge in his chair.

'I'm terribly sorry,' the voice on the phone said slowly. 'Freddy's a wonderful boy.'

'You're his friend?'

'Yes, we're friends.'

'Then, could you come over? You see, we've got to get a terrible idea out of his head. He thinks a man across the street poisoned his dog on purpose. Miss Dana, *he has no doubt!* And he doesn't cry.' She gasped again. 'Greenwood Lane,' he said, 'and Hannibal Street – the southeast corner.'

She said, 'I have a car. I'll come as soon as I can.'

Russell turned and caught the judge biting his lips. 'Am I making too much of this, sir?' he inquired humbly.

'I don't like the boy's stubborn conviction.' The judge's voice was dry and clear. 'Any more than you do. I agree that he must be brought to understand. But . . .' The old man shifted in the chair. 'Of course, the man, Matlin, is a fool, Mike. There is something solemn and silly about him that makes him fair game. He's unfortunate. He married a widow with a crippled child, and no sooner were they married than *she* collapsed. And he's not well off. He's encumbered with that enormous house.'

'What does he do, sir?'

'He's a photographer. Oh, he struggles, tries his best, and all that. But with such tension, Mike. That poor misshapen girl over there tries to keep the house, devoted to her mother. Matlin works hard, is devoted, too. And yet the sum comes out in petty strife, nerves, quarrels, uproar. And certainly it cannot be necessary to feud with children.'

'The kids have done their share of that, I'll bet,' mused Mike. 'The kids are delighted – a neighbourhood ogre, to add the fine flavour of menace. A focus for mischief. An enemy.'

'True enough.' The judge sighed.

'So the myth is made. No rumour about ole Matlin loses anything in the telling. I can see it's been built up. You don't knock it down in a day.'

'No,' said the judge uneasily. He got up from the chair.

The young man rubbed his dark head. 'I don't like it, sir. We don't know what's in the kids' minds, or who their heroes are. There is only the gang. What do you suppose it advises?'

'What could it advise, after all?' said the judge crisply. 'This isn't the slums, whatever Matlin says.' He went nervously to the window and fiddled with the shade pull. He said suddenly, 'From my little summer house in the back yard you can overhear the gang. They congregate under that oak. Go and eavesdrop, Mike.'

The young man snapped to attention. 'Yes, sir.'

'I . . . think we had better know,' said the judge, a trifle sheepishly.

The kids sat under the oak, in a grassy hollow. Freddy was the core. His face was tight. His eyes never left off watching the house of the enemy. The others watched him, or hung their heads, or watched their own brown hands play with the grass.

They were not chattering. There hung about them a heavy, sullen silence, heavy with a sense of tragedy, sullen with a sense of wrong, and from time to time one voice or another would fling out a pronouncement which would sink into the silence, thickening its ugliness . . .

The judge looked up from his paper. 'Could you—?'

'I could hear,' said Mike in a quiet voice. 'They are condemning the law, sir. They call it corrupt. They are quite certain that Matlin killed the dog. They see themselves as Robin Hoods, vigilantes, defending the weak, the wronged, the dog. They think they are discussing justice. They are waiting for dark. They speak of weapons, sir – the only ones they have. B.B. guns, after dark.'

'Great heavens!'

'Don't worry. Nothing's going to happen.'

'What are you going to do?'

'I'm going to stop it.'

Mrs Somers was cooking supper when he tapped on the screen. 'Oh, it's you. What do you want?'

'I want your help, Mrs Somers. For Freddy.'

'Freddy,' she interrupted loudly, with her nose high, 'is going to have his supper and go to bed his regular time, and that's all about Freddy. Now, what did you want?'

He said, 'I want you to let me take the boy to my apartment for the night.'

'I couldn't do that!' She was scandalised.

'The judge will vouch—'

'Now, see here, Mr What's-your-name – Russell. This isn't my house and Freddy's not my boy. I'm responsible to Mr and Mrs Titus. You're a stranger to me. As far as I can see, Freddy is no business of yours whatsoever.'

'Which is his room?' asked Mike sharply.

'Why do you want to know?' She was hostile and suspicious.

'Where does he keep his B.B. gun?'

She was startled to an answer. 'In the shed out back. Why?'

He told her.

'Kid's talk,' she scoffed. 'You don't know much about kids, do you, young man? Freddy will go to sleep. First thing he'll know, it's morning. That's about the size of it.'

'You may be right. I hope so.'

372

Mrs Somers slapped potatoes into the pan. Her lips quivered indignantly. She felt annoyed because she was a little shaken.

Russell scanned the street, went across to Matlin's house. The man himself answered the bell. The air in this house was stale, and bore the faint smell of old grease. There was over everything an atmosphere of struggle and despair. Many things ought to have been repaired and had not been repaired. The place was too big. There wasn't enough money, or strength. It was too much.

Mrs Matlin could not walk. Otherwise, one saw, she struggled and did the best she could. She had a lost look, as if some anxiety, ever present, took about nine-tenths of her attention. May Matlin limped in and sat down, lumpishly.

Russell began earnestly, 'Mr Matlin, I don't know how this situation between you and the boys began. I can guess that the kids are much to blame. I imagine they enjoy it.' He smiled. He wanted to be sympathetic toward this man.

'Of course they enjoy it.' Matlin looked triumphant.

'They call me the Witch,' the girl said. 'Pretend they're scared of me. The devils. I'm scared of them.'

Matlin flicked a nervous eye at the woman in the wheelchair. 'The truth is, Mr Russell,' he said in his high whine, 'they're vicious.'

'It's too bad,' said his wife in a low voice. 'I think it's dangerous.'

'Mama, you mustn't worry,' said the girl in an entirely new tone. 'I won't let them hurt you. Nobody will hurt you.'

'Be quiet, May,' said Matlin. 'You'll upset her. Of course nobody will hurt her.'

'Yes, it is dangerous, Mrs Matlin,' said Russell quietly. 'That's why I came over.'

Matlin goggled. 'What? What's this?'

'Could I possibly persuade you, sir, to spend the night away from this neighbourhood? And to depart noisily?'

'No,' said Matlin, his ego bristling, 'no, you cannot! I will under no circumstances be driven away from my own home.' His voice rose. 'Furthermore, I certainly will not leave my wife and stepdaughter.'

'We could manage, dear,' said Mrs Matlin anxiously.

Russell told them about the talk under the oak, the B.B. gun.

'Devils,' said May Matlin, 'absolutely.'

'Oh, Earl,' trembled Mrs Matlin, 'maybe we had all better go away.'

Matlin, red-necked, furious, said, 'We own this property. We pay our taxes. We have our rights. Let them! Let them try something like that! Then, I think the law would have something to say. This is outrageous! I did not harm that animal. Therefore, I defy . . .' He looked solemn and silly, as the judge had said, with his face crimson, his weak eyes rolling.

Russell rose. 'I thought I ought to make the suggestion,' he said mildly, 'because it would be the safest thing to do. But don't worry, Mrs Matlin, because I—'

'A B.B. gun can blind,' she said tensely.

'Or even worse,' Mike agreed. 'But I am thinking of the—'

'Just a minute,' Matlin roared. 'You can't come in here and terrify my wife! She is not strong. You have no right.' He drew himself up with his feet at a right angle, his pudgy arm extended, his plump jowls quivering. 'Get out,' he cried. He looked ridiculous.

Whether the young man and the bewildered woman in the wheelchair might have understood each other was not to be known. Russell, of course, got out. May Matlin hobbled to the door and as Russell went through it she said, 'Well, you warned us, anyhow.' And her lips came together sharply.

Russell plodded across the pavement again. Long enchanting shadows from the lowering sun struck aslant through the golden air and all the old houses were gilded and softened in their green setting. He moved toward the big oak. He hunkered down. The sun struck its golden shafts deep under the boughs. 'How's it going?' he asked.

Freddy Titus looked frozen and still. 'Okay,' said Phil Bourchard with elaborate ease. Light on his owlish glasses hid the eyes.

Mike opened his lips, hesitated. Suppertime struck on the neighbourhood clock. Calls, like chimes, were sounding.

'. . . 's my mom,' said Ernie Allen. 'See you after.'

'See you after, Freddy.'

'Okay.'

'Okay.'

Mrs Somers' hoot had chimed with the rest and now Freddy got up stiffly.

'Okay?' said Mike Russell. The useful syllables that take any meaning at all in American mouths asked, 'Are you feeling less bitter, boy? Are you any easier?'

'Okay,' said Freddy. The same syllables shut the man out.

Mike opened his lips. Closed them. Freddy went across the lawn to his kitchen door. There was a brown crockery bowl on the back stoop. His sneaker, rigid on the angle, stepped over it. Mike Russell watched, and then, with a movement of his arms, almost as if he would wring his hands, he went up the judge's steps.

'Well?' The judge opened his door. 'Did you talk to the boy?'

Russell didn't answer. He sat down.

The judge stood over him. 'The boy . . . The enormity of this whole idea *must* be explained to him.'

'I can't explain,' Mike said. 'I open my mouth. Nothing comes out.'

'Perhaps *I* had better.'

'What are you going to say, sir?'

'Why, give him the facts,' the judge cried.

'The facts are . . . the dog is dead.'

'There are no facts that point to Matlin.'

'There are no facts that point to a tramp, either. That's too sloppy, sir.'

'What are you driving at?'

'Judge, the boy is more rightfully suspicious than we are.'

'Nonsense,' said the judge. 'The girl saw the dog's body before Matlin came home.'

'There is no alibi for poison,' Mike said sadly.

'Are you saying the man is a liar?'

'Liars,' sighed Mike. 'Truth and lies. How are those kids going to understand, sir? To that Mrs Page, to the lot of them, truth is only a subjective intention. "I am no liar," sez she, sez he. "I *intend* to be truthful. So do not insult me." Lord, when will we begin? It's what we were talking about at lunch, sir. What you and I believe. What the race has been told and told in such agony, in a million years of bitter lesson. *Error*, we were saying. Error is the enemy.'

He flung out of the chair. 'We know that to tell the truth is not merely a good intention. It's a damned difficult thing to do. It's a skill, to be practiced. It's a technique. It's an effort. It takes brains. It takes watching. It takes humility and self-examination. It's a science and an art . . .

'Why don't we tell the *kids* these things? Why is everyone locked up in anger, shouting liar at the other side? Why don't they automatically know how easy it is to be, not wicked, but mistaken? Why is there this notion of violence? Because Freddy doesn't think to himself, "Wait a minutes. I might be wrong." The habit isn't there. Instead, there are the heroes – the big-muscled, noble-hearted, gun-toting heroes, blind in a righteousness totally arranged by the author. Excuse me, sir.'

'All that may be,' said the judge grimly, 'and I agree. But the police know the lesson. They—'

'They don't care.'

'What?'

'Don't care enough, sir. None of us cares enough – about the dog.'

'I see,' said the judge. 'Yes, I see. We haven't the least idea what happened to the dog.' He touched his pince-nez.

Mike rubbed his head wearily. 'Don't know what to do except sit under his window the night through. Hardly seems good enough.'

The judge said simply, 'Why don't you find out what happened to the dog?'

The young man's face changed. 'What we need, sir' said Mike slowly, 'is to teach Freddy how to ask for it. Just to ask for it. Just to want it.' The old man and the young man looked at each other. Past and future telescoped. '*Now*,' Mike said. 'Before dark.'

Suppertime, for the kids, was only twenty minutes long. When the girl in the brown dress with the bare blonde head got out of the shabby coupé, the gang was gathered again in its hollow under the oak. She went to them and sank down on the ground. 'Ah, Freddy, was it Bones? Your dear little dog you wrote about in the essay?'

'Yes, Miss Dana.' Freddy's voice was shrill and hostile. *I won't be touched!* it cried to her. So she said no more, but sat there on the ground, and presently she began to cry. There was contagion. The simplest thing in the world. First, one of the smaller ones, whimpering. Finally, Freddy Titus, bending over. Her arm guided his head, and then he lay weeping in her lap.

Russell, up in the summerhouse, closed his eyes and praised the Lord. In a little while he swung his legs over the railing and slid down the bank. 'How do? I'm Mike Russell.'

'I'm Lillian Dana.' She was quick and intelligent, and her tears were real.

'Fellows,' said Mike briskly, 'you know what's got to be done, don't you? We've got to solve this case.'

They turned their woeful faces.

He said, deliberately, 'It's just the same as a murder. It *is* a murder.'

'Yeah,' said Freddy, and sat up, tears drying. 'It was ole Matlin.'

'Then we have to prove it.'

Miss Lillian Dana saw the boy's face lock. He didn't need to prove anything, the look proclaimed. He knew. She leaned over a little and said, 'But we can't make an ugly mistake and put it on Bones's account. Bones was a fine dog. Oh, that would be a terrible monument.' Freddy's eyes turned, startled.

'It's up to us,' said Mike gratefully, 'to go after the real facts, with real detective work. For Bones's sake.'

'It's the least we can do for him,' said Miss Dana, calmly and decisively. Freddy's face lifted.

'Trouble is,' Russell went on quickly, 'people get things wrong. Sometimes they don't remember straight. They make mistakes.'

'Ole Matlin tells lies,' said Freddy.

'If he does,' said Russell cheerfully, 'then we've got to *prove* that he does. Now, I've figured out a plan, if Miss Dana will help us. You pick a couple of the fellows, Fred. Have to go to all the houses around here and ask some questions. Better pick the smartest ones. To find out the truth is very hard,' he challenged.

'And then?' said Miss Dana in a fluttery voice.

'Then they, and you, if you will—'

'Me?' She straightened. 'I am a schoolteacher, Mr Russell. Won't the police—'

'Not before dark.'

'What are *you* going to be doing?'

'Dirtier work.'

She bit her lip. 'It's nosey. It's – well, it's not done.'

'No,' he agreed. 'You may lose your job.'

She wasn't a bad-looking young woman. Her eyes were fine. Her brow was serious, but there was the ghost of a dimple in her cheek. Her hands moved. 'Oh, well, I can always take up beauty culture or something. What are the questions?' She had a pad of paper and a pencil half out of her purse, and looked alert and efficient..

Now, as the gang huddled, there was a warm sense of conspiracy growing. 'Going to be the dickens of a job,' Russell warned them. And he outlined some questions. 'Now, don't let anybody fool you into taking a sloppy answer,' he concluded. 'Ask how they know. Get real evidence. But don't go to Matlin's – I'll go there.'

'I'm not afraid of him.' Freddy's nostrils flared.

'I think I stand a better chance of getting the answers,' said Russell coolly. 'Aren't we after the answers?'

Freddy swallowed. 'And if it turns out that—?'

'It turns out the way it turns out,' said Russell, rumpling the towhead. 'Choose your henchmen. Tough, remember.'

'Phil. Ernie.' The kids who were left out wailed as the three small boys and their teacher, who wasn't a lot bigger, rose from the ground.

'It'll be tough, Mr Russell,' Miss Dana said grimly. 'Whoever you are, thank you for getting me into this.'

'I'm just a stranger,' he said gently, looking down at her face. 'But you are a friend and a teacher.' Pain crossed her eyes. 'You'll be teaching now, you know.'

Her chin went up. 'Okay, kids. I'll keep the paper and pencil. Freddy, wipe your face. Stick your shirt in, Phil. Now, let's organise . . .'

It was nearly nine o'clock when the boys and the teacher looking rather exhausted, came back to the judge's house. Russell, whose face was grave, reached for the papers in her hands.

'Just a minute,' said Miss Dana. 'Judge, we have some questions.'

Ernie Allen bared all teeth and stepped forward. 'Did you see Bones today?' he asked with the firm skill of repetition. The judge nodded. 'How many times and when?'

'One. Er . . . shortly before noon. He crossed my yard, going east.'

The boys bent over the pad. Then Freddy's lips opened hard. 'How do you know the time, Judge Kittinger?'

'Well,' said the judge, 'hm . . . let me think. I was looking out the window for my company and just then he arrived.'

'Five minutes of one, sir,' Mike said.

Freddy flashed around. 'What makes you sure?'

'I looked at my watch,' said Russell. 'I was taught to be exactly five minutes early when I'm asked to a meal.' There was a nodding among the boys, and Miss Dana wrote on the pad.

'Then I was mistaken,' said the judge thoughtfully. 'It was shortly before one. Of course.'

Phil Bourchard took over. 'Did you see anyone go into Matlin's driveway or back lot?'

'I did not.'

'Were you out of doors or did you look up that way?'

'Yes, I . . . When we left the table. Mike?'

'At two thirty, sir.'

'How do you know that time for sure?' asked Freddy Titus.

'Because I wondered if I could politely stay a little longer.' Russell's eyes congratulated Miss Lillian Dana. She had made them a team, and on it, Freddy was the How-do-you-know-for-sure Department.

'Can you swear,' continued Phil to the judge, 'there was nobody at all around Matlin's back lot then?'

'As far as my view goes,' answered the judge cautiously.

Freddie said promptly, 'He couldn't see much. Too many trees. We can't count that.'

They looked at Miss Dana and she marked it down on the pad.

'Thank you. Now, you have a cook, sir? We must question her.'

'This way,' said the judge, rising and bowing.

Russell looked after them and his eyes were velvet again. He met the judge's twinkle. Then he sat down and ran an eye quickly over some of the sheets of paper, passing each one to his host.

Startled, he looked up. Lillian Dana, standing in the door, was watching his face.

'Do you think, Mike—?'

A paper dropped in the judge's hand.

'We can't stop,' she challenged.

Russell nodded, and turned to the judge. 'May need some high brass, sir.' The judge rose. 'And tell me, sir, where Matlin plays golf. And the telephone number of the Salvage League. No, Miss Dana, we can't stop. We'll take it where it turns.'

'We must,' she said.

It was nearly ten when the neighbours began to come in. The judge greeted them soberly. The chief of police arrived. Mrs Somers, looking grim and uprooted in a crêpe dress, came. Mr Matlin, Mrs Page, Mr and Mrs Daugherty, a Mr and Mrs Baker, and Diane Bourchard who was sixteen. They looked curiously at the tight little group, the boys and their blonde teacher.

Last of all to arrive was Mr Russell, who slipped in from the dark veranda, accepted the judge's nod, and called the meeting to order.

'We have been investigating the strange death of a dog,' he began. 'Chief Anderson, while we know your department would have done so in good time, we also know you are busy, and some of us,' he glanced at the dark windowpane, 'couldn't wait. Will you help us now?'

The chief said genially, 'That's why I'm here, I guess.' It was the judge and his stature that gave this meeting standing. Naïve, young, a little absurd it might have seemed had not the old man sat so quietly attentive among them.

'Thank you, sir. Now, all we want to know is what happened to the dog.' Russell looked about him. 'First, let us demolish the tramp theory.' Mrs Page's feathers ruffled. Russell smiled at her. 'Mrs Page saw a man go down Matlin's drive this morning. The Salvage League sent a truck to pick up rags and papers which at ten forty-two was parked in front of the Daughertys'. The man, who seemed poorly dressed in his working clothes, went to the tool room behind Matlin's garage, as he had been instructed to. He picked up a bundle and returned to his truck. Mrs Page, the man was there. It was only your opinion about him that proves to have been, not a lie, but an error.'

He turned his head. 'Now, we have tried to trace the dog's day and we have done remarkably well, too.' And he traced it for them, some faces began to wear at least the ghost of a smile, seeing the little dog frisking through the neighbourhood. 'Just before one,' Mike went on, 'Bones ran across the judge's yard to the Allens' where the kids were playing ball. Up to this time no one saw Bones *above* Greenwood Lane or *up* Hannibal Street. But Miss Diane Bourchard, recovering from a sore throat, stayed at home today. After lunch she sat on her porch directly across from Mr Matlin's back lot. She was waiting for a few minutes since she expected her friends to come by.

'She saw, not Bones, but Corky, an animal belonging to Mr Daugherty, playing in Matlin's lot at about two o'clock. I want your opinion. If poisoned bait had been lying there at two, would Corky have found it?'

'Seems so,' said Daugherty. 'Thank God that Corky didn't.' He bit his tongue. 'Corky's a show dog,' he blundered.

'But Bones,' said Russell gently, 'was more like a friend. That's why we care, of course.'

'It's a damned shame!' Daugherty looked around angrily.

'It is,' said Mrs Baker. 'He was a friend of mine, Bones was.'

'Go on,' growled Daugherty. 'What else did you dig up?'

'Mr Matlin left for his golf at eleven thirty. Now, you see, it looks as if Matlin couldn't have left poison behind him.'

'I most certainly did not,' snapped Matlin. 'I have said so. I will not stand for this sort of innuendo. I am not a liar. You said it was a conference.'

Mike held the man's eye. 'We are simply trying to find out what happened to the dog,' he said. Matlin fell silent.

'Surely you realise,' Mike went on, 'that, human frailty being what it is, there may been other errors in what we were told this afternoon. There was at least one more.

'Mr and Mrs Baker worked in their garden this afternoon. Bones abandoned the ball game to visit the Bakers' dog, Smitty. At three o'clock the Bakers, after discussing the time carefully, in case it was too late in the day, decided to bathe Smitty. When they caught him, for his ordeal, Bones was still there. . . . So, you see, Miss May Matlin, who says she saw Bones lying by the sidewalk *before three o'clock*, was mistaken.'

Matlin twitched. Russell said sharply, 'The testimony of the Bakers is extremely clear.' The Bakers, who looked alike, both brown, outdoor people, nodded vigorously.

'The time at which Mr Matlin returned is quite well established. Diane saw him. Mrs Daugherty, next door, decided to take a nap, at five after three. She had a roast to put in at four thirty. Therefore, she is sure of the time. She went upstairs and from an upper window she too saw Mr Matlin come home. Both witnesses say he drove his car into the garage at three ten, got out, and went around the building to the right of it – *on the weedy side*.'

Mr Matlin was sweating. His forehead was beaded. He did not speak.

Mike shifted papers. 'Now, we know that the kids trooped up to Phil Bourchard's kitchen at about a quarter of three. Whereas Bones, realising that Smitty was in for it, and shying away from soap and water like any sane dog, went up Hannibal Street at three o'clock sharp. He may have known in some doggy way where Freddy was. Can we see Bones loping up Hannibal Street, going *above* Greenwood Lane?'

'We can,' said Daugherty. He was watching Matlin. 'Besides, he was found above Greenwood Lane soon after.'

'No one,' said Mike slowly, 'was seen in Matlin's back lot, except Matlin. Yet, almost immediately after Matlin was there, the little dog, died.'

'Didn't Diane—?'

'Diane's friends came at three twelve. Their evidence is not reliable.' Diane blushed.

'This – this is intolerable!' croaked Matlin. 'Why *my* back lot?'

Daugherty said, 'There was no poison lying around my place, I'll tell you that.'

'How do you know?' begged Matlin. And Freddy's eyes, with the smudges under them, followed to Russell's face. 'Why not in the street? Or from some passing car?'

Mike said, 'I'm afraid it's not likely. You see, Mr Otis Carnavon was stalled at the corner of Hannibal and Lee. Trying to flag a push. Anything thrown from a car on that block he would have seen.'

'Was the poison quick?' demanded Daugherty.

'It was quick. The dog could not go far after he got it. He got cyanide.' Matlin's shaking hand removed his glasses. They were wet.

'Some of you may be amateur photographers,' Mike said. 'Mr Matlin, is there cyanide in your cellar darkroom?'

'Yes, but I keep it . . . most meticulously . . .' Matlin began to cough. When the noise of his spasm died, Mike said, 'The poison was embedded in ground meat which analysed, roughly, half beef and the rest pork and veal, half and half.' Matlin encircled his throat with his fingers. 'I've checked with four neighbourhood butchers and the dickens of a time I had,' said Mike. No one smiled. Only Freddy looked up at him with solemn sympathy. 'Ground meat was delivered to at least five houses in the vicinity. Meat that *was* one-half beef, one-quarter pork. one-quarter veal, was delivered at ten this morning to Matlin's house.'

A stir like an angry wind blew over the room. The chief of police made some shift of his weight so that his chair creaked.

'It begins to look—' growled Daugherty.

'Now,' said Russell sharply, 'we must be very careful. One more thing The meat had been seasoned.'

'Seasoned!'

'With salt. And with . . . thyme.'

'Thyme,' groaned Matlin.

Freddy looked up at Miss Dana with bewildered eyes. She put her arm around him.

'As far as motives are concerned,' said Mike quietly, 'I can't discuss them. It is inconceivable to me that any man would poison a dog.' Nobody spoke. 'However, where are we?' Mike's voice seemed to catch Matlin just in time to keep him from falling off the chair. 'We don't know yet what happened to the dog.' Mike's voice rang. 'Mr Matlin, will you help us to the answer?'

Matlin said thickly, 'Better get those kids out of here.'

Miss Dana moved, but Russell said, 'No. They have worked hard for the truth. They have earned it. And if it is to be had, they shall have it.'

'You know?' whimpered Matlin.

Mike said, 'I called your golf club. I've looked into your trash incinerator. Yes, I know. But I want you to tell us.'

Daugherty said, 'Well? Well?' And Matlin covered his face.

Mike said gently, 'I think there was an error. Mr Matlin, I'm afraid, did poison the dog. But he never meant to, and he didn't know he had done it.'

Matlin said, 'I'm sorry . . . It's . . . I can't . . . She means to do her best. But she's a terrible cook. Somebody gave her those . . . those herbs. Thyme . . . thyme in everything. She fixed me a lunch box. I . . . couldn't stomach it. I bought my lunch at the club.'

Mike nodded.

Matlin went on, his voice cracking. 'I never . . . You see, I didn't even know it was meat the dog got. She said . . . she told me the dog was already dead.'

'And of course,' said Mike, 'in your righteous wrath you never paused to say to yourself, "Wait, what *did* happen to the dog?" '

'Mr Russell, I didn't lie. How could I know there was thyme in it? When I got home I had to get rid of the hamburger she'd fixed for me – I didn't want to hurt her feelings. She tries . . . tries so hard . . .' He sat up suddenly. '*But what she tried to do today,*' he said, with his eyes, almost out of his head, '*was to poison me!*' His bulging eyes roved. They came to Freddy. He gasped. He said, 'Your dog saved my life!'

'Yes,' said Mike quickly, 'Freddy's dog saved your life. You see, your stepdaughter would have kept trying.'

People drew in their breaths. 'The buns are in your incinerator,' Mike said. 'She guessed what happened to the dog, went for the buns, and hid them. She was late, you remember, getting to the disturbance. And she did lie.'

Chief Anderson rose.

'Her mother . . .' said Matlin frantically, 'her mother . . .'

Mike Russell put his hand on the plump shoulder. 'Her mother's been in torment, tortured by the rivalry between you. Don't you think her mother senses something wrong?'

Miss Lillian Dana wrapped Freddy in her arms. 'Oh, what a wonderful dog Bones was!' She covered the sound of the other voices. 'Even when he died, he saved a man's life. Oh, Freddy, he was a wonderful dog.'

And Freddy, not quite taking everything in yet, was released to simple sorrow and wept quietly against his friend . . .

When they went to fetch May Matlin she was not in the house. They found her in the Titus back shed. She seemed to be looking for something.

Next day, when Mr and Mrs Titus came home, they found that although the little dog had died, their Freddy was all right. The judge, Russell, and Miss Dana told them all about it.

Mrs Titus wept. Mr Titus swore. He wrung Russell's hand. '. . . for stealing the gun,' he babbled.

But the mother cried, 'And for showing him, for teaching him . . . Oh, Miss Dana, oh my dear!'

The judge waved from his veranda as the dark head and the blonde drove away.

'I think Miss Dana likes him,' said Ernie Allen.

'How do you know for sure?' asked Freddy Titus.

Michael Gilbert

The Conspirators

Every August, whilst Patrick Petrella was a detective-constable up at Highside, the Circus and Funfair appeared on the Heath. If duty took him there, Petrella cut his visit as short as possible. Otherwise, his colleagues noticed, he avoided it altogether. Later, when he was promoted, and married, his wife remarked on the same peculiarity. He had not bothered to explain it to his colleagues at Highside. And he hesitated to do so even to his wife, from whom he had few secrets. In the end, he did tell her about it.

They were motoring in France, and had stopped in a village to buy stores for their midday meal. On the whitewashed wall, outside the Mairie, a poster, faded by the hot sun of Provence, advertised the Cirque Jacquetti.

'Goodness,' said Petrella. 'I wonder if Sam Borner still runs it. I don't think he can do. He must be eighty, if he's still alive.'

'Please tell me about Sam,' said Jane, in her most irresistible voice.

Still Petrella hesitated. For it had all happened a long time ago. And it had been the first time he had grasped the fact that hate can be more compelling than love; and the first time that he had seen, in action, a conspiracy to kill. The passage of time had buried these events deep, but small things, the distant roar of a caged lion, a clockwork clown tumbling about the pavement, a tattered circus poster – still had the power to twitch at his nerves.

'I'll tell you when we stop for lunch,' he said. 'It was my first murder. I was eleven years old at the time.'

When you are young, each summer holiday hangs on a thread of remembrance. A sight, a sound, a smell. To Patrick Petrella, that prewar summer at Perpignan, hung on a poster. Not faded and fly-blown like the one he had just seen, but eye-catching in its glorious colours, it depicted two white horses, in harness of black leather and trappings of gold, cantering round a sawdust ring, each ridden by a slender, graceful, grave-eyed lemur, dressed in a lady's riding-habit with a tiny crimson cap on one side of its furry head.

Patrick was vague as to why his family were in Perpignan – as vague as to why they had spent the summer before that in Casablanca. He knew that his father worked for the Spanish Government, and he surmised that it was government business which had brought them to the French side of the Pyrenees. It was something to do with refugees, and every now and then they would go for long drives through the mountains, meeting French and Spanish policemen and shepherds and muleteers on both sides of the frontier. But for the most part his father was closeted with Monsieur le Commissaire Theron, in the police station, and Patrick was free to amuse himself.

As well as his native Spanish he spoke street boy Arabic and French, and he slipped about the sunlit streets of Perpignan, a thin, dark, friendly shadow, making new acquaintances along the river front, dropping one, picking up another, listening more than he spoke. It did not take him long to discover the Cirque Jacquetti in the Champ des Martyrs, the little plateau on the inland side of the City where the dragoons had shot and sabred more than a hundred unarmed Huguenots during the Repression.

The Champ des Martyrs was the permanent base of the Jacquettis. It was from there that its component parts, the first and second-ring circuses, and the fun fairs, sometimes operating marches, south to the Rock of Gibraltar, north as far as Bruges and Ostend, where they met, but did not trespass on the territory of the other great European troupe, the German Muller-hilde. Perpignan was their base. Patrick liked it best when, as now, it was almost empty. August was the peak of the trouping season. All that was left behind, inside the high wire perimeter, was a shed full of old funfair machinery, a row of caravans, most of them empty, the cages where the big cats lived, the stables for the horses, the kennels for the dogs, and a handful of people.

Manfredo and Ramon were called Brothers, although, in complicated in-breeding of circus life no one quite knew whether brothers, half brothers, or cousins. Both were swarthy, handsome and attractive, and both were bullies, in the way that men who spend their lives controlling big cats often are.

Domenico Stromboli, who came from Naples, looked after the dogs. Or, to be truthful, the dogs looked after Stromboli. He was a cripple. Polio had reduced his arms and one of his legs to withered sticks. The circus had built him a little padded carriage, which two of the six

Alsatians took turns to pull. He had first appeared, to Patrick's fascinated gaze, driving at a hand-canter across the wide and dusty compound with two Alsatian dogs running escort in front of him and two more behind, surrounded by a tumbling, snapping, skirmishing pack of poodles.

Patrick had got into the closely guarded enclosure by the kindness of his special friend, Auguste. Auguste was a stand-in clown. He looked after the horses. His particular charges were Rosalie and Marguerite, the beautiful white thoroughbreds, whose likeness Patrick had so often admired on the poster. They were resting for a few weeks. Sam Borner, who had married twenty years before into the Jaquetti family, and had now the controlling voice in the circus, knew the virtue of not over-driving a willing and successful turn.

'That's his caravan,' said Auguste. 'Would you like to have a peep at it?'

'I'd like to very much,' said Petrella. 'If he wouldn't mind.'

'He's in town with Donna. Nina may be there. She won't tell on us.'

They climbed the stairs and opened the door, cut in two halves, heavy as a lock gate, built to last, like everything in that wonderful vehicle.

Patrick thought he had never seen anything so entrancing in his whole life. It was at once snug and spacious, and entirely beautiful.

Everything that could shine, shone. The polished teakwood tables, settles and built-in cupboards; the brass fittings of the lamps, and the window and door-fittings, and the ship's chronometer above the stove, itself a gleaming altar of glazed brick and winking steel. In one corner stood the cage where Leopold and Lorenzo, the riding lemurs lived. They sat on a log and stared back at Patrick as he gazed, round-eyed, at them.

Lorenzo wrinkled up his eyes and lifted his upper lip.

'He's laughing at me,' said Patrick.

'Laughing at me,' agreed a gruff voice behind him. Patrick swung round.

The largest parrot he had ever seen was sitting on a table behind the door.

He was dark bottle-green, all over, except for plum-coloured ruffs around his legs. His head was cocked on one side, and a single round yellow eye was fixed on the boy.

'Oh,' said Patrick. 'Oh, what a beauty.'

'What a beauty,' said the bird complacently. It swung down neatly from the rail on top of the cupboard and waddled along the window-seat.

'Stand still,' said Auguste. 'Quite still. He likes you, I think.'

'W-what,' said Patrick, 'w-would he do if he didn't?'

'Bite your ear off,' said Auguste. 'Just you ask Ramon or Manfredo. It's war to the knife between them and Nestor. They used to tease him – pull his tail feathers out. He bit Manfredo through the thumb. Nearly cut it off.'

Patrick watched the parrot, scarcely daring to breathe. It sidled along the table top towards him, still transfixing him with one unwinking yellow eye. Then it dipped its green head suddenly forward, caught the corner of Patrick's handkerchief, and whipped it out of his pocket.

'Hey!' said Patrick.

'Hey,' said the parrot, dropped the handkerchief and broke into a scream of laughter.

'He does like you, see,' said a long-legged, dark-haired girl. She had come out of the back part of the caravan, where she had been tidying and cleaning the bedroom. 'If he takes something of yours, it shows he likes you.'

She picked up the parrot without fuss, held it in one hand, and smoothed its head feathers with the other. The parrot preened itself.

'This person is Nina,' said Auguste. 'She is a wonderful girl. She is loved by all creatures, and fears none.'

Although he was only eleven Patrick was an observant boy, and when Auguste said 'creatures' it occurred to him that he might be including two-legged creatures as well. She was a very attractive girl.

The week that followed was a week of unmixed delight. Tolerated by old Stromboli, encouraged by Auguste and Nina, he explored every corner of the Jacquetti encampment. He avoided Ramon and Manfredo and studied the great Sam Borner, owner and boss of the Jacquettis, and his wife Donna from a respectful distance. But these were only the humans. It was the animals which entranced him. The six great Alsatian dogs, who were the policemen of the kingdom, and the tumbling crowd of poodles who formed the C.I.D. – sharp-eyed, sneaky, ubiquitous.

The old circus horses, their working life over, which lived at ease, grazing behind the caravans by day and stabled by night in the shed opposite Sam Borner's caravan. Rosalie and Marguerite, queens of the ring, each with a stall of her own, with her name on a shingle nailed over it; the great cats, in their cages at the far end of the enclosure, to be watched like Ramon and Manfredo, but not approached. White doves which lived on the rafters of the pony shed, and would come to Nina when she whistled. A marmoset which shared Auguste's caravan, and spent its day vainly trying to catch the pigeons. Leopold and Lorenzo the lemurs, who could ride and look after horses as well as any stable boy, who lived in Sam Borner's caravan, and were taken out of their cage by Nina every afternoon for a walk, on long leather leads, and Nestor the parrot, said to be more than a hundred years old, and very wise.

It was at the end of that week, on the Sunday morning, that Monsieur Theron came to call on Patrick's father.

Their talk took place in the front sitting-room, a place of peculiar French rectitude and gloom. M. Theron was a middle-aged Basque with a short brown beard and a deceptively mild appearance. It was later to deceive the Germans to their undoing. Patrick sat, unnoticed, in a corner behind a table covered with family photographs. He listened, in growing horror, to what was being recounted.

'Dead,' said M. Theron. 'The skull fractured by a single blow.'

'How long?'

'Discovered at six o'clock this morning. The doctor said that death must have occurred at least five hours before. Not more than seven.'

'Died about midnight, then,' said Patrick's father.

Patrick had heard only scraps of the earlier conversation. He had thought they were talking about refugees. Now he wished that he had listened. Because it was to do with the circus. Someone had been killed.

'We have held his brother for questioning.'

So! It was Manfredo or Ramon. Patrick felt a sense of relief. It would have been terrible if it had been one of his friends, Auguste, or Nina, or Stromboli. Even the majestic Sam Borner, or his kindly little wife. If someone had to be dead, better one of the savage Spaniards.

'It will be difficult to prove anything,' said M. Theron, and then stopped. It had occurred to him that what he was about to say might not, in the circumstances, be very tactful.

'Can behave like wild beasts,' agreed Patrick's father, smoothly. 'But there is usually some particular reason for a killing as cold-blooded as this would seem to have been.'

'The brothers were drinking in the Café d'Algérie – it is a riverside drinking place – until close on eleven o'clock. They were excited, and shouting. They left separately. So far that is all we have established.'

When M. Theron had departed, Patrick said to his father, 'It is not true.'

'What is not true, Patrick?'

'It is not true that anyone from outside could get over the wire fence and into the field of the circus. By day, it would be difficult. By night, impossible.'

'How so?'

'Because of the dogs. Would you like to try?'

Patrick's father looked at him seriously. He said, 'I have no official standing here. M. Theron consults me because he is friendly, and, I suspect, a little out of his depth with a case which involves two Spaniards, a Yorkshireman with a Milanese wife, a Neopolitan, a Belgian, and a local girl.'

Patrick's mouth opened.

'B-but,' he said, 'how do you know about these people?'

'You have talked to me about them, many times.'

'I talked to you,' said Patrick, 'but you didn't listen.'

'When you grow up, and become a policeman,' said his father, 'you will find that it is a great advantage not to appear too attentive. As I was saying, I have no status in this matter. But if what you tell me is true, it is clearly a fact of importance, which should be established in a proper scientific manner. We will take a walk together, this evening, after dinner.'

They approached the Champ des Martyrs with due precaution, from the back. It was a soft night, with the moon half full. Ahead of them loomed the bulk of the machinery shed, concealing them from view. The corner of the wire fence was supported here by an upright of iron angle-bar.

'This would be the best place,' said Patrick's father. He spoke in a whisper. 'Will you go over, or shall I?'

'I'd better,' said Patrick. 'They know me.'

He gripped the stanchion, and climbed up, easily enough, using the strands of the wire as steps. He had reached the top, and was steadying himself, with one hand on the roof of the shed, when a shrill yap sounded. As Patrick dropped to the ground, two dark forms materialised at the corner of the shed.

Patrick moved out from behind the shed, into the moonlight. The Alsatians were uncertain. The boy looked, and smelled, like someone they knew, but was behaving suspiciously. A small black dog ran up. Patrick stooped, and it jumped into his arms and started licking his face. The Alsatians lost interest. If Kiki vouched for the stranger, he was all right. Patrick walked back to his father, put the toy poodle gently down and climbed out.

'You see?' he said.

'Yes,' said his father. 'I see.'

The processes of the law are never quick. It was nearly a week later that Sam Borner's wife called on them. Donna Borner had been fifteen, a promising equestrienne, when Sam had married her; years of married life and the rearing of three sons had rounded out her figure and engraved some wrinkles on her face, but, until that black week, life had treated her kindly.

Now she was frightened.

She said, in an account in which her north Italian consonants mixed curiously with broad Yorkshire vowels, 'They have taken Sam for questioning. They took him this morning. They will not let me see him. It is a terrible mistake.'

Patrick's father made her sit down. He talked to her, and Patrick admired the skill with which he extracted the facts without seeming to ask any questions at all.

The police, at first, had suspected Ramon. He was a violent man, he had been drinking, he had been the last person seen with Manfredo. But he could have had no hand in the killing. When he left the café he had caused an uproar by trying to break into the house of a girl he knew. The police had been called. He had been arrested, and had spent the night in one of the police lockups. As soon as this was established he had, of course, to be released.

'I should not have let him go quite so quickly,' said Patrick's father. 'I should like to know exactly at what time he caused this convenient uproar.'

Donna Borner was uncertain. What she did know was that Ramon, exculpated, had turned inquisitor. He had vowed to find the killer of his brother. And the possible suspects were so very few. The killing had occurred just outside the pony-shed. Inside the camp, it was not at all easy for an outsider to get in undetected because of the dogs.

Patrick's father nodded. He said that he knew about the dogs. Who could have been in the camp, legitimately, that night?

The answer was simple. Stromboli, neither of whose arms was strong enough to lift a tack-hammer, let alone a sledge hammer. Auguste, who had a caravan in the middle of the line of caravans. Donna herself, and her husband. They had the caravan at the end, nearest to the pony-shed. The other caravans belonged to people who were out on circuit, and they were empty. Ramon and Manfredo had a caravan at the far end, near the cages of the big cats who were in their charge.

Patrick's father had a pencil in his hand, and was drawing a little sketch as she spoke, marking in the stables, the dog kennels, the machine-sheds and the cages, round three sides of a square, and the line of caravans along the top.

He said – 'And Nina?'

'How did you know about Nina?' asked Donna. 'Oh, I see—' She had spotted Patrick, in his favourite place in the corner. 'The boy told you. He is friends with all at the camp. It could not have been Nina. She is a local girl. She sleeps at home.'

Patrick's father was drawing a series of little arrows on his diagram. One ran from the corner behind the shed to the dog-kennels; a second from the kennels to the pony stables; a third from the stables to the line of caravans.

'So,' he said at last. 'Auguste – or your husband.'

'Certainly, it could have been Auguste,' agreed M. Theron. 'Although, he is thin as a rush, he is tough as a rush, too, and has very strong wrists and forearms. All clowns have. It is their early training in tumbling. Certainly he had a motive also. Not long ago he interfered to defend Nina, when Manfredo was being offensive, and received a thrashing for his pains.'

'Then—?' said Patrick's father.

'Fortunately for him – unfortunately for Monsieur Borner – Auguste can show that he was nowhere near the camp that night.' He looked out of the corner of his eye at Patrick, and said – 'Auguste spent that night with Nina, in her house.'

Patrick's father said to him, 'I think you'd better buzz off, old boy.'

'Oh, nonsense,' said Patrick impatiently. 'We all knew that Auguste was Nina's lover. That's why he stuck up for her, and got knocked about by Manfredo. Manfredo wanted her himself. I didn't say anything about it because I wasn't sure whether it was a terribly good alibi. After all, if she was fond of him, she'd say he was there, wouldn't she.'

M. Theron smiled, and said, 'Very true. But in this case the concierge of the house where Nina lodges confirms it. Auguste arrived at ten o'clock in the evening, and did not leave until six o'clock the following morning.'

'A concierge is a zealous watch dog,' said Patrick's father. 'But even she must sleep sometimes.'

'Agreed,' said M. Theron. 'But this one did not go to bed before one o'clock. Until that time she could hear the man and girl laughing and talking in their room. Manfredo, remember, was dead by one o'clock.'

'Did she see Auguste? Or simply hear his voice?'

'Heard him,' said M. Theron. 'What was in your mind?'

'He has a funny high-pitched voice. Easy to imitate.'

'That's true enough,' said Patrick. 'I've heard Nestor – he's the Borner's parrot – imitate him exactly. But then, he can take off all of them.'

M. Theron was frowning.

'I am a man of logic,' he said. 'If it be accepted that no one except its regular inmates could enter the camp after dark without being detected by the dogs, we have the following position. A man is struck down and killed, with a heavy instrument – most probably of metal and circular in shape, according to the autopsy – a sledge hammer, perhaps. The man who is killed was a bully, and a lecher. Any one of his fellows might have had cause to strike the blow. When was the blow struck? Between eleven o'clock and one o'clock, says the doctor. But we can be more precise than that. The man Stromboli heard Manfredo come back to the camp.'

Patrick and his father looked up quickly.

'Yes. That is so. We learned it only this morning. The old man sleeps with his dogs. The sharp-eared caniches! They woke him at midnight. He heard Manfredo. The inmates, when they come in late, they do not use the gate. There are places at the back where they climb through the wire.'

'He knew it must be one of the regulars,' said Patrick's father. 'But how did he know it was Manfredo?'

'He heard him. Manfredo was intoxicated. And he was talking to himself – loudly.'

'Did Stromboli go out to see?'

'He says no. He would not interfere with Manfredo sober. Certainly not when he was intoxicated.'

Patrick's father had taken out his sketch plan. Now he marked a spot behind the row of machinery-sheds.

'Manfredo would climb in on the south side, behind the machinery-sheds – here? Emerge by the end of the sheds, pass Stromboli and the dogs – so? And make his way across the open centre of the compound, towards the row of caravans on the north side.'

M. Theron nodded. 'And these caravans, remember, Signor Petrella, at that precise moment, were all empty, save one. The large caravan at the end, occupied by Borner and his wife. Let us suppose that Borner hears this sot approaching. Staggering across the open. He sees his chance. He picks up a heavy iron tent hammer. He creeps up behind him. One blow, and it is finished.'

'But why? Why would he do it?'

'He had a reason. All the circus knew it. I have no doubt your boy knows it, too.'

Patrick looked at his father, who said, 'Tell me.'

'It was about ten days ago,' said Patrick unhappily. 'Three days before Manfredo was killed. Nina was taking Leopold and Lorenzo for their afternoon walk – they are the lemurs, who live in Sam Borner's caravan and ride the ponies. Lorenzo slipped his leash, got into Manfredo's caravan and stole an orange. They're both terrible thieves. Manfredo chased him out, and Lorenzo got into a tree, and started to eat the orange and throw the peel at Manfredo. Everyone was laughing – except Manfredo. He was mad. He got his long whip, the one he uses on his cats, and flicked Lorenzo with it. It nearly cut his tail off.'

'And do you think,' said his father, 'that that would be sufficient provocation—?'

'Circus people think of their animals as children,' said M. Theron. 'If someone flicked your child with a whip—?'

'They're terribly valuable, too,' said Patrick. 'They ride Rosalie and

Marguerite, you see. It's one of the main attractions of the circus. They're awfully clever with them. Just like real jockeys. It's taken Sam fifteen years to train them.'

Patrick broke off. It suddenly occurred to him that he might be talking too much. His father had returned to his sketch plan.

'One thing puzzles me,' he said. 'Manfredo was found in the entrance of the stable.'

'If you are thinking,' said M. Theron, with a smile, 'that one of the horses may have kicked him, I can assure you that it is impossible. Unless it had legs of elastic! The nearest horse was tethered in its stall a full ten paces from the door.'

'I wasn't thinking of that. I was wondering what he was doing there at all. His caravan is at the other end of the line. Crossing the open compound he would go to the right to get to it. Why did he bear left-handed towards the stables?'

'Who knows?' said M. Theron. 'He was drunk. He may have lost direction.'

'He might,' said Patrick's father. 'It's curious, all the same.' He was frowning in a way that Patrick recognised. He said, 'I too, am a man of logic. I will concede to you that Borner is the only man who could have done this thing by himself. His wife would be a tacit accomplice, but we need not concern ourselves with her. Have you, however, considered that it could have been done, quite easily, by two people in concert – a conspiracy.'

It was clear that M. Theron had not thought about it.

'I will suggest two possible combinations. There may well be more. Clearly Auguste and Nina could have worked it. No one saw Auguste after eleven o'clock. The concierge heard his high-pitched voice. A voice which, as we have heard, even the parrot could imitate. If a parrot, how much more easily could a clever girl do so?'

M. Theron frowned and said, 'Auguste seems to me – somehow – psychologically an unlikely murderer.'

'Agreed. Then let me suggest a second one. Ramon. Who knows what tensions may grow between brothers. Did not Cain kill Abel?'

'But—'

'But Ramon was in a police-station cell by midnight. Agreed. But suppose he followed his brother back to the circus, killed him at half-past eleven, and immediately took steps to have himself arrested. That trouble he stirred up – it seemed to me a little obvious even at the time.'

'But—'

'But we are told that Manfredo was alive at twelve. Who by? By Stromboli. But who knows that he may not be in this, with Ramon, the two of them together—'

'A conspiracy,' said M. Theron. He sounded unhappy; as a man may, who has arrived at what seems to be the unique solution of a problem, perceived that it may, at best, be one of three.

'I worked out a fourth possibility,' said Patrick's father, 'involving Ramon, Stromboli and Sam Borner.'

'No, no,' said M. Theron. 'Three is enough. You have said quite sufficient to make me doubt my own diagnosis. Possibly I ought to let Mr Borner go? It is not right to detain a man who might be innocent. On the other hand, it might be wise to detain him for his own protection. That brute, Ramon, has sworn to avenge his brother.'

He took himself off, a worried frown on his good-natured face. After he had gone, Patrick said to his father, 'Did you really believe any of those ideas, or did you make them up to get Sam out of a hole?'

'Didn't they sound convincing?'

'Oh yes. They were terribly convincing.'

Patrick's father looked hard at him. If his son was capable of pulling his leg, he must be growing up.

'But I gather that they didn't convince you.'

'They were quite all right,' said Patrick. 'Quite logical. They could have planned it like that. The thing is, though, that they wouldn't. Auguste isn't the sort of person to kill anyone. And Ramon bickers a lot with Manfredo, but he wouldn't kill him. Manfredo was killed by someone who hated him. I'm positive of that.'

'By Sam Borner, then?'

'Not by Sam,' said Patrick. He said it in such an odd tone, that his father looked at him again. The boy had gone white.

The idea had not come to him suddenly. It had grown, from little things; things noticed, things heard, half observation, half impression. It was not a logical solution. It was more like a picture. He saw Manfredo, full of wine, muttering and stumbling, climbing through the wire perimeter at the well-known place, steering an unsteady course across the dusty, moon-lit compound, towards his caravan and bed. And then – his father had noticed that Manfredo drifted off course. A drunken man has a compass which takes him to his own bed. Something had attracted him to the front of the pony-shed and, inside that dark entrance, the murderer was crouched, ready to kill.

It might be proved, too. Only the time was short, and getting shorter.

In three or four days, the main circus would be back, the camp would be full of shouting, working, jostling people; the lights would be on most of the night as they repaired, against time, machinery and equipment for the autumn circuit. The caravans would all be occupied, the clues would be trampled underfoot and the scent would be cold. Also his mother would be back.

She had been in England, choosing a school for him. She was the daughter of an English colonel, and had a greater belief in the virtues of English boarding-schools than either Patrick or his father. When she was back, his liberty would be severely curtailed.

He spent the next two days on the quayside. Anyone will talk to a polite good-looking eleven-year-old boy. Patrick listened. There was a single piece of information that he needed. It was late on the evening of the second day – after nine o'clock – that the son of the proprietor of one of the water-side cafés brought him the news. Patrick went back with him, to confirm it. He wanted no slip-up. The boys stood and peered through the bead-curtained window. Ramon was sitting at a table, staring at the wall. There was a half-empty bottle on the table.

'It's his second,' said the boy. 'If he makes trouble, my father and his brother will handle him. Shall we stay to watch?'

'No,' said Patrick. 'I must telephone.'

'Why waste money?' said the boy. 'Use ours. It is in the passage. I will show you.'

Patrick spoke to the housekeeper. His father was out, and would not be back until late.

'When he comes,' said Patrick, 'tell him – tell him that I am going with some of my friends for a moonlight picnic—'

He cut short her protests by ringing off.

Ten minutes later, he was climbing, alone, into the circus enclosure. When the poodles had inspected him, and the Alsatians had sniffed, and passed him, he walked round the perimeter of the enclosure, keeping as much as possible in the shadows, until he came to the line of caravans. Here he moved very cautiously. He was making for an empty caravan, next to the Borners', at the end of the line. There was a light in the sleeping quarters of the Borners' van. That would be Donna. Even when she got into bed and turned out her light, she would probably not sleep very soundly. She would be worrying about Sam.

Great care was necessary.

Patrick fitted into the lock of the empty caravan the key which Nina had very unwillingly lent to him, eased it round gently, and went in. It was not elaborately equipped as the Borners' caravan, but was constructed on the same lines. There was a cushioned couch under the side window. Patrick climbed onto it, and opened the window.

It was a night of magic. The full face of the moon looked down from a sky of black velvet. It was so bright that it seemed to be generating a light and heat of its own.

And it was very quiet. Patrick could hear the clack of sharp little hoofs on the concrete as Rosalie or Marguerite moved in her stall, and, away on the far side of the compound, a throaty rumble as Rosso the lion dreamed of the forests of his youth.

From where he knelt, every detail of the living room of the Borners' caravan was picked out in the cold white moonlight. Opposite to him, on his perch by the open window, sat Nestor, the big green parrot. His eyes were shut. Of Nestor, alone among all the birds and animals of the circus, Patrick was afraid. He had been afraid since he had discovered, in a book of his father's, that Nestor was his real name. *Nestor notabilis*, the sheep-killing parrot of Australia and New Zealand. He had read how they would fly on to a terrified and cornered sheep and peck through its back, into its liver. He had read, too, how the enraged farmers tried to trap them and how the parrots, endowed with human cunning and calculation, had avoided all the snares that were set for them, and even set traps themselves in return.

Nestor had opened his eyes. For a moment, Patrick thought he had seen him; that he was going to open his hooked beak and scream out a warning to the camp. Then he saw that Nestor had his head cocked and was listening.

The next moment, Patrick heard it too. It was the sound of Ramon returning.

Nestor sidled along his perch towards Leopold and Lorenzo. Patrick could see that they, too, were awake, moving like shadows noiselessly, from side to side in their cage.

The door of the cage was fastened with a simple bolt, set well out of reach of the lemurs' arms. Nestor reached with his beak, lifted the arm of the bolt, and struck it. There was a tiny, metallic clang as the door swung open, and the monkeys were gone, out of the cage, and out of the window. Nestor hopped on to the sill, and the next moment, he was gone, too. Only the door of the cage swinging open, showed Patrick that he had not imagined the whole thing.

As he climbed the steps of the caravan he could see Ramon clearly. The man had come out from behind the shed, and was tacking, unsteadily, across the open, moonlit square.

Then the voice of Auguste spoke from the shadows by the stable. It called out 'Ramon'. The imitation was so perfect, that even Patrick, who knew it was Nestor, was deceived for a moment.

Ramon swung to his left. The voice added three unforgivable words in gutter Spanish. Ramon broke into a shambling run. Patrick was close enough to see the moonlight glinting from the knife which he carried, blade upwards, Spanish-fashion, in his left hand. Patrick padded after him, his plimsolls noiseless in the dust. As he rounded the corner, the voice of Auguste spoke for the third time. It came from inside the stable now, rather high up, towards the right.

The moonlight illuminated a small area in the mouth of the shed. In the middle, Ramon stood swaying. On the left – Patrick's heart missed a beat as he saw it – was the pony Rosalie. She had been moved by the lemurs out of her stall, and now stood, fastened only by her head rope, to a ring just inside the door. Leopold sat astride her, jockey-wise, Lorenzo crouched on the edge of the stall by her head. For a heartbeat, no one moved. Then Lorenzo bent forward and bit Rosalie's ear. At the same moment, Ramon stumbled. The stumble saved his life. Rosalie's steel tipped hoof, lashing out, missed his head, but hit him, with a splintering crack, in the left shoulder. He went down, rolled like an acrobat, and came up on his feet again. The crack must have been his collar-bone going, for his left arm was hanging limp. The shock had knocked all the drink out of him.

Rosalie was whinnying and stamping behind him, but he ignored her. He was staring, his face was pale as the moon itself, at the rafter above his head.

Nestor was sitting there. She stared down at him with unblinking yellow eyes. It was a battle of wills, and the stronger will prevailed. Ramon turned on his heel, and walked away. As he went the great green parrot gave a scream of derision and triumph.

Ramon broke into a shambling run.

'So,' said M. Theron. 'The brother, Ramon, has taken himself off. He crossed the frontier, illicitly, in the early hours of the morning. A guardia saw him, and shot at him, but could not stop him.'

'Do we want to stop him?' asked Patrick's father. 'Going off like that – it amounts to an admission of guilt. You will have to let Mr Borner go, now.'

'Of course. I have done so,' said M. Theron. 'It is unsatisfactory, all the same. I like a case to be neatly rounded. All the strings tied up. I should like to know why he killed his brother, and what he did it with. And who helped him. For it must have been the work of confederates.'

'I don't suppose we shall ever know the real truth,' said Patrick's father. And to Patrick, after M. Theron had taken himself off, he said, 'You're looking absolutely done. You must have been out very last late night. I didn't hear you come in.'

'I was a bit late,' said Patrick.

'It was a last fling,' said his father. 'Your mother's back today. I've had a letter from her. She's chosen the school. She enclosed the prospectus. It's on the South Downs. Association football in the Christmas term and Rugby football in the Easter. Two headmasters and a qualified matron. It sounds a splendid place.'

It sounded splendid to Patrick, too.

Roy Vickers

Double Image

There are some truths which the public invariably labels fictional. For instance, the Fanshaw murder mystery pivoted on the murderer being so like Julian Fanshaw that the latter's wife, Elsa, could fail to notice the difference. The public, bypassing the evidence, said that no wife could make that mistake and wondered why the police believed such a childish tale. The police, of course, do not commonly accept a tall tale in lieu of an alibi . . .

Seen from the outside, the Fanshaws were an ordinary young couple who lived in the well-appointed suburb of Rubington. They had a pleasant eight-room house, with more than half an acre of garden. A strange talent for getting and keeping competent help insured a smooth domesticity.

In the first week in October, Elsa announced at breakfast that she was going to Town for a day's shopping.

Her husband said he would squeeze in the time to have lunch with her at Blainley's Restaurant, at one o'clock. On the train she fell in with a neighbour, Gwenda Blagrove, and eventually brought her along to Blainley's believing that her husband would be pleased, as Gwenda's husband had been of use to Fanshaw in the city.

The Fanshaws' marriage had been satisfactory, so far. Elsa was sufficiently good-looking to seem beautiful to any man who liked her mental and emotional makeup. She kept her moods to herself. So did her husband. True, they had settled into a jog trot of absent-minded affection. He had ceased to notice her dress and she had taught herself to laugh at the right time without actually listening to his stories. For five years they had rippled along, stretching their income but avoiding really dangerous debt. A substantial sum, which would revert to Julian on the death of an uncle, discouraged saving.

The two women turned up at the restaurant ahead of time. At eleven minutes to one they were waiting in the entrance hall, which was somewhat crowded. At nine minutes to one Elsa exclaimed, 'There's Julian! He hasn't seen us, but he's coming this way.'

Julian Fanshaw was easy to pick out of a crowd, so Elsa always saw him before he saw her. He was taller than most men and he had the well-developed chest and overdeveloped shoulder muscles that come from rowing for one's university. His face was large, lean, and amiable, with a dimple in his chin. He went to a good tailor and his lounge suits were always on the same steely grey – the precise shade of which, Elsa said, she had never seen on any other man. His lightweight overcoats were cut from the same material. There was a touch of individuality even in his broad-brimmed homburg.

'He has seen you, but not me,' corrected Gwenda – a trivial remark which later acquired a certain importance. 'We'd better stand still, or we shall be dodging each other.'

The tall man with the steely grey clothes and the dimpled chin was weaving toward them.

'Julian! I've persuaded Gwenda to join us for lunch. We were both—'

The man she addressed did not ignore her. He seemed to assume that she was speaking across him to someone else. He looked into her eyes, doffed his hat, gave her a stranger's smile, murmured, 'Sorry!' and moved toward the cloakroom, leaving Elsa to gape at the overdeveloped shoulder muscles under the grey overcoat. The overcoat seemed to be not quite the same, but she couldn't be sure.

Gwenda was muttering to herself. Elsa looked frightened.

'You thought it was Julian, too,' Elsa almost whispered. 'You were just going to speak to him.'

'It *was* Julian! You can't mistake another man for your own husband!'

'But I did! Though when he turned his back I did think the overcoat was of a different material, even if it was practically the same shade.'

'His overcoat! Has Julian a twin brother?'

'No. He is a twin, but the other died when they were babies. It must be his double.'

'Nobody can be as double as that!'

Yet, there it was. Elsa felt as many have felt immediately after an accident – that she must force herself backward in time to the moment before it happened. Gwenda was still explaining about doubles when – at six minutes to one – Elsa felt a hand on her arm.

Julian again? Or just Julian?

'Julian! I've persuaded Gwenda to join us for lunch.' She was saying it over again. 'We were both going to the same shops—'

'Splendid! Sorry you've been waiting but I'm still five minutes to the good. I'll just dump my coat.'

After a civil exchange with Gwenda he hurried off before they could tell him about the other Julian. Elsa brought it up at lunch. In spite of Gwenda's corroboration, it sounded like a small-talk exaggeration. Julian mumbled politely about it.

'But don't you see it's terrific!' cried Gwenda. 'Elsa was as sure as I were that it was you! She says you actually are a twin.'

'Yes, that does give a tang to it,' grinned Julian. 'Unfortunately, my twin lived for only two days, statutory – my father told me it was twenty-six hours.'

'Were you born at home?'

'We were born at St Seiriol's.'

'Where hundreds are born every day.'

'Not hundreds every day – tens, perhaps. I can guess what you're thinking. But a mix-up of babies is such a likely thing to happen that it would be happening almost daily – it they didn't have a foolproof system for tabbing them. Nothing there!'

At home that evening Elsa's chatter lost its bubble.

'What's on your mind, darling? You were shopping today. If someone has stopped your credit we can probably fix it up.'

'It's that double of yours. You didn't really listen when Gwenda and I told you about him. He almost brushed against me. Our eyes met and I *still* thought he was you. He said "Sorry" in the same muttering tone you use. And he was dressed in exactly your grey, with the same cut, though the material itself may have been different. It's as if he must have been your identical twin.'

Julian frowned. 'Apart from anything else, we have no evidence that my twin brother was an identical. So, darling, you won't start something on that, will you? I mean the one about the nurses having changed the babies and one day the true earl turns up to claim the titles and estate. At the moment we have neither title nor estate for a missing heir to claim. Anyway, I am the older brother.'

'You're laughing at me!'

'Just a little. I don't believe your yarn. Only, there's nothing we can do about it except keep on agreeing that it's most extraordinary. So let's forget it.'

On the evening of the following day Julian, who was very regular in his habits, failed to appear at the usual time. Within an hour Elsa was waiting on the porch.

'Julian! Has something awful happened?'

'My dear girl! I'm barely an hour late. Just missed the train, that's all. I had a slack afternoon, so I thought I'd pop around the corner for a heart-to-heart talk with Uncle Ernest. The awful thing – if any – is that he is in rude health. We shall be middle-aged before we benefit.'

Later in the evening he expanded. 'Things have been rather tight the last six months. Some of my best clients are asking for longer credit, and they ought to have it. Obviously, the sensible thing is for me to realise at least part of my interest under the reversion. I can't do it without Uncle Ernest's consent. So I offered to pay him five hundred if he would authorise me to borrow ten thousand. It's pure gain for him – he loses nothing and risks nothing.'

'How did he take it?'

'He was very sour. Gave me a pijaw about living too extravagantly. I told him we didn't – because we don't!'

'I could manage with only Mrs Benson. And we could do nearly all the gardening ourselves.'

'We could not. And it isn't necessary. There's no crisis. It's simply that I'm pegged down for lack of a spot of extra capital.'

Which was only a different way of putting it, thought Elsa.

'Julian! Never mind how silly I am, please answer! If that man really is your twin – in spite of all the reasons why he can't be – would he share in the money on your uncle's death?'

'If I had a brother, which I have not, we would split.' Julian was scornful. 'On the utterly fantastic premise that my brother is alive, why doesn't he show up and make a fuss about it? Why lurk about and dress like me and play bogeyman at you?'

They talked no more about the double until the following evening, when Mrs Hebbleton rang Elsa.

To the extent that Rubington possessed a social leader, Mrs Hebbleton filled the role. Of moderate intelligence and immoderate energy she became president or secretary of most local activities, and enjoyed every minute of it.

'Mrs Hebbleton says she buttonholed you near the railway station yesterday evening—'

'She did not!'

'—that you had come off the 6:05 as usual, that you accepted for us to dine there next Thursday, and that she handed you the nominal roll of the tennis club to give to me, and I'd promised to do some of the letters.'

Julian was obliged to admit that this must be the handiwork of the double.

'That chap,' said Julian, 'is playing a game of his own. Turning up at Blainley's when you were there *and* doing this stunt in Rubington where we live – both can no longer be chance. Why didn't he tell Mrs Hebbleton his name isn't Fanshaw?'

'But supposing it is?'

'Don't bring that up again, darling. Whatever his name is, we're going to look silly.'

Next day, over morning coffee, Mrs Hebbleton came to the point.

'Gwenda told me an extraordinary story about your mistaking another man for your husband, though what use our nominal roll can be to him if he is *not* your husband—'

'Gwenda mistook him, too,' put in Elsa.

'In a crowded restaurant, perhaps,' conceded Mrs Hebbleton. 'But I'm sure that you will understand that I must ask you to prepare another nominal roll.'

'I will, with pleasure. But Gwenda was as close to him as I was.'

'It's all very peculiar indeed, but I shall expect you both on Thursday, all the same,' said Mrs Hebbleton magnanimously. 'If there really is a double impersonating your husband I imagine you will take steps.'

'I don't see what we can do.'

'Do you think it's ever true that one can do nothing?' said Mrs Hebbleton. 'Why not apply to the police for protection? Superintendent Norris is a very capable man. If you care to mention my name I'm sure he'll do something for you.'

Thus goaded, Elsa unfolded her tale to the superintendent, who disconcerted her by making notes.

'Let's take the restaurant incident first, Mrs Fanshaw. Between the two appearances, you tell me, there was an interval of three minutes. In that time Mr Fanshaw could – I don't say he did, mind – I say he *could* have gone out by a side door and come in again by the main door. To play a practical joke on you ladies. And he might have been continuing the joke with Mrs Hebbleton. By the way, I suppose Mr Fanshaw hasn't a twin brother?'

'He did have' – and Elsa told the tale about the short-lived baby.

'Then that's out of it,' said the superintendent, nevertheless making a note of it.

'Mrs Hebbleton,' said Elsa to her husband that night, 'thinks she runs Rubington, because she's rumoured to be a cousin of the Duke of Sheffield. Before marriage her name was Jennifer Maud Carmaenham. I wish you'd look her up in *Who's Who* – there's sure to be a copy at your club.'

'Aren't you being catty, darling?'

'Yes, and I'm liking it. She as good as said that there's no double – that it's only you playing the fool. And she practically forced me to go to the local police.' She added an account of her interview with the superintendent.

Julian's reaction was disappointing. In silence he took a postcard from his pocket, on which the made calculations of time.

'The superintendent is on solid ground,' he pronounced. 'The attitude of that woman is asinine, of course, but we can't defend ourselves. I can't prove I was somewhere else at the relevant times.' He added gloomily, 'This might damage us quite a lot. If that chap crops up again, I shall consider asking legal advice.'

The next incident touched on the business relations of the Fanshaws, uncle and nephew.

Julian was a slow-transport agent. If you wished to move a wardrobe or a ton of fertiliser or whatnot to the next town, or to an obscure island in the Pacific, without incurring the cost of express delivery, Julian Fanshaw was your man. He had maps and technical charts showing the most inexpensive way of sending goods from almost any spot on earth to almost any other.

Ernest Fanshaw, who was a fuel agent specialising in the less common fuels, occasionally employed the services of his nephew. As their offices were within a minute's walk they were in the habit of calling on each other and doing their business personally to preserve the family courtesies.

John Thwaites, Ernest Fanshaw's elderly head clerk, who had many of the qualities of a family retainer, was shocked when Julian presented himself at three in the afternoon and asked if his uncle were disengaged.

Mr Thwaites looked surprised.

'But Mr Julian! He's very busy just now, and he wasn't really pleased when you dropped in this morning to see him.'

'But I did *not* drop in this morning!'

The clerk, after careful scrutiny, could find no sign of excessive drinking.

'Mr Julian, I myself showed you in.'

'Mr Thwaites, this is damned serious!'

Julian strode into the private office and opened the door. Ernest Fanshaw, who had been dozing in his chair, opened his eyes and blinked.

'Sorry, Uncle. Thwaites says he showed me into this room this morning. I was not here this morning. I have been impersonated. I'll tell you all about it—'

After some confusion they reached bedrock.

'Let us be precise,' said Ernest Fanshaw. 'On Tuesday afternoon you called here to make an improper offer about the reversion. This morning, sitting where you are sitting now, you tried a new approach to the same subject. Before you left this room I produced your account for the sum of forty-three pounds, twelve shillings, apologising for having neglected to settle it before, and gave you a cheque for that amount. Are you telling me you have forgotten? Feel in your pocket.'

'Uncle Ernest! If it was a cheque made out to cash, you've probably lost your money. If it was a cheque made out to me, phone the bank now and have it stopped.'

When the bank had been warned, Julian told his tale, to which his uncle listened with impatience.

'I've never heard anything so damned ridiculous! This double – as you call him – how the devil could he know anything about that reversion?'

'I haven't the ghost of a notion, but I do know that he has nosed out a lot of details of my business and domestic affairs. He has made a fool of me in Rubington, impersonating me to our friends.'

It was his nephew's tone that impressed Ernest and inclined him to take notice.

'Julian, it has suddenly struck me – d'you think it possible that something slipped in the hospital and that your twin brother—'

'I've given up guessing. After this I shall see my lawyer and hit back if I can.'

Julian told Elsa about it – then slipped in the unwelcome information that *Who's Who* fully authenticated Mrs Hebbleton's claim to be the cousin of a duke.

'Anyhow, she'll have to believe now that there's a double, duke or no duke.'

A couple of days later, Miss Hackett, Julian's secretary, came into his room looking slightly offended. He had first met Miss Hackett when he was a small boy on a visit to the office. On his father's sudden death, while Julian was at Cambridge, she had proved herself a very competent manager. She was content to continue as Julian's secretary and office aunt.

'Mr Thwaites has been on the phone with a very mysterious message,' she said, with disapproval. 'Your uncle asks you to meet him at his bank in ten minutes. It's very urgent. And there is no explanation.'

In the bank manager's room Julian was shown the cheque for £43 12/- which had been cashed through a Post Office savings account.

'The endorsement certainly looks like my signature. But I know that I did not endorse that cheque, and anyway I have no Post Office account, so I declare the endorsement a forgery.'

The bank manager, applying a routine test, agreed that the signature had been traced and insisted on calling the police. Julian, eager to cooperate, volunteered to go with the police to the branch Post Office, warning them that he would be identified as the forger. They were so alike, he told them, that his own wife had made a mistake.

Pursuing the twin-brother theory the police visited St Seiriol's Hospital, Westminster, where Julian had been born. The records showed that there had been five male babies born within an hour of the twins and a total of eleven males and seven females – with one male death – within 26 hours. But the routine for preventing a confusion of babies was so thorough that the possibility of a mistake was untenable.

There remained the thin chance that a nurse might have tampered with the routine, robbing the mother of twins in pity for the bereaved mother of a singleton. So the police worked on the list of nurses and patients of 29 years ago. Five of the nurses had died, and more than half the number of parents were untraceable.

They interviewed Elsa and were impressed. Gwenda Blagrove's testimony added nothing. Mrs Hebbleton challenged them to explain why the double should want the nominal roll of the tennis club. The local superintendent agreed that it was incredible that Mr Fanshaw should play such a clownish trick on his uncle, and promised to keep a sharp lookout in Rubington.

After a blank week the papers of the case came before Chief Inspector Thurtle, who sent a courteous request to Julian to call at Scotland Yard.

Thurtle had the appearance of a prosperous family man who is bullied by his daughters. Many of his earlier successes were due to his talent for inspiring confidence.

'Our chief difficulty is that all roads lead back to you, Mr Fanshaw – such as that Post Office clerk identifying you yourself as the double. I thought pr'aps you'd like to let us have your fingerprints – for your own sake.'

Julian thanked him and had his prints taken.

'Forty-three quid odd,' resumed Thurtle, 'seems a very poor target for an elaborate stunt like this. He dresses himself up like you, and that alone would cost more than thirty. And why does he force himself on your wife's attention at a restaurant? And why the practical joke on Mrs Hebbleton? Of course, we have to deal with the fact of forgery. But, between you and me, it looks more like a hoax. That suggests he may be your twin brother nursing a grievance, in spite of what the hospital people say.'

Julian was unresponsive. 'If he's my brother, why doesn't he show up in a friendly way? He would have a strong moral claim on us.'

'Would he be entitled to any money?'

'There's no immediate money. But there's a reversion on my uncle's death – about fifty thousand pounds – which he would share equally with me.'

Thurtle said this was important and took a note of details.

'We have to find a means of separating your movements from his, Mr Fanshaw. Now, he was getting that cheque out of your uncle at about twenty past twelve on the morning of the fourteenth. You were in your office at that time, I suppose?'

'Probably – just a minute!' Julian produced a pocket diary. 'The fourteenth . . . I have an entry – *Who's Who*—' He smiled. 'My wife had asked me to look up a social reference. So I went to my club, leaving the office at twelve. I walked, so I must have got there – the Junior Commonwealth, Mendover Street – about ten past.'

'Can you give me something to check on, just for the record?' Then Thurtle added, 'That's a large club and I don't suppose the staff ticks off every member – there'd be a good many coming in at that time. You had lunch with somebody?'

'N-no, I had a standup in the snack bar – don't remember running into any of my own clique there. On the way to the reading room I nodded to one or two acquaintances. I doubt if they'll remember.'

They did not remember. Thurtle's checkup at the club yielded no one, of membership or staff, who could state positively that Julian Fanshaw was or was not there on the fourteenth.

Thurtle followed with inquiries in Rubington, intensive but fruitless. He called on Ernest Fanshaw and enlisted the latter's cooperation. Then he sent Fanshaw another equally courteous request to call at the Yard.

When Julian had seated himself and accepted a cigarette, Thurtle reported his total lack of progress in any direction – then waited for Julian to say something.

'Awkward for me.' Julian braced himself. 'Let's face it, Inspector. Like Mrs Hebbleton, you suspect that I have played my own "double" as a practical joke?'

'Not as a practical joke.'

Julian looked puzzled.

Thurtle went on: 'Take the buildup of this "double" of yours – or identical twin, if you like. He must have staged the incident at Blainley's Restaurant – same applies to Mrs Hebbleton and her tennis papers – and to that prank with the forty-three quid cheque. Builds up a half lunatic who might do anything.' Thurtle paused. 'For instance, he might murder your uncle – and leave you to collect the fifty thousand quid.'

Julian removed his cigarette and stared at it.

'Let's take this slowly, Inspector. You don't believe this fellow exists. You suggest that "he" might murder my uncle – meaning that *I* might murder my uncle—'

'Put it this way, Mr Fanshaw. I'm warning you that if you have any such fantasy in your brain you'd do well to get rid of it.'

Julian laughed loudly and long.

'It's a great idea, Inspector! I scupper Uncle Ernest and plant the murder on a ghost!'

'Just so. Our job is to prevent crime, when we can.'

'You do it very thoroughly,' sighed Julian. 'If I had had any such plan – fantasy, you rightly called it – you would have dished it.'

He got up and moved toward the door.

'The police have done a lot of work on this job – which you believe to be a hoax on my part. Am I to be charged with "creating a public mischief" – if that's what it's called?'

'We have no immediate intention of making that charge, Mr Fanshaw.'

'Haven't you?' Julian smiled. '*I wonder why!*'

There were no developments during the next fortnight. Elsa no longer asked every evening if there was news of the double. Routine was restored. Fifteen days after the incident of the forged cheque Julian announced that he intended to go to Manchester the following afternoon – a Tuesday – in hope of nailing an important new client, and that he would stay overnight, returning home at the usual time on Wednesday evening.

In the middle of Tuesday afternoon Elsa heard a latchkey and ran into the hall.

'Julian! I thought you were going to Manchester today?'

'Washout. Phone call just as I was leaving the office. I had made arrangements with Miss Hackett, so I thought I'd knock off work just the same.'

'What've you done with your suitcase, Julian?' Her voice was the least bit unsteady.

'Damn! Left it at the office.'

Mrs Benson was making a clatter in the kitchen. Even so, she would hear a scream. Elsa saw that he had guessed her thought. He looked angry, but she did not flinch.

'How do I know you *are* Julian?'

'You don't, I guess. And you never will know, because there's no means of telling you. "I am myself" – what the devil does it mean? Nothing!' His anger seemed to be lost in self-pity. 'I am not just like one man but thousands. My conversation is the same as theirs, my habits, my very gestures. And we all whisper the same things to our wives. Why is it remarkable that some of us should have the same face?' He laughed as a man who laughs at himself. 'But if it's the problem of my face that's worrying you, perhaps you noticed at breakfast this morning that I had nicked myself while shaving. Look closely – left side, near the ear – and if you can find a trace of the nick, treasure it. It's my solitary claim to individuality.'

'Don't work yourself up over nothing, Julian.' Elsa felt ashamed of herself. 'After all, I was wrong about you once.'

'Sorry, darling. It was your question that upset me. I thought you meant it seriously. Perhaps you did – don't tell me! The truth is, this wretched "double" business is getting us down. Let's snap out of it for a few hours. I vote we have a nice, noisy evening in Town. Elsa – *Elsa!*' His voice pushed aside the five years of jog-trot, leaving her dizzy.

They used the car, to eliminate the rush for the last train. Neighbours, the Brigstocks, saw them dining at Blainley's, and thought that they seemed absorbed in each other – which was true.

They went to a musical show and afterward to a night club. He noticed her dress. She listened to his stories and laughed because she was amused. She set herself to engage his whole attention. When they had returned to Rubington she was still effervescent. They were acutely conscious of each other.

Next morning he was the first up and about. By the time Elsa came downstairs Mrs Benson had brought in breakfast and placed his overcoat and hat in readiness for him in the hall – the staff was always devoted to Julian. A thin beam of sunlight, filtering through the glass panel in the front door, rested on the overcoat.

Elsa looked at the coat – then passed on as if she had not seen it. On the hall table, as usual, was a copy of the *Times*. She opened a drawer, took out an ancient pair of scissors with which she would often cut out the crossword puzzle before Julian whisked it off to the office – and the next instant turned back to the coat. It was the right shade; but the material, she thought was different – the same difference she had noted in the coat of the 'double' that day at Blainley's Restaurant.

'How utterly ridiculous! It's the effect of the sun on it!' The thought was unspoken, but she laughed aloud – laughed a second time as she stopped herself from fingering the material. She positively bounced into breakfast.

She began to chatter. She made a casual remark about one of their friends. His mumbled answer confused her by its irrelevance. Her thoughts flew back to the coat in the hall. In the next few seconds she felt the blood rushing in her head. She steadied herself, pushed back her chair. The same words came unbidden.

'How do I know you *are* Julian?'

Their eyes met, fanning her panic.

'You can say that to me, Elsa, after all that has passed between us – since yesterday afternoon?'

'*You're stalling!*' It was almost a whisper. 'If you're Julian, tell me the name of my bridesmaid – the pet name we've always used.'

'A test question!' He laughed. 'After five years and two months of marriage you need a password to tell you the difference between your husband and another man of the same appearance. It proves what I was saying yesterday—'

'Why don't you answer?'

'For one of two reasons. Either I am not your husband and don't know the answer. Or I am your husband and see no point in answering. Think it over, Elsa, and you'll find that it doesn't matter a damn to you whether I'm Julian Fanshaw or his twin brother.'

He got up and walked out.

Elsa sagged in her chair. Had she insulted both Julian and herself? It was one thing to mistake the other man for Julian for a few seconds in Blainley's Restaurant. But last night! As if she could have the slightest doubt! Why, the thing was a psychological absurdity! She did not move until Mrs Benson came in to clear the breakfast table.

Toward the end of the morning it dawned on her that she could remove all doubt by ringing his office. But she must choose her words carefully. Secretaries were very careful of what they said to wives about husbands.

She looked up the train schedule to Manchester. There was a dining-car express arriving in London at 2:45. Julian would take that train – *if* he were in Manchester.

'Oh, Miss Hackett!' she was saying at a few minutes past two. 'Is Julian back yet?' – a question which might have referred to lunch.

'No, Mrs Fanshaw. He said he would probably take the mid-day expresss from Manchester, so he should be here about three. Shall I ask him to ring you?'

'No, thanks – it's of no importance, and I shall be out at three.'

So much for the psychological absurdity! All emotion had spent itself and she faced with detachment the riddle of what to say to Julian.

Actually, she said nothing. Julian came home at the usual time. Watching him from the window she thought he looked haggard. When she met him in the hall he burst into a heartiness that was wholly unconvincing.

'Hullo, darling! Had a good day? I came down with Brigstock. Says he saw us at Blainley's last night – they were three tables away, apparently – couldn't catch our eye – eyes, I mean. I told him you and I were having an evening out together for a change. Not a bad evening either, eh? Shan't be long.'

He hurried upstairs, carrying his suitcase. She had said nothing, and he had not noticed her silence.

He had picked up the truth from Brigstock, she concluded, and wished to spare her feelings. But perhaps that was not quite his style – in their five years, all his little kindnesses had been trumpeted. More probably he found the facts humiliating to himself and wished to avoid discussion. She would play along.

On the last Monday in November, six weeks after the incident of the forged cheque, Ernest Fanshaw's head clerk overheard what he took to be the voice of Julian Fanshaw speaking to the reception girl. Through the window he noted the steely grey overcoat and the wide-brimmed homburg affected by Julian Fanshaw, and under his arm a folded newspaper, obviously the *Times*. The clocks were striking eleven.

'Good morning, Mr Thwaites. Do you think Uncle Ernest could spare me five minutes, or are you working him too hard?'

'Ah! Your uncle doesn't need anybody to make him work.' He spoke on the office telephone. 'Mr Julian is here, sir . . . Very good, sir. Will you go right through, Mr Julian.'

Ernest Fanshaw had been compelled by the logic of events to accept the idea of 'the double' – which was repugnant to him. But as his inner door opened he forgot the double and saw only his nephew. He also forgot the arrangement made with Inspector Thurtle – which Thwaites was at the moment putting into action.

'Well, Julian. I hope you haven't come to talk about that reversion again?'

'Not literally, Uncle. The reversion can remain in the background of our thoughts.' Julian spoke with one eye on the inner door, as if he expected interruption. 'I want you to make me a personal loan of a thousand pounds.'

The proposition was not fully expanded before the head clerk came in without knocking. He handed his employer a folded slip.

Ernest Fanshaw studied the slip with undisguised astonishment. He stared at his caller. Then he stared at his clerk.

'All right, Thwaites. Go ahead.'

Before the clerk had shut the door, the slip, which had been refolded, was snatched from Ernest Fanshaw's fingers.

'What have we here, Uncle?' He read the message aloud: ' "By phone as directed: Miss Hackett states that Mr Julian Fanshaw is in his office at this moment. J. Thwaites." I guessed it – your face gave you away. So Thwaites is ringing the police, eh?'

'What happens to you will depend largely on the evidence I give about that cheque. You're Julian's twin, aren't you?'

'So I believe. Taking myself at my face value and adding a few dates and places.' He began to open out the copy of the *Times* which he had brought with him. 'There's an article here—'

'Sit down, sir! No doubt you believe yourself to have been ill-used. You may have been, but not by our family. In the circumstances I am prepared to—'

The extent of Ernest Fanshaw's intended benevolence was never known, because, at that moment, he died in mid-sentence without even an audible groan. He was killed with an Army dagger, by the commando technique employed when it is necessary that an enemy sentry shall die before he can make any sound whatever.

The murderer had been wearing cuffed cleaning gloves and had used the open copy of the *Times* to try to protect his clothes. But the cuff of the right-hand glove became bloodstained nevertheless. He shook the glove into the wastepaper basket. Then, with a quick intake of breath, he noticed a bloodstain on his overcoat too – close to the second button.

The stain was slight, but recognisable, and had obviously been made by contact with the cuff. He glanced round the room, picked up a copy of a magazine, leaving the *Times* on Ernest Fanshaw's desk. With his gloved left hand he then unlocked the door that gave on to the outside corridor. He shut and locked the door behind him. He folded the key in the left-hand glove and put it in a side pocket of his overcoat. The magazine, carried in a sufficiently natural manner, concealed the bloodstain near the second button.

It was now eight minutes past eleven.

Like any other murderer he had to escape from the scene of the crime before the police arrived. He achieved this purpose when he entered the taxi that was waiting for him.

'Back to where you picked me up – you remember – just round the corner.'

But like no other murderer he wished to draw attention to his movements – for the next few minutes only. The taxi itself would be useful. No ordinary businessman would take a taxi for so short a distance, and keep it waiting to boot.

The taximan stopped outside the building containing Julian Fanshaw's office, where he had originally picked up his passenger. The meter registered two shillings. The taximan was handed a ten-shilling note.

'Keep the change.'

The taximan would remember. But some taximen were very clever at keeping out of the witness box. Luck produced a squad of window cleaners about to enter the building.

'Are you the foreman? My name is Fanshaw – you'll see it on the doors upstairs. I want you to do my windows last.'

The foreman was given a pound note. Twenty shillings, where five would have been adequate. The foreman would remember.

And there was more luck coming. On the staircase he met a man coming down. The latter happened to be Marberry, whose office was on the third floor, a personal acquaintance of Julian Fanshaw's.

'Hullo, Fanshaw! Looks as if you were right about Pretty Polly!'

'Hope so. I'm backing her to win.'

Marberry blinked as the other passed on. 'Pretty Polly' was not a racehorse, but their own nickname for Pritt-Polson, owner of the building, whom they had been pressing for improvements.

Now the luck was petering out. In the hall below there was a mild commotion. The window cleaner's voice and then Marberry's, explaining – obviously to the police. He caught the words 'Pretty Polly.' The taxi driver was chipping in, too.

He had not expected the police here for at least another twenty minutes. He would have to hurry.

The fatal slip, of tradition, is often the result of an unconscious habit, a foible, an affection which leads to identification and eventually to the gallows. The same principle operates, of course, in reverse – sometimes shielding the guilty, sometimes saving the innocent from arrest.

Julian might well have had no substantial alibi but for an odd little trick of carrying in his pockets unstamped postcards, on which he would make notes – both business and personal.

On the day of the murder he had arrived at his office half an hour earlier than usual. A client, who had bought a furniture business in bankruptcy, required two thousand items of furniture to be transported from Plymouth to London within seven months, and was clamouring for an estimate on slow delivery.

'This Baverbridge estimate will keep us on the hop,' Julian said, when he and Miss Hackett had hurried through the morning mail. 'I made some notes at home last night – and some more in the train, with some queries for you.' He flicked out half a dozen postcards, held them fanwise like a poker hand, then put them back in his pocket. 'Now where the devil did I put those notes—?'

'In your overcoat pocket, I expect. Shall I look?'

'Please.'

Julian's room was of the seedy type often affected by prosperous businessmen to convey that overhead costs are cut to a minimum for the benefit of the customer. The steely grey overcoat and wide-brimmed homburg hung inelegantly on the wall between an early-model rolltop desk and a gaunt metal closet some six feet high, deemed to be fireproof. The walls were quite clean, but the carpet was nearly threadbare and one of the floorboards creaked.

Miss Hackett felt in the breast pocket of the overcoat and produced another poker hand of postcards.

'That's it. You might pencil in the answers, in case I get an idea when I'm not in the office. I'll be in the chart room if anything really urgent crops up.'

The chart room was the powerhouse of the firm. It was lined with wall maps, several of which Julian now removed to the long table.

There were special filing cabinets for the charts, a couple of fireproof cupboards, and a single chair. Considered as a room, it was the best in the suite, with an inner and outer door, whereas Julian's room was a mere annex of Miss Hackett's, with no outer door.

Thus Julian went through Miss Hackett's room, across the interior corridor containing a peephole window labeled *Inquiries*, through the typists' room to the chart room. He always went that way to the chart room and always made the return journey through the outer door of the chart room and the outer corridor, thereby completing a loop when he reached the interior corridor – another little idiosyncrasy which Miss Hackett had noted with aunt-like indulgence.

In half an hour – that is, by eleven o'clock – Miss Hackett had looked up the references and filled in the blanks and queries on the overcoat postcards. She took the cards into Julian's room and put them on his desk. Then, reminding herself that he would probably drop something on top of them and leave the office without them, she picked up the cards again and put them back in the breast pocket of his overcoat. The telephone rang as she returned to her own room.

'Good morning, Miss Hackett, Mr Thwaites speaking for Mr Ernest Fanshaw. Is Mr Julian in the office, please?'

'Yes, Mr Thwaites. He's in the chart room. I can't switch you through, as there's no extension. If you'll wait a minute—'

'Don't disturb him, please. My chief only wishes to know if he is there. I think he will call on Mr Julian later in the morning. Thank you, Miss Hackett.'

At eleven ten a junior typist brought Miss Hackett a glass of milk which she took in obedience to her doctor, disliking it. She started on a letter. One paragraph, one gulp. As she finished the milk she was again interrupted.

'Everything okay, Miss Hackett?'

It was a meaningless question. Julian, she told herself, was getting flustered over this Baverbridge estimate.

'I've been over your notes and I've put the cards back in your overcoat pocket.' Then she added, 'Your uncle is coming to see you some time today.'

'We're too busy. Ring him back, but be diplomatic. Say I'll look in on him on my way up tomorrow.'

He passed on to his own room, shutting the door behind him. Miss Hackett dialed Ernest Fanshaw, but the number was busy. She was halfway through the next letter when she heard steps in the reception corridor which did not stop at *Inquiries*. Her door was opened by a man in early middle-age and of benign appearance.

'I am Detective Inspector Thurtle. May I speak to Mr Fanshaw, please?'

'I'll tell him you're here.' Miss Hackett went into Julian's room, closely followed by Thurtle. The room was empty.

'Did you expect Mr Fanshaw to be in this room, Miss Hackett?'

'Yes. He came here from the chart room a few minutes ago. He spoke to me, then went into his room. He must have gone back to the chart room while I was on the telephone and I didn't notice. Will you follow me, please.'

She took him through the typists' room. When she opened the inner door of the chart room Julian did not look up. He was seated sideways at the long table, a writing pad on his knee since there was no room for it on the table, which was covered with maps now opened out and fluttering in the draft.

'I believe we can do the whole job by – hullo, Inspector.'

'Good morning, Mr Fanshaw.'

Miss Hackett retired, shutting the door behind her. Julian tore a sheet from the writing pad, clipped it to similar sheets of notes.

'Take this chair, Inspector,' he invited, rising.

Thurtle did not move. He was gazing at the other with something approaching awe. He meant to be curt and official, but he actually spoke like a human being.

'*Why* didn't you take my warning? It was madness to go through with it.'

'Last time we met, Inspector,' said Julian, with controlled exasperation, 'you told me you believed that I had faked my own "double." And you warned me not to murder my uncle. Are you now telling me that my uncle *has* been murdered – and that I have murdered him?'

'If you want to play it that way – yes, to both questions.'

'Well, I'm damned! Poor old Uncle Ernest! As you don't believe the double exists you've come to arrest me?'

'Unless you can account for your movements between eleven o'clock this morning and the present moment – and answer my questions satisfactorily.'

'I turned up here about nine thirty and I haven't left the office. Doesn't leave much scope for questions, does it?'

Thurtle shrugged. His familiar task had suddenly become distasteful.

'To save a lot of cross-talk I'll tell you what you're up against.' Thurtle told him about the taxi, about Thwaites, about the latter telephoning Miss Hackett – about the window cleaners' foreman and the encounter with Marberry.

'Marberry spoke to you. And you gave him a funny answer about "Pretty Polly" – a clever touch that, to clinch the "double" idea. And you gave it more and more buildup by leaving a trail through the taximan and the window cleaners – to suggest that if you were the

murderer you wouldn't be such a fool as to leave a trail of your movements at the most dangerous time.'

'Of course I wouldn't!' laughed Julian. 'How does it go on?'

'The man who got out of that taxi and came into this building is still
in this building – and he can't get out.'

'Meaning me?' Julian offered his wrists, as if for handcuffs. 'What
are you waiting for?'

'All right, if you want to drag it out! How long had you been sitting
in that chair when Miss Hackett brought me in here?'

'I haven't left this room since I entered it about ten thirty.'

'Miss Hackett says you were talking to her in her room a few minutes
before I turned up.'

'I was not!' cried Julian. 'But if Miss Hackett said it, she *believed* it to
be true. Did she say that I left her and went back to this room?'

'She said you went into that inner room off hers – she thought you
were still there.'

'And she went into that inner room?'

'Of course she did! So did I. It was empty.'

'Did you look in the fireproof closet? It's big enough to hold a man.'
Thurtle turned sharply to the door, then checked himself.

'There was no man in that closet, Fanshaw. You're trying to suggest
it was the "double" who spoke to Miss Hackett?'

'What for? In the hope of convincing you?'

'You're not bothering about me – you're setting the stage for the jury.'
When Julian made no answer, Thurtle went on, 'We can't search this
building properly until the office workers have left. So you can go on
stalling until about seven this evening.'

Thurtle left the chart room by the outer door and waited in the corridor
until Sergeant Boyce reported.

'Four floors and a basement. Total of six offices. We've been through
them all, everybody cooperating. The basement gives on to a blind wall
approached through the caretaker's living quarters. So the only way
out is by the front. Window cleaners will be here most of the day. I've
asked 'em to keep their eyes open.'

News of the murder had by now reached Julian's staff. Thurtle found
it necessary to console Miss Hackett – whereupon she recovered her
office manner and proved herself an ideal witness. Like many of her kind
she was time-conscious. She explained that the routine had been slightly
affected by the Baverbridge estimate.

'It was close to half-past ten when Mr Fanshaw went to the chart room.
By eleven I had finished working on his notes. I made the entries on his
postcards' – Miss Hackett smiled on the word – 'then took them into his
room. Then Mr Thwaites rang – that would be a minute or so after

eleven – asking if Mr Julian were in the office. Next, the junior brought me my glass of milk – it ought to have been brought at eleven punctually, but it was nearer ten past. I had just finished the milk when Mr Fanshaw came in from the chart room and spoke to me and then went into his room.'

Thurtle decided not to raise the issue of the 'double.'

'And what time was that?'

'It would have been – twelve to fifteen minutes past eleven.'

Near enough to the time when Marberry and the foreman of the window cleaners were giving their information to Boyce and himself, noted Thurtle.

'Check this, please, Miss Hackett. Between ten thirty and eleven fifteen you do not know for certain that Mr Fanshaw was in the chart room – the whole of that time? You only *infer* that he must have been there?'

'If you wish to split hairs it's possible that he *might* have gone up to see Mr Marberry for a few minutes – they're putting pressure on the landlord – but it's extremely unlikely, as we are working against time. Anyhow, I know he didn't leave the building—'

'How do you know that?'

'Because he never goes out without his overcoat after the first of October' – again the indulgent smile – 'and his overcoat was hanging up, as it is at this moment.'

She got up and opened the communicating door, Thurtle followed her and contemplated the steely grey overcoat surmounted by the broad-brimmed homburg.

'He always hangs it there, Miss Hackett? But you don't notice it *every* time you come into the room?'

'I do not,' agreed Miss Hackett. 'But on this occasion I did – I had to.' She told him how she had first put the postcards on the desk. 'Then I thought they would be safer in his pocket. So I put them there.' She thrust her hand into the breast pocket of the overcoat. 'And here they are.'

That was conclusive. Thwaites had stated that the murderer was wearing a grey overcoat and wide-brimmed homburg. And the taximan, Marberry, and the foreman of the window cleaners had said the same.

For the first time in his official life Thurtle caught himself trying to shirk a fact because it menaced a theory. It would be absurd to believe that Miss Hacket was lying – making herself an accessory. And Miss Hackett was proving that Julian Fanshaw could not have been the murderer seen by Thwaites and the others – in short, that the 'double' did exist, and the 'double' had killed Ernest Fanshaw.

There was still one loophole – the possibility that Fanshaw was using a duplicate coat and hat. In which case he must have hidden the duplicates in the building.

Thurtle was staring at the postcards which Miss Hackett had handed him. As the sense of shock weakened he studied the notes on the postcards, then returned them to Miss Hackett, who put them back in the pocket of the overcoat.

Before leaving the room Thurtle lifted the coat from its peg, looked it over, back and front, and replaced it. He did the same with the homburg, studying the inside, noting that there was no mark of ownership on the inner band. Next, his eye rested on a metal closet near the window.

'What do you keep in there?'

'Any special documents to be protected from fire, but it's been out of use for the last three months. It you want to look inside I'll have to ask Mr Fanshaw for the key – oh! – it's not locked – it's not even properly shut!'

She opened the door, revealing an empty interior. If the 'double' existed, that closet would have been large enough to hide him. And so would the similar closets in the chart room.

While explaining Julian's routine and recent movements Miss Hackett had made use of the diary.

'I see, Miss Hackett, that Mr Fanshaw went to Manchester on the fifth and stayed overnight. To meet a client, I suppose?'

'I don't know if it was a definite client. He may have gone with the general idea of seeking new business. He gave me no details.'

Thurtle thanked Miss Hackett, then went back to the chart room – in search of a duplicate coat and hat.

'I'd like to have a look round, Mr Fanshaw, especially in those closets.'

'Go ahead,' said Julian, without looking up. 'Nothing is locked.'

The first was little more than nests of deep metal drawers, of which three were empty and two contained account books. The second closet was grooved for shelves, but all the shelves had been taken out. It could have concealed an overcoat – or a man, for that matter – but it was empty. The drawers of the filing cabinet were too small even for the hat – as were the drawers in the long table.

Downstairs, Thurtle found Sergeant Boyce in the hall. Two men were guarding the doors. Thurtle spoke to Boyce.

'Grey overcoat and broad-brimmed homburg. See that they don't leave the building on anybody or are carried away by anybody. Examine all outgoing bags and parcels big enough to contain either or both.'

Thurtle left the building and walked round the corner to the late Ernest Fanshaw's office, where he received a detailed report from Rouse, the inspector in charge.

He was shown the copy of the *Times* which had been brought in by the murderer and used in the murder. Rouse turned to the page – unstained – which is allotted to small advertisements. Near the centre of one column about two inches had been somewhat clumsily cut out.

'Thought you'd like to have a look at this, sir – I've never seen a cluer clue, myself!' chuckled Rouse. 'Jagged edge and all – so when we find the missing bit we can fit it in and know we've found *the* missing bit.'

'That sort of thing does happen sometime.' Thurtle grinned. 'What's the missing bit about?'

'Just what you'd expect, when you come to think of it.' Rouse produced a complete copy of the same edition and read aloud: ' "Legacies. Reversions. Missing relatives. Genealogies traced. Identification formalities executed. Write for appointment. Guardian Agency, 15 Tinbury, E.C.2." I've phoned the agency that we want a list of those answering this ad as soon as possible.'

'Anything else?'

'Not a thing. The glove – you can buy 'em in any of the chain stores. The commando knife – thousands of 'em have been smuggled out of the Army as souvenirs. Tidiest job on record, I'd say.'

In the early afternoon Inspector Thurtle returned to Julian Fanshaw's office. The guard in the hall reported all quiet. Julian Fanshaw had lunched in the office. On the landing Thurtle came upon Sergeant Boyce talking to a junior typist who had been in charge of the office while the staff was out at lunch.

Thurtle learned from the girl that she had taken the lunch tray to Mr Fanshaw in the chart room. She had seen him again when he came through the typists' room, on the way to his own room. He had been carrying a metal drawer, apparently full of papers. It was a big drawer and she had opened the doors for him. There was no further information, except that the window cleaners had been at work most of the time.

In the office Miss Hackett reported that Mrs Fanshaw had come, following a telephone message, and was now with her husband in the chart room.

Thurtle, interviewing Elsa in Julian's room, was favourably impressed by the frankness of her answers about their home life.

'So your routine went on very much as usual these last three months?' When Elsa agreed he asked, 'Was your husband absent from home on the night of the fifth of this month?'

The rather beautiful mouth was distorted in a sudden twitch. The answer was a long time coming.

'*Yes.*' It was a strained whisper, as if a damaging admission had been dragged from her. 'But there's no reason why I should make a fuss about it – to a police officer.' She took a grip of herself. 'To the best of my belief my husband spent that night at Manchester. On the other hand, some neighbours of ours – Mr and Mrs Brigstock – will tell you that, they saw him dining with me at Blainley's Restaurant that night. For all I know, the Brigstocks – or somebody else – may have seen us going home in the car at about one in the morning. I tell you – I suppose I'd better keep saying "to the best of my belief" – I tell you that it was *not* my husband! It was this murderer who took me out – and came home with me.'

Thurtle was thunderstruck.

'Mrs Fanshaw! A man spent all that time with you! And you failed to perceive that he was not your husband – until the following morning!'

She flushed, but she still gave the impression that she was telling the truth.

'You think a woman couldn't possibly make a mistake like that? I thought so, too – in a way, I still think so. I know that sounds like nonsense – oh, please try to look at it from my point of view, Inspector! Julian – that is, the other man – came home in the middle of the afternoon. He said that the trip had been cancelled.'

'One minute! With all this double stuff you'd been hearing about, weren't you suspicious?'

'Of course I was! I actually said, "How do I know you *are* Julian?" I forgot how he answered – I forgot even that I had asked him. We had a jolly evening in Town.'

Thurtle was convinced that she believed her own tale. He beamed like an uncle and encouraged her to give a detailed account of the evening, up to the return home. She added that she had telephoned Miss Hackett at two the following afternoon.

'And when your husband came home that evening he told you he had spent the previous night at Manchester?'

'No, he didn't. He referred to "our" evening in Town. But I could tell he was pretending. He had met Brigstock on the train, and Brigstock had mentioned that he had seen "us" at Blainley's. Julian guessed what had happened and wanted to save my face.'

That was a nuisance, reflected Thurtle; if Julian had stuck to the Manchester story it would have been easy to check.

'Let's get this clear, Mrs Fanshaw. You had a suspicion the moment he turned up on Tuesday afternoon. He talked you out of that. But you must have become suspicious a second time or you wouldn't have rung Miss Hackett.'

'Quite true. At breakfast next morning I panicked. I challenged him with a question which only my husband could answer. He was evasive.

And when I pressed him for an answer, he was deeply offended and walked out of the house.'

'What started the panic?'

'His overcoat, Inspector. When I came downstairs, his coat was in the hall. The sun was on it. And I thought it seemed very slightly different – like the coat I saw on the "double" at Blainley's – though, even then, I wasn't sure.' Her eyes turned to the coat hanging on the peg, beneath the homburg. 'If you'll look closely at my husband's coat you'll see that the fabric—'

She stopped short, staring at the coat on the wall, her eyes wide with fear. 'It was *that* coat!' The words came in a whsiper. 'That is the murderer's coat!'

'No need for alarm, Mrs Fanshaw. I think you're mistaken, but we'll soon make sure. Don't touch it, please.' Keeping one eye on Elsa he opened the communicating door.

'Miss Hackett! Will you kindly ask Mr Fanshaw to come here – and please come back with him yourself. And I'd be very grateful if you'd send someone to get Sergeant Boyce.'

Elsa was sitting at the desk. She was leaning back in the swivel chair her eyes closed. Thurtle thought might have fainted, and he touched her wrist. She opened her eyes as Julian came in. They waited in silence until Miss Hackett arrived, with Boyce.

Thurtle turned to Julian.

'Mr Fanshaw. This morning Miss Hackett made some notes for you on postcards. May I see the notated postcards, please?'

'Certainly.' He moved toward the desk.

'I put them in the breast pocket of your overcoat,' said Miss Hackett, annoyed because he had apparently forgotten.

'Then they'll still be there.' Julian felt in the breast pocket of the overcoat. As he withdrew his hand, empty, he touched the cloth, fingered it, then peered at it.

'This is not my overcoat!'

'Right! Stand away from it, please.'

The left side pocket bulged. Thurtle drew out a cleaning glove with a long cuff – fellow to the bloodstained glove found in the wastebasket in Ernest Fanshaw's office. From the folds of the glove a key fell to the floor. Thurtle picked it up with his handkerchief.

'Evidence, Inspector?' asked Julian.

'That's a left-hand glove. A right-hand glove, similar in every way, was found in your uncle's office, bloodstained.'

Thurtle lifted the coat from its peg, turned it, revealing the bloodstain near the second button.

'Better look at the hat, too, Mr Fanshaw.'

'Not mine! This one has initials on the inside band. *J.F.* – standing presumably for "Julian Fanshaw." I had no initials in my hat.'

Thurtle remembered that the hat he himself had taken from that peg had no initials. And that the overcoat had nothing in the side pockets, and no bloodstain.

'That's the murder coat, all right!' put in Boyce.

'Maybe. But there's a catch in it,' said Thurtle. 'It's not the coat and hat I examined in this room – hanging on that peg – in Miss Hackett's presence this morning.'

'A catch in it!' Julian laughed. 'You'll find the same catch in all your evidence, Inspector, until you admit you've made a fool of yourself in accusing me of faking my own double. To everyone else it will be obvious that he walked in here – as me – and planted that coat.'

'It's horrible!' cried Elsa. 'Things are creeping up behind us and strangling us. Julian, I told Inspector Thurtle that you were in Manchester that night and that the other man was with me.'

'That just about puts the lid on!' Julian dropped into a chair, straddlewise. 'Inspector, my wife has been torturing herself with this nightmare until she has come to believe it. I was *not* in Manchester – I was with her.'

'Miss Hackett!' boomed Thurtle over Elsa's protest. 'Can you contribute anything?'

'I can only say that Mr Fanshaw left the office with a suitcase at about two thirty on the Tuesday afternoon and that he returned with the suitcase at about three on Wednesday.'

'That doesn't prove that I went to Manchester. I changed my mind after leaving the office and put my suitcase in a cloakroom. I did so precisely because I was afraid my double might turn up and make love to Elsa.'

Thurtle glanced as Elsa and received the impression that she believed Julian.

'And where did you happen to be, Mr Fanshaw, between breakfast time and three o'clock on Wednesday?'

'Walking the streets of London in a state of advanced nervous depression, due to my wife's inability to tell me from another man – and in a general blue funk about this whole twin-brother-double business. Ask me if I met anybody. I didn't. I can't prove any of it. And I don't have to!'

To Elsa his outburst registered as a cry for help.

'I can help you prove you were with me – if you were, Julian. I told the Inspector everything we did. You've only to repeat it.'

'I don't see how that will help,' muttered Julian. 'But here goes. We dined at Blainley's. Brigstock and his wife saw us.'

'And after Blainley's, Julian?' Her eagerness revealed that she had changed ground and was ready to believe Julian had been with her in spite of everything, including the coat in the hall.

'After Blainley's we went to a show, but I can't remember which. Nothing sticks out in particular – there was the usual scramble to get out before the curtain calls, to make sure of the last train.'

The last train! There came a low moan from Elsa. Julian did not even know that they had gone from the theatre to a night club – and then on home in the car, long after the last train.

Without a word to anyone she walked out of the room, out of the suite. Julian abandoned a half-hearted attempt to follow her. He ignored the others, absorbed in his own thoughts.

'If you don't want me for anything else, Inspector, I'll get back to the chart room,' he said absently. 'All these upsets are putting me behind in my work.'

At five the various staffs began to leave. By half-past six Julian – still in the chart room wrestling with estimates – was the only office worker left in the building. Thurtle came in without knocking.

'We shan't be very long now,' he announced. 'There aren't many spots in this building where a man can hide himself.'

'I don't think you'll find him,' said Julian indifferently. 'He probably planted that coat in my room during lunch hour.'

Thurtle found himself staring at the long table, still cluttered with wall maps, as it had been when he first saw it. Why should a man want to take a lot of maps from the wall and jumble them all up on the table?

'During lunch hour – yes,' said Thurtle. 'But you planted the coat yourself. When you came into this room this morning from your uncle's office you hid that coat and hat under those maps there on the table. During lunch hour you carried the coat and hat into the other room in one of those big metal drawers, covering the top with papers to prevent the girl seeing anything.'

'You're letting this become an obsession, Thurtle. I thought you'd drop it after our little get-together with my wife – and the coat and the bloodstain and whatnot.'

'*And* the visit to Manchester,' said Thurtle. 'Were you in Manchester that night?'

'No.'

'Exactly! You tell us – truthfully – you were not in Manchester, because you know we could check. You tell your wife you were not in Manchester in such a way as to make her certain that you're lying. You worked up suspicion at home by dodging her test question. And this afternoon you *deliberately* fluffed – by leaving out that you went on to the Mignon night club and that you went home in your own car. Result:

she's ready to swear that she was in the company of the double!'

Julian stared at Thurtle. 'In short, everything I say and do is a fake – even if there's no evidence of a fake. You see what I mean by obsession? My dear fellow, talk it over with your sergeant! He'll tell you that the expert searching of this building is sheer footle. He'll tell you that my double planted the coat, removed mine, and then walked out of the building more or less disguised as a window cleaner.'

Thurtle looked blank. He had forgotten those window cleaners.

Julian went on, 'I don't suppose your men looked very closely at the window cleaners. Under your obsessional orders they were concentrating on me.'

Obsession! Thurtle admitted to himself that the word made him wince. He had certainly formed a theory early in the case – not that you could ever really string facts together without making a theory of some sort!

'If he got himself up as a window cleaner, what did he do with the coat and hat he took off your peg?'

'Obviously he hid them. You'll almost certainly find them somewhere in this office. Now I come to think of it there's a loose floorboard in my room – parallel with my desk and close to the back. It's been like that for years.'

Some five minutes later Julian was invited into his own room. Thurtle and Boyce stood by while one of the searchers raised the loose floorboard.

'What do you see, Mr Fanshaw?'

'My overcoat and hat, by the look of it.'

Thurtle bent down. There was a clearance of only about three inches between the floorboards and the reinforced concrete. The overcoat had been spread under the adjoining boards and the hat had been flattened. Thurtle coaxed the coat free and held it up.

'Is that your coat?'

'It appears to be. Try the pocket for those cards Miss Hackett put there.'

Thurtle withdrew with cards and recognised them from his previous inspection. He laid the coat on a chair and retrieved the hat.

'I'm glad I was right!' chirped Julian.

Boyce and the searchers left the room.

'May I have my hat and coat – they aren't evidence of anything, are they?'

Thurtle felt in the other pockets, which were empty, then handed over the coat. Julian took a clothes brush from a drawer and used it. Then he put on the coat and the hat.

'If I can't be of any further use to you, Inspector, I think I'll go home.'

'I can't stop you.'

'I gather the murderer has got clean away?'

Their eyes met. Thurtle could only see a man of iron nerve, stimulated by bravado – a man enjoying his own peril.

'Maybe he thinks he got clean away!'

'I have to remember that he will probably turn out to be my twin brother. All the same, I hope you catch him. But even if you don't it won't prove that he doesn't exist. I mean – how *can* you prove that a man does *not* exist? Think it over, Inspector. Good night!'

The police obtained an adjournment of the inquest after formal evidence had been given. Two days after the funeral Julian Fanshaw, as beneficiary under the reversion with an approximate value of £50,000, filed proof of his uncle's death. The Guardian Agency had received 34 answers to its advertisement in the *Times* and the police had checked the list without result.

'Looks like a dead case, Thurtle,' said the assistant commissioner – by which he meant that they had already obtained all the evidence that was obtainable. 'This twin business! I confess I'm keeping an open mind. Like you, of course, I always disbelieve those yarns about identical twins. But some of the yarns are true. Anyhow, we'll send the papers in and see what happens.'

The director of public prosecutions sent the papers back – but he sent with them one of the brighter members of his staff, a man named Mawson, to soften the blow.

'We can't charge Fanshaw as a principal, because we can't prove that the twin – or double – has no existence. Equally, he could not be charged as accessory, principal unknown, because there is no evidence that the two men ever met or communicated with each other.'

'Are you breaking it gently to us,' asked the assistant commissioner, 'that Fanshaw is going to get away with the murder?'

'That's my opinion – I'm not quoting anybody, mind! The strength of Fanshaw's position lies in the evidence his wife will give – that she let the other man spend the evening with her, believing him to be her husband.'

'But Fanshaw himself denies it,' objected Thurtle.

'Fanshaw denies it to you because you would check and prove he was not in Manchester. But at the trial Fanshaw would obviously exercise his right to *keep out of the witness box*. His wife's evidence would therefore stand. Without some rebutting evidence – which you cannot produce – her evidence would establish the existence of the – call him the Twin. That, in turn, would strengthen the already strong alibi given by Miss Hackett.'

Mawson bowed himself out, leaving the two officials in the dumps.

'The funny thing about these office lawyers, sir, is that after a few years of it they know a lot about the law and nothing about anything else, if you understand.'

'Got an idea, Thurtle?'

'You could hardly call it an idea, sir. I'm pretty sure the wife is playing straight – doesn't know she's being used. And I don't think she'll be very pleased when I tell her so.'

He went down to Rubington after lunch, trying to work out a tactful approach. It was a distasteful job. He thought of Elsa as a featherhead, but a good woman at heart who deserved a better man.

In the front yard of the Fanshaws' house was a real estate agent's notice advertising a sale by auction.

'Mr Thurtle!' She greeted him almost as an old friend. 'Have you some good news?'

'Nothing much. I've come down on the chance of picking up something from you.' He declined an offer of coffee and said it was too early for tea. 'I see you're moving?'

'It's awful here,' she admitted. 'People don't exactly cut us outright. But they simply don't believe in the twin.'

'You can't blame them,' he said sympathetically. 'You didn't altogether believe in him yourself after that first encounter at Blainley's. Did you?'

'I suppose I didn't, really. It's sort of too much to believe suddenly, isn't it?'

'But by the time of the Manchester incident you believed absolutely in a twin, didn't you?'

'Y-yes, I had to. But it was all loose ends. I didn't say "because this, therefore that" – the way you do. I had proved to my own satisfaction that it was not Julian who took me out that night. A couple of days later I sort of stood a long way off and looked at the whole thing. It seemed then that I couldn't possibly have mistaken another man for Julian. I believed one thing – then I believed the opposite – then back again. It was muddled and silly, but that was how I felt. And I don't mind telling you now that I thought the police were cheating.'

'Well, I'm jiggered! How did we manage to cheat?'

'I thought that you weren't really trying to find the twin because, like the local superintendent, you didn't really believe in him. So after a day or two I went to a private detective.'

'And he charged you a lot and told you nothing?'

'That's spiteful, Inspector,' she smiled. 'He only charged me three guineas and he refused to go on with the case after he had been to the hospital to inquire – where they made him believe that a mistake would have been impossible.'

That gave Thurtle an inspiration – the first one he had in the entire case.

'Don't mind my feelings,' he said. 'You were disappointed with us. And then you went to one of those agencies that offer to trace missing relatives?'

'How did you know?'

'Hasn't anyone ever told you that your policemen are wonderful? I can even give you the name. The Guardian Agency, in Tinbury.'

'I think that was the name. Only, you see, I didn't go. Nothing came of it because, before I had mailed the letter, Miss Hackett rang up telling me about Uncle Ernest. I knew then that you'd *have* to try and find him.'

'I'd like to know what you said to the agency. It might give me a new angle.'

'I didn't say much – the advertisement said to write for an appointment. Now that I think of it I don't remember tearing up the letter.'

She went to an escritoire. Thurtle held his breath while she opened a drawer and rummaged around. Then she looked under the blotter.

'Here it is. It's sealed but not stamped – I remember I didn't have a stamp.'

She handed him the envelope. He took out the letter.

Dear Sir: In answer to the enclosed advertisement in todays' Times—

Pinned to the notepaper was the advertisement, clumsily cut, with a jagged edge.

'Are you sure you cut it from the *Times*, as you say in the letter?'

'It's delivered here every morning. I cut it out before Julian took it to the office.'

Thurtle's sense of triumph was dampened by pity. There was still a nasty little bit of work to be done.

'I'm glad you happened to show me this, Mrs Fanshaw.' He took out his fountain pen. 'It's evidence, among other things, that you believed in the twin and were trying to help the police to find him. I'd like to show it to my chief. Just sign your name on the advertisement, will you – write it so that your signature runs over onto the notepaper.'

When she had signed he gently waved the paper to dry the ink – reflecting that there was no longer any means by which he could soften the blow that must come to her. He chattered himself out of the house.

On arriving at the Yard the Inspector was startled to learn that Mr Fanshaw had asked to see him and was in the waiting room. Ten minutes later – after Thurtle had checked the advertisement with the copy from which it had been cut – Julian was being shown in.

'Good afternoon, Inspector.' Julian's face was flushed and the heartiness was self-conscious. 'My wife rang me up to say you had seen her and that you were rather enthusiastic over a clipping from a newspaper.

Can I be of any help?'

'You can,' said Thurtle. 'On the day your uncle was murdered you left home carrying a copy of that day's *Times*. *Did you give that copy to your twin brother before eleven o'clock – so that he could use it while committing the murder?*'

Julian sighed. For a long moment he looked haggard, then he bucked back to heartiness.

'I guessed what had happened when she told me you'd made her sign the clipping. Odd thing, Inspector, I suddenly became terrified of Miss Hackett – thought I'd sneak round here and get it over with quietly. I'll sign a confession. But you've won on a fluke, you know.'

'Fluke be damned!' cried Thurtle. 'If you hadn't dragged your wife in as an unconscious accomplice – upset the poor girl's nerves by making her think you were in Manchester that night – she'd never have cut out that advertisement!'

Roald Dahl

Lamb to the Slaughter

The room was warm and clean, the curtains drawn, the two table lamps alight – hers and the one by the empty chair opposite. On the sideboard behind her, two tall glasses, soda water, whisky. Fresh ice cubes in the Thermos bucket.

Mary Maloney was waiting for her husband to come home from work.

Now and again she would glance up at the clock, but without anxiety, merely to please herself with the thought that each minute gone by made it nearer the time when he would come. There was a slow smiling air about her, and about everything she did. The drop of the head as she bent over her sewing was curiously tranquil. Her skin – for this was her sixth month with child – had acquired a wonderful translucent quality, the mouth was soft, and the eyes, with their new placid look, seemed larger, darker than before.

When the clock said ten minutes to five, she began to listen, and a few moments later, punctually as always, she heard the tyres on the gravel outside, and the car door slamming, the footsteps passing the window, the key turning in the lock. She laid aside her sewing, stood up, and went forward to kiss him as he came in.

'Hullo, darling,' she said.

'Hullo,' he answered.

She took his coat and hung it in the closet. Then she walked over and made the drinks, a strongish one for him, a weak one for herself; and soon she was back again in her chair with the sewing, and he in the other, opposite, holding the tall glass with both his hands, rocking it so the ice cubes tinkled against the side.

For her, this was always a blissful time of day. She knew he didn't want to speak much until the first drink was finished, and she, on her side, was content to sit quietly, enjoying his company after the long hours alone in the house. She loved to luxuriate in the presence of this man, and to feel – almost as a sunbather feels the sun – that warm male glow that came out of him to her when they were alone together. She loved him for the way he sat loosely in a chair, for the way he came in a door, or moved slowly across the room with long strides. She loved the intent, far look in his eyes when they rested on her, the funny shape of the mouth, and especially the way he remained silent about his tiredness, sitting still with himself until the whisky had taken some of it away.

'Tired, darling?'

'Yes,' he said. 'I'm tired.' And as he spoke, he did an unusual thing. He lifted his glass and drained it in one swallow although there was still half of it, at least half of it left. She wasn't really watching him, but she knew what he had done because she heard the ice cubes falling back against the bottom of the empty glass when he lowered his arm. He paused a moment, leaning forward in the chair, then he got up and went slowly over to fetch himself another.

'I'll get it!' she cried, jumping up.

'Sit down,' he said.

When he came back, she noticed that the new drink was dark amber with the quantity of whisky in it.

'Darling, shall I get your slippers?'

'No.'

She watched him as he began to sip the dark yellow drink, and she could see little oily swirls in the liquid because it was so strong.

'I think it's a shame,' she said, 'that when a policeman gets to be as senior as you, they keep him walking about on his feet all day long.'

He didn't answer, so she bent her head again and went on with her sewing; but each time he lifted the drink to his lips, she heard the ice cubes clinking against the side of the glass.

'Darling,' she said. 'Would you like me to get you some cheese? I haven't made any supper because it's Thursday.'

'No,' he said.

'If you're too tired to eat out,' she went on, 'it's still not too late. There's plenty of meat and stuff in the freezer, and you can have it right here and not even move out of the chair.'

Her eyes waited on him for an answer, a smile, a little nod, but he made no sign.

'Anyway,' she went on, 'I'll get you some cheese and crackers first.'

'I don't want it,' he said.

She moved uneasily in her chair, the large eyes still watching his face. 'But you *must* have supper. I can easily do it here. I'd like to do it. We can have lamb chops. Or pork. Anything you want. Everything's in the freezer.'

'Forget it,' he said.

'But, darling, you *must* eat! I'll fix it anyway, and then you can have it or not, as you like.'

She stood up and placed her sewing on the table by the lamp.

'Sit down,' he said. 'Just for a minute, sit down.'

It wasn't till then that she began to get frightened.

'Go on,' he said. 'Sit down.'

She lowered herself back slowly into the chair, watching him all the time with those large, bewildered eyes. He had finished the second drink and was staring down into the glass, frowning.

'Listen,' he said. 'I've got something to tell you.'

'What is it, darling? What's the matter?'

He had now become absolutely motionless, and he kept his head down so that the light from the lamp beside him fell across the upper part of his face, leaving the chin and mouth in shadow. She noticed there was a little muscle moving near the corner of his left eye.

'This is going to be a bit of a shock to you, I'm afraid,' he said. 'But I've thought about it a good deal and I've decided the only thing to do is tell you right away. I hope you won't blame me too much.'

And he told her. It didn't take long, four or five minutes at most, and she sat very still through it all, watching him with a kind of dazed horror as he went further and further away from her with each word.

'So there it is,' he added. 'And I know it's kind of a bad time to be telling you, but there simply wasn't any other way. Of course I'll give you money and see you're looked after. But there needn't really be any fuss. I hope not anyway. It wouldn't be very good for my job.'

Her first instinct was not to believe any of it, to reject it all. It occurred to her that perhaps he hadn't even spoken, that she herself had imagined the whole thing. Maybe, if she went about her business and acted as though she hadn't been listening, then later, when she sort of woke up again, she might find none of it had ever happened.

'I'll get the supper,' she managed to whisper, and this time he didn't stop her.

When she walked across the room she couldn't feel her feet touching the floor. She couldn't feel anything at all – except a slight nausea and a desire to vomit. Everything was automatic now – down the steps to the cellar, the light switch, the deep freeze, the hand inside the cabinet taking hold of the first object it met. She lifted it out, and looked at it. It was wrapped in paper, so she took off the paper and looked at it again.

A leg of lamb.

All right then, they would have lamb for supper. She carried it upstairs, holding the thin bone-end of it with both her hands, and as she went through the living-room, she saw him standing over by the window with his back to her, and she stopped.

'For God's sake,' he said, hearing her, but not turning round. 'Don't make supper for me. I'm going out.'

At that point, Mary Maloney simply walked up behind him and without any pause she swung the big frozen leg of lamb high in the air and brought it down as hard as she could on the back of his head.

She might just as well have hit him with a steel club.

She stepped back a pace, waiting, and the funny thing was that he remained standing there for at least four or five seconds, gently swaying. Then he crashed to the carpet.

The violence of the crash, the noise, the small table overturning, helped bring her out of the shock. She came out slowly, feeling cold and surprised, and she stood for a while blinking at the body, still holding the ridiculous piece of meat tight with both hands.

All right, she told herself. So I've killed him.

It was extraordinary, now, how clear her mind became all of a sudden. She began thinking very fast. As the wife of a detective, she knew quite well what the penalty would be. That was fine. It made no difference to her. In fact, it would be a relief. On the other hand, what about the child? What were the laws about murderers with unborn children? Did they kill them both – mother and child? Or did they wait until the tenth month? What did they do?

Mary Maloney didn't know. And she certainly wasn't prepared to take a chance.

She carried the meat into the kitchen, placed it in a pan, turned the oven on high, and shoved it inside. Then she washed her hands and ran upstairs to the bedroom. She sat down before the mirror, tidied her face, touched up her lips and face. She tried a smile. It came out rather peculiar. She tried again.

'Hullo Sam,' she said brightly, aloud.

The voice sounded peculiar too.

'I want some potatoes please, Sam. Yes, and I think a can of peas.'

That was better. Both the smile and the voice were coming out better now. She rehearsed it several times more. Then she ran downstairs, took her coat, went out the back door, down the garden, into the street.

It wasn't six o'clock yet and the lights were still on in the grocery shop.

'Hullo Sam,' she said brightly, smiling at the man behind the counter.

'Why, good evening, Mrs Maloney. How're *you*?'

'I want some potatoes please, Sam. Yes, and I think a can of peas.'

The man turned and reached up behind him on the shelf for the peas.

'Patrick's decided he's tired and doesn't want to eat out tonight,' she told him. 'We usually go out Thursdays, you know, and now he's caught me without any vegetables in the house.'

'Then how about meat, Mrs Maloney?'

'No, I've got meat, thanks. I got a nice leg of lamb, from the freezer.'

'Oh.'

'I don't much like cooking it frozen, Sam, but I'm taking a chance on it this time. You think it'll be all right?'

'Personally,' the grocer said, 'I don't believe it makes any difference. You want these Idaho potatoes?'

'Oh yes, that'll be fine. Two of those.'

'Anything else?' The grocer cocked his head on one side, looking at her pleasantly. 'How about afterwards? What you going to give him for afterwards?'

'Well – what would you suggest, Sam?'

The man glanced around his shop. 'How about a nice big slice of cheesecake? I know he likes that.'

'Perfect,' she said. 'He loves it.'

And when it was all wrapped and she had paid, she put on her brightest smile and said, 'Thank you, Sam. Good night.'

'Good night, Mrs Maloney. And thank *you*.'

And now, she told herself as she hurried back, all she was doing now, she was returning home to her husband and he was waiting for his supper; and she must cook it good, and make it as tasty as possible because the poor man was tired; and if, when she entered the house, she happened to find anything unusual, or tragic, or terrible, then naturally it would be a shock and she'd become frantic with grief and horror. Mind you, she wasn't *expecting* to find anything. She was just going home with the vegetables. Mrs Patrick Maloney going home with the vegetables on Thursday evening to cook supper for her husband.

That's the way, she told herself. Do everything right and natural. Keep things absolutely natural and there'll be no need for any acting at all.

Therefore, when she entered the kitchen by the back door, she was humming a little tune to herself and smiling.

'Patrick!' she called. 'How are you, darling?'

She put the parcel down on the table and went through into the living-room; and when she saw him lying there on the floor with his legs doubled up and one arm twisted back underneath his body, it really was rather a shock. All the old love and longing for him welled up inside her, and she ran over to him, knelt down beside him, and began to cry her heart out. It was easy. No acting was necessary.

A few minutes later she got up and went to the phone. She knew the number of the police station, and when the man at the other end answered, she cried to him, 'Quick! Come quick! Patrick's dead!'

'Who's speaking?'

'Mrs Maloney. Mrs Patrick Maloney.'

'You mean Patrick Maloney's dead?'

'I think so,' she sobbed. 'He's lying on the floor and I think he's dead.'

'Be right over,' the man said.

The car came quickly, and when she opened the front door, two policemen walked in. She knew them both – she knew nearly all the men at the precinct – and she fell right into Jack Noonan's arms, weeping hysterically. He put her gently into a chair, then went over to join the other one, who was called O'Malley, kneeling by the body.

'Is he dead?' she cried.

'I'm afraid he is. What happened?'

Briefly, she told her story about going out to the grocer and coming back to find him on the floor. While she was talking, crying and talking, Noonan discovered a small patch of congealed blood on the dead man's head. He showed it to O'Malley who got up at once and hurried to the phone.

Soon, other men began to come into the house. First a doctor, then two detectives, one of whom she knew by name. Later, a police photographer arrived and took pictures, and a man who knew about fingerprints. There was a great deal of whispering and muttering beside the corpse, and the detectives kept asking her a lot of questions. But they always treated her kindly. She told her story again, this time right from the beginning, when Patrick had come in, and she was sewing, and he was tired, so tired he hadn't wanted to go out for supper. She told how she'd put the meat in the oven – 'it's there now, cooking' – and how she'd slipped out to the grocer for vegetables, and come back to find him lying on the floor.

'Which grocer?' one of the detectives asked.

She told him, and he turned and whispered something to the other detective who immediately went outside into the street.

In fifteen minutes he was back with a page of notes, and there was more whispering, and through her sobbing she heard a few of the whispered phrases – '. . . acted quite normal . . . very cheerful . . . wanted to give him a good supper . . . peas . . . cheesecake . . . impossible that she . . .'

After a while, the photographer and the doctor departed and two other men came in and took the corpse away on a stretcher. Then the finger-print man went away. The two detectives remained, and so did the two policeman. They were exceptionally nice to her, and Jack Noonan asked if she wouldn't rather go somewhere else, to her sister's house perhaps, or to his own wife who would take care of her and put her up for the night.

No, she said. She didn't feel she could move even a yard at the moment. Would they mind awfully if she stayed just where she was until she felt better? She didn't feel too good at the moment, she really didn't.

Then hadn't she better lie down on the bed? Jack Noonan asked.

No, she said. She'd like to stay right where she was, in this chair. A little later perhaps, when she felt better, she would move.

So they left her there while they went about their business, searching the house. Occasionally one of detectives asked her another question. Sometimes Jack Noonan spoke to her gently as he passed. Her husband, he told her, had been killed by a blow on the back of the head administered with a heavy blunt instrument, almost certainly a large piece of metal. They were looking for the weapon. The murderer may have taken it with him, but on the other hand he may've thrown it away or hidden it somewhere on the premises.

'It's the old story,' he said. 'Get the weapon, and you've got the man.'

Later, one of the detectives came up and sat beside her. Did she know, he asked, of anything in the house that could've been used as the weapon? Would she mind having a look around to see if anything was missing – a very big spanner, for example, or a heavy metal vase.

They didn't have any metal vases, she said.

'Or a big spanner?'

She didn't think they had a big spanner. But there might be some things like that in the garage.

The search went on. She knew that there were other policemen in the garden all around the house. She could hear their footsteps on the gravel outside, and sometimes she saw the flash of a torch through a chink in the curtains. It began to get late, nearly nine she noticed by the clock on the mantel. The four men searching the rooms seemed to be growing weary, a trifle exasperated.

'Jack,' she said, the next time Sergeant Noonan went by. 'Would you mind giving me a drink?'

'Sure I'll give you a drink. You mean this whisky?'

'Yes, please. But just a small one. It might make me feel better.'

He handed her the glass.

'Why don't you have one yourself,' she said. 'You must be awfully tired. Please do. You've been very good to me.'

'Well,' he answered. 'It's not strictly allowed, but I might take just a drop to keep me going.'

One by one the others came in and were persuaded to take a little nip of whisky. They stood around rather awkwardly with the drinks in their hands, uncomfortable in her presence, trying to say consoling things to her. Sergeant Noonan wandered into the kitchen, came out quickly and said, 'Look, Mrs Maloney. You know that oven of yours is still on, and the meat still inside.'

'Oh *dear* me!' she cried. 'So it is!'

'I better turn it off for you, hadn't I?'

'Will you do that, Jack. Thank you so much.'

When the sergeant returned the second time, she looked at him with her large, dark, tearful eyes. 'Jack Noonan,' she said.

'Yes?'

'Would you do me a small favour – you and these others?'

'We can try, Mrs Maloney.'

'Well,' she said. 'Here you all are, and good friends of dear Patrick's too, and helping to catch the man who killed him. You must be terrible hungry by now because it's long past your supper time, and I know Patrick would never forgive me, God bless his soul, if I allowed you to remain in his house without offering you decent hospitality. Why don't you eat up that lamb that's in the oven? It'll be cooked just right by now.'

'Wouldn't dream of it,' Sergeant Noonan said.

'Please,' she begged. 'Please eat it. Personally I couldn't touch a thing, certainly not what's been in the house when he was here. But it's all right for you. It'd be a favour to me if you'd eat it up. Then you can go on with your work again afterwards.'

There was a good deal of hesitating among the four policemen, but they were clearly hungry, and in the end they were persuaded to go into the kitchen and help themselves. The woman stayed where she was, listening to them through the open door, and she could hear them speaking among themselves, their voices thick and sloppy because their mouths were full of meat.

'Have some more Charlie?'

'No. Better not finish it.'

'She *wants* us to finish it. She said so. Be doing her a favour.'

'Okay then. Give me some more.'

'That's the hell of a big club the guy must've used to hit poor Patrick,' one of them was saying. 'The doc says his skull was smashed all to pieces just like from a sledge-hammer.'

'That's why it ought to be easy to find.'

'Exactly what I say.'

'Whoever done it, they're not going to be carrying a thing like that around with them longer than they need.'

One of them belched.

'Personally, I think it's right here on the premises.'

'Probably right under our very noses. What you think, Jack?'

And in the other room, Mary Maloney began to giggle.

Roald Dahl

The Way up to Heaven

All her life, Mrs Foster had had an almost pathological fear of missing a train, a plane, a boat, or even a theatre curtain. In other respects, she was not a particularly nervous woman, but the mere thought of being late on occasions like these would throw her into such a state of nerves that she would begin to twitch. It was nothing much – just a tiny vellicating muscle in the corner of the left eye, like a secret wink – but the annoying thing was that it refused to disappear until an hour or so after the train or plane or whatever it was had been safely caught.

It was really extraordinary how in certain people a simple apprehension about a thing like catching a train can grow into a serious obsession. At least half an hour before it was time to leave the house for the station, Mrs Foster would step out of the elevator all ready to go, with hat and coat and gloves, and then, being quite unable to sit down, she would flutter and fidget about from room to room until her husband, who must have been well aware of her state, finally emerged from his privacy and suggested in a cool dry voice that perhaps they had better get going now, had they not?

Mr Foster may possibly have had a right to be irritated by this foolishness of his wife's, but he could have had no excuse for increasing her misery by keeping her waiting unnecessarily. Mind you, it is by no means certain that this is what he did, yet whenever they were to go somewhere, his timing was so accurate – just a minute or two late, you understand – and his manner so bland that it was hard to believe he wasn't purposely inflicting a nasty private little torture of his own on the unhappy lady. And one thing he must have known – that she would never dare to call out and tell him to hurry. He had disciplined her too well for that. He must also have known that if he was prepared to wait even beyond the last moment of safety, he could drive her nearly into hysterics. On one or two special occasions in the later years of their married life, it seemed almost as though he had *wanted* to miss the train simply in order to intensify the poor woman's suffering.

Assuming (though one cannot be sure) that the husband was guilty, what made his attitude doubly unreasonable was the fact that, with the exception of this one small irrepressible foible, Mrs Foster was and always had been a good and loving wife. For over thirty years, she had served him loyally and well. There was no doubt about this. Even she, a very modest woman, was aware of it, and although she had for years refused to let herself believe that Mr Foster would ever consciously torment her, there had been times recently when she had caught herself beginning to wonder.

Mr Eugene Foster, who was nearly seventy years old, lived with his wife in a large six-storey house in New York City, on East Sixty-second Street, and they had four servants. It was a gloomy place, and few people came to visit them. But on this particular morning in January, the house had come alive and there was a great deal of bustling about. One maid was distributing bundles of dust sheets to every room, while another was draping them over the furniture. The butler was bringing down suit-cases and putting them in the hall. The cook kept popping up from the kitchen to have a word with the butler, and Mrs Foster herself, in an old-fashioned fur coat and with a black hat on the top of her head, was flying from room to room and pretending to supervise these operations. Actually, she was thinking of nothing at all except that she was going to miss her plane if her husband didn't come out of his study soon and get ready.

'What time is it, Walker?' she said to the butler as she passed him.

'It's ten minutes past nine, Madam.'

'And has the car come?'

'Yes, Madam, it's waiting. I'm just going to put the luggage in now.'

'It takes an hour to get to Idlewild,' she said. 'My plane leaves at eleven. I have to be there half an hour beforehand for the formalities. I shall be late, I just *know* I'm going to be late.'

'I think you have plenty of time, Madam,' the butler said kindly. 'I warned Mr Foster that you must leave at nine fifteen. There's still another five minutes.'

'Yes, Walker, I know, I know. But get the luggage in quickly, will you please?'

She began walking up and down the hall, and whenever the butler came by, she asked him the time. This, she kept telling herself, was the *one* plane she must not miss. It had taken months to persuade her husband to allow her to go. If she missed it, he might easily decide that she should cancel the whole thing. And the trouble was that he insisted on coming to the airport to see her off.

'Dear God,' she said aloud, 'I'm going to miss it. I know, I know, I *know* I'm going to miss it.' The little muscle beside the left eye was twitching madly now. The eyes themselves were very close to tears.

'What time is it, Walker?'

'It's eighteen minutes past, Madam.'

'Now I really *will* miss it!' she cried. 'Oh, I wish he would come!'

This was an important journey for Mrs Foster. She was going all alone to Paris to visit her daughter, her only child, who was married to a Frenchman. Mrs Foster didn't care much for the Frenchman, but she was fond of her daughter, and, more than that, she had developed a great yearning to set eyes on her three grandchildren. She knew them only from the many photographs that she had received and that she kept putting up all over the house. They were beautiful, these children. She doted on them, and each time a new picture arrived she would carry it away and sit with it for a long time, staring at it lovingly and searching the small faces for signs of that old satisfying blood likeness that meant so much. And now, lately, she had come more and more to feel that she did not really wish to live out her days in a place where she could not be near these children, and have them visit her, and take them for walks, and buy them presents, and watch them grow. She knew, of course, that it was wrong and in a way disloyal to have thoughts like these while her husband was still alive. She knew also that although he was no longer active in his many enterprises, he would never consent to leave New York and live in Paris. It was a miracle that he had ever agreed to let her fly over there alone for six weeks to visit them. But, oh, how she wished she could live there always, and be close to them!

'Walker, what time is it?'

'Twenty-two minutes past, Madam.'

As he spoke, a door opened and Mr Foster came into the hall. He stood for a moment, looking intently at his wife, and she looked back at him – at this diminutive but still quite dapper old man with the huge bearded face that bore such an astonishing resemblance to those old photographs of Andrew Carnegie.

'Well,' he said, 'I suppose perhaps we'd better get going fairly soon if you want to catch that plane.'

'*Yes*, dear – *yes!* Everything's ready. The car's waiting.'

'That's good,' he said. With his head over to one side, he was watching her closely. He had a peculiar way of cocking the head and then moving it in a series of small, rapid jerks. Because of this and because he was clasping his hands up high in front of him, near the chest, he was somehow like a squirrel standing there – a quick clever old squirrel from the Park.

'Here's Walker with your coat, dear. Put it on.'

'I'll be with you in a moment,' he said. 'I'm just going to wash my hands.'

She waited for him, and the tall butler stood beside her, holding the coat and the hat.

'Walker, will I miss it?'

'No, Madam,' the butler said. 'I think you'll make it all right.'

Then Mr Foster appeared again, and the butler helped him on with his coat. Mrs Foster hurried outside and got into the hired Cadillac. Her husband came after her, but he walked down the steps of the house slowly, pausing halfway to observe the sky and to sniff the cold morning air.

'It looks a bit foggy,' he said as he sat down beside her in the car. 'And it's always worse out there at the airport. I shouldn't be surprised if the flight's cancelled already.'

'Don't say that, dear – *please.*'

They didn't speak again until the car had crossed over the river to Long Island.

'I arranged everything with the servants,' Mr Foster said. 'They're all going off today. I gave them half pay for six weeks and told Walker I'd send him a telegram when we wanted them back.'

'Yes,' she said. 'He told me.'

'I'll move into the club tonight. It'll be a nice change staying at the club.'

'Yes, dear. I'll write to you.'

'I'll call in at the house occasionally to see that everything's all right and to pick up the mail.'

'But don't you really think Walker should stay there all the time to look after things?' she asked meekly.

'Nonsense. It's quite unnecessary. And anyway, I'd have to pay him full wages.'

'Oh yes,' she said. 'Of course.'

'What's more, you never know what people get up to when they're left alone in a house,' Mr Foster announced, and with that he took out a cigar and, after snipping off the end with a silver cutter, lit it with a gold lighter.

She sat still in the car with her hands clasped together tight under the rug.

'Will you write to me?' she asked.

'I'll see,' he said. 'But I doubt it. You know I don't hold with letter-writing unless there's something specific to say.'

'Yes, dear, I know. So don't you bother.'

They drove on, along Queens Boulevard, and as they approached the flat marshland on which Idlewild is built, the fog began to thicken and the car had to slow down.

'Oh dear!' cried Mrs Foster. 'I'm *sure* I'm going to miss it now! What time is it?'

'Stop fussing,' the old man said. 'It doesn't matter anyway. It's bound to be cancelled now. They never fly in this sort of weather. I don't know why you bothered to come out.'

She couldn't be sure, but it seemed to her that there was suddenly a note in his voice, and she turned to look at him. It was difficult to observe any change in his expression under all that hair. The mouth was what counted. She wished, as she had so often before, that she could see the mouth clearly. The eyes never showed anything except when he was in a rage.

'Of course,' he went on, 'if by any chance it *does* go, then I agree with you – you'll be certain to miss it now. Why don't you resign yourself to that?'

She turned away and peered through the window at the fog. It seemed to be getting thicker as they went along, and now she could only just make out the edge of the road and the margin of grassland beyond it. She knew that her husband was still looking at her. She glanced at him again, and this time she noticed with a kind of horror that he was staring intently at the little place in the corner of her left eye where she could feel the muscle twitching.

'Won't you?' he said.

'Won't I what?'

'Be sure to miss it now if it goes. We can't drive fast in this muck.'

He didn't speak to her any more after that. The car crawled on and on. The driver had a yellow lamp directed on to the edge of the road, and this helped him to keep going. Other lights, some white and some yellow, kept coming out of the fog towards them, and there was an especially bright one that followed close behind them all the time.

Suddenly, the driver stopped the car.

'There!' Mr Foster cried. 'We're stuck. I knew it.'

'No, sir,' the driver said, turning round. 'We made it. This is the airport.'

Without a word, Mrs Foster jumped out and hurried through the main entrance into the building. There was a mass of people inside, mostly disconsolate passengers standing around the ticket counters. She pushed her way through and spoke to the clerk.

'Yes,' he said. 'Your flight is temporarily postponed. But please don't go away. We're expecting this weather to clear any moment.'

She went back to her husband who was still sitting in the car and told him the news. 'But don't you wait, dear,' she said. 'There's no sense in that.'

'I won't,' he answered. 'So long as the driver can get me back. Can you get me back, driver?'

'I think so,' the man said.

'Is the luggage out?'

'Yes, sir.'

'Good-bye, dear,' Mrs Foster said, leaning into the car and giving her husband a small kiss on the coarse grey fur of his cheek.

'Good-bye,' he answered. 'Have a good trip.'

The car drove off, and Mrs Foster was left alone.

The rest of the day was a sort of nightmare for her. She sat for hour after hour on a bench, as close to the airline counter as possible, and every thirty minutes or so she would get up and ask the clerk if the situation had changed. She always received the same reply – that she must continue to wait, because the fog might blow away at any moment. It wasn't until after six in the evening that the loudspeaker finally announced that the flight had been postponed until eleven o'clock the next morning.

Mrs Foster didn't quite know what to do when she heard this news. She stayed sitting on her bench for at least another half-hour, wondering, in a tired, hazy sort of way, where she might go to spend the night. She hated to leave the airport. She didn't wish to see her husband. She was terrified that in one way or another he would eventually manage to prevent her from getting to France. She would have liked to remain just where she was, sitting on the bench the whole night through. That would be the safest. But she was already exhausted, and it didn't take her long to realise that this was a ridiculous thing for an elderly lady to do. So in the end she went to a phone and called the house.

Her husband, who was on the point of leaving for the club, answered it himself. She told him the news, and asked whether the servants were still there.

'They've all gone,' he said.

'In that case, dear, I'll just get myself a room somewhere for the night. And don't you bother yourself about it at all.'

'That would be foolish,' he said. 'You've got a large house here at your disposal. Use it.'

'But, dear, it's *empty*.'

'Then I'll stay with you myself.'

'There's no food in the house. There's nothing.'

'Then eat before you come in. Don't be so stupid, woman. Everything you do, you seem to want to make a fuss about it all.'

'Yes,' she said. 'I'm sorry. I'll get myself a sandwich here, and then I'll come on in.'

Outside, the fog had cleared a little, but it was still a long, slow drive in the taxi, and she didn't arrive back at the house on Sixty-second Street until fairly late.

Her husband emerged from his study when he heard her coming in. 'Well,' he said, standing by the study door, 'how was Paris?'

'We leave at eleven in the morning,' she answered. 'It's definite.'

'You mean if the fog clears.'

'It's clearing now. There's a wind coming up.'

'You look tired,' he said. 'You must have had an anxious day.'

'It wasn't very comfortable. I think I'll go straight to bed.'

'I've ordered a car for the morning,' he said. 'Nine o'clock.'

'Oh, thank you, dear. And I certainly hope you're not going to bother to come all the way out again to see me off.'

'No,' he said slowly. 'I don't think I will. But there's no reason why you shouldn't drop me at the club on your way.'

She looked at him, and at that moment he seemed to be standing a long way off from her, beyond some borderline. He was suddenly so small and far away that she couldn't be sure what he was doing, or what he was thinking, or even what he was.

'The club is downtown,' she said. 'It isn't on the way to the airport.'

'But you'll have plenty of time, my dear. Don't you want to drop me at the club?'

'Oh, yes – of course.'

'That's good. Then I'll see you in the morning at nine.'

She went up to her bedroom on the second floor, and she was so exhausted from her day that she fell asleep soon after she lay down.

Next morning, Mrs Foster was up early, and by eight thirty she was downstairs and ready to leave.

Shortly after nine, her husband appeared. 'Did you make any coffee?' he asked.

'No, dear. I thought you'd get a nice breakfast at the club. The car is here. It's been waiting. I'm all ready to go.'

They were standing in the hall – they always seemed to be meeting in the hall nowadays – she with her hat and coat and purse, he in a curiously cut Edwardian jacket with high lapels.

'Your luggage?'

'It's at the airport.'

'Ah yes,' he said. 'Of course. And if you're going to take me to the club first, I suppose we'd better get going fairly soon, hadn't we?'

'Yes!' she cried. 'Oh, yes – *please!*'

'I'm just going to get a few cigars. I'll be right with you. You get in the car.'

She turned and went out to where the chauffeur was standing, and he opened the car door for her as she approached.

'What time is it?' she asked him.

'About nine fifteen.'

Mr Foster came out five minutes later, and watching him as he walked slowly down the steps, she noticed that his legs were like goat's legs in those narrow stovepipe trousers that he wore. As on the day before, he paused halfway down to sniff the air and to examine the sky. The weather was still not quite clear, but there was a wisp of sun coming through the mist.

'Perhaps you'll be lucky this time,' he said as he settled himself beside her in the car.

'Hurry, please,' she said to the chauffeur. 'Don't bother about the rug. I'll arrange the rug. Please get going. I'm late.'

The man went back to his seat behind the wheel and started the engine.

'*Just* a moment!' Mr Foster said suddenly. 'Hold it a moment, chauffeur, will you?'

'What is it, dear?' She saw him searching the pockets of his overcoat.

'I had a little present I wanted you to take to Ellen,' he said. 'Now, where on earth is it? I'm sure I had it in my hand as I came down.'

'I never saw you carrying anything. What sort of present?'

'A little box wrapped up in white paper. I forgot to give it to you yesterday. I don't want to forget it today.'

'A little box!' Mrs Foster cried. 'I never saw any little box!' She began hunting frantically in the back of the car.

Her husband continued searching through the pockets of his coat. Then he unbuttoned the coat and felt around in his jacket. 'Confound it,' he said, 'I must've left it in my bedroom. I won't be a moment.'

'Oh, *please!*' she cried. 'We haven't got time! *Please* leave it! You can mail it. It's only one of those silly combs anyway. You're always giving her combs.'

'And what's wrong with combs, may I ask?' he said, furious that she should have forgotten herself for once.

'Nothing, dear I'm sure. But . . .'

'Stay here!' he commanded. 'I'm going to get it.'

'Be quick, dear! Oh, *please* be quick!'

She sat still, waiting and waiting.

'Chauffeur, what time is it?'

The man had a wristwatch, which he consulted. 'I make it nearly nine-thirty.'

'Can we get to the airport in an hour?'

'Just about.'

At this point, Mrs Foster suddenly spotted a corner of something white wedged down in the crack of the seat on the side where her husband had been sitting. She reached over and pulled out a small paper-wrapped box, and at the same time she couldn't help noticing that it was wedged down firm and deep, as though with the help of a pushing hand.

'Here it is!' she cried. 'I've found it! Oh dear, and now he'll be up there for ever searching for it! Chauffeur, quickly – run in and call him down, will you please?'

The chauffeur, a man with a small rebellious Irish mouth, didn't care very much for any of this, but he climbed out of the car and went up the steps to the front door of the house. Then he turned and came back. 'Door's locked,' he announced. 'You got a key?'

'Yes – wait a minute.' She began hunting madly in her purse. The little face was screwed up tight with anxiety, the lips pushed outward like a spout.

'Here it is! No – I'll go myself. It'll be quicker. I know where he'll be.'

She hurried out of the car and up the steps to the front door, holding the key in one hand. She slid the key into the keyhole and was about to turn it – and then she stopped. Her head came up, and she stood there absolutely motionless, her whole body arrested right in the middle of all this hurry to turn the key and get into the house, and she waited – five, six, seven, eight, nine, ten seconds, she waited. The way she was standing there, with her head in the air and the body so tense, it seemed as though she were listening for the repetition of some sound that she had heard a moment before from a place far away inside the house.

Yes – quite obviously she was listening. Her whole attitude was a *listening* one. She appeared actually to be moving one of her ears closer to the door. Now it was right up against the door, and for still another few seconds she remained in that position, head up, ear to door, hand on key, about to enter but not entering, trying instead, or so it seemed, to hear and to analyse these sounds that were coming faintly from this place deep within the house.

Then, all at once, she sprang to life again. She withdrew the key from the door and came running back down the steps.

'It's too late!' she cried to the chauffeur. 'I can't wait for him, I simply can't. I'll miss the plane. Hurry now, driver, hurry! To the airport!'

The chauffeur, had he been watching her closely, might have noticed that her face had turned absolutely white and that the whole expression had suddenly altered. There was no longer that rather soft and silly look. A peculiar hardness had settled itself upon the features. The little mouth, usually so flabby, was now tight and thin, the eyes were bright, and the voice, when she spoke, carried a new note of authority.

'Hurry, driver, hurry!'

'Isn't your husband travelling with you?' the man asked, astonished.

'Certainly not! I was only going to drop him at the club. It won't matter. He'll understand. He'll get a cab. Don't sit there talking, man. *Get going!* I've got a plane to catch for Paris!'

With Mrs Foster urging him from the back seat, the man drove fast all the way, and she caught her plane with a few minutes to spare. Soon she was high up over the Atlantic, reclining comfortably in her aeroplane chair, listening to the hum of the motors, heading for Paris at last. The new mood was still with her. She felt remarkably strong and, in a queer sort of way, wonderful. She was a trifle breathless with it all, but this was more from pure astonishment at what she had done than anything else, and as the plane flew farther and farther away from New York and East Sixty-second Street, a great sense of calmness began to settle upon her. By the time she reached Paris, she was just as strong and cool and calm as she could wish.

She met her grandchildren, and they were even more beautiful in the flesh than in their photographs. They were like angels, she told herself, so beautiful they were. And every day she took them for walks, and fed them cakes, and bought them presents, and told them charming stories.

Once a week, on Tuesdays, she wrote a letter to her husband – a nice, chatty letter – full of news and gossip, which always ended with the words 'Now be sure to take your meals regularly, dear, although this is something I'm afraid you may not be doing when I'm not with you.'

When the six weeks were up, everybody was sad that she had to return to America, to her husband. Everybody, that is, except her. Surprisingly, she didn't seem to mind as much as one might have expected, and when she kissed them all good-bye, there was something in her manner and in the things she said that appeared to hint at the possibility of a return in the not too distant future.

However, like the faithful wife she was, she did not overstay her time. Exactly six weeks after she had arrived, she sent a cable to her husband and caught the plane back to New York.

Arriving at Idlewild, Mrs Foster was interested to observe that there was no car to meet her. It is possible that she might even have been a little amused. But she was extremely calm and did not overtip the porter who helped her into a taxi with her baggage.

New York was colder than Paris, and there were lumps of dirty snow lying in the gutters of the streets. The taxi drew up before the house on Sixty-second Street, and Mrs Foster persuaded the driver to carry her two large cases to the top of the steps. Then she paid him off and rang the bell. She waited, but there was no answer. Just to make sure, she rang again, and she could hear it tinkling shrilly far away in the pantry, at the back of the house. But still no one came.

So she took out her own key and opened the door herself.

The first thing she saw as she entered was a great pile of mail lying on the floor where it had fallen after being slipped through the letter box. The place was dark and cold. A dust sheet was still draped over the grandfather clock. In spite of the cold, the atmosphere was peculiarly oppressive, and there was a faint and curious odour in the air that she had never smelled before.

She walked quickly across the hall and disappeared for a moment around the corner to the left, at the back. There was something deliberate and purposeful about this action; she had the air of a woman who is off to investigate a rumour or to confirm a suspicion. And when she returned a few seconds later, there was a little glimmer of satisfaction on her face.

She paused in the centre of the hall, as though wondering what to do next. Then, suddenly, she turned and went across into her husband's study. On the desk she found his address book, and after hunting through it for a while she picked up the phone and dialled a number.

'Hello,' she said. 'Listen – this is Nine East Sixty-second Street. . . . Yes, that's right. Could you send someone round as soon as possible, do you think? Yes, it seems to be stuck between the second and third floors. At least, that's where the indicator's pointing. . . . Right away? Oh, that's very kind of you. You see, my legs aren't any good for walking up a lot of stairs. Thank you so much. Good-bye.'

She replaced the receiver and sat there at her husband's desk, patiently waiting for the man who would be coming soon to repair the lift.

Avram Davidson

The Necessity of his Condition

Sholto Hill was mostly residential property, but it had its commercial district in the shape of Persimmon Street and Rampart Street, the latter named after some long-forgotten barricade stormed and destroyed by Benedict Arnold (wearing a British uniform and eaten with bitterness and perverted pride). Persimmon Street, running up-slope, entered the middle of Rampart at right angles, and went no farther. This section, with its red brick houses and shops, its warehouses and offices, was called the T, and it smelled of tobacco and potatoes and molasses and goober peas and dried fish and beer and cheap cookshop food and (the spit-and-whittle humourists claimed) old man Bailiss' office, where the windows were never opened – never had *been* opened, they said, never were *made* to be opened. Any smell off the street or farms or stables that found its way up to Bailiss' office was imprisoned there for life, they said. Old man Bailiss knew what they said, knew pretty much everything that went on anywhere; but he purely didn't care. He didn't have to, they said.

J. Bailiss, Attorney-at-Law (his worn old sign said), had a large practice and little competition. James Bailiss, Broker (his newer, but by no means new, sign), did an extensive business; again, with little competition. The premises of the latter business were located, not in the T, but in a whitewashed stone structure with thick doors and barred windows, down in the Bottom – as it was called – near the river, the canal, and the railroad line.

James Bailiss, Broker, was not received socially. Nobody expected that bothered him much. Nothing bothered old man Bailiss much – Bailiss, with his old white hat and his old black coat and his old cowhide shoes that looked old even when they were new – turned old on the

447

shoemaker's last (the spit-and-whittle crowd claimed) directly they heard whose feet they were destined for.

It was about twenty-five years earlier, in 1825, that an advertisement – the first of its kind – appeared in the local newspaper.

'*Take Notice!* (it began). James Bailiss, having lately purchased the old arsenal building on Canal Street, will henceforth operate it as a Negro Depot. He will at all times be found ready to purchase all good and likely young Negroes at the Highest Price. He will also attend to Selling Negroes on Commission. Said Broker also gives Notice that those who have Slaves rendered unfit for labour by yaws, scrofula, chronic consumption, rheumatism, & C., may dispose of them to him on reasonable terms.'

Editor Winstanley tried to dissuade him, he said later. 'Folks,' he told him, 'won't like this. This has never been said out open before,' the editor pointed out. Bailiss smiled. He was already middle-aged, had a shiny red face and long mousy hair. His smile wasn't a very wide one.

'Then I reckon I must be the pioneer,' he said. 'This isn't a big plantation state, it never will be. I've give the matter right much thought. I reckon it just won't pay for anyone to own more than half a dozen slaves in these parts. But they will multiply, you can't stop it. I've seen it in my law work, seen many a planter broke for debts he's gone into to buy field hands – signed notes against his next crop, or maybe even his next three crops. Then maybe the crop is so good that the price of cotton goes way down and he can't meet his notes, so he loses his lands *and* his slaves. If the price of cotton should happen to be high enough or him to pay for the slaves he's bought, then, like a dumned fool' – Bailiss never swore – 'why, he signs notes for a few more. Pretty soon things get so bad you can't *giv* slaves away round here. So a man has a dozen of them eating their heads off and not even earning grocery bills. No, Mr Winstanley; slaves must be sold south and southwest, where the new lands are being opened up, where the big plantations are.'

Editor Winstanley wagged his head. 'I know,' he said, 'I know. But folks don't like to say things like that out loud. The slave trade is looked down on. You know that. It's a necessary evil, that's how it's regarded, like a – well . . .' He lowered his voice. 'Nothing personal, but . . . like a sporting house. Nothing personal, now, Mr Bailiss.'

The attorney-broker smiled again. 'Slavery has the sanction of the law. It is a necessary part of the domestic economy, just like cotton. Why, suppose I should say, "I love my cotton, I'll only sell it locally"? People'd think I was just crazy. Slaves have become a surplus product in the Border States and they must be disposed of where they are not produced in numbers sufficient to meet the local needs. You print that advertisement. Folks may not ask me to dinner, but they'll sell to me, see if they won't.'

The notice did, as predicted, outrage public opinion. Old Marsta and Old Missis vowed no Negro of *theirs* would ever be sold 'down the River.' But somehow the broker's 'jail' – as it was called – kept pretty full, though its boarders changed. Old man Bailiss had his agents out buying and his agents out selling. Sometimes he acted as agent for firms whose headquarters were in Natchez or New Orleans. He entered into silent partnerships with gentlemen of good family who wanted a quick return on capital, and who got it, but who still, it was needless to say, did not dine with him or take his hand publicly. There was talk, on and off, that the Bar Association was planning action not favourable to Bailiss for things connected with the legal side of his trade. It all came to nought.

'Mr Bailiss,' young Ned Wickerson remarked to him one day in the old man's office, 'whoever said that "a man who defends himself has a fool for a client" never had the pleasure of your acquaintance.'

'Thank you, boy.'

'Consequently,' the young man continued, 'I've advised Sam Worth not to go into court if we can manage to settle out of it.'

'First part of your advice is good, but there's nothing to settle.'

'There's a matter of $635 to settle, Mr Bailiss.' Wickerson had been practicing for two years, but he still had freckles on his nose. He took a paper out of his wallet and put it in front of them. 'There's this to settle.'

The old man pushed his glasses down his nose and picked up the paper. He scanned it, lips moving silently. 'Why, this is all correct,' he said. 'Hmm. To be sure. "Received of Samuel Worth of Worth's Crossing, Lemuel County, the sum of $600 cash in full payment for a Negro named Dominick Swift, commonly called Domino, aged thirty-six years and of bright complexion, which Negro I warrant sound in mind and body and a slave for life and the title I will forever defend. James Bailiss, Rutland, Lemuel County." Mmm. All correct. And anyway, what do you mean, six hundred and *thirty-five* dollars?'

'Medical and burial expenses. Domino died last week.'

'Died, now, did he? Sho. Too bad. Well, all men are mortal.'

'I'm afraid my client doesn't take much comfort from your philosophy. Says he didn't get two days' work out of Domino. Says he whipped him, first off, for laziness, but when the doctor – Dr Sloan, that was – examined him, Doctor said he had a consumption. Died right quickly.'

'Negroes *are* liable to quick consumptions. Wish they was a medicine for it. On the other hand, they seldom get malaria or yella fever, Providence.'

He cut off a slice of twist, shoved it in his cheek, then offered twist and knife to Wickerson, who shook his head.

'As I say, we'd rather settle out of court. If you'll refund the purchase price we won't press for the other expenses. What do you say?'

Bailiss looked around the dirty, dusty office. There was a case of law books with broken bindings against the north wall. The south wall had a daguerreotype of John C. Calhoun hanging crookedly on it. The single dim window was in the east wall, and the west wall was pierced by a door whose lower panels had been scarred and splintered by two generations of shoes and boots kicking it open. 'Why, I say no, o' course.'

Wickerson frowned. 'If you lose, you know, you'll have to pay *my* costs as well.'

'I don't expect I'll lose,' the old man said.

'Why, of course you'll lose,' the young man insisted, although he did not sound convinced. 'Dr Sloan will testify that it was *not* "a quick consumption." He says it was a long-standing case of Negro tuberculosis. And you warranted the man sound.'

'Beats me how them doctors think up long words like that,' Bailiss said placidly. 'Inter'sting point of law just come up down in N'Orleans, Ned. One of my agents was writing me. Negro brakeman had his legs crushed in a accident, man who rented him to the railroad sued, railroad pleaded "negligence of his fellow-servant" – in this case, the engineer.'

'Seems like an unassailable defence.' The younger lawyer was interested despite himself. 'What happened?'

'Let's see if I can recollect the court's words.' This was mere modesty. Old man Bailiss' memory was famous on all matters concerning the slave codes. 'Mmm. Yes. Court said: "The slave status has removed this man from the normal fellow-servant category. He is fettered fast by the most stern bonds our laws take note of. He cannot with impunity desert his post though danger plainly threatens, nor can he reprove free men for their bad management or neglect of duty, for the necessity of his condition is upon him." Awarded the owner – Creole man name of Le Tour – awarded him $1300.'

'It seems right, put like that . . . but now, Dr Sloan—'

'Now, Neddy. Domino was carefully examined by *my* doctor, old Fred Pierce—'

'Why, Pierce hasn't drawn a sober breath in twenty years! He gets only slaves for his patients.'

'Well, I reckon that makes him what they call a specialist, then. No, Ned, don't go to court. You have no case. My jailer will testify, too, that Domino was sound when I sold him. It must of been that whipping sickened him.'

450

Wickerson rose. 'Will you make *partial* restitution, then?' The old man shook his head. His long hair was streaked with grey, but the face under it was still ruddy. 'You *know* Domino was sick,' Wickerson said. 'I've spoken to old Miss Whitford's man, Micah, the blacksmith, who was doing some work in your jail a while back. He told me that he heard Domino coughing, saw him spitting blood, saw you watching him, saw you give him some rum and molasses, heard to say, "Better not cough till I've sold you, Dom, else I'll have to sell you south where they don't coddle Negroes." This was just before you *did* sell him – to my client.'

The old man's eyes narrowed. 'I'd say Micah talks overmuch for a black man, even one of old Miss Whitford's – a high and mighty lady that doesn't care to know me on the street. But you forget one mighty important thing, Mr Wickerson!' His voice rose. He pointed his finger. 'It makes no difference what Micah heard! Micah is property! Just like my horse is property! And property can't testify! Do you claim to be a lawyer? Don't you know that a slave can't inherit – can't bequeath – can't marry nor give in marriage – can neither sue nor prosecute – and that it's a basic principle of the law that a slave can never testify in court except against another slave?'

Wickerson, his lips pressed tightly together, moved to the door, kicked it open, scattering a knot of idlers who stood around listening eagerly, and strode away. The old man brushed through them.

'And you'd better tell Sam Worth not to come bothering me, either!' Bailiss shouted at Wickerson's back. 'I know how to take care of trash like him!' He turned furiously to the gaping and grinning loungers.

'Get away from here, you mudsills!' He was almost squeaking in his rage.

'I reckon you don't own the sidewalks,' they muttered. 'I reckon every white man in this state is as good as any other white man,' they said; but they gave way before him. The old man stamped back into his office and slammed the door.

It was Bailiss' custom to have his supper in his own house, a two-storey building just past the end of the sidewalk on Rampart Street; but tonight he felt disinclined to return there with no one but rheumaticky old Edie, his housekeeper-cook, for company. He got on his horse and rode down toward the cheerful bustle of the Phoenix Hotel. Just as he was about to go in, Sam Worth came out. Worth was a barrel-shaped man with thick short arms and thick bandy legs. He stood directly in front of Bailiss, breathing whiskey fumes.

'So you won't settle?' he growled. His wife, a stout woman taller than her husband, got down from their wagon and took him by the arm.

'Come away, now, Sam,' she urged.

'You'd better step aside,' Bailiss said.

'I hear you been making threats against me,' Worth said.

'Yes, and I'll carry them out, too, if you bother me!'

A group quickly gathered, but Mrs Worth pulled her husband away, pushed him toward the wagon; and Bailiss went inside. The buzz of talk dropped for a moment as he entered, stopped, then resumed in a lower register. He cast around for a familiar face, undecided where to sit; but it seemed to him that all faces were turned away. Finally he recognised the bald head and bent shoulders of Dr Pierce, who was slumped at a side table by himself, muttering into a glass. Bailiss sat sat down heavily across from him, with a sigh. Dr Pierce looked up.

'A graduate of the University of Virginia,' the doctor said. His eyes were dull.

'At it again?' Bailiss looked around for a waiter. Dr Pierce finished what was in his glass.

'Says he'll horsewhip you on sight,' he muttered.

'Who says?' Bailiss was surprised.

'Major Jack Moran.'

Bailiss laughed. The major was a tottery veteran of the War of 1812 who rode stiffly about on an aged white mare. 'What for?' he asked.

'Talk is going around you Mentioned A Lady's Name.' Pierce beckoned, and at once a waiter, whose eye old man Bailiss had not managed to catch, appeared with a full glass. Bailiss caught his sleeve as the waiter was about to go and ordered his meal. The doctor drank. 'Major Jack says, impossible to Call You Out – can't appear on Field of Honour with slave trader – so instead will whip you on sight.' His voice gurgled in the glass.

Bailiss smiled crookedly. 'I reckon I needn't be afraid of him. He's old enough to be my daddy. A lady's name? What lady? Maybe he means a lady who lives in a big old house that's falling apart, an old lady who lives on what her Negro blacksmith makes?'

Dr Pierce made a noise of assent. He put down his glass. Bailiss looked around the dining room, but as fast as he met anyone's eyes, the eyes glanced away. The doctor cleared his throat.

'Talk is going around you expressed a dislike for said Negro. Talk is that the lady has said she is going to manumit him to make sure you won't buy him if she dies.'

Bailiss stared. 'Manumit him? She can't do that unless she posts a bond of a thousand dollars to guarantee that he leaves the state within ninety days after being freed. She must know that free Negroes aren't allowed to stay on after manumission. And where would she get a thousand dollars? And what would she live on if Micah is sent away? That old lady hasn't got good sense!'

'No,' Pierce agreed, staring at the glass. 'She is old and not too bright and she's got too much pride on too little money, but it's a sis' – his tongue stumbled – 'a singular thing: there's hardly a person in this town, white or black or halfbreed Injun, that doesn't *love* that certain old lady. Except you. And *no*body in town loves *you*. Also a singular thing: here we are—'

The doctor's teeth clicked against the glass. He set it down, swallowed. His eyes were yellow in the corners, and he looked at Bailiss steadily, save for a slight trembling of his hands and head. 'Here we are, heading just as certain as can be towards splitting the Union and having war with the Yankees – all over slavery – tied to it hand and foot – willing to die for it – economy bound up in it – sure in our own hearts that nature and justice and religion are for it – and yet, singular thing: nobody likes slave traders. Nobody likes them.'

'Tell me something new.' Bailiss drew his arms back to make room for his dinner. He ate noisily and with good appetite.

'Another thing,' the doctor hunched forward in his seat, 'that hasn't added to your current popularity is this business of Domino. In this, I feel, you made a mistake. *Caveat emptor* or not, you should've sold him farther away from here, much farther away, down to the rice fields somewhere, where his death would have been just a statistic in the overseer's annual report. Folks feel you've cheated Sam Worth. He's not one of your rich absentee owners who sits in town and lets some cheese-paring Yankee drive his Negroes. He only owns four or five, he and his boy work right alongside them in the field, pace them row for row.'

Bailiss grunted, sopped up gravy.

'You've been defying public opinion for years now. There might come a time when you'd want good will. My advice to you – after all, your agent only paid $100 for Domino – is to settle with Worth for five hundred.'

Bailiss wiped his mouth on his sleeve. He reached for his hat, put it on, left money on the table, and got up.

'Shoemaker, stick to your last,' he said. Dr Pierce shrugged. 'Make that glass the final one. I want you at the jail tomorrow, early, so we can get the catalogue ready for the big sale next week. Hear?' the old man walked out, paying no attention to the looks or comments his passage caused.

On his horse Bailiss hesitated. The night was rather warm, with a hint of damp in the air. He decided to ride around for a while in the hope of finding a breeze stirring. As the horse ambled along from one pool of yellow gaslight to another he ran through in his mind some phrases for inclusion in his catalogue. *Phyllis, prime woman, aged 25, can cook, sew, do fine ironing . . .*

When he had first begun in the trade, three out of every five Negroes had been named Cuffee, Cudjoe, or Quash. He'd heard these were days of the week in some African dialect. There was talk that the African slave trade might be legalised again; that would be a fine thing. But, sho, there was always such talk, on and off.

The clang of a hammer on an anvil reminded him that he was close to Black Micah's forge. As he rounded the corner he saw Sam Worth's bandy-legged figure outlined against the light. One of the horses was unhitched from his wagon and awaited the shoe Micah was preparing for it.

A sudden determination came to Bailiss: he would settle with Worth about Domino. He hardly bothered to analyse his motives. Partly because his dinner was resting well and he felt comfortable and un-expectedly benevolent, partly because of some vague notion it would be the popular thing to do and popularity was a good thing to have before and during a big sale, he made up his mind to offer Worth $300 – well, maybe he would go as high as $350, but no more; a man had to make *some*thing out of a trade.

As he rode slowly up to the forge and stopped, the blacksmith paused in his hammering and looked out. Worth turned around. In the sudden silence Bailiss heard another horse approaching.

'I've come to settle with you,' the slave trader said. Worth looked up at him, his eyes bloodshot. In a low, ugly voice Worth cursed him, and reached his hand toward his rear pocket. It was obvious to Bailiss what Worth intended, so the slave trader quickly drew his own pistol and fired. His horse reared, a woman screamed – did *two* women scream? Without his meaning it, the other barrel of his pistol went off just as Worth fell.

'Fo' gawdsake don't kill me, Mister Bailiss!' Micah cried. 'Are you all right, Miss Elizabeth?' he cried. Worth's wife and Miss Whitford suddenly appeared from the darkness on the other side of the wagon. They knelt beside Worth.

Bailiss felt a numbing blow on his wrist, dropped his empty pistol, was struck again, and half fell, was half dragged, from his horse. A woman screamed again, men ran up – where had they all come from? Bailiss, pinned in the grip of someone he couldn't see, stood dazed.

'You infernal scoundrel, you shot that man in cold blood!' Old Major Jack Moran dismounted from his horse and flourished the riding crop with which he had struck Bailiss on the wrist.

'I never – he cussed me – he reached for his pistol – I only defended myself!'

Worth's wife looked up, tears streaking her heavy face.

'He had no pistol,' she said. 'I made him leave it home.'

'You said, "I've come to get you," and you shot him point-blank!' The old major's voice trumpeted.

'He tried to shoot Miss Whitford too!' someone said. Other voices added that Captain Carter, the high sheriff's chief deputy, was coming. Bodies pressed against Bailiss, faces glared at him, fists were waved before him.

'It wasn't like that at all!' he cried.

Deputy Carter came up on the gallop, flung the reins of his black mare to eager out-thrust hands, jumped off, and walked over to Worth.

'How was it, then?' a scornful voice asked Bailiss.

'I rode up . . . I says, "I've come to settle with you" . . . He cussed me, low and mean, and he reached for his hip pocket.'

In every face he saw disbelief.

'Major Jack's an old man,' Bailiss faltered. 'He heard it wrong. He—'

'Heard it good enough to hang you!'

Bailiss looked desperately around. Carter rose from his knees and the crowd parted. 'Sam's dead, ma'am,' he said. 'I'm sorry.' Mrs Worth's only reply was a low moan. The crowd growled. Captain Carter turned and faced Bailiss, whose eyes looked at him for a brief second, then turned frantically away. And then Bailiss began to speak anxiously – so anxiously that his words came out a babble. His arms were pinioned and he could not point, but he thrust his head toward the forge where the blacksmith was still standing – standing silently.

'Micah,' Bailiss stuttered. 'Ask Micah!'

Micah saw it, he wanted to say – wanted to shout it. *Micah was next to Worth, Micah heard what I really said, he's younger than the major, his hearing is good, he saw Worth reach . . .*

Captain Carter placed his hand on Bailiss and spoke, but Bailiss did not hear him. The whole night had suddenly fallen silent for him, except for his own voice, saying something (it seemed long ago) to young lawyer Wickerson.

'*It makes no difference what Micah saw! It makes no difference what Micah heard! Micah is property! . . . And property can't testify!*'

They tied Bailiss' hands and heaved him onto his horse.

'*He is fettered fast by the most stern bonds our laws take note of . . . can't inherit – can't bequeath . . . can neither sue nor prosecute—*'

Bailiss turned his head as they started to ride away. He looked at Micah and their eyes met. Micah knew.

'. . . it's basic principle of the law that a slave can never testify in court except against another slave.'

Someone held the reins of old man Bailiss' horse. From now on he moved only as others directed. The lights around the forge receded. Darkness surrounded him. The necessity of his condition was upon him.

Jay Wilson

The Unsuspected

A thing about murder is that you go for broke – alone. There are no rehearsals, no retakes, no changes in bits of business to make them fit – no changes in the cast. When the victim gurgles his last, the curtain goes up. The killer is at centre stage, alone with a cast that has not read his script.

Mr Piper was thoroughly aware of this. He had considered it most carefully. Because murder seemed to be the quickest, easiest, and, really, the safest solution to a problem which had become more urgent the past few years.

At fifty-five, Mr Piper was nearing retirement. On the surface he was an affable, pink-cheeked, slightly plump little man who looked some years younger than his age. He appeared so because he had lived a pleasant life. A bachelor, he bought good Scotch, enjoyed the theatre, played week-end golf on public courses, and maintained a better-than-average little apartment. A man who had only himself to consider could afford these little pleasures and luxuries on even a bank teller's salary. But, of course, they took most of that salary. What little he could save additionally, even as senior teller in the uptown branch of the New Amsterdam Trust Company, went for little extras such as hopeful long shots at the track or the more consoling ministrations of demoiselles of the evening.

Such indulgences are habit-forming. Mr Piper had come to regard them as no more than a reasonable compensation for the monotony of a banking career which had reached its zenith at a considerably lower altitude than he had once anticipated. His problem was the continuance of his pleasures on funds supplemental to the meagre pension which would shortly be his sole means of support.

Mr Piper had often considered using money out of his cash trays to make quick little profits on the stock market, with no harm done as long as he returned the bank's money before it was missed. If he made enough quick profits, he would accumulate some capital which, in turn, could be speculated into further capital until there was enough to spread out over the years, over and above his pension, to make the difference between survival and a life worth living. The thought of bank examiners had always deterred Mr Piper.

Murder, as a safer solution, occurred to Mr Piper after George Manetti became a depositor and began making his deposits and withdrawals at Mr Piper's station. Manetti's mistake was in taking a liking to Mr Piper and talking too much. This was because the calculating meanness of Mr Piper's inner being did not show through his affable exterior, and because during business hours Manetti could not afford to like anyone, and the less he said the better. It would have shaken what little trust Manetti had in mankind to have known that Mr Piper came to view him with cold objectivity as no more than the means for Mr Piper's old-age comfort.

Manetti was carried on the bank's books as a green-goods broker. Mr Piper became quickly aware of the pattern of Manetti's withdrawals and deposits. The withdrawals were usually just before bank-closing time Friday afternoons when Manetti would present a cheque to cash for five, ten or fifteen thousand dollars. The deposits were usually Monday mornings, and averaged more than with withdrawals.

'You gave me all new bills Friday,' Manetti said one Monday morning. 'They kept sticking together and I was tossing more than I wanted in the pot. Always give me used fifties.'

Mr Piper looked across the counter at the burly, olive-hued young man. 'You are a gambler?' he inquired.

Manetti's bland features became animated in a genial grin. 'Only technically, Mr Piper. Gamblers are guys who think money talks. Poker players listen to the cards. I'm a poker player. I make a living playing poker with gamblers.'

It had been the protective instinct of kind for kind that had made Mr Piper glance sideways to see if the next teller had heard. Apparently he had not. He said, 'If you want to keep your account in this bank, Mr Manetti, you'd best not discuss your – uh – profession quite so loudly.'

Manetti was in Mr Piper's hands from that moment. Manetti's grin spread. 'Yeah. I forgot. Thanks, Mr Piper. You're a right guy. I picked this place to bank because nobody would figure I would. I like privacy when I put the take.'

Manetti, unfortunately for Manetti, continued to think of Mr Piper as a right guy – and to talk. Successful, he needed to brag a little. 'One of my secrets, Mr Piper, is training. Most of these guys I do business with drink. I don't. From here I always go to my place and get some sleep before I meet them. By the time they can't tell treys from aces I'm still alive in there and sandbagging them.'

The thought of killing Manetti was born and fed by envy. Mr Piper watched Manetti's account grow. Here was a young man who was easily and steadily building a small fortune, while he, Mr Piper, after more than thirty years of exemplary service, protecting more money than Manetti would ever dream of, would soon be retired on a pittance pension. He would be expected to retire gracefully and gratefully after the customary office banquet, at which they would present him with the customary engraved watch with the customary jocular remark that it would measure out all the good time he had to loaf in while his old friends would still be watching the clock in the bank.

Mr Piper began to wonder how long Manetti's luck would hold out. How long would it be before someone who had been sandbagged once too often decided to break it off and do a little sandbagging of his own on a dark street? Gone would be Manetti, and his money with him – doing Manetti not one bit of good. Not anywhere near what it could do for Mr Piper.

Once born, it was a thought that would not die. Nor did Mr Piper want it to. Rather, he nourished it as he sat in his chair, evenings, sipping Scotch and soda. With ten or fifteen thousand dollars he could, on retirement, become a silent partner in some promising little business that needed a shot in the arm. It would return him the income he would need to supplement his pension. That was all Mr Piper asked – the means to continue his pleasant way of living. Mr Piper knew a thing or two about contracts. He would see to it that the contract under which he bought into the promising little business would provide a way to freeze out the other owner if it began really to prosper – or if a quick sale of assets should be indicated.

To get the money in the first place, of course, he would have to get rid of Manetti. A prime consideration was whether or not he could safely do this. Could he, for instance, gain access to Manetti in his apartment while he was resting before a game?

Mr Piper found himself casing the joint. He stood across the street from the apartment house in which Manetti lived. It was a middle-class building. There was no doorman. The people who went in either used a key or pressed a buzzer button in the foyer. Between five-thirty and six-thirty scarcely anyone went in or out. The white-collar folk who lived there were reading their newspapers, watching TV or eating dinner.

Mr Piper crossed the street and entered the foyer. George Manetti was listed as occupying a second-floor apartment. A man emerged, opening the foyer door, as Mr Piper stood there. He hurried out into the street, not looking at Mr Piper. The tenants in that building took little or no notice of one another. They preferred to remain invisible to one another. Entrance and exit could be safely made.

The script developed as Mr Piper sat in his rooms and sipped his good Scotch. Certain things were in his favour. Highly important, Manetti trusted him. Manetti would believe any plausible excuse Mr Piper might make to come up and see him. Mr Piper would know when to strike. It would be after Manetti had made one of his larger withdrawals. Mr Piper possessed a small pistol which could never be traced to him by ballistics experts. He had bought it several years ago in another state while on a vacation. Fired while thrust hard against Manetti, it would make very little noise. Later it could be dropped from a ferryboat into the middle of the river. There would be any number of far more logical suspects in the gambling fraternity than a respectable senior teller with over thirty years of impeccable service in the New Amsterdam Trust Company. A reflection against Mr. Piper would be a reflection against the New Amsterdam Trust Company. The police would think several times before they risked the wrath of that mighty institution over the demise of a small-time gambler. Because Manetti was far from really big time, there would be no stir if the police simply wrote the case off – as they very likely would, Mr Piper decided, if they did not quickly find a shady character who could not clear himself.

The other side of the coin appeared to offer few risks. There was a minimum chance of being seen entering or leaving or, if seen, of being later identified. A killer not associated with the bank would not bother to remove any chequebooks or statements connecting Manetti with the bank. Therefore Mr Piper had better leave any such records to be found. It meant the police would quickly find out that Mr Piper knew about the cash Manetti had withdrawn but which was missing when Manetti was found. But, after all, how could he help knowing as he had known about Manetti's many previous withdrawals? It would be best to play this straight. The bank would learn about Manetti's death anyway, check the account, and report the withdrawal to the police. It could tend to point to a bank employee trying to cover his trail if no evidence of Manetti's association with the bank was found on the scene. It would tend to indicate innocence if such normal evidence was found. Nor could Mr Piper afford the risks of a manufactured alibi. If questioned he would simply claim to have been at home reading a book. Without strain he stood an innocent man against whom nothing could be proved. The weakness or two in his position would actually turn into strengths.

That was the important thing – to be able to weather any routine questioning without strain. To be able to answer truthfully to everything except for one simple lie – that he had been at home.

Then there was the matter of what to do with the money. Mr Piper pondered this carefully. A safe-deposit box in a suburban bank seemed the best bet. It should be rented in advance, of course. He could open a small savings account under an assumed name and, under those cordial conditions, rent a box without being questioned or thought about. He would have to remember only to go there and pay the annual box rental before a bill was mailed to a non-existent person. He would not touch the money until after retirement.

That left only the problem of what to do with the money until he could get it to the safe-deposit box. If the big event took place on a Friday evening he would be unable to get the money to its hiding place until Monday morning. But it would be highly important that he be at his station promptly Monday morning as he had been for years. Any deviation could be suspect when related to other factors. He would have to wait to get to his suburban bank. In fact, there was the possibility he might have to wait several days. If that was the way the ball happened to bounce, it would also be dangerous to hide a packet of bills unguarded in his apartment. Mr Piper chuckled and had another drink when he thought of the solution to this final problem. Placed with the other bills in his cash trays at the bank the money would become utterly invisible. Immediately that it was safe he would get it off to the waiting safe-deposit box.

Mr Piper was fascinated by his plan: the script of the play he had written for himself. The action was simple, the lines few and easy. Manetti had become less than human. He was no more than a stage prop necessary for Mr Piper's star role. It was too bad, Mr Piper thought, that there would be no audience to applaud.

Two weeks later Manetti made his largest withdrawal. The cheque he pushed across the counter towards Mr Piper was for twenty-five thousand. Mr Piper stared at the cheque.

George Manetti laughed. 'That still leaves a couple of hundred in the account, Mr Piper. Make it the usual fifties in a package.'

'I – I'll have to get some from the vault, Mr Manetti.'

Manetti grinned. 'Rub it for luck, Mr Piper. One of those Wall Street tycoons is sitting in tonight. A real big shot. I'll double my lettuce before I quit and let the gamblers fight it out.'

Maybe he would and maybe he wouldn't double it, Mr Piper thought in the vault. If he did, maybe fifty thousand would be enough to get Manetti followed home. Manetti could be dead or broke – or both – before morning. But before either happened, Manetti would be at home with ten thousand more in cash than Mr Piper had planned to go into action for.

Mr Piper knew that if his play was to go on stage at all, this was curtain time.

At precisely six o'clock that evening Mr Piper's cotton-gloved finger pressed the buzzer button to Manetti's apartment.

Presently Manetti's voice spoke sleepily from the foyer speaker. 'Yeah? Whossit?'

'Piper. You know. Piper at the bank. I hate to bother you, but I've got to see you for a moment.'

'Huh? Piper? Bank? Oh, yeah! Hey, what's up?'

'I think I overpaid you this afternoon. Can I please come up and verify? I mean, I'm short in my cash tally and the examiners are just about due. They could be in first thing Monday morning.'

'Oh. Sure, Mr Piper. Come on up. I'll push the door button.'

Mr Piper removed the cotton gloves as he walked along the corridor from the self-operated elevator. TV sounds came from the doors he passed – shots, shouts and loud voices. The Western programmes were on the air. It was an assistance Mr Piper had not counted on.

Manetti was waiting at the door to his apartment. He was in pyjama trousers and a T-shirt. For a moment Mr Piper knew dismay. Would a tiny bullet destroy that powerful body? Quickly enough, that is, so there would be no final struggle?

'Come on in, Mr Piper!' Manetti said cordially and loudly.

'Please, Mr Manetti!' Mr Piper pleaded, moving quickly into the apartment. 'Not so loud! I mean, you know how it is with the bank. I shouldn't be here at all.'

'Huh? Oh, yeah.' Manetti laughed as he closed the door. 'You got this Mrs Grumpy watching all the time. You know, Mr Piper, you got a dog's life.'

Mr Piper smiled. 'It has its advantages, Mr Manetti. A dog is allowed one bite.'

Manetti placed a powerful arm around Mr Piper's soft shoulders. 'Well, don't waste that bite on me, Mr Piper,' he said genially. 'I didn't mean anything. Now, what's this about you being short?'

'Well, I must have put one too many thousand-dollar packets in the package I gave you. I counted it out very quickly. I mean, that's what I'm short in my cash tally.'

'Well, now, that's easy, Mr Piper. We'll just count the packets and see.'

No one saw Mr Piper leave. He left Manetti dead with two bullets through his upper spine. There had been hardly any sound; only a grunt of surprise when Mr Piper had pressed the little pistol hard into

Manetti's back, then two muffled reports that blended in with the TV sounds. Mr Piper had put on the cotton gloves and left no fingerprints.

Back in his apartment Mr Piper put the pistol and the brown-paper package of money in his dresser drawer. He didn't bother to count the money. He knew it was all there. He needed a drink. A stiff one. He poured it and collapsed in his favourite chair. It had been something of an ordeal. His nerves needed steadying. He needed for the while not to think. He needed to drink himself quietly into oblivion – to forget the horribly quiet way Manetti had sagged to the floor.

Mr Piper awakened the next morning sprawled across his bed, still fully dressed. His head ached horribly and he had no recollection of when he had come to bed. He remained perfectly still, combating a raw, inner emptiness and a nightmarish apprehension of having passed some sort of a point of no return. Then memory flooded back.

For a while longer Mr Piper remained motionless on the bed, intuitively shrinking from facing both physical distress and an assessment of his situation at the same time. Finally, having re-run the film of memory several times, Mr Piper stumbled to his feet. He went to his dresser. The money and the pistol were there in the drawer. The ball had indeed bounced.

A shower. He needed a shower – and a shave. He needed food. He needed a drink. Mr Piper shuddered. No, not a drink! He needed to clear his head. Until he could do that he needed once more not to think.

Restored once more to a state of convalescence, Mr Piper sat down in his favourite chair and endeavoured to estimate his situation calmly. Nowhere could be recall anything going in the least amiss. Manetti had died quite easily when he had turned his back to Mr Piper; so easily that Mr Piper knew he would soon be able to put the scene quite out of mind. He had only to take a ferryboat ride to New Jersey and drop the pistol in a paper bag off the stern into the middle of the river. Monday morning he would put the money in his cash tray. He was in! In with a twenty-five-thousand-dollar nest egg to keep life beautiful!

Mr Piper got up and made himself a Bloody Mary. He drank a silent toast to the success of his plan and the manner in which he had carried it out.

Manetti's death was reported in the Sunday paper. It was only a short item on an inner page. George Manetti, a known card player, had been found shot in his apartment the previous evening. A cocker spaniel, being taken out for a walk, had sniffed and fussed at the door to Manetti's apartment. The spaniel's owner had called the superintendent, who had opened the apartment. The police said there was evidence of murder for robbery.

Mr Piper read the item carefully. So they had found a chequebook showing Friday's withdrawal and, of course, not the money. Mr Piper shrugged. This he had anticipated. All it meant was that the police would come to the bank to verify the withdrawal. He, Mr Piper, had nothing to hide. That was the beauty of it all. He could tell the truth, almost the whole truth, and scarcely anything but the truth.

Mr Piper turned to the sporting section of the paper. The thing to do was to get back into his normal routine. There was a double-header that afternoon. A very good double-header too. And that evening, he mused, perhaps Fern would be free. Mr Piper chuckled. He was indeed a man of many parts.

No one at the bank, it seemed, had noted the item about Manetti in the Sunday paper. Mr Piper had not the slightest difficulty in cashing the money with the rest that was in his cash trays Monday morning.

Detective Sergeant Henderson arrived as the doors opened for the day's business. A few minutes later Mr Piper was summoned to the branch manager's office. The manager, Mr Farnsworth, was young, Ivy League, and hoping for an early vice-presidency. In college he had been known as Duke – a title bestowed in recognition of suave competence. He did not rise from behind his desk when Mr Piper entered. He had the slightly dazed look of a sea captain whose first command had just stove in her bow on a submerged derelict. He waved to a burly man seated in the chair beside his desk.

'Piper, this is Sergeant Henderson. Police. It – it seems that one of our depositors has been murdered!'

Sergeant Henderson did not rise. He acknowledged Mr Piper with a nod. If there was a crucial moment, Mr Piper thought, this would be it. He could tell nothing from Henderson's expressionless features. He felt the palms of his hands become slightly moist. He forced himself to return the policeman's steady gaze for a moment, then turned to Mr Farnsworth. The truth, he reminded himself, only one small lie, and he was safe.

'Yes, sir. I read it in the paper yesterday. The name stood out because Manetti always came to my station. I was just about to come in and tell you about it when you sent for me.'

'What we found,' Sergeant Henderson said, 'was a chequebook of this bank. The last stub showed a cheque to cash for twenty-five thousand. The money wasn't in the apartment.'

Mr Piper nodded. 'Yes, sir. He cashed a cheque for that amount Friday afternoon. I gave it to him in fifties. There is only a hundred or so left in the account.'

'Do you have the serial numbers?'

'No, sir. I mean, Mr Manetti made frequent deposits and withdrawals.

Besides, he preferred used bills. We put those up in packets of five hundred and a thousand dollars, but we don't note serial numbers ordinarily.'

Sergeant Henderson sighed. 'Well, at least we can establish that he left here Friday afternoon with twenty-five thousand on him.' He looked at Mr Piper. 'And right now you're the only one we know who knew he had it.'

This was it! Mr Piper stiffened with a show of indignation. 'Well! I could hardly be expected not to know, could I? I also knew of several other depositors who left the bank with considerable amounts of cash!'

Sergeant Henderson raised a large, placating hand. 'O.K., O.K. Don't get sore. A cop has to collect facts. For instance, where were you Friday night, say, between five P.M. and ten?'

'In my apartment, reading a book!' Mr Piper snapped.

'Now, just a minute!' Farnsworth cut in. 'Piper here has been with this bank for more than thirty years! He has an impeccable record! He'll retire on a good pension. Of course he knew this man had that money. And why shouldn't he be home reading a book? And if you are, by the slightest chance, suggesting Piper might have done this, would he have left that chequebook there to lead you here? Besides, you said Manetti was a gambler. You have a world of more likely suspects!'

Mr Piper exulted inwardly that Mr Farnsworth should point out all these things to Henderson.

Sergeant Henderson grinned. 'Don't get excited, Mr Farnsworth. Nobody over at Manetti's place saw anything, nobody heard anything, and nobody left any fingerprints that hadn't ought to be there. Ballistics probably won't be able to trace the weapon. On the face of it, Mr Piper could have done it as easy as anyone else. Only he didn't. Nobody that's been a bank teller over thirty years has got it left in him to leave himself so wide open. We'll just go about it the usual way – pass the word around and wait until somebody begins flashing fifty-dollar bills.' Henderson stood up. He nodded to Mr Piper. 'Well, thanks for the information – and I didn't mean to get you shook up.'

'Don't mention it!' Mr Piper said. 'After this I'll be sure to have a witness ready to testify that I'm behaving myself.'

'That's when I'll be looking twice at you, Mr Piper.'

Mr Farnsworth said, 'Uh – would it be possible not to publicise the bank in this? I'm sure there will be some way we can show our appreciation.'

'There wouldn't be any way you could do that, Mr Farnsworth,' Henderson replied coolly. 'If we could keep the bank's name out of it we would. But when we catch the guy, we'll have to establish that

Manetti had the money – and that brings you people into it. So long.'

And that was that, Mr Piper thought jubilantly. The police would putter around among Manetti's associates until they got tired of it and wrote the case off as not important enough to waste any more money or effort on.

Mr Piper turned to find Mr Farnsworth glaring at him across his wide desk. 'This is bad, Piper,' he said. 'Very bad. It is going to be bad for us to have accepted an account from such a fellow.'

Mr Piper couldn't have cared less. He said, 'But it was a good account, Mr Farnsworth.'

'Not that good, Piper! Not that good at all! And suppose that detective reports that I tried to bribe him?'

'He won't,' Mr Piper said reassuringly. Mr Piper was inwardly amused. Mr Farnsworth was more perturbed over the superficialities than he, Mr Piper, was concerned over the deed itself. He went on, 'They may never catch anyone. In that case if we just keep quiet no one need know anything about it.'

'Don't be an ass, Piper! You know perfectly well I've got to report this downtown – and then try to explain why we accepted this account!' Mr Farnsworth groaned. 'This will fix my chances but good!'

'Oh, come, Mr Farnsworth! I'm sure you're making a mountain out of a molehill.'

Mr Farnsworth glowered. 'You think so? You think they select vice-presidents from among branch managers whose depositors get murdered? Even the way we carried him will make it worse – green-goods broker!'

Mr Piper felt it was time to soothe Mr Farnsworth and get back to a normal routine. 'But you could hardly be expected to know what kind of green goods, Mr Farnsworth. They'll understand.'

'They'll understand nothing!' Mr Farnsworth rasped. 'They'll understand only that I didn't know who I was doing business with!' Mr Farnsworth's eyes narrowed. 'You said he always came to your station. Do you mean to tell me that there was nothing about this account to give you an inkling about Manetti? To support the suspicion you should have had when he preferred used fifties?'

Mr Piper thought rapidly. The branch manager could check records and learn the pattern of Manetti's withdrawals and deposits. In his present frame of mind he would leap to the conclusion that only an utter fool would not have identified Manetti as an unusual type of depositor, one whose account should at least have been brought to the attention of the branch manager. For over thirty years Mr Piper had a record of astuteness and meticulous regard for the bank's interests.

'Piper! I asked you a question! I want an answer!'

Mr Piper assumed a slightly hurt expression. 'Perhaps I did have intimations, Mr Farnsworth. Perhaps Manetti did say things now and then that may have made me slightly suspicious. But it was a good and growing account on the books. It was helping the branch standing. That was good for you, Mr Farnsworth. Naturally you would have had to close it out if you had personally suspected anything. If I did wrong in keeping my suspicions to myself I did so with the best of intentions.'

Mr Farnsworth was not impressed. He snapped, 'You know what the road to hell is paved with, don't you?'

Mr Piper was becoming annoyed. There wasn't a thing this whipper-snapper could do to him. It was time he was told. 'I think, Mr Farnsworth,' he said quietly, 'that you are exceeding good taste and your authority. I have had over thirty years' service with the New Amsterdam Trust Company. You just stated it was an impeccable record. I have never been reprimanded. If a reprimand is called for in this case I will be ready to accept it from those who have known me much longer than you have.'

Let young Farnsworth chew on that! Mr Piper thought.

Young Farnsworth regarded Mr Piper with fury in his eyes. 'What it boils down to,' he said, 'is that you did not report an account about which you were suspicious. Now you're standing on your record and claiming the right to one mistake, eh?' Mr Farnsworth leaned across his desk and waggled a long finger at Mr Piper. 'Well, I've got news for you! I've got absolutely nothing to lose and perhaps a great deal to gain by taking decisive action, now that I've found out about the Manetti account! You, Piper, are fired!'

'You can't make it stick!' Mr Piper retorted, not fully understanding yet what being fired could mean to him. 'My record—'

'Blast your record!' Mr Farnsworth raged. 'Maybe you didn't blast Manetti, but you've certainly blasted me! Can't make it stick, eh? Well, we'll see!' He reached for the telephone on his desk. He glared coldly at Mr Piper as he said, 'Give me Martinson . . . Hello? Martinson? As of this minute you are head teller. Go tally out Piper's cash!'

Stanley Ellin

You can't be a little girl
all your life

It was the silence that woke her. Not suddenly – Tom had pointed out more than once with a sort of humorous envy that she slept like the dead – but slowly; drawing her up from a hundred fathoms of sleep so that she lay just on the surface of consciousness, eyes closed, listening to the familiar pattern of night sounds around her, wondering where it had been disarranged.

Then she heard the creak of a floorboard – the reassuring creak of a board under the step of a late-returning husband – and understood. Even while she was a hundred fathoms under, she must have known that Tom had come into the room, must have anticipated the click of the bed-light being switched on, the solid thump of footsteps from bed to closet, from closet to dresser – the unfailing routine which always culminated with his leaning over her and whispering, 'Asleep?' and her small groan which said yes, she was asleep but glad he was home, and would he please not stay up all the rest of the night working at those papers.

So he was in the room now, she knew, but for some reason he was not going through the accustomed routine, and that was what had awakened her. Like the time they had the cricket, poor thing; for a week it had relentlessly chirped away the dark hours from some hidden corner of the house until she'd got used to it. The night it died, or went off to make a cocoon or whatever crickets do, she'd lain awake for an hour waiting to hear it, and then slept badly after that until she'd got used to living without it.

Poor thing, she thought drowsily, not really caring very much but

468

waiting for the light to go on, the footsteps to move comfortingly between bed and closet. Somehow the thought became a serpent crawling down her spine, winding tight around her chest. *Poor thing*, it said to her, *poor stupid thing – it isn't Tom at all!*

She opened her eyes at the moment the man's gloved hand brutally slammed over her mouth. In that moment she saw the towering shadow of him, heard the sob of breath in his throat, smelled the sour reek of liquor. Then she wildly bit down on the hand that gagged her, her teeth sinking into the glove, grinding at it. He smashed his other fist squarely into her face. She went limp, her head lolling half off the bed. He smashed his fist into her face again.

After that, blackness rushed in on her like a whirlwind.

She looked at the pale balloons hovering under the ceiling and saw with idle interest that they were turning into masks, but with features queerly reversed, mouths on top, eyes below. The masks moved and righted themselves. Became faces. Dr Vaughn. And Tom. And a woman. Someone with a small white dunce cap perched on her head. A nurse.

The doctor leaned over her, lifted her eyelid with his thumb, and she discovered that her face was one throbbing bruise. He withdrew the thumb and grunted. From long acquaintance she recognised it as a grunt of satisfaction.

He said, 'Know who I am, Julie?'

'Yes.'

'Know what happened?'

'Yes.'

'How do you feel?'

She considered that. 'Funny. I mean, far away. And there's a buzzing in my ears.'

'That was the needle. After we brought you around you went into a real sweet hysteria, and I gave you a needle. Remember that?'

'No.'

'Just as well. Don't let it bother you.'

It didn't bother her. What bothered her was not knowing the time. Things were so unreal when you didn't know the time. She tried to turn her head toward the clock on the night table, and the doctor said, 'It's a little after six. Almost sunrise. Probably be the first time you've ever seen it, I'll bet.'

She smiled at him as much as her swollen mouth would permit. 'Saw it last New Year's,' she said.

Tom came around the other side of the bed. He sat down on it and took her hand tightly in his. 'Julie,' he said. 'Julie, Julie, Julie,' the words coming out in a rush as if they had been building up in him with explosive force.

She loved him and pitied him for that, and for the way he looked. He looked awful. Haggard, unshaven, his eyes sunk deep in his head, he looked as if he were running on nerve alone. Because of her, she thought unhappily, all because of her.

'I'm sorry,' she said.

'Sorry!' He gripped her hand so hard that she winced. 'Because some lunatic – some animal—!'

'Oh, please!'

'I know. I know you want to shut it out, darling, but you mustn't yet. Look, Julie, the police have been waiting all night to talk to you. They're sure thay can find the man, but they need your help. You'll have to describe him, tell them whatever you can about him. Then you won't even have to think about it again. You understand, don't you?'

'Yes.'

'I knew you would.'

He started to get up, but the doctor said, 'No, you stay here with her. I'll tell them on my way out. Have to get along, anyhow – these all-night shifts are hard on an old man.' He stood with his hand on the doorknob. 'When they find him,' he said in a hard voice, 'I'd like the pleasure—' and let it go at that, knowing they understood.

The big, white-haired man with the rumpled suit was Lieutenant Christensen of the police department. The small, dapper man with the moustache was Mr Dahl of the district attorney's office. Ordinarily, said Mr Dahl, he did not take a personal part in criminal investigations, but when it came to – that is, in a case of this kind special measures were called for. Everyone must cooperate fully. Mrs Barton must cooperate, too. Painful as it might be, she must answer Lieutenant Christensen's questions frankly and without embarrassment. Would she do that?

Julie saw Tom nodding encouragement to her. 'Yes,' she said.

She watched Lieutenant Christensen draw a notebook and pad from his pocket. His gesture, when he pressed the end of the pen to release its point, made him look as if he were stabbing at an insect.

He said, 'First of all, I want you to tell me exactly what happened. Everything you can remember about it.'

She told him, and he scribbled away in the notebook, the pen clicking at each stroke.

'What time was that?' he asked.

'I don't know.'

'About what time? The closer we can pin it down, the better we can check on alibis. When did you go to bed?'

'At ten-thirty.'

'And Mr Barton came home around twelve, so we know it happened between ten-thirty and twelve.' The lieutenant addressed himself to the notebook, then pursed his lips thoughtfully. 'Now for something even more important.'

'Yes?'

'Just this. Would you recognise the man if you saw him again?'

She closed her eyes, trying to make form out of that monstrous shadow, but feeling only the nauseous terror of it. 'No,' she said.

'You don't sound so sure about it.'

'But I am.'

'How can you be? Yes, I know the room was kind of dark and all that, but you said you were awake after you first heard him come in. That means you had time to get adjusted to the dark. And some light from the streetlamp outside hits your window shade here. You wouldn't see so well under the conditions, maybe, but you'd see something, wouldn't you? I mean, enough to point out the man if you had the chance. Isn't that right?'

She felt uneasily that he was right and she was wrong, but there didn't seem to be anything she could do about it. 'Yes,' she said, 'but it wasn't like that.'

Dahl, the man from the district attorney's office, shifted on his feet. 'Mrs Barton,' he started to say, but Lieutenant Christensen silenced him with a curt gesture of the hand.

'Now look,' the lieutenant said. 'Let me put it this way. Suppose we had this man some place where you could see him close up, but he couldn't see you at all. Can you picture that? He'd be right up there in front of you, but he wouldn't even know you were looking at him. Don't you think it would be pretty easy to recognise him then?'

Julie found herself growing desperately anxious to give him the answer he wanted, to see what he wanted her to see; but no matter how hard she tried, she could not. She shook her head hopelessly, and Lieutenant Christensen drew a long breath.

'All right,' he said, 'then is there anything you can tell me about him? How big was he? Tall, short or medium?'

The shadow towered over her. 'Tall. No, I'm not sure. But I think he was.'

'White or coloured?'

'I don't know.'

'About how old?'

'I don't know.'

'Anything distinctive about his clothes? Anything you might have taken notice of?'

She started to shake her head again, then suddenly remembered.

'Gloves,' she said, pleased with herself. 'He was wearing gloves.'

'Leather or wool?'

'Leather.' The sour taste of the leather was in her mouth now. It made her stomach turn over.

Click-click went the pen, and the lieutenant looked up from the notebook expectantly. 'Anything else?'

'No.'

The lieutenant frowned. 'It doesn't add up to very much, does it? I mean, the way you tell it.'

'I'm sorry,' Julie said, and wondered why she was so ready with that phrase now. What was it that *she* had done to feel sorry about? She felt the tears of self-pity start to rise, and she drew Tom's hand to her breast, turning to look at him for comfort. She was shocked to see that he was regarding her with the same expression that the lieutenant wore.

The other man – Dahl – was saying something to her.

'Mrs Barton,' he said, and again, 'Mrs Barton,' until she faced him. 'I know how you feel, Mrs Barton, but what I have to say is terribly important. Will you please listen to me?'

'Yes,' she said numbly.

'When I talked to you at one o'clock this morning, Mrs Barton, you were in a state – well, you do understand that I wasn't trying to badger you then. I was working on your behalf. On behalf of the whole community, in fact.'

'I don't remember. I don't remember anything about it.'

'I see. But you undersand now, don't you? And you do know that there's been a series of these outrages in the community during recent years, and that the administration and the press have put a great deal of pressure – rightly, of course – on my office and on the police department to do something about it?'

Julie let her head fall back on the pillow, and closed her eyes. 'Yes,' she said. 'If you say so.'

'I do say so. I also say that we can't do very much unless the injured party – the victim – helps us in every way possible. And why won't she? Why does she so often refuse to identify the criminal or testify against him in cases like this? Because she might face some publicity? Because she might have started off by encouraging the man, and is afraid of what he'd say about her on the witness stand? I don't care what the reason is, that woman is guilty of turning a wild beast loose on her helpless neighbours!

'Look, Mrs Barton. I'll guarantee that the man who did this has a police record, and the kind of offences listed on it – well, I wouldn't even want to name them in front of you. There's a dozen people at headquarters right now looking through all such records, and when they find the right one it'll lead us straight to him. But after that you're the only one who can help us get rid of him for keeps. I want you to tell me right now that you'll do that for us when the time comes. It's your duty. You can't turn away from it.'

'I know. But I didn't see him.'

'You saw more than you realise, Mrs Barton. Now, don't get me wrong, because I'm not saying that you're deliberately holding out, or anything like that. You've had a terrible shock. You want to forget it, get it out of your mind completely. And that's what'll happen, if you let yourself go this way. So, knowing that, and not letting yourself go, do you think you can describe the man more accurately now?'

Maybe she had been wrong about Tom, she thought, about the way he had looked at her. She opened her eyes hopefully and was bitterly sorry she had. His expression of angry bewilderment was unchanged, but now he was leaning forward, staring at her as if he could draw the right answer from her by force of will. And she knew he couldn't. The tears overflowed, and she cried weakly; then magically a tissue was pressed into her hand. She had forgotten the nurse. The upside-down face bent over her from behind the bed, and she was strangely consoled by the sight of it. All these men in the room – even her husband – had been made aliens by what had happened to her. It was good to have a woman there.

'Mrs Barton!' Dahl's voice was unexpectedly sharp, and Tom turned abruptly toward him. Dahl must have caught the warning in that, Julie realised with gratitude; when he spoke again his voice was considerably softer. 'Mrs Barton, please let me put the matter before you bluntly. Let me show you what we're faced with here.

'A dangerous man is on the prowl. You seem to think he was drunk, but he wasn't too drunk to know exactly where he could find a victim who was alone and unprotected. He probably had this house staked out for weeks in advance, knowing your husband's been working late at his office. And he knew how to get into the house. He scraped this window sill here pretty badly, coming in over it.

'He wasn't here to rob the place – he had the opportunity but he wasn't interested in it. He was interested in one thing, and one thing only.' Surprisingly, Dahl walked over to the dresser and lifted the framed wedding picture from it. 'This is you, isn't it?'

'Yes,' Julie said in bewilderment.

'You're a very pretty young woman, you know.' Dahl put down the picture, lifted up her hand mirror, and approached her with it. 'Now I want to show you how a pretty young woman looks after she's tried to resist a man like that.' He suddenly flashed the mirror before her and she shrank in horror from its reflection.

'Oh, please!' she cried.

'You don't have to worry,' Dahl said harshly. 'According to the doctor, you'll heal up fine in a while. But until then, won't you see that man as clear as day every time you look into this thing? Won't you be about to point him out, and lay your hand on the Bible, and swear he was the one?'

She wasn't sure any more. She looked at him wonderingly, and he threw wide his arms, summing up his case. 'You'll know him when you see him again, won't you?' he demanded.

'Yes,' she said.

She thought she would be left alone after that, but she was wrong. The world had business with her, and there was no way of shutting it out. The doorbell chimed incessantly. The telephone in the hall rang, was silent while someone took the call, then rang again. Men with hard faces – police officials – would be ushered into the room by Tom. They would duck their heads at her in embarrassment, would solemnly survey the room, then go off in a corner to whisper together. Tom would lead them out, and would return to her side. He had nothing to say. He would just sit there, taut with impatience, waiting for the doorbell or telephone to ring again.

He was seldom apart from her, and Julie, watching him, found herself increasingly troubled by that. She was keeping him from his work, distracting him from the thing that mattered most to him. She didn't know much about his business affairs, but she did know he had been working for months on some very big deal – the one that had been responsible for her solitary evenings at home – and what would happen to it while he was away from his office? She had only been married two years, but she was already well-versed in the creed of the businessman's wife. Troubles at home may come and go, it said, but Business abides. She used to find that idea repellent, but now it warmed her. Tom would go to the office, and she would lock the door against everybody, and there would be continuity.

But when she hesitantly broached the matter, he shrugged it off. 'The deal's all washed up, anyhow. It was a waste of time. That's what I was going to tell you about when I walked in and found you like that. It was quite a sight.' He looked at her, his eyes glassy with fatigue. 'Quite a sight,' he said.

And sat there waiting for the doorbell or telephone to ring again.

When he was not there, one of the nurses was. Miss Shepherd, the night nurse, was taciturn. Miss Waldemar, the day nurse, talked.

She said, 'Oh, it takes all kinds to make this little old world, I tell you. They slow their cars coming by the house, and they walk all over the lawn, and what they expect to see I'm sure I don't know. It's just evil minds, that's all it is, and wouldn't they be the first ones to call you a liar if you told them that to their faces? And children in the back seats! What is it, sweetie? You look as if you can't get comfy.'

'I'm all right, thank you,' Julie said. She quailed at the thought of telling Miss Waldemar to please keep quiet or go away. There were people who could do that, she knew, but evidently it didn't matter to them how anyone felt about you when you hurt their feelings. It mattered to Julie a great deal.

Miss Waldemar said, 'But if you ask me who's really to blame I'll tell you right out it's the newspapers. Just as well the doctor won't let you look at them, sweetie, because they're having a party, all right. You'd think what with Russia and all, there's more worthwhile things for them to worry about, but no, there it is all over the front pages as big as they can make it. Anything for a nickel, that's their feeling about it. Money, money, money, and who cares if children stand there gawking at headlines and getting ideas at their age!

'Oh, I told that right to one of those reporters, face to face. No sooner did I put foot outside the house yesterday when he steps up, bold as brass, and asks me to get him a picture of you. Steal one, if you please! They're all using that picture from your high school yearbook now; I suppose they want something like that big one on the dresser. And I'm not being asked to do him any favours, mind you; he'll pay fifty dollars cash for it! Well, that was my chance to tell him a thing or two, and don't think I didn't. You are sleepy, aren't you, lamb? Would you like to take a little nap?'

'Yes,' said Julie.

Her parents arrived. She had been eager to see them, but when Tom brought them into her room the eagerness faded. Tom had always despised her father's air of futility – the quality of helplessness that marked his every gesture – and never tried to conceal his contempt. Her mother, who had started off with the one objection that Tom was much too old for Julie – he was thirty to her eighteen when they married – had ultimately worked up to the point of telling him he was an outrageous bully, a charge which he regarded as a declaration of war.

That foolish business, Julie knew guiltily, had been her fault. Tom, who could be as finicky as an old maid about some things, had raged at her for not emptying the pockets of his jackets before sending them to the tailor, and since she still was, at the time, more her mother's daughter than her husband's wife, she had weepingly confided the episode to her mother over the telephone. She had not made that mistake again, but the damage was done. After that her husband and her parents made up openly hostile camps, while she served as futile emissary between them.

When they all came into the room now, Julie could feel their mutual enmity charging the air. She had wistfully hoped that what had happened would change that, and knew with a sinking heart that it had not. What it came to, she thought resignedly, is that they hated each other more than they loved her. And immediately she was ashamed of the thought.

Her father weakly fluttered his fingers at her in greeting, and stood at the foot of the bed looking at her like a lost spaniel. It was a relief when the doorbell rang and he trailed out after Tom to see who it was. Her mother's eyes were red and swollen; she kept a small, damp handkerchief pressed to her nose. She sat down beside Julie and patted her hand.

'It's awful, darling,' she said. 'It's just awful. Now you know why I was so much against your buying the house out here, way at the end of nowhere. How are you?'

'All right.'

Her mother said, 'We would have been here sooner except for Grandma. We didn't want her to find out, but some busybody neighbour went and told her. And you know how she is. She was prostrated. Dr Vaughn was with her for an hour.'

'I'm sorry.'

Her mother patted her hand again. 'She'll be all right. You'll get a card from her when she's up and around.'

Her grandmother always sent greeting cards on every possible occasion. Julie wondered mirthlessly what kind of card she would find to fit this occasion.

'Julie,' her mother said, 'would you like me to comb out your hair?'

'No, thank you, Mother.'

'But it's all knots. Don't those nurses ever do anything for their money? And where are your dark glasses, darling? The ones you use at the beach. It wouldn't hurt to wear them until that discolouration is gone, would it?'

Julie felt clouds of trivia swarming over her, like gnats. 'Please, Mother.'

'It's all right, I'm not going to fuss about it. I'll make up a list for the nurses when I go. Anyhow, there's something much more serious I wanted to talk to you about, Julie. I mean, while Dad and Tom aren't here. Would it be all right if I did?'

'Yes.'

Her mother leaned forward tensely. 'It's about – well, it's about what happened. How it might make you feel about Tom now. Because,

Julie, no matter how you might feel, he's your husband, and you've always got to remember that. I respect him for that, and you must, too, darling. There are certain things a wife owes a husband, and she still owes them to him even after something awful like this happens. She's duty-bound. Why do you look like that, Julie? You do understand what I'm saying, don't you?'

'Yes,' Julie said. She had been chilled by a sudden insight into her parents' life together. 'But please don't talk about it. Everything will be all right.'

'I know it will. If we aren't afraid to look our troubles right in the eye, they can never hurt us, can they? And, Julie, before Tom gets back, there's something else to clear up. It's about him.'

Julie braced herself. 'Yes?'

'It's something he said. When Dad and I came in we talked to him awhile and when – well, you know what we were talking about, and right in the middle of it Tom said in the most casual way – I mean, just like he was talking about the weather or something – he said that when they caught that man he was going to kill him. Julie, he terrified me. You know his temper, but it wasn't temper or anything like that. It was just a calm statement of fact. He was going to kill the man, and that's all there was to it. But he meant it, Julie, and you've got to do something about it.'

'Do what?' Julie said dazedly. 'What can I do?'

'You can let him know he mustn't even talk like that. Everybody feels the way he does – we all want that monster dead and buried. But it isn't up to Tom to kill him. He could get into terrible trouble that way! Hasn't there been enough trouble for all of us already?'

Julie closed her eyes. 'Yes,' she said.

Dr Vaughn came and watched her walk around the room. He said, 'I'll have to admit you look mighty cute in those dark glasses, but what are they for? Eyes bother you any?'

'No,' Julie said. 'I just feel better wearing them.'

'I thought so. They make you look better to people, and they make people look better to you. Say, that's an idea. Maybe the whole human race ought to take up wearing them permanantly. Be a lot better for their livers than alcohol, wouldn't it?'

'I don't know,' Julie said. She sat down on the edge of the bed, huddled in her robe, its sleeves covering her clasped hands, mandarin style. Her hands felt as if they would never be warm again. 'I want to ask you something.'

'All right, go ahead and ask.'

'I shouldn't, because you'll probably laugh at me, but I won't mind.

It's about Tom. He told mother that when they caught the man he was going to kill him. I suppose he was just – I mean, he wouldn't really try to do anything like that, would he?'

The doctor did not laugh. He said grimly, 'I think he might try to do something exactly like that.'

'To *kill* somebody?'

'Julie, I don't understand you. You've been married to Tom – how long is it now?'

'Two years.'

'And in those two years did you ever know him to say he would do something that he didn't sooner or later do?'

'No.'

'I would have bet on that. Not because I know Tom so well, mind you, but because I grew up with his father. Every time I look at Tom, I see his father all over again. There was a man with Lucifer's own pride rammed into him like gunpowder, and a hair-trigger temper to set it off. And repressed. Definitely repressed. Tom is, too. It's hard not to be when you have to strain all the time, keeping the emotional finger off that trigger. I'll be blunt, Julie. None of the Bartons has ever impressed me as being exactly well-balanced. I have the feeling that if you gave any one of them enough motive for killing, he'd kill, all right. And Tom owns a gun, too, doesn't he?'

'Yes.'

'Well, you don't have to look that scared about it,' the doctor said. 'It would have been a lot worse if we hadn't been warned. This way I can tell Christensen and he'll keep an eye on your precious husband until they've got the man strapped into the electric chair. A bullet's too good for that kind of animal, anyhow.'

Julie turned her head away and the doctor placed his finger against her chin and gently turned it back. 'Look,' he said, 'I'll do everything possible to see Tom doesn't get into trouble. Will you take my word for that?'

'Yes.'

'Then what's bothering you? The way I talked about putting that man in the electric chair? Is that what it is?'

'Yes. I don't want to hear about it.'

'But why? You of all people, Julie! Haven't you been praying for them to find him? Don't you hate him enough to want to see him dead?'

It was like turning the key that unlocked all her misery.

'I do!' she said despairingly. 'Oh, yes, I do! But Tom doesn't believe it. That's what's wrong, don't you understand? He thinks it doesn't matter to me as much as it does to him. He thinks I just want to forget all about it, whether they catch the man or not. He doesn't say so, but

478

I can tell. And that makes everything rotten; it makes me feel ashamed and guilty all the time. Nothing can change that. Even if they kill the man a hundred times over, it'll always be that way!'

'It will not,' the doctor said sternly. 'Julie, why don't you use your head? Hasn't it dawned on you that Tom is suffering from an even deeper guilt than yours? That subconsciously he feels a sense of failure because he didn't protect you from what happened? Now he's reacting like any outraged male. He wants vengeance. He wants the account settled. And, Julie, it's his sense of guilt that's tearing you two apart.

'Do you know what that means, young lady? It means you've got a job to do for yourself. The dirtiest kind of job. When the police nail that man you'll have to identify him, testify against him, face cameras and newspapermen, walk through mobs of brainless people dying to get a close look at you. Yes, it's as bad as all that. You don't realise the excitement this mess has stirred up; you've been kept apart from it so far. But you'll have a chance to see it for yourself very soon. That's your test. If you flinch from it, you can probably write off your marriage then and there. That's what you've got to keep in mind, not all that nonsense about things never changing!'

Julie sat there viewing herself from a distance, while the cold in her hands moved up along her arms, turning them to gooseflesh. She said, 'When I was a little girl I cried if anybody even pointed at me.'

'You can't be a little girl all your life,' the doctor said.

When the time came, Julie fortified herself with that thought. Sitting in the official car between Tom and Lieutenant Christensen, shielded from the onlooking world by dark glasses and upturned coat collar, her eyes closed, her teeth set, she repeated it like a private *Hail Mary* over and over – until it became a soothing murmur circling endlessly through her mind.

Lieutenant Christensen said, 'The man's a janitor in one of those old apartment houses a few blocks away from your place. A drunk and a degenerate. He's been up on morals charges before, but nothing like this. This time he put himself in a spot he'll never live to crawl away from. Not on grounds of insanity, or anything else. We've got him cold.'

You can't be a little girl all your life, Julie thought.

The lieutenant said, 'The one thing that stymied us was his alibi. He kept telling us he was on a drunk with this woman of his that night when it happened, and she kept backing up his story. It wasn't easy to get the truth out of her, but we finally did. Turns out she wasn't near him that night. Can you imagine lying for a specimen like that?'

You can't be a little girl all your life, Julie thought.

'We're here, Mrs Barton,' the lieutenant said.

The car had stopped before a side door of the headquarters building, and Tom pushed her through it just ahead of men with cameras who swarmed down on her, shouting her name, hammering at the door when it was closed against them. She clutched Tom's hand as the lieutenant led them through long institutional corridors, other men falling into step with them along the way, until they reached another door where Dahl was waiting.

He said. 'This whole thing takes just one minute, Mrs Barton, and we're over our big hurdle. All you have to do is look at the man and tell us yes or no. That's all there is to it. And it's arranged so that he can't possibly see you. You have nothing at all to fear from him. Do you understand that?'

'Yes,' Julie said.

Again she sat between Tom and Lieutenant Christensen. The platform before her was brilliantly lighted; everything else was in darkness. Men were all around her in the darkness. They moved restlessly; one of them coughed. The outline of Dahl's sharp profile and narrow shoulders were suddenly etched black against the platform; then it disappeared as he took the seat in front of Julie's. She found that her breathing was becoming increasingly shallow; it was impossible to draw enough air out of the darkness to fill her lungs. She forced herself to breathe deeply, counting as she used to do during gym exercises at school. *In-one-two-three. Out-one-two-three—*

A door slammed nearby. Three men walked onto the platform and stood there facing her. Two of them were uniformed policemen. The third man – the one they flanked – towered over them, tall and cadaverous, dressed in a torn sweater and soiled trousers. His face was slack, his huge hand moved back and forth in a vacant gesture across his mouth. Julie tried to take her eyes off that hand and couldn't. Back and forth it went, mesmerising her with its blind, groping motion.

One of the uniformed policemen held up a piece of paper.

'Charles Brunner,' he read loudly. 'Age forty-one. Arrests—' and on and on until there was sudden silence. But the hand still went back and forth, growing enormous before her, and Julie knew, quite without concern, that she was going to faint. She swayed forward, her head drooping, and something cold and hard was pressed under her nose. Ammonia fumes stung her nostrils and she twisted away, gasping. When the lieutenant thrust the bottle at her again, she weakly pushed it aside.

'I'm all right,' she said.

'But it was a jolt seeing him, wasn't it?'

'Yes.'

'Because you recognised him, didn't you?'

She wondered vaguely if that were why. 'I'm not sure.'

Dahl leaned over her. 'You can't mean that, Mrs Barton! You gave me your word you'd know him when you saw him again. Why are you backing out of it now? What are you afraid of?'

'I'm not afraid.'

'Yes, you are. You almost passed out when you saw him, didn't you? Because no matter how much you wanted to get him out of your mind, your emotions wouldn't let you. Those emotions are telling the truth now, aren't they?'

'I don't know!'

'Then look at him again and see what happens. Go on, take a good look!'

Lieutenant Christensen said, 'Mrs Barton, if you let us down now, you'll go out and tell the newspapermen about it yourself. They've been on us like wolves about this thing, and for once in my life I want them to know what we've up against here!'

Tom's fingers gripped her shoulder. 'I don't understand, Julie,' he said. 'Why don't you come out with it? He is the man, isn't he?'

'Yes!' she said, and clapped her hands over her ears to shut out the angry, hateful voices clamouring at her out of the darkness. 'Yes! Yes!'

'Thank God,' said Lieutenant Christensen.

Then Tom moved. He stood up, something glinting metallically in his hand, and Julie screamed as the man behind her lunged at it. Light suddenly flooded the room. Other men leaped at Tom and chairs clattered over as the struggle eddied around the around him, flowing relentlessly toward the platform. There was no one on it when he was finally borne down to the floor by a crushing weight of bodies.

Two of the men, looking apologetic, pulled him to his feet, but kept their arms tightly locked around his. Another man handed the gun to Lieutenant Christensen, and Tom nodded at it. He was dishevelled and breathing hard, but seemed strangely unruffled.

'I'd like that back, if you don't mind,' he said.

'I do mind,' said the lieutenant. He broke open the gun, tapped the bullets into his hand, and then, to Julie's quivering relief, dropped gun and bullets into his own pocket. 'Mr Barton, you're in a state right now where if I charged you with attempted murder you wouldn't even deny it, would you?'

'No.'

'You see what I mean? Now why don't you just cool off and let us handle this job? We've done all right so far, haven't we? And after Mrs Barton testifies at the trial, Brunner is as good as dead, and you can forget all about him.' The lieutenant looked at Julie. 'That makes sense, doesn't it?' he asked her.

'Yes,' Julie whispered prayerfully.

Tom smiled. 'I'd like my gun, if you don't mind.'

The lieutenant stood there speechless for the moment, and then laid his hand over the pocket containing the gun as if to assure himself that it was still there. 'Some other time,' he said with finality.

The men holding Tom released him and he lurched forward and caught at them for support. His face was suddenly deathly pale, but the smile was still fixed on it as he addressed the lieutenant.

'You'd better call a doctor,' he said pleasantly. 'I think your damn gorillas have broken my leg.'

During the time he was in the hospital he was endlessly silent and withdrawn. The day he was brought home at his own insistence, his leg unwieldy in a cast from ankle to knee, Dr Vaughn had a long talk with him, the two of them alone behind the closed doors of the living room. The doctor must have expressed himself freely and forcefully. When he had gone, and Julie plucked up the courage to walk into the living room, she saw her husband regarding her with the look of a man who had had a bitter dose of medicine forced down his throat and hasn't quite decided whether or not it will do him any good.

Then he patted the couch seat beside him. 'There's just enough room for you and me and this leg,' he said.

She obediently sat down, clasping her hands in her lap.

'Vaughn's been getting some things off his chest,' Tom said abruptly. 'I'm glad he did. You've been through a rotten experience, Julie, and I haven't been any help at all, have I? All I've done is make it worse. I've been lying to myself about it, too. Telling myself that everything I did since it happened was for your sake, and all along, the only thing that really concerned me was my own feelings. Isn't that so?'

'I don't know,' Julie said, 'and I don't care. It doesn't matter as long as you talk to me about it. That's the only thing I can't stand, not having you talk to me.'

'Has it been that bad?'

'Yes.'

'But you understand why, don't you? It was something eating away inside of me. But it's gone now, I swear it is. You believe that, don't you, Julie?'

She hesitated. 'Yes.'

'I can't tell whether you mean it or not behind those dark glasses. Lift them up, and let's see.'

Julie lifted the glasses and he gravely studied her face. 'I think you do mean it,' he said. 'A face as pretty as that couldn't possibly tell a lie. But why do you still wear those things? There aren't any marks left.'

She dropped the glasses into place and the world became its soothingly familiar, shaded self again. 'I just like them,' she said. 'I'm used to them.'

'Well, if the doctor doesn't mind, I don't. But if you're wearing them to make yourself look exotic and dangerous, you'll have to give up. You're too much like Sweet Alice. You can't escape it.'

She smiled. 'I don't tremble with fear at your frown. Not really.'

'Yes, you do, but I like it. You're exactly what Sweet Alice must have been. Demure, that's the word, demure. My wife is the only demure married woman in the world. Yielding, yet cool and remote. A lovely lady wrapped in cellophane. How is it you never become a nun?'

She knew she must be visibly glowing with happiness. It had been so long since she had seen him in this mood. 'I almost did. When I was in school I used to think about it a lot. There was this other girl – well, she was really a wonderful person, and she had already made up her mind about it. I guess that's where I got the idea.'

'And then what happened?'

'You know what happened.'

'Yes, it's all coming back now. You went to your first country club dance dressed in a beautiful white gown, with stardust in your hair—'

'It was sequins.'

'No, stardust. And I saw you. And the next thing I remember, we were in Mexico on a honeymoon.' He put his arm around her waist, and she relaxed in the hard circle of it. 'Julie, when this whole bad dream is over we're going there again. We'll pack the car and go south of the border and forget everything. You'd like that, wouldn't you?'

'Oh, very much.' She looked up at him hopefully, her head back against his shoulder. 'But no bullfights, please. Not this time.'

He laughed. 'All right, when I'm at the bullfights you'll be sightseeing. The rest of the time we'll be together. Any time I look around I want to see you there. No more than this far away. That means I can reach out my hand and you'll always be there. Is that clear?'

'I'll be there,' she said.

So she had found him again, she assured herself, and she used that knowledge to settle her qualms whenever she thought of Brunner and the impending trial. She never mentioned these occasional thoughts to Tom, and she came to see that there was a conspiracy among everyone who entered the house – her family and friends, the doctor, even strangers on business with Tom – which barred any reference to the subject of Brunner. Until one evening when, after she had coaxed Tom into a restless sleep, the doorbell rang again and again with maddening persistence.

Julie looked through the peephole and saw that the man standing outside was middle-aged and tired-looking and carried a worn leather portfolio under his arm. She opened the door with annoyance and said,

'Please, don't do that. My husband's not well, and he's asleep. And there's nothing we want.'

The man walked past her into the foyer before she could stop him. He took off his hat and faced her. 'I'm not a salesman, Mrs Barton. My name is Karlweiss. Dr Lewis Karlweiss. Is it familiar to you?'

'No.'

'It should be. Up to three o'clock this afternoon I was in charge of the City Hospital for Mental Disorders. Right now I'm a man without any job, and with a badly frayed reputation. And just angry enough and scared enough, Mrs Barton, to want to do something about it. That's why I'm here.'

'I don't see what it has to do with me.'

'You will. Two years ago Charles Brunner was institutionalised in my care, and, after treatment, released on my say-so. Do you understand now? I am officially responsible for having turned him loose on you. I signed the document which certified that while he was not emotionally well, he was certainly not dangerous. And this afternoon I had that document shoved down my throat by a gang of ignorant politicians who are out to make hay of this case!'

Julie said incredulously, 'And you want me to go and tell them they were wrong? Is that it?'

'Only if you know they *are* wrong, Mrs Barton. I'm not asking you to perjure yourself for me. I don't even know what legal right I have to be here in the first place, and I certainly don't want to get into any more trouble than I'm already in.' Karlweiss looked over her shoulder toward the living room, and shifted his portfolio from one arm to the other. 'Can we go inside and sit down while we talk this over? There's a lot to say.'

'No.'

'All right, then I'll explain it here, and I'll make it short and to the point. Mrs Barton, I know more about Charles Brunner than anyone else in the world. I know more about him than he knows about himself. And that's what makes it so hard for me to believe that you identified the right man!'

Julie said, 'I don't want to hear about it. Will you please go away?'

'No, I will not,' Karlweiss said heatedly. 'I insist on being heard. You see, Mrs Barton, everything Brunner does fits a certain pattern. Every dirty little crime he has committed fits that pattern. It's a pattern of weakness, a constant manifestation of his failure to achieve full masculinity.

'But what he is now charged with is the absolute reverse of that pattern. It was a display of brute masculinity by an aggressive and sadistic personality. It was the act of someone who can only obtain emotional and physical release through violence. That's the secret of such a personality – the need for violence. Not lust, as the Victorians used to preach, but the need for release through violence. And that is a need totally alien to Brunner. It doesn't exist in him. It's a sickness, but it's not his sickness!

'Now do you see why your identification of him hit me and my co-workers at the hospital so hard? We don't know too much about various things in our science yet – I'm the first to admit it – but in a few cases we've been able to work out patterns of personality as accurately as mathematical equations. I thought we had done that successfully with Brunner. I would still think so, if you hadn't identified him. That's why I'm here. I wanted to meet you. I wanted to have you tell me directly if there was any doubt at all about Brunner being the man. Because if there is—'

'There isn't.'

'But if there is,' Karlweiss pleaded, 'I'd take my oath that Brunner isn't guilty. It makes sense that way. If there's the shadow of a doubt—'

'There isn't!'

'Julie!' called Tom from the bedroom. 'Who is that?'

Panic seized her. All she could envision then was Brunner as he would walk down the prison steps to the street, as he would stand there dazed in the sunlight while Tom, facing him, slowly drew the gun from his pocket. She clutched Karlweiss's sleeve and half dragged him toward the door. 'Please, go away!' she whispered fiercely. 'There's nothing to talk about. Please, go away!'

She closed the door behind him and leaned back against it, her knees trembling.

'Julie, who is that?' Tom called. 'Who are you talking to?'

She steadied herself and went into the bedroom. 'It was a salesman,' she said. 'He was selling insurance. I told him we didn't want any.'

'You know I don't want you to open the door to any strangers,' Tom said. 'Why'd you go and do a thing like that?'

Julie forced herself to smile. 'He was perfectly harmless,' she said.

But the terror had taken root in her now – and it thrived. It was fed by many things. The subpoena from Dahl which Tom had her put into his dresser drawer for safekeeping and which was there in full view every time she opened the drawer to get him something. The red circle around the trial date on the calendar in the kitchen which a line of black crosses inched toward, a little closer each day. And the picture in her mind's eye which took many forms, but which was always the same picture with the same ending: Brunner descending the prison steps, or Brunner entering the courtroom, or Brunner in the dank cellar she saw as his natural habitat, and then in the end Brunner standing there, blinking stupidly, his hand moving back and forth over his mouth, and Tom facing him, slowly drawing the gun from his pocket, the gun barrel glinting as it moved into line with Brunner's chest—

The picture came into even sharper focus when Dr Vaughn brought the crutches for Tom. Julie loathed them at sight. She had never minded the heavy pressure of Tom's arm around her shoulders, his weight bearing her down as he lurched from one room to another, hobbled by the cast. The cast was a hobble, she knew, keeping him tied down to the house; he struggled with it and grumbled about it continually, as if the struggling and grumbling would somehow release him from it. But the crutches were a release. They would take him to wherever Brunner was.

She watched him as he practiced using the crutches that evening, not walking, but supporting himself on them to find his balance, and then she helped him sit down on the couch, the leg in its cast propped on a footstall before him.

He said, 'Julie, you have no idea how fed up a man can get, living in pajamas and a robe. But it won't be long now, will it?'

'No.'

'Which reminds me that you ought to give my stuff out to the tailor tomorrow. He's a slow man, and I'd like it all ready when I'm up and around.'

'All right,' Julie said. She went to the wardrobe in the hall and returned with an armful of clothing, which she draped over the back of an armchair. She was mechanically going through the pockets of a jacket when Tom said, 'Come here, Julie.'

He caught her hand as she stood before him. 'There's something on your mind,' he said. 'What is it?'

'Nothing.'

'You were never any good at lying. What's wrong, Julie?'

'Still nothing.'

'Oh, all right, if that's the way you want it.' He released her hand and she went back to the pile of clothing on the armchair, sick with the feeling that he could see through her, that he knew exactly what she was thinking, and must hate her for it. She put aside the jacket and picked up the car coat he used only for driving. Which meant, she thought with a small shudder of realisation, that he hadn't worn it since *that* night. She pulled the gloves from its pocket and tossed the coat on top of the jacket.

'These gloves,' she said, holding them out to show him. 'Where—?'

These gloves, an echo cried out to her. *These gloves,* said a smaller one behind it, and *these gloves, these gloves* ran away in a diminishing series of echoes until there was only deathly silence.

And a glove.

A grey suède glove clotted and crusted with dark-brown stains. Its index finger gouged and torn. Its bitter taste in her mouth. Its owner, a stranger, sitting on the couch, holding out his hand, saying something.

'Give that to me, Julie,' Tom said.

She looked at him and knew there were no secrets between them any more. She watched the sweat starting from his forehead and trickling down the bloodless face. She saw his teeth show and his eye stare as he tried to pull himself to his feet. He failed, and sank back panting.

'Listen to me, Julie,' he said. 'Now listen to me and take hold of yourself.'

'You,' she said drunkenly. 'It was you.'

'Julie, I love you!'

'But it was you. It's all crazy. I don't understand.'

'I know. Because it was crazy. That's what it was, I went crazy for a minute. It was overwork. It was that deal. I was killing myself to put it across, and that night when they turned me down I don't know what happened. I got drunk, and when I came home I couldn't find the key. So I came through the window. That's when it happened. I don't know what it was, but it was something exploding in me. Something in my head. I saw you there, and all I wanted to do – I tell you I don't even know why! Don't *ask* me why! It was overwork, that's what it was. It gets to everybody nowadays. You read about it all the time. You know you do, Julie. You've got to be reasonable about this!'

Julie whispered, 'If you had told me it was you. If you had only told me. But you didn't.'

'Because I love you!'

'No, but you knew how I felt, and you turned that against me. You made me say it was Brunner. Everything you've been doing to me – it was just so I'd say it and say it, until I killed him. You never tried to kill him, at all. You knew I would do it for you. And I would have!'

'Julie, Julie, what does Brunner matter to anybody? You've seen what he's like. He's a degenerate. He's no good. Everybody is better off without people like that around.'

She shook her head violently. 'But you knew he didn't do it! Why couldn't you just let it be one of those times where they never find out who did it?'

'Because I wasn't sure! Everybody kept saying it was only the shock that let you blank it out of your mind. They kept saying if you tried hard enough to remember, it might all come back. So if Brunner – I mean, this way the record was all straight! You wouldn't have to think about it again!'

She saw that if he leaned forward enough he could touch her, and she backed away a step, surprised she had the strength to do it.

'Where are you going?' Tom said. 'Don't be a fool, Julie. Nobody'll believe you. Think of everything that's been said and done, and you'll see nobody would even *want* to believe you. They'll say you're out of your mind!'

She wavered, then realised with horror that she was wavering. 'They will believe me!' she cried, and ran blindly out of the house, sobbing as she ran, stumbling when she reached the sidewalk, so that she fell on her hands and knees, feeling the sting on the scraped knee and she rose and staggered farther down the dark and empty street. It was only when she was at a distance that she stopped, her heart hammering, her legs barely able to support her, to look at the house. Not hers any more. Just his.

He – all of them – had made her a liar and an accomplice. Each of them for his own reason had done that, and she, because of the weakness in her, had let them. It was a terrible weakness, she thought with anguish – the need to have them always approve, the willingness to always say yes to them. It was like hiding yourself behind the dark glasses all the time, not caring that the world you saw through them was never the world you would see through the naked eye.

She turned and fled toward lights and people. The glasses lay in the street where she had flung them, and the night wind swept dust through their shattered frames.

Anthony Gilbert

A Day of Encounters

I noticed the woman the minute she came into the clinic – St Barnabas'
Eye Clinic where I go every six weeks about a little trouble I have. I'm
Martita Browne and you've probably seen my books all over the place.
Eggheads despise them, but I consider myself a benefactress. Even in the
Affluent Society lots of women lead pretty dreary lives. So my books are
like a magic mirror that reflects them as they see themselves, not as they
appear to husbands or families – beautiful, loyal, courageous, even
though they may scream at the sight of a mouse, and above all irresistible
to men; and, naturally, only to be had at the cost of a wedding ring.
Services like that are worth paying for, and, to do my readers justice,
they pay at the rate of substantial royalties to me every year.

This newcomer – I realised at once I'd never seen her before, you
get to know the regulars – didn't resemble my heroines in any way. For
one thing, she was past forty, not good-looking, though she had a lively
face that was somehow demure, too, which wasn't without attraction.
But though her clothes were good – her crocodile bag alone had set
someone back about £60, her scarf was pure heavy silk, and her shoes
handmade – she lacked something, a kind of vitality perhaps. There was
a man with her, presumably her husband, a fair, quiet sort of fellow,
but not living on the breadline – far from it. An expensive house in
the suburbs, I thought, with central heating, a double garage, storm
windows, at least one trip abroad every year, and not a package tour
at that.

I usually sit in a sort of alcove that holds only three or four chairs, and
hardly anyone else ever chooses them. The patients have an idea that
if they sit in the middle of the room they'll be seen sooner, but, of course,
it doesn't help; it's all poppycock – you're seen when the doctor's ready

489

for you and not before. I'd brought the proofs of my new book with me –
Not Wooed but Won – and I thought I might get quite a lot of work done
while I waited. I could see it was going to be a busy clinic this afternoon.

I was a bit surprised when the newcomer came to sit beside me. 'Is it
always as crowded as this?' she asked. 'Willy said he'd be back in an
hour and he does hate waiting.' Then before I could reply she saw the
proofs on my lap – I hadn't begun, so the title page was on top. 'Are
you Martita Browne?' she asked. 'Did you write that?'

I knew what was coming, of course. She'd always longed to write,
but there'd never been time; her life story would make a wonderful
plot, and since she'd never use it – and of course I'd disguise the names.
If I've heard that once, I've heard it a hundred times. I was wondering
how I could suggest that none of my readers would be interested in a
woman in her forties when she gushed on, 'People say that sometimes
your heroes are too good to be true, but of course that's nonsense. I
know because – well, you might say I married one of them. You might
have taken Victor for your model.'

'I thought you said his name was Willy,' I murmured.

'Victor was my first husband. Willy's as different as chalk from cheese.
Victor had everything – good looks, a marvellous figure, tall, dark,
alluring – it wasn't surprising all the women were after him. I'm sure
they must all have gasped when they heard it was me he was going to
marry. I wasn't even young – twenty-eight – you'd never have a heroine
of twenty-eight, would you, Miss Browne?'

Well, she knew I wouldn't. My readers never see themselves as more
than twenty-five at the very most.

'I wasn't in the least like one of your heroines,' the voice babbled on.
'My father – he was a minister with a great sense of fun – everyone said
so – used to call me Miss Brains-Before-Beauty. Count your blessings,
he'd say. Brains are often a better investment. And I put mine out to
usury like that man in the Bible, whose ten talents turned into twenty
talents. I never really thought I'd get married.'

'But there was Victor?' I remarked.

'Yes. He came into this office where I was working – actually, it was
my own business – and it was like the sun coming in. He was a bit
younger than me, but he said he preferred mature women. Girls never
had any conversation except hairdos and what he called "parish pump"
subjects.'

'What was his job?' I asked. It was quite automatic. I couldn't have
even a minor character in a story without knowing his background, and
obviously Victor wasn't going to be minor.

'Oh!' For the first time she sounded evasive. 'He was a sales representative – went round to the big industrial houses.'

'A success?' I bored on. You might say it was none of my business, but the woman had thrust herself on me and I had a right to some return. Anyway, you can never be sure where you'll find plot and character ideas.

'You'd have thought with those looks and that charm he couldn't fail, though he always warned me it was cut-throat competition, and I suppose he wasn't ruthless enough. Still, at first everything went all right, and then he started going "on the road." You know what that means? The firms – and they weren't always the same firms – sent him to the outlying districts. He made a joke of it. Someone's got to carry news to the heathen, he'd say, but – oh, Miss Browne, it was like playing Shaftesbury Avenue and then finding yourself sent out with a second-class repertory company. Luckily I wasn't called Miss Brains-Before-Beauty for nothing. I'd sold my business when I got married, so I had a nice little nest egg put by, and believe me, it came in very useful.'

Candidly, I didn't think this was getting me anywhere. A plain woman had been married for her money – that's what it amounted to. But of course there had to be a third party, otherwise there was no story at all. And even I couldn't believe *she* would turn up with a lover.

'So what happened?' I encouraged.

Her reply startled me. 'Oh, he died.'

'Victor died?'

'Yes. It was a bit sudden.'

I had a fresh idea. 'Sudden enough to attract the attention of the police?'

She took off her handsome gloves and folded them carefully on her knee. Her rings would have paid my rent for a year.

'Anyone could tell you *are* a writer. You know all the answers.'

But did I? There'd been an odd note in her voice when she said, 'Oh, he died.' Not grief, not relief either, but a sort of lack of confidence, as if she couldn't be certain. But that was nonsense. You either know your husband's dead or you don't. Or perhaps she knew he wasn't, and he was blackmailing her. It seemed pretty obvious she'd struck it rich in her second marriage. I was so deep in calculations that I missed the next few sentences, but what I did hear nearly blew me out of my chair.

'You couldn't call it murder, could you?' the voice pleaded. 'I've waited eight years to hear someone say that, only there was never anyone to tell. I don't even have a sister.'

And wouldn't tell her if you had, I thought grimly. Not if you've got the sense you were born with.

I realised now, of course, that she had no doubts about dear Victor's death – a posh funeral and wreaths three foot deep, most likely. No, it was the way of it that worried her. But – murder? I hadn't time to think straight.

'What did the police make of it?' I asked. 'I mean, who mentioned murder?'

'There were only three alternatives – accident, suicide, or murder – and no one could believe it was an accident.'

'Why should it be a suicide?'

'Well, there was this girl – Elizabeth Sinclair.'

Inwardly I heaved a sigh of relief. So we'd got to the heart of the story at last – the third side of the triangle, without which there's no story at all.

'People used to ask me sometimes – aren't you afraid of someone trying to steal your handsome husband now that he's away from home so much? But I wasn't. Oh, there might be incidents, but a sensible wife shuts her eyes to them. He was away three or four days on end sometimes. Frankly, I didn't see how he could afford to leave me. It's a cruel thing to say about a dead man, Miss Browne, but – well, charm's like anything else: it gets tarnished, and thirty-six is different from twenty-four, which was his age when we married. It appeared he'd met this girl – she was barely twenty-one – and it had been love at first sight for both of them.'

'I thought you said he couldn't afford to keep a wife. Or did Elizabeth have money?'

'She was the only daughter of a very rich man – the only child – and she'd get everything.'

'Unless Daddy married again.' I took for granted he was a widower.

Her mouth hardened. 'You didn't know Victor. He'd have insisted on a prenuptial settlement – and he'd have got it. I don't say Daddy would have approved, but Elizabeth was the kind no man can resist. Now, *there* was a heroine for you, Miss Browne. Dark and slender and – glowing. You remember Shelley's moon-maiden, with white fire laden? She made me think of that. I only saw her the once, you know.'

'You mean he brought her?' Victor was proving himself less and less like one of my heroes.

'She brought herself. "I thought if I came in person, perhaps you'd understand," she said. "Oh, how can you want to hold onto him when you know it's me he loves? Why won't you divorce him, Mrs Hughes? You've had twelve years—"

'And, of course, Victor could live another thirty. But not with this girl, I decided. If I'd been tempted to yield before, I was iron-hard now.

' "Surely she made you see—" That was Victor talking, when he came home.

' "So it was your idea?" I said. "I might have guessed it. You must be mad if you think I'd make it possible for you to ruin that girl's life," I said warmly. "She's made for better than secondhand goods."

' "I won't give her up," Victor said.

' "There's no law to stop your setting up house," I agreed. "But would Daddy like that?" He raged, but he didn't move me. "You'll only marry her over my dead body," I said. Have you ever noticed, Miss Browne, how often clichés come home to roost?'

'But it was Victor's dead body,' I pointed out.

'Yes.'

'And there was talk of murder.'

'It's what the police would have liked to believe,' she said bitterly. 'I suppose you can hardly blame them. You don't get promotion by arresting motorists for illegal parking.'

'You want to be careful,' I advised her sharply. 'You never know who may be sitting next to you in a place like this. There's an ex-Superintendent Humbolt who comes here sometimes.' He was one of the few useful contacts I'd made at the clinic; he'd helped me out of knotty problems once or twice when my heroines had been more feather-brained than usual. I knew what he'd say about Victor. Never trust charm, it's the most powerful weapon in the devil's armoury. I've heard him say that more than once. 'But why should anyone think it was murder?'

She went off at a bit of a tangent. 'If you saw someone who'd cheated you sitting on a balcony, say, and a chimney pot started to topple, and you knew it would hit him and you didn't yell out, would that make you a murderer?'

It wasn't the sort of problem I've ever been called on to solve. Murder's taboo in my kind of tale. 'Accessory before the fact?' I hazarded.

'Ah, but whose accessory? You can't be accessory to a force of nature – but what else caused the chimney pot to fall?'

'A good question,' I agreed. I wondered what the pious would say. An Act of God? Not very complimentary to God, of course. Not that I supposed a chimney pot had actually played any part in this story. And of course it turned out to be just an analogy.

But talk about clichés! The truth was almost as incredible – the truth as she told it, that is.

It seems that it was Victor's custom to make their after-dinner coffee.

'And you let him do it, even after you'd refused him a divorce?' My most addle-pated heroine would have had more sense than that.

'If he'd meant to – to do away with me – he'd never have chosen anything so obvious.'

'Sometimes the most obvious thing is also the most subtle.'

'Anyway, that night – it was a few days after our conversation about Elizabeth and I thought he was accepting the situation – he'd just brought in the coffeepot and tray when the phone rang. I went to answer it, expecting it to be for me. But it was for Victor. When I came in he'd just poured out the coffee. "Well, that was quick," he said. "Or was it a wrong number?" "It's for you," I told him.

' "Chaps do choose the most inconvenient times," he grumbled, looking at his coffee. "He might have waited another five minutes."

' "It'll take five minutes to cool – or are you afraid I might lace it with arsenic while you're out of the room?" I said.

'He stared. "That's a nice thing for a wife to say to her husband." He jammed the cup down. "Don't let yours grow cold. I poured it out" – and he went off, shutting the door behind him. It's funny, Miss Browne, how trifles can hold your attention. I hadn't thought anything about his pouring out both cups till he called my attention to it, and it made me wonder. You see, he knows – knew – I love everything piping hot, and if it had been Leila Hope on the phone – the call I'd expected – well, it's always ten minutes before she hangs up.

'I'd picked up my cup, but now I put it down and crept over and opened the door. The telephone was in an alcove in the hall, so that I could hear without being seen. Victor was laughing and joking, then suddenly his voice changed. "I'm very anxious about her," he said. "She gets these moods, you can't reason with her, and she's inclined to be morbid. I can neither laugh nor argue her out of it."

'I shut the door and came back to my chair. So that was his game, I thought. I was to be represented as being eccentric, so that anything might be expected of me. Automatically I picked up the coffee, and then the notion came to me. I'm not a writer, Miss Browne, though I'm quite a reader. And being alone so much I'd had time to think. And I wondered why he'd been so anxious that I drink my coffee hot. It wasn't like him to worry about things like that. And then his saying I was morbid.'

I interrupted rather brutally. 'So you decided he'd poisoned the coffee and then gone off to telephone. But how did he know it was going to ring then?'

'He could have arranged it, knowing I'd probably answer. Oh, I didn't think he intended murder. He knew the surviving partner would be the first suspect, and there was no one but ourselves in the house. But don't you see, that meant he could tell any story he liked! I thought he'd put in enough of whatever it was to make it necessary to call a doctor, who'd say it was attempted suicide, and then later, if, for instance, I fell under a subway train or something – I don't drive a car – everyone would remember the first time.'

'Why didn't you pour the coffee out of the window?' I suggested sensibly.

'I didn't think of that, only of upsetting the table, and that would have meant breaking the cups; but then I'm not clumsy, so I'd have aroused his suspicions at once. Besides, I didn't see why he shouldn't be – what's the phrase?'

'Hoist on his own petard?'

'That's it. Biter bit. So – oh, Miss Browne, I switched the cups. I thought it would serve a dual purpose – make him uncomfortable and let him see I knew what he was up to. I thought of it as a self-protective measure.'

'And when he came back?'

'I'd finished my cup, and he drank his – well, mine really. Then we each had a refill, and soon after he said he was tired and how about bed? Happy dreams, he said. Those were the last words I ever heard from him. When I went in next morning with a cup of tea – we had separate rooms by then, since I'd found out about Elizabeth – oh, it was clear he wasn't going to be interested in tea any longer.

'The doctor said he must have been dead for quite some time; and he couldn't give a death certificate, he'd have to inform the coroner. That's when the horror suddenly became real. You're very clever, Miss Browne, not to have crimes in your books. People who like violence can get it in the newspapers. The police were in and out of that house like – like mites in a cheese.'

'What was it he'd taken?'

'One of the barbiturates. I don't understand about medicine – I'm never ill, neither of us ever was. I hardly take an aspirin six times a year. Of course, they searched everything, almost took the paper off the walls, but they couldn't find even an empty vial. And seeing that I practically never went to a doctor they couldn't have traced the stuff to me, however much they'd wanted to.'

'Where did they think he got it from?'

'No one knows, but he did travel for a firm of pharmaceutical chemists at one time. He could easily have got it that way, though I've heard you *can* get hold of drugs even without a doctor's prescription. But that was only the beginning. Accident was ruled out – which left suicide or murder. Everyone said he wouldn't have committed suicide, and I didn't think he would myself.'

She paused, but I wasn't letting her stop there. It's not often an hour-and-a-half wait in a clinic can bring you a plum like this. 'So it *had* to be murder?'

'Only it couldn't be. What advantage did I gain from his death, I asked them. I didn't inherit a penny – in fact, after the funeral I had to pay a large tailor's bill – he was very dandified about his clothes. If I'd wanted to be rid of him I had only to walk out. I had my own means, you know.'

'You didn't think of telling them the simple truth?'

Her eyes stared at me, as round as pennies. 'Well, naturally I thought of it; and naturally I held my tongue. There was no proof and if I let them know I had a suspicion – well, there was only my word for it that *I* hadn't doped the coffee. They wouldn't have got a conviction. I know that, but the mud would have stuck to me for life. Anyway, the verdict was death from barbiturate poisoning, with insufficient evidence to show how it had been administered.

'But that was bad enough. I was conscious of very odd looks wherever I went, and people in shops suddenly and mysteriously didn't have the things I wanted. A little later I changed back from Ruth Hughes to Ruth White – they're neither of them conspicuous names, are they? – and I came south. In London they might never have heard of Victor Hughes and quite likely they hadn't. Anyway, it's like that hymn you learn at school. "They fly forgotten as a dream—" '

'And in London you met Willy?'

'Well, that was three years ago. I still had my capital and I went into partnership with a woman who ran an agency. I supplied the competence and she supplied the charm, which seemed to me quite a fair division of labour. When I met Willy – he was so different from Victor they might hardly have belonged to the same species.'

'And yet they say that when people marry again, they always choose the same type,' I reminded her.

'I suppose there has to be an exception to every rule. Victor had been so popular, but Willy seemed so – so neglected. He'd been a widower for years, had a bookshop, and was the studious type. The shop had great potentialities, but, oh, Miss Browne, the confusion in it, everything so hugger-mugger it would take a week to find anything a customer wanted. Willy lived – very uncomfortably – in two rooms above the shop. The first time I invited him back to my apartment for a meal he said, "This is what I call a home. I've seen nothing like it since Edna died fifteen years ago."

'He was so vague – if he'd been in Victor's shoes the police wouldn't have found any trouble at all in believing he'd taken the stuff himself thinking it was saccharine. I had a sense of responsibility towards him. That was the start. Of course, it was never like Victor, but I was forty-five by then, an age when your ardour has cooled off. And then, when once you've been married – even if it hadn't worked out too well – well, it seems unnatural to be living alone.

'Anyway, we got married. I kept up my interest in the business – Willy had the shop, you see, and it wasn't as though we were likely to have a family – and weekends we worked among the books. I tell you, Miss Browne, you wouldn't recognise the place now. It's got quite a reputation. We can tell customers right away if we've got what they want in stock, and, if not, where we can get it and how long they must wait. A few months ago we put in a manager, a very capable fellow of about forty-five – sometimes I say to Willy, I don't know how we'd get on without Mr Brett. It means Willy isn't tied down so much, he can go to book sales, have a bit of private life. Mr Brett's a bachelor – it doesn't seem to matter to him how long hours he works.'

I only had time for one more question before her name was called. 'Did you tell Willy about Victor?'

She looked astounded, as though her eyes would drop out of her head.

'Of course not! All that happened to Mrs Victor Hughes, and to me at least she's as dead as her husband. Nothing whatever to do with Willy.'

Then her name was called and she jumped up with the eagerness of all new patients. I saw that she'd left her umbrella leaning against the chair, but I supposed she'd come back for it. I got down to my proofs at last; a while later I heard a creak as some heavy body descended alongside mine.

A voice said, 'Well, Miss Browne, still at it, I see?'

I looked up and there was my old friend, ex-Superintendent Humbolt, though he doesn't insist on his former title any more. Pulling rank, he calls it.

'This is a day of encounters,' I said. 'I haven't seen you for a long time.'

'Come for my semi-annual checkup,' he told me. 'Fact is, my sight's not what it used to be. There's one disease none of the doctor's can cure, and that's *Anno Domini*. And a good thing for the race it can't. We'd all be living in trees like chimps – there wouldn't be anywhere else to live.'

'Oh, come on,' I jollied him. 'You're not that old. I was wondering if you could give me some advice.'

'I knew it,' he said mournfully. 'All you ever want of me is a chance to pick my brains.'

'It's a point arising from a story,' I explained, carefully not saying it was one of mine. 'If you'd been married to a man who tried to murder you, and later on you decided to marry again, would you tell Husband Number Two about Number One?'

'I'd never put the notion of murder in any husband's mind,' he replied promptly.

'That solves my problem,' I told him, and then he shook out his newspaper and I got to work.

A bit later a rather diffident voice said, 'I was looking for my wife, and I believe this is her umbrella.' And I looked up to see the rather vague-looking man who'd come with the 'late' Mrs Victor Hughes.

'It's quite a relief,' he told me. 'I thought I'd lost her.'

An odd sound, like a bear chuckling to itself in a sardonic sort of way, came from behind the open newspaper.

'You want to be careful you don't make a habit of it, Willy.' The newspaper was lowered. Ex-Superintendent Humbolt might appear to be grinning but his voice was the voice of Jehovah. 'This 'ud be the third, wouldn't it? It nevers pays to overdo things. People get such strange ideas. Funny, you know.'

'I don't call that very funny,' said Willy. 'I'm surprised at you, Mr Humbolt.'

'Your wife's seeing one of the doctors,' I intervened quickly. 'I don't suppose she'll be long.'

'Don't want to get caught up in the rush hour on the underground,' Humbolt went on, and Willy said, 'I've got the car. We live out at Sheepshot now, and Ruth doesn't drive. Still, it's a nice house and a big garden. My wife enjoys gardening.'

'Nothing wrong with gardening so long as you don't dig too deep.' I had never thought that Humbolt could be so malicious. And then *she* came hurrying back, saying, 'Oh, Willy, did I keep you long? I had to wait, and the doctor thinks I should come again in six weeks.'

'It'll be Harley Street for you next time, my dear,' said Willy.

'You must meet Miss Browne, Martita Browne, the famous writer. You know.' She didn't pay any attention to Humbolt. After all, she'd never set eyes on him before.

'Why did you say that, about losing wives?' I demanded, as soon as the couple was out of earshot. I simply had to know. If an angel had summoned me with a trumpet at that moment, I wouldn't have heard.

'The object of the police is to try and prevent crime,' Humbolt said in his deceptively quiet way. 'Poor Willy! He's lost a couple of wives already. Such a careless fellow – or could I be wrong? I mean, no doctors, no deathbeds. Number One was drowned in the South of France. They'd only been married two years. Something went wrong, the boat overturned, he keot swimming round and diving for her; they saw him from the shore, but he couldn't find her. She was under the boat, and they said she must have hit her head on something that knocked her out.

'Then about three years later he married again. It was the Costa Brava this time, and he was miles away, sunbathing. She'd taken the car – she brought that and some other very nice bits of goods you'd not turn your nose up at, Miss Browne, to the marriage – and had gone to visit friends. When she didn't come back he got anxious, phoned the friends' house, but she'd never arrived. Then he called the authorities, but you know how it is in Spain. *Mañana!*' He looked at me questioningly.

'I understand,' I assured him. 'Never do today what you can put off till tomorrow.'

'She'd been dead for hours when they found her, under the wreck of the car. One of the Spanish police said, "What a waste! Such a beautiful motor!" Nothing about the lady, but I daresay when they found her she wasn't so beautiful.'

'What did they think had happened?'

'No one could tell for sure, the car being in the state it was – something gone wrong with the steering, perhaps. Only – she had been proud of that car, had had it completely overhauled only the week before, when they'd left England. Still, there were no witnesses and a car can't talk. The advantage of coming to a sticky end in a warm foreign climate is you can't hang about waiting for relatives—'

'You mean, she was buried in Spain?'

'Both wives were buried abroad. Good sense really. The authorities make a lot of hoo-ha about shipping a corpse home – much less trouble and, of course, much more economical to have it buried on the spot. Wonder if the new Mrs Willy likes to travel.'

'I don't think she said. Just that she'd met him by way of business. Gone to his shop to buy a book, I suppose.' That surprised me. She looked the sort who would expect to get her reading from the Public Library.

Humbolt shook his head. 'They met at her place of business, not his.'

'She said she ran some sort of agency with another woman.'

'That's right. Marriage bureau. Fact, Miss Browne. They'll tell you there's one born every minute, and you don't have to be a policeman to know it's true. Convenient for chaps like Willy: you get all the statistics about the lady, age, looks – they have to supply a photograph and not one taken twenty years ago at that – financial position – the agency does all your homework for you. It's my belief if a chimp walked into one of those places they'd match him up with a woman chimp.'

He thought a moment, then went on, 'I suppose it occurred to Willy he could hardly do better than to marry the boss. To my way of thinking he's no matinee idol, but somehow he gets the women. That quality called charm, I suppose. She kept on with her interest in the agency, and he had the shop – got a very good name now, I understand, quite a little gold mine.'

'I thought you were retired,' I remarked maliciously.

'Once a copper always a copper. I'll retire when they start ringing the church bell for me. Still, as you say, no skin off my nose.'

'It proves one thing,' I said. 'Women do always go for the same type. Willy may not look remotely like Victor, but they're chips from the same block.'

I saw I'd really got his attention now. 'Who's Victor?'

'Victor Hughes – her first husband.'

'First time I heard she had one before she married Willy. Sure she's not pulling your leg?'

'After he died—'

'How was that?'

'You could call it a sort of accident.'

'With or without wifely assistance?' The Day of Judgment will hold no shocks for that man.

'Let's say that she took a chance and it came off.' I told him in detail about her switching the cups. 'And if you don't believe me,' I said, 'there's bound to be a record. I'm not sure where it happened, but somewhere up north.'

He shook his head. 'Not me, Miss Browne. You've just reminded me, I'm retired and if there wasn't a trial – or was there?'

'There wasn't enough evidence to charge her. They never seemed to think of the fourth alternative – that he might have been the one with the murderous impulse.'

'You bet they thought of it, but the police can't go on feminine intuition, not the way ladies do. No witnesses, no proof she'd ever handled a barbiturate in her life, and, like she said, no motive. Anyway, it wasn't my manor and the Chief Constable wouldn't thank me for taking up an old case. I've no fresh evidence. You might say it's a good thing she knows how to take care of herself, seeing who she's married to now.'

'But you can't leave it at that,' I exclaimed. 'She could be in danger this very minute.'

Humbolt has one of those India-rubber faces that can change under your eyes. Now he looked like a bloodhound – sad, a bit bloodshot, long drooping jowls. 'You don't have to worry about her Miss Browne, now that Willy knows we've met her. Even he 'ud be hard put to it to explain a third tragedy. Of course, if I was to drop dead, or you – but you take it from me, there'll be no need to search the newspapers for her name this side of Christmas.'

Only the ex-superintendent was wrong. About four months later I picked up my *Morning Argus* – the posh papers are no good to writers like me – and there he was on the front page: *Well-Known Bookseller Falls to His Death.* It was in France – that was true to type, I thought – they'd been staying in one of these big old-fashioned hotels with a balcony and steps leading to a courtyard, a fountain, flowers, that sort of thing.

There was a gate in the trellis you could unbolt if you wanted to go down. The widow said they'd been talking and she went back into the bedroom for a cigarette, and the next minute she heard a scream and a sort of muffled crash and the trellis gate was swinging. It was two stories to the courtyard and Willy never recovered consciousness.

Everyone in the hotel was shocked – such an affectionate couple! Only they changed their tune when some busybody dug up the story of his previous wives. Then they started to talk about the mills of God grinding slowly, Providence seeing to it that he'd fallen into the pit he'd dug – meaning he'd opened the gate intending to give her a fatal shove, and then forgotten he'd opened it.

Her story was they'd been in the courtyard earlier, looking at the fish in the fountain, and he must have forgotten to bolt the gate after them. No, there was no family tomb, and burial on the spot, she was sure, was what he'd have preferred.

A few weeks ago I happened to be passing the bookshop. It was just about closing time, and Ruth came out with a tall dressy sort of fellow – forty-five or forty-six, I'd say.

When she saw me Ruth said, 'Fancy meeting you again! Do you still go to that eye clinic? Do you remember me telling you about Mr Brett? You did read about Willy, I expect? Wasn't it terrible? But he was always so absent-minded. I don't know what I'd have done without Malcolm.'

It was easy to see who Malcolm was – easy, too, to realise she probably wasn't going to have to do without him.

I haven't seen Mr Humbolt since – perhaps he doesn't come to the clinic any more. Of course, I'm only a writer of romantic tales, not works of logic or mystical speculation; but I do sometimes wonder, if there really is a Hereafter, what Victor and Willy are thinking now.

Brian Cleeve

Foxer

Mr Francis O'Reilly, known to a wide circle of enemies as Foxer, lay on his narrow prison bed thinking of old age and death. Tomorrow he would be seventy-eight! It had crept up on him unawares – like a policeman in the night. He had grown old, and never realised it. He had known, naturally enough, that he was growing older. But not that he was already old. Very old. Too old. He stroked his beard, soft as white silk, luxuriously spread on the coarse prison blanket, wavy, sumptuous, so convincingly old and virtuous that he had never thought of it as a sign of true old age, but merely as a tool of his trade, a means of convincing victims that a man with a beard like that could not conceivably be telling them a string of expensive lies.

He had had it for twenty years, tended it, loved it, seen it grow from mere pale grey to pure, angelic white, defended it with a terrible fury from a series of prison doctors and barbers, stolen the most delicate shampoos for it, kept it in defiance of reason, when its mere appearance in any police district was enough to get him arrested. In fact many a poor old bearded clergyman, going about his heavenly business in London, or Manchester, or Dublin, had suddenly become aware of some large man in plain clothes taking an unnatural interest in his innocent old face, and had felt vaguely guilty, until the detective realised it wasn't Foxer, and had turned away.

For Foxer specialised in clergymen. Catholic priests, Church of England parsons, Congregational ministers, Unitarians – he was entirely ecumenical. But at home in Ireland he was always a priest. From the Foreign Missions. It might be South Africa. Or South America. Or China. He liked variety. And prided himself on giving spiritual value. Many a gull who had already parted with his five-pound donation to the building fund of the Mission Church in M'Wanga, or the Convent in San Felipe in Uruguay, or the Seminary in Pei Pei, somewhere to the north of Ping Ping, had been entertained for an hour afterwards with fearsome stories of pagan darkness in Pei Pei, of the awful threat of Communistic atheism in San Felipe, or of the dreadful fate of female orphans among the Abongas. Many a hard-headed commercial traveller had wiped away a tear as he put down his contribution to the M'Wanga mission on his expenses sheet, suitably disguised as 'entertainment'.

And it was not entirely lies on Foxer's part. He had truly been in San Felipe. He had spent a fortnight in gaol there until he bribed his way out. And once he had actually adopted a female Abonga orphan. At least she was female, and probably an orphan. And if she wasn't an Abonga she was certainly black, and strikingly handsome in a dark and lissom way. He had found her in Liverpool, and spent three months of absolute felicity with her in Manchester, until an interfering police-man raked up an old unpleasantness and saw him off to Strangeways Gaol for two and a half years. But that was life.

His at any rate, and he had few regrets. Of the past fifty-seven years he might have, indeed he had, spent thirty-seven in various prisons, from Wandsworth to Sing-Sing, but when he considered the way he had spent the remaining twenty years of his adult life he had no regrets at all. 'Oh boy,' he might have said, 'the times I've had.' Now, though, he had grown old and all the times were behind him, and only death in front, and it was time to make an end of folly and face the facts.

'You've got to face up to it,' the Governor had said. 'You're too old for it.' And taking him by his frail elbow the Governor had steered him to the barred window of the Governor's office and pointed to the neat row of wooden crosses in the cemetery plot. 'Unless you want to join them out there, you'll have to go straight from here on, old friend, you really will.' And he had looked quite sad. Because although he was a comparatively young man – barely sixty – he and Foxer had known each other for a very long time; since the days when Foxer still worked the race trains and the Governor was a junior screw.

'You don't want to die in here, do you, Foxer?' the Governor had said, because he didn't want to die in there himself, and sometimes he was afraid he would. And, indeed, neither did Foxer want to die in prison, although for rather different reasons from the Governor's. Foxer's were purely snobbish. He had been so long connected with the clergy that he had very little faith in a heavenly life beyond the grave. The grave itself was all a man could be sure of, and he had no wish to spend eternity beside some gas-meter pilferer or defaulting debtor. For years he had had his mind's eye fixed on a charming little plot in Glasnevin near the poet's corner, where his neighbours were certain to be people of intellect and conversation. All that he needed was the price of it, and his last little escapade had been connected with that very thing. . . .

He had been spending the summer working the tourist resorts of the South West, modestly but profitably. He hadn't touched the South West for twenty-five years, and he hadn't had a beard then, so that between the natural generosity of holiday-makers, and the profound respect of Irish hoteliers for the holy cloth – perhaps they hope that it will be counted to them in Heaven against their various little occupational peccadillos, like serving the worst coffee west of Kamchatka – he had done quite well. But collecting donations for non-existent missions, while very safe, is also a very slow way of conning gulls, and it is almost impossible, given the cost of living, to accumulate much capital like that. By the end of the summer Foxer had enough to get him through the winter, or a fair part of it, but not a penny more. And it was then, in Tralee, in late September, that the thought of the little plot in Glasnevin came back to him. A mere hundred pounds would secure it. But it might as well have been a thousand. Nearly all the tourists had gone home.

Which meant the Bishop's Party racket. Just once more. For the plot in Glasnevin. And then, as God was his witness, never again. It had already cost him two years in Sing-Sing, three and a half in Wandsworth, and two stretches in the 'Joy'. But after all he had never worked it in the South West.

The next day, therefore, he went into the local branch of the Bank of Ireland, deposited five pounds, and acquired a cheque book. He then went to the largest hotel, booked a room with a private bath, had the finest dinner that the hotel could provide, order a bottle of twelve-year-old whiskey, and begged the manager to join him for a night-cap. He had already armed himself with a good deal of local clerical knowledge.

The manager came, and for half an hour was treated to a virtuoso display of conning – the fruit and essence of more than fifty years of expertise. Female orphans in Abonga, heart-rendingly grateful babies in Pei Pei, pathetically devout Indianos in San Felipe, held out their black and yellow and brown hands to the manager until the tears sprang to his eyes and his hand sprang to his pocket-book.

But Foxer merely shook a reproachful head. 'My dear fellow,' he said, 'do you think I invited you up here to get a subscription for my orphans? Another time perhaps, but tonight allow me to lay aside my shepherd's cares and play host for once. Even a missionary grows tired of begging, you know, even for Holy Charity.' And he tipped the last of the whiskey into the manager's glass with a sly wink of hospitality.

'And talking of playing host, I find that I am an old' – he stroked his beard – 'a *very* old friend of your bishop, the good Doctor McGurk.' For that was in fact the bishop's name. 'We were in Maynooth together – oh, half a century ago, alas for vanished youth, vanished ambitions. *Eheu, fugaces, tempus fugit*, as our old professor of philosophy would say. Little we knew, ah little indeed, young skipping lambs of the Good Shepherd's, how it would *fugit*. And now the good Aloysius McGurk wears the purple, may God deal gently with him always, and I – I am what you see, my dear fellow: a humble missionary priest, begging bread for his orphans in the four corners of this generous land. But just for once, for old times' sake, I would dearly love to play host to my old friend, and his cathedral clergy. And indeed' – he winked broadly – 'I am not entirely disinterested in this, for the good Doctor can, if he wishes, favour my mission field in many ways, such as directing the thoughts of young seminarians towards the spiritual needs of my pagan orphans. Alas, we doves must be wiser than serpents if we are to survive in this world.'

Which in a way was very true. And so first Foxer planned with the manager a most elaborate feast that would melt any bishop's charitable old heart – beginning with oysters and carrying on through a dozen courses to peaches *flambées* in kirsch *à la maréchale*, God forgive Foxer; accompanied by enough wines of France and the Rhineland, not to speak of twelve-year-old whiskey and ancient brandy, to sink the clergy of the entire diocese into a fit of the DTs.

'There will,' said Foxer, 'be about a dozen of us. Say fourteen. I would,' he added roguishly, 'say thirteen, if that did not verge on blasphemy. But there is one thing more. I wish to make this little party a memorable one for my old friend, and *his* old friends, for God knows whether we shall meet again this side of Paradise. And while he is certain of his entry, I, alas. . . .' And he struck his breast.

'No, no,' cried the manager, entirely overcome. 'May God spare you both to us for many years yet; may you give many more such little parties.' As well the manager might wish, for his profit on this one looked like being in the neighbourhood of fifty pounds. He and Foxer were both on the edge of weeping, and Foxer had barely voice enough left to call for another bottle. It came, was opened, sampled, approved.

'You were saying?' prompted the manager. 'You wanted to make this occasion truly memorable for our beloved bishop?'

'Ah yes!' cried Foxer, striking his forehead. 'I'm glad you reminded me. I wish to buy a few little gifts for my guests, trifles of course, a missionary's wallet is seldom filled with anything but crumbs' – a sad smile – 'but trifles of taste. Pray tell me, what is the best establishment for such gifts in this estimable town?'

The manager looked extremely thoughtful, fondled his chin, and suggested a local jeweller of excellent stock and standing. The bottle was finished. And both manager and missionary – after his share of two bottles of twelve-year-old Irish whiskey Foxer *was* a missionary, heart, soul and body – both these old men toddled off to bed and slept the sleep of the truly satisfied.

Next morning Foxer strolled gently down to the recommended jewellers, told the necessary part of his story, bought a handsome pectoral cross for the bishop; a snuff box, gold and enamel, for the canon; a gold cigarette lighter for Monsignor O'Flaherty; and so on through the list of his clerical guests, to the amount of about three hundred pounds.

When all was parcelled and totted he produced his cheque book, gave the Bank of Ireland and the hotel manager as his references – not to speak of the bishop, or his own appearance – paid, if that is the word, for his purchases, and walked blithely out of the shop with the loot that, properly flogged in the right quarters of Dublin, would net him a hundred cold smackers in cash. He thought he might even keep the pectoral cross for himself.

Ten yards down the street he was arrested.

When he gave evidence against Foxer at the trial, the hotel manager almost wept again – with unkind laughter. Thirty years before, he said, choking back his revengeful mirth, Foxer had caught him and the local jeweller in exactly the same way. He had been under-manager then, in a large hotel in Roscommon, and to make it worse, the jeweller had been his cousin. That time Foxer had got clean away with one hundred and fifty pounds worth of jewellery, a four-day hotel bill, five bottles of whiskey and a set of hotel towels. This time Foxer got two years in Mountjoy, the two years he was just finishing in time for his seventy-eighth birthday.

That was one of the things that had made Foxer realise that he was indeed far too old for the profession and should retire. A con man who can no longer recognise a client he has already gulled, even thirty years earlier, has no right to stay in the business. And not much chance to, either.

The other element in Foxer's decision to retire, apart from the fear of being buried in the prison cemetery, was family feeling. It was a comparatively new growth, but with roots in an incident of almost forty years before.

He had met in London an Irish widow, handsome, well-set-up in flesh and bank account, and in a weak moment married her. The marriage, like her bank account, had lasted about a month. A sports car, a honeymoon in Antibes ... moonlight on the Riviera, Monte Carlo ...

ah, the delights of marriage. But an angry man in Monte had recognised him and he had fled with the sports car and the remains of the bank account, and he'd never seen his wife again. And to tell the truth, he hardly ever thought of her.

Until about a year ago, a middle-aged woman with vaguely familiar features came to visit him in Mountjoy, and introduced herself as his daughter. On a later visit she brought her husband, who was a doctor of psychology and an amateur criminologist, with advanced theories of penal reform and the underlying causes of recidivism.

The doctor fell in love with Foxer at once, seeing in him the material for several papers to learned societies, and even a book on *The Latent Schizophrenia of Confidence Tricksters*. It was the doctor indeed who had persuaded his wife to visit her disgraceful old father, once the newspaper publicity had reminded him of the relationship. The wife herself, Foxer's daughter, was a dull woman, with none of Foxer's dash and imagination. But she was good-hearted, and when her husband suggested that they should make a home for Foxer she reluctantly agreed.

'What shall we tell the two boys?' was all she said, referring to Patrick and Martin, twelve and ten. 'They must never know the truth.' As for little Grace, five and a half, the very thought of her baby ever hearing such words as 'prison' and 'crime' made her blood run cold.

'We will tell them he is your great-uncle from South America,' the doctor said. His mouth twitched. 'He is probably well-enough used to supporting such stories with a wealth of circumstantial detail.'

And so Foxer went to live with his daughter, his son-in-law and his three grandchildren, taking to retirement with something approaching contentment. It was pleasant to stroll aimlessly in the sun, to greet the neighbours with no ulterior motives, to look young policemen fearlessly and even forbiddingly in the eye, to be able to speak of 'my daughter', 'my son-in-law', 'my little grand-daughter, Grace'. Especially her. To be no longer the lone wolf, but a belonging sheep. It was a great and oddly pleasant change. He found himself sinking into Number Ten Acacia Avenue like a tired athlete sinking into a warm bath.

And there, but for little Grace, he might well have stayed for ever. Or at least until the plot in Glasnevin received him. He was clean and quiet about the house. He gave immensely good value to the doctor, helped his daughter with the washing-up, and entertained the children at their bedtimes with elaborate stories about South America – not missionary stories, naturally, and again, he found it a relief after so long in Holy Orders to be a layman. He described lost Inca civilisations that he happened to have found, drawing on years of serious travel reading – mainly for professional purposes – in a dozen well-stocked prison libraries. He told of fantastic alligator hunts in the upper waters of the

Amazon, where the piranhas ate the alligators as fast as he shot them, which was why he had failed to bring home an alligator handbag for their mother, or even a stuffed baby alligator for Little Grace.

But the stories the children liked best were connected with The Treasure. 'You might say,' he told them, 'that I have spent my life searching for that treasure.' And he stroked his beard and described to them the fabled treasure-lake of the Incas high up in the Andes, still as melted glass, cold as ice, deep as the Pit of Hell itself, and guarded by monstrous swimming serpents with sabre teeth and horned, scaly heads.

'Now, now, Uncle,' his daughter said, coming briskly in with Grace's cocoa – half water, half milk so as not to give her indigestion – 'you'll be giving her bad dreams.' And Foxer was gently but firmly ushered off to the kitchen, where there was a great deal of washing-up.

These interruptions began to happen more and more regularly. It was as though her mother's instinct dreaded the effects of fantasy on her precious chicks. Fantasy for boys meant insecurity, losing jobs, going to prison. For girls it meant bad marriages, the stage, journalism, God knew what. Although obedient to her husband, she was still a mother, and determined not to see her children ruined. She began to drop little hints to them that their South American great-uncle, while a dear, sweet old man, was sometimes a trifle – well, imaginative.

'You mean he tells lies?' Martin said scornfully, adding. 'Of course he does.' And for obscure reasons this easy acceptance by the boys worried her still more.

Only Grace was both shocked and incredulous. 'Oh no!' she cried. 'He's true, always. He promised me. And when his money comes from South America he says he'll buy me a beautiful gold ring, just like The Treasure rings.'

Indeed, Foxer had promised exactly that, in a weak moment. And he overheard this particular conversation. It worried him very much. Like two small pebbles in an otherwise very comfortable pair of shoes – his daughter's coolness, understandable, he told himself sadly, quite understandable, and his grand-daughter's expectancy, also understandable, women feeling as they do about promises, even from their earliest years. But worrying to an old man whose every comfort depended increasingly on these two females. On his daughter to cook and provide for him, make his bed, mend his shirts, iron his tie (he had always been a dandy, and now that he could wear a collar and tie he liked both to be smart) and perform those thousand little functions for which God designed the female creature, and without the proper and willing performance of which a home is not much better than a prison cell, and much less peaceful. And on Grace for two or three small luxuries which he could get in no other honourable way.

He could not ask the boys to steal their father's cigars because they would have thought it wrong; but Grace thought it great fun. And for much the same reasons, and because they would have eaten all the proceeds themselves, he could not ask the boys to get him chocolate biscuits on their mother's account in the grocer's. Grace got them for him on a fifty-fifty basis, and he paid her in more and more lavish promises. A gold necklace, a doll that said, 'Hello', and 'Goo Goo, Mamma'. A doll's house. Once, when the boys almost caught the pair of them with half a pound of chocolate wafers, he turned the threatened investigation aside with talk of an electric train.

'When?' said Patrick.

And with the biscuits melting stickily under his chair cushion Foxer said, 'Christmas', without realising that Christmas was less than a month away.

From then on life became more and more difficult. Patrick reported the promise to his mother. His mother warned him to disregard it. Martin repeated the warning to Foxer with a certain unkind mockery that cut the old man to the quick and sent Grace into hysterics. When Martin had gone, Foxer quietened Grace with more promises. And lay down that night with the realisation that if, by Christmas, he reneged on his promises, he could never face the children again. And that while the loss of Martin's and Patrick's never-very-real respect would merely hurt his pride, the loss of Grace's belief in him would be something else again.

Martin and Patrick were entirely their parents' children. But in Grace he could see, dimly and childishly, but yet distinctly, a great deal of himself. He saw it in the casual efficiency with which she robbed her father's cigar cabinet, abstracting the key from his desk almost under his nose, and returning it with one hand while stroking his work-tired brow with the other. He saw it in her mature discretion about the biscuits, never too many, never a kind her mother didn't buy for herself in case the grocer should be suspicious. He had begun to think quite seriously of passing on his immense store of experience to this grandchild of his heart and blood. Even her eyes were like his, round and blue and innocent as cornflowers. And he too had once had curly golden hair. He stroked his beautiful beard. A woman confidence trickster. Starting at twenty with the benefit of nearly sixty years' experience behind her. She would be unique.

'Little Grace,' he whispered to her one December evening over chocolate biscuits and warm milk, 'would you like me to teach you how to be a student of human nature?'

She nodded carelessly, dropping chocolate crumbs on her tartan frock. But in spite of her apparent carelessness a swiftly accurate finger wet its pink tip on her tongue and picked up every last tell-tale crumb.

'Born to it,' the old man breathed. 'In the blood.' She'd be able to play a Missionary Sister, or a Mother Superior, to perfection. 'We'll begin after Christmas,' he whispered. But for lessons to be of value, the pupil must have faith in the teacher. And it was almost Christmas.

Obviously he had to keep his promises. And equally obviously, with the three and sixpence a week pocket-money that his daughter allowed him, there was only one way to do it. One last fling, before respectability claimed and tamed him for ever. He found suddenly that he was feeling ten years younger. Ten? He hadn't felt like this since he was sixty. He went to bed for the whole weekend in order to think, undisturbed by washing-up.

Another bishop's party was out of the question. His daughter had burned his clerical gear the night he arrived and he had no money to get any more. Besides, the Archbishop of Dublin – no, not a dinner party. Then what?

Again, Grace was the finger pointing the way. Tiptoeing into his room with a book of raffle tickets from her school. Three tickets for sixpence, seven for a shilling, with a seventeen-pound turkey as first prize. 'You just give me sixpence, and put your full name on that bit of the ticket there,' Grace said, pointing at the counterfoil.

Your full name. Light dawned, and Foxer fell asleep with his plan already perfected.

On Monday morning, two days before Christmas, he began to operate it.

Ever since he came to the district he had gathered local gossip of a particular kind, not with any real motive, but simply out of the habit of a lifetime. Know the countryside. And among the snippets he had collected was that a certain shopkeeper in the next suburb kept his main supply of working cash not in his shop, which had once been successfully burgled, but in his private house, in a heavy safe, to which his wife had the keys during the day. In this way his cash was never left unattended. By day his wife cared for it. By night he slept beside it. And if he needed it during the day – more, that is, than the smallish float he carried to the shop each morning and home each night – he sent a messenger to his wife to fetch it to him. His business was antique furniture and expensive *bric-à-brac* which he occasionally bought in the shop itself from callers. Hence the messages to his wife for cash. It was not the wisest system perhaps, but what system is? His name was Henry Molloy. His wife's was Margaret.

At 10.30 a.m. on the Monday morning before Christmas, Foxer took Grace out on the pretext of buying her a Christmas present with his weekly three and sixpence, and from across the road loosed her, with her raffle tickets, at Mr Molloy's antique shop.

'Whatever you do,' he emphasised, 'sell one to Mr Molloy himself. Just think if one of his assistants won a turkey and he didn't!'

Five minutes later he had Mr Henry Molloy's full signature and handwritten address on a raffle ticket counterfoil, and was rewarding Grace with a banana split. It crossed his mind briefly that here was a whole new line of country to exploit – but he realised sadly in the next minute that there is a limit to the number of raffle tickets which even the most angelic little girl could sell in one day. Even at a shilling a time the turnover would be minute. In fact, considering the price of banana splits, one would very likely operate at a considerable loss. As it was, he barely had the bus fare home, because Grace refused to give him Mr Molloy's shilling. But at least he had the ticket. And all that night he practised the signature and the address. The style of handwriting was quite simple and straightforward.

Next morning he presented himself to Mr Molloy in the guise of an elderly American on a visit to relations. But alas, his visit was about to end, his age told him that he would not pass this way again – how true! – and he desired, indeed he aimed, to take back a few little souvenirs of his delightful stay to dear old Joliet – er, Illinois. Like, for example, that silver teapot.

When he began, Foxer intended to be modest. Say twenty pounds. But why be modest on a last fling? Good God, a man would have to be pretty mean-spirited to restrain his last fling to twenty pounds. 'And that li'l old silver tray – is that the real McCoy?'

By the time he was done, the total of his purchases came to one hundred and ninety-seven pounds. He added a little fireside screen. 'For my delightful hostess in this beautiful old city of yours, sir,' to make it a nice round two hundred guineas, and came to business.

Stroking his luxurious beard he said to the obsequious Mr Molloy: 'Waal sir, two hundred guineas is a fair sum of money, such as an old man like me would be afraid to carry through the streets.'

'How wise of you, sir,' said Mr Molloy.

'Equally, I guess, I cannot expect a stranger in a strange town, who happens to be leaving for the li'l ol' United States this very afternoon, to be allowed to pay such an account by cheque. . . .' Mr Molloy made deprecatory noises.

'But if you would provide me with a piece of that stationery I see lying there, I will scribble a note to my niece and hostess, who is minding my little supply of cash. And then, if by chance you have a messenger who could save my old shanks a journey . . . ?'

'Why yes!' cried Mr M. His never-very-dormant suspicions had been sharply aroused by the beginning of this long spiel, but they had, happily, been laid to rest by the promise of cash.

'Pray take this sheet of paper, if you will forgive it being headed by my shop address. In fact I myself can type the note for you – unless, of course, it is of too personal a nature?'

'How kind!' cried Foxer. 'Just say, "Dear Margaret," which is my niece's Christian name—'

'What a coincidence,' said Mr M. 'It's also my wife's name!'

'Then she must be a thoroughly good and delightful woman,' cried Foxer. 'I just know it. But I am keeping you too long,' he whispered, seeing the blue shape of a policeman stroll past the door.

'Just write that I've found a couple of small bargains and need two hundred guineas. Use your own words, sir; I'm no hand at composing letters, being a self-educated mill – I mean man.'

'A millionaire!' breathed Mr M., to himself. 'How could I have suspected this sweet old gentleman?' And hastily using the formula that he used when writing to his own Margaret, typed, *Dear Margaret, I have just been offered some rather interesting items. Please let me have two hundred guineas by bearer Your loving—* and gave it to Foxer, who swiftly signed it *Henry*, casually shading the flowing signature with his cupped hand.

'And the address?' asked Mr M., eagerly producing an envelope.

'Why, this one in my pocket will do,' said Foxer. 'Waste not, want not.' And producing a bundle of old letters, selected an envelope from among them.

Swiftly taking the note, he tucked it into the envelope on which he had already written Mrs Molloy's name and address in Henry Molloy's handwriting, copying all from Grace's counterfoil.

Mr M. called forward a spotty and cretinous messenger boy, too stupid to be dishonest or even lazy, which was why Mr M. employed him, and Foxer, who had strolled away in order to consider an antique Windsor chair, beckoned the boy towards him.

'Take this letter to this address,' he said, giving the boy the note, together with a half-crown filched from Grace's piggy bank. 'And if you are back here in ten minutes, why boy, I'll make it an even dollar.'

The boy sped off, not at all surprised to be sent to his master's house for it was an errand he ran at least once or twice a week.

Foxer stayed admiring this and that for a minute or two more, pleading another errand in the neighbourhood and, promising to be back in two shakes of a donkey's tail, toddled out of the shop.

'A millionaire!' breathed Mr M. again. 'And so unaffected!'

Ten minutes later Foxer waylaid the returning messenger fifty yards up the street, took the thick envelope addressed to Henry Molloy by his loving safe-keeping Margaret, gave the boy Grace's remaining half-crown, and disappeared at a surprising speed for a man of seventy-eight.

He spent the afternoon shopping, after a long and sumptuous champagne lunch in an excellent restaurant. He bought gold rings and a necklace, electric trains, a doll's house with twenty rooms and running water, two dolls that danced and one that said 'Peek-a-boo' as well as 'Mamma'; he bought tea sets, copper saucepans, delicious and exotic foods for his daughter; and two dozen Havanas and a pure silk dressing-gown for his son-in-law. He bought himself a gold cigarette lighter, and an ivory brush-and-comb set especially for his beard. When he got home that night he had four and elevenpence. He slipped it unobtrusively into Grace's piggy bank and went to bed.

The next day was Christmas Eve. And from midday onwards a succession of respectful messengers delivered a series of richly wrapped parcels to the astonished family at Number Ten Acacia Avenue.

'Open Them!' cried Foxer.

And by six that evening the house was filled with coloured wrappings, squeaking children, speechless parents, and a beaming, benevolent Father Christmas of a Foxer. Water gushed out of the doll's house. Dolls cried 'Peek-a-boo!' and danced on the table. Electric trains encircled the floor at ever increasing speeds. The air was rich with Havana smoke and the subtle and exotic scents of unusual cooking.

'My life savings,' Foxer breathed to his daughter, 'but why save them?'

'A little legacy,' he murmured to his son-in-law. 'Totally unexpected.'

'Football pools,' he confided to Patrick and Martin. 'Quite a stroke of luck.'

And to Grace: 'My money from South America.'

At half-past six a large man in plain clothes knocked heavily at the door. Foxer answered it.

'How did you know?' he said sadly.

'The beard, Foxer,' the detective said, almost equally sadly. 'You're getting senile, that's what it is. As soon as old Molloy described the beard. . . .'

'Be discreet,' pleaded Foxer. He went inside, packed his spare false teeth, his gold cigarette lighter, his ivory brush-and-comb set, his socks and a flannel, and was ready.

To tell the truth he wasn't entirely broken-hearted. He was thoroughly sick of washing-up. And rather tired of respectability.

'Just slipping out with a friend for a moment,' he murmured to the adults. 'A visitor from South America,' he whispered to Grace. 'He wants to talk to me about The Treasure.'

'I have tried my hardest,' the judge said, 'to find extenuating circumstances in your case, your age, the pleas of your daughter,' – not very passionate ones, it must be admitted – 'the partially generous motives of your crime; but when I consider your truly appalling record. . .

Everyone thought he was extremely lucky to get off with eighteen months. Mr Molloy wrote an indignant letter to his parliamentary representative about it.

By the end of January Foxer was lying in his old cell, stroking his beard.

A slip of a young warder put his head round the door. 'Barber, Foxer?' he cried jokingly.

'Why yes,' Foxer said. 'I think I will. I find this beard *is* inclined to irritate my chin at times.'

And as he sat in the barber's chair, submitting to the razor, his mind was already eighteen months ahead. . . .

Eric Parr

Special Release

When Maxie Winters was nicked for the theft of £350,000 worth of scrap platinum from the office of a Birmingham bullion dealer, everyone tipped him for fifteen years.

Actually he went down for ten which was a comparatively lenient sentence in view of the fact that not one single ounce was ever recovered.

What surprised both friend and foe alike was that Maxie didn't bat an eyelid when the judge weighed him off. He just shrugged his shoulders, turned on his heels and walked down the steps towards the cells. This from a man who cried like a baby some three years ago when he was sentenced to twelve months under Section 7 of the Prevention of Crimes Act.

But Maxie could have told them the answer to this riddle. Three years ago he didn't have three hundred and fifty grand's worth of platinum stowed away in a safe hideout, and what was more important, he hadn't met the Fixer.

The word 'met' is hardly a true statement for nobody met the Fixer, who was a shy retiring character who shunned the limelight and carried out negotiations through one of his many contacts.

He it was who arranged the unofficial release of Hymie Myers from Pentonville Prison by the simple method of using a helicopter to pluck Hymie off the exercise ring one bright Sunday morning when the nick was running on a skeleton staff.

Hymie was sorted out from among the other three hundred prisoners who were enjoying God's fresh air and sunlight for the simple reason that Hymie, like Maxie, was a lone wolf who had the Countess of Bevington's diamonds which, for the purposes of insurance, were valued at £250,000, tucked away in cold storage.

There were one or two other lone wolves who, by various ingenious methods, never repeated twice, were sprung from their cages by the Fixer. His fee for this service was always the same: Fifty per cent of the take. Half the entire sum the gear would fetch from a buyer of stolen property. That the Fixer was also the biggest receiver in England was beside the point. Half the crooked market value or no dice. Few refused for the Fixer had a lot to offer and he always honoured his end of the bargain to the letter.

His client might have to lie in gaol for a year of his sentence until such time as the Fixer could guarantee a certain way out but during that waiting period he would want for nothing.

Within a few days of his reception he would receive a visit from someone belonging to the small percentage of prison officers who traffic with prisoners and who, in the curious, caustic jargon of the Fraternity, are classed as 'straight screws'.

This straight screw would at regular intervals hand over a small parcel containing such luxuries as tobacco, chocolates and the occasional quarter bottle of whisky.

This straight screw would also arrange, through other straight screws, that his protégé would be speedily transferred to a cushy working party, and Maxie Winters was delighted when he was called before the Governor who informed him that from henceforth he would be a member of the outside painter's party which, as the straight screw mentioned afterwards, was a better way of passing the time than sitting on his arse in the mailbag shop sewing eight stitches to the inch.

This tale of graft and corruption would have astounded and horrified Mr Cromby-Withers, for Cromby-Withers was a do-gooder.

Whenever his benevolent-looking face appeared in Maxie's doorway, Maxie used to sigh and resign himself to half an hour of platitudes and exhortations to 'give up this way of life, which can only lead to sorrow and degradation'.

Maxie's philosophy was live and let live. He realised that there are some people in life who must of necessity give up a lot of their time in an effort to 'spread the light' and Mr Cromby-Withers was one of them. Three evenings a week he visited one prison within a radius of two hundred miles which made him the most energetic official prison visitor on the registers of the Prison Commission.

The screws used to grin to each other at the sight of Mr Cromby-Withers in a shabby mackintosh, large-brimmed trilby from under which a pair of eyes short-sightedly blinked from behind a pair of pebble-lensed spectacles.

An extremely absent-minded man with no sense of direction. Quite often he would be discovered by the duty Principal Officer roaming around those parts of the prison which were out of bounds to every one except the official staff.

It was the standing joke of the prison officers' club that it would be no surprise to any one of them one day to discover Mr Cromby-Withers sitting at the governor's desk waiting to take applications.

He means well was the consensus of opinion amongst the prisoners, and the man who has been in prison many times develops a good-humoured tolerance for those characters who are not quite in this world.

So Maxie used to recline on his bed and patiently listen to Mr Cromby-Withers' exhortations to look at his sentence as a just punishment for the wrong he had committed. To be a model prisoner and earn all his remission.

After his visitor had gone, Maxie would dig into his mattress and toast the parting guest in contraband Scotch whisky.

Now Maxie was as highly-sexed as the next athletic man of 34, and on his daily trips outside the prison he found himself agreeing with the proverb that in the night 'all cats are grey'. Even some of the middle-aged ladies with whom he came into contact during his job of decorating the prison officer's quarters seemed to take on the desirability of starlets.

There wasn't much chance of a stray affair although Maxie could sense that one or two of these dames given half the chance would welcome a quick tumble with a randy young prisoner.

Unfortunately the fly in the ointment was the Chief Officer. In any nick the real power behind, and sometimes in front of the throne, is the Chief and this one was no exception.

He was always bobbing up in the most unexpected places and consequently he had his staff on the hop. He had only been at this nick for a few months. His record showed that he had made many moves during the past five years but this was not unusual for a zealous officer seeking a governorship.

He had the curious and intimidating habit of staring at a prisoner for about three minutes. He wouldn't utter a word but as one man put it 'I could feel him counting the spots on my liver'. A hard man with only one weak spot and that was the girl he had married and who was twenty-five years his junior. He made this poor bird's life a minor hell. Even the milkman couldn't give her a second glance.

Maxie caught a glimpse of her one day as they were returning to the prison and as far as Maxie was concerned she was for him. He forgot the loot he had stowed away and all the plans that were being made on his behalf. All he could see in his mind's eye was a mass of red hair, a wide mouth and legs that ran Dietrich a close second. He found himself constantly on the look-out for her.

Now an obsession like this has to come to a head. Had Maxie been on the outside he would have known what to do about a bird who was married to a man many years her senior and who, judging by the sidelong glances she gave the prisoners, was a case of hot pants.

Unfortunately for Maxie he was in the nick and the only sex outlet in prison, apart from what the Jesuits at my school used to describe as 'the solitary sin', was the taking up with a queer.

There's nothing strange in this, for many long-sentence men who, outside the walls, live a perfectly normal sex life, think nothing of having sexual relations with a queer. A relationship that begins with their first months of imprisonment and ends the day they are discharged.

Men have fought until one of them is lying on the ground unconscious while the object of their affections stood by and watched the bloody battle for 'her' favours.

It doesn't always stop with the prisoners for screws also succumb to this temptation. Only a few weeks before Maxie's reception a certain prison officer had been caught 'bang to rights' in, of all places, the Jewish synagogue.

The Rabbi took one look at the two figures of a screw and a prisoner with their trousers actually and not metaphorically down, and rang the alarm bell.

Anyway Maxie found himself drifting into an association with a young man whose homosexuality was obvious. The danger of a prison relationship with a type like this is that he invariably becomes very possessive. Soon Maxie was lumbered. This kid had gone overboard for him and God help any outside interference, for the homosexual has all of a woman's vices and not all her virtues.

To Maxie this relationship was an outlet; sandwiches for the journey; but to his partner this was it.

Then came a red-letter day in Maxie's life. The Chief's house was next on the list for redecorating and what was more the Chief was away on a governor's course.

Everything went well for Maxie that first week. The 'straight' screw was in charge of the party and Maxie had a certain amount of licence.

He made a point of being in the right place at the right time and the right place was wherever the Chief's wife would be.

Now Maxie was a very good-looking chap. One who always caused a throb in feminine hearts whenever he walked into a room.

The Chief's wife was no exception. She fluttered her eyes in his direction and one day while he was painting the staircase she walked past him on her way to the bathroom and if ever a woman laid it out on a plate this one did.

She was wearing a housecoat and just as she had passed Maxie the housecoat opened and she dropped her towel. As she bent down to pick it up Maxie was presented with a view of a long leg and a breast firm like a pear. What was more he realised that she was completely naked under the housecoat and that she was a true redhead.

She ascended the stairs with the air of the queen making an entrance and as she reached the top of the stairs she turned her head, grinned mischievously at Maxie and put out the tip of her tongue. Then she entered the bathroom.

It took Maxie a long time to paint the sides of two stairs. The bent screw looked in to see how he was getting on and Maxie whispered in his ear.

'You mind how you go,' said the screw, 'I know she's hot stuff and that one or two screws have had a go at her. But you're a prisoner and she's the Chief's old woman.'

Maxie grabbed his arm.

'This,' he said, 'is worth a century to me. Just keep me isolated from the rest of the party until it's time to go back to the nick and I'll give you the address of a club where you can collect a hundred nicker on my note of hand.'

The screw's beady eyes glittered. He thought for a moment. 'Right,' he said finally, 'you've got until four o'clock. I'll see you're not disturbed but remember this. If she complains that you've molested her I'll have to nick you. Understood?'

Maxie grinned.

'She won't complain,' he said.

Maxie perched himself on the top stair immediately outside the bathroom.

He waited feverishly for the door to open and then suddenly she appeared. She stood for a moment looking at him and then she disappeared into a bedroom. Maxie swallowed hard in excitement when he noticed that she had left the door half open.

He approached nearer and found himself looking into a long mirror which was at the end of the bedroom.

She stood there looking at her reflection and for a full five minutes Maxie stared at her young body, white as only the body of a true redhead can be. Then she turned round. Maxie entered the room and closed the door. He advanced towards her and she was in his arms.

'I thought you were never going to make your mind up,' she whispered as Maxie picked her up and laid her on the bed. . . .

When it was over she stroked his hair.

'I've never had things like that done to me before,' she murmured. 'I've read about them but I never realised that they could really happen.'

'I've only started,' said Maxie.

Well, of course, that was it as far as Maxie's queer partner was concerned. No man can serve two masters especially when one of them is a mistress with an insatiable sexual appetite. Had Maxie been living on the farinaceous diet which is standard in all British prisons he would never have lasted the course. His bent screw worked overtime bringing him in nourishing foods.

Make an enemy of a queer and you can expect the worst. Maxie's protégé took his neglect very badly. His quietness should have warned Maxie, who by this time only had one thought in mind and that was to spend as much time as possible with the Chief's wife.

But this time they were making arrangements to live together as soon as Maxie was free. He hinted to her they would have no financial worries and that something might happen which would hasten the happy event.

And then one evening while Maxie was in his cell, the message came from the Fixer.

All Maxie knew was that his door was unlocked and Maxie looked for a screw to walk in. Instead a uniformed arm reached inside the door and from its hand dropped a piece of paper. The door was then slammed to and Maxie listened to the footsteps fading away down the cell landing before he opened the note.

Cryptic but the the point.

'Be ready after lights out.'

This was a tonic which Maxie was badly in need of. That day the Chief had returned and there were no more intoxicating half-hours.

In the intervals of making love Maxie and the bird had talked quite a bit about her husband. His name was Charles. She'd met him at a dance and married him on the rebound, having just been ditched by one of the local talent.

'He's hard as nails and mean as mud,' she said. 'Would you believe it, he's got four banking accounts. I found out one day, when he'd left the keys of his desk behind.'

'How much was in them?' Maxie asked.

'I don't know. He came back just as I was having a squint. I only saw one figure but there were four noughts on the end. Stingy bastard! I tried to get him to raise my housekeeping money. Not he. The only person he cares about is his bloody brother. Thick as thieves they are.'

'What does the brother do? Not another screw, is he?'

'No fear. Some sort of salesman, I'd say. He's always travelling. God knows what he sells. Corn plasters, I should think. He's a funny old-fashioned looking little guy.'

Maxie grinned as he lay back on his bed waiting for operation jail break to be set in motion. He knew some screws were making a packet but this was the first one he had come across who had four bank accounts.

He wondered just how much the Fixer had tucked away. He must be making a bomb with very little risk attached. All his staff work was carried out by the underlings, for the Fixer never showed himself.

Take his, Maxie's case. The Fixer's cut out of this was £100,000 payable in advance, for you had to trust the Fixer completely. Maxie had no worries there for the Fixer was known to be a man of his word. He paid all expenses from the moment his client was remanded at the first hearing. Passage to any country, his client's share of the loot in whatever currency he desired or a letter of credit drawn on a foreign bank. And no worries about passports.

Maxie heard the click of the light switches outside each cell door as the night patrol made his rounds. Fully dressed, he snuggled down in his blankets and all the eye through the Judas hole could see was an apparently sleeping figure.

Maxie waited, chain-smoking, as he heard the prison clock chime each passing hour. Then, soon after 1 a.m., his cell door was quietly opened.

'Put on your cell slippers and walk straight ahead in the direction of E Wing. I'll be right behind you. Keep close to the wall and don't look round. When I touch you on the shoulder stop dead in your tracks and wait for my next move.'

Maxie slipped through the door and walked towards E Wing hugging the wall like a shadow.

Suddenly the Chief Screw's hand squeezed his shoulder. He came to a full stop. The Chief Screw stepped in front of him and pointed to a small door in the corridor. He opened it with his master key and motioned to Maxie to go through. Maxie found himself outside in the night, in a part of the prison grounds which, at first, he didn't recognise. The Chief led him to another small door in a blank-sided building. He unlocked this with his key and flashed his torch.

'You know where you are now?'

'The flipping topping shed!' Maxie said. 'What sort of a bloody lark is this?'

'Not to worry, boy, no one will look for you here. Just you stay put while I make sure your transport is on the spot. We're a shade early. Here, take my torch.'

Maxie found himself in a little chamber not much bigger than a cupboard. Above his head was the trap. He could see the dividing line that marked the opening. He was in the pit of the 'topping-shed' or execution chamber.

The execution routine is like this. The condemned man is in the condemned cell. There is a door in the wall of the condemned cell which opens onto the scaffold. The famous 9 o'clock walk from condemned cell to scaffold is in fact only a few feet and takes, if all goes well, a matter of seconds. For the moment the hangman and his assistant enter the condemned cell until the prisoner, pinioned, with a white sack over his head, is placed on the execution platform, with the noose around his neck, and the trap is sprung, often takes not much more than 90 seconds. Sometimes the trap is sprung before the prison chaplain has finished reading the burial service. The body of the hanged man is inspected by the prison's medical officer who enters the pit below by the little door through which the Chief Screw had gently pushed Maxie.

Maxie sat down on his haunches and lit a cigarette. Time passed very slowly. What the hell, he thought. He supposed there had been a hitch. Anyway, he was safe enough and could leave it all to the Fixer.

The situation amused him. He was, in effect, buying the Chief Screw's wife for a hundred grand. Did he really want her? There would be plenty of time to find out.

The door opened quietly and the Chief Screw beckoned to him. 'Okay now,' he said.

Maxie looked out and saw the stars. The next moment he saw a lot more stars. When he recovered consciousness he was sitting on the trap. His arms were tied tightly behind his back. The Chief Screw was standing a little to one side holding in his hand the noose of the rope. Beside him stood a familiar figure, an elderly man wearing a mackintosh and a trilby. It was Mr Cromby-Withers, the prison visitor.

'I dare say you often wanted to meet the Fixer,' the Chief Screw said. 'Here he is. My brother. And he's the last person you ever will meet on this earth. You've been had for a mug, Maxie. It might have been all right to double-cross me with that little bitch of a wife of mine, but you shouldn't have let that boy-friend of yours find out.'

Mr Cromby-Withers spoke for the first time. 'Brother Charles,' he said, 'I think the honour is yours.'

'Thank you, brother,' said the Chief Screw. 'I've always wanted to spring the trap. I think I know how to do it by now.'

The next morning the landing screw found Maxie in his cell hanging from an old piece of rope that had been tied to the window-grating.

Mr Cromby-Withers, the prison visitor, made a special representation to the Governor and wrote a letter to *The Times* protesting against the barbarous practice of inflicting long prison sentences on men who, despite their criminal way of life, could yet be redeemed by more lenient corrective remedial training methods.

Julian Symons

Love Affair

From the beginning of their marriage it had always been Don who made the decisions and, as Moira told their friends, this was not because he was aggressive or domineering, it was just that both of them thought it right and natural for things to be that way. When, after a year of marriage, he suggested that it was time they moved from the little flat in Kilburn to a district where you could see a bit more of God's green earth and sky, she agreed at once.

He ticked off on his fingers just what they wanted: a three- or four-bedroom house, central heating, a garden big enough to sit in, and of course the whole thing set in a nice place with neighbours who were their own sort.

She agreed with it all. But wouldn't a garden mean a lot of work?

'I'll look after it. Always fancied myself with the old spade and trowel.' Tamping down the tobacco in his pipe, not looking at her, Don said, 'And you need a bit of garden for the kids.'

'But you said we ought to wait.'

'Got a bit of news. MacGillivray's retiring. I get a step up next month.'

'Oh, Don! Why didn't you tell me?'

'Best not to say anything till you're sure. What you don't know won't hurt you, that's my motto.' He had got his pipe going. 'I've been in touch with a few real-estate agents already.'

It proved more difficult than they had expected to find exactly what they wanted, but when they saw the house at Gainham Woods they knew it was just the thing. It was a new development – you didn't call it an estate any more – but the thing that made this particular house a snip, as Don said, was its position on a corner, so that you faced two ways, had more windows than your neighbours, and a bigger garden as well.

523

There was an attached garage, which Don said would come in handy as a workshop or playroom since they had no car. Gainham Woods was half an hour from central London by train, but Don worked out that the cost of extra fare would be balanced by the fact that living would be less expensive. And, of course, the house would run itself, so that Moira could keep her secretarial job.

'For the time being,' Don said with a smile. 'Later on you'll have your hands full.'

She did stay in the job until she was nearly three months pregnant. After that she had rather a bad time, with a good deal of morning sickness, so she gave up the job. At six months she had a miscarriage. She was disturbed, partly because she felt it showed her incompetence, but Don was very sympathetic and told her to look on the bright side. Perhaps it would have been a bit soon anyway, and they were still young, they would try again.

When she had her second miscarriage he said that perhaps they weren't meant to have children. She had not gone back to her job because it hardly seemed worthwhile, and after the second miscarriage she found that she didn't really want to work again.

It was at this point that Tess arrived. She was a nice little black sedan, three years old but for that reason a real bargain. Don lifted the hood and expatiated on the cleanliness of what lay inside.

'It's lovely.' Then Moira added doubtfully, 'But can we afford it?'

'Have I ever bought anything we couldn't afford?' Don asked, and it was perfectly true that he never had. It turned out that he had received another minor promotion and was now an Assistant Personnel Officer in the large corporation for which he worked. He proudly showed her the name 'Tess' which he had stuck onto the side of the car with plastic letters. It was one of several names they had talked about for the baby.

There could be no doubt that Tess was a boon and a blessing. They took her occasionally on trips to the seashore, and were able to visit Don's family on week-ends. His father was a retired bank manager and lived with his wife in a semidetached house in Elmers End, a pleasant enough house but, as Don said every time they left, you couldn't compare Elmers End with Gainham Woods.

Sometimes Don's brother and sister also came to Elmers End. They were both married, and it was a real family party. Moira had no family, or none that was ever mentioned. Her father, a grocer, had gone off with another woman when Moira was in her teens, and after his departure her mother had taken gas. Of course, Moira could not be held responsible for any of this, but she always felt that the Bradbury's thought their son had married beneath him.

Don had already passed his driver's test – one of the things Moira had admired about him from their first meeting at the Conservative Club dance was his competence in practical matters; but she couldn't drive. As he said, there was no point in wasting money going to a school when he could easily teach her how. It would be a pleasure, he said, and on the first day that she sat in the driver's seat, with Don beside her explaining the gears and saying that there was nothing to it, not really, but it *was* just a bit tricky going from third down to second gear. She thought it might be a pleasure too, but this did not prove to be the case.

Don was immensely patient – that was another of the things she had always admired in him – but it took her a long time to understand just when and how to shift gears. First gear was close to reverse, and she frequently engaged one when she meant to use the other. And somehow Don's habit of treating every drive as an adventure didn't help.

'You see that Austin up ahead there,' he would say. 'Just crawling along. We're going to pass that fellow. Get ready now. Up into high, arm out to show you're passing, and away we go! No, steady now, something coming the other way, tuck yourself in behind him – right. Now, road's clear, give her all you've got.' And as they passed the car he would beam. 'Managed that all right though you went out too far, nearly had us in the ditch.'

'I'm sorry.'

'Nothing to worry about. Turn down this side road – no, left, not right. And you didn't give an arm signal.'

'I shall never be able to do it! There's so *much* to remember.'

'Don't worry. If at first you don't succeed, try, try again – as Confucius says. Now, this road takes us back into town and when we're back we'll try some low-gear practice.'

After six weeks of lessons he said she was ready to take her test. A day or two before it was due, however, she misinterpreted something he told her, turned left instead of right, and then stalled the engine. When she started up again, she confused reverse with first and drove straight into a tree. While Don got out to look at the damage she sat over the steering wheel and wept.

'Poor old girl.' He was addressing the car. 'She's had a nasty knock. Buckled her fender.' He came back and patted Moira's shoulder. 'Never mind. Worse things happen at sea. Shall I drive back?'

She got out. 'I never want to drive that bloody car again!'

'Now, now, it's not her fault.' He patted the hood, got in, and turned on the ignition. The motor hummed. 'She's a good old girl, Tess is.'

It proved possible to beat out the buckled fender, and when it was resprayed you couldn't tell that anything had happened. At least, that was what Don said, but she caught him occasionally giving comparative glances at the fenders, and she knew that for him the repaired one was not *quite* the same colour as the rest of the car. When he mentioned her taking the test she shook her head. 'No, I won't take it. I don't want to drive that car, ever – I hate it!'

'You're being hysterical.' It was his severest term of condemnation. 'But perhaps it would be a good thing to delay taking the test for the time being.'

'I shall never drive it again.'

Four years had passed since then and Moira had kept her word. They still had Tess – who was getting, as Don said, a bit long in the tooth but was a gallant old girl. He spent a good deal of time with the car, cleaning it inside and out every week, making adjustments in the carburettor, checking the spark plugs. She was in beautiful condition, except that the gears had become a little dicky. They had a tendency to slip, and there were even a couple of occasions when Don himself had shifted into reverse instead of into first, although he always caught himself in time. He was shocked when she suggested that they should buy another car.

'Get rid of Tess, you wouldn't want to do that! There's a lot of life in her yet, before she's ready to be put on the junk heap.'

But although Moira had not driven Tess again, she had passed the driving test. She saved a pound a week of the money Don gave her every month for household expenses, took lessons at a neighbourhood driving school, and passed the test the first time. She never told him about this, partly because he would have been upset, partly because – well, she couldn't have said exactly why, but it was a thing she had done entirely on her own and she wanted to nurse her feeling of achievement.

It was after this small achievement that she found herself looking at her husband with a more critical eye. She became conscious of the fact that his sandy hair was rapidly thinning, and what had once appeared to her as profound or witty remarks now seemed obvious clichés, and his devotion to doing everything in a certain way ('there's one right way and a thousand wrong ones') which she used to admire so much, now seemed to her a childish insistence on routine. Why, for example, did he always come home on the 6:15 train, she asked, why not sometimes take an earlier one? He assumed what she regarded as his wounded expression.

'There's work to be done, my dear. A.H. himself never leaves before five-thirty.'

'Just sometimes – say, once a month. You can't tell me A.H. would mind that?' A.H. was Head of Personnel.

'I daresay not. But it wouldn't be quite the thing.'

'Or catch a later one then – have a drink with the boys.'

'I don't see the point. The next one's the six-forty-seven, and the six-fifteen's a better train. Mind you, if there's a reason why I should get off earlier one day I can manage it – no problem there. Did you have something in mind?'

'No, no, nothing at all. It doesn't matter.'

You've become middle-aged at thirty, she thought, and I'm still young at twenty-seven. The mirror, which showed a neat little figure and a pretty, slightly discontented, and somehow unused face, did not contradict her. She had hair which Don had called titian when they first met, and a white milky skin.

In Gainham Woods, where she saw nobody except the neighbours, most of whom had children, these things were being wasted, but when she suggested that they might move nearer to London he was astounded. It was healthy out here, the neighbourhood was pleasant, you could see green things growing. They would never get a place with such a good garden. He had become devoted to gardening and had recently bought a whole set of gleaming new chromium-headed tools, including a special hoe and a rake whose sharp tines shone like silver. These tools hung neatly on the rear wall of the garage, just behind the car. What was the point of moving? he asked. Besides, they couldn't afford it.

'What about when you get moved up to become A.H.'s deputy?' Two years earlier he had told her that this was highly probable.

'Yes, well.' He hesitated.

'You'll get more money then.' He said nothing. 'You mean you won't get the job?'

'Salisbury's had a step up.'

Salisbury was another Assistant Personnel Officer, and Don's deadly rival.

'He's been made Deputy?' she persisted.

'In a way. There's been a reorganisation.'

'But he's moved up and you stay where you are.'

'At the moment. I think A.H. may have something special in mind for me. In my position you're really dealing with people, man to man. That's my strength, as A.H. says. Salisbury's really just an administrator.'

'But he gets more money?'

'I tell you, there may be something special ahead for me. In a year or two.'

He looked away as he spoke and she knew that there was nothing special ahead for him, that he was a nonentity who had climbed the short way he would ever go up the ladder of success. When he added that he would get his yearly increase and that the corporation had a wonderful pension scheme, she had a vision of herself in Gainham Woods forever, seeing the same people, being driven in Tess every other

Sunday to see Don's father and mother, going to the pictures once a week, having sex once a month, going in Tess to an English seaside resort for a holiday once a year. The car seemed the symbol of this terrible routine.

'When shall we get rid of that car?'

'Tess? She may need a new battery soon, but she's running beautifully now I've tuned up the motor.'

'Shall we still have her when you're pensioned off? Perhaps she'll outlive us and come to the funeral?'

'If that's meant to be funny I think it's a very poor joke.'

A few weeks later Moira had a letter from a solicitor telling her that her father had died out in New Zealand. It seemed that he had done rather well out there, and although he had married the woman he went off with and she got most of his money, he had remembered Moira in his will to the tune of £3,000.

She spoke to Don again about moving, saying that they could use her money as deposit on a new house. He positively refused. It was her money, and he wouldn't think of using it for any such purpose.

'After all, I'm the breadwinner, my dear, and that's how it should be. I'm quite able to support us both.'

He had taken to calling her 'my dear' lately, but she did not say how middle-aged it made her feel, or how much it irritated her.

'Couldn't we at least use the money, some of the money, to get another car? A new one.'

His mouth turned down in the expression that she had once thought conveyed strength of character. Now it just seemed to her to show weak, pouting obstinacy.

'I shouldn't think of getting rid of Tess.'

'I could buy a car of my own.'

He looked at her in astonishment. 'Where should we keep it? I couldn't turn Tess out of the garage. And anyway, my dear, your driving—'

He did not finish the sentence. It was on the tip of her tongue to say that she had passed her test with flying colours, but what was the use? It was true they had only a one-car garage, and if she bought a car it would not be allowed to stand in the road.

So she said nothing further. Don read all the financial columns to discover the safest forms of investment, and consulted Mr Bradbury who advised putting the inheritance into National Savings. It stayed on deposit in the bank.

Twice a year Don went away on group study courses to which the corporation sent their personnel officers. The courses lasted five days, and it was during one of his absences that she went to Marjorie Allenden's party. Marjorie had been to school with Moira, and they had met in a department store when Moira went up to London to do some shopping. Marjorie worked on a fashion magazine and was married to Clive, who worked in some editorial capacity on a glossly weekly.

The Allendens had a flat just off Earl's Court Road. It was furnished with brightly coloured sofas and eccentrically shaped chairs. There were lots of paintings on the walls, most of them abstracts. Moira was very impressed. It was just the kind of place she would have liked, although she did not say so. The mantelpiece was quite bare except for a large Victorian teapot, and Marjorie drew the attention of all her visitors to this.

'Clive picked it up in the Portobello Road for thirty bob,' she said in the high emphatic voice she seemed to have acquired. 'Don't you think it's too fascinatingly hideous?'

'Just hideous,' a voice behind Moira murmured. It belonged to a dark young man of about her own age who wore narrow light-blue trousers, a dark-blue jersey, and the small gold-rimmed spectacles that she knew were the latest thing. When he smiled at her she smiled back.

His name was Louis and he was a partner in a photographic agency. While they drank some kind of rather potent reddish liquid they talked – rather, he talked and she listened. Through the hum of noise she heard that he was an American who had been in London for two years now, and wasn't going back.

'I've always wanted to go to New York,' she said.

'Beside London it's just dead, baby – but dead.'

'It's not your scene,' she ventured. It was a word she had often heard used by young people on television; but perhaps she used it wrongly, because he laughed.

'You're wonderful.' He looked at her through those fascinating little gold-rimmed glasses. 'Look, this is strictly from Deadsville. What do you say we get out of here and eat? I know a nice little place.'

His car was parked just outside the house, ignoring the forbidding double yellow lines, and she gasped when she saw it. It was long, sleek, low, and immensely wide, and seemed to be totally enclosed in glass. When she ducked down into the passenger seat she had the double feeling of being almost on the ground because the car was so low, and of being on the bridge of a ship with total visibility all round her. He dropped into the seat beside her, gunned the motor, and she felt the surge of power as they drove away.

She asked what make of car it was and he said casually it was Italian, a Ghiani-Lucia, a make she had never heard of. 'Felix Ghiani's a friend of mine, asked me to try it out.'

They reached the restaurant and she felt that people were looking at her as they got out of the gleaming monster. Louis was known, a doorman rushed forward to greet him, and inside the restaurant everybody knew him; the headwaiter left another table to come over and shake hands.

Afterward she tried to remember what they ate and drank, but although she clearly recalled the long menu and could even see the mauve ink in which it was written, she had not the faintest recollection of any of the dishes or the wines. But she could afterward remember talking about herself, about Don and the boredom of life in Gainham Woods, and possibly – she was not quite sure of this – about her hatred of Tess.

Once or twice she had caught him looking at her through his gold rims with a speculative gaze, as though she were a creature of some new species to whom he was giving coolly sympathetic consideration. At the end of the meal he said, 'Coffee at my pad, as you cool young hipsters put it?'

'You're laughing at me,' she said happily. She longed to be back inside the Ghiani-Lucia, to feel the exhilarating movement of it beneath her.

The drive was all that she had expected and when they reached his flat she was a little drunk, just enough to make the outlines of everything seem faintly hazy – but not so drunk that she failed to look forward with excitement to the prospect of making love. Yet in the end the exciting prospect turned into something rather dismayingly practical and even disappointing when he said that he thought every woman should remember the Boy Scouts' motto, 'Be Prepared,' before going to a party, and then seemed to take for granted a great deal that was strange and uncongenial to her. Afterward she looked at his dark hairy body, thought of the clean metallic power within the Ghiani-Lucia, and shuddered slightly. At the same time it occurred to her that Don might phone home, and she was suddenly eager to be back.

'Okay, I'll ring for a taxi.' She had hoped he would take her in the car, but did not say so. 'I'd take you myself, but it's been a hard day.'

'It's not very far.' She wanted very much to ride in the car again.

His gaze was mocking. 'Gainham Woods? Baby, I've never been that far in my life.'

On the way back she cried, although she could not have said exactly why. The taxi took her home and she paid the man off at the end of the road. In the house she looked at everything as though it belonged to a stranger, then went out into the garage, turned on the light, and stared at the dull black car. Don did not phone.

She telephoned Louis the next day, not because she particularly wanted to see him, but because she wanted to experience again the excitement she had felt in the car. He said that he was going out of town and wasn't sure when he would be back. 'Don't call me, baby, I'll call you,' he said. She put down the phone without saying goodbye.

Two days later, on Friday night, Don returned. The group study course had been pretty exhausting, he said, had anything happened in his absence? Yes, she said, she had something to tell him. She showed him her driver's license and he was as surprised as she had expected. He agreed that she could drive Tess, but she sensed his lack of enthusiasm.

On Saturday morning she sat in the driver's seat. But Tess would not start.

Don had the hood up in a flash, but soon closed it. 'Battery's almost dead. Perhaps if I push her out she might start. You guide her.'

She nodded. It was a small garage and he had to squeeze round to get between the car and the rear wall. The gleaming row of garden instruments was directly behind him. He levered himself against the wall and pushed the car ahead of him two or three yards, then indicated that she should try again to start it. She turned the ignition and the motor came to life.

Don raised a thumb. 'Good old girl. Now back her out.'

She put the car into reverse (as she explained to a sympathetic coroner at the inquest) and released the clutch. But it moved forward instead of back. She lost her head, tried to brake, instead pushed the accelerator harder, and then . . .

The sympathetic coroner spared her the necessity of going on. Don was standing directly in front of the rake. He was transfixed by the sharp new tines like a piece of bread on a toasting fork. But if the rake had not been there, the coroner said consolingly, he would undoubtedly have been crushed to death against the wall.

An expert motor-car engineer gave evidence. He said that the car was very old and badly needed new gears. You hardly needed to depress the clutch to move from one gear to another. It was the easiest thing in the world to slip into first instead of into reverse.

Friends and neighbours were very sympathetic, like the coroner. Don Bradbury had made himself known and respected in Gainham Woods, and indeed they were a most devoted couple. 'He was a real member of our community,' the vicar said to Moira at the funeral.

Afterward she got rid of Tess. As she explained to Marjorie Allenden, she couldn't keep a car that had killed her husband. It was Marjorie who helped her to find a nice little flat in Camden Town, which at least wasn't in the heart of deadly exurbia like Gainham Woods.

And a week after moving in she bought a Ghiani-Lucia.

Elizabeth Ferrars

Scatter his Ashes

On nights like tonight, about the beginning of December, I often suffer from an attack of depression and insomnia and find myself wandering about the house, feeling that there's something special that I ought to be doing, but not knowing what it is. I find myself wanting a cigarette, although normally I'm a non-smoker. I start wanting to ring up friends on the telephone for no particular reason.

My husband understands these moods of mine and doesn't interfere with me. He's a very kind and tolerant man. He knows that the moods generally come on about the anniversary of the night my father died. That's how I like to put it to myself. I think, I speak, of the night he died, or passed on, or passed away, and my husband does the same. But both of us know, of course, that what we are doing is only avoiding saying 'the night he was killed, the night he was murdered'. Time doesn't soften the brutality of those words. If anything, it makes them crueller. After twenty years I find I shrink from using them even more than I did at the time, when there was no evading them.

Tonight my mood is an especially bad one, which is why I have started to try to write down some of my feelings. I'd like to be rid of the past, and perhaps writing of it may help. I've heard people say it does, and at least it's something that I've never tried before. I've tried travel, drink, even drugs. But the ghosts always return and while they're with me they utterly destroy the orderly contentment of my life, which I value beyond everything.

I know that the weather tonight is half the trouble. All day long it's looked as if it were going to snow, yet no snow has fallen. That's how it was on that day twenty years ago. About half-way through the morning the daylight grew murky and as I went about my usual work in the

532

house I started turning on lights in all the rooms. My father shouted at me from his downstairs bedroom that this was another example of my recent insane extravagance, but really I couldn't see without the lights. Thick clouds had spread quickly over the sky. It was dark grey and looked like a dirty old pillow, ready to burst and spread its white feathers all over the city.

Feathers. . . .

There I go, thinking of them again.

I had a dream about them last night. I dreamt that I'd bought a new fur coat. As it happens, I already have four, my new ocelot that my husband gave me for my birthday, and my old mink, which was one of the first things I bought for myself when I inherited my money, and a very smart short black sealskin jacket, which is about two years old now, and the musquash, which my father let me buy I don't know how many years ago, which won't wear out and which I still keep for running around the shops. But last night, in my dream, I bought a fifth coat. I don't know what I thought the fur was, but it was dark grey and soft and silky. And then, when I got home, I found that the coat wasn't made of fur at all, but all of feathers. Nothing but feathers. For some reason, this was terrifying. The dream turned into a nightmare and I woke up, shivering with panic.

My father had been sleeping in that downstairs bedroom for several years before his death. He had bad arthritis, a bad heart, some trouble with his kidneys and had had a slight stroke. Our doctor once said to me jovially that Mr Greenbank had at least six illnesses which ought to have killed him, but that he'd probably outlive us all. I almost believed this. I saw him as indestructible. Half helpless as he was, he clung to life with a kind of ferocity, growing murderously angry with anything that struck him as a threat to his security. I think, in his situation, I should have been glad to die, but his limited, crippled life was astoundingly precious to him.

He was sure, from the start, that my marriage threatened him. I told him. I swore to him, that I'd never leave him as long as he needed me, that Garry was going to move into the house with us and that that would mean that my father would have more help than before, not less. He only muttered some of the ugly words that he liked to use and asked me jeeringly if I really didn't know that Garry was only marrying me for the money that would one day be mine, and was he likely, that being so, to trouble himself much about my poor old father?

Perhaps I should explain here that my father couldn't stop the money coming to me. I'm sure he would have, if he could. But it had been my mother's, most of it willed to my father only for his lifetime, and when he died it would be mine. I sometimes think that that will of my mother's may have been one of the reasons why he had that bitter determination to live on and on. For when he died he would lose all his power over me, except through what he had managed to make of me while he was alive. And that was the only power he had left over anyone. He had once been managing director of a big firm that manufactured woollen goods, and had had a lot of power over a great many people, but now his world had shrunk to me and the few old cronies who still came to see him sometimes.

I was thirty-two when I married Garry. My mother had died when I was fifteen, so my father had had seventeen years in which to mould my character. Garry was three years younger than I was. He was a small man, which for ɔme reason I found intensely attractive. I was big myself, tall and lumpy, rather like my father, with an indifferent complexion and thin, mouse-brown hair. The sort of good-natured charm that I'm told I possess now had had no chance to develop then, because I was about as lacking in self-confidence as a young woman can be.

Garry's hair was fair and curly and his eyes were a vivid blue. All his movements were quick, vigorous and decisive. He had immense vitality. And he had a number of habits which I thought of as wholly, uniquely masculine and so accepted as somehow peculiarly endearing. He was extremely untidy. If he opened a drawer to take something out, he never thought of shutting it again, but assumed that someone would always be there to do it for him. When a shirt, or socks, or his underwear were soiled, he simply dropped them on the floor, knowing that I'd pick them up and put them in the linen basket. He was a chain-smoker, and used only to aim his cigarettes in the vaguest way in the direction of an ashtray. But he never said anything wounding or spiteful. He was generous with presents. And as for his having married me for my money, he had a good job with a big firm of estate agents in our Northern town, and soon after moving into our house, he took to paying the house-keeping bills himself, to save me the humiliation, so he told me, of having to ask my father for the money. Also, Garry paid for our wedding reception, when, of course, my father should have done it.

My father wouldn't come to the wedding, and wouldn't have the reception in our house.

'I don't want a lot of people here whom I don't know from Adam,' he said, 'eating and drinking and making a racket. It wouldn't be good for me. If you want to do such a damnfool thing, go on and do it, I can't stop you. But count me out of it.'

So we had the reception in an hotel, and there, for the first time, I met Garry's brother, Alec.

If there was one thing from the first that I didn't like about Garry, it was Alec. I know that sounds absurd. A man's brother is not a part of him. Yet, as it happens, Garry and Alec were more a part of one another than brothers usually are. Both their parents had died when they were boys, leaving them very badly off, and Alec, who was five years older than Garry, had always looked after him until he was able to stand on his own feet. So I did my best to see the good in Alec. It must be there, I thought, if Garry could be so fond of him. He was in the habit of consulting Alec about everything. He used to quote the things Alec said, kept telephoning him and from time to time, if some specially difficult problem connected with his work came up, went up to London to stay with him overnight. For Alec was in the London headquarters of the same firm as Garry, and had helped him to get his job with them.

But Alec was a noisy, vulgar man, red-faced, thick-necked, burly, with sly little eyes under thick lids with hardly any eyelashes, and he thought it was funny to be rude and ask such things as whether I couldn't find a wife for him just like myself, rich and beautiful. He was drunk by the time he said it, and I could see how embarrassed Garry was, because even he never made out that I was a beauty. So I pretended to be amused and said that I'd do my best, at which Alec flung an arm round me, gave me a great kiss on my cheek and said, 'Ah, there aren't any more like you, love!'

Garry and I had no honeymoon, as my father couldn't be left alone for long enough for us to go away. Mrs Clarke, our daily, who didn't mind coming to sit with him on the evenings when I went out to the Townswomen's Guild or to a concert, couldn't possibly have looked after him for a whole week-end. So as soon as the reception was over, Garry and I went back to the house and began our life together there. Garry went to the office on Monday morning, and I went on doing the cooking, as I always had, as well as a fair amount of the housework. Mrs Clarke, who came for three hours each morning, was too old, and the house was too big and inconvenient, for her to be able to manage it by herself. Garry asked me once if I wouldn't like to have someone younger to work for me, or even a maid who lived in, but I knew what an upheaval like that would do to my father, after the shock of my marriage, so I said I was perfectly happy with things as they were.

In fact, I was unbelievably happy. I'd never minded doing the cooking and the housework. I'd never been trained for anything else. And I went out so seldom that if I hadn't had some kind of work to do, I'd long ago have died of boredom. And now I had Garry to cook for and look after, and for the first time in my life had the glorious experience of hearing my cooking praised when I'd taken the trouble to make something specially good, and of being thanked for doing little things for him, so little that sometimes I was hardly aware I'd done them.

What a lot Garry taught me about living! I discovered my own body through him. There I was, thirty-two, and I'd never known before what a body was meant for. It was like being given the gift of life for a second time. I also learnt how much two people can enjoy themselves just talking together over a bottle of good sherry in the evenings, telling each other things which I'd never dreamt it was possible to share with a single soul. You had no need of other friends if you could do that. There was also the joy of being told, not that I was incompetent, lazy and indifferent to the sufferings of others, but too kind for my own good, sweet-natured, gentle and in need of cherishing.

And always there was the delight of simply seeing Garry about the house, small, taut, vital, male. I loved simply to sit and look at him and think of nothing but him.

The flaws in my happiness were Alec and the silent war between Garry and my father. It became a silent war, not an open one, very quickly, when my father discovered that Garry never answered back. To sarcasm, unkind innuendoes and violent tirades, his only answer was a rather odd smile, as if he were enjoying a joke that couldn't be shared with anyone, not even with me. Then he'd go out of the room and quietly do whatever he'd meant to do all along. So Garry was always easily the victor and my father learnt to avoid quarrels which he was sure to lose.

Garry tried to teach me the trick of it. He said, 'A man on crutches or in a wheelchair can't follow you all over the house, so when he annoys you, why don't you simply leave the room?'

'But he doesn't often exactly *annoy* me,' I said. 'It's much more complicated than that.'

'I know,' Garry said. 'He frightens, bullies, hypnotises you, so you think you have to stay there and take it. But you haven't really, you know. He hasn't any power over you. It's you who have power over him. You can leave him any time you choose, and at the back of his mind he knows it.'

'But he's very fond of me in his own way, don't you see?' I said. 'I couldn't hurt him.'

'I wonder if he is fond of you,' Garry said, 'or ever has been of anyone. I can't see him caring for anyone but himself.'

'Oh, he adored my mother,' I said. 'He simply worshipped her.'

'That's what he says now,' said Garry. 'But I wonder what she'd have told you herself, if you'd been old enough to ask her.'

This was such a shocking thought to me that I was silent. My whole relationship with my father had been built on the assumption that he had loved my mother with all his heart and that it had been his hideous suffering on her early death that had warped what had once been a fine and generous nature. For she must once have found him worth loving, after all, and my memory of her was of someone who had a lot of rich affection to give and cheerfulness and charm.

'Have you ever thought,' Garry went on, 'that he may have married her for her money and that that's why he's so certain I married you for yours?'

I looked at him stupidly. I've always had a slow mind and it takes me time to assimilate a new idea.

He gave his easy-going laugh.

'You don't think I don't know that's what he thinks about me, do you?' he said. 'He came straight out with it the very first time we met. He doesn't bother with subtleties.'

'Well, anyway,' I said after a moment, 'I could never leave him. It wouldn't be right. I told you that before we married.'

'Good lord, I wasn't talking about *leaving* him,' Garry said. 'Not leaving the house, moving away. I understand how you feel about that and it's quite all right with me. No, I just meant, when he says something that gets under your skin and makes you go dead white – do you know you do that? – just get up and walk out. Out of the room. Let him stew in his own juice for a little. That's all I meant.'

'Oh, I see,' I said, relieved, because I dreaded an argument with him.

'Only you'll never do it,' Garry said with a smile and reached out and punched my cheek lightly with his fist. 'You're too damned easily put upon. You just ask to be trodden on. Well, don't ever let me do it. If ever you find me treading on you, my darling, yell.'

The funny thing was that I wanted to yell, though of course I never did, at his devotion to Alec, at his clinging to him even now that he was married, his dependance on him or whatever it was. Actually I was never quite sure which brother was more dependent on the other. It must have begun by the older brother supporting the younger, but by now Garry was so much the more intelligent and wide-awake of the two that I thought perhaps this had been reversed. In any case, I hated the relationship between them. Even if Alec had been a person for whom I could have felt some affection, I should have hated it. I wanted Garry all to myself.

I used always to feel nervous and restless during the long telephone conversations that he and Alec used to have with one another. There was nothing private about these conversations. The telephone was in the sitting-room and Garry used to sit comfortably on the sofa with his feet up and the telephone to his ear, smoking cigarette after cigarette and spraying ash on the carpet and chatting on and on to Alec. Sometimes it was about something that had happened in the office, some mistake that Garry had made and was worrying about, or something that a client had said. Sometimes it was about nothing in particular. And as I listened a weird sort of feeling that was almost like hatred used to well up in me, hatred not of Alec, which would have been silly but understandable, but of Garry himself. I used to get stiff and cramped in my chair with the effort of fighting the violence of the feeling. It frightened me a good deal.

But I felt even worse when Garry went to London to see Alec. On those occasions Garry never stayed away for more than one night and he always telephoned me in the evening from Alec's flat and had a long conversation with me, of much the same kind as he had with Alec. But every time that he went away I became possessed by an utterly irrational, feverish anxiety that I would never see him again. I used not to show it. I would kiss him good-bye quite calmly, tell him in an unemotional, automatic way to drive carefully and go back into the house and shut the door before the car was even out of sight. But then I would go frantic.

I wouldn't sit down and cry, though I always felt as if I should like to. Instead, I'd start to rush about the house, doing all sorts of unnecessary jobs, turning out drawers, moving pieces of furniture, and, as likely as not, breaking something. I would polish, scrub, rearrange books, clean windows and cook enough to last the household for at least the next three days. I would keep this up until the evening, when Garry's telephone call came through.

Usually this was at about ten o'clock. If it was much later than that I would go up to my room, because my father became fractious if he could hear me moving about downstairs when he wanted to go to sleep, and I would take the call on the extension up there. At last then I would be at peace. I would take my sleeping pill and sleep soundly. I didn't normally take sleeping pills, but on those nights when Garry was away and my mind became obsessed, you might say almost unhinged, with terrifying premonitions of disaster, I used to take three grains of sodium amytal and have a quiet night.

At this distance, it all seems so ridiculous. I can't think of anything whatever that would make me act like that now.

My fears of disaster didn't take any specific form. They were like a child's fears of the dark, in which the special terror is that the perils thronging it are unimaginable. I didn't see, oh no, my God, I did not see even a shadow of what was actually to happen!

It began one day in early December, when Garry set off on one of his visits to Alec in London. It was bitterly cold. The sky was the colour it's been all day today, that dirty grey that threatens snow, and it seemed to have sunk down so low that it almost rested on the roofs of the houses. There was black ice on the garden path.

It was after lunch that Garry set off for London. It was a six hour drive. I warned him that the roads would be treacherous and as usual I begged him to drive extra carefully. He patted my shoulder, kissed me and told me not to worry. He was a good driver, wasn't he, he asked me. I agreed that he was. I didn't, as a matter of fact, worry much about his having a crash on the road. I didn't imagine the car going into a skid, shooting over the edge of a bank, turning over and over and bursting into flames, or else perhaps going head-on at seventy into a lorry. I wasn't afraid of anything so rational. As he got into the car I turned back into the house and quietly shut the door behind me.

Soon I began to wish that the snow would come, although I knew that it would be unpleasant for him to drive through, because there was a curious tension in waiting for it. It gave me the feeling that time had stopped and that the day and the solitary night ahead of me would never come to an end. But by the time that full darkness came and I went round the house, drawing the curtains, no snow had fallen yet. There was no wind either, but only a silent, lifeless chill that seeped into our big, old-fashioned rooms through the chinks round the badly fitting sash windows and the great blank panes of glass.

My father and I had steak and kidney pudding for dinner, followed by apple charlotte and custard and biscuits and cheese. Afterwards my father hobbled into the sitting-room on his crutches to watch television for a while before going to bed, and when I had done the washing-up I joined him. But the programme he was watching wasn't one I cared about, and my usual devil of restlessness entered into me and I returned to the kitchen.

I made a chocolate cake of which Garry was particularly fond. I made a trifle with plenty of brandy in it. I made a chicken casserole with mushrooms, which I thought we could have for dinner the next evening. I made a plum tart, using some plums I'd bottled in the summer. I made an apricot flan. By then the kitchen was wonderfully warm from the heat of the oven, and full of good smells, but it was ten minutes to ten and Garry hadn't rung up yet.

I leafed through one of my cookery books, looking for something new to try. Then all of a sudden I decided I'd had enough of cooking and would vacuum the sitting-room carpet instead and give the furniture an extra good polishing. I knew my father would have gone to bed by then and the room would be empty.

I did the polishing first. There's something to be said for that heavy old mahogany. It does show results when you polish it. I quite enjoyed doing it. Then I got out the vacuum cleaner and went to work on the carpet. I'd all but finished when I realised that the door had opened and that my father, in his dressing-gown and leaning on his crutches, was in the doorway.

There was a puzzled sort of fury on his face. He said something to me that I didn't hear because of the buzz of the vacuum cleaner. I switched it off and in the silence the sound of his voice burst on me like a shout.

'You're mad!' he roared at me. 'Do you know that? That man's driven you mad. You were always weak in the head, but now you're actually insane. What time do you think it is?'

'I'm sorry,' I said. 'I'm afraid I wasn't thinking. It's just that I get restless when Garry goes away. I never get used to it.'

'You were used to it for long enough before you got married, weren't you?' my father said. 'You didn't seem to mind being alone in those days. You didn't start using that damned machine in the middle of the night.'

'It isn't actually the middle of the night,' I said. 'It's only a little after half past ten. I didn't think you'd want to go to sleep yet.'

'Who said I wanted to go to sleep?' he demanded. 'I want to read and I want to read in peace. I can't do it with that devil's racket going on.'

'But you always read the paper while Mrs Clarke uses the vacuum in the mornings,' I said.

He answered, 'Of course I do. I know she's got to use it. I know the house has to be kept clean and you can't get a woman to go down on her knees nowadays and do a job of work like her mother did. I know all that. I'm not unreasonable. But there's a time for everything. At half past ten at night I expect quiet. I've a right to quiet – even if I haven't many other rights left in this house.'

'I'm sorry.' It occurred to me that half the things I said to my father used to begin with those words.

'Oh, you're sorry.' His big, sallow face began to crumple as if he were about to cry. It sometimes did that in his attacks of self-pity, though tears never actually came. 'D'you know what, you aren't sorry at all. You've no heart. You do things like that on purpose, just to goad me, just to try to make me get angry. You know it isn't good for me to get angry. You know about my heart. You know about my arteries. You know anything could happen to me any time if I ever lost control of my feelings. And you say you're sorry!'

It was at times like this that I went silent. Something seemed to lock up everything inside me. I'm sure my face turned white, as Garry had told me it used to. I stood there, holding the handle of the vacuum cleaner, thinking of all the things I might have done if I'd been a different kind of woman. For, big as he was, my father was really very helpless. He was a great, half-lifeless, ruined hulk of a man. He was at my mercy. He had been for years. But I just stood there, silent.

He began to turn away, moving clumsily on his crutches. But then he paused and looked straight into my face with his puzzled, fierce eyes.

'You'll never understand,' he said. 'You haven't the brains to understand, and I'm not good at putting things. But I've always tried to do what was best for you. I've thought of you before anything else. I promised your dear mother I would, and I have, I swear to God I have. I tried as hard as I could to save you from getting into the clutches of that cheap little crook you've married, and I'm trying still. I'm trying to go on living, though I'm pretty sick and tired of it, let me tell you, to stop him getting his hands on your money. Because you'll give it all to him, every penny you've got, you're so simple-minded. And as soon as you do, you'll have seen the last of him. That'll be the end for you. That'll be the end of your fine daydream. But tell you that – what's the use?'

I came to my senses then. It was the attack on Garry that did it. I remembered what he'd told me to do. Quietly I wound up the flex of the vacuum cleaner, wheeled it past my father out of the room, put it away in the cupboard under the stairs and went up to my room.

My father called something after me, but I didn't listen. I closed the door behind me, threw myself down on the bed and found that I was shaking all over. But inside I was joyful. I had won. I had been all by myself, scared, but I had won. Garry was right, I could always win. When I heard my father's crutches thumping slowly across the hall downstairs as he returned to his room, I had to jam some of the eiderdown into my mouth to stop myself laughing aloud.

An eiderdown is full of feathers. . . .

When I think of it I can still feel the rasp of the rose-coloured satin against my lips. The feathers seem to be choking me. I want to be sick.

It was nearly eleven o'clock and I was in bed reading when the telephone rang. I picked it up and the operator said, 'Mr Willis is calling you from London and wishes you to pay for the call. Will you accept the charge?'

Garry always did that when he rang me up from Alec's flat, so that the cost would go on our bill and not on Alec's.

I said impatiently, 'Yes, please go ahead.'

There was the usual click, then Garry's voice said, 'Darling? I'm sorry it's so late, but Alec insisted on taking me out to dinner and a theatre he'd got tickets for and we've only just got in. How are things?'

'Fine,' I said. 'Wonderful.'

'Now what's all this?' he said. 'Things aren't supposed to be fine when I'm away. You're supposed to worry all the time. Or haven't I understood you in the past?'

'Ah, of course you have,' I said. 'I've been on edge all day, just as usual. But what I meant was, my father came and talked to me all about you, and I simply walked out. He said horrible things about you, and I simply walked out.'

'Now that really *is* fine,' Garry said. 'I'll make an adult woman of you yet. What were the horrible things he said about me? Just the usual?'

'Oh, don't let's talk about them,' I answered. 'None of it matters. I'm beginning to grasp that things that simply aren't true don't matter. You can laugh at them. Tell me about the play.'

'It's not worth talking about either. It was just a lot of nonsense about people popping in and out of bed with the wrong people, and losing their trousers and falling over the furniture. I found it hard work to raise a laugh, even to please Alec, but he seemed to enjoy it. Then he wanted to drop into a pub on the way home, so I couldn't help being late, could I?'

'It doesn't matter,' I said.

'I thought perhaps I shouldn't call you at all,' he said. 'I thought perhaps you'd have taken your sleeping-pill already and gone to sleep.'

I answered, 'I never take it till after you've rung. If you hadn't, I'd just have lain here awake, waiting.'

'Well, take it now and have a good night.'

'Yes, I will. And you take care, driving home tomorrow, won't you?'

'Of course. I always do. Good night, darling. I love you.'

'Oh, Garry....' My voice broke and I couldn't get out what I wanted to say. There was too much love in me for me to be able to direct a trickle of it into something so small as the mouthpiece of a telephone. I held it tightly for a moment, then gave a deep sigh and put it down. Reaching out for the capsule that I'd put ready on the bedside table with a glass of water, I swallowed the pill, turned off the light, lay back on my pillows and slept deeply and dreamlessly.

The alarm clock woke me at seven o'clock. I always got up then to make my father his morning tea. Then I would have a bath, get dressed and cook the breakfast. It was still dark. It was still very cold too. Going to the window, I expected to see the pale glitter of snow in the darkness, but everything was utterly black. I didn't like it. There was something eerie and threatening about that icy barrenness. I put on my dressing-gown and slippers, went downstairs, made the tea and carried it into my father's room.

I know I'm very slow in my reactions. Some people take this for stupidity. Cleverer people realise that I'm simply very slow. I need time to put together what I see, what I think and what I feel. I need time to understand. But in the end I do. Indeed, I do.

What I saw as I stood there in the doorway was whiteness. It was all over the bed and the carpet and the furniture. Also I saw a great jagged hole in the plate glass of the window, through which a freezing draught was blowing in. It was as if the draught had blown a snowstorm into the room, although there was no snow outside in the garden. The white-ness stirred gently here and there in the current of air from the window.

Of course, it wasn't snow. It was feathers. Someone had pressed a pillow down over my father's face and the pillow had burst and the draught had carried the blizzard of little downy feathers all over the room. But the pillow had done its work. My father was dead.

Because I am so slow, I stood there for some seconds before, quite gently, I let the tea-tray slide out of my hands and fall with a crash. Hot tea splashed over my feet and bare ankles. I began to scream. Naturally, there was no one to hear me. After a moment I stopped. I didn't go near the bed, for I knew my father was dead and that there was nothing I could do for him. There was a feather on his face, just by one of his nostrils, and it was motionless.

Turning, holding to the wall as I went, because I was so dizzy, I went to the sitting-room, dropped on to the sofa and picked up the telephone.

I was going to dial 999.

But just before I started, I noticed a disconcerting thing. It caught my attention, made me wonder, frown, then thoughtfully put the telephone down again.

On the carpet, close to where I was sitting, was a little heap of cigarette ash.

It was on just about the spot where Garry had a habit of letting his ash fall during those long conversations that he used to have with Alec. But I'd been over that part of the carpet the evening before with the vacuum cleaner. I knew I had. I remember moving the sofa so that I could clean the spot where it usually stood, as well as all round it. Moving that heavy old sofa was a thing that you remembered.

But now there was a little heap of ash where there couldn't be one.

My first impulse was to put my slipper down on it and flatten it into the carpet and forget about it. For ever. But then my mind began to work. Thoughts began to come to me. Slow, slow thoughts.

At first only one was clear. Garry had been here last night.

It wasn't easy to believe, but it was easier than to look at that heap of ash and convince myself that I'd missed it with the vacuum cleaner, or simply that it didn't exist. I had to face it, he had been here, had sat just here where I was sitting and had smoked a cigarette.

Drawing my feet up under me on the sofa, I clasped my arms tightly round me to try to keep out the awful chill of the room. But the chill was in my own blood, seeping out of my bones. I started shivering and found I couldn't stop it.

I started thinking of all sorts of unimportant things, like the chocolate cake I'd made, and a pink feather hat I'd bought a few weeks before that Garry had said he liked, and some gold cuff-links that I'd seen in a shop a day or so ago which I'd thought of buying for him, but hadn't, because I was too unsure of his tastes. I often wanted to buy things for him and then didn't, because I never trusted myself to guess what he'd like. I'd had very little experience of buying presents for anyone, and was so nervous of choosing the wrong things, which he'd only thank me for out of politeness, that possibly I'd appeared ungenerous. That was a wretched thought. I brooded on it for a while as I sat there and shivered.

Then, with a jolt, I thought again that last night Garry had sat here in this room. He had smoked a cigarette. He had talked to me on the telephone.

But how can you ring up a person on an extension of the telephone you're using yourself?

I began to think that I would like a cup of tea. I went out to the kitchen, where the kettle that I'd used to make the tea for my father was still warm, and made another pot of tea and took it back to the sitting-room and sat down on the sofa again.

By then I understood how the telephone call had reached me. It had been Alec who had telephoned from London and asked the operator for that transferred charge call. Then, as soon as it had rung here and I'd picked up the telephone by my bed, Garry had picked up this one. And so we had been connected and had been able to talk to one another. He must have been sitting here quietly, waiting for the call to come through, for some time, and smoking as usual and forgetting to notice where his ash fell. All as usual. It was such a familiar scene, I could see him doing it. How could he know that the last thing I'd do before going to bed would be to vacuum the carpet?

The trouble about thinking is that you can't always stop when you want to. I shut my eyes and pressed my knuckles against them.

I thought, 'My father was right all along. Garry and Alec, they had it all planned from the beginning. A convenient marriage to a lonely, unwanted woman who would be rich when her sick old father died. A simple murder. And now. . . . I wonder what they've got planned for me now.'

I opened my eyes again and gazed at the little heap of cigarette ash.

It was so small that the first policeman who came into the room might easily put his foot on it and tread it into the carpet.

Hesitatingly my hand went out to the silver cigarette box near the telephone. I took out a cigarette, put it between my lips and lit it. It made me cough and the smoke got into my eyes and brought tears to them. I'd smoked only one cigarette before in my whole life. That was when I was sixteen and wanted not to be left out among the other schoolgirls. But I hadn't liked it and had never smoked again. I didn't like it now. But I smoked that cigarette from beginning to end, adding to the little heap of ash on the carpet and scattering the rest of the ash carelessly about, some on the sofa, some actually in an ashtray, and finally taking the stub to the lavatory and flushing it down the drain, in case it had fingerprints, or traces of my saliva, or something like that on it, which would show it hadn't been Garry who'd smoked it.

Then I dialled 999.

I told the police, when they questioned me later, about having vacuumed the carpet in the evening, but I never said anything about the ash. But of course they saw it, and worked out for themselves what it meant, and once their suspicions were aroused, it didn't take them long to break down Garry's alibi. They explained it all to me after they'd proved that he hadn't been in the theatre with Alec, and that neither of them had been to the public house where Garry said they'd gone for a drink, and that someone had seen him in a café on the road to London, where he'd been stupid enough to stop for a snack in the early morning. He hadn't in fact been in London at all the day before. He'd actually stayed hidden in our garage, where he'd known I'd have no reason to go, since he had the car. Then when he'd seen the light go on in the bedroom and known I'd gone to bed at last, he'd let himself quietly into the house and gone into the sitting-room to wait for Alec's call. It had been made specially late on purpose so that he and Alec could be sure that I'd be waiting for it in bed and not downstairs. And after Garry had talked to me, he'd gone to my father's room and smothered him. Smothering can sometimes be mistaken for a natural death, particularly with someone as old and ill as my father. Of course it had been intended to look like a natural death. But the pillow had burst and the feathers had floated all over the room, so there had been no hope of disguising the fact that it was murder. So then Garry had smashed the window, to make it look like a case of breaking and entering, and had taken my father's wallet and his gold watch and chain. But he'd thrown them over some hedge on the way to London, where he'd gone straight after the murder, and where, by the time I discovered it, he'd been in bed, asleep.

In those days they still had hanging.

It wasn't long before I was a widow and a rich widow too. I sold the house and moved away, and I reassumed the name of Greenbank, though I stuck to the title of Mrs I had some bad times at first, because I hadn't any friends or outside interests, and sometimes I used to drink too much by myself and take too many barbiturates. Then one day I bought myself that mink coat I mentioned.

It was a gesture of liberation. After it I began to find it easier to spend money on myself and to start doing things I'd only had dreams of before. It was about a year after my father's death that I went to a travel agent and made arrangements to take a trip round the world. I bought a lot of new clothes for it, all totally different from anything I'd ever worn before, and I had my hair cut short and tinted. I was feeling like an exciting stranger to myself when I set off, with my mind full of all the new sights I was going to see, and the new people I'd meet, and the friends I'd make.

What actually happened is that before we'd even reached Madeira I met the man who later became my second husband. We were drawn to each other from the first, and spent a great deal of time in each other's company throughout the voyage. There was no question of falling in love. I suppose there never has been. But we have a great deal of affection for one another, we trust each other and enjoy being together. He is twenty years older than I am, has more money than I have and suffers from rather poor health, which makes him require a good deal of looking after. But with my experience, that isn't too much of an effort. He was a widower when we met, whose first wife, whom he'd worshipped, had recently died. So in some ways, I suppose, you could say I'm almost back where I started.

The difference is that my husband, compared with my father, is a kind and considerate man, who makes me feel that he likes me and values what I do for him. I consider myself, on the whole, a very lucky woman. We've spent almost eighteen years together. It's only occasionally, on a day like today, about this time of year, that I feel all sorts of disturbing emotions stirring inside me, and a kind of wildness threatens to do strange things to my brain.

The real tragedy, of course, is that it was all so unnecessary. If Garry had ever loved me as he pretended he did, if he'd relied on me instead of on Alec, if he'd trusted me, he need never have tried to deceive me. We could have worked together. Among my daydreams there'd often been one of getting rid of my father and being finally free to be myself, and with Garry's initiative and forcefulness behind me, I might really have done something about it. And I shouldn't have blundered as he did. I am a more capable woman than people realise. At least, if I'd used a pillow, it wouldn't have been one that would burst, spilling those horrible feathers everywhere. The death would really have looked like a natural death. Or natural enough to deceive that silly old doctor of ours, who thought that my father ought to be dead anyway of six different diseases. There would have been no difficulties about a death certificate. Everything would have gone smoothly and we could have been so happy. . . .

But Garry never loved me. That's the thought I have to concentrate on when my mind starts to run on in this way and a sort of grinding pain starts up in my heart. Everything he said to me, everything we did together, was founded on lies. All our happiness was only something he let me imagine for a little. My father was right about him from the start. Garry himself proved it to me. He showed me up to myself as everything my father had always said I was. I suppose that was why I killed him.

Hugh Pentecost

Jericho and the Two Ways to Die

The place probably had a name, Jericho thought, like Lookout Point or High View or something equally imaginative. The road wound around the side of the mountain, with vertical cliffs on one side and a drop into space on the other. From this particular point there was an incredibly beautiful view of a wide valley below: farming country with fenced-in fields that made it look like a nonsymmetrical checkerboard; cattle looking like tiny toys in the distance and grazing languidly. And colour! Autumn glory was at its peak, gold and red and russet brown and the dark green of pines and fir trees.

Jericho had discovered this spot a few days ago and his painter's eye had been caught and held. He'd taken a room in a motel in the nearby town of Plainville and come here each of the last three days with his easel and painting gear.

The town fathers of Plainville had obviously been aware of all this magnificence. The two-lane road had been widened so that visitors in cars could pull out to the very edge of the drop, guarded by a steel-cable fence, park, and take in God's handiwork at their leisure. Jericho had chosen a spot above the road, above the lookout point, to do his painting. He had found a place to pull his red Mercedes off the road, had scrambled up the bank with his equipment, and set himself up for the day. Unless someone was searching for his car or craning his neck to look straight up, his presence would remain unknown.

He was sitting with his back propped against a huge boulder, filling a black curve-stemmed pipe from an oilskin pouch, when he first saw the small sports car with the girl at the wheel. She was driving up from the town, hugging the inside of the road. The car's top was down and he was attracted by the bright blonde hair of the driver that blew around her face, wondering idly if the colour was real or if it came out of a bottle. While he watched, the girl stopped the car directly below him and got out. A very short skirt and very nice legs, he thought, and an exquisite figure. She was wearing a pair of amber-tinted granny glasses.

She walked across the road to the lookout area, reached the steel cable of the fence, and instead of looking out at the view she leaned forward and looked down. Some people are fascinated by dizzying heights. She stood there for a full minute, gazing down. Then she came back to the car, got in, and started the motor. She started, faster than was good for the motor or tyres, swung the wheel to the left, and aimed directly at the spot where she'd been standing.

Jericho pushed himself up on his haunches and his mouth opened to shout when she came to a sudden skidding stop, the front bumper of the sports car hard against the steel-cable fence.

'Idiot!' Jericho said out loud, standing up.

The girl got out of the car and went to the fence – staring down again. Slowly she came back and got into the car. She backed across the road, almost in her own tracks, and stopped where she had first parked. Then she started up again, with a spray of gravel from the rear tyres, and once more headed straight for the fence. And once again she stopped, just in time.

Jericho went sliding down the bank, braking with his heels. He reached the car and stood gripping the door on the passenger's side, towering over the girl. He was a giant of a man, standing six feet four and weighing about 240, all muscle. He had flaming red hair and a buccaneer's red beard and moustache.

'There are two ways to die,' he said in a conversational tone. 'One is to give up and kill yourself; the other is to go down fighting whatever it is that has you up a tree.' He smiled. 'The second way, there's a chance you won't have to die at all.'

The eyes behind the granny glasses were wide, frightened. He couldn't tell their colour – they were shielded by the amber lenses. The mouth was wide, drawn down at the corners. The face was classic: high cheekbones, straight nose, eyes set nicely apart. She would have been beautiful if something like terror hadn't contorted the features. Her hands gripped the wheel of the car so tightly her knuckles were white knobs.

'Oh, God!' she said in a strangled whisper.

Jericho opened the car door and got in beside her. 'This isn't a very heavy car,' he said. 'I don't know if you could plow through that steel cable or not.' He took his pipe out of his pocket and held his lighter to it. 'Want to talk about it?'

Her head was turned away toward her target at the lookout point. 'You're John Jericho, the artist, aren't you?'

'How did you know?'

'Plainville is a small town. You're a celebrity. Word gets around.' Her voice was low and husky. She was fighting for control.

'And you are Miss—?'

'Mrs Virgil Clarke,' she said. She turned to him. 'You've heard of my husband?'

He looked at her ringless fingers. 'Famous trial lawyer,' he said. 'You live in Plainville?'

'We have a home here, an apartment in New York, an island in the West Indies.'

'Nobody can say that crime does not pay,' Jericho said. Fragments of memory were falling into place. Virgil Clarke was endlessly in the headlines. His Lincolnesque face was as familiar as a movie star's. He was the Clarence Darrow of the 1970s, the hero of people with lost causes. He must be, Jericho thought, sixty years old, at least twice the age of the girl who sat gripping the wheel of the sports car.

Memory again: a girl charged with murder; a brilliant defence; an acquittal; a headline romance and marriage. It was the first marriage for the noted lawyer; the bride was a widow, accused and acquitted of having murdered her husband.

'You've remembered,' she said.

He nodded, his strong white teeth clamped on the stem of his pipe. 'Care to tell me why?' he asked.

'Why?'

'Why you were contemplating a plunge into oblivion?'

She looked at him, forcing a smile. 'You thought I meant to—?'

'Didn't you?'

'I – I'm not a very good driver,' she said. 'I wanted to turn around. I couldn't seem to figure out how to – how to do it.'

'Have it your way,' Jericho said. 'It's really none of my business.' He opened the car door, swung his long legs out, and stood looking down at her. 'At least you've had a chance to think about it twice.' His smile was mirthless. 'Pull back, cut your wheels right, back up some more, then head for – wherever you're headed for, Mrs Clarke.'

About a hundred yards from Jericho's motel, down the main street of Plainville, was a delightful small country inn. Jericho had tried to get a room there when he decided to stay over but the inn was full. He had discovered, however, that they had an excellent kitchen.

He dined there the evening of the day he encountered the girl at Lookout Point. He had a dry martini, a shrimp cocktail, a very good brook trout helped along by a small white wine, a delicious mixed green salad. He was debating a homemade lemon meringue pie when the boy from the motel came to his table.

'Mrs Clarke left a note for you, sir,' he said. 'I knew you were having dinner here.'

Jericho opened the pale blue envelope.

Dear Mr Jericho:

I tried to reach you on the phone without any luck. We are having an open house party tonight and my husband and I would be delighted to have you join us and our guests at any time after eight o'clock.

Janice Clarke

P.S. I hope you won't mind being lionised. Incidentally, anyone can tell you where we live.

People who behave strangely and without explanation were irresistible to Jericho. He went back to the motel, changed into slacks, a blue blazer, and a yellow turtlenecked sweatershirt. At about 8:30 he drove through the big stone gates that guarded the entrance to the Clarke estate. In the moonlight he saw the old Colonial house ideally situated on a hillside, with its magnificent lawns, shrubbery, and gardens. The house was brilliantly lighted and as he came close he saw this was not a small party. There were more than thirty cars parked along the side of the wide circular driveway.

The sound of music and laughter drifted toward Jericho as he approached the front door. The music was loud – rock rhythm. He was admitted by a uniformed maid and found himself in an enormous living room which seemed to occupy most of the ground floor of the house. All the furniture had been pushed to the sides of the room and the floor space was crowded with jumping, gyrating couples. The music came from a bearded trio in a far corner – two electric guitars and drums. There was a bar, loaded with every conceivable kind of liqour. There were two bartenders in scarlet shirts and leather vests. The dancing couples wore every conceivable kind of mod dress.

Jericho, looking around for his hostess, spotted his host standing at the far end of the room, his back to a blazing fire in a huge fieldstone fireplace. Virgil Clarke was unmistakable, tall, angular, with a lock of hair drooping over his broad forehead. He looked wildly out of place in this gathering in his dark business suit, button-down white shirt, and black knitted tie. His attention was focused on his wife who was dancing with a long-haired, not unhandsome young fellow wearing a batik shirt that hung loose outside his trousers. Virgil Clarke's face looked carved out of rock. What he was seeing obviously gave him no pleasure.

Watching the dancers, Jericho thought how things had changed in the last twenty years. When you danced, back then, the music was soft and you held your girl close. Now the music was deafening and the couples danced apart from each other, not touching, each performing a kind of individual war dance.

Jericho's attention was diverted by a luscious blonde girl, not more than twenty, he thought. She was wearing a startling peek-a-boo dress that revealed almost everything of her gloriously suntanned young body.

'Jericho!' There was delight in the young voice and she was instantly clinging to his arm. 'Jan is a genius! How did she manage to get you here? I'm Dana Williams, by the way. My father owns two of your paintings.'

'Bless your father. And Mrs Clarke didn't have to be a genius to get me here. She invited me and I came.'

'We've been trying to guess how to meet you for the last three days without barging up and brazenly thrusting ourselves on you. How did Jan manage it?'

'She brazenly thrust herself at me,' Jericho said, 'which is the best and quickest way.'

'Does she know you're here? She'll be wild when she sees I've glommed onto you first. Oh, there she is, dancing with Roger.'

'Who is Roger?'

'Roger Newfield. He's one of the young lawyers who works in Virgil's office. You'd better have a drink. You're way behind everyone here.'

They fought their way around the edge of the dancing throng to the bar. So far Janice hadn't noticed him. She was totally concentrated on the young man opposite whom her body twisted and turned.

Jericho ordered a Jack Daniels on the rocks and Dana a vodka martini. Watching the dancers again, Jericho found himself puzzled. They were all young. There seemed no one here even approaching Virgil Clarke's generation. Jericho suspected that he, at forty, came closest to his host in years. It was odd, he thought, that in the home of a famous man there seemed to be no other famous people, no sycophants, no hangers-on, no yes-men. Clarke, moving away from the fireplace as Jericho watched, seemed out of place in his own home.

'Shall we dance, Jericho?' Dana asked, smiling at him over the rim of her glass.

'It reveals my antiquity,' he said, 'but I don't – can't – do this modern stuff.'

'You want to hold me close we can go out on the terrace,' the girl said.

'To dance?'

'No, silly, to hold me close. I like older men, Jericho. Ask and ye shall receive.'

'You ought to have your backside paddled,' Jericho said.

'Oh, please! I'd love that!'

Before he could reply to that gambit Jericho felt a hand on his arm. He turned to face the uniformed maid.

'Mr Clarke hopes you will join him in his study for a moment, sir,' she said.

'A summons from the All Highest,' Dana said. 'Maybe he wants to buy a painting, maestro. I'll be waiting on the terrace. You be thinking about what you want to ask me to do.'

'I'll be thinking,' Jericho said, thinking about a number of ungallant suggestions. He liked to make his own passes.

The maid led him away from the bedlam of the dancers and down a short corridor to an oak door. She knocked and a deep voice invited them in. Virgil Clarke was standing by a far window and looking out over the moonlit lawn.

'Mr Jericho,' he said, as he turned. 'Thank you, Millicent.'

The maid left, closing the door behind her. The jumping rock rhythms were suddenly silenced. Jericho realised that this room was sound-proofed. 'Good evening, sir,' he said.

At close quarters Clarke was even more impressive. The deep lines at the corners of his mouth were lines of character. The mouth was firm and uncompromising without suggesting vanity or inflexibility. The eyes were deep and dark and somehow tragic, as if he couldn't shake the memory of a thousand violences. Fighting against violence had been his lifework.

'We've never met, Mr Jericho, but I have been an admirer of yours for some years.'

Jericho had noticed the absence of any art in the house. 'I hadn't thought of you as being interested in painting, sir.'

'I'm not,' Clarke said. 'Never had a chance to develop a taste for it. I've never seen one of your paintings to know it. I've admired you since the trial of the Faxon brothers.'

Jericho frowned. A good part of his own life had been devoted to travelling to the scenes of violence and trying to put on canvas his outrage at man's inhumanity to man. The Faxon Brothers had murdered two civil-rights demonstrators. Jericho had been a witness for the prosecution.

'I don't recall your being connected with the case, sir,' he said.

'I wasn't, except as a spectator,' Clarke said. 'I was interested in the defence counsel. I thought of asking him to become a partner in my firm. You broke his back in this case. You stood up under a damn good cross-examination and you broke his back.'

'I told the truth.'

'You convinced the jury it was the truth.'

'It was. Did you hire your man?'

'I did not,' Clarke said. 'He committed the cardinal sin of getting to admire you while trying to break you down. I would have beaten you, I think, because I wouldn't have allowed myself that luxury. But as a spectator I admired you. There is a good honest man, I told myself. Honest and strong.'

'A nice compliment,' Jericho said, wondering.

Clarke gestured toward a comfortable armchair. 'Can I get you a drink? I noticed you were drinking Jack Daniels out there.' He had noticed from across the room. 'I'll join you in fruit juice, if you don't mind. I have hours of work ahead of me tonight.'

'Lucky your study is soundproofed,' Jericho said, smiling. 'Thanks. Jack Daniels on the rocks would be fine.'

Clarke went to a small sideboard, made Jericho's drink, and poured himself some cranberry juice. He handed Jericho his glass and said, 'Why, if I may seem to be impertinent, are you here?'

'Because I was asked,' Jericho said.

'What I would like,' Clarke said, 'is that you, without asking for any explanation, leave this room, go out to your car, and return to your lodgings.'

'If you, my host, ask me to leave I will,' Jericho said, 'but I damn well want to know why. I'm entitled to that, I think.'

'I am not your host,' Clarke said. 'Janice evidently invited you here.'

'She did.'

'Then go,' Clarke said, his voice raised. 'You have been asked here to be used. Janice never does anything without a purpose. If you imagine it is your maleness that's attracted her, forget it. Her tastes lie in areas which I suspect would bore you. She has some other reason. I would dislike seeing you used, Mr Jericho.'

'That's a rather extraordinary thing for you to say to a stranger about your wife,' Jericho said.

'If you were to say that in front of Janice or that little tramp Dana, you would promptly be labelled a square,' Clarke said. His face looked haggard, and there was a kind of frightening bitterness in his voice. Jericho felt acute embarrassment. The man was revealing some kind of deep unhealed wound without hinting how it had been inflicted. Perhaps it was just age, the inexorable process of growing old surrounded by a desirable young wife and her young friends.

But there had been Lookout Point and Janice Clarke's tentative exercise in suicide.

'Perhaps I should tell you how I came to meet your wife, Mr Clarke,' Jericho said. So he told the lawyer about Lookout Point and the little car and the frightened girl and the preparations to die which he had been lucky enough to forestall.

Clarke listened attentively, and when Jericho finished, the lawyer said, 'I saved her once and I have been laughed at ever since – betrayed and laughed at. And now, if you don't leave, you will be betrayed and laughed at too. You have already sprouted donkey's ears, Jericho. You have been deliberately made to feel that you were Sir Galahad saving the desperate princess. The next step will be some grotesque practical joke that will have them all laughing at you.'

'Why?' Jericho asked.

'It is their prime pleasure,' Clarke said.

'Why me?' Jericho asked.

'Because you are a famous man. Because you are a crusader for decency and fair play – causes that seem antiquated to them. Because you are over thirty and your generation must be discredited. Because it will delight them to show you up as a romantic square, to show you up publicly.'

Jericho looked at his pipe which rested, cold, in the palm of his hand. 'Your wife must be reaching that thirty deadline,' he said.

'Which is why she will go to any lengths to show that she is still part of that young world – go to any outrageous lengths, I tell you!'

Jericho looked at the haggard face. 'Why do you put up with it?'

'I was once Sir Galahad,' Clarke said. 'I defended her against a murder charge. I set her free. I was bewitched by her youth, her helplessness, and I wanted to protect her forever. I persuaded her to marry me. And then – then I was laughed at because I couldn't begin to satisfy her needs. Everyone out there knows that, in her terms, I am an inadequate lover. I have no taste for orgies, which makes me a square.'

'Why haven't you walked out on her? Your values are sound and you know it. You are miserable, so why do you put up with it?'

'Because there is a bigger joke,' Clarke said. 'I defended her in court because I believed in her innocence.'

Jericho drew a deep breath. 'Are you telling me—?'

'That she was guilty,' Clarke said, grinding out the words. 'I, the Great Defender, was suckered into believing in her innocence. I married her. I showered her with luxuries. I was fooled, blinded.'

'But if that's so, she must be ready to do anything you ask. She can't risk your displeasure.'

'Double jeopardy,' the lawyer said. 'There is no new evidence. She can't be tried again. I can bear to be laughed at for my personal inadequacies but there is one area where I can't face public laughter.'

'Your legal reputation?'

'It's all I have,' Clarke said.

The study door burst open and Janice Clarke swept into the room.

'Jericho!' she cried out. 'I've been looking for you everywhere! How selfish of you to keep our celebrity to yourself, Virgil.' She appropriated Jericho, her arm linked in his. 'It's my turn now.'

Jericho glanced at the lawyer. Virgil Clarke had turned away. He had revealed himself and issued his warning. Now it appeared he couldn't bear to confront his wife.

Jericho was led out into the hall and instantly assailed by the cacophony of the rock group and the shouting, laughing dancers.

'Take me for a ride in your car,' Janice Clarke said. 'I need to get away from this for a bit.' She looked up at him with a wan smile. 'It's been something of a day.'

Either Clarke was a vicious liar or this girl deserved an Oscar for her acting talent, Jericho thought. He had a deep instinct for the fake, the phony, but the instinct was blurred at the moment. Someone had lied to him, he knew – either the lawyer in his study tonight or the girl with her performance at Lookout Point this afternoon.

They walked across the lawn to where the red Mercedes was parked. She was hanging onto his arm as though terrified of being separated from him. He helped her into the car and walked around to the other side.

'Where to?' he asked as he settled behind the wheel.

'Anywhere. Just away from here for a while.'

'Won't your boyfriend miss you?'

She looked up at him, her eyes wide. 'Virgil's been talking to you! Who is alleged to be my boyfriend tonight?'

'My own guess,' Jericho said. 'The young man you were dancing with when I came in.'

'Roger Newfield?' She laughed, a harsh little sound. 'Roger is a lawyer on Virgil's staff. He's one of the family. He worships Virgil, not me.'

Jericho started the motor and drove the car slowly down the drive and out through the stone gates. He turned right for no particular reason. He wondered if this was part of the 'practical joke' that Virgil Clarke had warned him about. Jericho wasn't afraid of laughter, so there was no reason for him to feel uneasy. Yet he did feel uneasy.

'You're too kind to ask me what you want to know,' Janice said after a bit.

'Oh?'

'About Lookout Point today. What could have – could have driven me to think – of – of what I was thinking.'

Jericho felt the small hairs rising on the back of his neck. 'I *was* wondering,' he said, looking straight ahead into the cone of light from the car.

'Virgil saved my life, you know,' she said, 'I owed him everything. I loved him for what he had done for me. I was deeply moved and deliriously happy when he asked me to marry him. I would have married him even if I hadn't loved him. I owed him anything he asked.'

'And he's given you a great deal – every luxury you could desire. But not love?'

'Have you never been astonished, Jericho, when the curtains are lifted and you can see inside the house? Virgil, so calm, so cool, so brilliant when he is onstage, turned out to be a sadistic monster in his private world. It is beyond endurance, and yet I owe him my life. Sometimes – and today was one of those times – it seemed I couldn't stand it any longer. If it hadn't been for you—'

Jericho's foot was on the brake. 'I think we'd better go back,' he said.

'Oh, not yet!' She glanced at her little diamond-studded wrist watch.

'Now,' Jericho said, and swung the car in a U-turn.

'Oh, please, Jericho! Let me have a little time to get hold of myself.'

The car leaped forward, back toward the stone gates. The girl glanced at her watch again.

'Please, Jericho, not just yet!' she cried out over the sound of the wind and the squealing tyres.

They cornered through the gates and up the drive, past the parked cars to the front door. Jericho sprang out of the car and ran into the house, leaving the driveway blocked. He heard the girl call out behind him but he paid no attention. The rock band belted at him, and the almost hysterical laughter.

He ran along the passage to Virgil Clarke's study and put his shoulder to the door as if he expected it to be bolted. There was a splintering sound and he hurtled into the room.

Virgil Clarke was sitting at his desk, his eyes wide with astonishment. Standing beside him was Roger Newfield, the young lawyer in the mod clothes.

'What in the name of—'

Clarke was staring at the door bolt which hung ripped from its fastenings.

'I'm afraid the joke – a very grim joke – was to be on you, sir,' Jericho said, rubbing his shoulder.

'Joke?'

'Death is a joke played on all of us, sooner or later,' Jericho said. He moved slowly toward the desk, aware that Janice Clarke had come through the door behind him. She was standing there, her face a white mask, gripping the doorjamb to steady herself.

'Do you own a gun, Mr Clarke?' Jericho asked.

'Why, yes, I do,' Clarke said, bewildered.

'Where do you keep it?'

'Here. Here in my desk.'

'May I see it?'

Clarke was not a man to take orders, but something of Jericho's violence had thrown him off balance. He opened the flat drawer of his desk and fumbled inside it. Then he looked up.

'It seems to be gone,' he said. 'I must have – misplaced it.'

Jericho took a stride forward and was facing Roger Newfield. He held out his hand. Newfield stared at him, a nerve twitching high up on his cheek. Then Jericho stepped in and started to pat at Newfield's batik shirt. The young lawyer sidestepped and swung at Jericho.

Jericho's left hand blocked the punch and his right swung with crushing force at Newfield's jaw. The young man fell, his eyes rolling up into his head. Jericho bent down, searched the pockets, and came up with a small handgun. He dropped it on the desk.

'Is that yours, Mr Clarke?' he asked.

The girl in the doorway screamed and ran to the fallen Newfield, crooning his name. 'Roger! Roger!'

Clarke had picked up the gun. 'It's mine,' he said, in something close to a whisper.

'Suicide is the name of the game,' Jericho said. 'A fake suicide. Two fake suicides, in fact.'

'I don't understand,' Clarke said. His eyes were fixed on his wife, fondling the unconscious Newfield.

'You and the Williams girl both told me something I wasn't supposed to know,' Jericho said, his voice hard. 'You both implied that Mrs Clarke was aware I was painting above the bank at Lookout Point. That meant the whole suicide gambit there was a fake, a setup. I was to stop her. I was to feel sorry for her. I would almost certainly be curious as to what had driven her to contemplate suicide, so I would accept her invitation to the party.

'You almost told me why, without knowing the reason yourself. I was to be the object of a practical joke, you said. But why me? Yes, I'm well known, but not to this crowd. What could she possibly do to me that would make me the butt of laughter? And then, when she asked me to take her away from here, I began to wonder. And when I suggested coming back she instantly looked at her watch. We hadn't, it seemed, been gone long enough. Long enough for what?'

'I don't follow you,' Clarke said.

'Why the elaborate scheme to get me here? What could my presence here tonight do for her? It suddenly hit me. I could provide her with an unbreakable alibi. Her friends might not be trustworthy. Her friends might be suspected of playing along with her, lying for her. But I,

God help me, am a solid citizen with a reputation. If I testified she was with me it would hold fast.'

'But why did she need an alibi?' Clarke asked.

'Because you were going to commit suicide, sir,' Jericho said. 'You were going to be found here, shot through the head with your own gun. The gun would be found in your hand with your fingerprints on it. But there was bound to be at least a faint suspicion. People close to you must know that your marriage isn't a happy one, and your wife was once charged with a murder. There are people who must still wonder if she was innocent of that crime or if it was your brilliance that set her free. They might ask if a woman who might have killed one husband might not have killed another. She didn't dare have that question asked. I could prevent it. I, the solid citizen, the stranger who had no past connections with her. I could have provided her with the perfect alibi if I hadn't insisted on coming home too soon.'

Janice Clarke looked up from where she was cradling Newfield in her arms. 'It isn't possible for you to prove a word of this insane theory,' she said. 'Surely, Virgil, you can't believe—'

'It's not my job to prove it, Mrs Clarke,' Jericho said. 'Your husband is the legal expert here. Maybe if he can stop feeling sorry for himself long enough, he'll know how to deal with you.'

Jericho turned toward the door and then backed again. 'You were right, Mr Clarke. I was asked here to be used. I trust my donkey's ears have disappeared.'

He walked out into the night, the rock band hurting his ears. He was eager to get away, as far and as fast as he could.

Christianna Brand

The Niece from Scotland

'Well, fancy meeting you again!' the pleasant stranger exclaimed, all flattering astonishment. (And about time, too, old girl! he thought to himself. Kept him hanging about a solid two hours for this 'chance' encounter.)

Gladys had first met him last week here in The Green Man at the mouth of the cul-de-sac. She'd been sipping a dry sherry before going home to cope with her ladyship and he'd happened to sit down at the same table. Such a nice man! He'd seemed so interested in her, thought her far too good to be just a housekeeper, wanted to know all about where she worked and for whom. She'd soon found herself pouring out all her little personal troubles; if Gladys had a fault it was perhaps that she was rather too unreticent about the problems of life with Lady Blatchett.

And now here he was, just dropped in for a quick one and insisted on her joining him. 'Well, all right, but I *must* be home on the hour. If I'm not she locks the door and then hides the key and by the time she's had a couple of drinks, she can't find it again and I'm done for.'

'Surely there must be other ways you could just nip in? You've got the run of the place. You could leave something unlocked.'

'Unlocked! She goes over every door and window even when I'm there; you never know when she'll go round checking. If I *wasn't* there . . . I tell you,' said Gladys, 'the house is like a beleaguered castle.' Guilelessly she described its inner fortifications. 'She lives in terror, poor old thing, especially after dark.'

It was all on account, it seemed, of Lady Blatchett's Past. She'd done something shady – fiddled a Trust or something – and so all the family money had come to her and now she went in fear of vengeance at the hands of cheated relatives. 'Especially one of them. "My niece from Scotland," she calls her. It must have been the niece who should have got most of the money. She's built up this niece into some sort of terrible ogre; I really think she believes she'll be murdered in her bed.' She supposed, said Gladys, that was what had turned her to drinking.

'A proper old lush, she sounds to me. I wonder you stay with her,' said the sympathetic stranger.

A new look came into Gladys' sad middle-aged eyes. 'I get very good wages. And I've got my poor brother, you see. I'm not having him put in any public institution. With his background and living with a lot of patients beneath his proper station—' She was back on a well-worn hobby-horse. Mr 'Smith' looked at his watch and warned her that the hour was approaching.

Patsy was waiting for Mr 'Smith' when he returned from seeing Gladys safely through the front door of Number 20, at the bottom of the cul-de-sac. Patsy looked exhilarated. Her blue eyes were shining, her feather-cap of dusty gold hair seemed to be standing on end with excitement and gaiety. 'You look somewhat lit,' he said, climbing into the driver's seat of the little car.

'Oh, Edgar, he's such a pet! And fallen for me like a ton of bricks; poor lamb – quite defenceless.'

'You are speaking of Dr Fable, I take it,' said Edgar, not quite so pleasant now.

'At Number 10 – slap opposite Lady Blatchett's. We did agree, dear heart, that I should go to work on him?'

'Well, you did go to work then? And it went off all right?'

'Like a bomb. I was the last patient, all as arranged. "Stay and have a glass of sherry, my dear Miss Comfort?" "Hey, hey," I said, "watch your doctor-patient relationship – it's slipping!" '

'Despite all this wit, however, you stayed for the sherry?'

'Yes, I stayed. And who else do you think stayed, too? The Desiccated Receptionist. Now, wasn't that a masterstroke? I made her join us; and now I've got not one of them eating our of my hand, but two.' She wriggled complacently in her seat. 'So how's about the housekeeper?'

Edgar told her his own news. 'It's true all right, blast it! The place is like a fortress. Bolts, keys – I heard the very rattle of the chains as the drawbridge went up. And what's worse, they've got it so fixed that once inside you can't get out again. Self-locking doors and whatnot. You have to have special keys.' Though why she should want to cage herself *in* with thieves and murderers, he couldn't imagine. 'I tried advising dear Gladys to leave a few orifices open, but she literally dared not. The old woman lives in terror.' He expanded on Lady Blatchett's reactions to her niece in Scotland.

'Oh, well, revenge is sweet, no doubt,' said Patsy equably. 'Personally, I'll be quite content with the pearls.'

'You'll have to be – everything else she's got is kept in the bank vault.' said Edgar.

Their plan went into operation the following evening. Gladys, patently rattled, answered the front door and beheld the friendly stranger from The Green Man. 'Do forgive my disturbing you at such an hour—' he began.

'You shouldn't be calling here at any hour,' said Gladys, glancing fearfully back to the closed drawing-room door.

'It was only that I mislaid my lighter last night. Sentimental value, you know; I couldn't bear to lose it. I wondered if by any chance you'd happened to notice—'

'I noticed nothing,' said Gladys, beginning to close the door.

'It's nowhere in the pub. I suppose—' He had unconsciously moved a step forward so that she could do nothing without physically pushing him backward. 'You couldn't possibly have picked it up, without thinking, and dropped it with your other things into your handbag?'

In his anxiety the gentleman had begun – quite unconsciously again, of course – to raise his voice. Gladys glanced back over her shoulder again. 'No, no, of course. No such thing!'

'If you wouldn't mind just looking? So sorry to trouble you.'

'*Please* keep your voice down; she'll be coming out into the hall.' Gladys dithered doubtfully. 'Well, I'll just go and make sure.'

She hurried off toward the kitchen and in her agitation she never thought of asking him to wait on the step outside. And extraordinary to relate, what he had suggested must have happened; for there at the bottom of her neat vinyl handbag was a rather cheap silver lighter.

He thanked her effusively and went away. She listened for a moment at the drawing-room door, but except for the clinking of glass against bottle all was peace.

Gladys' room was on the third floor; her ladyship never climbed that high – couldn't manage the stairs, these days; and one way and another Gladys had got it very comfortable and cosy. With an occasional glance down from the top landing to see that all was well, she spent the rest of the evening with her knitting and the television.

Patsy slipped out of the dining room, once Gladys was gone, and went quietly up to the second floor. She located her ladyship's bedroom – really, the amount Edgar had got out of that housekeeper! – and inspected the others. There were two unused rooms, their keys in the doors. She chose the more remote, went in, locked the door behind her, and put herself very comfortably to bed. There would be the whole night to wait; and who ever looked into a locked spare room?

At midnight Lady Blatchett, propelled by the patient Gladys, reeled uncertainly up to bed. She would remain there till lunchtime – so Gladys had confided to her sympathetic friend in the pub – 'She never thinks *I've* got to get up, after waiting up for her till all hours!' Patsy did not hear them. She was snuggled up under the spare-room eiderdown, deep in untroubled slumber.

At eleven the next morning Gladys, according to her custom, inched open the bedroom door and peeked in, before going to the kitchen for coffee and a biscuit. Lady Blatchett was still fast asleep and snoring. The pearls were kept under her pillow but in her late-evening condition her ladyship hadn't been too careful about concealing them; Gladys could see their gentle gleam, tumbled half out from under the crumpled linen. A choker of pearls, not many of them and not very large – but perfectly matched, they said, of a wonderful quality and worth a small fortune.

At that moment Gladys heard the milkman's knock and went down to the back door. Patsy had checked on this being settling-up day. Gladys would be kept occupied for several minutes.

Gladys came back into the house to hear muffled squeals and the sound of her ladyship's bell ringing violently. Lady Blatchett had been shocked awake to find her head and shoulders enveloped in a tangle of draperies; and by the time she managed to get free to summon help, the front door had closed and the pearls were gone.

Gladys spent some time in calming her ladyship's agitations, which centred largely on the threat of the niece from Scotland, and then she telephoned the police.

The station was at the mouth of the cul-de-sac, just opposite The Green Man; and a constable on duty outside was able to report that though many people had gone in and out of the cul-de-sac in the course of the morning, in the few minutes since the theft of the pearls, not a soul had left it. Unless egress had been effected through one of the other houses – which on a rapid mental reconnaissance seemed most unlikely – it was safe to assume that both the plunder and the plunderer were still safely bottled up inside. A police officer made good time to the scene of the crime.

Patsy, meanwhile, had trotted calmly out of the front door of Number 20 (it now being daylight, its defences were down) and across to the front door of Number 10.

The Desiccated Receptionist was all of a flutter. "Oh, Miss Comfort, you're early.'

'Am I?' said Patsy. 'That's not like *me*. I'm usually late.'

'Well, you aren't due today until half-past eleven.'

'Oh, aren't I?' said Patsy. 'Well, never mind. I'll just have to sit in your lovely waiting room and wait.'

She was at leisure, therefore, to observe the antics of the patient who emerged from Dr Fable's consulting room five minutes later and she could therefore describe them in full when the police subsequently made their inquiries.

In the interim, however, she had been in to see Dr Fable and assure that infatuated practitioner that her headaches were, alas, no better. He showed no marked distress at this information and agreed that she'd have to come back several times – several times – for more treatment. Meanwhile: 'Have you got another box of the pills for me, like you promised? Oh, you *are* a sweetie! – lovely sample ones again so I shan't have to pay for those either?'

He handed them over in their round white cardboard box, faintly rattling, the box plastic-covered and sealed. "It'll have to be a prescription after this, I'm afraid,' he said. 'That's the last of the lot they sent me. Let me know next time how much good they've done you.'

'I'll make it an evening appointment and scrounge another drink from you,' said Patsy, cheerfully departing. 'With you and your nice Miss Hodge,' she added, just loud enough for nice Miss Hodge to hear.

What with putting down her gloves on Miss Hodge's desk while she ruffled through her handbag for her diary, and riffling through the diary for a suitable date for the evening appointment, it was not surprising that when at last she left, in a near hysteria of jokes and farewells and thank-yous, Miss Comfort should have forgotten to take her box of pills with her. She was making such good time up the cul-de-sac that Miss Hodge could not catch her. The receptionist put the box on her shelf where it merged very nicely into the clutter of professional samples common to any doctor's office – and forgot all about them.

The police intercepted Patsy at the mouth of the cul-de-sac. She was highly entertained to learn of the theft of pearls from the house opposite the doctor's: just like on the telly, she said – weren't they all thrilled, right here under the nose of their own dear little police station, in their own dear little cul-de-sac? Was she a suspect? Were they going to search her? She simply longed to be searched – only promise not to tickle!

The police compromised by inviting her into their own dear little station where a young policewoman obliged with the searching. Neither Miss Comfort's charming person nor her handbag offered up anything of interest, except that, mixed up with the exotic clobber in the latter, there appeared a round white box of pills. The police broke the seal and glanced at the pills, even breaking one or two of them across; but they proved to be just pills. Since they showed so little eagerness, Patsy apparently thought it not worth while to mention that while one pillbox now appeared in her handbag, another had been left behind on Miss Hodge's desk. Instead she trailed a pretty little red herring.

'I suppose the thief must have been the funny man with the medicine?'

What funny man with what medicine?

'Well, he came out of Dr Fable's examining room while I was waiting, but instead of leaving he sat down while Miss Hodge was busy with the next patient and pulled a bottle of pink medicine out of his pocket and started taking it. I mean, poured it down his throat straight out of the bottle.'

Police interest perked up. The man was still in the station, having just come through, unscathed, a fairly thorough searching.

'Yes, and then he jumped up and went over to one of the pictures on the wall and began looking at it, terribly intent – I mean, sort of looking at the frame and feeling behind it in a funny sort of way. A frightful picture, too! Personally, I think Dr Fable's got it upside-down, poor love. Perhaps the man thought so, too. Anyway, he took some more medicine and then went away.'

The officers went away, too, legging it down the cul-de-sac as fast as they could. The picture was there all right and, upside-down or not, simply covered with glove prints, the gloves having been liberally dribbled over with the pink medicine. Apart from these, however, it all proved unrewarding.

There seemed little doubt about the genuineness of Lady Blatchett's loss. The police went about the busy elimination of suspects. Gladys the housekeeper had an unsullied ten-year record and a further twelve years to her credit of faithful if not devoted service to her ladyship.

Dr Fable appeared to be a blameless practitioner, debonair and extremely well-to-do, hardly susceptible to suspicion of an elaborate and well-planned theft.

Desiccated Miss Hodge had been twenty years in the service of this doctor or that, without a blot on her escutcheon.

Inquiries in neighbouring houses were in progress, of course; but meanwhile all that remained was the little clutch of patients. And one was Miss Comfort, limpidly innocent; one was an ultra-respectable mother-to-be from an address in Kensington; and the third was the funny man with the bottle of pink medicine. The police may be forgiven for concentrating with some intensity on the man, and since he had not gone at all into Miss Hodge's room, for saving this sanctum to the very last in their investigations of Dr Fables' premises.

Miss Comfort slid up close to Miss Hodge as they sat awaiting dismissal from the police station. 'I say, Miss Hodge, it's a little bit awkward. But I seem to have left my pills in your room.'

'Yes, I found them,' said Miss Hodge. 'I put the box on my shelf.'

'The thing is – well, it's because of Dr Fable,' said Patsy, raising troubled blue eyes to Miss Hodge's sharp, grey, elderly ones. 'I mean, they're – well, you know, sort of pep pills. I don't think he really ought to have given them to me only I – I pleaded with him. I'm trying to fight it. I told him – well, he doesn't know I'm not supposed to be on them.' She insisted: 'It would be so awful if through helping me he got any kind of horrid publicity. You know how ugly it can be and the reporters will be swarming around here soon.'

'What can *I* do about it?' said Miss Hodge.

'If you just wouldn't mention my having left them? Could you perhaps sort of whisk them out of sight before they start looking round your office? It's for his sake, you know. I do like him so much. And I think you do, too?' said Patsy, half tender, half teasing.

'I'll see that it's all right,' said Miss Hodge gruffly.

'And not say a word to him? I swore to him I wouldn't tell a soul, not even you.'

'I'll keep it to myself,' said Miss Hodge.

A further examination, increasingly penetrating, produced nothing in the man that might have been 'taken internally' along with the pink medicine. His fingerprints on the other hand were highly revealing. For Mr Smith, the agreeable stranger of The Green Man, proved to be none other than Edgar Snaith, jewel thief, with a long and unbeautiful history behind him.

He appeared to have arrived but recently in London, though he had a familiar face – and a set of fingerprints – farther up north. Usually he worked with accomplices, varying them frequently. Certainly he was not known ever to have associated with Dr Fable, Miss Hodge, the pregnant patient, or Miss Comfort. He had, however, scraped up an acquaintance with the now deeply penitent Gladys (currently under notice of dismissal) and had certainly elicited from her a great deal of information about Lady Blatchett's ménage and regime.

Witnesses attested to his having been seen at Gladys' front door the previous evening, but agreed with her indignant avowal that he had been (almost) immediately sent away; and both Gladys and Lady Blatchett herself could testify to the pearls having been in her ladyship's possession long after he had gone. He had turned up at Dr Fable's two mornings earlier, declaring himself the victim of mysterious pains, his regular doctor having been left behind when Snaith came south. He had been a little insistent on a second appointment being fixed for eleven o'clock this morning.

By this time it was not remarkable that the vivacious and gregarious Miss Comfort, still caged up – though with all courtesy – at the police station, had fallen into a chat with her fellow sufferers. The pink-medicine man, however, proved impervious to her blandishments. 'A fine mess of things you've made for *me*, Miss! The pain come on frightful and I took a swig of me stuff to ease it. What else do I carry it around for? And as for the picture, it's my belief he's got it upside-down, so I was trying to see how it'd look if I righted it.'

Miss Comfort sh'sh'd him, to the great disappointment of everyone else present, and his voice died away to a reproachful grumble. Miss Comfort seemed to be defending her actions. In fact, she was whispering, 'It all went fine, Edgar. The Desiccated One's got them. You've drawn off the hunt beautifully.'

'When can you get hold of them?'

'As soon as the police stop harassing *you*. And they soon must – there's nothing to hold you on. Get in touch like we arranged and we can get on with it.'

'No tricks meanwhile,' warned Edgar.

'Of course not,' said Patsy warmly. And she meant it. He deserved his share.

When some days later she judged the time was ripe, she went back to Dr Fable's office. Miss Hodge was in the act of shrugging on her outdoors coat. 'The doctor's left, I'm afraid.'

Patsy knew that. She had not come to see Dr Fable.

Miss Hodge took off her coat and led the way to her back room. 'You've come for the pills?'

'I've tried to hold out. But the craving – it's terrible,' said Patsy, going into her act. 'I just simply must have them.'

'No doubt,' said Miss Hodge. She had turned and now half sat on the edge of her desk and was looking straight at Patsy. 'You see, Miss Comfort, I know what the pills are.'

Patsy played for time. 'Well, I explained to you—'

'I mean I know that they're *not* pills,' said Miss Hodge.

'Oh,' said Patsy. It did seem rather final.

'You see,' said Miss Hodge, 'you made one small mistake. Yes, I am in love with Dr Fable; to anyone of your age, no doubt that's very amusing. But it does mean something: it means that Dr Fable knows he can trust me, that I'd never let him down. He would never in his life have warned you not to tell *me*.'

So she'd looked in the box. But having looked there, reflected Patsy, taking heart, she had done nothing – hadn't gone at once to the police. Perhaps even the Miss Hodges of this world had their price? 'Have you told this to anyone?' Patsy asked.

'No, I haven't,' said Miss Hodge. (Was the glass of sherry paying dividends?) 'I thought – well, you have shown yourself very – friendly –

towards me, Miss Comfort. And I know Lady Blatchett, she's a patient of ours – and I know she's a horrid old woman. So I thought I'd wait and hear your side of the story.'

'Let's sit down and have a nice natter, Miss Hodge,' said Patsy, and she began to explain. 'You see, Lady Blatchett is my aunt. And when my uncle died she sort of fiddled things – nothing illegal that anyone could get hold of – just worked on our doddering old family solicitor till she'd done us out of something like twenty thousand pounds. Well, that was too bad; but now my father's dead and my mother's ill – so beautiful, she is, Miss Hodge, and still quite young – and so dreadfully ill! And twenty thousand pounds – or ten thousand or five, for that matter – might make all the difference in her living a little longer and living that little in comfort. So . . .

'Well, one day our little house in Scotland was burgled and I caught the thief – no one more surprised than I was, unless it was him! – and I locked him up in a room. And then, instead of sending for the police, I had a little chat with him. I mean, suddenly I saw that if I could bring in a professional I might get some of my own back – and I do mean that, Miss Hodge,' said Patsy, 'get my *own* back. The pearls would be only a part of the value of what she's robbed us of. So we went into partnership. His name, no doubt you realise, was Edgar Snaith.'

And Patsy went off into fits of giggles describing the alternative plans she and Edgar had devised for drawing the fire of the police. '*He's* safe enough. He never touched the pearls, and they can't pin anything on him for drinking pink medicine and staring at a picture. Unless, of course,' she asked, raising her sweet blue eyes, half alarmed, half smiling, 'you're going to give us away?'

'You mean,' said Miss Hodge, 'that I'm simply to hand over the pearls to you!'

Patsy half opened her mouth to propose a cut, but knew better and closed it again. 'Would you – please?' she said.

Miss Hodge got up and fetched the round white box with its green lettering. She sat nursing it in her hand. Then she suggested pleasantly, 'Fifty-fifty?'

'Fifty-fifty!' said Patsy.

'Twenty-five percent for you and the same for Mr Snaith. The other half to me.'

Patsy made a wild snatch at the box. It was empty. 'I was expecting that,' said Miss Hodge. She added that Miss Comfort need not worry; the pearls were quite safe – but not where Miss Comfort could ever find them.

'Fifty-*fifty*?' said Patsy.

'Make up your mind,' said Miss Hodge.

Patsy's quick little mind shifted – she had spotted a discrepancy. 'Possession is nine points of the law,' she said. 'You have possession of the pearls. Why divvy up? Why not scoop the lot for yourself?'

'I am not an habitual criminal,' said Miss Hodge simply. 'I wouldn't know how to dispose of them.'

'Impasse,' said Patsy.

'Impasse,' agreed Miss Hodge.

And yet, not quite.

'Possession's nine points of the law,' said Patsy again. 'But the law will not allow you to keep possession of Lady Blatchett's pearls. Suppose I cut my losses and inform the police?'

'You do just that,' said Miss Hodge, growing alarmingly less desiccated every minute, 'and see where it will get you.'

'It won't get me anywhere, except one up on *you*. And if I can't have my proper share of the pearls that'll do next best for me. Twenty-five percent of what a fence will give for them! – it'll be worth that much to me to see you doing time. And don't think you won't. You can say what you like to them about me – I haven't got them, I'm in the clear; they don't even know I know Edgar.

'But Edgar was at that house last night and he was here the next morning. You wait till Edgar starts coming clean to the police – how you bribed him to take care of the sale of the pearls, which you'd already stolen on one of the old woman's visits here, replacing them with false ones; perfectly easy while the doctor was examining the patient. You'd have told Edgar to look for them behind the picture frame,' said Patsy, warming to her theme, 'and to swallow them down with some medicine and so smuggle them out.'

Patsy shrugged. 'Lots of holes, but Edgar will stop them up, never fear! He's a past-master, is Edgar, at conning the police. And there'll still be nothing against him – he won't ever have touched the pearls; he'll tell them you have them, and that'll be true. And against me – also nothing.'

'Except, of course,' said Miss Hodge, 'that the most casual inquiry will reveal that you are the niece from Scotland, with a grudge against Lady Blatchett and a well-founded conviction that whatever she possesses is rightfully yours.'

'Oh, that!' said Patsy. 'No dice there, I'm afraid, love! You didn't really fall for that, did you?'

'Well, no,' said Miss Hodge. 'You cooked it all up on the spur of the moment from what poor Gladys had confided to your friend, Mr Snaith. You thought such a story surely must win my sentimental spinster's heart and that I'd turn over the pearls to you.'

'But you didn't believe it?'

'Lady Blatchett is an old woman,' said Miss Hodge. 'So odd for her to have a niece of your generation, especially as your poor dying mother is still so young.' She smiled at Miss Comfort with the smile of a crocodile. 'So much more likely, don't you think, that the niece from Scotland is by now at least a middle-aged woman.'

Miss Comfort saw the light immediately. 'Like you?'

'That's right, my dear,' said Miss Hodge. 'Like me.'

The niece from Scotland: obliged to earn her own living, wangling herself at last with her excellent references into a position where she might observe the old aunt at close quarters, might even ingratiate herself into her favour. The older one became, the more frequent one's visits to the doctor – chosen because his office was so conveniently just across the way – and the more necessary the attentions of the doctor's kindly receptionist.

Miss Comfort bowed to necessity. '*You* are the niece from Scotland.'

'And *you* are a professional thief,' said Miss Hodge, 'and that's that.' She rose, dusted her charmless dress. 'So I think fifty-fifty is a very fair division. Where do we begin?' she said.

At Number 20, Lady Blatchett rang the bell for Gladys. She continued a serial lecture on the sins and follies of careless talk in public. 'But I have decided after all to retain you.'

Gladys was not exactly astonished; not for nothing had she made herself indispensable over all these years. She said, 'Thank you, my lady.'

'I have had a nice cheque from the insurance people, so I feel rather better.'

'Oh, I *am* glad,' said Gladys, much relieved. 'Now your ladyship can have some pearls again.' Then she said humbly for in some mysterious way the theft was acknowledged to have been all her fault, 'Always seeing you with them – I've missed them, my lady.'

'I hadn't intended—' But Lady Blatchett looked into the mirror. 'Perhaps I do need something.'

Bare, ancient, crepey throat, where the dewlap hung unlovely and the 'bracelets' deepened with each succeeding year.

'I was even thinking that your ladyship might get a double row, this time. You'll never match the last, I know, but perhaps two rows not quite so good—?'

Her ladyship thought that might be a good idea. After all, a nice bit of jewellery was better for her, really, than all that money lying in the bank.

Better for Gladys, too. What a blessing the burglary had been! Not that she hadn't been, for simply ages, working toward something of the sort – all that carefully indiscreet talk in the pub! She'd been beginning to feel a bit desperate by the time Mr 'Smith' turned up; the money from the first pearls wouldn't last forever – and if she died for it, her poor brother wasn't going to be moved to some public institution where he wouldn't have his proper privacy; a man of his background mixing with just ordinary patients – no, it just wouldn't do.

Behind the shop front of a respectable jeweller's, Miss Hodge, Miss Comfort, and Mr Snaith stood aghast at an offer of £25 for some nice cultured pearls; and up in her comfortable room Lady Blatchett's well-paid housekeeper was writing off to an address in Scotland.

Dick Francis

Carrot for a Chestnut

Chick stood and sweated with the carrot in his hand. His head seemed to be floating and he couldn't feel his feet on the ground, and the pulse thudded massively in his ear. A clammy green pain shivered in his gut.

Treachery was making him sick.

The time: fifty minutes before sunrise. The morning: cold. The raw swirling wind was clearing its throat for a fiercer blow, and a heavy layer of nimbostratus was fighting every inch of the way against the hint of light. In the neat box stalls round the stable yard the dozing horses struck a random hoof against a wooden wall, rattled a tethering chain, sneezed the hay dust out of a moist black nostril.

Chick was late. Two hours late. He's been told to give the carrot to the lanky chestnut at four o'clock in the morning, but at four o'clock in the morning it had been pouring with rain – hard, slanting rain that soaked a man to the skin in one minute flat, and Chick had reckoned it would be too difficult explaining away a soaking at four o'clock in the morning. Chick had reckoned it would be better to wait until the rain stopped, it couldn't make any difference. Four o'clock, six o'clock, what the hell. Chick always knew better than anyone else.

Chick was a thin, disgruntled nineteen-year-old who always felt the world owed him more than he got. He had been a bad-tempered, argumentative child and an aggressively rebellious adolescent. The resulting snarling habit of mind was precisely what was now hindering his success as an adult. Not that Chick would have agreed, of course. Chick never agreed with anyone if he could help it. Always knew better, did Chick.

He was unprepared for the severity of the physical symptoms of fear. His usual attitude toward any form of authority was scorn (and

authority had not so far actually belted him one across his sulky mouth).
Horses had never scared him because he had been born to the saddle
and had grown up mastering everything on four legs with contemptuous
ease. He believed in his heart that no one could really ride better than
he could. He was wrong.

He looked apprehensively over his shoulder, and the shifting pain in
his stomach sharply intensified. That simply couldn't happen, he thought
wildly. He'd heard about people getting sick with fear. He hadn't
believed it. It couldn't happen. Now, all of a sudden, he feared it could.
He tightened all his muscles desperately, and the spasm slowly passed.
It left fresh sweat standing out all over his skin and no saliva in his
mouth.

The house was dark. Upstairs, behind the black open window with
the pale curtain flapping in the spartan air, slept Arthur Morrison,
trainer of the forty-three racehorses in the stables below. Morrison
habitually slept lightly. His ears were sharper than half a dozen guard
dogs', his stable hands said.

Chick forced himself to turn his head away, to walk in view of that
window, to take the ten exposed steps down to the chestnut's stall.

If the guv'nor woke up and saw him. . . . Gawd, he thought furiously,
he hadn't expected it to be like this. Just a lousy walk down the yard to
give a carrot to the gangly chestnut. Guilt and fear and treachery. They
bypassed his sneering mind and erupted through his nerves instead.

He couldn't see anything wrong with the carrot. It hadn't been cut in
half and hollowed out and packed with drugs and tied together again.
He'd tried pulling the thick end out like a plug, and that hadn't worked
either. The carrot just looked like any old carrot, any old carrot you'd
watch your Ma chop up to put in a stew. Any old carrot you'd give to
any old horse. Not a very young, succulent carrot or a very aged carrot,
knotted and woody. Just any old ordinary *carrot*.

But stranger's didn't proposition you to give any old carrot to one
special horse in the middle of the night. They didn't give you more than
you earned in half a year when you said you'd do it. Any old carrot
didn't come wrapped carefully alone in a polythene bag inside an
empty cheese-cracker packet, given to you by a stranger in a car park
after dark in a town six miles from the stables. You didn't give any old
carrot in the middle of the night to a chestnut who was due to start
favourite in a high-class steeplechase eleven hours later.

Chick was getting dizzy with holding his breath by the time he'd
completed the ten tiptoed steps to the chestnut's stall. Trying not to
cough, not to groan, not to let out the strangling tension in a sob, he
curled his sweating fingers around the bolt and began the job of easing
it out, inch by frightening inch, from its socket.

By day he slammed the bolts open and shut with a smart practiced flick. His body shook in the darkness with the strain of moving by fractions.

The bolt came free with the tiniest of grating noises, and the top half of the split door swung slowly outward. No squeaks from the hinges, only the whisper of metal on metal. Chick drew in a long breath like a painful, trickling, smothered gasp and let it out between his clenched teeth. His stomach lurched again, threateningly. He took another quick, appalled grip on himself and thrust his arm in a panic through the dark, open space.

Inside the stall, the chestnut was asleep, dozing on his feet. The changing swirl of air from the opening door moved the sensitive hairs around his muzzle and raised his mental state from semiconsciousness to inquisitiveness. He could smell the carrot. He could also smell the man: smell the fear in the man's sweat.

'Come on,' Chick whispered desperately. 'Come on, then, boy.'

The horse moved his nose around toward the carrot and finally, reluctantly, his feet. He took it indifferently from the man's trembling palm, whiffling it in with his black mobile lips, scrunching it languidly with large rotations of jaw. When he had swallowed all the pulped-up bits he poked his muzzle forward for more. But there was no more, just the lighter square of sky darkening again as the door swung shut, just the faint sounds of the bolt going back, just the fading smell of the man and the passing taste of carrot. Presently he forgot about it and turned slowly round again so that his hindquarters were toward the door, because he usually stood that way, and after a minute or two he blinked slowly, rested his near hind leg lazily on the point of the hoof and lapsed back into twilight mindlessness.

Down in his stomach the liquid narcotic compound with which the carrot had been injected to saturation gradually filtered out of the digesting carrot cells and began to be absorbed into the bloodstream. The process was slow and progressive. And it had started two hours late.

Arthur Morrison stood in his stable yard watching his men load the chestnut into the motor horse box that was to take him to the races. He was eyeing the proceedings with an expression that was critical from habit and bore little relation to the satisfaction in his mind. The chestnut was the best horse in his stable: a frequent winner, popular with the public, a source of prestige as well as revenue. The big steeplechase at Cheltenham had been tailor-made for him from the day its conditions had been published, and Morrison was adept at producing a horse in peak condition for a particular race. No one seriously considered that the chestnut would be beaten. The newspapers had tipped it to a man and the bookmakers were fighting shy at 6-4 on. Morrison allowed himself a glimmer of warmth in the eyes and a twitch of smile to the lips as the men clipped shut the heavy doors of the horse van and drove it out of the yard.

These physical signs were unusual. The face he normally wore was a compound of concentration and disapproval in roughly equal proportions. Both qualities contributed considerably to his success as a racehorse trainer and to his unpopularity as a person, a fact Morrison himself was well aware of. He didn't in the least care that almost no one liked him. He valued success and respect much more highly than love and held in incredulous contempt all those who did not.

Across the yard Chick was watching the horse van drive away, his usual scowl in place. Morrison frowned irritably. The boy was a pest, he thought. Always grousing, always impertinent, always trying to scrounge up more money. Morrison didn't believe in boys having life made too easy: a little hardship was good for the soul. Where Morrison and Chick radically differed was the point at which each thought hardship began.

Chick spotted the frown and watched Morrison fearfully, his guilt pressing on him like a rock. He couldn't know, he thought frantically. He couldn't even suspect there was anything wrong with the horse or he wouldn't have let him go off to the races. The horse had looked all right, too. Absolutely his normal self. Perhaps there had been nothing wrong with the carrot. . . . Perhaps it had been the wrong carrot, even. . . . Chick glanced around uneasily and knew very well he was fooling himself. The horse might look all right but he wasn't.

Arthur Morrison saddled up his horse at the races, and Chick watched him from ten nervous paces away, trying to hide in the eager crowd that pushed forward for a close view of the favourite. There was a larger admiring crowd outside the chestnut's saddling stall than for any of the other seven runners, and the bookmakers had shortened their odds. Behind Morrison's concentrated expression an itch of worry was growing insistent. He pulled the girth tight and adjusted the buckles automatically, acknowledging to himself that his former satisfaction had changed to anxiety. The horse was not himself. There were no lively stamping feet, no playful nips from the teeth, no response to the crowd; this was a horse that usually played to the public like a film star. He couldn't be feeling well, and if he wasn't feeling well he wouldn't win. Morrison tightened his mouth. If the horse were not well enough to win, he would prefer him not to run at all. To be beaten at odds-on would be a disgrace. A defeat on too large a scale. A loss of face. Particularly as Morrison's own eldest son Toddy was to be the jockey. The newspapers would tear them both to pieces.

Morrison came to a decision and sent for the vet.

The rules of jump racing in England stated quite clearly that if a horse had been declared a runner in a race, only the say-so of a veterinarian was sufficient grounds for withdrawing him during the last three-quarters of an hour before post time. The Cheltenham racecourse veterinarian came and looked at the chestnut and, after consulting with Morrison, led it off to a more private stall and took its temperature.

'His temperature's normal,' the veterinarian assured Morrison.

'I don't like the look of him.'

'I can't find anything wrong.'

'He's not well,' Morrison insisted.

The veterinarian pursed his lips and shook his head. There was nothing obviously wrong with the horse, and he knew he would be in trouble himself if he allowed Morrison to withdraw so hot a favourite on such slender grounds. Not only that, this was the third application for withdrawal he'd had to consider that afternoon. He had refused both the others, and the chestnut was certainly in no worse a state.

'He'll have to run,' the veterinarian said positively, making up his mind.

Morrison was furious and went raging off to find a steward, who came and looked at the chestnut and listened to the vet and confirmed that the horse would have to run whether Morrison liked it or not. Unless, that was, Morrison cared to involve the horse's absent owner in paying a heavy fine?

With the face of granite Morrison resaddled the chestnut, and a stable lad led him out into the parade ring, where most of the waiting public cheered and a few wiser ones looked closely and hurried off to hedge their bets.

With a shiver of dismay, Chick saw the horse reappear and for the first time regretted what he'd done. That stupid vet, he thought violently. He can't see what's under his bloody nose, he couldn't see a barn at ten paces. Anything that happened from then on was the vet's fault, Chick thought. The vet's responsibility, absolutely. The man was a criminal menace, letting a horse run in a steeplechase with dope coming out of its eyeballs.

Toddy Morrison had joined his father in the parade ring and together they were watching with worried expressions as the chestnut plodded lethargically around the oval walking track. Toddy was a strong, stocky professional jockey in his late 20s with an infectious grin and a generous view of life that represented a direct rejection of his father's. He had inherited the same strength of mind but had used it to leave home at 18 to ride races for other trainers, and had only consented to ride for his father when he could dictate his own terms. Arthur Morrison, in consequence, respected him deeply. Between them they had won a lot of races.

Chick didn't actually dislike Toddy Morrison, even though, as he saw it, Toddy stood in his way. Occasionally Arthur let Chick ride a race if Toddy had something better or couldn't make the weight. Chick had to share these scraps from Toddy's table with two or three other lads in the yard who were, though he didn't believe it, as good as he was in the saddle. But though the envy curdled around inside him and the snide remarks came out sharp and sour as vinegar, he had never actually come to hate Toddy. There was something about Toddy that you couldn't hate, however good the reason. Chick hadn't given a thought to the fact that it would be Toddy who would have to deal with the effects of the carrot. He had seen no further than his own pocket. He wished now that it had been some other jockey. Anyone but Toddy.

The conviction suddenly crystalised in Chick's mind as he looked at Toddy and Morrison standing there worried in the parade ring that he had never believed the chestnut would actually start in the race. The stranger, Chick said to himself, had distinctly told him the horse would be too sick to start. I wouldn't have done it, else, Chick thought virtuously. I wouldn't have done it. It's bloody dangerous, riding a doped steeplechaser. I wouldn't have done that to Toddy. It's not my fault he's going to ride a doped steeplechaser, it's that vet's fault for not seeing. It's that stranger's fault, he told me distinctly the horse wouldn't be fit to start. . . .

Chick remembered with an unpleasant jerk that he'd been two hours late with the carrot. Maybe if he'd been on time the drug would have come out more and the vet would have seen. . . .

Chick jettisoned this unbearable theory instantly on the grounds that no one can tell how seriously any particular horse will react to a drug or how quickly it will work, and he repeated to himself the comforting self-delusion that the stranger had promised him the horse wouldn't even start – though the stranger had not in fact said any such thing. The stranger, who was at the races, was entirely satisfied with the way things were going and was on the point of making a great deal of money.

The bell rang for the jockeys to mount. Chick clenched his hands in his pockets and tried not to visualise what could happen to a rider going over jumps at thirty miles an hour on a doped horse. Chick's body began playing him tricks again: he could feel the sweat trickling down his back and the pulse had come back in his ears.

Supposing he told them, he thought. Supposing he just ran out there into the ring and told Toddy not to ride the horse, it hadn't a chance of jumping properly, it was certain to fall, it could kill him bloody easily because its reactions would be all shot to bits.

Supposing he did. The way they'd look at him. His imagination blew a fuse and blanked out on that picture because such a blast of contempt didn't fit in with his overgrown self-esteem. He could not, could *not* face the fury they would feel. And it might not end there. Even if he told them and saved Toddy's life, they might tell the police. He wouldn't put it past them. And he could end up in the dock. Even in jail. They weren't going to do that to him, not to *him*. He wasn't going to give them the chance. He should have been paid more. Paid more because he was worth more. If he'd been paid more, he wouldn't have needed to take the stranger's money. Arthur Morrison had only himself to blame.

Toddy would have to risk it. After all, the horse didn't look too bad, and the vet had passed it, hadn't he, and maybe the carrot being two hours late was all to the good and it wouldn't have done its work properly yet, and in fact it was really thanks to Chick if it hadn't; only thanks to him that the drug was two hours late and that nothing much would happen, really, anyway. Nothing much would happen. Maybe the chestnut wouldn't actually *win*, but Toddy would come through all right. Of course he would.

The jockeys swung up into their saddles, Toddy among them. He saw Chick in the crowd, watching, and sketched an acknowledging wave. The urge to tell and the fear of telling tore Chick apart like the Chinese trees.

Toddy gathered up the reins and clicked his tongue and steered the chestnut indecisively out on to the track. He was disappointed that the horse wasn't feeling well but not in the least apprehensive. It hadn't occurred to him, or to Arthur Morrison, that the horse might be doped. He cantered down to the post standing in his stirrups, replanning his tactics mentally now that he couldn't rely on reserves in his mount. It would be a difficult race now to win. Pity.

Chick watched him go. He hadn't come to his decision, to tell or not to tell. The moment simply passed him by. When Toddy had gone he unstuck his leaden feet and plodded off to the stands to watch the race, and in every corner of his mind little self-justifications sprang up like nettles. A feeling of shame tried to creep in round the edges, but he kicked it out smartly. They should have paid him more. It was their fault, not his.

He thought about the wad of notes the stranger had given him with the carrot. Money in advance. The stranger had trusted him, which was more than most people seemed to. He'd locked himself into the bathroom and counted the notes, counted them twice, and they were all there, £300 just as the stranger had promised. He had never had so much money all at once in his life before. . . . Perhaps he never would again, he thought. And if he'd told Arthur Morrison and Toddy about the dope, he would have to give up that money, give up the money and more. . . .

Finding somewhere to hide the money had given him difficulty. Three hundred used £1 notes had turned out to be quite bulky, and he didn't want to risk his Ma poking around among his things, like she did, and coming across them. He'd solved the problem temporarily by rolling them up and putting them in a brightly coloured round tin which once held toffees but which he used for years for storing brushes and polish for cleaning his shoes. He had covered the money with a duster and jammed the tin back on the shelf in his bedroom where it always stood. He thought he would probably have to find somewhere safer, in the end. And he'd have to be careful how he spent the money – there would be too many questions asked if he just went out and bought a car. He'd always wanted a car . . . and now he had the money for one . . . and he still couldn't get the car. It wasn't fair. Not fair at all. If they'd paid him more. . . . Enough for a car. . . .

Up on the well-positioned area of stands set aside for trainers and jockeys, a small man with hot dark eyes put his hand on Chick's arm and spoke to him, though it was several seconds before Chick started to listen.

'. . . I see you are here, and you're free, will you ride it?'

'What?' said Chick vaguely.

'My horse in the Novice Hurdle,' said the little man impatiently. 'Of course, if you don't want to. . . .'

'Didn't say that,' Chick mumbled. 'Ask the guv'nor. If he says I can, well, I can.'

The small trainer walked across the stand to where Arthur Morrison was watching the chestnut intently through the race glasses and asked the same question he'd put to Chick.

'Chick? Yes, he can ride it for you, if you want him.' Morrison gave the other trainer two full seconds of his attention and glued himself back on to his race glasses.

'My jockey was hurt in a fall in the first race,' explained the small man. 'There are so many runners in the Novice Hurdle that there's a shortage of jockeys. I just saw that boy of yours, so I asked him on the spur of the moment, see?'

'Yes, yes,' said Morrison, ninety per cent uninterested. 'He's moderately capable, but don't expect too much of him.' There was no spring in the chestnut's stride. Morrison wondered in depression if he was sickening for the cough.

'My horse won't win. Just out for experience you might say.'

'Yes. Well, fix it with Chick.' Several other stables had the coughing epidemic, Morrison thought. The chestnut couldn't have picked a worse day to catch it.

Chick, who would normally have welcomed the offer of a ride with condescending complacency, was so pre-occupied that the small trainer regretted having asked him. Chick's whole attention was riveted on the chestnut, who seemed to be lining up satisfactorily at the starting tape. Nothing wrong, Chick assured himself. Everything was going to be all right. Of course it was. Stupid getting into such a state.

The start was down the track to the left, with two fences to be jumped before the horses came past the stands and swung away again on the left-hand circuit. As it was a jumping race, they were using tapes instead of stalls, and as there was no draw either, Toddy had lined up against the inside rails, ready to take the shortest way home.

Down in the bookmakers' enclosure they were offering more generous odds now and some had gone boldly to evens. The chestnut had cantered past them in his way to the start looking not his brightest and best. The bookmakers in consequence were feeling more hopeful. They had expected a bad day, but if the chestnut lost, they would profit. One of them would profit terrifically – just as he would lose terrifically if the chestnut won.

Alexander McGrant (Est. 1898), real name Harvey Buskins, had done this sort of thing once or twice before. He spread out his fingers and looked at them admiringly. Not a tremble in sight. And there was always a risk in these things that the boy he'd bribed would get cold feet at the last minute and not go through with the job. Always a gamble, it was. But this time, this boy, he was pretty sure of. You couldn't go wrong if you sorted out a vain little so-and-so with a big grudge. Knockovers, that sort were. Every time.

Harry Buskins was a shrewd middle-aged East End Londoner for whom there had never been any clear demarcation between right and wrong and a man who thought that if you could rig a nice little swindle now and then, well, why not? The turnover tax was killing betting . . . you had to make a quick buck where you could . . . and there was nothing quite so sure or quick as raking in the dough on a red-hot favourite and knowing for certain that you weren't going to have to pay out.

Down at the post the starter put his hand on the lever and the tapes went up with a rush. Toddy kicked his chestnut smartly in the ribs. From his aerie on top of the stand the commentator moved smartly into his spiel. 'They're off, and the first to show is the grey. . . .' Arthur Morrison and Chick watched with hearts thumping from different sorts of anxiety, and Harry Buskins shut his eyes and prayed.

Toddy drove forward at once into the first three, the chestnut beneath him galloping strongly, pulling at the bit, thudding his hooves into the ground. He seemed to be going well enough, Toddy thought. Strong. Like a train.

The first fence lay only one hundred yards ahead now, coming nearer. With a practiced eye Toddy measured the distance, knew the chestnut's stride would meet it right, collected himself for the spring and gave the horse the signal to take off. There was no response. Nothing. The chestnut made no attempt to bunch his muscles, no attempt to gather himself on to his haunches, no attempt to waver or slow down or take any avoiding action whatsoever. For one incredulous second Toddy knew he was facing complete and imminent disaster.

The chestnut galloped straight into the three-foot-thick, chest-high solid birch fence with an impact that brought a groan of horror from the stands. He turned a somersault over the fence with a flurry of thrashing legs, threw Toddy off in front of him and fell down on top and rolled over him.

Chick felt as if the world were turning grey. The colours drained out of everything and he was halfway to fainting. Oh God, he thought. Oh God. *Toddy*.

The chestnut scrambled to his feet and galloped away. He followed the other horses toward the second fence, stretching out into a relentless stride, into a full-fledged thundering racing pace.

He hit the second fence as straight and hard as the first. The crowd gasped and cried out. Again the somersault, the spread-eagled legs, the crashing fall, the instant recovery. The chestnut surged up again and galloped on.

He came up past the stands, moving inexorably, the stirrups swinging out from the empty saddle, flecks of foam flying back now from his mouth, great dark patches of sweat staining his flanks. Where the track curved round to the left, the chestnut raced straight on. Straight on across the curve, to crash into the rail around the outside of the track. He took the solid timber across the chest and broke it in two. Again he fell in a thrashing heap and again he rocketed to his feet. But this time not to gallop away. This time he took three painful limping steps and stood still.

Back at the fence Toddy lay on the ground with first-aid men bending over him anxiously. Arthur Morrison ran down from the stands toward the track and didn't know which way to turn first, to his son or his horse. Chick's legs gave way and he sagged down in a daze on to the concrete steps. And down in the bookmakers' enclosure Harry Buskins' first reaction of delight was soured by wondering whether, if Toddy Morrison were badly injured, that stupid boy Chick would be scared enough to keep his mouth shut.

Arthur Morrison turned toward his son. Toddy had been knocked unconscious by the fall and had had all the breath squeezed out of him by the chestnut's weight, but by the time his father was within 100 yards he was beginning to come round. As soon as Arthur saw the supine figure move, he turned brusquely round and hurried off toward the horse: it would never do to show Toddy the concern he felt. Toddy would not respect him for it, he thought.

The chestnut stood patiently by the smashed rail, only dimly aware of the dull discomfort in the foreleg that wouldn't take his weight. Arthur Morrison and the veterinarian arrived beside him at the same time, and Arthur Morrison glared at the vet.

'You said he was fit to run. The owner is going to hit the roof when he hears about it.' Morrison tried to keep a grip on a growing internal fury at the injustice of fate. The chestnut wasn't just any horse – it was the best he'd ever trained, had hoisted him higher up the stakes-won list than he was ever likely to go again.

'Well, he seemed all right,' said the vet defensively.

'I want a dope test done,' Morrison said truculently.

'He's broken his shoulder. He'll have to be put down.'

'I know. I've got eyes. All the same, I want a dope test first. Just being ill wouldn't have made him act like that.'

The veterinarian reluctantly agreed to take a blood sample, and after that he fitted the bolt into the humane killer and shot it into the chestnut's drug-crazed brain. The best horse in Arthur Morrison's stable became only a name in the record books. The digested carrot was dragged away with the carcass but its damage was by no means spent.

It took Chick fifteen minutes to realise that it was Toddy who was alive and the horse that was dead, during which time he felt physically ill and mentally pulverised. It had seemed so small a thing, in the beginning, to give a carrot to the chestnut. He hadn't thought of it affecting him much. He'd never dreamed anything like that could make you really sick.

Once he found that Toddy had broken no bones, had recovered consciousness and would be on his feet in an hour or two, the bulk of his physical symptoms receded. When the small trainer appeared at his elbow to remind him sharply that he should be inside changing into colours to ride in the Novice Hurdle race, he felt fit enough to go and do it, though he wished in a way that he hadn't said he would.

In the changing room he forgot to tell his valet he needed a lightweight saddle and that the trainer had asked for a breast girth. He forgot to tie the stock round his neck and would have gone out to ride with the ends flapping. He forgot to take his watch off. His valet pointed everything and thought that the jockey looked drunk.

The novice hurdler Chick was to ride wouldn't have finished within a mile of the chestnut if he'd started the day before. Young, green, sketchily schooled he hadn't even the virtue of a gold streak waiting to be mined: this was one destined to run in the ruck until the owner tired of trying. Chick hadn't bothered to find out. He'd been much too pre-occupied to look in the form book, where a consistent row of noughts might have made him cautious. As it was, he mounted the horse without attention and didn't listen to the riding orders the small trainer in-sistently gave him. As usual, he thought he knew better. Play it off the cuff, he thought scrappily. Play it off the cuff. How could he listen to fussy little instructions with all that he had on his mind?

On his way out from the weighing room he passed Arthur Morrison, who cast an inattentive eye over his racing colours and said, 'Oh yes . . . well, don't make too much of a mess of it. . . .'

Morrison was still thinking about the difference the chestnut's death was going to make to his fortunes and he didn't notice the spasm of irritation that twisted Chick's petulant face.

There he goes, Chick thought. That's typical. *Typical.* Never thinks I can do a bloody thing. If he'd given me more chances . . . and more money . . . I wouldn't have given. . . . Well, I wouldn't have. He cantered down to the post, concentrating on resenting that remark, 'don't make too much of a mess of it,' because it made him feel justified, obscurely, for having done what he'd done. The abyss of remorse opening beneath him was too painful. He clutched at every lie to keep himself out.

Harry Buskins had noticed that Chick had an unexpected mount in the Novice Hurdle and concluded that he himself was safe, the boy wasn't going to crack. All the same, he had shut his bag over its swollen takings and left his pitch for the day and gone home, explaining to his colleagues that he didn't feel well. And in truth he didn't. He couldn't get out of his mind the sight of the chestnut charging at those fences as if he couldn't see. Blind, the horse had been. A great racer who knew he was on a racetrack starting a race. Didn't understand there was anything wrong with him. Galloped because he was asked to gallop, because he knew it was the right place for it. A great horse, with a great racing heart.

Harry Buskins mopped the sweat off his forehead. They were bound to have tested the horse for dope, he thought, after something like that. None of the others he'd done in the past had reacted that way. Maybe he'd got the dose wrong or the timing wrong. You never knew how individual horses would be affected. Doping was always a bit un-predictable.

He poured himself half a tumbler of whisky with fingers that were shaking after all, and when he felt calmer he decided that if he got away with it this time he would be satisfied with the cleanup he'd made, and he wouldn't fool around with any more carrots. He just wouldn't risk it again.

Chick lined up at the starting post in the centre of the field, even though the trainer had advised him to start on the outside to give the inexperienced horse an easy passage over the first few hurdles. Chick didn't remember this instruction because he hadn't listened, and even if he had listened he would have done the same, driven by his habitual compulsion to disagree. He was thinking about Toddy lining up on this spot an hour ago, not knowing that his horse wouldn't see the jumps. Chick hadn't known dope could make a horse blind. How could anyone expect that? It didn't make sense. Perhaps it was just that the dope had confused the chestnut so much that although its eyes saw the fence, the message didn't get through that he was supposed to jump over it. The chestnut couldn't have been really blind.

Chick sweated at the thought and forgot to check that the girths were still tight after cantering down to the post. His mind was still on the inward horror when the starter let the tapes up, so that he was caught unawares and flat-footed and got away slowly. The small trainer on the stand clicked his mouth in annoyance, and Arthur Morrison raised his eyes to heaven.

The first hurdle lay side-by-side with the first fence, and all the way to it Chick was illogically scared that his horse wouldn't rise to it. He spent the attention he should have given to setting his horse right in desperately trying to convince himself that no one could have given it a carrot. He couldn't be riding a doped horse himself . . . it wouldn't be fair. Why wouldn't it be fair? Because . . . because . . .

The hurdler scrambled over the jump, knocked himself hard on the timber frame, and landed almost at a standstill. The small trainer began to curse.

Chick tightened one loose rein and the other, and the hurdler swung to and fro in wavering indecision. He needed to be ridden with care and confidence and to be taught balance and rhythm. He needed to be set right before the jumps and to be quickly collected afterwards. He lacked experience, he lacked judgement and he badly needed a jockey who could contribute both.

Chick could have made a reasonable job of it if he'd been trying. Instead, with nausea and mental exhaustion draining what skill he had out of his muscles, he was busy proving that he'd never be much good.

At the second fence he saw in his mind's eye the chestnut somersaulting through the air, and going round the bend his gaze wavered across to the broken rail and the scuffed-up patches of turf in front of it. The chestnut had died there. Everyone in the stable would be poorer for it. He had killed the chestnut, there was no avoiding it anymore, he'd killed it with that carrot as surely as if he'd shot the bolt himself. Chick sobbed suddenly, and his eyes filled with tears.

He didn't see the next two hurdles. They passed beneath him in a flying blur. He stayed on his horse by instinct, and the tears ran down and were swept away as they trickled under the edge of his jockey's goggles.

The green hurdler was frightened and rudderless. Another jump lay close ahead, and the horses in front went clattering through it, knocking one section half over and leaving it there at an angle. The hurdler waited until the last minute for help or instructions from the man on his back and then in a muddled way dived for the leaning section, which looked lower to him and easier to jump than the other end.

From the stands it was clear to both the small trainer and Arthur Morrison that Chick had made no attempt to keep straight or to tell the horse when to take off. It landed with its forefeet tangled up in the sloping hurdle and catapulted Chick off over its head.

The instinct of self-preservation which should have made Chick curl into a rolling ball wasn't working. He fell through the air flat and straight, and his last thought before he hit was that that stupid little sod of a trainer hadn't schooled his horse properly. The animal hadn't a clue how to jump.

He woke up a long time later in a high bed in a small room. There was a dim light burning somewhere. He could feel no pain. He could feel nothing at all. His mind seemed to be floating in his head and his head was floating in space.

After a long time he began to believe that he was dead. He took the thought calmly and was proud of himself for his calm. A long time after that he began to realise that he wasn't dead. There was some sort of casing round his head, holding it cushioned. He couldn't move.

He blinked his eyes consciously and licked his lips to make sure that they at least were working. He couldn't think what had happened. His thoughts were a confused but peaceful fog.

Finally he remembered the carrot, and the whole complicated agony washed back into his consciousness. He cried out in protest and tried to move, to get up and away, to escape the impossible, unbearable guilt. People heard his voice and came into the room and stood around him. He looked at them uncomprehendingly. They were dressed in white.

'You're all right, now,' they said. 'Don't worry, young man, you're going to be all right.'

'I can't move,' he protested.

'You will,' they said soothingly.

'I can't feel . . . anything. I can't feel my feet.' The panic rose suddenly in his voice. 'I can't feel my hands. I can't . . . move . . . my hands.' He was shouting, frightened, his eyes wide and stretched.

'Don't worry,' they said. 'You will in time. You're going to be all right. You're going to be all right.'

He didn't believe them, and they pumped a sedative into his arm to quiet him. He couldn't feel the prick of the needle. He heard himself screaming because he could feel no pain.

When he woke up again he knew for certain that he'd broken his neck.

After four days Arthur Morrison came to see him, bringing six new-laid eggs and a bottle of fresh orange juice. He stood looking down at the immobile body with the plaster cast round its shoulders and head.

'Well, Chick,' he said awkwardly. 'It's not as bad as it could have been, eh?'

Chick said rudely, 'I'm glad you think so.'

'They say your spinal cord isn't severed, it's just crushed. They say in a year or so you'll get a lot of movement back. And they say you'll begin to feel things any day now.'

'They say,' said Chick sneeringly. 'I don't believe them.'

'You'll have to, in time,' said Morrison impatiently.

Chick didn't answer, and Arthur Morrison cast uncomfortably around in his mind for something to say to pass away the minutes until he could decently leave. He couldn't visit the boy and just stand there in silence. He had to say *something*. So he began to talk about what was uppermost in his mind.

'We had the result of the dope test this morning. Did you know we had the chestnut tested? Well, you know we had to have it put down anyway. The results came this morning. They were positive. . . . *Positive*. The chestnut was full of some sort of narcotic drug, some long name. The owner is kicking up hell about it and so is the insurance company. They're trying to say it's my fault. My security arrangements aren't tight enough. It's ridiculous. And all this on top of losing the horse itself, losing that really great horse. I questioned everyone in the stable this morning as soon as I knew about the dope, but of course no one knew anything. God, if I knew who did it I'd strangle him myself.' His voice shook with the fury which had been consuming him all day.

It occurred to him at this point that Chick being Chick, he would be exclusively concerned with his own state and wouldn't care a damn for anyone else's troubles. Arthur Morrison sighed deeply. Chick did have his own troubles now, right enough. He couldn't be expected to care all that much about the chestnut. And he was looking very weak, very pale.

The doctor who checked on Chick's condition ten times a day came quietly into the small room and shook hands with Morrison.

'He's doing well,' he said. 'Getting on splendidly.'

'Nuts,' Chick said.

The doctor twisted his lips. He didn't say he had found Chick the worst-tempered patient in the hospital. He said, 'Of course, it's hard on him. But it could have been worse. It'll take time, he'll need to learn everything again, you see. It'll take time.'

'Like a bloody baby,' Chick said violently.

Arthur Morrison thought, a baby again. Well, perhaps second time around they could make a better job of him.

'He's lucky he's got good parents to look after him once he goes home,' the doctor said.

Chick thought of his mother, forever chopping up carrots to put in the stew. He'd have to eat them. His throat closed convulsively. He knew he couldn't.

And then there was the money, rolled up in the shoe-cleaning tin on the shelf in his bedroom. He would be able to see the tin all the time when he was lying in his own bed. He would never be able to forget. Never. And there was always the danger his Ma would look inside it. He couldn't face going home. He couldn't face it. And he knew he would have to. He had no choice. He wished he were dead.

Arthur Morrison sighed heavily and shouldered his new burden with his accustomed strength of mind. 'Yes, he can come home to his mother and me as soon as he's well enough. He'll always have us to rely on.'

Chick Morrison winced with despair and shut his eyes. His father tried to stifle a surge of irritation, and the doctor thought the boy an ungrateful little beast.

Patricia McGerr

This one's a beauty

'This one's a beauty,' Captain Rogan said cheerfully as he climbed into the car beside Sergeant Pringle.

It was an odd term to apply to a murder, but the sergeant nodded agreement. By Homicide Squad definition it described any investigation that could be wrapped up without overtime. And the case they were headed toward on this crisp January evening was, it appeared, right at the top of that category. The desk man had recorded the call at 7:47.

'This is Horace Sanderson,' the authoritative voice at the other end had announced. 'I want to report a murder. I've shot a man in my office.'

So all they needed to do was visit the scene, hear his confession, and bring him in. As the captain said, 'This one's a beauty.'

'Sanderson,' Pringle ruminated while he eased the car away from the curb. 'Don't I know that name from somewhere?'

'You should,' Rogan returned. 'If he's never made a monkey of you on the witness stand, you're a lucky exception.'

'Oh, sure, the big defence lawyer. No, I haven't testified in any of his cases, but I've heard plenty from those who have. They say he gets an extra charge out of making our guys sweat.'

'Too right.' Rogan's lips twisted wryly in personal recollection. 'On cross-examination he can turn you around till you misspell your own name. But now it's our turn. I'm going to like seeing Mr Horace Sanderson in the dock.'

'Weird, isn't it, that after all the raps he's beaten for other people he'd turn himself in without a fight.'

'It has to mean the evidence against him is airtight,' Rogan said with satisfaction. 'Sanderson knows criminal law up and down, backwards

588

and sideways. If he could've seen the smallest loophole he'd never have started off by admitting he did it.'

'Maybe he'll claim self-defence,' the sergeant suggested.

'On the phone he called it murder. He knows every meaning of that word and it doesn't include justifiable homicide.'

'How about not guilty because of temporary insanity?'

'That's one he might try,' Rogan conceded, 'but it won't affect our schedule. All we want are the facts. If he decides to take the psycho route it'll be the D.A.'s headache. Unless the lab boys slow us down, we'll be drinking squad-room coffee again before ten o'clock tonight.'

It was a short ride to the building that housed the Sanderson law offices. Pringle parked in front and the two men rode the elevator to the fourth floor. The only door that showed a light was lettered 'Sanderson, Sanderson & Sanderson, Attorneys-at-Law.' At Rogan's sharp rap it was opened by a tall broad-shouldered man of sixty-odd whose physique, grooming, and general air of affluence fitted him to intimidate the most hostile witness.

'You made fast time, gentlemen,' he complimented them. 'Captain Rogan, I believe.' He paused to nudge his recollection. 'Ah, yes, you were the arresting officer in the Hutchins murder, weren't you? A pity you got the wrong man. And your colleague—' He looked questioningly at Pringle. 'I don't believe our paths have crossed before.'

'This is Sergeant Pringle,' Rogan snapped. Acquittal of the man he was sure had killed Tom Hutchins was still a rankling memory. 'It's my duty to inform you that you are not required to answer—'

'Skip the litany,' Sanderson cut him off. 'I'm well informed as to my rights and I'm already represented by counsel. If you'll come into the next room I'll show you the corpse and tell you what happened.'

A cool, cool customer, Rogan thought with reluctant admiration. His head's halfway in the noose, but he's the same take-charge guy as he is in the courtroom.

Sanderson crossed the reception room to open an inner door. He passed through it, then stepped aside to unblock the view. Sprawled on the dark green rug of what appeared to be a conference room was a man's body.

Rogan dropped to one knee beside it. Lifting the left wrist he felt for a pulse, though he was sure he wouldn't find one. The blood-matted hair at the back of the head indicated that a bullet must have entered the brain to bring instant death.

'D.O.A.,' he told Pringle. 'We'll want the technical unit and the morgue wagon.'

'Use the phone on the desk in the corner, Sergeant,' Sanderson said helpfully.

Rogan straightened and looked down at the dead man. He had fallen forward, but the face was turned to rest on one cheek. Rogan felt a glimmer of recognition.

'An old friend, Captain?' Sanderson asked. 'His name is – or was – Chet Tankersley.'

Gambler, confidence man, jack-of-many-crooked-trades. The computer in Rogan's head punched the appropriate slots. No loss to society. He liked the case even better.

'You shot him?' he asked.

'With this gun.' Sanderson stepped around the body to approach the long table that filled two thirds the length of the room and pointed to the weapon that lay on its mirror-bright surface. 'I have a licence for it, of course. A criminal practice can bring in some rough characters, so I keep it loaded and ready in my desk.'

Is he laying a basis for self-defence after all, Rogan wondered, then looked again at the victim and was reassured. The shot had come from behind and the position of the body showed that Tankersley had been on his way out of the office.

Pringle had finished telephoning. 'They're on the way, Captain,' he reported.

'Fine. Now we'd better hear your story, Mr Sanderson.'

'I'm waiting to tell it,' he assured him. 'I want my lawyers present, of course.'

Three private offices were connected to the conference room. On each was a name. Horace T. Sanderson, Sr., Horace T. Sanderson, Jr., Paul A. Sanderson. The lawyer walked to the centre door – his own – and opened it to say, 'Come out, boys, I need you.'

'My sons and legal counsel,' he introduced the two young men who answered the summons. 'Horace, Junior, and Paul.' Paul, the younger one, was a slim replica of his father, while Horace, Jr., slightly overweight, with narrow eyes and soft lips, showed no sign of the hard courage and sharp intelligence that marked the other two. Junior must favour the maternal line, Rogan decided. If the firm is to go on, it will be Paul who takes the old man's place.

'Sit down, gentlemen.' Sanderson took a seat at the end of the table farthest from the body, with one son on each side. Sergeant Pringle stayed at a desk near the door. Rogan turned one of the chairs around and straddled it to retain a sense of mobility.

'I'll get right to the point.' Sanderson, Sr.'s tone seemed more suited to chairing a board meeting than to confessing a crime. 'This afternoon, Sonny – that is, Horace, Junior – told me he was being blackmailed. Tankersley had a certain document bearing Horace, Junior's signature that could, if made public, lead to his disbarment. Tankersley asked twenty-five thousand dollars and was coming here today after office hours to collect.

'Sonny had managed to raise fifteen thousand on his own and asked me for the balance. I advised him not to give the man one cent and said that I would deal with him myself. My two sons, therefore, left the office at five-thirty, the usual time, and drove home together. I stayed behind and was alone when Tankersley arrived.

'I told him there would be no payoff, now or ever, and threatened him with arrest for blackmail unless he immediately gave me the incriminating document. It was, I admit, a bluff and it failed. That paper, as Tankersley well knew, would not only end my son's career but cast doubt on the integrity of our law firm. He grew abusive and said I had until noon tomorrow to change my mind. If by that time he did not receive the entire sum, the document would be delivered to the secretary of the Bar Association.

'Well, gentlemen, what could I do? I looked at that miserable creature who held in his hand my family name, my son's future, the professional reputation I'd built with such care.' His voice rose to the dramatic height that had swayed so many juries. 'Something exploded in my brain.'

He paused and Rogan exchanged a quick glance with the sergeant. So it was to be a plea of temporary insanity.

'He walked out of my office. I took the gun from my drawer, followed him into this room, and shot him. Then I phoned my own house. Paul answered. I said I wanted them both here and they drove right back. I explained what had happened and, as my counsel, they advised me to notify the police and make a clean breast of it. Which I have just done.'

'And the document that Tankersley was holding?' Rogan asked.

'I took it from the dead man's pocket, tore it into small pieces, burned the pieces, and flushed away the ashes. I apologise for destroying evidence, but I believe my motive is clear enough without making public what I've killed a man to keep secret.'

Before Rogan could answer, a rap on the outer door signalled the arrival of the technical unit. Admitted by Pringle and instructed by Rogan, they set about their routines with camera and other equipment. The captain returned to the three Sandersons.

'I appreciate your giving us such a straightforward story,' Rogan told the father.

'I like to make your job easy when I can, Captain,' Sanderson, Sr., returned with sham geniality. 'Besides, I really have no choice. The body is in my office. The bullet came from my gun. Tankersley may even have told someone about his appointment with Sonny. I know better than to try to buck those odds.'

'Then the next step is to go to headquarters, get your statement typed and signed, and—'

'I'm familiar with the procedure,' Sanderson reminded him. 'And I'm sure you'll follow all the rules. We can't charge police brutality tonight, can we, boys?'

'No, we can't,' Paul answered for them both. His glance at Rogan held the same glint of mockery as his father's. 'Our client's statement was freely given and is correct in almost every detail.'

'Almost?' Rogan felt a stir of apprehension on the edge of his complacency.

'He's made one significant error,' Paul continued. 'Sonny didn't say anything to Dad about being blackmailed. Sonny told me.'

'Oh? Then you passed it on to your father?'

'Certainly not. I agreed with my brother that we'd better keep it to ourselves. So I told Dad I had some work to finish, and he and Sonny left together. After that everything happened just as my father reported it – except it was I who waited here for Tankersley. I'm the one who shot him.'

'You—' Rogan left the sentence suspended.

'It's his word against mine, Captain,' Sanderson, Sr., said. 'Which of us do you believe?'

'I'll get that answer from your other son.' Rogan's eyes moved to Horace, Jr. 'Did you tell your father or your brother about the blackmail? Which one rode home with you?'

Sonny's gaze stayed on the tabletop. His voice was low, with each word forced through stiff lips.

'I didn't tell anybody,' he answered. 'And I didn't go home. I said *I* had work to finish and let Dad and Paul leave without me. When Tankersley came I told him I had only fifteen thousand. He said it wasn't enough, he was sure my father would give me the rest sooner than see me disgraced. I said I didn't want Dad to know and he laughed at me. He said I had until twelve o'clock tomorrow noon to raise the whole twenty-five thousand or – as Dad told you – he'd turn the paper over to the Bar Association. I couldn't let that happen. So when he started to go, I – I shot him.'

'Where did you get the gun?'

'Out of Dad's drawer. I know where he keeps it.'

'Let's see if I have the picture straight. Tankersley left your office, you ran into your father's room, took his gun, and—'

'No,' Sonny interrupted. 'I was already in Dad's room when I talked to Tankersley. I'd put the money in his safe and wanted to be where I could get it out right away if he agreed to settle for what I had.'

'And you?' He turned to the younger brother. 'Where did you

conduct the interview?'

'I'm the junior junior partner,' Paul returned smoothly. 'My room is small and my desk cluttered. When Dad's away I take my visitors into his office.'

Very carefully arranged, Rogan thought glumly. Tankersley's fingerprints will show up only in the father's office – just as all three stories indicate.

'We're a close-knit family,' Sanderson explained. 'I told my two sons that I was guilty and that they shouldn't interfere. But you know how it is with young people nowadays. No respect.'

'One of you killed Tankersley.' Rogan organised his thinking out loud. 'Then he called the other two back to the office. The three of you talked it over and cooked up this round robin.'

'Exactly.' Sanderson beamed at him. 'So you have two confessions left over. Untidy, isn't it? If one of us is charged, each of the other two will swear he did it. You haven't a prayer of getting an indictment, much less a conviction.'

'Don't bet on it, Mr Sanderson,' Rogan said. 'You've wasted your time and mine with your phony confessions.'

'Only two are phony,' Paul murmured. 'One of us is telling the truth.'

Rogan ignored the interruption. 'Now we'll get on with our work, just as we would if all three of you had denied it. We solve a fair number of cases without anybody coming forward to say he did it.' He could not resist the sarcasm. 'Sometimes we even convict one of your clients.'

'Indeed you do,' Sanderson agreed heartily. 'The city has a very efficient force and I'll observe your work with great interest.' He looked beyond Rogan to watch the morgue men cover the body preparatory to its removal. 'I don't usually get to see the start of an investigation. But I'm afraid the evidence you'll collect here won't be very helpful. Fingerprints, for instance. I know how important they can be. But we were a bit nervous while we waited for you and we wandered about opening doors and drawers. As a result you'll find all three sets of prints in random order all over the place.'

'In other words,' Rogan interpreted, 'the one who committed the crime gave the other two a step-by-step account of his actions from the moment of Tankersley's arrival. Then the other two reenacted the crime, taking care to touch all pertinent surfaces. No doubt all three of you handled the weapon.'

'Naturally.' Sanderson's face burlesqued repentance. 'I'm afraid we did something even more reprehensible. I call your attention to the holes in the wall near the ceiling. The two of us who aren't guilty both took a shot up there. Very bad for the panelling, but tests will show that all three of us recently fired a gun.'

The old sod's enjoying this, Rogan thought sourly. He's used to being called in to pick up the pieces after his client has made a mess of it and the police have all the evidence. For the first time he's been on the scene ahead of us, able to set the stage to show exactly what he wants us to see. He's handled more murder cases than most policemen and can anticipate all our moves, plus some we might not think of.

'Worried, Captain?' the senior Sanderson prodded.

'Just trying to work out a timetable.' Rogan left his chair and walked to the head of the table to place himself between father and older son. 'You said your sons left here at five-thirty.' He focused on the father. 'How long does it usually take to get home?'

'In normal traffic, twenty-five minutes.'

'And what time did you phone them?'

'Six-fifteen. My interview with Tankersley was brief.'

'Then I can assume they got back here at six-forty. Right?'

'Give or take five minutes, that's correct.'

'That gave you a full hour to discuss the situation, make a plan, and arrange the – er – stage effects. I'm inclined to agree with you, Mr Sanderson, that we won't find evidence here to point to the one who actually committed the murder.' He waited for the other man's lips to curve into a satisfied smile before adding, 'It may be easier to discover which two went home.'

Rogan whirled to face Horace, Jr., and leaned down till their noses were only inches apart. 'Tell me, Sonny,' he barked, 'who drove the car home?'

'Dad always—' The young man broke off, gulped air. 'I mean, I don't know who drove tonight. I didn't go home. I told you, I stayed here. I—' His eyes darted to his father, seeking rescue.

'Don't bully the boy,' Sanderson said softly. 'He's already told his story.'

'But he was about to tell a different one. He started to say that you drove home and he rode beside you. That places Paul in the office at the time of the murder.'

'So it does,' Paul agreed. 'You see, I was telling the truth all the time.'

'Don't talk nonsense, Captain,' Sanderson ordered. 'What Sonny started to say was 'Dad always drives.' And that's true. When the three of us are together, I'm always the driver. But I wasn't in the car this evening, so I presume Paul took the wheel. That's how it usually is, isn't it, Sonny?'

'Yes, I – I don't care much for driving.'

And you don't care much for this game of bait-the-cop either, Rogan added mentally. Sanderson, Sr., and Paul are riding every wave, but Sonny looks as if he's about to go under. Judging by the way he acts, he's guilty as hell, but that doesn't move me forward. Unquestionably he's guilty of falling into a blackmail trap – which makes him responsible for what happened tonight, even if someone else did the shooting.

Rogan walked down the table to confer with Sergeant Pringle, then returned to the Sandersons.

'Thought of some more questions, Captain?' the father asked.

'The same one,' Rogan answered. 'Which of you three killed him? We're going to look for the answer in places where you didn't have time to doctor the evidence. Your house and your car, for instance.'

'Good thinking,' Sanderson applauded. 'Since you can't find the guilty one, maybe you can pin down the two who are innocent. The car's parked in the garage under this building, but I doubt if it will yield any secrets. Will it, Paul?'

'No, Dad,' the younger son answered confidently. 'You see,' Paul told Rogan, 'after I asked my father and brother to come back here, it occurred to us that you'd be curious about who drove and who was in the passenger seat. So I went down with a clean cloth and wiped off the wheel, the door handles – did a general cleanup job. Your fingerprint man is going to draw another blank.'

'But you didn't go all the way home with your clean cloth, did you?' Rogan asked. 'Or did you alert someone there to take care of it?'

'No,' Paul conceded. 'Mom's out of town and we're batching it this week. You'll get a fine collection of prints at home. But since that's where the three of us live, I don't know what you expect them to prove.'

'Don't underestimate the captain's intelligence,' his father advised. 'He's thinking of spots like doorknobs which might indicate who was the last man to go in or out.'

'How disappointing for you,' Paul said. 'There's an electric gadget in the car that opens the garage door. The stairs go right into the centre hall with no need to turn any knobs.'

'Don't overlook the telephone,' Sanderson suggested. 'If it was Paul who answered my call, as I said he did, his prints will be on top. Unless he was in his own room at the time, in which case the prints won't prove anything.'

'No more,' Paul seconded, 'than can be proved if Dad took my call on his bedside phone.'

'Just to complete the circle, Sonny,' Rogan asked without enthusiasm, 'who answered the phone when you called home?'

'Paul did. But I asked him to let me talk to Dad.'

'You're not forgetting,' Sanderson put in, 'the possibility of witnesses?'

'I'm sure you didn't forget it, either,' Rogan returned.

'The boys assured me there was no one else in the elevator or in the garage when they left here and, of course, by the time they got back, the building was empty. If we weren't sure of that we wouldn't be taking this line.'

'But the streets and sidewalks weren't deserted,' Rogan reminded him. 'There's no way on earth you can be sure that someone won't come forward who saw you somewhere along the way.'

'No doubt many people saw the car,' Sanderson agreed. 'But it was dark by five-thirty and I challenge anybody to make positive identification in a moving vehicle under those conditions. Especially when there's such a strong family resemblance.'

So now, Rogan told himself, we're back to Go. Sanderson has foreseen every possible move. He reads my thoughts even before I think them.

Rogan left them to pace restlessly around the table. Since Sanderson is so knowledgeable about how the official mind works, I'd better stop thinking like a police officer and try to get inside the murderer. There must be some place he's slipped up.

He looked back at his antagonists. Sanderson, Sr., and Paul were talking in low tones. Sonny watched them warily. Who scares Sonny most, Rogan wondered, his father or me? Is he shaking because he may be tagged for murder or because he may not be able to stick to the lie the old man's making him tell? Junior's getting closer and closer to the edge. If I could talk to him alone, he'd break. But the other two won't let that happen.

Rogan went into the office marked with the name of Horace, Jr., and sat down at a desk whose bare top could indicate either extreme efficiency or that he was given very little to do. An inspection of the nearly empty drawers tended to support the second theory. Sergeant Pringle came in to report that the car, as predicted, showed no clue as to its most recent occupants.

'Tough going, Captain,' the sergeant commiserated. 'You got a favourite?'

'I like Sonny for it,' Rogan answered. 'His father and brother are the smart ones, the glib ones, the two who can stick to a lie and sidestep any trap that might give them away. If one of them had killed Tankersley, it's not likely they'd set up an escape route that would be shut off if Sonny broke under pressure. But with Sonny as the killer, the three-way confession lets him tell nothing but the truth. That way Sonny knows the answer to every question we ask and only the other two need to be quick-witted.'

'He looks like a very nervous boy,' Pringle said. 'Too bad you can't lean on him a little.'

'Maybe I can. I'm thinking about a breath test.'

'The kind the traffic squad uses on drunk drivers?'

'That's it. Can you get a machine up here in a hurry?'

'Right away.' Pringle looked puzzled, but he didn't ask any more questions. While he telephoned, Rogan moved on to the office of Sanderson, Sr., where the technicians were turning up an abundance of prints that pointed nowhere. Then he looked into Paul's room, which confirmed the younger son's statement about its smallness and clutter. When the sergeant announced the arrival of an officer with a breath machine, Rogan escorted all of them to the table.

'You don't seem to be making much progress, Captain,' Sanderson jibed.

'I'm still trying to eliminate the two who are lying,' Rogan answered. 'We've established that they arrived home about twenty minutes before the phone call that brought them back. The question is, how did they spend that time at home?'

'An intriguing question,' Sanderson said. 'Unfortunately, since none of us admit having gone home, there's no one to answer it.'

'So I'll have to guess. What does a successful lawyer do at the end of a hard day's work? I think he unwinds over a drink. Am I right?'

'Absolutely,' Sanderson agreed. 'My personal preference is a very dry martini. But I don't see how that's relevant.'

'I'm going to ask you to cooperate in an experiment. We have here a machine that measures blood alcohol content. If three of you blow into it and two register a recent intake of alcohol – well, you follow my reasoning, I'm sure.'

'You'll put it down that those two were relaxing at home while the third was committing murder. Very ingenious.' Sanderson's tone was indulgent. 'I've never seen one of these before. Always been curious about how they work.'

The officer placed the box-like machine in front of Sanderson, twisted a dial, and put a narrow tube into his hand.

'Just blow into it,' Rogan directed. 'The needle will tell us if you've had a drink.'

Sanderson followed instructions. The needle stayed at zero. The officer turned the machine to Paul, who provided a breath sample with the same result.

'Another good idea gone wrong,' Sanderson said in mock sympathy as the machine was moved in front of Sonny. 'There's one flaw in your reasoning, Captain. We're civilised people who treat our before-dinner drinks with ceremony. We don't rush from car to bar.' He looked at his older son who was regarding the machine with a suspicious scowl. 'Go ahead, Sonny. It won't bite.'

'This is stupid,' Sonny said.

'Play the game,' his father ordered. 'Give the captain his full quota of hot air.'

The officer lifted the tube to Sonny's mouth. His scowl deepened, but he gave a quick exhalation. The needle moved to the left.

'Alcoholic content point zero eight,' the officer read. 'At his weight that's about four ounces.'

'What?' Sanderson exploded. 'That's impossible. Sonny wasn't even—' He broke off, clamped his lips shut.

'Go on,' Rogan prodded. 'Finish the sentence. "Sonny wasn't even at home tonight!" Of course he wasn't. You wouldn't have been so willing to take the test if you weren't sure there were no drinks taken at your house. What you didn't allow for was the possibility that Sonny gave you a censored account of his activities after you left the office. He probably has a habit of not telling you things you'd disapprove of.'

'I don't know what you're getting at,' Sanderson said. 'Your machine's obviously broken.'

'That can be checked,' Rogan said impassively. 'You've been a step ahead of me all the way, Mr Sanderson. Too bad you don't have as thorough an understanding of your older son. He had a twenty-five-minute wait from the time he killed Tankersley until you two got back here. He was alone with a dead body, facing a murder charge and – maybe worst of all – about to have to explain it all to you. It should have occurred to you that he'd need a stiff drink to steady his nerves. Then you'd have found the vodka bottle he has hidden in his desk and fitted it into your triple confession. You see, Sonny, it doesn't pay to lie to your father.'

'Why, you—' Sonny made a huge lunge toward Rogan.

'Shut up, you fool,' his father barked. 'Sit still and keep your mouth shut.'

'*You* told me to blow in his machine.' Sonny turned furiously on his father. 'I didn't want to do it, but you think you're so damn smart. I shouldn't have phoned you. I should have taken my fifteen thousand and headed for Mexico. I knew your fancy scheme would never work.'

'It came close,' Rogan said pleasantly. 'Do you and Paul want to withdraw your confessions now?' he asked Sanderson. 'Or will you wait until you're charged as accessories after the fact?'

Helen Neilsen

The Perfect Servant

Lieutenant Brandon was trying to bridge a generation gap when the woman walked into the police station and deposited a wad of currency on the counter. The trio of teen-agers he had charged with collecting hubcaps that belonged to irate citizens seemed unimpressed with the idea that they had committed theft, and then the woman, who was in her middle forties, shabbily dressed and wearing a look of quiet despair in her eyes, relinquished a cheap money clip containing the bills and said, 'Please, who is the officer I see about this?'

Brandon nodded for a uniformed officer to take away the teen-agers, grateful for a release from the pointless conversation, and asked the woman to state her problem.

'I was walking down the street – down Broadway,' she stated, 'and I saw this on the sidewalk. I picked it up. It is money.'

Brandon pulled the bills out of the slip. There were three twenty-dollar bills, three tens, and two fives. 'One hundred dollars,' he said.

'Yes,' the woman agreed. 'I counted, too. That's a lot of money for someone to lose.'

It was a lot of money, and the woman looked as if she had never had her hands on that much at any one time in all her life. Brandon called the desk sergeant to fill out a report and explained to the woman that the money would be held for thirty days, during which time the real owner could report his loss, describe the bills and the clip, and have the money returned, or, failing a claimant, the money would then become the property of the finder.

'Your name?' asked the sergeant.

She hesitated. 'Maria,' she said. 'Maria Morales.'

'Occupation?'

'I have no work now. When I work I am a domestic.'

'Address?'

She gave the number of a cheap roominghouse in the Spanish-speaking section of town. She told them she was very poor, unemployed, and without any property of her own. When the report was offered for her signature she placed both hands on the desk. A plain gold band adorned the third finger of her left hand.

'Just sign here, Miss Morales,' the sergeant said.

'Mrs Morales,' she corrected. 'I am a widow.'

Brandon caught the desk sergeant's eye and shook his head in wonder.

'You should get those cocky young kids back in here to see this,' the sergeant suggested.

'Waste of time,' Brandon answered. 'They wouldn't appreciate anything this square. Don't forget now, Mrs Morales, in thirty days you check back with us. Chances are you'll get the money – or at least a reward.'

'Thank you,' she said in a very soft voice, 'but I would rather have a job.'

A young reporter from the Tucson daily came into the station just as Maria Morales was leaving, and Brandon, the bitter taste of the cynical teen-agers still in his mouth, related the incident of the honesty of Maria Morales. It was a slow day on the newsfront and when the morning papers came out, the story of the unemployed widow and the $100 was written up in a neat box on the front page.

By noon Lieutenant Brandon was flooded with calls from people who claimed the money, and also with job offers for Maria Morales. Having developed a protective interest in the widow, he took it upon himself to screen the offers and decided that the best prospect was Lyle Waverly, a bachelor and a physician with a lucrative practice among the country-club set.

Waverly needed a housekeeper he could trust. He owned a fine home in one of the better suburbs and entertained a well-heeled social set. He offered Maria a home, a good salary, and free medical care for as long as she remained in his employ.

Brandon approved the credentials and gave Waverly the woman's address, feeling the kind of inner warmth he always got from delivering Christmas parcels to the Neediest Families.

Maria Morales was extremely pleased with young Dr Waverly. He was easy to work for. The house was large but new, and there was a gardener to help with the heavy work. She was an excellent cook but, aside from breakfast, the doctor seldom dined in. He was a busy man in more ways than one, which was only natural for one so attractive and increasingly affluent.

It soon became apparent that the doctor's love life was divided between two women: Cynthia Reardon, who was twenty-three and the sole heir of Josiah Reardon of Reardon Savings and Loan, and Shelley Clifford, ten years older, who had an additional handicap of being already married to Ramsey Clifford, the owner of Clifford Construction Company. Clifford was a huge burly man of fifty who had too little time to spend with a lovely wife who liked younger men.

Maria observed these things with professional silence, and long before Dr Lyle Waverly was aware of his destiny, she knew that Cynthia had the inside track and would eventually get her man.

Life was pleasant in the Waverly house and Maria had no desire to return to the kind of employment she had recently known. She began to plot a campaign of self-preservation. When the doctor gave her an advance on her salary, she purchased fitted uniforms with caps and aprons for the frequent cocktail parties he gave for his wealthy friends and patients.

He soon learned that a caterer was no longer necessary. Maria's canapés became the envy of every hostess, and she herself became a topic of conversation not unwelcome in the tension created whenever Cynthia and Shelley were present on the same occasion. Shelley had the prior claim – a fact made obvious by the way she took over as hostess. She was the 'in' woman fighting against the inevitable successor, and only Clifford's preoccupation with business could blind him to what anyone else could see. Of the two women, Maria preferred Shelley, who was no threat to her own position as mistress of the house. Shelley wanted only Lyle Waverly; Cynthia wanted his name, his life, and his home.

'Maria is a miracle,' Shelley explained at the second party. 'Imagine finding someone with her divine talent who is honest as well. Why, she's a perfect servant!'

'An honest woman?' Cynthia echoed. 'Impossible! No woman can be honest and survive! Maria must have a few secrets.'

Maria smiled blandly and continued to serve the canapés.

'I refuse to believe it!' Dr Waverly announced. 'All my life I've searched for a pure woman and this is she!'

'Perhaps you'd better marry her, darling,' Shelley said. 'You could do worse.'

That remark was aimed at Cynthia, and Maria didn't wait to hear the reply. She returned to the kitchen and began to clean up the party debris. It was sometime later, after most of the guests had gone home and even Ramsey Clifford had taxied off to catch a late plane for a business appointment, that she heard Shelley berating Dr Waverly for his interest in Cynthia Reardon. Maria returned to the living room to collect abandoned glasses and saw them alone.

'You needn't think I don't know what you're doing,' Shelley was saying. 'You needed me when you were beginning your practice – you needed my contacts and influence. Now you want a younger woman.'

'Shelley, please,' the doctor begged.

'No, I'm going to have my say! You want a younger and a richer woman, don't you, darling? What better catch than Josiah Reardon's sexy daughter? You'll never hold her, Lyle. She'll wear you like a pendant until she's bored with you. She's used up half a dozen handsome young men already.'

'I'm not a child!' Waverly protested.

'No. You're a man and vain enough to think you can use Cynthia Reardon. I'm warning you, you'll be the one who gets used!'

'You're jealous,' Waverly said.

'Of course I'm jealous. I love you, and I need you, Lyle. Now *I* need *you*—'

Maria retreated quickly to the kitchen before she was noticed. Sometime later the doctor came in carrying the glasses. All the guests were gone. He loosened his tie and drew a deep breath. 'The things they don't teach you in medical school!' he sighed. 'Maria, you are the only sane person on earth. You must never leave me.'

'I'll fix you a hot milk,' Maria said.

'Oh, no—'

'A bromide?'

'Brilliant idea. Are you sure you never worked the social route before?'

Maria's face darkened. 'I worked for women,' she said. 'I didn't like it. They talk about you in front of others. "You just can't trust anyone these days," she said with savage mockery. "They'll steal you blind and expect to get paid besides!"'

Waverly laughed. 'I think I understand why honesty is so important to you. By the way, the thirty days are up. Did you ever go back to claim that hundred dollars?'

'Tomorrow,' Maria said. 'Tomorrow I go.'

'Good! I hope it's there. If it isn't I'll give you a bonus to make up for losing it.'

Maria returned to the police station the next day. Lieutenant Brandon gave her a paper to sign and then handed her the money, which was still held in the money clip made of cheap metal with a silver dollar for decoration. None of the claimants could identify the exact denominations of the bills or describe the clip, so the money was now legally hers.

'How's the job?' Brandon asked.

'The best one I ever had,' Maria said.

'Now, that's what I like to hear! There's some justice in the world after all.'

'Yes,' Maria said, and slipped the money into her handbag.

Her position at the Waverly house continued to improve. She had her own room and, with an adequate household budget, was able to buy food less fattening than the starchy diet of the poor. She soon replaced her uniforms with a smaller size and had her hair done once a month. She was beginning to feel and look more like a woman. Waverly soon took notice.

'Maria,' he said, 'you never told me about your husband. He was one lucky guy. What was his name?'

'Wa—' she began.

'Juan?'

She smiled softly. 'Yes,' she said, 'his name was Juan.'

'Handsome?'

'Of course!'

'And a passionate devil, I'll bet! What do you have going for you now? There must be a boyfriend somewhere.'

The doctor had been drinking. He slipped a friendly arm about her shoulder.

'No boyfriend,' Maria said.

'No? That's a shame! What's the matter? With legs like yours you could still do a fancy fandango. I'll bet you've done many a fancy fandango in your day.'

'In my day – yes,' Maria admitted.

'Then get back in circulation. Take a night off once in a while. Take tonight off. I'm going out with Miss Reardon.'

'In that case, I think I should make you another bromide.'

'No, you don't! I'm just a teensy-weensy bit drunk and I need much more fortification tonight. I'm going to ask Miss Reardon to marry me.'

'She will accept,' Maria said flatly.

'That's what I'm afraid of. You see, Maria, I've never been married. I'm afraid of marriage. I like women but I like my freedom better.'

'Then why—?'

'Why marry? Because it's the thing to do. It's stabilising. It builds character. It's what every rising young doctor should do, Maria, but I'm still scared. I don't like to be dominated.'

'Then don't be dominated,' Maria said. 'Be the boss.'

Waverly picked up his glass. 'I'll drink to that,' he said.

But it was Maria who feared the marriage more than Waverly. No sooner was the engagement announced than Cynthia began to re-organise the household, and Maria began to worry again about her security. Waverly caught her reading the want ads and demanded an explanation.

'What's the matter? Aren't you happy here?' he asked. 'Do you want more money?'

'No,' Maria said.

'Then what's wrong?'

'Things will change after you marry.'

'What things? Don't you like Miss Reardon?'

'It's not what I like. It's what Miss Reardon likes.'

'Stop worrying. Nobody's going to treat you the way you were treated before I found you. I like you and that's all that matters. I'll tell you something I was going to keep secret. I've had my lawyer draw up a new will – a man does that when he gets married. I've made a five-thousand-dollar bequest in your behalf. Now do you feel more secure?'

Maria was reassured, but she had lived long enough to take nothing for granted except money in the bank. Dr Waverly was impulsive and generous, but Cynthia Reardon was a spoiled, strong-willed girl and Shelley Clifford's description of her character was more accurate than anything a prospective bridegroom was likely to see. What's more, Shelley didn't give up the battle simply because the engagement was announced. The mores of Dr Waverly's social set, Maria learned, were more liberal than her own.

Shelley immediately developed symptoms requiring the doctor's professional attention at indelicate hours – particularly when her husband was away on business. There were surreptitious calls going both ways. When Waverly finally refused to go to see Shelley again, she came to see him. Travelling over an unpaved, circuitous drive, Shelley's small imported coupé made the trip between the Clifford estate and the doctor's house with increasing frequency.

It was a shameful thing, Maria reflected, for a woman to cling so to a man. As much as she had loved her husband, she would have let him go the minute he no longer wanted her. But no matter how many women Walter might have had before their marriage, he was faithful to his vows. Walter – not Juan. Juan Morales was the name of the father Maria barely remembered. Walter Dwyer was the name of the man she had wed. But when one must work as a domestic for the Anglos, it seemed better not to let it be known that she had once been married to an Anglo, had once lived like a lady.

She had been hardly twenty when Walter married her, but Walter was a gambler and gamblers die broke. After settling with the creditors, there was nothing for the widow Dwyer to do but return to Tucson and again become Maria Morales, domestic.

She had nothing left of the past but what Walter had called her 'Irish luck,' but her mind was no longer servile. She saw things now with the eyes of Mrs Walter Dwyer, and what she saw was troubling. When a woman lost at love it was the same as when a man lost at cards. If she cried, she cried alone. What she could never do was cling to anything that was finished.

If Cynthia Reardon knew what was going on, she showed no outward sign. She might even be enjoying Shelley's humiliation. If Ramsey Clifford knew what was going on, he was indifferent. Eventually Dr Waverly had it out with Shelley in a verbal battle over the telephone. Maria didn't eavesdrop. It was impossible not to hear him shouting in his study.

'No, I won't come over tonight!' he shouted. 'There's nothing wrong with you, Shelley, and I won't come over tonight or any other night! I suggest that you get another doctor. I have no time for a chronic neurotic.'

It was cruel, but it seemed to work. The telephone calls stopped. Two weeks before the scheduled wedding, Cynthia Reardon moved into the doctor's house and Maria's moral values were again updated. It seemed to be accepted practice in the young doctor's circle and Maria made no comment.

But her worst fears about her future status were soon confirmed. She couldn't please the new mistress, who took Maria to task on the slightest provocation. The good days were finished. Cynthia was vicious. She would get whatever she wanted on her own terms either by using her sex or the lure of Josiah Reardon's wealth and prestige. If there was any doubt of who would rule the Waverly manse, it was decided the night of Josiah Reardon's prenuptial dinner party.

Once a week Dr Waverly spent a day at the local free clinic, and, because Cynthia didn't care about these things, he sometimes talked about this work with Maria. It was the one thing of which he was genuinely proud, and because of it she was proud of him. A twelve-year-old Mexican boy had been under his care for some time. Minor surgery had been performed and confidence carefully built for the major surgery which, if successful, would restore him to a normal life. Half of the battle, Waverly assured her, was in the rapport he had established with the frightened boy. On the evening before the scheduled major surgery Reardon gave his dinner party. Maria heard the doctor try to get Cynthia to change the date.

'I have nine-o'clock surgery,' he said. 'It's imperative that I get my rest.'

'You're not the only doctor at the clinic!' Cynthia scoffed.

'But this is a special case!'

'And Daddy's dinner isn't, I suppose! Lyle, you must be mad. You know Daddy doesn't change his plans for anyone, and this is a very special occasion. You see, darling, you're the first man I've ever known that Daddy liked. He thinks you're a stabilising influence for me. I happen to know what his wedding present is going to be. What would you think of fifteen percent of the Reardon Corporation?'

Dr Waverly thought through a few moments of absolute silence. 'You're dreaming.'

'Then I must have dreamed the papers I saw Daddy's lawyer drawing up. That's what the dinner is for tonight – the presentation of the gift. Now I know you can get somebody else to take over for you tomorrow. It's not as if you had a paying patient. It's just one of those clinic cases.'

Maria held her breath and said a silent prayer, but she lost. Waverly went to the dinner with Cynthia. It was almost two A.M. when he returned and, minutes later, Cynthia was at the door. Maria heard them laughing in the entry hall.

'You shouldn't have come here,' Waverly said. 'The old boy doesn't know we've jumped the gun, and he might not like it.'

'He would loathe it – but who cares? Darling, isn't it wonderful? You see, I didn't lie to you. We've got something to celebrate.'

'It's so late—'

'A little nightcap – please.'

Maria, listening from the kitchen, sighed and went back to bed. In the morning she arose, made a pot of coffee, and carried it up to Waverly's room. He was asleep. Cynthia opened one eye and then threw a pillow at her.

'Nobody called you!' she whispered angrily.

'The doctor has a hospital call—'

'Cancel it! Tell them he's sick or something. Can't you see that he's asleep? If you don't call the hospital this minute, I will!'

Maria retreated from the room. She went downstairs and phoned the hospital to inform them that Dr Waverly couldn't perform the nine-o'clock operation. It was noon before the doctor came downstairs and that was just a few minutes after the hospital called to tell him that the boy had died on the operating table. It was a small event in the life of a young doctor who was slated to become the most popular society doctor in the area, but it destroyed Maria's last vision of Camelot.

She remembered that Walter, who was crude and uneducated, had once left a game during a winning streak – and that was the one thing he had taught her a gambler should never do – to donate blood to the black porter who parked his car at the casino each night. The friend who took over Walter's hand had lost everything, but that hadn't mattered because the porter lived and Walter came back as happy as a schoolboy playing hookey. And so Maria was thoroughly disenchanted with her position at the Waverly house even before the night that Shelley Clifford returned.

It was four nights before the wedding. Cynthia, tired from rehearsals of the ceremony, had gone up to bed and taken two sleeping pills. The doctor was preparing a deposit slip for the visit to the bank that he wanted Maria to make for him in the morning. Maria went to the front door when the bell rang and there was no way to keep Shelley out of the house. She had been drinking and was hysterical. One eye was blackened and she had a cut on one cheek. Her husband, she explained when Waverly hurried out of the study, had learned of their relationship and beaten her. Her story might be true or untrue, but the doctor's reaction was firm.

'You can't stay here!' he insisted.

'Just for tonight,' she begged. 'Ram's been drinking, too. I'm afraid to go home.'

'I don't believe you,' Waverly said. 'Ram Clifford doesn't drink.'

'He did tonight. I'm afraid, Lyle. I'm afraid he'll kill me!'

Maria watched the doctor's face. He looked as if he thought that might be a good solution. Firmly he took Shelley by the shoulders and turned her back toward the door.

'Then go to a hotel,' he said.

'Why can't I stay here?'

'Because I won't let you.'

Waverly was trying to keep his voice down. When Shelley noticed him glance apprehensively toward the stairs, she sensed immediately what he was trying to hide. Her eyes widened. '*She's* here, isn't she? Cynthia's *here!*' And then she laughed and pushed Waverly away from her. 'You couldn't even wait for the marriage! Oh, that's beautiful! Now wouldn't old Josiah Reardon love to know about this! His daughter may be a swinger, but the old boy's a stickler for the proprieties! And there's nothing more conservative than a savings and loan corporation, darling. When they hear about this you may not get that partnership and seat on the board of directors.'

'Get out of the house!' Waverly ordered.

'Oh, I will, I will – just as soon as I've run upstairs to check—'

She lunged past him and started to run up the stairs. Waverly was about two steps behind her when the liquor, the shock, and the injuries caught up with Shelley. She was more than halfway up the stairway when she stumbled and fell against the railing. She shrieked and grabbed at the air and then, as both Waverly and Maria watched in horror, she plummeted over the railing and fell to the marble floor of the entry hall. There was a sickening sound as her head struck the marble. She was dead when Dr Waverly reached her.

For a few moments he was too stunned to speak. Then he turned to Maria. 'You've got to help me,' he said.

'What do you mean?' Maria asked.

'You saw what happened. It was an accident – she killed herself. But I can't have her found in my house like this. Can you drive a car, Maria?'

'Yes.'

'Good. Cynthia's asleep. The pills I gave her will last until morning. I'll get my car out of the garage and you follow me in it. I'll take Mrs Clifford's body in her car and leave it out on that shortcut she uses.'

Maria hesitated.

'Do you understand what I've said?' Waverly asked.

'I understand,' Maria said, 'but suppose the police come—'

'Out on that unpaved stretch? No chance. Anyway, I'll be the one taking the risk. I'll have the body with me. If you see a police car, just keep going.'

'Still, there could be trouble,' Maria said.

'Maria, there's no time to argue! I'm not going to hurt Mrs Clifford – she's already dead. But I can't afford a scandal now. This is a matter of self-preservation!'

'With me, too, it is a matter of self-preservation,' Maria said coldly.

It took the doctor a few seconds to understand Maria's words. He had taken her for granted too long a time to make a sudden change without a certain anguish. When he finally did understand, he asked how much self-preservation she had in mind.

'A will is risky,' she said. 'Wills can be changed. Five thousand dollars in cash is more reliable.'

'I don't have that much money in the house,' he protested.

'I'll take a cheque,' Maria said.

Minutes later, the doctor's cheque tucked away in her handbag, Maria drove Waverly's sedan at a safe distance behind Mrs Clifford's little sports car. There was no traffic at all on the narrow road. When they reached a wide shoulder forming a scenic view over a ravine, Waverly stopped the small car and parked off the roadway. Maria stopped the sedan and watched him carry Shelley Clifford's body to the edge of the shoulder and toss it into the shrubbery.

Waverly then returned to the car and emptied Shelley Clifford's handbag of all cash and credit cards. Leaving the emptied purse on the seat, and pocketing the items that a robber would steal, he then took out his pocketknife and jammed it between the treads of one rear tyre, letting out the air. The scene was set: a flat tyre on a seldom-used road; a passing car hailed and a grim harvest of murder and robbery.

Waverly folded his pocketknife and walked to the waiting sedan. He drove the car back to the house himself and then he and Maria scrubbed away the bloodstains on the marble entry floor.

When they had finished, Waverly said, 'Nothing happened here tonight.'

'Nothing,' Maria agreed, 'except that there's a bloodstain on your coat sleeve, Doctor. Give me the coat and I'll sponge out the stain before I go to bed.'

Waverly pulled off his suit coat and gave it to her without hesitation. 'Don't call me in the morning,' he said. 'I'm going to take a couple of sleeping pills myself.'

Maria took the coat to her room but she didn't sponge out the blood. She turned off the light and tried to sleep. When that didn't work, she got up and packed her bag. In the morning she got the doctor's bank deposit from his study, the suitcase and the stained coat from her room, and then, because the keys were still in the ignition, drove the doctor's car to the bank. Ordinarily she would have taken the bus. Today was urgent. Because she was so well known at the bank, and particularly after having made the doctor's deposit, she had no difficulty cashing the cheque for $5,000.

On the return trip she took the unpaved shortcut. No other cars passed and she reached Mrs Clifford's abandoned coupé unseen Drawing alongside, she tossed Dr Waverly's coat into the front seat, and then drove on.

Both Waverly and his fiancée were still asleep when Maria returned the doctor's sedan to the garage. Then, bag in hand, she walked to the bus stop.

Shelley Clifford's body was found early in the afternoon. The story of her death was on the evening television newscasts. An apparent victim of a casual murderer, her death inspired urgent editorial demand for increased police patrols and an end to permissive education. Ramsey Clifford offered a $10,000 reward for the apprehension and conviction of her murderer. It wasn't until the third day after Shelley's body was found that Lieutenant Gannon came to Dr Waverly's house. He carried a small bundle wrapped in brown paper.

'I've been doing some checking, Doctor,' he said. 'I understand that you and the late Shelley Clifford were very good friends.'

'You've picked up some gossip,' Waverly stated.

'I don't think so. We didn't release all the evidence we had in her death when the body was found. We needed a little time to check out something that was found on the seat of her car—' Gannon ripped open the package and held up Waverly's suit coat. 'We've traced this to your tailor, Dr Waverly, and we've matched the bloodstains to Mrs Clifford's. Now all we want from you is an explanation of what it was doing in her car.'

On the fourth day after Shelley Clifford's death a smartly dressed, middle-aged woman checked into a hotel on the Nevada side of Lake Tahoe. She signed the register as Mrs Walter Dwyer and then took a stroll through the casino because the atmosphere of a gambling town made her feel closer to Walter. Later, upstairs in her room, she studied the Tucson newspaper she had picked up in the lobby and was amused to learn that the police of that area were conducting an intensive search for her body.

Confronted with his blood-stained jacket, Waverly had told the truth – but he wasn't believed. When it developed that his housekeeper had last been seen on the morning of Mrs Clifford's death cashing a $5,000 cheque at Waverly's bank, Lieutenant Gannon formed the theory that Waverly had used Maria Morales to get him some ready cash in the event the doctor was linked to Mrs Clifford and had to leave the country, and had then disposed of the woman so she wouldn't talk.

It was all nonsense, of course, and Maria was sure that Gannon could prove nothing. No crime had been committed. The worst that could happen to Dr Waverly was that his marriage would be called off. That was a little sad since he deserved Cynthia Reardon as much as she deserved him. The other thing that would happen – and this was the reason she had placed the doctor's coat in Mrs Clifford's car – was that the community would be made aware of Waverly's true character. This was imperative, in Maria's mind, in view of the nature of his profession.

Mrs Dwyer remained at the hotel for several weeks. By that time the Tucson papers no longer referred to the Shelley Clifford affair, and she could assume that it was in a state of permanent limbo with no need for her reappearance to save Waverly from a murder charge.

Before leaving the resort, Mrs Dwyer put a down payment on a smartly furnished condominium apartment which, the salesman assured her, would bring prime weekly rental in high season. Mrs Dwyer explained that she travelled in her work and would occupy the apartment only a few months of the year, but that it was nice to have roots somewhere and a woman did need a good investment for her retirement years.

A few days later, a shabbily dressed woman, wearing a look of quiet despair in her eyes entered the Tahoe bus station. She carried a cheap suitcase and a handbag containing $100 in a money clip. The bills were old – in fact, they were the same bills, in the same money clip, that Maria Morales, who was then nineteen and the prettiest cocktail waitress on the Strip, saw drop from Walter Dywer's pocket as he bent over a casino gambling table. Maria had nothing of her own but a $10 advance on her salary, and when she returned the $100 to Dwyer he was so impressed by her honesty, and other attributes, that he took her to dinner. A week later they were married and the marriage was for love – not the cheap bargain that Dr Lyle Waverly had tried to make with Cynthia Reardon. The money and the clip had been Walter's wedding present.

'Keep it for luck,' he said. 'Your Irish luck.'

In the bus station Maria bought a ticket to Sacramento, the state capital of California. There would be many wealthy people in that area who were so nervous about their own corruption that they would be eager to hire a housekeeper honest enough to go to the police station with $100 found on the street while looking for a job.

Walter had taught her never to walk out on a winning streak.

Mary Kelly

Judgement

Anyone who has never experienced coincidence please write to me. I
don't put it the other way round for fear of being flooded with letters.
Coincidence happens; and *nil humanum alienum*, et cetera. Yet someone
speaking to me about a book I'd written said, 'Wasn't it rather a coincidence that the girl arrived just as the man was coming down the stairs?
Now if I'd been reading that for your publisher I wouldn't have passed
it.'

Three Octobers past I experienced a coincidence of meeting that was
linked to one I'd experienced thirty years ago; doubly linked, because
the people involved were related to each other and because on both
occasions I condoned a crime – or at least an act punishable by law.
In my judgement crime names only acts against the person; blackmail,
cruelty, violence, murder. However, I leave you to judge for yourself
what these acts were.

On an afternoon of golden motes I walked home from shopping. I
turned into the drive and saw a white BMW parked by the entrance to
flat two. A woman was sitting in the driver's seat, a stranger, someone's
visitor. I walked past the car towards the front porch; before I'd reached
it a voice called my name.

The woman had opened the door of the car and was leaning out,
smiling at me: rather a wolfish grin. I took a few steps towards her.
Petals of silver-pink hair curved round her tanned face. Her eyes were
brown. Her nose was high-boned, slightly crooked. She could have been
my age, more or less.

She said, 'Don't you know me, then?'

The deep husky voice, the grin with a hint of bravado or mockery –

they took me back years, decades. I said hesitantly, unbelieving, 'Dinah? Dinah!'

Three decades back.

We were eight or nine years old then, the two of us, kneeling side by side in the school corridor in front of a large statue of Our Lady of Lourdes. We'd got back late after going home to dinner. If you missed prayers you had to say them on your own before joining your class. A sight we must have looked, kneeling there in short gym tunics and wellingtons.

Upstairs in my flat I said to Dinah, 'How did you know me? Don't tell me I haven't changed.'

'Course you have. There's something about you that hasn't though. Dunno what. Perhaps it's your eyes. Have you lived here long?'

'Five years.'

'You married?'

'Yes. But he's away at a conference till Sunday.'

Dinah had a trim figure, big bones, good legs. She was wearing snakeskin shoes that matched her handbag, and she'd carried up from the car a pale fur coat that looked to me quite opulent. She flung it down with fine carelessness on the *chaise longue* by the window.

I got out the last two Copenhagen cups and the silver teaspoons my aunt Elsie left me. Dinah was inspecting the furniture, the carpet, my pictures.

She said, 'You don't go out to work, then.'

'I work at home. Writing.'

'I'm not surprised. There was an air about you – I always expected you to do something impractical.' She laughed. What hadn't changed about Dinah was her voice; it was deep and full of lung power.

I'd seen that she wore no wedding ring. I said, 'What do you do, Dinah?'

'I'm a vocalist. I sing with Jeff Ravel.'

The name used to appear in the old-style *Radio Times*. He had some sort of band – dance orchestra, he called it. I'd have pronounced his name like the French composer's, but that was wrong, it seemed: Dinah rhymed it with travel. She was telling me about her life, her tours in Holland, Germany, Spain.

In 1938 or 1939 – walking about the streets one summer evening I passed Dinah's house and on an impulse called in.

She was practising a song and dance in their living-room. Her mother, watching critically, nodded to me as I opened the door from the backyard. Dinah rolled her eyes without interrupting the routine. She held a cane or short walking stick. She wore white gloves and a top hat, her cotton frock and ankle socks. I can't have paid much attention to the song, I don't remember any words; only Dinah's voice baying out, her swaggering strides as she twirled the cane.

Her mother wasn't satisfied. She said, 'Oh come on, Di, for goodness' sake, put a kick in it.'

Dinah broke off and complained in her ordinary voice, 'Oh – I don't feel like it.'

'Never mind what you feel like, you've got to do it,' her mother said severely. She turned to me with a gesture of despair. 'I don't know – this show's supposed to be going on on Saturday.'

The show would have been for the working men's club in the Victoria Rooms, or perhaps for the Constitutional Club which met in rooms at the back of the Duke of Cambridge.

Dinah sipped the tea as if she needed it. She said, 'Well – aren't you dying to know what I'm doing here?'

Thinking of the fur, the BMW, I said, 'Are you the company that owns the flats?'

She smiled. 'No, love. I've been seeing my brother. Flat eight.'

But Dinah had no brother. And flat eight was Dave Close-shave, as my husband calls him, Fly Dai; I say simply Flash. Realising that I hadn't kept astonishment off my face I tried to account for it respectably by saying, 'But his name isn't Harker.'

'No, Mum remarried and they adopted him. I was twenty-one by then, so they didn't adopt me.'

'Did your father get killed? In the raids?'

'No, no. They just divorced.'

'But when was your brother born? I don't remember—'

'You wouldn't, love. I was sixteen when he arrived. Mum must have slipped up. I expect it was the war. Things were hard to come by, weren't they, rubber goods, what have you. She was thirty-eight. Didn't do her any harm though. And then she did quite well for herself.'

I couldn't help wondering if Flash were Dinah's full brother. It wasn't impossible. Five years between his birth and his adoption by the new husband. Five years was plenty of time to fall out of one marriage into another. What made me wonder was that I could see no likeness between the tenant of flat eight and Dinah, none between him and my memories of his parents.

'More tea, Dinah?'

'No thanks. You smoke?' She lit a cigarette.

'Do you see your father at all?'

'He died a couple of years ago. You don't remember him, do you, surely?'

'I saw him once or twice.'

She shook her head. 'He was no good, you know. Useless.'

'What do you mean?'

'Well – he didn't give Mum much of a home.'

'Perhaps it wasn't all his fault. There was the Depression till the war, wasn't there?'

'Oh, it would have been all the same. There was plenty of work when the war started. But he . . .'

Each time Dinah took the cigarette out of her mouth her lips made a small smacking noise. She was not just inhaling smoke but dragging on the cigarette itself.

She said abruptly, 'Dad nearly went to prison in the war, did you know?'

I was very much startled; in fact, for a reason you'll later understand, I blushed. 'What for?'

'Oh – typical. He stole a bale of cloth from Keele's, brought it home to Mum. Supposed to be for a summer dress. You never saw such rubbish. Fray in the first wash. And such a colour – just like French mustard, with a thin black check. You wouldn't want it even without paying. Mind you, someone had bought a bit. It wasn't a whole bale.'

'What do you mean, he *nearly* went to prison?'

'They caught up with him, but he was only put on probation. I expect they wanted to keep down the numbers they'd have to feed free.'

There were two or three pops as Dinah took the cigarette out of her mouth. She seemed preoccupied. After a minute she said, 'Dave takes after him, you know. He never keeps a job. He doesn't get sacked, he just gives up. Nothing suits his ideas. He can't be bothered.'

'How does he live? The rent here—'

'Oh, he gets money from Mum. I told you she did quite well for herself the second time. She gives him something. And then he gambles. He has the devil's own luck. Eleven hundred pounds he won the other week.'

I'd never seen such a sum in my life. No doubt it was peanuts to Dinah. I said to her, 'Where do you live?'

'We stay in hotels when we're touring. I've been spending a couple of days with Mum. We haven't got a show till Saturday.'

Show. Vocalist. Dinah seemed to have realised some glamorous fiction of her teens, which time meanwhile had outmoded.

A few months earlier I'd happened to meet (more true coincidence) another former schoolfellow. All she seemed to think about, still, was dating Air Force officers.

Perhaps the same thing had happened to me; though I don't turn out the sort of book that at fifteen I thought the most accomplished kind of writing in the world.

Dinah put down her cup. 'Must fly, love. Thanks for the tea.'

'I'm glad I happened to walk by at the right moment.'

'Nice to see you again after all these years. I'm glad you got on.' Dinah stood up and looked round the room. 'This is a good conversion, isn't it? And you've got the flat looking nice.' She went across to the *chaise longue* and picked up her fur. She glanced out of the window and paused. 'Yes, very nice,' she said absently. 'I think if you don't mind I'd better use your toilet. I've got a long drive.'

I showed her where the lavatory was and hurried to fetch a clean towel to put in the bathroom. I couldn't stop wondering over the revelation that Flash in flat eight was Dinah's brother. He lived there with the thinnest shrimp of a girl I'd ever seen. She wore a minidress before anyone else. When I first saw it I thought she'd had a nervous breakdown and walked out in her underwear, because the skirt wasn't just mini, it was divided. Except for the long sleeves the dress looked exactly like what used to be sold in the thirties as camiknickers; only shorter. Flash's girl wore platform soles and silver eyelashes and tendril wigs – anything that was going before it had even got started.

Flash came to borrow a funnel from us one Sunday; no one else in the flats was at home. Something was wrong with the engine of his ten-year-old resprayed Zodiac. Flash spoke in quick bursts, blinking his thick lashes; they were so long they brushed the lenses of his glasses, which had mahogany-coloured frames swept round his temples. His skin was pale, dusted with big yellow freckles.

When he brought back the funnel he seemed to feel he should make some return for the loan. He told us several stories one after the other. Here is an example. (You can skip to the asterisk if you like.)

A new officer joins the unit. The CO says to him, 'You'll soon feel at home here, Carruthers. We've got entertainment laid on for every night of the week. Sundays, of course, we have to toe the line and read a book – but we reckon we've got the liveliest library in the command. Mondays we have a poker table.'

'I'm sorry, sir, I don't gamble.'

'Oh. Well, Tuesdays we all go down to the village pub.'

'I'm sorry, sir, I don't drink.'

'Really? Well, Wednesdays the locals put on a concert for us.'

'I'm sorry, sir, I'm tone deaf.'

'That's a pity. Thursdays there's a dance at the roadhouse.'

'I'm sorry, sir, I don't dance.'

'Goddamn it, man! Well, at least you'll like Friday. Friday we have exclusive use of the local brothel.'

'I'm not interested in women, sir.'

'Not interested in women, eh? Queer, are you?'

'Certainly not, sir.'

'Ah. You're going to hate Saturday.'

*

That was the style and level of Flash's stories. He told them with a wide frog grin interrupting the spasms of speech, shrugging his shoulders and gesturing with overlarge white hands.

Our silence was a mistake. When embarrassed one should plug all pauses with one's own voice; otherwise the embarrasser will seize them.

I hoped Dinah wouldn't mention to her brother that we'd been at school together; or if she did that he wouldn't think it any reason to pay us extra attention. Maybe he'd change house as often as he changed job; he hadn't lived long in flat eight.

Dinah protested so much against my coming down to the porch that it was simpler not to insist. However, I went to the window and knelt on the *chaise longue* to wave goodbye.

There was a police car parked outside the door. The driver glanced at Dinah as she walked to her BMW, then went back to reading a newspaper.

I thought at once: they've come to see Flash. I went to wave to Dinah, then hesitated. I wondered if she'd had the same thought about the police. She couldn't miss seeing the car and she'd spoken about her brother without illusion. But if the thought did cross her mind that he might be in trouble she obviously didn't want to be involved. She got in the BMW without looking up at his outside stair or my window, and drove away.

If Flash had been mixed up in anything illegal it would have been through inertia. Long before Dinah had told me about him I'd judged him with words like feckless, shiftless, degenerate – but not depraved. The impression he gave was of moral exhaustion, using moral in the sense of capable of choice in action or conduct.

I settled myself comfortably on the *chaise longue*, resting my head on my arms on the window-ledge in a position from which I could watch the police car. We had no muslin screens at the window; we hadn't needed them for privacy since we were on the first floor and not over-looked. I'd never imagined I might want to spy out unobserved. So I had to kneel.

That time I'd knelt with Dinah in wellingtons, catching up on our missed prayers. Normally you just bobbed down in the empty corridor, skipped through a Hail Mary and got into class unnoticed at the beginning of the lesson.

That afternoon the corridor wasn't empty. Miss Docherty, headmistress, and Father Aloysius, parish priest, were walking towards us. I closed my eyes and lingered through three silent Hail Marys, hoping they'd walk right past us deep in talk. Dinah's prayers were evidently long ones too, for the same reason.

As I started the lengthier Hail Holy Queen, Miss Docherty behind us said with sarcasm, 'What very devout girls we have here, Father.'

I didn't mind trying to keep out of trouble, it was only natural. I didn't want Miss Docherty to think I had any opinion of her at all. I broke off the prayer at *thine eyes of mercy towards us*, stood up, turned round. But Dinah out of subtler bravado prayed on.

My people hadn't encouraged my friendship with Dinah. They wanted me to make friends with 'nice girls' and 'good Catholics'. A good Catholic went to early Mass on Sundays to take Communion. Dinah was usually sent alone at twelve o'clock, to the last. (The built-in penalty for lazy rising was the sermon, preached only at twelve o'clock Mass.) The Catholicism of Dinah's father was pretty nominal; her mother wasn't a Catholic at all. It was a trial and bewilderment to my people that all my school friends were children of mixed marriages, and that I was attracted to the Protestants who lived in our road – girls with 'hard' names like Valerie, Beryl, Joyce, Phyllis, Brenda. 'Nice girls' were called Mary, Bernadette, Teresa, Cecilia or at a pinch Maureen, Kathleen, Sheila (it being next to mortal certainty that these were Irish). Josephine and the like were slightly suspect; although they incorporated saints' names they had been filtered through loose-living free-thinking France. And Old Testament names were given to Jews.

I didn't choose friends on purpose to be awkward. I had no quarrel with the Church, only indifference to her doctrine and impatience with some of its side effects in practice. But I was fond of our parish church, the building.

It had risen on the swell of the Oxford Movement and Irish immigration. It could hold over a thousand people and on great feasts it did. There was a big high altar and two side altars, a Lady chapel, three shrines, a baptistery. The roof was painted, so were spaces between the pointed arches of the aisles. There was plenty of stained glass, especially in the rose window above the high altar; this held the last glow of a winter sunset when everything below was gloom, and the sanctuary lamp just a solitary red gleam that shed no light.

I liked the church at a solemn High Mass, blazing with candles and sunlight, blue with incense smoke that smelled so exotic and tickled the nose; when the parish choir sang florid 'secular' masses and the chapter interposed yearning plainchant, and three priests in cloth-of-gold copes moved about the altar among servers and acolytes wearing surplices hemmed with deep bands of crochet.

Equally I liked the church silent and empty in dusk, when I would slip in alone after school. I never felt frightened, always at ease. No one would have been surprised to see me there, wondered what I was doing. Anyone might go in at any time to say a prayer or meditate; it was understood. The church was never shut till late at night.

The Lady chapel was the darkest spot in the building, at the altar end, behind the row of confessional boxes. Its two narrow north windows were protected on the outside with wire screens; they were the pieces of stained glass nearest the road. Beyond them was a six-foot closeboard fence and beyond that one of the pollarded limes which were planted regularly along our streets. The walls of the chapel were panelled in dark wood that matched the screen behind its altar. The shrine itself was painted midnight blue with gold stars, and carved into dozens of knobbly pinnacles which were gilded. The statue of Our Lady wore a deep blue mantle and a glittering crown. The altar cloth was blue, and the carpet on the altar steps, and the glass devotional lamp that hung by chains from the dark ceiling. To sit in the Lady chapel on a fine day and look through two ranks of pillars to the nave was like being in a camera obscura. But there was nothing dingy about the chapel; it was complicated and rich. And there was usually a taper burning on the candle stand by the altar rail.

Perhaps you don't know what a candle stand looked like: like a music stand with small metal cups, fifty or more, fixed to its tilted bars, which were sometimes the same in pattern as a music stand's and sometimes arranged in concentric circles. Just above the tripod two metal boxes were attached to the frame. One was open; it held white wax candles six inches long and half an inch thick. The other box was locked; into a slot in its lid you put your money for candles – a penny each, they used to cost, but there was no upwards limit on price. The object of lighting a candle was to signal seriousness of a good intention or a prayer. After the earlier Masses on Sunday the stands were incandescent forests, but by the end of the morning, nearing one o'clock, they looked debauched, with the candles dead or guttering convulsively or drunk and maudlin. Children loved lighting candles, of course, just for the fun of it; but no child to my knowledge ever lit one without paying.

In the winter of 1938 or 1939 I went into the Lady chapel one afternoon. Junior school used to stop later than it does now; at quarter past four. (We had a longer break at midday to let us all get home to dinner and back – I for example walked a mile each way.) Probably by the time I got into the chapel it was half past four.

Father Anselm was playing the organ, which was a fine one that wouldn't have sounded puny in the Albert Hall. He was not messing about with the *vox humana*; he liked *diapason*, thunder rolls, niagaras of music.

There were only two low candles flickering on the stand. I went into a bench near the back of the chapel, right along to the end of it against the wall. There I knelt down, resting my bottom on the edge of the seat to spare my bony knees. I laid my face on my folded arms on the prayer-book rest. I was sure the bench was vibrating to Father Anselm's thunders. I said a Hail Mary; perhaps another. Then I got lost in sound. From time to time I'd make a vague gesture of good-will in my mind, think snatches of litany, hymns, prayers. Mystical Rose, Mother of Mercy. Refuge of Sinners. To thee do we cry, poor banished children of Eve. O clement, O loving.

I walked four miles a day and it was dark and I felt at home. I must have fallen into a doze.

When I woke up Father Anselm was making the organ ring like a high trumpet. The candles on the stand had gone out. No they hadn't. Someone was kneeling to say a prayer before lighting one and the dark stooping shape had hidden the flames for a moment. I wondered how long I'd slept. I thought I'd better go. I stood up, moved out of the bench and made a genuflexion towards the high altar. The person lighting a candle was a man. He seemed to be having trouble getting his money in the box. Perhaps he was putting in half a crown and it was stuck in the slot. And how odd – a small shock went through me: the man hadn't taken off his hat. As a mark of reverence to the Most Holy Presence.

I walked past the empty confessional boxes, the baptistery, the statue of St Peter. Under the organ loft the noise was incredible. I dipped my hand in the holy water stoup. There was only a mingy bit of wet at the bottom; I liked a brimming stoup you would splash your face from. As I made my last (quite unnecessary) genuflexion I saw a slight movement in the dimness by the confessionals. The man who'd forgotten to take off his hat must have succeeded in getting his money in the box and lit his candle. I couldn't see the little flame; a big nave pillar was in the way.

I stood for a moment or two on the porch. It was raining softly. There was more light in the sky than you'd have thought from the gloom in the church. I turned round as the man came quickly out of the door behind me. He gave a great jump. It was Dinah's father.

I said, 'Hullo, Mr Harker.'

He brushed past me and ran down the steps. He crossed the wide yard to the gate walking very fast yet stiffly, a most odd walk – it looked almost as if he'd done something—

Before I could stop myself I'd had a thought that was coarse and improper considering I was almost inside the church. I rushed down the steps as if speed would retroactively clear me.

I knew then that Dinah's father hadn't been lighting a candle. He'd been forcing open the money box. I knew about conscience: I'd been confessing for three years. I'd seen his shock, the alarm on his pale face; his guilt in short.

He'd been frightened enough at being seen outside the church. What would he have felt if he'd known I'd also seen him at the candle stand? He wouldn't have seen me, bowed at the end of a back bench in the dark chapel. A navy-blue beret covered my hair. I wore a navy-blue coat and knitted gloves. Father Anselm's music would have drowned my footsteps when I moved. Anyway, my people always had rubber heels put on my shoes to make them last longer.

I walked home. I said nothing about what I'd seen.

I knew that what Dinah's father had done was judged wrong. I just felt repugnance for telling. I knew the church wouldn't miss the money – if he succeeded in getting any. No, no. God saw everything, they said, though we couldn't see him. Let God deal with it, then. Stealing was a sin, and sin was God's province, not mine.

When the war came Dinah and I were eleven. We were due to go to different schools that September. We were evacuated to different places.

When most of us drifted home later I saw Dinah again from time to time; we'd wave to each other across the road. I suppose I saw her last when we were eighteen. Until this afternoon.

Two policemen appeared on the drive below my window, they'd come from round the corner of the house. They wore flat hats, of course, not helmets; they were walking towards the car. Just as I'd thought; they'd been to see Flash. The only entrance on that side of the house was the iron stair to flat eight.

With some disappointment I watched the car drive away with them. I suppose I'd imagined I might see Flash brought down manacled. But because a person is feckless, keeps no job and gambles it doesn't follow that he will ever cross the line into positive crime. He may make it easier for himself to do this, but it is not inevitable.

My reverie on the *chaise longue* had lasted some time. I went along to the lavatory. As soon as I'd closed the door I noticed that the cistern lid had a grey line under it. When I looked close I saw that it had got shifted on the tank. Dinah must have leaned against it or somehow knocked it. The grey line was the rough unglazed edge of the porcelain tank, darkened with dried condensation. Actually Dinah couldn't have knocked the lid back to where it was, though there was a little play to its fit on the tank. It was completely askew; the back was raised on the wooden strut that supported the tank on the wall. The lid couldn't get up there without being lifted.

Why should anyone do such a thing?

I lifted it myself and looked inside the tank. There was something dark at the bottom, between its side and the foot of the overflow pipe, in the shadow of the ball. At a quick glance it might have been one of the stains on the base of the tank. I pushed the handle to release the water. The last two inches never run out. I reached down and pulled up a soggy, closed leather notecase.

I thought casually: if it had been plastic it wouldn't have come to any harm, I'd have wiped it on a towel. The wet leather was slimy, and when it dried it would be stained and stiff.

There was no money inside the case. Folded very small at the bottom of the back pocket was a slip of thin paper: a London hotel bill, two months old, paid, obviously overlooked when the notecase was emptied because it was so slight.

I remembered that I'd heard the lavatory flushed twice. Perhaps some scraps of driving licence and credit card had survived the first deluge. Dinah had looked out of the window as she picked up her fur from the *chaise longue*. I'd thought she was admiring the autumn colour of the trees that screened the drive. But the police car must have been there already.

Of course I speculated on exactly what had happened, who had done what. There's no need to review all the permutations; you can see them for yourself. I also thought that the owner of a good leather notecase who could afford to stay in that London hotel would only have to go to his bank, or ring up his bank, for money to replace what he'd lost; though very likely the sum would be more than a candle box would hold. There was no upward limit to price, but most people had only paid their penny.

In 1938 or 1939 four pennies bought a large loaf or a pint of milk or a large tin of beans.

I must have made my first visit to Dinah's house in 1937; we were still in Miss O'Donnell's class. The house had two entrances, one from an alley at the back. This gave it interest in my eyes. In a grid of terraces it is a distinction to possess a side or back door. Dinah's was set in a five-foot creosoted fence. When I saw the garden on the other side I was shocked. Most of it was covered with concrete. There were two beds of caked earth filmed with mould, and a sycamore growing out of the back fence. A clothes-line stretched the length of the little yard; a shrunk mauve jumper of Dinah's hung in the cold air.

I knew Mrs Harker from having seen her meet Dinah outside school. She had a thin sad face (I mean I thought then that it was sad). Her lank hair was worn rather long, curled at the ends; its colour was that metallic red dyes used to give to brown hair. She seemed tired that day. When Dinah asked if she could show me 'your things' Mrs Harker just answered with a nod.

We went in the front bedroom of the house. Dinah pulled a cardboard box from under the double bed. As she lifted the quilt I saw a row of shoes standing in fluff on the linoleum: once pink mules, a pair of court shoes, winter boots, all worn and battered. Dinah said, 'D'you want to try them on?' She pushed the court shoes towards me. They had high heels. I put my feet inside them. The inner soles were pressed into lumps and ridges.

Out of the cardboard box Dinah brought items for my admiration – a mother of pearl cardcase without a lid, a piece of net embroidered with sequins, a Japanese paper fan, an ostrich feather.

Those were some of them.

When we went downstairs a man was sitting in the living-room. Dinah said, 'Hullo, Dad,' and he answered listlessly, 'Hullo.'

I liked Dinah's mother but her father seemed strange. He hadn't the frankness of my father and uncles, their straightforward smiles. He looked as if he couldn't smile. His face was pasty pale and flabby. His eyes were black. He wore a thin moustache. He'd sat down on one of three wooden chairs without taking off his overcoat; it hung open over a chalk-stripe suit.

Dinah's mother sent her to empty the cold leaves from the teapot. The kettle was coming to the boil in their kitchen that was more like what we called a scullery. Mrs Harker put down a fourth cup on the table in the living-room that was also a dining-room. (I learnt later that they rented only half the house, sharing the kitchen.) She went to a cupboard in the corner of the room, opened its door wide and stood back as if inviting the man, Dinah's father, to look inside. Although he didn't look he gave a small shrug. From where I sat I could see that there was nothing in the cupboard but a few empty jam jars. After a moment Dinah's mother shrugged too and shut the door.

I wondered why Mr Harker wasn't still at work; it was only half past four.

'What are we going to have for tea?' Dinah said; and as there was no answer in a couple of seconds she went on, 'Will you make pancakes, Mum? Go on. Oh go on.'

Her mother went out to the kitchen-scullery and moved about with a pan and spoon.

Dinah skipped round by her father's chair and made to sit on his knee. He pushed her aside, not roughly. 'Lay off, kid,' he said. 'I'm tired.'

Dinah sat beside me on a tottery settee. We looked at a treasure of hers, an old book of verse; the pages were covered with small print and brown spots. Dinah said, 'Look – this one's good. "How does the water come down at Lodore?" '

Her father had closed his eyes. His mouth had dropped open a little way. Dinah told me later that he'd been tramping about trying to find a job.

Mrs Harker came in with a frying pan in her hand. She glanced at her husband, then turned to me. She said sadly, 'Would you like a little pancake too?'

'Yes, please.'

I didn't realise how short they were. Not that I blame myself, a child of eight, for not recognising something beyond my experience. I loved pancakes, with lemon and sugar, soft and juicy, brown and crisp rolls – or sometimes for fun you flattened them out to cover the plate. And then you had the next one, and the next.

The single pancake Mrs Harker gave me was a white scorched disc the size of a crumpet. I know now that she only had flour and milk to make it with, and practically no fat for frying.

Anyway, Dinah thought it was tasty.

Of course the pancake was then; the notecase was now.

Making choices on the basis of what one feels is a form of sentimentality. I know the argument against it – feeling is too easy and too fickle: it's just as easy to feel rage as tenderness. So one should act according to one's reason. But what is reason? Judgement? That is, experience, guesswork and self interest.

I can understand people falling back in despair on formulae, precedents, principles, dogma; the technology of morals.

I went down to the garden and found a large stone. I brought it upstairs and fastened the wet notecase round it with rubber bands. Later that evening, when it was dark, I drove to the river and dropped the bundle in. Not because I felt anything for Dinah now, still less on account of Flash; not because I had a normal repugnance for informing; but because in my judgement, my guess, my hope, suppression would do least damage all round.

There were two people, Dinah and Flash, living in society, maybe not contributing any outstanding service to it, but not grossly violating its fabric. They were not in prison nor as far as I knew even on probation.

The longer they stayed that way the better. And if you think they should have been nipped in the bud, given a sharp lesson to prevent them going on to worse, I can only say that I disagree with you. Why add resentment to fecklessness? Then it would be surprising if you didn't find you'd brewed a worse poison than either.

They say that if theft were not crime no one would pay, no one could work, we should be back to the jungle not just as a figure of disgust, but truly. Law protects property (they say) not in a conspiracy of greed but to protect security, as far as such a thing is possible. Isn't it as much a crime to injure people's minds (they say) as their bodies? And what else does a threat to security do?

In that case I can think of plenty of people, governments, institutions, that ought to be languishing in jail.

The next morning I found out who was Jeff Ravel's agent; it took me forty minutes of telephoning to establish that on Saturday Jeff Ravel would be playing at – well, it really doesn't matter about the name: a town roughly on the Lodore latitude.

On Saturday that's where I went. There would be plenty of time for me to get back early on Sunday. And I had in mind to tell Dinah what I'd found. I didn't want her to think she or Flash could treat my lavatory cistern as a dump for anything they ever needed to be rid of. I wasn't free to come and go, without ties, to please myself. I was one half of a social unit, a household, a partnership. One can't expect to be protected without in turn protecting.

Jeff Ravel was playing for a dinner dance at the Mount Pleasant Hotel. I decided after all not to book in for the night. I wasn't tired. I meant to have dinner, a long break, then drive home after seeing Dinah; and that wouldn't be till she'd finished her work for the evening; I didn't want to upset her performance.

I watched the dinner-dance crowd going into the banqueting room. All the girls wore short silk dresses with full skirts, some of which had large bows above the seat. A woollen cardigan was draped on nearly every girl's shoulders; its back hem was lifted by the swell of the skirt or bow, like a blanket over a horse's tail.

The ordinary dining-room was empty apart from one old resident and myself. Pockmarked waiters stood round the trolley on which a spirit stove gushed flame all the time I was there and presumably all evening. I ate two small tough lamb cutlets. Through an open arch to the banqueting room came a hum of voices and the thump and clash and wheeze of a band. While I was eating tinned fruit salad (knowing that it would be tinned but preferring it to any other thing offered) I heard Dinah: a deep husky voice thrown right out from her chest. She was singing a song that was popular when I was in the sixth form. 'Tonight' – (da da, da da) – 'my heart cries out for Lydia' (da da, da da)—

I remembered that when I'd first heard it I'd thought the words were *heart cries out 'Perfidia!'*

I left the sour boiled coffee after two sips. As I went out of the dining-room I looked through the arch. Dinah was wearing a skin-clinging silver dress, a glittering bracelet. The cardigan girls and their escorts were spooning up fruit salad and ice cream, talking energetically between mouthfuls. No wonder Dinah bawled.

I asked at the reception desk what time the dance was expected to end and what room the singer had.

'Oh, they don't stay here,' the girl said, affronted.

The dance was to end at half past twelve. I walked round the town. I went for a drive. I got out and walked in pitch black silence along a lane in the middle of fields.

At twenty past twelve I came back to the hotel. There was scarcely a car in its forecourt, and no white BMW. The lights in the vestibule were dimmed, the reception desk looked shut for the night. No sound came from the banqueting room. I looked inside. On the platform two men were packing up a piece of percussion. I said to them, 'Where's your singer?'

'Just gone, Reg, hasn't she? Dinah gone?'

'Only this minute. She may be still in the car outside.'

I ran back to the yard.

Someone was standing by a Dormobile van which had its door open and its inside light on. Another figure blocked the window, moving about in the van. Light from a street lamp fell on the person standing outside. For a moment I thought it was Dinah's mother; then I realised that I was looking at Dinah. She'd taken off the silver-pink wig. Lank dark hair hung at the sides of her face. She was smoking. Over her silver dress she wore a cotton raincoat with brass buttons.

Perhaps the fur had been hired. And the BMW. If you can't afford the truth buy make-believe for an hour to two.

'Dinah,' I said.

She didn't move.

I said, 'I won't keep you, you must be tired. I just wanted to let you know I've dealt with the plumbing. Everything cleared up. Rolling down the river to the sea. It isn't a job I'd like to do twice. But it's all right for now.'

After a moment she said, 'Clever to find me.' Pause. 'Did you see the show?'

'Not really. I was in the next room.'

She drew on the cigarette, popped her lips. A rough cough shook her.

I said, 'I don't want to keep you out in the cold. I'm sorry. I just wanted to tell you. You needn't worry.'

She nodded. 'You mean you don't want to worry. Well, you needn't.'

She opened the door of the Dormobile and got in without saying goodbye.

Miles Tripp

Fixation

It was Freddie, my oldest friend, who dragged me out of a sinking spiral of depression following my mother's death. He wouldn't accept my refusal to go out for a drink and when we were sitting in a pub he asked what the trouble was. I told him there was no trouble. He didn't reply. He simply rested his hand on the sleeve of my coat for a few seconds and then removed it. He still didn't speak. It was obvious he didn't intend to speak. 'I'm beginning to wonder if I'm quite normal,' I burst out.

He didn't laugh. He didn't look surprised. He said, 'Don't we all sometimes wonder whether we're normal?' and took a long drink.

It was difficult to believe the implication of his remark. What worries could Freddie have? He was happily married, he had three daughters, a splendid home and he was senior partner in a well-established legal firm. To all appearances he lived a full and successful life. 'You are certainly normal,' I stated.

'Am I? What is normal?'

'That's not easy. Not in a few words.'

'What is abnormal then?' he asked.

'Isn't it a bit abnormal,' I asked, 'for a man of forty-two to have spent all his life with his mother and when she has gone to realise that his life has been devoted to performing for her, to winning praise and approval? Is that abnormal or normal?'

'I'll answer that,' he said, 'by telling you of the time when I wondered whether I was normal.' And he told me of a period when he had quarrelled violently, and every day, with one of his daughters until the stage was reached when he felt unsafe to be alone with her in case he strangled her. Fortunately one of his clients was a psychiatrist who had told him the border between normality and abnormality would only be crossed if, once the daughter started going out with boy-friends, Freddie still continued the warfare. It was a certainty that the girl wouldn't continue once she had a boy-friend.

Freddie gave me a quick glance. 'It seems that fathers and daughters can have pretty complicated relationships under the surface, but these are quite normal. I was normal.'

It was astute of him to make the observation about fathers and daughters because there had been times when I had wondered – never very coherently and with thoughts quickly suppressed – about mothers and sons. References in books and newspaper articles to the Oedipus complex have always made me feel uncomfortable, particularly since my father's death was inadvertently caused by me when I was a small boy. I fell off a pier into the sea. My father, who couldn't really swim, jumped after me and was drowned. I was saved by a local lifeguard.

'So you see,' Freddie continued, 'we all get these times of doubt. You are as normal as the next man but I'd like to give you a bit of advice. It's free. No professional charge.'

'I know. I need a holiday. No thanks, Freddie.'

'Get married.'

I had to laugh. I know it was impolite, but I couldn't help it. What woman would look twice at a man of my age, whose face had never been his fortune, and who held a humdrum job as an executive in a firm of chartered accountants.

'I know of a marriage bureau,' he said, 'where they interview you very carefully and then get a computer to work out what sort of partner is likely to be compatible. I'm told it works very well.'

Sometimes, in the quiet of my flat, I had wondered about consulting a marriage bureau but could never nerve myself to take the plunge.

'Don't forget,' he said, 'you'll not only be doing yourself a good turn, you'll be doing someone else a good turn. Someone who at this very moment is probably sitting alone wondering whether her loneliness will ever end.'

Although it was a busy pub and there was noise and movement all around I felt as though I was sitting in a sealed capsule. I was an astronaut on a launch pad and it was for me, and only me, to decide whether the infinite sky should be explored.

'All systems go,' I said.

He grinned. 'That's more like it. I'll arrange the interview for you. Can't do more than that, I'm afraid.'

I had a snatch of awful hesitation. 'Not this week,' I said.

'I'll arrange it tomorrow and don't tell me you can't take a couple of hours away from adjusting other people's tax returns, because I know you can . . . Have another?'

'It's not Dutch courage I need at this moment.'

'You'll be all right. Damn it, what have you got to lose?'

I had no answer.

'You can only gain,' he said.

I was interviewed, documented, tabulated, coded and programmed into a computer.

Two weeks later I was looking at a photograph of Kay. A little white triangle of a face with big, staring eyes, and hair torn back from temples and forehead. I remember thinking, 'She looks quite pretty,' and then, 'Why has she found it hard to get married?'

She was thirty-five, an audio-typist in the personnel department of a London store, and her interests were reading, crocheting and walking. She liked to go on day trips to the country and would try to identify and name all the wild flowers and grasses she saw. She enjoyed listening to classical music, and cooking French regional dishes. She usually took her holidays in France.

The computer had done its work well.

We could have met in the bureau's office but it was suggested that I should ring her for a date for an evening meal. A particular restaurant was recommended where the service and food was excellent, and we could be sure of special attention if I mentioned the bureau when making the reservation. It was important that slow service or indifferent waiting should not spoil the evening.

A timid voice answered the telephone and when I announced my name and asked if we could have a meal together the voice became slightly breathless, but the date was made and two evenings later we met.

She was small and fragile and looked like a sparrow that might dart into flight if anyone came too close.

We shook hands and I asked if she would like a drink or whether she would prefer to go straight in for a meal.

'I'd like a gin and tonic,' she said.

We sat opposite each other at a small table. A waiter swooped and was an attentive parrot to my order. I began to feel more confident.

'It looks like rain,' I said.

'I listened to the forecast before I came out.' She paused and gathered breath. 'They expect a cold front bringing rain to reach London during the night.'

'The farmers need rain.'

'Yes.'

'Not that there are many farmers in London,' I said. It was meant as a little joke, but she gave the futile remark a sort of strained and serious attention.

'No,' she said, after a pause.

'What I mean is that the rain tonight in London won't mean much to farming communities.' Although the tiny joke was dead I was parading its corpse. And even as I spoke I realised the phrase 'farming communities' was one I had never used before. Hearing my own voice was rather like overhearing a pedantic stranger talking about the most boring triviality imaginable. And then my mind went utterly blank. All the conversational gambits I had rehearsed were scattered to the four corners of my unconscious mind. If she didn't speak we should sit here for ever, figures trapped in an engraving of embarrassment.

'Have you had a holiday this year?' she asked.

She had produced one of my lost gambits.

'Not yet. I suppose I should plan something but since my mother's death . . . We used to go on a cruise each August . . . How about you?'

'I used to go away with a girl-friend. But the last of my single girl-friends got married in March and . . . I don't fancy going on my own.'

The waiter arrived with our drinks.

I lifted my glass to her. 'Cheers.'

'Cheers,' she replied, and her hand was shaking so much as she raised her glass that she had to use the other hand to steady it. When she drank it was as though she was holding a chalice.

Then she put down the glass and said, 'Look, if you would sooner finish these drinks and say goodbye, we can. The meal hasn't been ordered.'

I felt as breathless as she sounded. Had she decided against me, having met and seen me? A voice which I scarcely recognised as my own said, 'I'm in no hurry to go. But how about you?'

She smiled for the first time, and if smiles were electrical discharges I should have become a pile of bemused ash. And when the enchanting, stunning smile faded, she said, 'I don't want to go. I like the view from where I'm sitting.' And she directed another smile at me.

It was at this moment we fell in love.

The following weeks were a dream but as the wedding date drew near I had misgivings, not about the marriage but about my competence. I was inexperienced.

Because this subject has some bearing on what follows I cannot gloss over it, but briefly, I had a word with Freddie about my fears and his advice was, 'For God's sake don't leave it to the first night of the honeymoon unless there's no alternative. Start now, and start slowly. Get to know each other gently. Don't worry if nothing happens on the first or second nights. It will. Leave it to Mother Nature, but don't try to push the old girl. Nothing good ever came of trying to push Mother Nature.'

Freddie's advice was absolutely right. What a splendid lawyer the man is.

By the time we went on honeymoon – to a little French village near the Pyrenees where the scent of flowers is so strong that it seems to pervade food and drink and even the pores of one's body – we were lovers, and completely attuned.

That was seven years ago.

Marriage didn't alter our lives. I continued to work in an accountant's office and Kay, after a six-month period of housekeeping, decided she preferred to be a working girl and went back to being an audio-typist. We changed physically, however. My scant hair accelerated its departure and within a year I was completely bald, and within two years I had a disgraceful paunch. Kay's appearance changed more dramatically. 'I used to be an undersized weakling,' she laughed. 'Now look at me!'

In her own words she was 'a tub on two matchsticks', and although this was a slur on her beautiful legs, she had certainly put on weight. Her face had filled out too; but I love her face and every surplus ounce on her. To someone looking at her objectively she would be a plump, ordinary, middle-aged women, but I cannot be objective about her although, in retrospect, I can see that when the trouble started I did act with admirable objectivity.

She would usually come home to our flat an hour before me and prepare the evening meal. It was on a perfect June evening as we were clearing away the plates that she said, 'Have I ever mentioned Wilson to you?'

'No. Who's Wilson?'

'He's fairly new. In the Buying Department. He's only about twenty.' She hesitated. 'He seems to have a ridiculous sort of crush on me.'

I asked what she meant and I felt mildly amused.

'He makes all sorts of excuses to come into our room. And he hangs about looking at me. Josie and Pat pull my leg about it.'

'He hasn't asked you for a date, then?' I asked jokingly.

'No. He seems too shy for that. He just stands. And looks. It's getting quite unnerving.'

'It's your fatal fascination,' I said.

Kay wasn't amused. 'It's absurd,' she said. 'I'm old enough to be his mother. There are dozens of young attractive girls around the place. Why pick on me to make sheep's eyes at?'

'If it bothers you, you can tell him to shove off,' I said, but immediately I had spoken I knew this would be difficult. Kay is incapable of being rude to anyone.

'Oh well,' she said, 'I expect he'll get tired of it when he sees he's getting nowhere.' And that, so far as I was concerned, was the end of Wilson.

But one evening during the next week, just after we had switched off the television and were preparing to go to bed, she said, 'There's something I must tell you.'

An anxious note in her voice made me stop whatever I was doing and look at her.

'It's been on my mind all evening,' she said.

'What has?'

'You remember I told you about Denis Wilson?'

I had to think. The name 'Denis' wasn't familiar.

'You know,' Kay said. 'The boy at our office.'

'Oh yes. What's he been up to now?'

'On Monday he was waiting for me at the main entrance when we were all leaving. I know it was me he was waiting for. He said, "Goodnight." It was the same yesterday, Tuesday. Today he came across and said, "May I speak to you?" '

'What did you say?'

'I asked what he wanted. Do you know what he said?'

How could I know? 'I've no idea,' I said rather brusquely.

'He asked if I'd have a drink with him in the lunch hour tomorrow.'

This jolted me. 'And what did you say?'

'I said, "No thank you," and hurried off. He didn't try to follow, but I felt very upset. I know it sounds stupid but when I stopped at the Underground to get a ticket my legs were shaking.'

I put my arms round her. 'Don't think anything more about it, darling. He probably had to get it out of his system and now that you've given him the brush-off he won't bother you any more.'

'I hope he doesn't,' she said. 'There's nothing wrong with him. To look at, I mean. But there's something about him that frightens me. Josie says I'm an idiot to worry about it. She says he'll soon get tired.'

'I'm sure she's right.'

'But I think even Josie and Pat are a bit puzzled by it. There are so many young and pretty girls he could choose from but he doesn't seem interested in any of them. I'm twice his age and not a beauty by any stretch of the imagination.'

I told her my imagination didn't need to stretch an inch to find her beautiful.

She nestled against me. 'You're different,' she said, and she added softly, 'Thank God.'

The following evening I asked whether the young fellow had troubled her. She said she hadn't seen him. But the next day, Friday, she told me she had seen a medical certificate for Wilson on the Personnel Manager's desk. He was suffering from gastric enteritis but expected to return to work early next week.

'No doubt caused by frustrated calf-love,' I said, trying to make a joke of it.

Kay said, 'I hope not,' and I was surprised to see that she had taken my remark seriously. 'I'd hate to be the cause of anyone's – pain,' she said.

'He's probably eaten too many green apples,' I said, but this time, although I meant it to sound reassuring, I had the first intimation, or perhaps it was an intuition, that I should take the Wilson business more seriously.

I suppose it was about two weeks later when we were walking home from the cinema that I asked, 'How's the Wilson boy these days?'

We had been walking slowly side by side, enjoying the mild evening, but she quickened her step. 'He's all right.'

'Not giving any trouble?'

'Not here,' she said. 'Wait till we get home.'

Ten minutes later, as she was making coffee, she said, 'It seems to be getting worse.'

'How do you mean?'

'He hangs round the main entrance to see me arrive in the morning, he comes into our room on the most feeble pretexts and he hangs around in the evening to say "Goodnight".'

'He hasn't asked you out for a drink again?'

'No. But I think he might have tonight only I had Pat with me and I sensed he was disappointed. He gave her a sort of look.'

'What sort of look?'

'I can't describe it. But she noticed it too. She said it made her feel like a gooseberry.'

She passed a mug of coffee. 'He makes me nervous,' she said. 'I get a terrible feeling of panic inside me when I see him. And then I tell myself he can't help what he's doing. I ought to feel sorry for him.'

I snorted into my coffee. 'Don't waste your emotions on him. He isn't worth it.'

'But if he's . . . I mean . . . People do get fixations, don't they?'

I don't know why this question, and the use of the word 'fixation' should have made me suddenly very annoyed, but it did. 'Is that what you think this is?' I asked. 'A fixation?'

She lowered her eyes. 'Josie said she read a letter in a woman's magazine some time ago about a similar sort of situation and the reply was that young men sometimes get fixations on older women. The thing is for the woman to give absolutely no encouragement. Eventually it fades or he gets fixated elsewhere.'

'You don't encourage him?'

She lifted her eyes, and to my dismay I saw they were filled with tears. 'Of course I don't,' she said. 'What sort of a woman do you think I am?'

Rather unhappily we went to bed. That night our love-making lacked something, not in technique (to use the textbook word) but in mental harmony. Afterwards we lay silent. Then, out of the darkness Kay said, 'I wonder if he thinks about me all the time or just when he's at work.'

I didn't reply but her words stabbed me with an arrow of anxiety. Kay soon went to sleep but dawn was creeping into the eastern sky before I drifted into a shallow loss of wakefulness.

It was on the following night that the telephone calls started. Kay answered, and I turned down the sound of the television.

'It is,' she said.

'Yes,' she said.

'What do you want?' she asked.

'Certainly not,' she said.

She hung up the receiver without saying goodbye.

'Not him,' I said incredulously.

'He must be mad,' she said. 'Ringing me here. He must know you'll be at home.'

'What did he want?'

'I asked him.'

'I heard you. What did he say?'

Kay flushed. 'He said, "You know what I want. Will you come out with me?" '

'Well, your reply should have given him the message. You sounded very firm.'

'I need a drink,' she said.

I got her a drink without question but it worried me that she should be so upset by the call that her first thought was for alcohol to steady her nerves.

The telephone rang again the next evening and I answered.

The caller rang off.

He rang again an hour later. Again I answered. Again he rang off.

The third time he rang Kay answered and I stood beside her.

'Yes,' she said.

'It's me,' said a man's voice.

'What do you want?' she asked, and I took the phone from her.

'Please come out with me. Just for a drink. I need to talk to you.'

'Look here,' I said. 'If you don't stop troubling my wife I shall call the police.'

He rang off when I reached the word 'wife'.

Kay gave me an agonised look. 'We can't go on like this,' she said. 'Every time the phone goes my heart seems to lurch.'

I thought for a few moments. 'Tomorrow I'll come with you to the store,' I said, 'and if he's there I shall tell him in no uncertain terms what I shall do if he persists in his conduct.'

I don't know what reaction I expected from Kay. A look of gratitude perhaps. I didn't expect her to groan, 'Oh no!'

'Why not?'

'I'm sure he can't help himself. It's something out of his control.'

'But not out of my bloody control,' I replied.

That night we didn't make love.

Kay's store is in Oxford Street. At nine in the morning the street is a rush of workers scurrying from buses and trains, most of them looking as though they are late for an urgent, but somewhat unpleasant, appointment. At least, the older ones look like this; the younger ones are more casual. They wander and seem to get in the way of the dedicated clockers-in.

'That's him,' whispered Kay.

She was gazing at a tall, thin youth. His pale face was fringed with dark hair which fell in curls to his shoulders. He had what used to be called 'poetic good looks' and I felt a twinge of jealousy.

'Please don't be unkind to him,' said Kay.

She had tried to dissuade me from coming along, and this final plea was very annoying. Why shouldn't I be unkind to him? He had been unkind to us.

'You go along,' I said. 'I'll see you tonight.' Later I realised that this was the first time we had ever parted without a kiss.

I made straight for the young man and said, 'Your name is Denis Wilson?'

He looked startled. 'That's right.'

'And you have been pestering my wife? Asking her to go out with you?'

'I only want to talk with her,' he said.

'She doesn't want to talk with you.'

He flinched. 'I'm sorry,' he said.

'I'm sorry too. This thing is becoming a nuisance to both of us. My wife and me.'

'I'm sorry,' he repeated.

'So you've already said. It's got to stop. If you bother her any more, hang around for her, speak to her or ring us up, I shall report this to your manager and to the police. Is that clear?'

He nodded, and I felt a sense of relief. All he needed was a straight talking to.

'I have your promise that you won't cause any more trouble?' I asked.

'What do you mean? Trouble?'

He looked at me with soft brown eyes.

'You know exactly what I mean.'

He gave a sigh. 'I love Kay,' he said.

What I did was inexcusable, but I don't regret it. I grabbed his shirt collar intending to shake him as one might shake a naughty pup, but as I tugged the collar his tie, a scarlet bow tie, came away in my hand. I gazed at it feeling somehow off-balance.

'If you like it, you can keep it,' he said, and before I could give him back the tie he turned and ran into the building.

Kay was standing on the steps. Our eyes met, and then she followed him inside.

That evening she said she had felt humiliated when she saw me grab at his collar. I asked whether he had been waiting for her when she left, and she said, 'No.'

'In that case,' I said, 'your humiliation was worth it. He's obviously seen the error of his ways.'

A few minutes later the telephone rang. I picked it up. 'Yes?'

'This is Denis,' said a voice.

'I warned you this morning to stop this nonsense.'

'May I speak to Kay? Just for a moment?'

'You may not,' I said and slammed down the phone. Turning to Kay I said, 'He's asking for it.'

She was apprehensive. 'What are you going to do?'

'There's no point in making threats if one isn't prepared to carry them out.'

'No. Please, no!'

'I'm sorry, Kay. I've had enough. I'm involved in this too.'

'Please, please!'

There is no point in relating word by word, phrase by phrase, how I slowly weakened. Nor how our love-making reached a new height that night. It is sufficient to say that at this stage I did nothing more than fix an appointment to see Freddie. I didn't tell Kay.

As ever, Freddie was the cheery, solicitous friend. 'What can I do for you, old chap?' he asked. 'By the look on your face it's not advice on a fortune you've inherited.'

He listened patiently to my account of the absurd infatuation of Denis Wilson for Kay. And yet it wasn't a resigned patience. Once or twice (it might have been my imagination) I thought he was on the verge of smiling. When I had finished he said, 'All this is a great compliment to Kay, and indirectly a compliment to you for choosing Kay.' He seemed to be speaking with perfect seriousness. 'I can understand that you might be aggravated,' he said, and then qualified this statement by adding, 'In a way, I can see it.'

'Wouldn't you be annoyed, Freddie?'

He picked up his pen and began to peck at the blotting pad on his desk. 'Perhaps I should,' he said. 'But you know Cynthia.'

I did know his wife but the implication escaped me.

'How do you mean?'

'Obviously Kay and Cynthia aren't the same. We're all different. But Cynthia would have frozen him off within ten seconds.'

'Kay finds it difficult to be – cold.'

'I know. I appreciate that. And I'm not saying that she's actively encouraging him . . .'

'I should hope not!'

'But a woman of Kay's years . . . How old is she?'

'Forty-two.'

'Women of forty-two usually know how to handle these situations.'

'Kay doesn't,' I said doggedly. 'And I want it to stop. How do I go about it?'

Freddie frowned slightly. 'My advice is – do nothing. You've already done enough. Technically you committed an assault on him. Tell Kay not to speak to him if he speaks to her, and if she's always with another woman he's bound to give up in the end. No man can persist against endless snubs.'

'Wilson can. What about reporting it to the police?'

He shook his head. 'What can they do? He isn't guilty of threatening behaviour. There's been no breach of the peace. The police will dismiss it as a domestic matter.'

'I'm sorry, Freddie. I want some action. What about suing him for invasion of privacy?'

He continued to prod the blotting pad with his pen. 'Not in this country, old chap,' he said. 'It might be different in the States, but the courts over here don't recognise what you call "invasion of privacy".'

'Can't you do anything?' I asked.

He put down the pen and looked me straight in the eyes. 'The fellow is obviously a bit of a pest but I wouldn't be optimistic about obtaining an injunction to restrain him from molesting Kay. And that's your only legal remedy. Look at the facts. He has hung around for her at her place of employment – but it is his place of employment too. He has telephoned your flat a few times, and these are admittedly annoyances. But would they amount to a nuisance in a court of law. I doubt it. This isn't a case of obscene calls. He's been quite well-mannered and polite, as I understand it. Apart from anything else an action on the grounds of nuisance – which I don't think this is – happens to be a lengthy and expensive process.'

'In other words, you don't want to act for me,' I said huffily.

To Freddie's credit he didn't greet this remark with the chill it deserved. He said, 'You can always count on me, old chap, but you said something earlier about not making threats unless you were prepared to carry them out. I feel the same. I could easily write to this man and say that my client has instructed me with regard to the unwelcome attention being paid to my client's wife, and unless these attentions cease we shall reluctantly be compelled to institute proceedings against him. I can say that, but I wouldn't want to carry it through. I don't think you've got a case. However, if you're not satisfied with my opinion, I could take counsel's opinion.'

I felt as though I was banging my head against a brick wall. I knew and respected Freddie well enough to realise that he was giving good advice.

'Try to treat the whole thing as a joke,' he said, 'even if it's a joke in rather bad taste.'

I stood up. 'I doubt if I can do that. I'm a bit old-fashioned. But thanks for the advice, Freddie.'

'Now don't go doing anything silly, will you? And for God's sake don't grab hold of him again. If you can treat it as a joke you'll find that it's become a joke. And I'll bet, six months from now, you'll have forgotten his name.'

Looking back, I can see that the sensible course would have been for Kay to leave the store and find a job elsewhere. But she liked the work and I felt that for her to resign would be a sort of defeat. Too often in life the innocent suffer through the actions of irrational and selfish people. Why should Kay be another victim?

I decided to take advantage of the Personnel Department summer party to approach Kay's boss about Wilson. These parties, sociable without being exciting, were normally held in the private bar of a pub to the rear of the store. The formula was the same this year. Members of the staff were each allowed to bring one guest. I was Kay's guest.

Her boss was an extrovert who answered to the name of 'Mr Forbes'. He was in his early fifties and with erect bearing and trim moustache he looked like a retired army officer.

When Kay was busy elsewhere I went across to him.

'Hello there,' he said. 'No spot prizes today!'

This was a reference to a prize Kay and I had won during a waltz at the Christmas dance.

'I wonder if I could speak to you for a few moments, Mr Forbes. Off the record, as it were.'

His smile vanished and he assumed the air of a man accustomed to being entrusted with important confidences. 'Something to do with Kay?' he asked.

'Yes.'

'Happy here, isn't she? We're all very fond of Kay.' He was annulling in advance any complaint that she was unhappy through neglect.

'Oh yes. She enjoys her work and likes her colleagues in Personnel. But there is a fly in the ointment.'

He listened to the story of Wilson. At first his forehead was furrowed with concern but gradually this expression changed to one of slight hostility.

'Sounds like a storm in a teacup,' he said when I had finished. 'Wilson's a very good man. Excellent progress reports.'

'I was hoping you might have a word with him.'

He shook his head. 'Let's be men of the world,' he said, and paused.

I had no objection to being a man of the world. If I am not a man of this world, of what world am I a man? I said I didn't understand what he was driving at.

'A young lad finds your wife attractive. Nothing criminal in that. Flattering, if anything. He asks her out for a drink. Nothing criminal in that either.' He lowered his voice. 'There are hundreds of friendships made in office hours. You know that. I know that. Nothing harmful. Just a couple of people who get along well having a drink or a meal together in the lunch hour. They may be married to other parties, but what's the harm? Anyway, where's the opportunity, even if harm crossed their minds?'

'That isn't the point.'

Forbes straightened his shoulders and looked very military. 'This is not a departmental problem,' he said. 'I'm sure Kay, or one of her friends, is capable of treading on Wilson's toes if he goes beyond the bounds. And, as I say, he has an excellent record here. The sort of man we don't want to lose.'

He meant, 'I don't give a damn how many married women Wilson seduces so long as his work is first-class.'

'So you won't do anything about it,' I asked.

He made an impatient gesture with his hand. 'It's nothing to do with me. We're not living in the reign of Queen Victoria now, you know.'

That was the end of the conversation. Later, Kay said, 'What were you and Mr Forbes talking about?'

I knew the truth would upset her and, feeling a curious mixture of cowardice and kindness, I told her we were discussing London's transport problems.

'How dull,' she commented and mercifully the subject was dropped.

I doubt if Forbes said anything to Wilson, or to Kay, but from that night things began to improve. When I asked Kay if she had been bothered by Wilson she would say, 'I didn't see him at all today,' or 'He was around when I left but I'm not sure whether he saw me.'

There was a change in her which was probably due to the ending of a period of tension. She had lost some weight and this made her look younger. Her eyes regained their sparkle and her skin looked softer. But although she seemed happy, the memory of the ridiculous affair lingered in my mind and was reinforced by practically everything I saw or read.

Articles in newspapers and magazines which presumably I had subconsciously avoided reading after my eyes had skated across the heading seemed preoccupied with 'the permissive society'. One couldn't turn a page without finding some reference to adultery, pregnant schoolgirls or 'the Pill'. I began to read the articles I had formerly ignored and when I was travelling I found myself examining posters on Underground platforms and escalators. Why hadn't I noticed before that everywhere there were invitations to the vacant-minded passer-by to think about sex. Had I been travelling in blinkers for the last decade?

And I began noticing the name 'Wilson'. It was on shop fronts, in references to the Labour leader, and most frequently of all in my local library. Whenever I glanced through the rack of recently returned books there seemed to be a work by one of the Wilson trinity – Angus, Colin and Edmund.

Sex and Wilson were inescapable. I began to wonder for the first time since my mother's death whether I was normal. I disliked what I saw and yet was strangely compelled to contemplate it. I was out of step with the times, but was I also out of step with normal behaviour? From what I read nobody seemed to care much if his wife committed adultery. Parties were even arranged where wives could be swapped like used postage stamps. It was commonplace for wives to conduct affairs under their husband's noses and with their husband's consent. This was inevitably referred to as 'civilised behaviour'.

And then I read a passage in a book which gave me comfort. It is from Aldous Huxley's *Brave New World Revisited*.

The really hopeless victims of mental illness are to be found among those who appear to be most normal . . . They are normal not in what may be called the absolute sense of the word; they are normal only in relation to a profoundly abnormal society. Their perfect adjustment to that society is a measure of their mental sickness.

I didn't fit in with modern society but this wasn't evidence of abnormality on my part. The abnormal ones were those who swapped
wives because it was fashionable to swap wives, and who regarded the
Pill as mankind's salvation. They were those who advocated promiscuity
as a norm and found it necessary to sell cars, chocolate and even kitchen
utensils by blatantly sexual advertisements. They were men like Forbes
who said, 'What's the harm?' and like Wilson who with fantastic
impudence could say 'I love Kay' to Kay's husband. These were the
new sick born of the permissive society. Thank God I was normal.

And then there occurred the incident of the carnations.

Many months before, we had booked to go on a cruise in August. It
was to be my first holiday afloat since my mother's death and the boat,
a luxury liner, was scheduled to make calls at Lisbon, Madeira, the
Canaries and Casablanca. A week before sailing we decided to catch an
early morning train on Saturday and go for a tramp on the Sussex
downs. Unfortunately when we woke it was raining heavily and the
forecast was for continuing rain. Even so, we almost went, but Kay
eventually decided the issue by saying, 'What if we catch colds? It
would ruin the start of the holiday.'

So we stayed in the flat. If we hadn't been at home we shouldn't
have heard the bell ring during the morning and answered it to find
a messenger boy on the doorstep with a dozen deep red carnations.

'Who on earth would send me these?' asked Kay when the boy had
gone.

I said it must be a mistake.

'It can't be,' she replied. 'It's my name and address. And here's a
card.' Her eyes were shining and I wished I had sent the flowers.

She read the card. 'Oh,' she said.

I took it from her.

TO KAY, WITH DEEPEST RESPECT AND ADMIRATION — DENIS

'The bastard,' I said.

'Aren't they lovely?'

I wondered for a split second if she had gone insane and then I took
the sheaf of carnations from her and hurried outside to the dustbin.

She ran after me calling, 'Have you gone mad?'

'I thought you had gone mad,' I said.

'What do you think you're doing,' she asked, retrieving the carnations
from the dustbin. 'These are *flowers*!'

Dear Kay. She is so sensitive and sympathetic towards flowers. To her they are as much creatures as animals are. What I had done was almost equivalent to putting a child in the dustbin.

'I'll put them in water,' she said, and I followed her back into the flat.

'I'd prefer not to be reminded of their provenance,' I said. 'If you must keep them, would you mind keeping them in the spare room?'

'Why? They're lovely to look at.'

'They have come from a young fool would who, if he could, wreck our marriage. It's not asking too much to have them kept out of sight.'

She looked at me in a way I shall never forget. It is said that one remembers only the pleasant things in life and forgets all else. I can only remark that this may be true for the majority but it is not true for me. Kay's disdainfully cold look was photographed on my memory. 'Very well,' she said. 'We'll keep them in the spare room.'

'You do understand?' I asked.

'I understand,' she said. 'Perfectly,' she added.

And she put them in a cut-glass vase in the spare room. I didn't know whether to be angry at her disregard for my feelings or to find her love of flowers so endearing as to erase my annoyance.

The carnations remained in the spare room until we sailed.

On boarding at Southampton we were shown to our cabin. It was compactly designed with separate berths covered in green and blue tartan overlays and with a wide dressing table between the bed-heads. Piped music drifted into the cabin and we had a choice of different radio channels so that, if we wished, we could listen to non-stop classical music instead of the pop which was playing on our arrival. The cabin had its own small bathroom. Kay peeped out of the porthole by her berth and said, 'This is going to be fun.'

After unpacking some luggage we went up to the restaurant to obtain a table number from the manager. Then we went aft to enjoy the sunshine on the quarter deck. The first meal was tea which could be taken in one of the lounges. As we sipped from our cups we watched the shore of the Isle of Wight slide slowly past.

I am a fairly good sailor but on my advice Kay had been inoculated against sea-sickness and although by dinner time there was a moderately heavy swell in the Channel we went to the restaurant, happy and hungry.

It is said that one never realises when one *is* happy only that one *was* happy. Happiness is in the wake. As we entered the restaurant I wasn't conscious of being happy (although at that moment I was happy) but the moment we sat down I was acutely aware of being suddenly unhappy. Directly across the aisle and gazing at a menu was Wilson.

I said, 'Good God,' and the words emerged aloud although I had meant to keep them under my breath.

'What's the matter?' asked Kay.

'Look!'

She had been slightly flushed but the blood faded from her cheeks. 'I can't believe it,' she said.

At that moment he looked up from the menu, saw us staring aghast at him and gave a timorous half smile.

'Did you know he would be on board,' I asked in a lowered voice.

'No. How could I?'

'He must have known you'd be on board.'

'Well, lots of people at the office knew about this trip. He could easily have heard about it.'

I said I was going to get our table changed.

'Please don't make a fuss,' she said. Kay dislikes fuss and scenes. 'Please!' she begged.

I looked around. Every table was full. It was unlikely that we could change now.

'Let's see what delicacies they have for us,' she said, trying to sound bright. 'I'm famished.'

My appetite had gone. I was thinking, 'Twelve days . . . Twelve days on the same ship with him!'

This was only the beginning. We should see him in the bars, as we move around the decks, as we lay sunbathing, as we ate, as we danced, as we debouched at each port of call; we were all captives in the same prison and my only escape was in the cell of our cabin.

I was glad Kay wanted to turn in early. I could hear her breathing in sleep on the far side of the cabin as a succession of furious thoughts tumbled through my mind. If Wilson had walked in through the cabin door I am certain I should have strangled him with my bare hands.

If he spoke to us, even to say 'Good morning', I should have to restrain myself. And there were twelve days of this accumulating tension.

Eventually my immediate fury burned itself out and I resolved to exercise iron self-control and to ignore the fellow if he spoke to us. If you discipline yourself to ignore an unpleasant fact of life it can sometimes happen that, except when your nose is rubbed in it, you can succeed in ignoring it.

At first it wasn't quite as bad as I expected; we managed to eat at different times from him and although we saw him about the ship he made no attempt to speak to us.

'Why the devil doesn't he get a girl,' I said. 'There are enough around for a thousand and one shipboard romances.'

'I feel rather sorry for him,' said Kay. 'He looks awfully lonely.' She adjusted her sun-glasses and lay back on a reclining chair. 'Isn't this wonderful,' she said. 'I'm going to get as brown as a berry.'

In the distance I could see Wilson leaning forlornly on the rail gazing out at a blue expanse of water and sky.

At Lisbon we didn't join an organised shore excursion but took a taxi to the top of Parque Eduardo VII and then strolled down past the little bird sanctuary with its splendid peacocks towards the main part of town. The day was warm without being too hot and we wandered along pavements that were diapered in black and white stones observing the lottery ticket sellers, the plethora of policemen, country-women with panniers on their heads, the numerous blind, the numerous shoe-shiners, the well-stocked shops; and thus idling we reached the Praco Rossio Don Pedro IV in time for lunch. In the afternoon we went to look at the castle district with its warren of narrow streets and ancient buildings. It was a delightful day and I hardly thought about Wilson whom we had seen earlier departing, glum-faced, on a coach tour for Estoril via Quelez and Sintra.

Kay and I are used to walking long distances without tiring and although we must have covered more than a dozen miles we walked all the way back from the castle district to the dock where our ship was berthed passing through fish and fruit markets on the way. Kay hugged my arm. 'Not a tourist in sight,' she said. 'We really are away from it all.'

The ship pulled out while we were having dinner and we watched the Salazar Bridge and the illuminated statue of Christ glide past as we sampled *espalada*, a fish caught off the Portuguese coast. There was no sign of Wilson. Perhaps he had got lost at Estoril, Quelez or Sintra. I hoped so.

'There's a dance tonight,' said Kay. 'Let's go, or are you too tired?'

A Spanish proverb has it that a gentleman is never tired and I quoted it to her.

'Good,' she said. 'I'll wear my long red dress.'

But, a couple of hours later, we were no sooner on the dance floor than I saw Wilson standing on his own at the bar. His face matched the colour of Kay's dress and he was wearing an orange kipper tie on a bilious yellow shirt. His suit was bright emerald green and he looked like a garish advertisement for poster paints.

'Look who's here,' said Kay, fashioning her body to the rhythm of a quickstep. 'Hasn't his face caught the sun?'

'I've seen him. A walking Joseph's coat of many colours.'

We danced, and we sat out, and we danced again, and then we were in a waltz with spotlights dappling the dancers. Wilson had disappeared. Perhaps he'd gone to bed.

'Excuse me,' said a voice. I felt a tap on my shoulder.

The dance was a gentlemen's excuse-me. I turned to see who had requested the pleasure of taking my place and before I could protest (or 'make a scene' as Kay would say) Wilson had whisked her into the splashes of moving light.

My first reaction was to re-excuse him, but I decided to ignore his unwanted intervention. I had planned to ignore him, and ignore him I would.

The dance seemed to last a long time. When Kay rejoined me she looked tense and I wondered what had upset her.

'Let me sit down,' she said. 'My feet are ruined. I don't think he's ever danced a waltz in his life.'

Shortly after this we left the dance, and while we were undressing in the cabin I asked what Wilson had talked about.

'He kept apologising for his steps. He needed to.' She gave a brief smile. 'He said, "They call me the octopus of the Buying Department – I've got four times the usual number of feet." ' She gazed down at her own small and pretty feet. 'They don't look too bruised and battered, do they?'

I moved towards her but she turned away. 'I'm dog-tired, darling. And we've been on our feet all day.'

I shrugged. 'All right . . . What else did you talk about?'

She scrambled into her bed. 'Nothing really.'

'He just kept saying that he was an octopus?'

'I'm too tired to remember,' she said and she switched off the bed-head light.

I suppose a normal man by the standards of the permissive society would have dropped the subject, or even said, 'You were slow, dear. Why didn't you go to his cabin?' but I am not normal by the standards of a sick society.

I got into my bunk and persisted with the question. 'He must have done more than apologise for bad dancing. You were a full three minutes together.'

'Three minutes!'

'What do you mean,' I asked, 'saying "three minutes" like that?'

She didn't reply.

'Kay. What did he say to you?'

'Please. I'm dreadfully tired.'

I switched off my light. The cabin was in darkness.

'Kay?'

'What?'

'Answer my question.'

She sighed loudly. 'How do you expect me to remember anything when you were sitting glowering at us?'

'I wasn't glowering. I was ignoring the whole thing.'

She gave a laugh.

'What's so funny?' I asked.

She gave no answer.

'I was watching,' I said. 'Not glowering. And he was talking a lot. What did he say?'

'What does it matter?'

'It matters to me.'

'You just want an excuse to make a scene with him.'

'Look, Kay, I swear I won't make a scene. I shall ignore the whole thing, but I do want to know what he said.'

She gave another sigh. 'We talked about Madeira. He asked what plans I had for the day ashore.'

'What did you say?'

'I said I left the planning to you.'

'What did he say to that?'

'Oh, please, can't we stop this? I really am whacked out.'

'What did he say, Kay?'

'I don't remember.'

'Of course you do. What did he say?'

'It was a joke.'

'Tell me the joke, Kay.'

'It was just a joke. He asked me to ditch you.'

'He asked you to ditch me?'

'Can I go to sleep – please?'

'What did you say? Did you say, "Well, I don't like making scenes so you can take me out if you like." '

Suddenly she was furious. Her voice came across the cabin like a whiplash. 'Yes, that's what I said. And I told him I'd do my best to ditch you. Now are you satisfied? Can I go to sleep?'

It was my turn to make no reply.

Within seconds she was snoring.

As I lay miserably awake in the darkened cabin I realised that Kay would not have said this, and she was only pretending to have said it to stop my incessant questions. I didn't hold her snappish reply against her, but I did hold Wilson responsible for an argument between man and wife, and I couldn't forgive the suggestion he had made to her. No wonder she had looked tense and distressed after dancing with him.

What else would happen in the days ahead? It was plain that Wilson would never give up his obsessive quest for Kay and I was beginning to wonder if his obsession might not, in the end, win the day. How does one fight a man who is utterly preoccupied with obtaining a woman's affections? How do you deal with a man whose *idée fixe* is far beyond reason, persuasion, threats of bodily violence or (provided he doesn't overstep certain bounds) the reach of the law?

Wilson would pursue his objective ruthlessly, never doing enough to condemn him in a legal tribunal, but he would erode my marriage by gifts of flowers, unstinted devotion and indelicate suggestions. Kay would gradually be attracted to him against her will and she would begin to regard me, and not him, as the enemy. Kay is gentle; Kay is kind. She can't even refuse a street flag-seller. Her life has been sheltered and she doesn't know how to cope with the harsher realities. How long would she be able to stand Wilson's pernicious pressures? One day a situation would arise when her fidelity would be tested beyond the limit. It might happen at her office. Pat and Josie would be out at lunch and Wilson would walk in. He would lock the door. Only a typewriter on a desk would be between them. Silently he would push the typewriter aside, vault the desk, and she would succumb to his overwhelming desires.

It is said by some philosophers that to understand a problem is also to know its solution. I understood the problem and the solution was obvious.

On the following day Kay seemed very subdued and all my efforts to cheer her failed.

There is no point in charting the various twists and turns of my mind on that unhappy day; it is sufficient to say that I wrote a note in a fair imitation of Kay's hand and slipped it under Wilson's cabin door, having first obtained the cabin number from the ship's telephone operator.

The note said: 'Meet me at 1.30 a.m. tomorrow morning at Station 5 on the Boat Deck. Urgent. Kay.'

She was asleep when I slid, fully dressed, off my bed and stole out of the cabin. The long narrow corridor was empty. I hurried to the elevator and ascended to the Boat Deck. As I stepped out, I looked around. Nobody in sight. I went to the door which opened onto the deck. It swung open silently. A cool salt breeze was blowing and the sky was milky with millions of stars. I walked to Station 5. I could see Wilson's outline. He was leaning on the rail and characteristically gazing out across the moon-washed sea.

I should never have a better opportunity. I crept up behind him. He didn't move. I bent down, pushed both arms between his thighs and bundled him over the rail. He let out a piercing, blood-curdling scream as he fell.

I heard the splash and was about to run away when I noticed a sandal on the deck. Somehow, one of his sandals had fallen off. It is very odd but that lone sandal looked more human than Wilson. I picked it up and tossed it over the side, but I knew I should always remember its shape and its feel.

Then I scampered back to the elevator, descended to our deck, ran along the empty corridor, tip-toed into our cabin, undressed and climbed into bed. The sheets were still warm. A moment later the ship's siren blew a long powerful blast.

I could feel a faint vibration running through the panels of the cabin. Was the ship stopping?

Kay woke and called my name. I gave a sleepy grunt.

'The siren's just gone,' she said. 'It woke me up. What do you think is happening?'

'Didn't hear it,' I mumbled.

A few minutes later she kneeled on her bunk, drew the curtain aside and peered out of the porthole. 'We've stopped,' she said.

'Stopped?'

'Come and look.'

She was right. The water around us was still. The ship might have been moored to a quay.

For half an hour we conjectured why the ship should have stopped in mid-ocean; then the engines started and we were on our way.

When the steward woke us with early morning tea I asked, 'Why did we stop in the night?'

He pulled a grim face. 'Man overboard, sir.'

'Good God. Was he saved?'

'They got a boat out to him with the ship's surgeon on board but he failed to respond to artificial respiration.'

'How did he fall?' I asked.

'No idea, sir.'

'Who saw him?'

'Someone on watch heard a scream, I think, sir. He looked over and saw what appeared to be a person in the water.' The steward edged towards the door. 'Very interesting manoeuvre the first officer made. Slowed the engines and did what we call a "Williamson Turn". Brings the ship back on a reciprocal course.' He left before I could ask more questions.

The day in Madeira was in contrast to the carefree day in Lisbon. Kay seemed unhappy and she didn't care for Funchal. She begged me to go sight-seeing without her; but I had to pretend Wilson was still alive and I said jocularly, 'Can't leave you alone with that young wolf around.'

She took a couple of aspirins and lay down on her bed. After a while she fell asleep and I went off to the coffee bar. I wanted to be on my own. Nobody could have seen me bundle Wilson overboard but they might find the note signed 'Kay'. But even if it was traced to us a hand-writing expert would confirm it wasn't in Kay's writing. There was nothing to fear. Wilson's death could not be attributed to me.

I felt no guilt or remorse. I had been provoked beyond endurance by a young man obsessively interested in my wife. I had acted as any normal man would. Only a permissive society could suggest that my action had been abnormal. Strangely, the single sandal worried me for a while. I knew Oedipus was a name meaning 'swollen foot' and I had an idea that this damned myth was haunting me. Did the oracle say that Oedipus would enter Thebes wearing one sandal? Luckily, the ship's library had a book on mythology and I soon realised I had been con-fusing Oedipus with Jason. It was Jason who lost a sandal in a muddy river and thereby began the fulfilment of an oracle.

To hell with Wilson; I had regained peace of mind.

If Kay hadn't been feeling so seedy I would have turned cartwheels all over the deck.

When she learned that Wilson had been the 'man overboard' she cried. I could understand her reaction. After all, she is a very sensitive woman and he was an office colleague.

Back in England her health did not improve. She went to a doctor who told her she had a mild depression and gave her drugs. The depres-sion persisted. Physically she melted away and became an undersized weakling again.

I was at my wits' end wondering how to help her when, after a fit of crying, she let slip the cause of her depression. She had convinced herself that Wilson had committed suicide.

'What if he did,' I asked. 'That's not your fault.'

'But it is,' she cried. 'That night at the dance when he asked me to ditch you, I steeled myself and told him I wouldn't look at him if he was the last man on earth.'

I was amazed. 'That isn't what you told me.'

'I only said what I did because I was fed up with all your questions. I wanted to be left alone. I knew if I told you the truth you'd want to make love to me, and I couldn't bear the thought of being touched. Can't you understand?'

I shook my head. 'Not really . . . And you didn't make him commit suicide.'

She looked at me with tear-filled eyes. 'I finished by telling him he could jump overboard for all I cared!'

Kay's health is slowly improving. I couldn't let her suffer for my actions and so I told her the truth. When the shock wore off she said we couldn't live the rest of our lives together with this secret between us. But if I gave myself up and took my punishment, she would wait for me, and one day we would start afresh.

Freddie has briefed counsel and has impressed on me that if we can make out that I was suffering from a temporary abnormality of mind the sentenc should be less and the reunion with Kay will be speedier.

I can see the force of his argument, but it goes against the grain that I, a man who has given the extreme proof of his normality, should have to parade himself to the world as a specimen of abnormality.

Wilson was the one with an abnormal fixation, not me.

John Garforth

A Quite Conventional Death

It was ten minutes to midnight when the girl's body plunged from the hotel window and smashed on to the roof of a new Mini Cooper. The street had been deserted, but almost at once people came running, doors opened and drivers stopped to form a crowd. They stared in silence at the broken mess of blood and crumpled flesh until someone thought of calling the police.

Charles Inman was sitting in his room on the eighth floor considering the problem of Macbeth with a glass of vintage port beside him. He thought he had heard a scream, but more likely it had been a cry in his own mind: 'Macbeth does murder sleep!' It was the closed-room problem, Charles Inman felt, which confronted Macbeth when he needed to kill Duncan. And instead of locks it had been bodyguards.

There seemed to be a lot of noise coming from the street, but that was probably the Porter drunkenly refusing to admit Macduff and Lennox. There was always so much coming and going after a murder. Charles Inman refilled his glass and wondered how Macbeth had thought he could get away with it. Any competent policeman would have pinned the murder on Macbeth within two minutes.

His concentration was disrupted by a hammering on the door. 'Knock, knock, knock,' he quoted fiercely. 'Who's there, i' the name of Beelzebub?' But he opened the door and scowled with Jacobean intensity at the hotel manager.

'I'm sorry, sir, but do you own a blue Mini Cooper?'

'Eh? Yes, of course I do. But I'm busy at the moment planning the perfect murder.' He turned away in search of the bottle of port. 'I suppose Macbeth was trying to commit an English murder; or do you think of him more as an American-style gangster?'

The manager blinked in surprise. 'I don't know, Mr Inman. I only came to tell you that a girl has just demolished the bonnet of your car. She jumped out of the window of the next room.'

Charles Inman hurried across the room and pulled back the curtains. 'My car?' he called in dismay. He peered down at the throng. 'What are they staring at? Haven't they seen a wrecked car before?'

Detective-Inspector Lawrence arrived at fifteen minutes past midnight. The corpse had been photographed, a chalk line indicated where she had bounced from the blue Mini Cooper, and an ambulance was waiting to take her away. The inspector remained in his car for a moment while he lit a cigar, then he wound down the window.

'Constable!' he rasped. 'Are all these people witnesses?'

While the constable tried to shoo away the sightseers Inspector Lawrence ambled across to the body. He crouched beside it, pulled back the sheet and glanced at the girl's face.

'She fell head first,' explained the constable. 'From the eighth floor.'

'Unh.' Lawrence wiped his hand clean on the edge of the sheet. 'Suicide?' He looked up at the black silhouette of the building. There was an open window high above them. 'Why should such a beautiful girl want to kill herself like this?'

'I don't know, sir,' said the constable. He paused while the ambulance drove away with the body and then visibly relaxed. 'She was a journalist up from London to cover the crime writers' convention. Name of Jennie Webster.' He held out the girl's crocodile-skin handbag, filled with the usual lipsticks, compact, keys, snapshots, and a reporter's notebook. 'She was staying in room 817, but we haven't been in there yet. Sergeant Green said to touch nothing until you arrived.'

'All right, so now I've arrived,' Lawrence said in the gravel voice that had terrified criminals and constables for the past twenty years. He was a large, overweight man with eyes that glowed threateningly behind the flabby mask of his face. 'Let's take a look at the girl's room. If it's suicide there might be a letter.'

He strode through the swing doors of the Esplanade Hotel and into the lift. 'Eighth floor,' he growled at the hotel manager, who was scurrying over to join them.

'Good evening, Inspector. My name is Weston. I'm the manager, and I don't need to tell you—'

'No, you don't.' He puffed irritably at his cigar. 'Crime writers' convention, eh? What the hell does that mean?'

'They seem to be meeting at the Spa Pavilion throughout the weekend, having dinners and lectures and choosing a famous president, that sort of thing. You know what conventions are like. There are novelists all over the town, and six of them are staying at this hotel.' The manager spoke too quickly and he ducked his head about, as if he expected to find a novelist lurking behind him taking notes. 'I didn't know there'd be trouble when I accepted their bookings.'

A uniformed policeman was standing guard outside Jennie Webster's room. He had obviously heard the clatter of the lift gates and he was standing rigidly to attention.

'Are you here for ceremonial purposes, constable?' snapped the Inspector. He jabbed his cigar at the door. 'Come along, man, let me in.'

'It's locked, sir,' said the policeman. But he stepped aside. 'I suppose the girl must have locked it from the inside when she decided to jump.' He smiled helpfully. 'Perhaps the manager has a pass key?'

Inspector Lawrence held up an imperious hand to prevent Mr Weston from unlocking the door. Then he fished about in the dead girl's handbag until he found a key labelled ESPLANADE HOTEL, 817. He opened the door with a disapproving grunt.

'They've taken the corpse away,' said Iain Stewart as he slipped back into his room. Philip Marshall was still there, sitting by the window. 'Now the police are coming up to investigate. Do you think we should dress?'

'You always want to put on your goddamned medals,' said Philip Marshall. He sank his hands into his dressing-gown pockets. 'I never wear anything except my dressing-gown back in California. It's the only way I can work comfortably.'

Iain Stewart braced his shoulders and tried to look like an officer and a gentleman. 'Ah yes,' he said incisively, 'but how often are you interviewed by the police in California?'

'Not often, but I've had my nose broken and three ribs bruised. Why should I dress for the law? A stiff shot of rye would be more appropriate.' He sat on the table beside the colour television set, looking like an old, discarded teddy bear. 'Do you think they'll reopen the bar?'

'I don't know.' Iain Stewart opened the door half an inch and squinted into the corridor. 'They've gone into the room at the end. Good Lord, Phil, you don't suppose the body belonged to anyone we know, do you?'"

He nodded gloomily. 'It was the dumb broad with all the upholstery.'

'Jennie Webster? The journalist with the breasts? My God.' He stared thoughtfully into the gilt-framed mirror above the fireplace and adjusted the lapels of his silk dressing-gown. 'Poor Jennie,' he muttered, 'what a tragedy.'

'Well, at least she smashed up Charlie Inman's car, so her death hasn't been altogether pointless.' He chuckled maliciously. 'I was telling him this evening that it isn't enough to be an effete academic concocting literary crossword puzzles during the long vacation. You have to walk with death through the mean streets, roll up your shirtsleeves and impose your will on the machinery and steel of our civilisation. That's the way to get the frisson of reality into a novel.' He grinned. 'Now perhaps he'll understand what I was talking about.'

'I doubt it,' said Iain Stewart. 'He'll simply claim on his insurance and write another book about identical twins running amok during the grouse season.'

'I suppose you don't have any more of that whisky?'

It was a normal, rather dowdy hotel room, sparsely furnished and impersonal. Some clothes neatly folded on a chair and a vase with tulips and daffodils were the only signs of human occupation. The bed had not been disturbed, and the lace curtains were flapping gently before the open window. Inspector Lawrence searched the room and went through the girl's luggage in less than ten minutes, but he found no suicide note.

'Mind if I use the phone?' he asked. He sat on the edge of the bed and picked up the receiver. 'Give me a line.' He dialled the number and then while he waited he emptied the girl's handbag on to the pillow. There was a holiday snap showing Jennie Webster on the beach, laughing in the required manner while a sea breeze blew through her long blonde hair. She had been a beautiful girl. Not a care in her head when the Instamatic camera had clicked for posterity. 'Sergeant Green? I need you here at the Esplanade. We seem to have a murder on our hands.'

The word murder drew the manager abruptly to his feet. 'Murder?' he repeated. 'But she couldn't have been murdered! The door was locked from the inside.' He looked desperately round the room. 'She committed suicide, didn't she? I mean, there's no sign of a struggle, is there? Why do you want to create a scandal in my hotel, Inspector? Nobody heard anything, did they? Has anybody come forward to suggest they heard Miss Webster arguing or quarrelling or crying? What are you trying to do to my hotel?'

Inspector Lawrence groaned. He disliked these wiry, eager little men who fell back so easily into hysteria. The man's head was glistening pinkly beneath the wisps of mouse-coloured hair. 'Sit down,' Lawrence waved his cigar at the armchair. 'My constable is going to take notes while you tell me what happened this evening.'

'Nothing happened this evening. Well, you know what I mean. Nothing unusual happened until just before midnight, when Miss Webster jumped out of that open window.'

The six crime writers and Miss Webster had arrived back from their evening session at half past nine, and as far as the manager knew they had all spent some time in the residents' bar before going upstairs to bed.

Miss Webster had gone to her room at around ten thirty.

'Alone?' asked Inspector Lawrence. He stubbed out his cigar in the ashtray and then eased his massive frame off the bed. 'I asked you a question.' The Inspector moved silently across the room towards the door.

Yes, she had been alone. The group had been absorbed and friendly, even excitable, but that doesn't mean . . . One doesn't encourage the guests to . . . I mean, we have a reputation, you know.

'Was she drunk?'

Inspector Lawrence stood carefully against the wall and lowered his hand on to the door knob while the manager gaped. Then with a sudden flick he threw open the door. A rather frail old lady stumbled into the room. With unexpected gallantry the Inspector caught her and held her upright.

'Miss Beech!' he said. 'You should be ashamed of yourself.'

Miss Beech was wearing a powder-blue dressing-gown and fluffy blue mules which matched perfectly the colour of her eyes and the blue rinse of her hair. 'I sleep very lightly,' she explained. 'And there seems to be so much going on.' She allowed the Inspector to lead her across to a chair. 'By the way, how do you know my name?'

The Inspector's jowls twitched with the suggestion of a smile. 'I've seen your photograph in the newspapers.' He forbore to mention that as a boy he had read many of her books; she was the *Grande Dame* of English crime fiction, and he didn't want to encourage her regal condescension. He wasn't going to be treated like one of her thick-headed policemen!

He turned abruptly to the hotel manager. 'That'll be all for the moment, Mr Weston. But I'd like a pot of coffee, milk, sugar, and cups for four people. When my sergeant arrives I want him shown straight up here, and first thing in the morning I'll need a complete guest list, staff duty roster, and all the details of their comings and goings that you can add. All right?' He turned away in dismissal. 'Thank you.'

The manager fled.

'Now, Miss Beech,' he said, gathering his features into an expression of avuncular charm, 'I gather you were one of the last people to see Jennie Webster alive.'

She fixed the inspector with a riveting stare. 'Tell me Inspector, are you married?'

'Yes,' he grunted.

'Happily married?'

'That's right,' He had been in bed when the call about the girl's death came through, watching his wife at the dressing-table. She was nearly fifty now and the preparations were taking longer and longer, with skin creams and strange lotions and hair brushing. But nothing could hide the thickening of her hips and the changes in her basic shape. It made him sad, sometimes, to watch Betty growing old; it was so much worse for a woman.

'I like to know whether people are human beings or not,' explained Miss Beech. 'If I can visualise you in the garden—'

'Miss Beech, what time did you retire this evening?'

'I went to bed at ten o'clock. When you're an old lady you need plenty of rest. We had such a tiring day.'

Lawrence wondered how Miss Beech had managed to preserve her delicate, bird-like shape. A constant preoccupation with bodies in the library, probably, and Mediterranean cruises in the winter. She had alert, questioning eyes. Would Betty, he wondered, be like this in twenty-five years?

'Did you go straight off to sleep?' he asked.

'No, I always read for an hour when I go to bed. My husband complains when I'm at home, but I find it relaxing, so useful for dismissing the day's problems.' She smiled. 'Why do you ask? I didn't hear the girl crying, if that's what you mean. Her room is directly below mine and I should certainly have heard anything like that. No, I don't think she was distressed this evening. She must have committed suicide on impulse.' Miss Beech leaned forward dramatically. 'There was no final letter, was there? So it was clearly unpremeditated. In my opinion there is only one possible explanation: LSD. She must have thought she could fly!'

Inspector Lawrence raised a sceptical eyebrow. 'I think she was murdered.'

'Nonsense, Inspector, you're being fanciful. The girl committed suicide.'

He shrugged his shoulders. 'Was she the type to take LSD?'

'Of course,' Miss Beech answered promptly, 'she was a typical modern girl. Self-possessed and extrovert, attractive but not, for my money, very feminine. She went after what she wanted instead of letting the world woo her.' She considered the characterisation for a moment and then added, 'Good at tennis, I should think, bad at bridge. Not the type to be murdered.'

'Did Miss Webster have any special friends up here, or any special enemies?'

Not, the doyenne of crime decided, more than most other journalists. 'One treats them with suspicion, of course, but Jennie Webster attached herself to our group. I believe she'd known Gilbert Wyatt vaguely for years, and she wrote a profile of Iain Stewart some weeks ago for her Sunday colour comic, so she was virtually *persona grata*. Iain Stewart,' she explained, 'he writes those rather technological thrillers full of machines and functional women. He describes sex in terms of putting guided missiles into orbit and he makes missiles sound like phallic symbols.'

Inspector Lawrence refrained from mentioning an agog train journey he had spent reading an Iain Stewart paperback. There was no point in antagonising Miss Beech. 'No other friends?' he asked. 'How did you all spend today?'

'Together, as a group. We had a forum on the closed-room murder – you know, where a death takes place in a locked room and nobody could possibly have got in or out to do it. We're supposed to be working hard on our solutions, and tomorrow afternoon we have the confrontation scene – that's when all the suspects are assembled together and the hero explains how it was done by the least probable person present.'

The Inspector was looking worried. 'But that's precisely what we have on our hands at the moment, Miss Beech, a closed-room murder!'

'Pure imagination, Inspector. I thought policemen were trained not to use their imaginations?'

There was a tap at the door and a waiter appeared with the coffee. Inspector Lawrence growled at the man and pushed him out of the room. He poured the cups of coffee himself. He didn't want nosey bloody waiters lurking about listening for gossip. Miss Beech took her coffee black.

'So who was the victim?' Inspector Lawrence asked her. 'At your forum this afternoon, who was killed?'

Miss Beech shrugged her thin shoulders. 'That isn't really important. Usually we choose somebody who is widely disliked. It helps with the motive and avoids any unpleasant problems about the fact of death.'

'Doesn't the motive come first?'

'Oh no. You can fill in the motive afterwards. Money, jealousy, ambition.' She waved her hands in vague disdain. 'Anything you like.'

'What', Inspector Lawrence persisted, 'was the motive this afternoon?'

'We decided on jealousy. The victim was a young girl, so sex was the obvious motive.'

'Which young girl?'

Her voice faltered for a moment. 'Well, actually, Miss Webster was helping us out.'

The room was in darkness except for a shaft of moonlight falling on the bleached face and shoulders of Veronica Carlton. 'You have to be so terribly careful,' she was saying theatrically. 'I once had a Swiss murderer, and I described him as a phlegmatic thick-set man with typically Swiss perseverance. Do you know that my Swiss publisher refused to take the book? He said it was inaccurate! And I'd been in bed the night before with a thick-set phlegmatic little Swiss! We made love for hours and he never said a word – it was murder! You have to be so careful about foreign sales. I remember my American publisher made me change—' She stopped in bewilderment. 'Darling, are you crying?'

'No,' whispered Gilbert Wyatt. But she could feel him trembling.

Veronica Carlton had been an actress until she found that writing novels was a more total way of controlling the creatures of her imagination. She had written five detective novels, murdering horribly the directors and stars she had once hated and enjoying the vicarious successes of her glittering casts. She was a thin, dramatic woman with a neurotic appetite for attention.

'You are crying,' she accused him, 'you're making my nightdress wet through!'

'I was only thinking – last night I was in bed with Jennie, and now she's dead.' He shuddered. 'Perhaps she knew that she was going to die. She kept on talking and talking.'

'Not at all what bed is about, darling.' She paused briefly. 'I was telling you about my American publisher. He insisted that I change a reference to the thin demanding thighs of American womanhood. Said that American women were buxom and generous. The fool! I told him I'd been to an orgy in Chicago the night before and all the girls were as skinny as mendicant nuns. But of course he knew the American market!'

Veronica soothed the lank head down in the shadows. He couldn't be expected to understand the labyrinth of overseas sales and subsidiary rights. Gilbert Wyatt had written a clutch of brilliant who-dunnits during his undergraduate days and had published nothing since. Veronica didn't understand why he had come to the crime writers' convention. But he was languidly good-looking in an aristocratic way, so she wasn't complaining. And he didn't try to steal the limelight.

It was growing late. Inspector Lawrence glanced at his watch and found that it was nearly three o'clock. Sergeant Green had arrived and he was establishing the groundwork for tomorrow's investigation: contact with the dead girl's employers and her family in London, requests for information on the key suspects, and of course a systematic dossier on the case. Lawrence yawned. There was nothing much else he could do until morning. Everybody except Miss Beech was in bed, and the post-mortem report would not be ready until seven. Time to snatch a few hours' sleep, he decided. He shared the last of the coffee with Miss Beech and then made to leave.

'By the way,' he said as an afterthought, 'I must know, Miss Beech. What is your solution to the closed-room murder?'

'Mine? I haven't really thought of one. I did wonder whether to falsify the time of death, so that in fact she was murdered an hour before the room was locked. It would mean storing the body in a freezer. I don't know whether that would work.'

Lawrence nodded. It had worked well enough in one of her earlier novels. The Inspector remembered all those irrelevant alibis and the cold-storage room. 'That brings us back to the question of when Miss Webster was last seen alive.'

'She went up to her room at half past ten and only the murderer will have seen her after that. But she was still alive an hour later. Phil Marshall was hammering at her door demanding to be let in.' She smiled sadly. 'Poor Mr Marshall, such polished style, but he drinks, you know, and he lives in America.'

The Inspector slipped Jennie Webster's notebook into his pocket. It might provide some light bedtime reading. 'Why was Mr Marshall hammering at her door?'

'Sex, Inspector, I presume. Phil was making such a fuss that I had to go down and ask him what was the matter. Apparently the girl was calling to him to sod off – as Mr Marshall put it.'

They went into the corridor together and along to the lift. 'But surely,' he said tactlessly, 'isn't Philip Marshall over sixty?'

Miss Beech gave a regal smile. 'My dear Inspector, I'm seventy-nine, but I still insist that my husband makes love to me once a month! Perhaps he would rather not, but I feel that we owe it to the people we once were.' She ran almost lightly up the stairs and turned back at the landing. 'Good night, Inspector.'

Inspector Lawrence was rusty on his shorthand, but he struggled through the notebook entry while his wife snored disconcertingly beside him.

The Spa Pavilion, Saturday. An aeroplane hangar of a building full of gently respectable people intent on my death. How will they murder me?

Ellen Beech, the death's head of the lady hawk moths, favoured an injection of air into an artery – as though nobody remembered that from Dorothy Sayers. Philip Marshall suggested a couple of rounds fired at close range from a Centennial .38 Special, which must be a gun. The conversation became very cerebral when Charles Inman insisted that the weapon had to be a dagger – his ivory tower is his own head. He baffled everybody with a lecture on 'The Ballad of Macdobeth', which apparently could have been a source book for Shakespeare's play. Charles Inman hadn't read it, we hadn't heard of it, and there was no record of what it was about. He eventually settled for a silver of ice as the murder weapon.

Veronica Carlton developed an obsession about 'the pill', which she thought could be switched for a cyanide tablet. 'It will illuminate the girl's character,' she claimed, 'the reader will think she's promiscuous.' We couldn't convince her that people don't take the wrong pills without noticing it; Veronica herself takes so many pills for so many things that food upsets her metabolism and often produces unexpected side effects.

'Couldn't she just be tossed from an eighth-floor window?' Gilbert Wyatt suggested airily.

The pill is a recurring theme at this convention. Iain Stewart clings to the last remaining playing-field of his bed, desperate to prove his masculinity, but he's a chauvinist. 'You girls have the pill on the National Health,' he said with a sneer, 'so there's no need to become pregnant unless you want a child.' There's a cruelty beneath his darned good looks.

They take the problem of killing me with chilling seriousness. As the afternoon wore on they began to hate me; except Gilbert, of course, the most original and creative of them all. I think he hates me already.

Inspector Lawrence put aside the notebook, turned out the bedside lamp, and stared sleeplessly at the ceiling.

It didn't surprise Inspector Lawrence to learn that Jennie Webster had been ten weeks pregnant, but he was disconcerted to hear that she had died from perforation of the brain by a spiked instrument. 'Stabbed with a long needle or some such,' the doctor explained, 'through the skull.'

'You mean she was dead before she was pushed from the window?'

'Undoubtedly.' He pulled back the sheet to demonstrate his argument, but Lawrence turned away.

'Would that be an easy way to kill her?'

'A four-year-old child could have done it,' the doctor said cheerfully, 'if he knew where to stick the needle. It has to be thrust up through here—'

'When? What was the time of death?'

'I couldn't say exactly. It might have been any time after eleven thirty.' He shrugged in apology. 'I should have taken her body temperature at once, but I didn't think the time of death was in dispute . . .'

Lawrence growled unforgivingly. 'What about the murder weapon?' he asked. 'Could it have been a hypodermic needle?'

'Yes, I suppose it could be. Yes, it would have been something very like a hypodermic needle.'

'Or a sliver of ice?'

The doctor gave a patronising smile. 'Now you're being imaginative, Inspector.'

Breakfast at the Esplanade Hotel was a heavy occasion. Philip Marshall sat at a table by the window and gazed accusingly at a cup of black coffee. Gilbert Wyatt and Veronica Carlton were drinking grapefruit juice in uneasy silence while Charles Inman was doing a crossword puzzle and ignoring breakfast altogether. He might as well, Inspector Lawrence felt, have stayed in his room until noon as Miss Beech intended to do. But the Inspector was feeling defensive. Everybody kept watching him as he ate his way through a bowl of porridge, a plate of bacon and eggs, and four slices of toast and marmalade. He was vastly relieved when Iain Stewart came in and ordered a two-minute-fifty-five-second egg with a slice of lightly done toast (bread two days old) and coffee made in an earthenware pot with the top of the milk.

'Beautiful morning,' Stewart announced briskly to the room at large. 'Anyone fancy a swim after breakfast?'

'You're mad,' muttered Philip Marshall.

'I mean to say,' Gilbert Wyatt exploded, 'Jennie was murdered last night!' He looked across to the Inspector and said more calmly, 'I suppose you'll be questioning us this morning?'

Inspector Lawrence nodded.

Iain Stewart sliced the top off his egg with a single blow. 'Getting oneself murdered at a crime writers' convention is in very poor taste,' he declared. 'But it's typical of Jennie, she had no sense of restraint. Lack of breeding, one is almost tempted to say.'

'No sense of direction,' Charles Inman said sadly. 'Did you know that she landed on my car? The second time it's happened. Last month a student ran into it with a bicycle.'

'I don't suppose she did it deliberately,' Veronica Carlton hissed angrily.

'I wouldn't be surprised. It wasn't her bicycle, and I'd irritated her by saying that *Gorboduc* is incompatible with the activities of Women's Lib. She was extremely militant.' He gathered up the several sections of his newspaper and folded them carefully under his arm. 'Oh well, I must be off.' But he paused by the Inspector's table. 'By the way, Sergeant, this newspaper girl. Remind me to tell you how she was killed when we have a little more time. It's perfectly simple.'

Gilbert Wyatt laughed. 'Don't tell us, it's all in *Macbeth*!'

'Precisely. "If chance will have me king, why, chance may crown me, without my stir." That gave me the clue.'

He left a stunned silence in the room behind him. Then gradually the sound of Inspector Lawrence chewing on his toast reasserted a kind of normality, until Gilbert Wyatt and Veronica Carlton felt they could leave without making an exit.

'We'll be in the hotel,' said Wyatt, 'just in case there's anything else you need to know.'

Lawrence finished his coffee and wiped his mouth with the table napkin. He folded it with great deliberation and replaced it in the pewter ring. 'Did you know that Miss Webster was ten weeks pregnant?' he asked at last.

Philip Marshall looked startled. 'No,' he said, 'but it would have been a waste for her to have died without a sex angle.' He glanced nervously at Iain Stewart. 'I wonder whether she was raped?'

'That would not have been necessary.' Stewart lit a cigarette and stood in a self-consciously relaxed pose by the window. 'Jennie was a typical modern girl, unscrupulous and over-sexed.'

I don't know anything about modern girls,' Philip Marshall said unhappily. 'But she had a nice turn of phrase. She called me a chocolate-coated character with a liqueur centre. I think that sums me up.'

Inspector Lawrence pushed back his chair and rose menacingly to his feet. 'Mr Marshall, I understand that you were the last person to speak to Miss Webster.'

'I was?' he said uncertainly.

'You were. At half past eleven last night. I'm told you were hammering on her door for admittance.'

'Ah, yes,' he said sadly. 'She suggested it half way through the afternoon, because I was flirting with her in a somewhat paternal fashion. I suppose she changed her mind.'

'She told you to sod off,' rasped Lawrence.

'Apparently.'

'What,' he said in exasperation, 'does apparently mean?'

'It means that I don't remember what happened last night. I was drunk, you see. But if Ellen Beech says I was hammering on the door then who am I to doubt it? All I remember is hearing a scream, and I was sitting on my bed. It must have sobered me up, because I hurried into the corridor and found Iain in his dressing-gown.' He pushed a worried hand through his grey hair. 'As a matter of fact I was wearing a dressing-gown as well. I must have undressed without knowing it.'

'So you wouldn't know,' Lawrence said harshly, 'whether you killed the girl or not.'

'Oh surely, Inspector,' Stewart interrupted hotly, 'one doesn't behave in a violently uncharacteristic way simply because one is under the weather!'

'Were you drunk as well last night?' asked Lawrence.

'Certainly not!'

'But you did spend the evening drinking with Mr Marshall?'

Iain Stewart fixed the Inspector with an expression of ice-cold hauteur. 'My dear man,' he snapped, 'I was a Commander in Her Majesty's Royal Navy for seventeen years. I drank my share of the Scotch last night, but I never lose control!'

Inspector Lawrence smiled happily. 'I'm pleased to hear it, Mr Stewart. I admire self-discipline. You're never sick on the carpet and you don't fall over and you don't get young girls in the family way, is that it?' He beamed with such an excess of friendliness that a lesser man than Iain Stewart would have been demanding the presence of a solicitor. 'All right, Mr Marshall, you can leave us. And perhaps you'd ask my constable to come in? I want a record of this conversation.'

Philip Marshall padded dejectedly from the room. 'Constable,' they heard him calling, 'Torquemada is asking for you. He needs someone to turn the screws!'

When the policeman was settled with his notebook in a corner Inspector Lawrence resumed. 'We were discussing the remarkable coincidence, I believe, that Miss Webster was ten weeks pregnant and ten weeks ago she was working on a profile of you, Mr Stewart.'

'She threw herself wholeheartedly into her work,' said Stewart.

'In her reporter's notebook Miss Webster recorded a conversation she had with you yesterday about the pill.'

'I told her she was careless.'

'Would you care to elaborate?'

'Not really,' said Stewart. 'I didn't preach a sermon to Jennie, so why should I want to convince you? It seemed to me that she had been irresponsible.'

'Was it your child?'

'It might have been.' He strolled across to the constable and peered down at the shorthand record. 'As you observed, the timing is consistent with such a possibility.'

'But you think it could equally have been somebody else's child?'

'Really, Inspector!' he said in exasperation. 'I don't like your imputation! Jennie herself told me that it might be my child, or her regular boyfriend's, or a foreign correspondent's whom she met in passing at a diplomatic reception. Jennie was an energetic girl.'

Inspector Lawrence breathed deeply with a sound suggestive of an elephant about to attack. 'Why did Miss Webster come to this convention, Stewart? Don't answer that question too quickly. Why did she attach herself to your group? And why did she discuss her pregnancy with you? What did she want, eh?'

The novelist laughed. 'I'll speak slowly, so that your constable can get it all down, Inspector. Are you ready? Jennie came to the convention to write a feature, she attached herself to our group because we are old friends, and she talked to me because she was a bloody chatterbox.' He paused. 'Now write this down as well. Miss Webster did not try to black-mail me, and I did not kill her. Miss Webster had every intention of marrying her regular boyfriend and bringing up the child as his, which in all probability it was.' He glanced at his watch. 'And now I see that the bar is open, so if you'll excuse me—'

'What time did you go to bed last night?'

'Eleven thirty,' he answered irritably. 'I came up with Phil Marshall and we parted in the corridor, outside Jennie's room. And please don't build any theories on that. Poor Phil would never have harmed the girl. He's absolutely terrified of women.'

'He was drunk,' snarled the Inspector.

'Quite. Much too drunk to have killed anybody. If he'd tried to draw the curtains he'd have fallen out of the window himself.'

Inspector Lawrence pushed back his chair and rose to his feet. 'That's all for the moment, Mr Stewart.' He held the door open and watched balefully as the man left. The arrogance of the bastard, he thought to himself, the arrogant bloody bastard!

Veronica Carlton was on the way down to a hairdressing appointment but she invited the inspector to accompany her. It would be a new experience in his sheltered life. Although one that he could have done without, he decided, as a row of faces beneath the driers gazed blankly at him. He didn't like the smell of soapless detergents either. He didn't like Veronica Carlton. She was wearing a vividly unsuitable vermilion trouser suit which made her look six feet tall and thin as lipstick.

'Gilbert and I went to bed at ten o'clock and we stayed together all night,' she declared. 'We heard the commotion, of course, the scream and the noise in the street, but there was nothing we could have done. I turned over and Gilbert made love to me again.'

Six soapy heads turned in astonishment and the eyes beneath the driers widened. 'I suppose,' Inspector Lawrence whispered, 'Mr Wyatt is an old friend of yours. I've been wondering—'

'I met him this weekend for the first time.' She laughed gaily. 'But I've known his work, of course. Such malicious ingenuity, don't you think?'

Lawrence sank lower into the chair by the washbasin. 'Too clever by half,' he muttered.

'I'm a very direct person,' Veronica confided resonantly. 'I saw Gilbert looking all willowy and handsome so I decided to have him. He's terribly versatile!' She smiled terrifyingly in the mirror at a young male assistant who was waiting to shampoo her hair. 'Unfortunately he was tied up with the journalist girl on the first night, but I soon cut him loose. Gilbert couldn't resist an experienced woman.'

Her head vanished into the bowl of water. Inspector Lawrence made his escape.

'Yes, I spent the first night here with Jennie. I was terribly fond of her. Known her on and off since I started on the book review treadmill. She was the clean-cut and athletic type, terribly wholesome and English.'

They were in the bar. Gilbert Wyatt was sipping Cinzano Bianco; across the room Philip Marshall and Iain Stewart were downing whiskies; Inspector Lawrence was holding half a pint of bitter.

'What I don't understand,' Lawrence said doggedly, 'is why you're at this conference at all. You haven't written a book for twenty years, have you?'

Gilbert Wyatt shrugged his shoulders. 'The public are still reading my works. A steady sale to the highbrow readership, you know.'

'I'm not satisfied with that answer.'

The languid features twitched in surprise. 'Just what is your case, Inspector? My books are all in print and I was invited to this convention by the organisers. Perhaps you'd be more explicit?'

'I wonder why you're here.' He swallowed a draught of beer and then wiped his mouth with a large, patterned brown handkerchief. 'I wonder what you've been doing these past twenty years.'

'I do this and that,' Wyatt answered with some hesitation. 'My criticism is quite influential and I do some journeyman work. There's more money in the byways of literature than in writing a detective novel every year till you die, unless you happen to be Ellen Beech.'

Inspector Lawrence went for a stroll along the seafront before lunch. He needed to clear his head. Crime writers were confusing people to have around at a murder investigation – they made it seem less than simple. A wind was whistling in from the Atlantic, dispelling the quirks and rivalries of his suspects and pounding the incoming tide on to the rocks. Lawrence enjoyed the power and the grandeur; they put his problems into perspective.

The problem. A female journalist had been murdered at half past eleven (or thereabouts), and it had been made to seem that she committed suicide half an hour later. Why? Because half an hour later her door had been locked.

It seemed a little improbable that any of the suspects would kill a girl. An Oxford don, an over-theatrical ex-actress, a languid young man left behind by the vanished age of country-house parties, an Anglo-American drunk – the only thing they had in common was that they murdered people with relish in their imaginations. Even Ellen Beech revealed a streak of gloating cruelty on the printed page. Perhaps the frequent contemplation of the unthinkable . . . But Inspector Lawrence was a plain thinker. He preferred to think that the only possible killer among them was the ex-naval commander, Iain Stewart.

The Inspector strolled back along the beach and sat on the seat opposite the Esplanade Hotel. It was a late Victorian building, grey, symmetrical, solid, like the Victorians themselves. The window on the eighth floor was closed now. He thought he could see Veronica Carlton watching from the third window along, and that looked like Miss Beech waving from the window above Miss Webster's.

Lawrence buttoned up his jacket. Perhaps it was too early in the summer for sitting by the sea. And he'd done all the thinking he needed. He knew how the murder had been done, but he would need to check on the motive. A telephone call to London, unless Sergeant Green had confirmation in his records. Lawrence crossed the road and went up the steps of the hotel.

'Hello, Inspector. I thought I saw you taking the air.' Miss Beech was coming through the swing doors in a hyacinth-blue spring coat and a striking wide-brimmed hat which was held in place with a diamond-crested hat pin. 'Have you solved our mystery yet?'

He nodded. 'I think I know who did it,' he said hesitantly. 'I suppose we'll make the arrest this afternoon. There are one or two details—'

'You'll make your arrest at the convention, of course, when we all present our closed-room solutions!'

'Well, no, I thought—'

'It's the only way to do it, Inspector. We've done it that way for a hundred years, assembling all the suspects and making a speech. I couldn't allow you to handle the climax in any other way.'

Inspector Lawrence had refused to conduct his forum on the closed-room mystery at the Spa Pavilion. He could just about allow the six suspects to sit and listen to his case, but there was no question of doing it before a full-scale audience. The trial judge later would make mincemeat of such proceedings! So they all sat in the late Jennie Webster's hotel room and six faces stared expectantly at the Inspector.

He lit a cigar and then nervously cleared his throat.

Gilbert Wyatt and Veronica Carlton were sitting on the bed looking, in spite of Veronica's new Sassoon hair-style, like two boys caught together after lights out. Iain Stewart was waiting in a characteristic pose against the mantelpiece, and Philip Marshall was slumped on a chair in the corner. Charles Inman had a file and a copy of *Macbeth* at the dressing-table, clearly intent on marking the inspector's performance with a beta plus at the most. Miss Beech was sitting commandingly in the high-backed armchair like a referee anxious to see the rules observed.

'Well, Inspector,' she whispered, 'you can start now. We're all assembled. Begin with the point which made you realise it was murder. What drew your attention to the crime?'

'The curious incident', he said self-consciously, 'of the girl's scream as she jumped.'

'The girl could not have screamed as she jumped,' Iain Stewart said stiffly.

'That was the curious incident.'

Miss Beech sat back in her chair and left the Inspector to his story. After that exchange she knew he could handle the scene.

'The other oddity was the girl's handbag,' he continued. 'I didn't believe that Jennie Webster would jump to her death with a handbag on her arm. It had to have been thrown out with her.'

'Good thinking,' muttered Gilbert Wyatt.

Inspector Lawrence prowled across to the bed and looked down at Gilbert Wyatt. He would have felt happier sitting down; but all the chairs were taken by the suspects. He pointed his cigar at Wyatt. 'You're at the centre of this, Mr Wyatt. I was puzzled by your twenty years of inactivity, because you're obviously so successful. You claim to write influential reviews and to dabble in the byways of literature. But according to Miss Webster you're the most creative and original mind in this room. She wrote that about you the day she died.'

Wyatt was suddenly very pale, but he said nothing.

'You obviously told Miss Webster more than you would tell me.' He smiled dangerously. 'But then you would, wouldn't you? You spent the night in her bed, didn't you?' Lawrence put the cigar back in his mouth and spoke round it. 'Mr Wyatt, what books have you written recently?'

Wyatt glanced around the room for help, but none was forthcoming. 'I can't tell you,' he said. 'I've ghosted one or two, but it wouldn't be proper for me to reveal—' He broke off in a pathetic gesture of honourable silence. 'I'm sorry.'

The Inspector found that he had lost his audience; they were all intently watching Ellen Beech. She was leaning forward and gently waving a frail hand as she picked up her wide-brimmed hat from the floor. 'It's all right, Inspector. Gilbert has written my more recent books.' She sighed. 'But, of course, you knew that already. So clever of you. Do tell me how you worked it out.'

'Your lack of invention gave me the clue,' he said apologetically. 'For the convention exercise you improvised a murder based on one of your early novels, and Jennie Webster noted in her diary that you were inventing a method of death which Dorothy Sayers had used. I know you're very alert for your years, very sprightly indeed. But a book every year requires more than alertness. The concentration, the attention to detail and the sheer deviousness – I thought they must be a little beyond you. I guessed that somebody must have helped you recently.'

'Gilbert is so clever,' sighed Miss Beech. She looked down at the hat in her lap and smiled. 'I could never understand why his own books didn't make him rich. My stuff is so much more straightforward – no literary references or tricks of style – yet our fifty-fifty partnership has made him a fortune. Gilbert really deserved to have his name on the title page, except that it would have killed the sales.'

Inspector Lawrence agreed. 'I know. You couldn't afford to let the secret out, could you? It would kill the sales and more importantly it would ruin your reputation as the *Grande Dame* of Detective Fiction.'

'Very true.' She carefully arranged the wide-brimmed hat on her head and pushed the diamond pin into place. 'Silly Miss Webster,' she murmured. 'Wanted to tell the world.' Her voice faded into nothing and she leaned back in the chair.

'Gilbert!' The summary tones of Veronica Carlton surprised everybody. 'Did you tell Jennie Webster that you were a ghost?'

He didn't look up. 'One says the wrong thing, sometimes, in bed. I didn't know she would decide it was immoral or insist on exposing Ellen to the world. These journalists have such funny ideas of integrity.'

'My God,' said Iain Stewart. 'I don't understand. Dammit, who did kill Jennie?'

Inspector Lawrence waved his cigar towards Miss Beech, but she was paying no attention. 'Jennie Webster went up to Miss Beech's room sometime between half past ten and half past eleven to discuss the story, and obviously they couldn't agree. In fact it must have been a hell of a row, because the doyenne of crime killed her.'

'No, no, that must be wrong,' Philip Marshall interrupted. 'I was talking to Jennie through this door at half past eleven last night, wasn't I?'

'You only have Ellen's word for that,' said Iain Stewart.

'That's true,' he said thoughtfully. 'So Jennie was already lying dead in the room above? And I suppose she was pushed out of Miss Beech's window? One more storey wouldn't make much difference.'

'That's damned clever!' said Gilbert Wyatt. 'Very,' said Veronica Carlton, 'but is it original?' Charles Inman nodded. 'I think so.'

Philip Marshall rose sadly to his feet. 'You were wrong about Ellen's inventiveness, Inspector,' he said. 'She must have come downstairs to open the window and lock the door, and that was when she found me bellowing through the keyhole. It must have been a nasty moment for the old girl.' He gave Miss Beech a sympathetic pat on the shoulder.

'Hey, is she all right?' snapped Iain Stewart.

Miss Beech looked as though she had fallen asleep. But when Philip Marshall shook her by the arms she toppled forward on to the floor. She was dead.

'I don't believe it!' Veronica Carlton cried. 'It isn't possible! What has she died of?'

Inspector Lawrence pointed dismally to the diamond hatpin. 'There's the weapon,' he said. 'That was what she used to kill Miss Webster.'

'I don't believe it,' said Veronica Carlton. 'Miss Beech just wasn't the type. Could she have produced that scream we heard? Such a sweet old lady—'

'She was a hard and vindictive old woman,' Gilbert Wyatt said, almost to himself. 'I believe it.'

The scene was over. Inspector Lawrence summoned his sergeant and the police constable to look after the details and see the latest body off the premises. It had been a tough eighteen hours and he was tired. It depressed him to think that the killer was the only person in the group he had liked.

'Good afternoon,' he said to the room in general. 'I hope you enjoy the rest of your convention.' It wouldn't deprive him too much if he never met another writer in his life. He tossed the cigar butt into the tray by the lift.

'Ground floor,' he snarled.

The liftman was waiting for somebody to catch up. Blast, the Inspector cursed audibly. It was Charles Inman loping up with an expression of button-holing eagerness. Lawrence tried to ignore the pompous smile of the academic.

'You weren't,' said Charles Inman as the lift descended, 'from your mother's womb untimely ripp'd.'

'That's true,' Lawrence agreed.

'Miss Beech only committed the murder, Inspector,' he said with the heavy patience which he reserved for the dimmer students. 'I told you at breakfast who was actually responsible.'

'A quote, wasn't it?' Lawrence growled. 'Shakespeare? Something about chance crowning Macbeth king so that he didn't have to work for it himself.'

'An excellent paraphrase, Inspector.'

The lift gates opened and they walked across the hotel foyer. The bloody don was staying with him! 'All right, so who's the king now that Miss Webster is dead? Miss Beech? Because she is dead now as well!'

'You don't understand, Inspector. Who is king, now that Miss Beech is dead? That's the question.' A black police car drew up by the steps and Lawrence climbed in the back. 'Gilbert Wyatt, the man who wrote her books for the past fifteen years, he is king, the man who told Jennie Webster the truth.' He leaned down and spoke through the window. 'By the way, Inspector, do you know the relationship between Wyatt and Jennie Webster?'

Lawrence swore violently. Then, 'No, I doubt whether I do.'

'They were going to be married,' said Inman. 'Until Wyatt discovered that she'd been to bed with Iain Stewart. There's a lot of professional jealousy among crime writers, Inspector.' He stood up and raised a hand in salute. 'Well, goodbye and congratulations on your success. Alpha minus, I think, for solid effort.' He turned and went back to the hotel.

'Station, sir?' asked the driver, 'or do you want to go home?'

'Neither,' he growled. He stayed thoughtfully in the car. He lit a cigar. So that was why Gilbert Wyatt had jumped into bed with the deplorable Miss Carlton. He was providing himself with an alibi and leaving the field clear for murder. 'On second thoughts,' he said at last, 'take me to the station. Radio the Chief Superintendent I need to see him.' He chewed angrily on the cigar. He listened to the thickheaded driver talking to the police station. Then he sighed. 'On third thoughts, take me home, will you? I'm tired.'

The car did a U-turn in the main road and sped off in the opposite direction. 'Anything the matter, sir?' the driver asked sympathetically.

'Yes,' he said theatrically. 'Somebody has just committed two perfect murders.'

The driver laughed. 'Ah well, you can't win them all, as they used to tell us at training college.' He would never know how close he was to unsubtle and bloody death.

P. D. James

The Victim

You know Princess Ilsa Mancelli, of course. I mean by that that you must have seen her on the cinema screen; on television; pictured in newspapers arriving at airports with her latest husband; relaxing on their yacht; bejewelled at first nights, gala nights, at any night and in any place where it is obligatory for the rich and successful to show themselves. Even if, like me, you have nothing but bored contempt for what I believe is called an international jet set, you can hardly live in the modern world and not know Ilsa Mancelli. And you can't fail to have picked up some scraps about her past. The brief and not particularly successful screen career, when even her heart-stopping beauty couldn't quite compensate for the paucity of talent; the succession of marriages, first to the producer who made her first film and who broke a twenty-year-old marriage to get her; then to a Texan millionaire; lastly to a prince. About two months ago I saw a nauseatingly sentimental picture of her with her two-day-old son in a Rome nursing home. So it looks as if this marriage, sanctified as it is by wealth, a title and maternity may be intended as her final adventure.

The husband before the film producer is, I notice, no longer mentioned. Perhaps her publicity agent fears that a violent death in the family, particularly an unsolved violent death, might tarnish her bright image. Blood and beauty. In the early stages of her career they hadn't been able to resist that cheap, vicarious thrill. But not now. Nowadays her early history, before she married the film producer, has become a little obscure, although there is a suggestion of poor but decent parentage and early struggles suitably rewarded. I am the most obscure part of that obscurity. Whatever you know, or think you know of Ilsa Mancelli, you won't have heard about me. The publicity machine has decreed that I be nameless, faceless, unremembered, that I no longer exist. Ironically, the machine is right; in any real sense, I don't.

I married her when she was Elsie Bowman aged seventeen. I was assistant librarian at our local branch library and fifteen years older, a thirty-two year-old virgin, a scholar manqué, thin faced, a little stooping, my meagre hair already thinning. She worked on the cosmetic counter of our High Street store. She was beautiful then, but with a delicate, tentative, unsophisticated loveliness which gave little promise of the polished mature beauty which is hers today. Our story was very ordinary. She returned a book to the library one evening when I was on counter duty. We chatted. She asked my advice about novels for her mother. I spent as long as I dared finding suitable romances for her on the shelves. I tried to interest her in the books I liked. I asked her about herself, her life, her ambitions. She was the only woman I had been able to talk to. I was enchanted by her, totally and completely besotted.

I used to take my lunch early and make surreptitious visits to the store, watching her from the shadow of a neighbouring pillar. There is one picture which even now seems to stop my heart. She had dabbed her wrist with scent and was holding out a bare arm over the counter so that a prospective customer could smell the perfume. She was totally absorbed, her young face gravely preoccupied. I watched her, silently, and felt the tears smarting my eyes.

It was a miracle when she agreed to marry me. Her mother (she had no father) was reconciled if not enthusiastic about the match. She didn't, as she made it abundantly plain, consider me much of a catch. But I had a good job with prospects; I was educated; I was steady and reliable; I spoke with a grammar school accent which, while she affected to deride it, raised my status in her eyes. Besides, any marriage for Elsie was better than none. I was dimly aware when I bothered to think about Elsie in relation to anyone but myself that she and her mother didn't get on.

Mrs Bowman made, as she described it, a splash. There was a full choir and a peal of bells. The church hall was hired and a sit-down meal, ostentatiously unsuitable and badly cooked, was served to eighty guests. Between the pangs of nervousness and indigestion I was conscious of smirking waiters in short white jackets, a couple of giggling bridesmaids from the store, their freckled arms bulging from pink taffeta sleeves, hearty male relatives, red faced and with buttonholes of carnation and waving fern, who made indelicate jokes and clapped me painfully between the shoulders. There were speeches and warm champagne. And, in the middle of it all, Elsie my Elsie, like a white rose.

I suppose that it was stupid of me to imagine that I could hold her.

The mere sight of our morning faces, smiling at each other's reflection in the bedroom mirror, should have warned me that it couldn't last. But, poor deluded fool, I never dreamed that I might lose her except by death. Her death I dared not contemplate, and I was afraid for the first time of my own. Happiness had made a coward of me. We moved into a new bungalow, chosen by Elsie, sat in new chairs chosen by Elsie, slept in a befrilled bed chosen by Elsie. I was so happy that it was like passing into a new phase of existence, breathing a different air, seeing the most ordinary things as if they were newly created. One isn't necessarily humble when greatly in love. Is it so unreasonable to recognise the value of a love like mine, to believe that the beloved is equally sustained and transformed by it?

She said that she wasn't ready to start a baby and, without her job, she was easily bored. She took a brief training in shorthand and typing at our local Technical College and found herself a position as shorthand typist at the firm of Collingford & Major. That, at least, was how the job started. Shorthand typist, then secretary to Mr Rodney Collingford, then personal secretary, then confidential personal secretary; in my bemused state of uxorious bliss I only half registered her progress from occasionally taking his dictation when his then secretary was absent to flaunting his gifts of jewellery and sharing his bed.

He was everything I wasn't. Rich (his father had made a fortune from plastics shortly after the war and had left the factory to his only son), coarsely handsome in a swarthy fashion, big muscled, confident, attractive to women. He prided himself on taking what he wanted. Elsie must have been one of his easiest pickings.

Why, I still wonder, did he want to marry her? I thought at the time that he couldn't resist depriving a pathetic, under-privileged, unattractive husband of a prize which neither looks nor talent had qualified him to deserve. I've noticed that about the rich and successful. They can't bear to see the undeserving prosper. I thought that half the satisfaction for him was in taking her away from me. That was partly why I knew that I had to kill him. But now I'm not so sure. I may have done him an injustice. It may have been both simpler and more complicated than that. She was, you see – she still is – so very beautiful.

I understand her better now. She was capable of kindness, good humour, generosity even, provided she was getting what she wanted. At the time we married, and perhaps eighteen months afterwards, she wanted me. Neither her egoism nor her curiosity had been able to resist such a flattering, overwhelming love. But for her, marriage wasn't permanency. It was the first and necessary step towards the kind of life she wanted and meant to have. She was kind to me, in bed and out, while I was what she wanted. But when she wanted someone else, then my need of her, my jealousy, my bitterness, she saw as a cruel and wilful denial of her basic right, the right to have what she wanted. After all, I'd had her for nearly three years. It was two years more than I had any right to expect. She thought so. Her darling Rodney thought so. When my acquaintances at the library learnt of the divorce I could see in their eyes that they thought so too. And she couldn't see what I was so bitter about. Rodney was perfectly happy to be the guilty party; they weren't, she pointed out caustically, expecting me to behave like a gentleman. I wouldn't have to pay for the divorce. Rodney would see to that. I wasn't being asked to provide her with alimony. Rodney had more than enough. At one point she came close to bribing me with Rodney's money to let her go without fuss. And yet – was it really as simple as that? She had loved me, or at least needed me, for a time. Had she perhaps seen in me the father that she had lost at five years old?

During the divorce, through which I was, as it were, gently processed by highly paid legal experts as if I were an embarrassing but expendable nuisance to be got rid of with decent speed, I was only able to keep sane by the knowledge that I was going to kill Collingford. I knew that I couldn't go on living in a world where he breathed the same air. My mind fed voraciously on the thought of his death, savoured it, began systematically and with dreadful pleasure to plan it.

A successful murder depends on knowing your victim, his character, his daily routine, his weaknesses, those unalterable and betraying habits which make up the core of personality. I knew quite a lot about Rodney Collingford. I knew facts which Elsie had let fall in her first weeks with the firm, typing pool gossip. I knew the fuller and rather more intimate facts which she had disclosed in those early days of her enchantment with him, when neither prudence nor kindness had been able to conceal her obsessive preoccupation with her new boss. I should have been warned then. I knew, none better, the need to talk about the absent lover.

What did I know about him? I knew the facts that were common knowledge, of course. That he was wealthy; aged thirty; a notable amateur golfer; that he lived in an ostentatious mock Georgian house on the banks of the Thames looked after by over-paid but non-resident staff; that he owned a cabin cruiser; that he was just over six feet tall; that he was a good business man but reputedly close-fisted; that he was methodical in his habits. I knew a miscellaneous and unrelated set of facts about him, some of which would be useful, some important, some of which I couldn't use. I knew – and this was rather surprising – that he was good with his hands and liked making things in metal and wood. He had built an expensively-equipped and large workroom in the grounds of his house and spent every Thursday evening working there alone. He was a man addicted to routine. This creativity, however mundane and trivial,

I found intriguing, but I didn't let myself dwell on it. I was interested in him only so far as his personality and habits were relevant to his death. I never thought of him as a human being. He had no existence for me apart from my hate. He was Rodney Collingford, my victim.

First I decided on the weapon. A gun would have been the most certain, I supposed, but I didn't know how to get one and was only too well aware I wouldn't know how to load or use it if I did. Besides, I was reading a number of books about murder at the time and I realised that guns, however cunningly obtained, were easy to trace. And there was another thing. A gun was too impersonal, too remote. I wanted to make physical contact at the moment of death. I wanted to get close enough to see that final look of incredulity and horror as he recognised, simultaneously, me and his death. I wanted to drive a knife into his throat.

I bought it two days after the divorce. I was in no hurry to kill Collingford. I knew that I must take my time, must be patient, if I were to act in safety. One day, perhaps when we were old, I might tell Elsie. But I didn't intend to be found out. This was to be the perfect murder. And that meant taking my time. He would be allowed to live for a full year. But I knew that the earlier I bought the knife the more difficult it would be, twelve months later, to trace the purchase. I didn't buy it locally. I went one Saturday morning by train and bus to a north-east suburb and found a busy ironmongers and general store just off the High Street. There was a variety of knives on display. The blade of the one I selected was about six inches long and was made of strong steel screwed into a plain wooden handle. I think it was probably meant for cutting lino. In the shop its razor sharp edge was protected by a strong cardboard sheath. It felt good and right in my hand. I stood in a small queue at the pay desk and the cashier didn't even glance up as he took my notes and pushed the change towards me.

But the most satisfying part of my planning was the second stage. I wanted Collingford to suffer. I wanted him to know that he was going to die. It wasn't enough that he should realise it in a last second before I drove in the knife or in that final second before he ceased to know anything for ever. Two seconds of agony, however horrible, weren't an adequate return for what he had done to me. I wanted him to know that he was a condemned man, to know it with increasing certainty, to wonder every morning whether this might be his last day. What if this knowledge did make him cautious, put him on his guard? In this country, he couldn't go armed. He couldn't carry on his business with a hired protector always at his side. He couldn't bribe the police to watch him every second of the day. Besides, he wouldn't want to be thought a coward. I guessed that he would carry on, ostentatiously normal, as if the threats were unreal or derisory, something to laugh about with his drinking cronies. He was the sort to laugh at danger. But he would never be sure. And, by the end, his nerve and confidence would be broken. Elsie wouldn't know him for the man she had married.

I would have liked to have telephoned him but that, I knew, was impracticable. Calls could be traced; he might refuse to talk to me; I wasn't confident that I could disguise my voice. So the sentence of death would have to be sent by post. Obviously, I couldn't write the notes or the envelopes myself. My studies in murder had shown me how difficult it was to disguise handwriting and the method of cutting out and sticking together letters from a newspaper seemed messy, very time consuming and difficult to manage wearing gloves. I knew, too, that it would be fatal to use my own small portable typewriter or one of the machines at the library. The forensic experts could identify a machine.

And then I hit on my plan. I began to spend my Saturdays and occasional half days journeying round London and visiting shops where they sold secondhand typewriters. I expect you know the kind of shop; a variety of machines of different ages, some practically obsolete, others comparatively new, arranged on tables where the prospective purchaser may try them out. There were new machines too, and the proprietor was usually employed in demonstrating their merits or discussing hire purchase terms. The customers wandered desultorily around, inspecting the machines, stopping occasionally to type out an exploratory passage. There were little pads of rough paper stacked ready for use. I didn't, of course, use the scrap paper provided. I came supplied with my own writing materials, a well-known brand sold in every stationers and on every railway bookstall. I bought a small supply of paper and envelopes once every two months and never from the same shop. Always, when handling them, I wore a thin pair of gloves, slipping them on as soon as my typing was complete. If someone were near, I would tap out the usual drivel about the sharp brown fox or all good men coming to the aid of the party. But if I were quite alone I would type something very different.

'This is the first communication, Collingford. You'll be getting them regularly from now on. They're just to let you know that I'm going to kill you.'

'You can't escape me, Collingford. Don't bother to inform the police. They can't help you.'

'I'm getting nearer, Collingford. Have you made your will?'

'Not long now, Collingford. What does it feel like to be under sentence of death?'

The warnings weren't particularly elegant. As a librarian I could think of a number of apt quotations which would have added a touch of individuality or style, perhaps even of sardonic humour, to the bald sentence of death. But I dared not risk originality. The notes had to be ordinary, the kind of threat which any one of his enemies, a worker, a competitor, a cuckolded husband, might have sent.

Sometimes I had a lucky day. The shop would be large, well supplied, nearly empty. I would be able to move from typewriter to typewriter and leave with perhaps a dozen or so notes and addressed envelopes ready to send. I always carried a folded newspaper in which I could conceal my writing pad and envelopes and into which I could quickly slip my little stock of typed messages.

It was quite a job to keep myself supplied with notes and I discovered interesting parts of London and fascinating shops. I particularly enjoyed this part of my plan. I wanted Collingford to get two notes a week, one posted on Sunday and one on Thursday. I wanted him to come to dread Friday and Monday mornings when the familiar typed envelope would drop on his mat. I wanted him to believe the threat was real. And why should he not believe it? How could the force of my hate and resolution not transmit itself through paper and typescript to his gradually comprehending brain?

I wanted to keep an eye on my victim. It shouldn't have been difficult; we lived in the same town. But our lives were worlds apart. He was a hard and sociable drinker. I never went inside a public house, and would have been particularly ill at ease in the kind of public house he frequented. But, from time to time, I would see him in the town. Usually he would be parking his Jaguar, and I would watch his quick, almost furtive, look to left and right before he turned to lock the door. Was it my imagination that he looked older, that some of the confidence had drained out of him?

Once, when walking by the river on a Sunday in early Spring, I saw him manoeuvring his boat through Teddington Lock. Ilsa – she had, I knew, changed her name after her marriage – was with him. She was wearing a white trouser suit, her flowing hair was bound by a red scarf. There was a party. I could see two more men and a couple of girls and hear high female squeals of laughter. I turned quickly and slouched away as if I were the guilty one. But not before I had seen Collingford's face. This time I couldn't be mistaken. It wasn't, surely, the tedious job of getting his boat unscratched through the lock that made his face look so grey and strained.

The third phase of my planning meant moving house. I wasn't sorry to go. The bungalow, feminine, chintzy, smelling of fresh paint and the new shoddy furniture which she had chosen, was Elsie's home not mine. Her scent still lingered in cupboards and on pillows. In these inappropriate surroundings I had known greater happiness than I was ever to know again. But now I paced restlessly from room to empty room fretting to be gone.

It took me four months to find the house I wanted. It had to be on or very near to the river within two or three miles upstream of Collingford's house. It had to be small and reasonably cheap. Money wasn't too much of a difficulty. It was a time of rising house prices and the modern bungalow sold at three hundred pounds more than I had paid for it. I could get another mortgage without difficulty if I didn't ask for too much, but I thought it likely that, for what I wanted, I should have to pay cash.

The house agents perfectly understood that a man on his own found a three bedroom bungalow too large for him and, even if they found me rather vague about my new requirements and irritatingly imprecise about the reasons for rejecting their offerings, they still sent me orders to view. And then, suddenly on an afternoon in April, I found exactly what I was looking for. It actually stood on the river, separated from it only by a narrow tow path. It was a one-bedroom shack-like wooden bungalow with a tiled roof, set in a small neglected plot of sodden grass and overgrown flower beds. There had once been a wooden landing stage but now the two remaining planks, festooned with weeds and tags of rotted rope, were half submerged beneath the slime of the river. The paint on the small veranda had long ago flaked away. The wallpaper of twined roses in the sitting-room was blotched and faded. The previous owner had left two old cane chairs and a ramshackle table. The kitchen was pokey and ill-equipped. Everywhere there hung a damp miasma of depression and decay. In summer, when the neighbouring shacks and bungalows were occupied by holidaymakers and week-enders it would, no doubt, be cheerful enough. But in October, when I planned to kill Collingford, it would be as deserted and isolated as a disused morgue. I bought it and paid cash. I was even able to knock two hundred pounds off the asking price.

My life that summer was almost happy. I did my job at the library adequately. I lived alone in the shack, looking after myself as I had before my marriage. I spent my evenings watching television. The images flickered in front of my eyes almost unregarded, a monochrome background to my bloody and obsessive thoughts.

I practised with the knife until it was as familiar in my hand as an eating utensil. Collingford was taller than I by six inches. The thrust then would have to be upward. It made a difference to the way I held the knife and I experimented to find the most comfortable and effective grip. I hung a bolster on a hook in the bedroom door and lunged at a marked spot for hours at a time. Of course, I didn't actually insert the knife; nothing must dull the sharpness of its blade. Once a week, a special treat, I sharpened it to an even keener edge.

Two days after moving into the bungalow I bought a dark blue untrimmed track suit and a pair of light running shoes. Throughout the summer I spent an occasional evening running on the tow path. The people who owned the neighbouring chalets, when they were there, which was infrequently, got used to the sound of my television through the closed curtains and the sight of my figure jogging past their windows. I kept apart from them and from everyone and Summer passed into Autumn. The shutters were put up on all the chalets except mine. The tow path became mushy with falling leaves. Dusk fell early, and the summer sights and sounds died on the river. And it was October.

He was due to die on Thursday October 17th, the anniversary of the final decree of divorce. It had to be a Thursday, the evening which he spent by custom alone in his workshop, but it was a particularly happy augury that the anniversary should fall on a Thursday. I knew that he would be there. Every Thursday for nearly a year I had padded along the two and half miles of the footpath in the evening dusk and had stood briefly watching the squares of light from his windows and the dark bulk of the house behind.

It was a warm evening. There had been a light drizzle for most of the day but, by dusk, the skies had cleared. There was a thin white sliver of moon and it cast a trembling ribbon of light across the river. I left the library at my usual time, said my usual good-nights. I knew that I had been my normal self during the day, solitary, occasionally a little sarcastic, conscientious, betraying no hint of the inner tumult.

I wasn't hungry when I got home but I made myself eat an omelette and drink two cups of coffee. I put on my swimming trunks and hung around my neck a plastic toilet bag containing the knife. Over the trunks I put on my track suit, slipping a pair of thin rubber gloves into the pocket. Then, at about quarter past seven, I left the shack and began my customary gentle trot along the tow path.

When I got to the chosen spot opposite to Collingford's house I could see at once that all was well. The house was in darkness but there were the customary lighted windows of his workshop. I saw that the cabin cruiser was moored against the boathouse. I stood very still and listened. There was no sound. Even the light breeze had died and the yellowing leaves on the riverside elms hung motionless. The tow path was completely deserted. I slipped into the shadow of the hedge where the trees grew thickest and found the place I had already selected. I put on the rubber gloves, slipped out of the track suit, and left it folded around my running shoes in the shadow of the hedge. Then, still watching carefully to left and right, I made my way to the river.

I knew just where I must enter and leave the water. I had selected a place where the bank curved gently, where the water was shallow and the bottom was firm and comparatively free of mud. The water struck very cold, but I expected that. Every night during that Autumn I had bathed in cold water to accustom my body to the shock. I swam across the river with my methodical but quiet breast stroke, hardly disturbing the dark surface of the water. I tried to keep out of the path of moonlight but, from time to time, I swam into its silver gleam and saw my red gloved hands parting in front of me as if they were already stained with blood.

I used Collingford's landing stage to clamber out the other side. Again I stood still and listened. There was no sound except for the constant moaning of the river and the solitary cry of a night bird. I made my way silently over the grass. Outside the door of his workroom, I paused again. I could hear the noise of some kind of machinery. I wondered whether the door would be locked, but it opened easily when I turned the handle. I moved into a blaze of light.

I knew exactly what I had to do. I was perfectly calm. It was over in about four seconds. I don't think he really had a chance. He was absorbed in what he had been doing, bending over a lathe, and the sight of an almost naked man, walking purposely towards him, left him literally impotent with surprise. But, after that first paralysing second, he knew me. Oh yes, he knew me! Then I drew my right hand from behind my back and struck. The knife went in as sweetly as if the flesh had been butter. He staggered and fell. I had expected that and I let myself go loose and fell on top of him. His eyes were glazed, his mouth opened and there was a gush of dark red blood. I twisted the knife viciously in the wound, relishing the sound of tearing sinews. Then I waited. I counted five deliberately, then raised myself from his prone figure and crouched behind him before withdrawing the knife. When I withdrew it there was a fountain of sweet smelling blood which curved from his throat like an arch. There is one thing I shall never forget. The blood must have been red, what other colour could it have been? But, at the time and for ever afterwards, I saw it as a golden stream.

I checked my body for blood stains before I left the workshop and rinsed my arms under the cold tap at his sink. My bare feet made no marks on the wooden block flooring. I closed the door quietly after me and, once again, stood listening. Still no sound. The house was dark and empty.

The return journey was more exhausting than I had thought possible. The river seemed to have widened and I thought that I should never reach my home shore. I was glad I had chosen a shallow part of the stream and that the bank was firm. I doubt whether I could have drawn myself up through a welter of mud and slime. I was shivering violently as I zipped-up my track suit and it took me precious seconds to get on my running shoes. After I had run about a mile down the tow path I weighted the toilet bag containing the knife with stones from the path and hurled it into the middle of the river. I guessed that they would drag part of the Thames for the weapon but they could hardly search the whole stream. And, even if they did, the toilet bag was one sold at the local chain store which anyone might have bought, and I was confident that the knife could never be traced to me. Half an hour later I was back in my shack. I had left the television on and the news was just ending. I made myself a cup of hot cocoa and sat to watch it. I felt drained of thought and energy as if I had just made love. I was conscious of nothing but my tiredness, my body's coldness gradually returning to life in the warmth of the electric fire, and a great peace.

He must have had quite a lot of enemies. It was nearly a fortnight before the police got round to interviewing me. Two officers came, a Detective Inspector and a Sergeant, both in plain clothes. The Sergeant did most of the talking; the other just sat, looking round at the sitting-room, glancing out at the river, looking at the two of us from time to time from cold grey eyes as if the whole investigation were a necessary bore. The Sergeant said the usual reassuring platitudes about just a few questions. I was nervous, but that didn't worry me. They would expect me to be nervous. I told myself that, whatever I did, I mustn't try to be clever. I mustn't talk too much. I had decided to tell them that I spent the whole evening watching television, confident that no one would be able to refute this. I knew that no friends would have called on me. I doubted whether my colleagues at the library even knew where I lived. And I had no telephone so I need not fear that a caller's ring had gone unanswered during that crucial hour and a half.

On the whole it was easier than I had expected. Only once did I feel myself at risk. That was when the Inspector suddenly intervened. He said in a harsh voice:

'He married your wife didn't he? Took her away from you some people might say. Nice piece of goods, too, by the look of her. Didn't you feel any grievance? Or was it all nice and friendly? You take her, old chap. No ill feelings. That kind of thing.'

It was hard to accept the contempt in his voice but if he hoped to provoke me he didn't succeed. I had been expecting this question. I was prepared. I looked down at my hands and waited a few seconds before I spoke. I knew exactly what I would say.

'I could have killed Collingford myself when she first told me about him. But I had to come to terms with it. She went for the money you see. And if that's the kind of wife you have, well she's going to leave you sooner or later. Better sooner than when you have a family. You tell yourself "good riddance". I don't mean I felt that at first, of course. But I did feel it in the end. Sooner than I expected, really.'

That was all I said about Elsie then or ever. They came back three times. They asked if they could look round my shack. They looked round it. They took away two of my suits and the track suit for examination. Two weeks later they returned them without comment. I never knew what they suspected, or even if they did suspect. Each time they came I said less, not more. I never varied my story. I never allowed them to provoke me into discussing my marriage or speculating about the crime. I just sat there, telling them the same thing over and over again. I never felt in any real danger. I knew that they had dragged some lengths of the river but that they hadn't found the weapon. In the end they gave up. I always had the feeling that I was pretty low on their list of suspects and that, by the end, their visits were merely a matter of form.

It was three months before Elsie came to me. I was glad that it wasn't earlier. It might have looked suspicious if she had arrived at the shack when the police were with me. After Collingford's death I hadn't seen her. There were pictures of her in the national and local newspapers, fragile in sombre furs and black hat at the inquest, bravely controlled at the crematorium, sitting in her drawing-room in afternoon dress and pearls with her husband's dog at her feet, the personification of loneliness and grief.

'I can't think who could have done it. He must have been a madman. Rodney hadn't an enemy in the world.'

That statement caused some ribald comment at the library. One of the assistants said:

'He's left her a fortune I hear. Lucky for her she had an alibi. She was at a London theatre all the evening, watching *Macbeth*. Otherwise, from what I've heard of our Rodney Collingford, people might have started to get ideas about his fetching little widow.'

Then he gave me a sudden embarrassed glance, remembering who the widow was.

And so one Friday evening, she came. She drove herself and was alone. The dark green Saab drove up at my ramshackle gate. She came into the sitting-room and looked around in a kind of puzzled contempt. After a moment, still not speaking, she sat in one of the fireside chairs and crossed her legs, moving one caressingly against the other. I hadn't seen her sitting like that before. She looked up at me. I was standing stiffly in front of her chair, my lips dry. When I spoke I couldn't recognise my own voice.

'So you've come back?' I said.

She stared at me, incredulous, and then she laughed:

'To you? Back for keeps? Don't be silly, darling! I've just come to pay a visit. Besides, I wouldn't dare to come back, would I? I might be frightened that you'd stick a knife into my throat.'

I couldn't speak. I stared at her, feeling the blood drain from my face. Then I heard her high, rather childish voice. It sounded almost kind.

'Don't worry, I shan't tell. You were right about him, darling, you really were. He wasn't at all nice really. And mean! I didn't care so much about your meanness. After all, you don't earn so very much do you? But he had half a million! Think of it, darling. I've been left half a million! And he was so mean that he expected me to go on working as his secretary even after we were married. I typed all his letters! I really did! All that he sent from home, anyway. And I had to open his post every morning unless the envelopes had a secret little sign on them he'd told his friends about to show that they were private.'

I said through bloodless lips.

'So all my notes—'

'He never saw them darling. Well, I didn't want to worry him did I? And I knew they were from you. I knew when the first one arrived. You never could spell communication could you? I noticed that when you used to write to the house agents and the solicitor before we were married. It made me laugh considering that you're an educated librarian and I was only a shop assistant.'

'So you knew all the time. You knew that it was going to happen.'

'Well, I thought that it might. But he really was horrible, darling. You can't imagine. And now I've got half a million! Isn't it lucky that I have an alibi? I thought you might come on that Thursday. And Rodney never did enjoy a serious play.'

After that brief visit I never saw or spoke to her again. I stayed in the shack, but life became pointless after Collingford's death. Planning his murder had been an interest, after all. Without Elsie and without my victim there seemed little point in living. And, about a year after his death, I began to dream. I still dream, always on a Monday and Friday. I live through it all again; the noiseless run along the tow path over the mush of damp leaves; the quiet swim across the river; the silent opening of his door; the upward thrust of the knife; the vicious turn in the wound; the animal sound of tearing tissues; the curving stream of golden blood. Only the homeward swim is different. In my dream the river is no longer a cleansing stream, luminous under the sickle moon, but a cloying, impenetrable, slow moving bog of viscous blood through which I struggle in impotent panic towards a steadily receding shore.

I know about the significance of the dream. I've read all about the psychology of guilt. Since I lost Elsie I've done all my living through books. But it doesn't help. And I no longer know who I am. I know who I used to be, our local Assistant Librarian, gentle, scholarly, timid, Elsie's husband. But then I killed Collingford. The man I was couldn't have done that. He wasn't that kind of person. So who am I? It isn't really surprising, I suppose, that the Library Committee suggested so tactfully that I ought to look for a less exacting job. A less exacting job than the post of Assistant Librarian? But you can't blame them. No one can be efficient and keep his mind on the job when he doesn't know who he is.

Sometimes, when I'm in a public house – and I seem to spend most of my time there nowadays since I've been out of work – I'll look over someone's shoulder at a newspaper photograph of Elsie and say:

'That's the beauuful Ilsa Mancelli. I was her first husband.'

I've got used to the way people sidle away from me, the ubiquitous pub bore, their eyes averted, their voices suddenly hearty. But sometimes, perhaps because they've been lucky with the horses and feel a spasm of pity for a poor deluded sod, they push a few coins over the counter to the barman before making their way to the door, and buy me a drink.

Jane Aiken Hodge

Suicide or Murder?

All night the wind had blown, savaging the house, tearing last leaves from the beech trees above it, slashing rain across the bedroom windows. Morning brought merely a slackening of darkness. 'I can't,' she said, when the alarm clock screamed on the far side of the bed.

'Again?' But he swung his legs out of bed and reached to turn on the overhead light.

'Don't. It hurts my eyes.'

James said something under his breath, picked up his clothes and vanished into the bathroom. Presently he would bring her a cup of tea, as he had on all the other mornings since her miscarriage, when she could not bring herself to get up, kiss her goodbye, and hurry down to get out the car for the drive to London. She ought to comb her hair, make herself presentable for him. But, 'I can't,' she told herself again, and pulled the bedclothes round her face.

When he brought the tea, she was half asleep, but pulled herself up reluctantly in the untidy bed. 'I didn't sleep all night,' she said. 'That wind. Put it on the table, would you?'

'Yes.' The saucer clicked sharply on the dusty table. 'Anything you'd like from town?'

'No thanks. What would I want? What shall I ever want?'

'God knows.' He picked up her old dressing-gown from the floor and dropped it on the bed. 'Have a good day. I'll be home about seven, I hope.'

'As late as that?' They had had this argument every day since she had left her job on doctor's orders and they had moved down here.

'I'm afraid so. Shall I take a run up to Smithfield at lunch time and get us a bit of steak?'

'Oh no,' she shuddered. 'Too bloody. I'm sure there's something in the freezer.'

'Another T.V. snack? Oh, very well . . . Goodbye.' He was gone. It was a minute before she realised that he had forgotten to kiss her. She cried a little, sorry for herself, found the tea was cold, and dozed off again. Presently it would be eleven o'clock; time to get up and have her first drink of the day. Her mind was just comfortably blurring into sleep again when Ginger landed with a thud on the bed. Ginger was hungry. James must have forgotten to feed him. Characteristic. Thoughtless; inconsiderate . . . Ginger meant to be fed. He walked round and round her head, purring, and making little passes at her with gentle paws. In the end, at half-past ten, she gave in and got up.

The face in the bathroom mirror was smeared with sleep and misery. Her hair needed cutting, reconditioning, everything . . . Why should she care? James never noticed, never took her anywhere. What was the use, marooned down here in the country? 'Six months,' she told the dismal face in the glass. 'Six months hard.' When had she started talking to herself?

Downstairs, a chair was pushed back from the kitchen table, a half-empty coffee cup sat in a saucer full of cigarette ends. James knew she hated that. How could he? She started through to the telephone in the hall, meaning to call him up and complain, then thought better of it. The last few times she had telephoned there had been something odd about Miss Minton's voice. She had never liked Miss Minton. Disastrous to have her down for that week-end. House-warming, indeed. To cheer her up. Miss Minton in one of her aprons being busy at the sink. Miss Minton oh so unobtrusively dusting the sitting-room. Miss Minton driving off with James to the Catholic church in the next village. Damn Miss Minton . . .

At least James had left some coffee in the pot. While it heated she opened a tin of cat-food and pacified Ginger. 'Cupboard love,' she grumbled at him. 'You don't care, so long as I feed you.' The cat glanced up nervously, then settled back to his food. He had taken to cringing away from her since that time she had kicked him on the stairs. Stupid.

The coffee was good, even if it had been reheated. She felt, for the moment, a little better. What had the doctor said? Make plans. Occupy herself. She reached for pad and pencil and made herself think about Christmas. But Christmas meant shopping, and shopping meant London, and how could she go to London? James would have to do the Christmas shopping. She must remember to make out a list for him at dinner tonight. He had been horrid about dinner. 'Another T.V. snack.' She got up and drifted over to the deep freeze. Steak in gravy. They had had that last night, and it had dried out because James was late. Fillets of cod in sauce. That was the night before. But down in the corner was one last packet of scampi. She would make her *scampi provençale*. James liked that.

Plan something. The doctor had been right. She felt better. She washed up the dishes, noticing that James seemed to have eaten nothing. Stupid. He would make himself ill, and then what would happen to her? She must speak to him about it. Call him up and urge him to have a proper lunch? This time she got half-way through dialling before she thought again and replaced the receiver. Anyway, it was after eleven o'clock. She went back to the kitchen, collected the sherry bottle and a glass and went through into the sitting-room.

It needed dusting. The roses James had bought for her birthday had dropped a trail of brown petals across the piano that she no longer played. Wind and rain lashed against the wide window. She shivered, went over to the thermostat, turned the heating up to seventy-four and listened with satisfaction as the boiler let out its willing roar in the cellar. James always turned the heat down when he got home. All right for him. He was out and about all day. Fresh air and exercise, the doctor had said. She looked down the rain-swept valley that showed no sign of human occupation. Not today, at all events.

It was well after eleven, and she had still not poured herself that life-saving first drink. Even after the coffee, her hand shook badly this morning, and when the telephone rang, she spilled the sherry and swore. James, no doubt: one of his anxious, boring calls. This time she would tell him he must do something about getting them twin beds. 'I can't stand it,' she told herself as she lifted the receiver.

But it was a woman's voice. Sally. Cheerful, stupid Sally from the magazine where she used to work. And she had left her sherry behind. How to cut her short? But Sally did not sound cheerful today. 'Look love, I'm calling from home. Got the day off. Wanted a chance to talk to you. How are you, by the way?'

The casual question infuriated her. 'I wish I was dead.'

'You've got to snap out of it, love. Honestly! I tell you, I saw James the other day.'

'Well?'

'In a restaurant. A good one. With that pretty secretary of his. Miss Minton. I warn you . . .'

'God damn you.' She slammed the receiver down on its rest. 'Trouble-making bitch.' She said it aloud, reaching a shaking hand for the sherry glass. She had really been feeling better, ready to get started, do something . . . And now Sally had spoiled it all. Jealous of course. They had all been jealous when she had married James. And no wonder. The taste of lost happiness was sour in her mouth. She and James had been so happy. Brilliantly, greedily happy, cramming more into their days and most especially into their nights than days or nights could hold.

James's fault that they had lost it. He had been the one who wanted the baby. Or said he did. Catholic nonsense. Her glass was empty, and she refilled it automatically. Absurd of him to think she could keep on her job through those dreadful early months of pregnancy. Sick, and sick and sick again, retching her heart out in the ladies' loo. Horrible. Never again. If that doctor said once more that all she needed was another baby, she would leave him. Men. How should they understand? And as for pretending the miscarriage was her fault . . . 'Balls!' She put her sticky glass down on the marquetry table James's mother had given them and thought with satisfaction how furious the mark would make him. House proud, that was James. Always fussing about something.

The telephone rang. Not Sally again. If it was, she would give her a piece of her mind. But it was Miss Minton, putting James through. She rather thought Miss Minton listened when she and James were talking, and felt a wild temptation to tell him of Sally's call. But it was all spiteful nonsense. She would not lower herself by mentioning it. And James was in a hurry; he sounded actually breathless. 'I've got a brute of a day, darling, and the worst of it is, I've got to dine a client at the end of it. God knows how late I'll be. I thought I might put up at the club.'

'Oh.' She had longed to have the wide bed to herself, but now felt curiously depressed at the prospect. 'I'd been planning to do my *scampi provençale*,' she said.

'Pity.' What was wrong with his voice? 'I say,' he went on in a rush. 'I meant to tell you, but you were asleep when I left. I thought I smelled gas in the downstairs hall. Better get on to the gas board and have them come out and check the boiler. They'll come at once if you tell them it may be a leak.'

Fussing again. Just like James. 'I haven't smelled anything.' They both knew that she had lost almost all sense of smell after a childhood illness. 'If I call them, they'll keep me waiting round all day.'

'Were you thinking of going out?'

She looked through the glass pane of the front door down the windy valley. 'You know the doctor told me to. Down to the village and back every day, he said. Sludge, sludge, sludge through the mud . . .'

'Mr James . . .' Miss Minton's voice. 'I have a call for you on the other line.' Since when had she called him 'Mr James'?

'Damn,' he said. 'Promise you'll phone them, darling. For my sake. I'll be worrying.'

'Oh, very well. Enjoy yourself at your "business dinner".' With Miss Minton? Mr James, indeed. Perhaps Sally had been right after all. 'Anyone I know?' she asked now, with spurious interest.

'No.' Shortly. He must have caught her note of irony. And then, 'Must go, darling. Don't forget the gas board.' He rang off without giving her time to answer.

Rude. Boorish. Tears of self pity stood in her eyes as she thought of the time when they were engaged, and talked, every day, so long on the telephone that they were the laughing-stock of both their offices. Two years ago? Two centuries.

The day yawned before her. She had been going to marinate the scampi, and make her special rice dish to go with them. And before that, she had meant to walk down to the village and buy garlic. No need to do that now. A boiled egg for lunch. Another one for supper? And blessed early bed, with the women's magazines James sneered at. As for the gas board; it was his idea; let him call them himself.

The sherry was making her rather pleasantly drowsy. Tonight, with no James to come fumbling to bed in the small hours, she would sleep and sleep and sleep . . . He would never understand how badly she slept, maintaining cheerfully that she was always out like a light when he came to bed. Well, of course she was, or pretended to be. They would have twin beds for Christmas, or, better still, she could keep the double and put a single in James's study. After all, if he wanted to stay up till all hours working, the study was the place for him. She got up, half-empty glass in hand and walked slowly across the hall. When had James taken to keeping the study door shut? It was ages since she had been in here. James had told her, rather rudely, she had thought, after the last cleaning woman had left, that he would look after it himself.

He had done so, too. The room was a surprise compared with the rest of the house. Even James's work table, about which she used to tease him so, was comparatively tidy. But what she noticed first was the one red rose in a tall wine glass by the typewriter. Not a late one from the garden. A florist's rose. One of a dozen James had given someone? Kept here where he knew she never came; or flaunted here because he wanted her to find it?

Or all a lot of nonsense? She had always had too much imagination for her own comfort. It had been one of her virtues as an editor. But it was queer. There was something queer about the whole room, come to think of it. It felt – ridiculous, of course – but it felt hostile. Suddenly dizzy, she sat down with a bump in James's chair. Her sherry glass landed half on, half off a pile of papers, tipped and spilled. Now James really would be angry. Luckily, she had never taken off her apron. She untied it and dabbed at the sticky liquid, which was seeping in among the sheets. At least it was nothing finished, just notes for a speech or something of the kind.

She turned the pile over, to mop underneath, 'Chapter One', she read. Good God, James was writing a book. Absurd. She was the one with literary talent in the family. It had been one of their jokes. Presently, she was going to write a best seller. She had actually started several, but there had always been so much else to do. Thinking this, she began idly to read poor James's attempt. 'Despair can be measured,' it began, 'by the quotient of lost happiness.' Oh, poor James indeed. He was trying to write one of those dreary modern novels he had taken to reading. He would never succeed, of course, not cheerful, extrovert James.

Cheerful? Well, they had neither of them been all that cheerful since the miscarriage. One must mourn one's dead. She had told him that when he tried to make a small festivity of her birthday. Pitiful, really. The champagne he had brought home had been warm, and half of it had fizzed out when the cork blew. And anyway, champagne with cod fillets. What a laugh. And, afterwards, inevitably, James's tentative, intolerable advances in bed. She looked about her. Plenty of room for a divan under the study window, and then, thank God, the argument would be over.

She did not think she wanted to read any more of James's depressing book. Besides, the dizziness was worse. She must be hungry. Just one more glass of sherry and she would boil herself two eggs. But first she must tidy up James's book. It was horrid of him to sit down here writing gloomy stuff like this, and pretending it was work he brought home from the office. No wonder she had felt the room hostile. And as for that rose . . . She felt a savage temptation to throw it away, but picked up her glass instead, and went through to refill it.

After lunch, she curled up on the sofa, and went off into a surprisingly heavy sleep, only to be wakened by Ginger, howling somewhere. 'What's the matter?' she called crossly, but he only howled louder, and finally she got sleepily up in her stockinged feet and found him sitting outside the cellar door. At sight of her he let out another banshee wail, almost as bad as the wind outside. 'Blast you.' She said it quite amiably. 'You woke me up. Think there's a mouse down there do you?' She opened the cellar door and heard the curious clicking, crackling noise the boiler made as it cooled off. But Ginger, who often went down to investigate this, had changed his mind, and backed away into the kitchen. 'Very well, then.' She shut the door with a bang and went back to the sofa.

This time her sleep was full of anxious dreams. She had watched a thriller on television a few nights before, where the bank robbers had been disguised as gas conversion crews. In her dream, she was one of them, on the run from the police, driving frantically down country lanes in her van with the gas board insignia. And all the time she knew, with that curious double vision of dreams, that the thing she was escaping was waiting for her at the end of the road. She heard the police siren . . .

No, it was the front door bell. 'Blast!' She sat up, running hands through untidy hair. But why answer it? It would be one of those dreadful, dauntless tweeded ladies who prowled the lanes collecting for their favourite charities. Nobody else came to the house. Or, worse still, a political canvasser? The bell rang again, loud above the howling of the wind.

It was November dusk already, and no lights on in the house. In a moment, they would go away. She settled back in her corner of the sofa. Much better not answer it. A woman alone in the house. Ridiculous to come collecting for charity so late. How was she to know it wasn't a hippy, a mugger, a maniac? She had meant to have a chain put on the door, but forgotten all about it. Certainly she would not go. Too late now, anyway. Whoever it was must have gone. And thank God for that. If it had been one of the local good ladies, she would have had to ask her in, offer her tea. Nothing to eat and the house full of dust. Quite impossible. James would simply have to put his mind on finding a new cleaning woman. He was the one who was in touch with the village. He went to the pub every Saturday and Sunday, and knew all about everyone.

She would speak to him about it tonight. Oh – he was staying in town tonight. Stupid to be so forgetful. A little frightening? Perhaps she would ask the doctor for some different pills. God, if only that wind would stop. The whole house was working with it, like a ship at sea. And dark, too. She peered at her watch. Only four o'clock, but night time just the same. She reached out and switched on the reading lamp, then got up and drew heavy curtains across the windows. That was better. That gave her a feeling of safety. If it had been violence, ringing at her door, she had shut it out now. No one could see her. And James was not coming home. Early supper and early bed. None of that dreary keeping things hot while she waited for the sound of the car on the hill.

She still felt a little dizzy. What she needed was a drink. After all, she was going to have supper early . . . Crossing the hall without bothering to turn on the light, she tripped over the cat, and swore. He would kill her one of these days, getting under her feet. What was he doing sleeping in the hall anyway? Still watching for his cellar mouse? At least he had gone out now, with a frantic slam of his cat door. Good riddance.

She had not washed the lunch dishes, so the sherry glass was still sitting on the dresser. The bottle was almost empty. James must have been drinking it at night. She fetched another from the store room and paused for a moment to listen to rain slamming on the corrugated iron roof. Horrible house. Horrible weather. Horrible life.

Ginger came flapping back in, golden fur sleek with rain, and tried to dry himself on her ankles. 'Blast you,' she said without heat, the first sip of sherry going blandly down. But she had hardly settled herself on the sofa when he started howling again, out in the hall, the almost Siamese screech mixing eerily with the wail of the wind outside. The telephone, adding its note, was almost a relief. James again, fussing about the gas board? No; it was a strange, rather diffident male voice, and identified itself quickly as belonging to Paul Marchant, the young vicar. 'You're all right?' he asked. 'I do apologise for bothering you, but I called on you earlier this afternoon, and got no answer. I was a little worried. Yours is such a lonely house . . .' His voice trailed off, apologetic, inconclusive.

She wanted to laugh at him down the telephone. All right, indeed. But instinct warned her that it might sound more hysterical than she would like. So he had been her mugger, her maniac. The vicar. And doubtless had been afraid that she really had been attacked. Or – not such a nice thought – had he thought that she might have taken an overdose? She might be a lapsed Catholic, but he ought to know she would never do that. 'Oh dear, I am so sorry,' she was pleased with the light note she achieved. 'I'm afraid I fell fast asleep this afternoon. It was such a brute of a night. I must have slept right through the door bell. I do apologise. I hope it wasn't anything important.'

'Oh, no,' he said. 'It just occurred to me that you might be lonely up there, on a day like this. No need to apologise; I enjoyed the walk. It's splendid out when you've got your teeth into it.'

'Rather you than me.' She was tired of the conversation now, and grateful when he rang off. Absent-mindedly, she reached for the sherry bottle and refilled her glass. Something odd about his calling? He had come when they first moved in, and she had given him a cup of tea and explained about being Catholics. Why come again? Did they get together, those men of religion, and compare notes? She doesn't come to my church, why don't you have a go? Or – she drank half a glass at one draft – had James said something to him? She knew they often met in the *Four Feathers* on Saturdays. Could James possibly have told that very young man that he was worried about her? Asked him to come and call? Involve her, perhaps, in some inspiring local activity? The Women's Institute, no doubt. Hardly the Mothers' Union.

She was crying again, hard tears that brought no comfort. If James had really done that to her; talked behind her back; betrayed her; she would . . . She would like to kill him. It would be the end of everything between them, except that it could not end, tied as they were by the iron bond of their Catholic marriage. Till death us do part. She had a sudden, horrible picture of herself, grinding up the sleeping pills the doctor handed out so lavishly, mixing them into . . . What would one mix them with?

Monstrous to be thinking like this. It was the wind, of course, and the loneliness, and the despair. Without James she would be lost, even more so than she was already. The thought brought her rather unsteadily to her feet. Memories of the red rose in the study had nagged at her all afternoon. Perhaps if she looked at more of that depressing book, it would tell her something about James. Because, suddenly, horribly, the thought of losing James had become a possibility, not remote, not hypothetical, but real.

Sally's telephone call. James lunching with Miss Minton. Giving her eleven red roses and keeping one for himself? Having an affair with her? Those late nights at the office? Not at the office at all? But – James? Pious, Catholic James, who had been so strait-laced before they were married? Impossible. Ludicrous. James and Miss Minton had gone to mass together, that week-end.

The bottle clicked against the glass as she crossed the hall to the study. Odd to be so unsteady on her feet. Something about her new lot of pills? She sat down in James's chair, put bottle and glass carefully on a sheet of rough notes, and picked up the typescript. 'Despair is the quotient of lost happiness.' Blast James. What did he know about despair? He had not lain, all alone, crying with pain, crying with fright, losing their child. Compared with hers, his despair was simply childish. She did not want to read about it, and, besides, the words blurred queerly before her eyes. Too hard work.

Could she be sickening for something? If she was really ill, James would have to stay at home and look after her. Get her help. Move into the study. Make life possible again. Or would life ever be possible again? Reaching for the bottle, she knocked over the wine glass with its single, mocking red rose. Water seeped across the typescript, but this time she did not do anything about it. She was savagely busy, tearing the rose petals into shreds; scattering them across the table.

Hail rattled on the uncurtained window. This room was horrible. It hated her. And she hated it right back. James would know that when he saw what she had done to his rose. Destroy the book, too? Her child. His book. She tore the first page across. But her hands shook. It was too much trouble. Let him keep his childish book. Besides, she wanted to get out of this hateful room, with its bleak, black windows. She was ill. She would go to bed, and James, when he got back tomorrow night, would be sorry. But, first, she must get herself a new bottle of sherry. Defiantly, she threw the empty one into James's waste-paper basket. That would teach him to badger her about how much she drank. In the store-room, rain on the iron roof ground at her nerves. 'I shall go mad,' she said. 'It's too much. I can't bear it.' And, from the hall, the cat howled again. 'Too much.' Quite slowly, full bottle in hand, she moved through the kitchen into the hall, where the cat, lying across the cellar door, raised its head a little and howled again, horribly.

'God damn you.' She threw the bottle. Had she assumed that the cat would run for it, as it always had before when she threw things? If so, she was wrong. The bottle hit Ginger squarely on the head, then shattered on the cellar door.

'Puss?' But the cat lay still, blood seeping into the flood of sherry, Horrible. An accident. What would James say? She felt too ill to care. Too ill even to get upstairs to her room. She staggered into the sitting-room, subsided on the sofa, and let the tears come.

And outside, in the double-glazed hall, the gas went on seeping, as it had all day, up from the cellar, where James had loosened one vital connection before he left for work.

Celia Fremlin

Accommodation Vacant

'I'm sorry. . . .' The woman's eyes slithered expertly down Linda's loose, figure-concealing coat, and her voice hardened. 'No, I'm sorry, the room's been taken. . . . No, I've nothing left at all, I'm afraid. . . . Good afternoon. . . .'

Familiar enough words by now. Goodness knows, we ought to be used to it, thought Linda bitterly, as she and David trailed together down the grimy steps. She dared not even look up at him for comfort, lest he should see the tears stinging and glittering in her eyes.

But he had seen them anyway. His arm came round her thin shoulders, and for a moment they leaned together, speechless, in the grey, mean street, engulfed by a disappointment so intense, so totally shared, that one day, when they were old, old people, they might remember it as an extraordinary joy.

'Lin – Lin, darling, don't cry! It'll be all right. I swear it will be all right! I promise you it will, Lin!'

The despairing note in his young voice, the pressure of his arm around her destroyed the last remnants of Linda's self-control. Burying her face against the worn leather of his jacket. She sobbed, helplessly, and hopelessly.

'It's my fault, David. It's all my fault!' she gulped, her voice muffled among the luxuriance of his dark, shoulder-length hair. 'It's my fault. It was me who talked you into it. You said all along we shouldn't start a baby yet, not until you've got a proper job—'

At this, David jerked her sharply round to face him.

'Lin!' he said. 'Never, never say that again! I want this baby as much as you do, and if I ever said different, then forget it! He's *our* baby, yours and mine! I'm his father, and I want him! Get it? I *want*

696

him! And I'm going to provide a home for him! A smashing home, too,'
he proclaimed defiantly into the dingy, uncaring street. 'A home fit for
my son! Fit for my wife and son . . .!' His voice trailed off as he glared
through the gathering November dusk at the closed doors, the tightly
curtained windows, rank on rank, as far as they could see. 'My God, if I
could only get a decent job!' he muttered; and grabbing Linda's hand
in a harsh, almost savage grip he hurried her away; back to the main
road, back to the lighted buses, back 'home'.

That's what they still called it, anyway, though they both knew it
wasn't home anymore. How could it be, when they had to steal in
through the front door like burglars, closing it in a whisper behind them,
going up the creaking stairs on tiptoe in the vain hope of avoiding Mrs
Moles, the landlady, with her guarded eyes and her twice-daily in-
quisitions: 'Found anywhere yet? Oh. Oh, I see. Yes, well, I'm sorry,
but I'm afraid I can't give you any more extension. Six months you've
had' (to the day, actually; Linda remembered in every detail that May
morning when she had come back from the doctor's bubbling over with
her glorious news, spilling it out, in reckless triumph, to everyone in the
house). 'Six months, and I could have got you out in a week if I'd been
minded! A week's notice, that's all I'd have to have given. It's not like
you're on a regular tenancy! Six months I've given you. It's not everyone'd be that patient, I can tell you! But I've had enough! I'm giving
you till Monday, understand? Not a day longer! I need that room.'

Sometimes, during these tirades, David would answer back. Standing
in front of Linda on the dark stairs, protecting her with his broad shoulders and his mass of tangled, caveman hair, he would storm at Mrs
Moles face to face, giving as good as he got; and Linda never told him
that it only made matters worse for her afterwards. His male pride
needed these shows of strength, she knew, especially now, when his
temporary job at the Rating Office had come to an end, and the only
money he could count on was from his part-time job at the cafeteria –
three of four afternoons at most.

If only he had finished his course and got his engineering degree
instead of dropping out half-way! Linda silenced the little stir of resentment, because what was the use? No good needling him *now* about his
irresponsible past. Poor Dave. Responsibility had caught up with him
now all right, and he was doing his best – his unpractised best – to
shoulder it. Doing it for *her*. For her, and for the baby. Recriminations
don't help a man who is already stretched to his limit. Besides, she loved
him.

Monday, though! Mrs Moles really meant it this time! *Monday*. Only
four days away! That night, Linda cried herself to sleep, with David's
arms around her, and his voice, still shakily confident, whispering into

her ear: 'Don't you worry, Lin! It'll be all right. I promise you it'll be all right.'

It wouldn't, though. How could it? They had been searching for months now, in all their free time and at weekends, lowering their standards week by week as the hopelessness of the search was gradually borne in on them. From a three-room flat to a two-room one; from one room with use of kitchen to anything, anything at all. If all these weeks of unflagging effort had produced nothing, then what could possibly be hoped for from four more days?

The next morning, for the first time since their search began, David set off for the estate agent's alone. After her near-sleepless night, Linda had woken feeling so sick, and looking so white and fragile, that David had insisted on her staying in bed – just as, a couple of weeks earlier, he had insisted on her giving up her job. Before he left, he brought her a cup of tea and kissed her goodbye.

'Don't worry, love, I'll come up with something *this* time, just you see!' – and Linda, white and weak against the pillows, smiled, and tried to look as if she didn't know that he was lying.

After he had gone she must have dozed off; for the next thing she knew, it was past eleven o'clock, pale November sunshine was glittering on the wet windows, and the telephone down in the hall was ringing . . . ringing . . . ringing. . . .

No one seemed to be answering. They must all be out. With a curious sense of foreboding (curious, because what bad news could there possibly be for a couple as near rock-bottom as herself and David?), Linda scrambled into dressing-gown and slippers, and hurried down the three flights of stairs.

'Darling! I thought you were never coming.' It was Dave's voice all right, but for a moment she hadn't recognised it, so long was it since it had sounded buoyant and carefree like that. 'Darling, listen! Just *listen*. You'll never believe it. . . .'

And she didn't. Not at first, anyway; it was just too fantastic; a stroke of luck beyond their wildest dreams. In those first moments, with the telephone pressed to her unbelieving ear, she couldn't seem even to take it in.

What had happened, she at last gathered, was this. David had been coming gloomily out of the estate agent's, with the familiar 'Nothing today, I'm afraid,' still ringing in his ears, when a young man, red-haired and rather tall, had stepped across the pavement and accosted him.

'Looking for somewhere to live, buddy?' he'd asked; and before David had got over his surprise the stranger was well and thoroughly launched on his amazing, incredible proposition.

A three-room flat, self-contained, with a balcony, and big windows facing the sun – all for five pounds a week!

'And he'd like us to move in *today*!' David gabbled joyously on. 'Just think of it, Lin! *Today!* Not even one more night in that dump! No more grovelling to the old Mole! God, am I looking forward to telling her what she can do with that miserable garret!'

'But – but, darling!' Linda could not help breaking in at this point. 'Darling, it sounds fantastic, of course it does! But – but, Dave, are you sure it's *all right*? I mean, why should this – whoever he is – why should he be letting the flat at such a ridiculously low rent? And—?'

'Just what *I* wanted to know!' David's voice came clear and exultant down the line. 'But it's quite simple really. He explained everything! You see, he's just broken up with his girl; she's gone off with another man; and he just can't stand staying on in the place without her. He's not thinking about the money, he just wants OUT – and you can understand it, can't you? I mean, he was nuts about this girl. They'd been together for over a year, and he thought she was just as happy as he was. The shock was just more than he could take—'

'Yes. . . . Yes, of course. . . .' Linda's excitement was laced with unease. 'But – David – I still don't quite understand. Why *us*? Why isn't he putting it in the hands of the agents?'

'Darling!' There was just the tiniest edge of impatience in David's voice now. 'Darling, don't be like that! Don't spoil it all! Anyway, it's all quite understandable really. Just think for a minute. A chap in that sort of emotional crisis – the bottom just knocked out of his life – the last thing he needs is a lot of malarky about leases and tenancy agreements and date of transfer and all the rest of it. So he decided to by-pass the whole estate-agent racket and simply—'

'So what was he doing, then, just outside an estate agent's?'

The words had snapped out before Linda could check them. She hated her own wariness, her inability to throw herself with total abandon into David's mood of unquestioning exultation.

But this time David seemed to enjoy her hesitation: it was as if she had played, unwittingly, the very card that enabled him to lay down his ace.

'*Aha!*' he said, and already she could hear the smile in his voice – the old, cheeky, self-congratulatory smile with which he used to relate the more outrageous exploits of that bunch of tearaways he used to go around with. '*Aha*, that was cleverness! Real cleverness. Just the sort of thing that *I* might have thought of.' How wonderful it was to hear his cocky, male arrogance coming alive again after all these months of humiliation and defeat! 'He did just the thing that *I* always do in a tricky situation. He asked himself the right questions! Like, what's the quickest way to clinch a deal – any deal? Why, find a chap who's desperate for what you've got to offer. And when the thing on offer is a roof over the head, then where do such desperate chaps come thickest on the ground? Why, outside an estate agent's, just after opening time! So that's what he did – just hung about outside waiting for someone to come out of the door looking really sick.'

It made sense. Sense of a sort, anyway. Linda felt her doubts beginning to melt. Joy hovered, like a bright bird, ready to swoop in.

'It – Oh, darling! It seems just too good to be true!' she cried. 'Oh, Dave, I'm so happy. And this young man – once we're settled, and you've got another job, we must insist on him taking more than five pounds – we mustn't take advantage of his misery! Not when *we're* so happy – so lucky! Oh, but we don't even know his name!'

'We do! It's Fanshawe!' David countered exultantly. 'It's on the name-slip outside the door: "R. Fanshawe". But I've changed it, darling. I'm right here, and I've changed it already! It says "Graves" now! "David and Linda Graves"! Oh, Lin, darling, how soon can you get here?'

It was bigger even than she'd imagined, and much more beautiful. It was on the fifth floor of a large modern block, and even now, in winter, the big rooms were filled with light. The sunshine hit you like a breaking wave as you walked in; and through the wide windows, far away above the roofs and spires of the city, you could see a blue line of hills.

Linda and David could hardly speak for excitement. They wandered from room to room as if in a trance, exploring, exclaiming, making rapturous little sounds that were hardly like words at all; more like the twittering of birds in the springtime, the joyous nesting time.

Deep, roomy shelves. Built-in cupboards and wardrobes. Bright, modern furniture – and not too much of it; there would be plenty of room for their own few favourite pieces.

'Your desk – it can go just here, Dave, under the window. It'll get all the light!' exclaimed Linda; and 'See, Lin, this alcove – I can build his cot to fit it exactly! This will be *his* room!'; and so on and so on, until, at last, exhausted with happiness, one of them – afterwards, Linda could never remember which, and of course, at the time, it did not seem important – one of them suddenly noticed the time.

'Gosh, look, it's nearly two!' exclaimed whichever one it was; and there followed quite a little panic. For by 2.30 David was supposed to be at the cafeteria, slicing hard-boiled eggs, washing lettuces, sweeping up the mess left by the lunchtime customers. It would never do for him to lose this job, too. Hand in hand they raced out of the flat, raced for the bus and managed to reach home in time to get David out of his leather jacket and into a freshly-ironed overall just in time to be not much more than ten minutes late for work. Kissing him goodbye, Linda was careful not to muss up his hastily smoothed hair: the curling, shoulder-length mane was a bone of contention at the cafeteria – as, indeed, it had been at all his other jobs – but *she* loved it.

At the door, he paused to urge her to rest while he was gone; to lie down and take things easy.

'You weren't too good this morning,' he reminded her, 'so, whatever you do, don't start trying to do any packing. We'll do it this evening, together. Oh, darling, just imagine Mrs M's face when she sees us bumping our suitcases down the stairs this very night! "Monday", indeed! *I'll* give her "Monday"!'

Obediently, after he'd gone, Linda pulled off her dress and shoes, and climbed into bed. It was quite true, she *was* tired. For a few minutes she lay, staring up at the ceiling, and trying to realise that she was looking at those familiar cracks and stains for the very last time. She couldn't believe it, really; the change in their fortunes had been so swift, so dreamlike somehow, that she hadn't really taken it in.

'Rest,' David had urged her; but it was impossible. Excitement was drumming in her veins; it was impossible to be still with all this happiness surging about inside her. She must *do* something. Not the packing – she'd promised to wait for David before starting on that; but there'd be no harm in getting things sorted out a bit – get rid of some of the rubbish. Those torn-off pages of Accommodation to Let, for a start: they'd never need *those* again!

Clumsily – for she was nearly eight months gone now – she heaved herself off the bed and, as she did so, David's leather jacket, hastily flung aside when he'd changed for work, cascaded off the bed on to the floor, with a little tinkling, metallic scutter of sound.

The keys, of course. The keys of the new flat; and as she picked them off the floor Linda was filled with a surge of impatience to see again her beautiful new home – 'home' already, as this place had never been. She ached to look once more out of the wide, beautiful windows, to gloat over the space, the light and the precious feeling that it was *hers*! Hers and David's, and the new baby's as well! She wanted to examine, at leisure and in detail, every drawer and cupboard; to make plans about where the polished wooden salad-bowl was to go, and the Israeli dancing girl . . . and the books . . . and the records. . . .

Well, and why not? The whole afternoon stretched ahead of her. David wouldn't be home till nine at the earliest. What was she waiting for?

The flat did not seem, this time, quite the palace of light and space that it had seemed this morning; but it was still very wonderful. The rooms were dimmer now, and greyer, because, naturally, the sun had moved round since this morning and left them in shadow.

But Linda did not mind. It was still marvellous. Humming to herself softly, she wandered, lapped in happiness, from room to room, peering into cupboards, scrutinising shelves and alcoves, planning happily where everything was to go.

What space! What lovely, lovely space! Opening yet another set of empty, inviting drawers, it occurred to Linda that, for a man with a broken heart, their predecessor had left things quite extraordinarily clean and tidy. In the turmoil of shock and grief, how on earth had he forced himself to clean up so thoroughly – to even vacuum the carpets, and dust out the empty drawers? Or maybe the defecting girl-friend had done it for him? A sort of guilt-offering to assuage her conscience?

Musing thus, Linda came upon a cupboard she had not noticed before – it was half-hidden by a big, well-cushioned armchair pulled in front of it. It looked as if it might be big enough to store all the things for the new baby in. Linda took hold of the handle and pulled – and straight-away she knew that it was locked. This, then, must be where the ultra-tidy Mr Fanshawe had stored away his things? Spurred on by curiosity, Linda tried first one and then another of the keys on the bunch David had been given – and at the third attempt the door gave under her hand. Gave too readily, somehow. It was as if it were being pushed from inside; a great weight seemed to be on the move; and just as the fear reached her stomach, making it lurch within her, the door swung fully open, and the body of a girl slumped out on to the floor. A blonde girl, probably pretty, but there was no knowing now, so pinched and sunken were the features, already mottled with death.

Linda stood absolutely still. Horror, yes. In her recollections after-wards, and in her dreams, horror was the emotion she remembered most clearly. And what could be more natural?

But not at the time. At the time, in those very first seconds, before she had had time to think at all, it was not horror that had overwhelmed her at all; it was fury. Sickening, stupefying fury and disappointment.

'Damn you, damn you, damn you!' she sobbed, crazily, at the silent figure on the floor. 'I *knew* it was too good to be true! I *knew* there would be a snag!' – and it was the sound of her own voice, raised in such blind, self-centred misery, that brought her partially to her senses.

She must *do* something. Phone somebody. Scream 'Murder!' out of the window. Get help.

Help with what? How can you help a girl who is already dead? With the strange, steely calm that comes with shock, Linda dropped to her knees and peered closely at the slumped, deathly figure. No breath stirred between the bluish lips; no pulse could be felt in the limp, icy wrist. The girl lay lifeless as a bundle of old clothes, ruining everything.

Because, of course, the flat was lost to them now – had, in fact, never been theirs to lose. The whole thing had been a trick, right from the beginning. What they had walked into, so foolishly and trustingly, was not a flat at all, but a dreadful crime. Presently the police would be here, cordoning everything off, hunting down the real owner of the flat, bringing him back for questioning. They would be questioning herself and David, too. That, of course, had been the whole point of the trick! Linda could see it all now. They had been lured here deliberately by the phoney offer of a home, in order that they should leave their finger-prints all over the place and be found here when the police arrived. A pair of trespassers, roaming without permission or explanation around someone else's flat! Because that's how it would look. Why should the police – or, indeed, any other sane person – believe such a cock-and-bull story as she and David would have to tell? A ridiculous, incredible tale about having been offered, by a total stranger, an attractive three-room flat in a pleasant neighbourhood for only five pounds a week! All that this Fanshawe man had to do now was to deny totally the encounter with David outside the estate agent's and it would be his word against David's – with, to him, the overwhelming advantage that his denials would sound immeasurably more plausible than David's grotesque assertions!

Neat, really. '*Aha*, that was cleverness!' as David had so light-heartedly remarked, only a few hours ago!

At the thought of all that happiness – of David's pride, his triumph, all to be so short-lived – a cold fury of determination seized upon Linda's still-shocked brain, and she knew, suddenly, exactly what she must do.

The dead cannot suffer. They are beyond human aid, and beyond human injury, too; so it wasn't really so terrible, what she was going to do.

Cautiously, and without even any great distaste, so numbed was she with shock, Linda got hold of the limp figure by the thick polo-neck of its woollen sweater and began to pull.

Luckily, at this dead hour of the afternoon, the long corridors were empty as a dream. The lift glided obediently, silently downwards with its terrible burden . . . down, down, past the entrace-floor, past even the basement . . . down, down to the lowest depths of all . . . and there, in an icy, windowless cellar, stacked with old mattresses and shadowy lengths of piping, Linda left her terrible charge.

It would be found – of course, it would be found – but now there would be at least a sporting chance that the clues – now so thoroughly scrambled – would no longer lead so inexorably to the fifth-floor flat into which the new tenants had just moved. It would be just one more of those unsolved murders. There were dozens of them, every year. Weren't there?

It would be all right. It *must* be all right. It must, it must.

All the same, Linda couldn't get out of the beautiful flat fast enough that afternoon. While the grey November day faded – she dared not switch on any lights for fear of advertising her presence there – she pushed the big chair back in front of the cupboard again, and set the room to rights. Then, still trembling, and feeling deathly sick, she set off for home. It was only five o'clock. Four whole hours in which to recover her composure before David got back from work.

And recover it she must. At any cost, David must be protected from all knowledge of this new and terrible turn of events. She recalled his triumphant happiness this morning, the resurgence of his masculine pride. She pictured how he would come bounding up the stairs this evening, three at a time; carrying a bottle of wine, probably, to celebrate.

And celebrate they would, if it killed her! Not one word would she breathe of her fearful secret – not one flicker of anxiety would she allow to cross her face.

Celebrate! Celebrate! Candles. Steak and mushrooms, even if it cost all the week's housekeeping! She would wash and set her hair, too, as soon as she got in, and change into the peacock-blue maternity smock with the Chinese-y neck-line. She thought of everything, in fact, hurrying home through the November dusk that evening, except the possibility that David would be in before her.

She stood in the doorway, clutching her parcels, speechless with surprise, and staring at him.

'*Where the hell have you been?*'

Never had she heard his voice sound so angry. How long had he been here? Why had he come back so early?

'I said you were to *rest*!' he was shouting at her. 'You promised me you'd stay here and rest! Where have you *been*? I've been out of my mind with worry! And where are the keys? The keys of the flat? They were here, in my pocket!'

He was sorry, though, a minute later, when she'd handed over the keys, and explained to him about her excitement, about the sudden, irresistible impulse to go and look at the beautiful new flat once more. He seemed to understand.

'I'm sorry, darling, I've been a brute!' he apologised. 'But you see it was so scary, somehow, coming in and finding the place all dark and empty! I was afraid something had happened. I thought, maybe, the baby. . . .'

The reconciliation was sweet; and if he questioned her a little over-minutely about her exact movements that afternoon, and exactly how she had found things in the flat – well, what could be more natural in a man thrilled to bits about his new home, into which he is going to move this very night?

And move that very night they did.

No more Mrs Moles! No more tiptoeing guiltily up and down dark stairs! Everywhere light and space and privacy! And on top of this a brand-new modern kitchen, and a little, sunny room exactly right for the baby – only a month away he was, now! For a day or so, Linda had feared that the birth might be coming on prematurely; she had been having odd, occasional pains since dragging that awful weight hither and thither along cement floors and through shadowy doorways. But after a few days it all seemed to settle down again – as also, amazingly, did her mind and spirits.

At first she had been full of guilt and dread; it was all she could do not to let David notice how she started at every footfall in the corridor, every soft moan from the lift doors as they closed and opened. Sometimes, too, she was aware – or imagined she was aware – of David's eyes on her, speculative, unsmiling. At such times she would hastily find occasion to laugh shrilly, clatter saucepans, talk about the baby. Anything.

But presently, as the days went by, and nothing happened, her nerves began to quieten. Indeed, there were times when she almost wondered whether she hadn't imagined the whole thing? Because there was nothing in the papers: nothing on the radio – though she'd listened, during those first few days, like a maniac, like a creature obsessed, switching on every hour on the hour.

Nothing. Nothing at all. Had the body, conceivably, not been found yet? Surely it was *someone's* business – caretaker, nightwatchman or someone – to go into that cellar now and again? Or was it possible that the murderer himself had discovered where it had been moved to – had, perhaps, even watched her moving it, from some hidden vantage-point? The lift, the corridors had all *seemed* to be totally deserted, but you never knew.

To begin with, weighed down as she was by guilt and dread, Linda had tried as far as possible to avoid contact with the neighbours; but inevitably, as the days went by, she found herself becoming on speaking terms with first one and then another of them. The woman next door; the old man at the end of the corridor; the girl who always seemed to be watering the rubber-plant on the second-floor landing. Bits of gossip came to her ears of tenants past and present, including, of course, snippets of information about her and David's predecessor in the flat; and slowly, inexorably, it was borne in upon her that practically none of it fitted with David's story in the very least degree. The previous tenant had been neither red-haired nor tall – hadn't, in fact, been a man at all, but a woman. A young, blonde woman, Linda learned, who had rather kept herself to herself. Oh, there's been goings-on, yes; but, there, you have to live and let live, don't you? Quite a surprise, actually, when the young woman gave up the flat so suddenly; no one had heard a thing about it; but there you are, the young folk are very unpredictable these days.

And it was now, for the very first time, that it dawned on Linda that she only had David's word that the bizarre and improbable encounter with 'Mr Fanshawe' had ever taken place at all. Or, indeed, that any 'Mr Fanshawe' had ever existed!

This terrible, traitorous thought slipped into her mind one early-December evening as she sat sewing for her baby. And, having slipped in, it seemed instantly to make itself horribly at home, as if, deep down in her brain, there had been a niche ready prepared for it all along.

Because everything now slid hideously into place: David's disproportionate anger when he found she had visited the flat by herself that first afternoon; his unexplained mysteriously early return from work on that same occasion. Perhaps, instead of going to the cafeteria, he had slipped off that working-overall the moment he was out of sight and gone rushing off to devise some means of disposing of the body. His preparations completed, he would have arrived at the flat, scared and breathless – to find that the body had already disappeared!

What then? Bewildered and panic-stricken, he would have hurried home – only to find that she, Linda, had been to the flat ahead of him! Had he guessed that she must have found the body? And, if so, what had he made of her silence all these days? What did he think she was thinking as she sat there, demure and smiling, evening after evening, sewing for the baby? No wonder he had been giving her dark, wary glances! What sort of a look would it be that he'd be giving her tonight, when he came in and saw the new, terrible fear in her eyes, the suspicion flickering in her face and in her voice?

Suspicion? No! No! She *didn't* suspect him. How could she? Not *David*! Not her own husband. The man she loved! How *could* she, even for an instant, have imagined that he might be capable of—!

Well, and what *is* a man capable of? A proud, headstrong young man who not so long ago was the daredevil leader of the most venturesome teenage gang in his neighbourhood? To what sort of lengths *could* such a young man go, under the intolerable lash of humiliation? He, who had set out in proud and youthful arrogance to conquer the world, and now finds he cannot even provide any sort of home for his wife and child? Such a young man – *could* he, in such extremities of shattered pride and of self-respect destroyed – *could* he simply walk into a strange flat, murder the occupant and coolly take possession?

And even if he couldn't – couldn't, and hadn't, and never would – what then? What about *her*? How could she, having once let the awful suspicion cross her mind, ever face him again? How was she to behave – look – when he came in from work tonight? What sort of supper should one cook for a suspected murderer?

And as she sat there, crouched in the beautiful flat, while outside the evening darkened into night, she heard the soft whine of the lift, the opening and closing of its doors.

And next – although it was only a little after five, and David shouldn't be home till nine – next there came, unmistakably, the sound of the key in the door.

Afterwards, Linda could never remember what exactly had been the sequence of her thoughts. '*Why?*' had been one of them, certainly. *Why* is he arriving home so early? And then, swift upon the heels of this, had come the blind, unreasoning panic. What is he *doing* out there? Why doesn't he come right in, shut the front door behind him? Why isn't he calling 'Lin, darling, I'm back'? the way he always does? Why is he being so quiet, so furtive? Lurking out there. Standing stock still, to judge by the waiting silence.

But after that, in Linda's jumbled memory, all was confusion. Had she recognised the blonde girl at once – so different as she now looked – or had there been several minutes of stunned incomprehension as they gaped at one another in the little hall, all at cross-purposes in their questions and ejaculations?

Because, of course, this was the rightful tenant of the flat. Rosemary Fanshawe by name; as astounded (on her return from a stay in hospital and a fortnight's convalescence) to find a strange girl in possession of her flat as Linda was at this sudden invasion by a stranger. Linda could never remember, afterwards, who it was who finally made coffee for whom, or in what order each had explained herself to the other; but in the end – and certainly by the time David got back at nine o'clock – all had been made clear, and a sort of bewildered friendship was already in the making.

For this bright, well-groomed girl was indeed the same that Linda had found and taken for dead; and there had indeed been a terrible lovers' quarrel, just as the red-haired young man outside the estate agent's had affirmed. What he had told David hadn't been a lie, exactly; rather a sort of mirror-image of the truth, with all the facts in reverse. Thus it had been he, not Rosemary, who had ended the relationship; it had been her heart, not his, that was broken. It was she, not he, who had declared that she couldn't bear to stay in the flat for so much as another day. Hysterically, she had flung her things into cases, ordered a car to take them to a friend's house and then, in less than an hour, had returned, half-crazy with grief and fury, to storm at him for not having tried to prevent her going. There had been a final, terrible quarrel, at the climax of which Rosemary had threatened dramatically to take a whole bottle of sleeping-pills. Enraged by this bit of melodramatic blackmail (as he judged it), the red-haired boy-friend – Martin by name – had slammed out of the flat; but later, growing scared, he had crept back, and found to his horror that she really *had* taken the pills, and was lying – dead, as he thought – on the floor. (Actually, as they'd explained to Rosemary in the hospital, she'd only been in a deep coma, but a layman could not be expected to realise this, as both breath and pulse would be too faint to be discerned.) Appalled – and terrified at the thought that he might be blamed – Martin had bundled the 'body' out of sight in the nearest cupboard, and set himself frantically to cleaning up the flat and removing all traces of their joint lives. All night it had taken him; and, while he packed and scrubbed, his brain had been afire with desperate schemes for shuffling off the responsibility – prefereably on to some anonymous outsider – while he, Martin, got clean away. By the time morning came, and his task was finished, his plans were also ready. He washed, shaved, and off he went to the estate agent.

And, in fact, it all worked out much as he had hoped – with the fortunate addition that, as it turned out, it was probably Linda's action in dragging the 'body' down to the basement that had saved Rosemary's life. The jolting, the knocking about, and the icy chill of the cellar had prevented the coma becoming so deep as to be irreversible. That same night, she had recovered consciousness sufficiently to stagger out into the deserted street and wander some way before being picked up and taken to hospital.

And David, when he came home and heard the whole story? He was unsurprised. David was no fool, and he had realised right from the start (despite his show of bravado) that there was something very phoney indeed about that offer outside the estate agent's; but had decided (being the kind of young man he was) to gamble on the chance of being able to cope with the tricksters, whatever it was they were up to, when the time came. However, with his mind full of the possible hazards of the venture, he had naturally been thrown into a complete panic by the discovery that Linda had gone off alone that first afternoon into what might well prove to be a trap of some kind; and even after his immediate fears had been set at rest he had not failed to notice, in the succeeding days, that Linda was oppressed and ill at ease. He knew nothing, of course, about the 'body', but he could see very well that there was *something*.

Now, he shrugged. He'd gambled and lost before in his short life.

'Oh, well. It's back on the road for us, then, Linda my pet,' he said, reaching out his hand towards her, but at that same moment Rosemary gave a squeal as if she'd been trodden on.

'Oh, *no*! Oh, *please*!' she cried. 'I can't possibly stay on in the flat by myself. I *must* have someone to share, now that . . .'

Of course, it wasn't quite the same as having the place to themselves; but it was much, much better than living at Mrs Moles'. And for Rosemary, likewise, it wasn't quite the same as having Martin there, but it was much, much better than having to pay the whole of the rent herself. She found, too, that she enjoyed the company; and when, soon after his son was born, David resumed his engineering studies and began bringing friends home from college she found she enjoyed it even more.

'Wasn't it *lucky* that I took all those pills just when I did?' she mused dreamily one evening, after the reluctant departure of one of the handsomer of the embryo engineers; and Linda, settling her baby back in his cot, had to agree that it was.

Indeed, when you thought of all the ways in which the thing *might* have ended, 'lucky' seemed something of an understatement.

James McClure

Scandal at Sandkop

Uncle Darvie was the progressive of Sandkop, a remote village in the bushveld north of Johannesburg. He believed that the Earth was round. And although many argued with him, and made him climb windmills to see how flat the horizon stayed, they could not alter his conviction.

Yet this did not mean he was an irreligious man, as a stranger might have supposed. Far from it: the Dominee regarded Uncle Darvie – whom he alone called Doctor Kruger, out of one professional's respect for another – as the fat-tailed ram of his flock. Some said that Uncle Darvie had not missed a single service in forty-three years, which went back before the Dominee's own time, but it was certainly true that he never missed a funeral, and that showed how clear his conscience was. In short, Uncle Darvie's devotion to both God and man so moved the Dominee that he was prompted to one of his rare smiles whenever they met over a deathbed.

Hettie Kruger, however, treated her husband with the loving contempt she thought he deserved.

'It's a scandal!' she said at the supper table one winter evening. 'Call yourself a doctor and a Christian and yet you let this happen!'

'Oh, ja?'

'Let a man murder his wife under your very eyes!'

Uncle Darvie nibbled off a whole row of pips from his mealie cob before bothering to look up. When he did, the melted butter ran down his chin and into his beard, which was modelled on that of his namesake.

'And you eat like a kaffir who doesn't wear shoes. Sis!'

'What did you say before that?' he asked, having only half-heard her because she began everything by saying what a scandal it was. Even the colour of a woman's hat would make her do it.

'Murder his wife.'

'Who?'

'Faanie Vermaak, that's who. And don't say I haven't told you this before.'

'I won't, love of my life, I won't.'

He began trimming the cob like a lathe.

'Well, Uncle Darvie?'

'Mmmm.'

'Motive. Faanie has a motive. When he was caught with that girl from the town who was staying at Uncle Jacobus's place, he said that one day he would find her. Do you remember that? When they put her in the Scotch cart and had the kaffir drive her away? Little hussy!'

'Spoken in the heat of the moment. Faanie's told me himself; he's very ashamed of the whole matter and just wants to forget it.'

'Huh!'

'A man can understand why he took a liking to her, she being of his own kind.'

'And young! And pretty! And as shameless as they come! A man may understand that, yes – but a woman wouldn't!'

'Mmmm.'

'And how do you think Emily Vermaak feels? Being told a thing like that? That he preferred one of his own kind?'

'You were the one so against him marrying her in the first place, woman. It was you who said no good could come of it if he took up with an English-speaker.'

'A long time ago, that was. Five years. Don't be unfair. How was I to know that Emily would learn to talk the *taal* so nice you need never worry she was English? And that's another mistake you keep making: she is real English, not just English-speaking. And what happens? She goes to all the trouble to be a proper wife to him and he wants to run away with—'

'He didn't run away,' said Uncle Darvie, tossing his cob over a shoulder and reaching for another.

'But he wants to – oh, ja. I know men. Secretly, that's what he wants. And the reason he's trying to poison poor Emily so an old fool like you won't notice.'

'What with?'

'Arsenic.'

'So, arsenic is it? We make progress.'

'Evidence,' said Hettie firmly, removing the pips from her cob with a knife which she had been taught by Emily Vermaak was more lady-like. 'We have *evidence* it's happening.'

'Evidence? Arsenic? Motive? Where have you been learning all these big lawyer's words? Has Sergeant Poolman been in Sandkop for the day again? For coffee and a show-off?'

'No. From Emily herself. Auntie Tina went to call on her again yesterday, to see if she was getting any better. She actually said she thought Faanie was trying to kill her.'

'It makes a good story.'

'Auntie Tina also points out,' Hettie continued icily, 'that Emily's sickness began when Faanie was found in that barn with Petronella Swart. From that very day.'

'But we locked him up in the pig sty for two nights.'

'All right then, but almost from that very day. Do you remember how she ran home and went to bed? Have you seen her out of it since? Have you?'

'Consumption,' said Uncle Darvie, picking his teeth with a chew of fingernail. 'That's the trouble with your Mrs Vermaak.'

'She says different. She says—'

'How come she knows what arsenic can do? Did you ask her that? What are the signs?'

'She knows them.'

'Ja, and I also know Faanie Vermaak. Don't forget, I brought him into this world. Never was a more honest boy born.'

'That sinner!'

'Almighty God, Hettie, we didn't catch him *doing* anything with Petronella, they were just *talking*. And he's repented. You'll see, given a little time—'

'And Emily will be dead! Ja, and Faanie can run off to his slut. Men! You are all the same, siding with each other.'

'Women,' he sighed, 'women talk far too much about things that aren't their business.'

'So it isn't our business that one of us is being slowly done to death?'

'No.'

'I wonder if the Dominee would agree?'

He knew he had given a silly answer, and now waited to pay for it. Reaching out for his snuff horn on the dresser.

'Have you forgotten what day it is?'

He had: it was the Sabbath. Divine retribution, no less.

'Why not tell me then?' he asked irritably. 'Why doesn't she? God in Heaven, don't I ride out to *Welkom* once a fortnight to see how she is getting on?'

'What she said to Auntie Tina was in strictest confidence.'

'In other words, she wanted the whole of Sandkop to know.'

'Uncle Darvie! Shame on you! You, an elder of the church, casting slander on a good woman like Auntie Tina! Three husbands she's had!'

He very nearly made a joking rejoinder, with a dark hint at who the real poisoner in their midst might be, but wisely checked himself in time.

'And so? What must I do about it?'

'You're to go and take a proper look at Emily. And then, if you see anything suspicious, you've got to tell the Dominee and Sergeant Poolman and—'

'I'll ride out tomorrow.'

'I'll see you do. And that's another thing: when are you going to get yourself a motor car like Dr Steenkamp in Blikkiesdorp? No wonder people are talking. No wonder.'

'I don't much mind,' replied Uncle Darvie, escaping on to the stoep.

He was too old a dog to learn new tricks, and besides, he was quite sure they were wrong about Emily Vermaak and poor old Faanie.

Being a man of his word, he was on the dirt track to *Welkom* soon after breakfast. As he passed over the cattle grid at the gate, he felt the usual sadness come upon him. Even after a two-year drought, the place should not have been in such a state. Barbed-wire fences falling down all over, and cattle roaming where they liked. If it had not been the thorn trees, he would have had difficulty in making out where the pastures ended and the veld began.

Not that anything like two years had passed since the scene at the barn – a matter of six months at most. But it was land that had been fought for, and land that you had to fight in turn, and keep on fighting, or the whole battle might as well have never begun. It was shocking, really.

Only the ridgeback bitch came out to greet him when he reached the long, low homestead built of mud bricks, with its tin roof that would rust if it was not painted again soon. Then, as he was tethering his horse, the Hottentot maid, whose face was truly like a yellow monkey's, appeared.

She told him her master was probably down at the dam, throwing sticks in the water. He told her to fetch him up directly as he wanted a word. He would find his own way in.

The Vermaak family bed almost filled the dim back room. It had been brought up from the Cape on the Great Trek itself, they said. A gigantic bed, made with stinkwood and leather thongs, that was ideal for the conception and delivery of gigantic sons – as Faanie had been. Yet he and Emily were still to be blessed, and that, Uncle Darvie considered, was at least half of their problem.

The farmer's wife looked very small and bony in it – like a panting springbok lying on its side at a dry waterhole. She had her back to him and was staring at a scruffy cat on the other pillow.

'Morning, Emily! How goes it? Just I was passing by and I thought

713

I'd stop in for a minute.'

She ignored him.

'It's all right then if I examine you?'

'What's left of me, you mean,' she said bitterly.

Uncle Darvie had been in half a mind to confront her outright with what had been reported to him, but now he was actually at her bedside, the very thought of it made him feel ridiculous. It was only hearsay, after all, and that from Auntie Tina, who was notoriously inventive.

So he elected to complete his observations first, and then see if there was any point in causing an upset. Everything he noted down had a simple, straightforward explanation without any sinister undertones – just as he had supposed. A layman, of course, with a list of symptoms for only one thing, and thinking they could therefore mean only one thing, might have been misled. But not Uncle Darvie, who already had a life-time of successful doctoring behind him.

And so, when it came to inspecting the scalp, he paused. Emily Vermaak was still English enough to practise a modesty uncommon among his own womenfolk of her years, and was wearing a night cap. Then, on the evidence already before him, he decided that asking her to remove it would be very unnecessary.

'Aren't you finished yet?'

'I am, I am – so sorry. Well, have you got anything to tell me? About how you are? Coughing much?'

'No more than you'd expect.'

'Good, good. Taking your medicine?'

'Of course.'

She still lay with her back to him – there was not really room around the other side of the bed for a man of his bulk. This was disconcerting, and made it difficult to find the right words for the question Hettie would undoubtedly expect him to ask. Then he had it.

'No special worries? You don't think something's – er, poisoning your system?'

She turned over to face him then, her brown eyes huge in the gaunt, spotty face.

'That's a funny thing to ask, Uncle Darvie. Isn't it you who's supposed to tell me what is the matter?'

How very right she was. He grunted apologetically, picked up his bag and stood a moment trying to think of something soothing to say. He felt a floorboard dip under the shift of his weight, and looked down to see they were all in bad condition – Faanie had even allowed the termites to make a start on his house. Disgraceful.

'God bless, Emily Vermaak,' said Uncle Darvie, and went outside to see if the erring husband had been found. He was glad to leave the room with all its smells, the sort you get with a very sick person, faintly rotten and sweet, and to which he had never grown accustomed. He was out in the fresh air too often for that.

Faanie was talking to Uncle Darvie's horse. Standing a good head above its own head, which just showed what a big fellow he was. Yet there was a stoop to his broad shoulders, and his mouth, pinky-grey in the black bush of his beard, was curiously slack.

'Uncle Darvie? How is—'

'No better, no worse, trust in the Lord, Faanie. But you, man, what is happening to you? Do you want me to give you something – a tonic?'

Faanie smiled crookedly. 'I'm all right, Uncle. There's nothing you can give me that will help. I'll get better when my love gets better – if she can, after what I've done to her.'

'And in the meantime?' Uncle Darvie said, hearing his own echo of Hettie's words. 'What happens to *Welkom*? Are you giving it back to the kaffirs or what? I saw some just now, sitting on their backsides, doing no work—'

'It is my fault, not theirs,' Faanie replied with his customary honesty – which not many men would have done where there were kaffirs concerned.

'Ja, maybe, but this is your heritage, man! You fully understand? It was Almighty God who led our forebears to this place. He who gave it to His Chosen People. To ignore the Will of the Lord is no light matter!'

'No, it isn't. I will try tomorrow.'

'May God give you a tomorrow, Faanie Vermaak.'

Uncle Darvie was pleased with the way he said this, from down deep in his chest, for it seemed to strike home at last. Faanie took his hand off the horse's nose and nervously picked his own.

'Petronella Swart. Is she what fills your mind night and day?'

'No, Uncle! That is not true! I know they say so in Sandkop, and I know Emily can never really believe me it was nothing, but—'

'What were you talking to her about?' asked Uncle Darvie, giving the foolish man his first-ever invitation to explain himself.

'About? About nothing. We were looking at the moon and wondering if—'

'It's round,' Uncle Darvie broke in. 'Round-shaped like the world we live on. But what sort of talk was this for a married man?'

'I don't understand.'

'These are scientific things you should say to your wife.'

'She was never interested. Whenever I wonder about anything, Emily says there are professors in England who already know—'

'Faanie, take a pull at yourself, man! Stop moping. Get *Welkom* back on its legs. And the Dominee and me want to see you in church this Sunday.'

Uncle Darvie brushed him aside and mounted his horse, heaving himself up in only one attempt. Then he remembered his original mission.

'Tell me, Faanie, do you take your wife her meals?'

The farmer reddened.

'Of course not! That's the Hott'not girl's work! I serve from the table and she takes them through.'

'I was just wanting to know if she eats properly, man.'

'Oh, I see. Usually the plate is empty when it comes back.'

'One more question, Faanie: do you hold any grudges about what happened at Uncle Jacobus's place? Are you sure? Not deep inside?'

There was a pause, and then Faanie Vermaak said: 'No, it was a just punishment you and the elders gave me in the sty.'

Which allowed Uncle Darvie to ride off in a much happier frame of mind than he had arrived in, feeling more convinced than ever that nothing untoward was taking place at *Welkom* – except to the land itself. And he had even done something about that.

Hettie Kruger, however, was not so easily persuaded. But that was her way.

'Of course, Emily wouldn't tell you what she told Auntie Tina,' she scoffed on his return. 'Trust a man to be so stupid and ask her outright.'

'I didn't exactly, I—'

'What if she was wrong? What if harm came to Faanie he did not deserve? She still loves that rubbish of a man or why would—'

'Last night, last night it was different, Hettie Kruger. Last night you said she actually told—'

'It seems all you care about is the farm!'

'Don't try to wriggle out of it, woman.'

'Me? Who's this doing the wriggling, may I ask? Tonight Auntie Tina can herself tell you of what passed between them.'

'No, I will not see her. I can't have my name—'

'Your name is in enough trouble already. We're trying to help you.'

'No.'

'Anyway, you can't refuse to see her.'

'Oh, no?'

'She has already made an appointment for her piles. That is something you cannot cancel.'

Uncle Darvie knew he was beaten. And for the rest of the day, went about his rounds with a face that intimated to his patients that they were not alone in their troubles. Several kindly offered him spoonfuls of their most dependable patent medicines, and one old dear tried to press on him a purge she had bought from a witchdoctor.

His surgery that evening was an equally gloomy business. Folk kept asking him how *he* was. What made it particularly difficult to bear was the fact that although Auntie Tina had been entered at the top of his list, she did not appear when he rang his small bell. The second person came instead, then the third, and so on. Finally, between acne and round worm, he put his stethoscope to the wall and confirmed his worst suspicions: Hettie and Auntie Tina were engaged in preliminary discussions in the front room.

He was devoutly praying for an emergency call as his last patient withdrew, when in she came with her usual vigour.

'Evening, you old layabout!'

'Auntie Tina. We must make haste, hey? I've just remembered noticing Gert van der Merwe wasn't looking too—'

Auntie Tina turned her back on him, hoisted up her black dress, bent over and backed towards the paraffin lamp shining on his desk.

'Emily Vermaak has all the symptoms, you know,' Auntie Tina stated with confidence, from round the other side.

'Feet a little wider apart, please.'

'She is wasting away, she vomits a lot and has diarrhoea, there's spots on her face, and her hands and feet itch. Also she feels sick all the time, her hair drops out in lumps – I've seen it – and her skin is that funny dark colour. Can you see them?'

'Man, I don't like talking like this,' Uncle Darvie protested plaintively. With a delighted laugh Auntie Tina dropped her skirt and turned around.

'I – I didn't mean—'

'Well? What do you think now? Haven't you even got a book that knows what it's doing?'

He had, right there on the desk before him, with the place marked. There was no need for him to open it though, because he could recall the paragraph vividly – especially now Auntie Tina had reminded him of its contents, virtually word for word.

'You have allowed yourself to become constipated again. I want you to take—'

'Well?' she repeated.

'Emily said nothing to me of vomiting and diarrhoea.'

'She's a lady, that's why. Haven't you smelt her room?'

'Ja, but—'

'Didn't she keep scratching while you were there?'

'No, not once.'

'It comes and goes; I've noticed. Saturday wasn't the only time I've been to *Welkom*, you know. Oh, no! *I* do what little I can for those who need help.'

That was very unjust of Auntie Tina.

'Spots can come from what you're eating!' he snapped.

'Exactly!'

Uncle Darvie glared at her.

'Her skin was always doing strange things. Remember how it burned when she first came here to work in Gert's shop? There is no sun in England, so they tell me.'

'Nor is there any in that room of hers. Besides, it's got a strange reddish tint that isn't natural.'

Uncle Darvie opened his book and looked again at the line referring to skin colour. A tanned, weatherbeaten appearance could be observed, it said, which was why it was put in some tonics. However, such a characteristic could place the entire community under suspicion of arsenical poisoning – the writer had not reckoned on the South African sun.

'And what about the hair, Uncle Darvie?'

'Look, you listen to me, there are many diseases that can—'

'My backside,' interrupted Auntie Tina. 'What are you going to do about it?'

For one joyous moment, Uncle Darvie thought she had changed subjects, reverting her concern to her own well-being. Then he saw the steely, selfless look in her eye.

'Emily told you these were the symptoms?'

'She read them to me out of a newspaper. It was all about a man who murdered his wife and nearly didn't get found out. They had even buried her first.'

'And why did he murder her?'

'Because of another woman he wanted to—'

'I thought so. And he used?'

'A white powder called arsenic he got from the chemist.'

'There is no chemist in Sandkop.'

Auntie Tina shrugged. Quite rightly – there were chemists in other places. Although Uncle Darvie could not imagine Faanie Vermaak leaving the farm in his condition.

'Where was this? I haven't seen such a story and—'

'It was a very old paper. Going a bit yellow.'

He decided against arguing this point any further. The truth was buying a paper was a recent thing in his life, which had started only when his name began to appear in a weekly list of contributors to the Blikkiesdorp Voortrekker Memorial Fund.

'Has it not occurred to you that this story in the paper is simply giving a poor, sick woman ideas?'

He had not consciously formulated that thought before uttering it, and sat back very proud to think his mind could be so brilliant.

'Er, come again?'

Uncle Darvie was pleased to: 'Seeing herself as the wife in the way of a man's desires, she begins to imagine—'

'Nobody can imagine their body wasting away!'

'What happened to Auntie Rentia when she thought she had pregnancy? Didn't she swell right up?'

'Huh! There is still the danger you could be wrong.'

'But—'

'Words, words, words! Men will play with words all day, thinking they are magic. We want to know what you intend to *do*.'

'We?'

The door opened without a knock first, and Hettie stumped in, halting at her friend's heaving side, arms akimbo.

'Well,' she asked, unabashed by what he might be thinking, 'what are you going to do, Darvie Kruger?'

They made a daunting couple. It had been only with women such as these in their laagers that his forebears managed to keep off otherwise overwhelming hordes of savages. Uncle Darvie wished that he, too, could turn and run.

'I tell you what, ladies,' he said, improvising desperately, 'if Emily Vermaak is indeed being given posion, then it is reaching her in her food.'

'He is quick, this one,' murmured Hettie.

'Tomorrow morning I will ride again to the farm. There I will speak to the Hott'not maid and give her special instructions. From now on, she must serve the food straight from the pot on to the plate in the kitchen – and then take it direct to her missus. Then, if we see an improvement in Emily's condition, I will see what steps must be taken to go more deeply into this matter.'

They looked at each other.

'What if Faanie wants to know why?' objected Auntie Tina.

'Then I tackle him there and then, face to face.'

'You will note,' muttered Hettie drily, 'that he has already found the courage to ask the *woman* straight out. But not the man, oh no.'

'It's different actually accusing—'

'The idea is good,' said Auntie Tina, giving one of those nods when she also sucked in her moustache. 'How long though will this take?'

'I would say a week from now. And "you will note", no harm can come to Emily in the mean time, not with this plan.'

'A week?' queried Hettie. 'Much can happen in a week. What if he tries some other way?'

Uncle Darvie had not thought of that, but somehow he had been given the gift of tongues.

'What is a poisoner – a *slow* poisoner? Someone who does not want to be found out. If she died any other way, there would be immediate suspicion – and, as you say, motive. He wants to dance with a pretty girl, not a rope.'

It was artful that, seeming to side with them. And his ploy clinched the matter. Without further ado, they plodded off to make some coffee.

And the following morning, Uncle Darvie did as he had promised. Putting the fear of God into the Hottentot maid, and not hearing a squeak out of Faanie whom he told it was for dietary reasons.

Not unnaturally, the news of sudden and violent death at *Welkom* proved a tremendous shock.

Uncle Darvie and the Dominee were walking home together after the second service that very next Sunday, speaking with humble pride of having had Faanie Vermaak among the congregation again that morning, when the farm's head boy came staggering towards them.

At first, they both thought he was drunk, as most kaffirs were on the Lord's Day, and merely readied themselves to belabour him with their sticks.

Then the man, coughing and gasping, near-winded by his long run, managed to say enough for them to realise there had been shooting.

'Come, come in my my motor car!' urged Gert van der Merwe, who was the only other person still abroad in the street, it being a very hot afternoon for winter. 'I can get you there much faster than the Devil can ride!'

The Dominee looked doubtful, and Uncle Darvie hesitated. Neither was very happy about motor cars. But then neither was dressed for riding, being in their long black frock-coats and white ties.

So off they went with Gert, who charitably allowed the head boy to stand on the back bumper, which pleased the simple creature immensely until he lost his grip going over the cattle grid.

The Dominee smiled his rare smile.

And Uncle Darvie drew the blanket up over the bloodied head of Faanie Vermaak whose soul had to be already well on its way to Hell by then. Faanie had died before they got to him, killed by his own hand.

'Man, may I see the note again?' Uncle Darvie asked politely, wiping his hand on the wall of the storeroom first.

'Certainly, my friend, but I say he does not repent in it.'

Uncle Darvie took the scrap of paper, torn from a crops ledger, and read the words scrawled across it:

To whom It May Concern

Almighty God have Mercy on Me. I do not know what to say so You will Understand. But I do know I Cannot Live with This Guilt. I cannot Live while I can hear my Brethren Accuse me Behind My Back as they did in Church Today. They Say I am killing My Love. Even Uncle Darvie and the Dominee ask Strange Questions when a man Thinks about them. I know None of it is True when I walk on my lands but I have Terrible Terrible Dreams when it seem to I wish harm to the Star in my Night Sky. Take Care of Her. I must Know the Truth of my Guilt and the Lord Will Tell Me. Please Forgive me. I remain, Your Obedient servant, F. J. Vermaak.

'He does ask us to forgive him,' Uncle Darvie murmured. 'Is that not repentance?'

'Well . . .'

'Dominee? Was it something else you had in mind? A full confession, maybe?'

'So, you have heard.'

'Of course.'

With the return of conversation, the air in that tiny room with its corrugated-iron walls baking under the sun, suddenly became almost as stifling as smoke. It also smelled like Swart's Flesh Shop, which was making the Dominee restless.

'Shall we talk on the stoep, Doctor?' he suggested, leading the way with a heavy clump of his boots. 'Or maybe you can wait in the kitchen while I first go and see how Gert is getting on with Mrs Vermaak.'

'Fine, tell her I'll be in again by and by.'

But Uncle Darvie did not go straight indoors; he had spotted the Hottentot maid standing drunkenly against the rainwater tank.

'Hey, where were you this afternoon?' he demanded.

'Making merry in my hut, baasie.'

'Oh, ja? Have you been doing as I told you?'

'True's God, baasie!'

'Take not the Name—' Uncle Darvie began, then found himself distracted. His mind filled with the horrific effect of a shotgun fired inside a man's mouth.

'Hey? When did you last give your missus a meal then?'

'Lunch time, my baas. Then she say I must go off same as all servants on Sunday afternoon time.'

The maid scuttled away as the Dominee came out of the house again.

'The widow is very calm,' he said. 'Gert is happy to stay with her while we decide what there is to do.'

'Shock,' grunted Uncle Darvie. 'That it should come to this.'

'You cannot blame yourself, Doctor.'

'Who told him to come to church? Who? It was me.'

'Perhaps this was the best way for it to end. The Almighty has in His Wisdom decided—'

'You can't say that until there's proof . . .' began Uncle Darvie, as they were walking into the kitchen, but his sentence remained forever unfinished.

There was the proof. Right there on the kitchen table: a large tin of sheep dip with its screw-top off. And beside it, a cup of coffee filled to the brim.

'Sheep dip!' exclaimed the Dominee. 'I thought I noticed something darker than blood on his clothes.'

'Sheep dip,' mourned Uncle Darvie. 'Now, why didn't I think of that? All the time I had in mind the white powder. Yes, it says so here on the label: Beware – Sodium Arsenite.'

He pressed the palm of his hand against the coffee pot.

'Still warm, Dominee. He must have been preparing it for her at tea time. Yes, the cup stinks of it.'

'But look here – and here, Doctor!'

Uncle Darvie's attention had been so taken up with the sheep dip, he had failed to note what else lay on the table top. There was a cut-throat razor, a short length of binding cord, and a stick of dynamite which Faanie must have had left over from blasting the dam. Even their separate properties as instruments of destruction were enough to make Uncle Darvie shudder – their combined effect so weakened his knees he had to sit down.

'What can this mean?' he said softly.

The Dominee picked up the cut-throat and turned to him, even more grim-faced than usual.

'I take it you do not miss its overall significance, Doctor, which is simply that the Lord God spared the life of Emily Vermaak this day not once but, in a manner of speaking, four times.'

'Five,' corrected Uncle Darvie, with whom accurate arithmetic was a habit. 'There's the gun.'

'Quite so even more for us to give thanks for. But to return to your question: you have been called to look into men's bodies; I, to look into their souls. And what I see here is one of those terrible dreams Faanie talks about in his letter to us. Only he woke up just in time, saw what he was about to do, wrote the note and very decently shot himself.'

'But *why*? Why all of a sudden?'

There was an odd glint in the Dominee's eye as he replied: 'Because all of a sudden, this slow poisoner was being thwarted by someone. He was being stopped from killing his victim, and could think of no other way except putting an end to her once and for all!'

'Which he realised he could no longer do with the sheep dip, because she'd smell it if he put in enough to kill her outright?'

'Right again, Doctor. So he explored what other means he had at his disposal, and I would suggest that slicing open, strangling—'

'Ja, ja, please—'

'The horror of it brought him to his senses,' the Dominee added, a little peevish at being cut short. 'Shall I send Gert for Sergeant Poolman to come now?'

Uncle Darvie stood up and barred his way to the bedroom, motioning with his hand for the right to think a moment before they did anything.

'Would it not be best,' he said, 'if we did not make our discoveries public?'

'That Faanie was poisoning his wife? Why, Doctor, I'm surprised at you! Anyone can make a mistake.'

'No, no, it wasn't that. I mean, in Heaven's Name, what good will it do? The Almighty has ordained that this should happen to spare Emily Vermaak suffering – but won't we be going against His Will in telling the police about the poison?'

'I cannot see how.'

'Sergeant Poolman can be trusted to be discreet in cases of simple suicide, as we both know from the past. But mention attempted murder, and those other ones, in the ordinary clothes who smoke cigarettes, will come down like vultures on Sandkop. Think of the distress that could cause Emily – all the pain and indignity of her having to tell strangers, outsiders, even newspaper reporters about what came between her and Faanie. Has the woman not suffered enough?'

The Dominee gave a little shrug.

'What will she feel if she *knows* Faanie was trying to kill her? We don't know, she might change her mind in time and think fondly of him – for her own sake, mind.'

Uncle Darvie was speaking with a desperation that he knew took its strength from the guilt large inside him. He tried once more to win his colleague round.

'All right, what about our part in this? Are you looking forward to seeing me admit at the inquest I made a mistake? Do you want to explain, under oath, how it was you, a leader of the community, disregarded the facts and treated them as gossip – thus endangering a woman's life?'

That was better. The Dominee closed his eyes and seemed to pray for a moment.

'Ja, I can see how this could be the Will of God also,' he said. 'What do we do? Destroy the note?'

'No, that would arouse suspicion. Few men don't explain their self-inflicted ends. The beauty of this one is that it can be read the other way – if you don't know about the poison, as the Sergeant doesn't, because Auntie Tina always insists that no outsider ever hears her stories, then it just sounds as if it's about Petronella Swart.'

'But—' began the Dominee.

'The Sergeant knows that already and can be discreet. No, all we do is put all this back where it belongs and say nothing.'

Uncle Darvie began to screw the lid on the can of sheep dip. He would put it back in the storeroom and perhaps sprinkle a little round to explain how it got on the clothes.

'Yes, this *is* right,' said the Dominee, coming to his side and coiling up the cord.

'You know, it's a funny thing,' Uncle Darvie murmured, happy that they were once again in accord, 'but I still can't believe this of Faanie. Truly, in my heart, that is. I still see him as the honest boy I pulled out backwards, and when I first saw him in the storeroom I thought—'

'What, old friend?'

'That – that he'd been murdered.'

'Doctor Kruger,' replied the Dominee, sparing one more smile, 'if ever a man was born stubborn and pig-headed, it was you! Only this time I don't have to make you go up a tree to see that.'

Two weeks later, Uncle Darvie suddenly rushed out of his surgery in the middle of rummaging for an ear syringe in a drawer, and went across to the manse.

Several things had happened since that dreadful Sunday afternoon out at *Welkom*. An inquest had been opened and closed on Faanie Vermaak, being held with unusual dispatch as it was important to know where to bury him. He had gone down deep into unconsecrated ground, and that had been one funeral both Uncle Darvie and even the Dominee missed, only Sergeant Poolman and two kaffirs with spades attended it. While Emily Vermaak had moved in with Uncle Jacobus and his family and was showing remarkable signs of recovery without any treatment at all, eating everything they put in front of her. There had been no buyer as yet for the farm, but hopes of a stranger becoming interested ran high.

Less happy, had been Uncle Darvie's loss of the peace of his mind. Which had given him no respite until he put his hand in that drawer.

Within minutes, the Dominee had been roused from his afternoon nap and bundled into Gert's Model T. Where he sat almost as bemused as Gert himself, while all three of them drove out to *Welkom*.

'I'm saying nothing,' Uncle Darvie informed them, 'nothing till I look in the dressing-table!'

Which he did shortly afterwards, with the Dominee peering over and seeing that it was naturally quite empty, save for its linings in each drawer.

'Right, that's one,' said Uncle Darvie, then began pulling up the floorboards on the far side of the big bed where a man could not fit himself unless it was moved.

'Sis!' said Gert, pinching his nose. 'What's down there?'

It was dark under the house, but soon a pale wriggle of maggots showed up, crawling over a mess of grey, slimy heaps sprinkled with sweet papers.

'So that's why he couldn't kill her – she was throwing her food away for fear of poison!' gasped the Dominee. 'No wonder she is fattening up so nicely.'

'No wonder,' echoed Uncle Darvie, his smile crooked as he noticed the other's air of romantic interest.

Then he dived for the door.

'Hey, but where are we going now?' Gert pleaded.

'To pay a call on a *very poisonous woman*,' Uncle Darvie said over his shoulder.

The Dominee cringed. That could mean only one person he knew. They were bound for Auntie Tina.

She sat very still, hands in her lap, as she listened to what her principal guest had to say. The Dominee, who found even a temporary boudoir an unnerving place to be, kept his eyes fixed out of the window.

'Isn't that a bit much?' Emily Vermaak asked Uncle Darvie.

'That is precisely my point. Does a man care very much how he kills, providing the killing is effective? Does he not just grab up the first thing that will do the job? Why should he care? It's not him that's going to suffer – to feel the pain.'

'Unless, of course, he means to kill himself.'

'Man,' Uncle Darvie said to her, 'I must say you are a very cool personality. Ja, that's the meaning of all those things on the kitchen table – Faanie was trying to decide which would be best for *him*.'

'Not for . . .' mumbled the Dominee, glancing across for a moment.

'Faanie Vermaak never ever intended his wife any harm,' Uncle Darvie growled. 'It was just the opposite: I let a woman murder a man under my nose! And how? By not seeing those symptoms were also symptoms of acute malnutrition, self-imposed, and helped along – in the case of the face sores – by too many of Auntie Tina's sweets!'

'She was very useful,' said Emily Vermaak.

'I'll say. Just a hint and you were vomiting all over the place in her mind. And the way she remembered the symptoms off pat. But that was where you made your big mistake!'

'Oh? Do tell me.'

'You missed one thing – you missed that when Auntie Tina tells a story that has scandal in it, she never leaves out a single detail.'

'Such as?'

'The fact you read aloud from the newspaper. When you want to convince somebody of something, you get them to read it themselves so they can see it down in black and white. You didn't because you knew she couldn't read English, and so you translated.'

'And we don't get English papers in Sandkop?'

'Ja, but first I thought of her saying it was "old and going yellow". What farmer's wife ever keeps a newspaper for so long as that without tearing it up to line her drawers and shelves? What other use is there for newspapers once you've read them – unless they're kept specially to remind you of something? Most probably something with which *you've* been connected.'

'I thought I'd never know why I did,' she said, pulling the paper out from under the cushion and handing it to him. 'Although now I wouldn't be without it.'

'The hair – how did you do that though?'

'Ringworm. The cat had it. I would have thought Sherlock of the Bushveld would have spotted that.'

'The Hereford Times,' Uncle Darvie read out. 'Major Herbert Rouse Armstrong T.D., sentenced to death for killing his wife in the Welsh border town of – hey, I see the date is 1922, five years ago. That's a coincidence, ja? Are you this Madame X involved?'

For the first time, Emily Vermaak showed emotion. She jumped up and kicked Uncle Darvie on the shins.

'You bastard! You bloody old peasant! I'll give you the "other woman"! I met the little rat at a Whitney dance, didn't I? Said he was a poor lonely widower. Said I was such a comfort to him in his grief – and that was *before* . . . Can't you see? I just wanted to get away as far as possible and find someone who would love me and—'

She slumped on her bed and began to cry.

The Dominee fled. Uncle Darvie, knowing there was no useful way of pursuing the matter, got wearily to his feet. Words were magic, but she could deny every last one used in her deadly spell.

'At least I kept my promise,' Emily Vermaak snuffled.

'Of sacred fidelity?'

'I mean when I promised Faanie he would *rot in Hell* for what he'd done to me! It wasn't hard to pretend I was dying – I'd died a little that night already. Then, when I saw what refusing my food was doing to me . . .'

'But you, woman,' Uncle Darvie said softly, 'won't you have to join him there some day? For what you've done?'

'I never thought of that,' she said in English. 'You're a funny old duffer. What really started you thinking there would be another side to it?'

'Ah,' said Uncle Darvie, taking off his hat again. 'All my life I've believed there was more to this world than meets the eye. Now, you tell me, my dear, what does an oblate spheroid mean to you?'

Ted Willis

The Man from the White Mountains

In one sense, of course, murder may be measured in moments. It takes only a split second after the squeezing of a trigger for a bullet to enter the brain or the heart, and only a fraction longer for a knife to slice into the soft flesh of the throat or penetrate a breast.

But to say this is to say little or nothing, the equivalent of asserting that love is no more than the fleeting moment of sexual climax.

A murderer – and, for that matter, his victim – is not made in a moment. He is the product of a long process, a combination of genes, background, upbringing, circumstances; in short, of his or her entire life. Luck can also play a vital part. There are many people, living innocent, respectable lives, who, in certain conditions, could and would commit murder, but who probably never will. It is their good fortune to escape the sequence of events which could drive them to kill. Others are not so lucky.

If, for example, we are to understand why a man called Marcos Kolomenos committed murder in Adelaide, South Australia, on March 17, 1972, it will be necessary to go back over forty years in time. The actual crime took only a few seconds, its preparation was a matter of careful planning over a period of months. But the seed of murder was planted in Marcos Kolomenos many years before, and ten thousand miles away, in the high White Mountains of Sphakia, to the west of the island of Crete.

It was there in the tiny village of Nigrita, on October 8, 1931, that a married woman named Lilika Kollias was taken, with her lover, in the act of adultery.

In accordance with the age-old custom of the mountain people, the woman was driven from the village with stones and left to fend for herself. In the weeks which followed she was seen from time to time on the outskirts of the village, a pathetic, starving, half-mad creature, trying desperately to get a glimpse of her children. No one spoke to her, no one fed her, no one lifted a little finger to help her. Eventually she was seen no more, but it was strongly rumoured that she had found her way to Athens and was working there in a hundred-drachma whore-house.

The man, Angelos, with whom she had sinned was left, according to custom, to the mercy of the husband and the brothers of the husband. For such a man castration was normally considered to be an apt punishment, but there was a complication. Angelos was a relative of the husband, a first cousin on the maternal side, and this made his betrayal of the unwritten code all the more serious.

The husband and the brothers sought the advice of Stavros Kontas, the oldest and wisest man in Nigrita. It was, after all, a question of the honour of the family. Stavros had to think for a long time and search his memory before he could give them an answer, for the problem was an unusual one. In his long life-time there had only been two instances of adultery in Nigrita, and since relatives were not involved, the customary punishment had been meted out. Expulsion for the woman, castration for the man.

And then Stavros remembered that his grandfather had once told him of a case in which a wife had betrayed her husband with his own brother. In such severe circumstances, the code decreed that the man should be put to death. It was a savage and primitive judgment but some deep instinct, centuries old, told the people that without such strict moral sanctions their isolated communities would degenerate and perish.

The following morning, as the sun was rising, Angelos was taken from the village into the mountains. He was stripped naked and while the three brothers held him, the husband castrated him. He was still screaming in agony as they carried him to a ledge and threw him on to the rocks eight hundred feet below. Then the husband broke Angelos' knife on a rock and threw the pieces after him. They left the body for twenty-four hours and then covered it with stones.

Marcos Kolomenos was five years old at this time. He heard the outcry in the village when the lovers were first discovered, and he realised from the behaviour of his elders that something of great importance and seriousness had taken place. Although he had been ordered to remain indoors, he crept out and from a discreet hiding-place watched the grim-faced women, his own mother among them, as they stoned Lilika Kollias and drove her away. He was appalled, yet excited by this strange game.

The next morning he saw four men leave the village with a fifth man, whose arms were tied behind his back. He recognised this man as Angelos, a person whom he had always admired. Angelos was tall and handsome, with white, flashing teeth and a fierce, manly expression. At first, Marcos had been afraid of him, but once Angelos had carried him on his shoulders up into the mountains for a long, long way and shown him the hidden entrance to a wonderful, secret cave; and on another occasion Angelos had made him a wooden knife, shaped just like the sharp, steel knife he carried in his own belt.

Marcos wondered what his friend had done to have his hands tied thus, and why he was being taken away. He wanted to call out to him but he was too frightened to do so. He was puzzled to see that Angelos was wearing his best clothes, just as though it were a Sunday or a feast-day, and to see the knife with its decorated handled in his belt. Angelos walked proudly, with his head high, looking neither to left nor right and Marcos watched until he was out of sight.

Marcos never saw Angelos again, but the incidents made a deep impression upon him. His life changed with the years, he became a different person, but there were times when the memory of Lilika and her lover echoed and surged in him like the sound of distant bells. Whenever he saw a man carrying a small boy on his shoulders, he would remember his friend. At such moments he imagined that he could smell, across the years, the strong, masculine scent – a blend of wine and old leather – which was his first experience of Angelos.

It wasn't until he was twelve years old that the full significance of what had happened was revealed to him. He did not question the judgment or the sentence. Both were just, they followed naturally from the unwritten code of the Cretan mountain people.

It was, after all, a simple question. Every man had the right and the duty to defend his honour. If he failed to do so he betrayed not only a code which had lasted a thousand years, but himself. Such a man was not fit to live.

In May, 1941, when Marcos Kolomenos was almost fifteen years of age, the Germans carried out a massive airborne invasion of the island and succeeded in occupying the main towns and the coastal plains. But the Cretans, helped by remnants of the British army, retreated to the mountains and carried on the resistance. The Germans turned in fury against village after village, but they were never able to break the spirit of a people for whom honour was more important than life.

This was a crucial time for Marcos. In a few weeks, even a few days, he became a man; with his father and his uncles, he joined the partisan forces. He saw many of his comrades die, and there were times when death brushed his own shoulder. He learned the art of survival the hard way. Older men came to admire and respect not his courage, for that in a Cretan was taken for granted, but his cunning, resourcefulness and adaptability.

He learned, also, that there was another world beyond the White Mountains and his village. He became friends with an Australian sergeant, a former school master, and in the long intervals between engagements the sergeant taught Marcos English and the elements of arithmetic. He talked to him for hours of other lands and other peoples, but most of all, he spoke of his native Australia, holding the boy fascinated with his tales of that immense brown country. By a strange coincidence, they spent most of their time together in the big, secret cave which Angelos had shown Marcos years before.

'When the war is over, you must leave,' the sergeant told Marcos. 'There is nothing for you here. Australia is the world's last frontier, it's a young man's country. You could make your mark there.' He said it time and time again.

The idea of leaving Crete shocked and frightened Marcos at first. He could not imagine himself living in any other place. In the event, it was the Germans who, inadvertently, settled the issue for him.

His mother was caught by an enemy patrol in the act of smuggling ammunition to the Resistance. She was stripped naked and hanged on a gallows in the village square as a deterrent to any others who might be tempted to follow her example.

The death of his wife changed Marcos' father. Normally a careful, slow-thinking man, he allowed anger and grief to overcome caution. At noon one day he went down to the nearest town with a British Sten gun concealed under his cloak. He sat on a bench in the little square and waited in the hot sun until a detachment of German soldiers came marching by on the way to the local barracks; then, quite calmly, he opened fire. Fourteen of the enemy were killed and seven wounded before the father was himself cut down.

From that point onwards, his comrades noted a new depth of ruthlessness in Marcos. It was as though all human pity had been drained from his soul. He rarely took prisoners, and those few enemy soldiers who did fall into his hands longed for death.

When the war was over, there was nothing to keep him in Crete. He had a brother, Alexander, who was seventeen years his junior, but there was no one else towards whom he felt any responsibility. In March, 1946, at the age of twenty, he emigrated to Australia. He left Alex with an aunt, promising to send for him as soon as he had settled in the new land.

He was still only twenty years of age, but he had the look and bearing of a man fifteen years older.

Marcos settled in South Australia, near the city of Adelaide, at a place called Paradise. The name appealed to him. But for the first year, his life was something less than Elysian.

He was employed as a labourer by a farmer named George Smith, a harsh, humourless man, who had a contempt for 'New Australians' and regarded them as a source of cheap labour. He worked Marcos as one would work an ox, housed and fed him little better than an animal. The young Cretan seemed to accept this patiently, even willingly; but underneath the resignation his spirit glowed fiercely, waiting like a fire which has been momentarily dampened but remains unquenched.

During those twelve months Marcos learned another valuable lesson – that patience can also be a weapon, that there are times when a man must simply wait and watch and learn. He perfected his knowledge of English (though he never completely lost his accent or the Cretan rhythm of speech) and he took the measure of this country in which he had decided to make his home. He saw that it was, indeed, a land of opportunity, and he knew, after only three months, that he could and would succeed there. This inner knowledge fortified him as the days of back-breaking labour passed; he had no doubts, his self-confidence was complete.

Quite suddenly, one morning, he decided he was ready. He had been into Adelaide the day before and seen the opportunity for which he had been waiting. He packed his few belongings, told Smith that he was leaving immediately and waited for the reaction. He did not wish to go quietly, he had a debt to pay and he was hoping that the farmer would give him an honourable opportunity to settle it. He was not disappointed. Smith began to rant and rave, piling the old familiar insults one on the other. He was a heavy man of formidable strength, but Marcos was confident.

He dropped his worldly possessions to the ground, stripped off his shirt and faced the astonished Smith. His right fist thudded into the farmer's beer-ripened belly, and as the big man gasped in anguish and doubled-up, Marcos linked his hands together and chopped down with pulverising force on Smith's neck. Smith fell to the ground, tried desperately to raise himself, and rolled over on his back. Marcos was angry that it had been so swift and easy a victory. He felt cheated on his revenge. He looked down at the farmer and, for a moment, he felt himself back in the White Mountains, standing over a fallen enemy, his hand reaching automatically for the knife in his belt. Smith must have read the intent in the Cretan's face, for he rolled his blue eyes imploringly and cried in fear.

'No, Marcos, no! No, no!'

Marcos steadied himself. He was not in Sphakia, there was no knife in his belt, the blubbering man at his feet was not a Nazi. He lifted a heavy boot and Smith whimpered in fear, then screamed as the boot crunched home. Marcos gave a grunt of contempt and spat at Smith; the spittle rolled slowly down the farmer's cheek, but he did not attempt to wipe it away.

Mrs Smith, a thin, scrawny woman in a shapeless dress, stood watching the scene from the homestead, her face like a sallow moon in the dark shade of the verandah. She made no move towards her husband, her eyes looked at Marcos without expression.

He picked up his things and walked away from Paradise without regret, and without once looking back.

The first thing Marcos did after this was to buy himself a hole in the ground. It was about two miles from the centre of Adelaide, a stretch of derelict and neglected earth, just over an acre in size, almost entirely made up of this huge, yawning hole. He bought the site for £90, which was half of what he had saved, and the man who sold it to him thought he was mad. But Marcos had seen, with the fresh eyes of a stranger, that Adelaide was growing, and that trucks, loaded with rubble from the demolition of old buildings, were being driven each day to tips on the city outskirts. He posted a notice inviting the demolition companies to dump their rubble on his site. Since, by so doing, the companies saved themselves time and mileage, they were quite happy to pay Marcos the nominal charge of £1 per truck-load which he imposed.

Within six months the hole was full and the site more or less levelled. Marcos sold it to a developer for £2,500, and with most of this capital he bought a half-share in a small building and construction company. His partner was Andy Byers, a small, genial, happy-go-lucky Australian who knew a great deal about building but very little about business. Marcos waited again, learning all he could from Byers, and at the end of two years he bought him out. Byers was drunk when he signed the contract of sale and on the following morning his wife tried to get Marcos to tear it up. He listened without emotion to her frantic pleading.

'Your husband is a good bricklayer, Mrs Byers,' he said. 'If he wishes to come back and work for me as a bricklayer, I will find him a place. But the business is mine. From now on, it is mine, please understand this.'

'You cheated him!' she screamed. 'He didn't know what he was doing, he was drunk. You made him drunk.'

'He has no head for drink and no head for business,' said Marcos calmly. 'Take my advice. Keep him away from both these things.'

A few months later, when he had run through his money, Andy Byers swallowed his pride and came back to Marcos for a job. He was made foreman-bricklayer on a big new development in the suburb of Springfield, a position which he accepted gratefully and humbly, and in which he served Marcos well.

It gave Marcos no satisfaction to take back his old partner on these terms. He valued pride in a man above all things, and the servile attitude of Byers offended him. Whenever they met – something he tried to avoid – Marcos found it difficult to conceal his contempt.

Shortly after taking over the construction firm Marcos Kolomenos changed his name to Mark Coleman. It was a difficult step to take, and one which he regretted, but he decided that it was essential to the success of the business. In any case, this was his country now, he knew he could never go back to the old life in Crete. When he had lived the statutory five years in Australia, he applied for and was granted naturalisation. He felt a surge of pride as he swore the oath of allegiance to the Queen and to his new country. He had left his old life behind forever, he was now an Australian, a man of substance.

In 1955 he built himself a new, modern house in Springfield, and sent for his younger brother, Alex, and his aunt, Amalia. He longed for their arrival, he wanted to have his own family around him, to show them what he had achieved. He had no interests outside the business, his one concession to his own nature was a weekly visit to a brothel in the port area of the town; but these cold encounters only served to sharpen his growing feeling of loneliness.

In the event, Aunt Amalia refused to leave Crete, and Alex, now a sturdy lad of twelve, travelled to Adelaide alone. He knew little or nothing of life outside Nigrita and the White Mountains and he was astonished by the sophistication and luxury which he saw around him. Most of all, he was enthralled by his brother, who seemed to be so much a part of this new environment, to be so confident, rich and successful. The house, the car, his bedroom with its own bathroom – the sheer space, the grandeur of it all took his breath away, it was like a dream.

But it wasn't a dream, it was astonishingly real. On that first evening Marcos said: 'All this is ours, Alex. Yours and mine. And believe me, it is only the beginning.'

Only the beginning? Alex was amazed. What could be better than this, how could a man want or have more? But he said nothing, only watched his brother with big, dark, wondering eyes.

'You will become an Australian like me,' Marcos continued. 'First, you will learn to speak the language. I've arranged all that. Then school, real school. And after that, university.' He spoke proudly.

'University?' It was a new word to Alex, he had never heard it before.

'You are tired. We will speak of it tomorrow – we shall have time enough to talk.' At the door, Marcos paused and looked back at his brother. 'Alex. Do you know what a millionaire is?'

'A rich man?'

'A very rich man. Like Onassis. I am going to be a millionaire, that is my plan. I shall achieve this in ten years.'

'Why do you want this?'

'Because it is important. Money is important.'

'But in this country it seems to me that everyone has money.'

'Not everyone. You will learn that. And it is the same here as it is back home. The rich give the orders and the poor obey. The greater the riches, the greater the power.' He moved in closer to the boy and put a hand on his shoulder. 'This is the way I see it, Alex. Our mother and our father did not die so that we should live for the rest of our lives taking orders from other people. I did not fight in the mountains for that either. Do you understand?'

Alex nodded, although he did not properly follow what Marcos was saying.

'The important thing is that you are now with me. We shall do well together.' Marcos embraced his brother and kissed him in the Cretan style. The boy was very near to tears but he held them back, knowing that it was unmanly to weep and that Marcos would not approve such weakness.

Marcos was as good as and better than his word. These were the lush, plush years when half the world seemed to be set on a course of endless growth, and whole nations nourished themselves on greed. Money made money and more money; the quick-witted and the corrupt fattened themselves on their easy killings. It was a time tailor-made for Marcos, a time for which all his background and experience had prepared him.

Within ten years he had expanded into real estate and mineral development; he had extensive interests in the wine districts of the Barossa Valley, he owned a television station in Adelaide, two radio stations in the country, and he was a major shareholder in several newspapers and leading industrial companies. He was a millionaire three times over, a powerful and influential figure, to whose views politicians and businessmen listened with respect, and even fear. Such was his reputation that he figured prominently in news stories and press cartoons; one satirical television programme (not on his own station) lampooned him at regular intervals.

This programme was to play an important part in later events.

What his critics did not understand was that Marcos seemed to take no joy from his success, no satisfaction from his conquests. Though few doors were closed to him, he found no pleasure in social life; he remained an enigma, a grim, solitary person for whom there was no existence outside his business. His one relaxation was an occasional weekend flight in his private plane to a small station he owned near Townsville, in North Queensland; but even on these occasions he took his working papers with him, and he was invariably alone.

This weekend hide-out was also destined to feature prominently in the unfolding pattern of the drama that was to come.

The force that continued to drive Marcos forward was disappointment.

TED WILLIS

As Alex grew older it became clear that he shared none of his brother' character or ambition. The simple truth was that he had been spoiled. Marcos had pampered the boy, giving him all he asked – and more – without question. Content to enjoy the fruits of the harvest, Alex gave nothing in return. He became notorious as a rich dilettante who was only protected from the consequences of his irresponsibility by the power and influence of his older brother. He developed artistic and literary pretensions, and openly mocked Marcos, making no secret of the fact that he regarded him as an uncultured moron whose horizons were bounded by balance-sheets. He returned cynicism for affection, coldness for warmth. The two men reached a point where they could hardly exchange a civil word and Alex left home.

Marcos continued to pay him an allowance, for to do otherwise would have been to deny his own roots. He was the eldest brother, he was still responsible. But beyond this there was nothing, only the business, into which he sank his energy and his bitter sense of loss.

And then fate or luck (aren't they, after all, the same thing?) made the final move in its long, remorseless buildup to inevitable tragedy.

It was as though Kristina Ayres had been kept waiting in the wings until the stage was set, and the other protagonists in position.

Marcos met her at one of his rare social engagements, a dinner party given by the Premier of South Australia to honour a group of visiting businessmen. The hostess paired her with Marcos and within a few minutes he was completely captivated by his dark-haired, vivacious and beautiful partner.

'Kristina?' he asked. 'It is a Greek name. Are you Greek?'

'I am Australian,' she answered with a smile. 'My father was English and mother Greek. I am called after her.'

He nodded with approval. Throughout the evening he watched her, noting her poise and sophistication, her humour and bright intelligence; above all, the odd, shy moments of innocence which showed in her big, dark expressive eyes. For the first time he felt his own lack of the social graces, his awkwardness. In her presence he felt like a thick-fingered peasant.

In a sense, it was for him a rebound from the crushing disappointment he had experienced with Alex. He needed someone as the centrepiece of his life, someone to show off his glittering wealth and thus give it purpose and meaning. And there was something more. She could give him a replacement for Alex, she could give him children, the sons he yearned for. Alex had been a sort of son, but that was ended, Marcos could take no pride in his brother. But with Kristina he could be proud again; to possess such a woman would make him the envy of other men, she would be a magnificent confirmation of his success and position.

736

What he felt for her could hardly be described as love, though he admired her body and desired to take her. It was as though he had seen something of extraordinary beauty and value in a shop-window and was desperate to own it. But this was the man he had become and he could think in no other terms. It was the nearest approach he could make to the concept of love; sadly, he knew no other way.

For weeks he laid siege to her, bombarding her with invitations and presents. She liked him, he amused her, and she was flattered to be courted by such a rich and famous man. And she was intrigued to find that, unlike other men, he made no sexual advances, there was no attempt to get her into bed. There were times when she wanted this herself, for she found him physically attractive; and she felt that only in this way, naked and in the act of love, would she discover the true Marcos, the man behind the image. But she held back, sensing that this would cheapen her in his eyes, that she was, in a sense, on trial.

Day by day, she saw herself coming more and more under the spell of his forceful personality. He wanted her, he was determined to have her, and any obstacles she erected were swept aside like so much chaff. He surrounded her, overwhelmed her, and she was helpless to resist.

They were married on August 2nd, 1970, a wedding of such magnificence that it made headlines in all the newspapers and was featured on television. Alex attended the reception, even putting on a suit for the occasion, and met Kristina for the first time.

'So you are his latest possession,' he said mockingly. 'Not bad, not bad. I've known him make worse bargains.'

She turned away from him in anger and distress, but she was to remember the words later, when the bitter truth they carried was stamped into her consciousness. Perhaps, in her heart, she had recognised some part of this truth from the beginning.

For truth it was. She was deeply fond of Marcos, she admired and respected him, and she told herself that this was enough, that she could build on this foundation and draw from him the response which would make her truly love him.

But it was a response of which he was incapable. He was generous and affectionate, proud of her, but that was all. She was, indeed, a possession, treasured as such and treated as such. And if the possession, at times, tried to assert her own individuality, to move beyond the mechanical role allotted to her, he rode over her with a ruthlessness which was frightening.

There was warmth between them, at least during the first year, but little tenderness. In bed, any veneer of sensitivity which he had acquired was left outside the sheets with his clothes; he coupled her as he had coupled the girls in the brothel, as though it was his right to do so, and he was only collecting what he had paid for. It was then that she felt most strongly that to him she was an ornament, an object, a possession.

Many women have suffered as much or more and have come to terms with their lives, content to accept half a loaf. It is possible that Kristina would have followed this path, for she was by nature an honest person with a strong dislike of intrigue or of anything that smacked of the underhand. Had she met and fallen in love with a stranger, her first instinct would have been to face Marcos with the fact, and to brave his inevitable wrath.

But, almost inevitably, the man who come into her life was Alex. He began to call at the big house in Springfield again, it seemed that he was prepared to make some sort of peace with Marcos. Kristina was forced to amend her first impression of Alex; as time went on she found his company amusing and relaxing. Marcos was pleased that this should be so and encouraged them to see more of each other; it relieved him of certain social duties which he found irksome.

He liked to see them laughing happily together, like children. In a way, that was how he looked upon them both. The change in Alex made him happy also; for the first time in months he began to feel something of the old warmth for his younger brother.

This was a time of deep content for Marcos. His business affairs were thriving, there was some talk that he might be recommended for a knighthood; his marriage, though not perfect, seemed to have settled into a secure pattern, and Alex was once more back in the family circle. The one disappointment was that Kristina had so far failed to produce the sons he wanted, but there was time for that, he told himself.

The contentment did not last long. One evening, working in his study on the first floor, he happened quite by chance to get up and look out of the window towards the large flood-lit swimming-pool. He smiled as he saw Alex and Kristina sporting together in the blue water, and he felt a touch of envy also. Kristina was seldom as relaxed and carefree with him. Perhaps it was his fault? He used the pool for exercise only, grimly swimming a statutory ten lengths each morning; to him it was a tool, useful for toning the muscles, not a playground.

The trouble was that he had gone from boyhood to manhood in one step. He had missed his youth – the best time of all. He was forty-five years of age, almost old enough to be their father – and at that moment, he felt the weight of the years that separated them. He would try to relax more. There was the yacht, moored in the harbour, idle for most of the year. He would take time off, he would take Kristina and Alex away for a long cruise, he would show them that he, too, knew how to enjoy life.

It was then that the incident occurred.

Alex was helping Kristina from the pool, pulling her up out of the water. He could see them clearly in the amber light, their bodies striking long shadows on the paved surface behind them. As Kristina straightened up, she stood close to Alex, and he put up a hand and held it against her cheek. It was more than a gesture, it was a caress as intimate and full of meaning as if he had touched her breast. They stood there motionless for a moment, not smiling, simply looking into each other's eyes, his hand still resting gently on her cheek. Then she pulled away abruptly and threw a warning look towards the house.

It was no more than that, a small, trivial thing. But watching them, Marcos felt a sudden, inexplicable apprehension of danger, manifested as in the old partisan days in the mountains, by a chill stiffening of his neck and spine.

He tried to set the thought aside, telling himself that the gesture was no more than a sign of friendship, that they were children, that it meant nothing, but it was useless. Fear and suspicion filled his mind, spreading like a virus in the bloodstream. He dared not watch Kristina too closely, lest she in turn should suspect, but as the days passed his torment grew. He feared to learn the truth but he knew that without it he would find no peace of mind.

At the end of a week, he hired a private detective agency to keep observation on his wife and Alex. They came back in five days with their report. She had visited Alex in his studio-apartment in South Adelaide three times during that period, and each visit had lasted for two hours or more. On one of those occasions she had told Marcos that she was visiting her dressmaker; and on another that she had driven up to Elizabeth to visit a girl-friend.

He put the issue to a further test. That weekend he flew up to the house in Queensland on one of his regular visits. On his return, a new report awaited him. Kristina visited Alex at his apartment on the Saturday evening. They went out to dinner and then returned to his place. She left him at 5 a.m. the next morning.

Marcos paid off the detective and dismissed him. His instinct had proved to be right – Kristina had lied to him, she was deceiving him with Alex, his own brother.

He instructed his secretary to block all calls and cancel his appointments. He was surprised at his own outward calmness; in that sense, at least, the truth had brought a certain peace. It was only later, as he sat at the big desk, with the light fading behind him, that the anger and bitterness crowded in on him. From that moment on, it could be said that the balance of his mind was disturbed, that he ceased to be a rational person.

Or perhaps it would be more accurate to say that Mark Coleman became more truly himself; the new Australian became once again the old Cretan, Marcos Kolomenos. Centuries of history, age-old instincts and concepts of honour stirred in his blood. He remembered Angelos and Lilika, he saw again as in a film, his own mother as she hurled a stone at the guilty woman, he saw Angelos being led from the village. The sharp scent of leather and wine came back to him across the years.

But this was not Sphakia, he knew that; there vengeance could be simple and direct, everyone would expect him to redeem his honour, they would see it as something obvious and inevitable, as natural as breathing. It was different in this new land; here they would not understand his motives; quite simply they would call it murder and instead of being honoured for the deed he would be hunted down as if he were the guilty party.

It would have to be done, there was no question about that, but it would have to be done in a different way. For why should he suffer, why should he throw away all he had worked for and achieved? He had done nothing wrong, he had been a faithful husband and brother. It was they, Kristina and Alex, who had brought dishonour to the family, not he.

And now all the sharp cunning and talent for organisation which Marcos had acquired over the years came to his aid. When he left the office it was quite dark, but the main outline of a plan was already clear in his mind.

It was not until one weekend, almost three months later, when all the pieces were in position, that he began to put the plan into operation.

It was nothing new for Marcos to fly to Queensland to spend a weekend alone with his papers, but Kristina was worried, on edge. During the past few weeks she had sensed a new tension in her husband and it frightened her. There was nothing she could put a finger on, no positive evidence; it was simply that he seemed to be burning with some secret, inner fierceness.

Nino and Faustina Silone, the Italian couple who looked after them, had gone to Melbourne and would not be back until Monday. There was nothing unusual in that, they had relations there whom they visited regularly, but their absence added to Kristina's foreboding. Even the air was heavy and oppressive, it weighed on her skin, as though warning that a storm was about to break. At least, it seemed so to her.

Alex laughed at her fears. He saw in the absence of Marcos and the servants a wonderful opportunity for them to be together. He wanted to spend the night with Kristina in the house, under his brother's roof: the thought of it gave him a peculiar satisfaction.

'Oh, come on, Kris,' he said petulantly. 'What's wrong?'

'I don't know. I wish I did. It's just this feeling. I can't explain it.'

She moved around restlessly. 'It's just – just that it is all too convenient. I mean – Marcos has a cold, a terrible cold, but he insisted on going. And then there's Nino and Faustina – they offered to cancel their trip, but he insisted they should go. He has been strange lately, Alex, he really has. I'm not imagining that.'

'You are! It's all in your mind!' Her attitude was making him irritable. 'Look, the main thing is – did he go or didn't he?'

'Yes,' she said listlessly. 'He left here at nine o'clock this morning.'

'Well, then!' he said as though that settled it. He tried to take her in his arms, but she eluded him with a frown.

'Yesterday,' she said thoughtfully, as though Alex hadn't spoken. 'Yesterday I was checking my make-up in the bedroom. Marcos came in, and I caught a glimpse of him in the mirror. It was only a flash, a moment, but the look in his eyes – it was terrible, Alex. I can't describe it – hate, madness, despair – all those things, but mainly hate.'

'Why should he suddenly hate you?'

'It could only be for one reason.'

'No,' he said firmly. 'Now you are imagining things. He trusts us. He goes out of his way to throw us together. This weekend is an example. He wouldn't go away if he suspected anything. Why, he even asked me to keep an eye on you! Which, of course, I said I would do with pleasure.'

He kissed her, but her response was cool. 'O.K.,' he said angrily, 'O.K. If that's how it's going to be, there's not much point in my staying!' He moved to the door, and she made no effort to stop him. 'Listen,' he said, from the doorway, 'is that place in Queensland on the telephone?'

'Of course.'

'Then ring Marcos. Put your mind at rest. Speak to him. Find out once and for all if he is there.'

'What shall I say?'

'God, you're his wife. Ask him about his cold – say you're worried – anything.' He went to the phone and picked it up. 'What's the number?'

'Greenvale, North Queensland 274. Area Code 032.'

He dialled the operator, gave her the area code and number, and asked for a personal call to Mr Mark Coleman. She took the phone from him, and he kissed her lightly on the cheek. 'Don't be frightened,' he said.

Relief showed in her eyes as she heard Marcos answer. She nodded towards Alex, who spread his hands as if to say, 'I told you so.'

'Marcos, it's Kristina. I – I just thought I'd ring to find how you were feeling. How's the cold?'

'It's much the same,' he answered abruptly. She could hear the slight hoarseness in his voice. 'Is everything all right at your end?' he continued.

'Yes, oh, yes. I was only concerned about you.'

'There is no need. I'm not going to die. I shall be back tomorrow as arranged. Goodbye.' There was a note of irritation in his tone.

She put the telephone down slowly. 'Yes,' she said, 'he's there. He's there, all right. His usual polite courteous self.' She went to Alex. 'Come on, let's go to bed.'

She spoke with bitterness, it was as if the need to spite Marcos was uppermost in her mind. They went up to the main bedroom.

She found little enjoyment in their love-making. She felt ill-at-ease lying in the bed which she had so often shared with Marcos and regretted the bitter impulse which had led her to take Alex there. And there was something in his attitude which disturbed her. He had taken her fiercely, swiftly, and when it was over he lay back smiling as though in triumph.

'That was the best ever,' he said with a deep sigh, 'the best ever. Great! In this bed, in this room! Great!'

'In his room, in his bed. Isn't that what you mean?'

'You've got to admit, it adds an edge to the situation. A certain flavour.'

There was a smugness in his voice which angered her. A sense of disgust, as much for herself as for him, rose in her throat like bile. She got out of bed and put on a robe.

'Oh, stay here, Kris,' he pleaded and his voice sounded like that of a spoiled child. 'Come back to bed.'

'Alex,' she said quietly, 'when Marcos comes back, I am going to tell him.'

'Oh, yes,' he said with a smile, 'I can just see you doing that.'

'I mean it. I shall tell him everything, and then I shall leave him.'

'You're out of your mind!' He sat up in the bed. 'You don't know Marcos. He won't just sit back and accept it. Kristina, come back to bed and don't be foolish.'

'Alex,' she said quietly, 'what is more important to you? Your love of me or your hatred of your brother?'

'What the hell are you talking about? Kris, for heaven's sake, what's wrong?'

'Nothing. Only, perhaps, that I don't like being used.'

'Used?'

'By Marcos. And by you against Marcos. Because that's what you've been doing, isn't it? Oh, I daresay you love me well enough in your spoiled, little-boy way, but that's not really what drives you, is it? You're using me to get back at Marcos. I'm just a—'

She stopped suddenly, holding her breath, listening. 'What was that?' she whispered.

'What?'

'I heard something. A door. Someone's in the house, Alex.'

'Oh, rubbish!' he said. But fear showed in her eyes and he rose from the bed quickly, reaching for his clothes.

'Listen! Listen!' she said urgently. He paused in the act of pulling on his shirt. Nothing at first, no sound, and then they heard it; the quiet, measured tread of someone mounting the stairs. Each step seemed to crack the silence like a football on ice.

Alex scrambled in panic for his jeans. 'Help me, help me, for Christ's sake!' he croaked. But Kristina was standing still and calm, as though she had anticipated this moment and was almost relieved that it had come.

The sounds stopped outside the door. A century passed, and then the handle began to turn, Alex, holding his jeans around his waist, his shirt flapping, snatched up the rest of his clothes and rushed for the bathroom, as the door opened.

'Marcos!' said Kristina, trying to keep the fear out of her voice. 'What is going on? I thought you were in Greenvale – I spoke to you on the phone only a half-hour ago. What are you up to?'

He looked at her in contempt and past her with the same contempt to the soiled and rumpled bed. His dark eyes glowed, he was breathing heavily; she caught in her nostrils a sour scent, as of an animal, and then he hit her. She cried out and fell across the bed. He looked down at her for a moment.

'Whore!' He ground out the word from behind his clenched white teeth.

'Marcos, please,' she whispered. 'Let me explain.'

'Explain? How do you explain this? And this?' He ripped the robe from her shoulder, tearing it to the waist; he plucked the blue sheet from the bed and tore at it with his great hands as though it were tissue. As he did so he kept repeating: 'Whore! Whore! Whore!'

He pulled her up, hit her again, and caught her as she fell unconscious into his arms.

In the darkness that surrounded her, Kristina heard the shot. It seemed to come from a long way off, and it took her a full minute to work out what it could be. She opened her eyes and saw that she was in one of the spare rooms. The full realisation of what had happened came as she looked at her tattered robe. She struggled painfully to her feet and stumbled to the door. It was locked on the outside; she wrenched at the handle, hammered feebly on the door-panels.

Quite suddenly it opened and she saw Marcos standing there. He seemed very calm now and when he put a hand on her arm his touch was gentle. She dimly registered the fact that he was wearing gloves.

'Now, Kristina,' he said evenly. 'Let us talk together for a moment or two.'

'Alex,' she said hoarsely, 'where is Alex?'

'Alex and I have reached an understanding,' he said, smiling. 'It was quite simple really. I offered him 50,000 dollars if he would clear off. He stuck out for double, and I agreed. After all, he is my brother. He left you a farewell note.'

Still dazed, she took the piece of paper he held out to her. 'Dear Kris,' she read, 'It is impossible for us to go on like this, so for your sake, I am doing the only thing possible in the circumstances. Please understand, and try to forget me. Goodbye, darling.' It was signed *Alex* and she knew that it was his handwriting.

'No, no,' she moaned, 'it isn't possible.' Her head cleared suddenly and she remembered the shot; pushing past Marcos, she ran to the bedroom. The door was open, the bitter smell of gun-fire hung in the air, and Alex was lying on the floor at the foot of the bed. There was a spreading crimson stain on the white carpet and half his face and head was missing. She turned on Marcos in horror and began to beat at him with her clenched fists, but he held her easily.

'I wasn't lying, Kristina,' he said. 'I told you the truth. He agreed to take 100,000 dollars and go to South America. That was your price. That was how much he loved you. He was a coward, he was a cheat. He had no true feeling for you.'

She wrenched herself free and ran like a mad thing, trying to reach the telephone at the side of the bed, but he was too quick for her. She stared past him towards the body; he took her chin and pulled her face close to his own. A trickle of sweat ran down his cheek.

'It had to be done, Kristina!' he shouted. 'Listen to me, listen! He should have respected and cherished you as a sister, as if you were of the same seed. Instead, he lay with you, he took you into my bed, he did this – this – dirty thing with you. He had to die, there was no other way.'

'They'll hang you!' she cried. 'They'll hang you or lock you up in a cell for the rest of your life!'

'Oh, no!' he said smoothly. 'That is not the way I have planned it. You see, I am not here. Have you forgotten so soon? You spoke to me on the telephone. I am in Queensland.'

'Who was that? Who did I speak to?'

'An actor. A drunken out-of-work actor. Very good at impersonation. He took me off several times on TV – do you remember? He is in my debt – and we agreed that this would be a good way to pay it off. Please Kristina, you surely know me by now. I like to organise things properly, thoroughly. You think I am standing here – but I am not. It is an illusion.' He glanced at his watch. 'As a matter of fact, at this moment, I am on my way into Greenvale to collect some supplies. I shall be seen by several people – it is what they call establishing an alibi, I believe.'

'They know you up there! They'll know it isn't you.'

'You under-estimate the acting ability of my friend. He really is very good. I took care to put on a cold to help him with the voice. As for the locals – well – they know I prefer to be alone. On my recent visits I've taken care to develop a reputation for surliness. Oh, I have no fears about that part of it, Kristina.'

She remembered the actor now although she couldn't put a name to him. His impersonation of Marcos on TV had been stunningly convincing, he had got the voice and the mannerisms exactly right. And he had managed to look so much like Marcos.

'The pilot!' she said suddenly. 'He knows you too well! You couldn't fool him!'

'Lockstey? Oh, he wasn't on duty today. He's on leave. I hired a temporary pilot. I went to the airport this morning. I met my actor friend in the gentlemen's lavatory, I gave him my coat and bag, and he took off in the plane while I stayed behind. All he had to do was pick up the car I keep at the Townsville airfield and drive to the house. He'll look after himself there as I always do. Tomorrow he'll drive back to Townsville, and take the plane back. I'll meet him as before, he'll hand back my identity and then disappear.'

'Suppose he decides to talk?'

'He won't,' he said blithely. 'I have, shall we say, strong reasons for believing that.'

'You blackmailed him!'

'It's a word. I prefer to think I persuaded him. So there you are, Kristina. It took weeks to perfect, but it was worth it. A good plan – I'm rather proud of it.'

'You haven't yet told me how I fit into it,' she said. 'I'm sure you can't have overlooked that.'

'Oh, not at all. The – what is the word they use? – scenario. The scenario runs as follows. You and Alex have been having an affair. You are madly in love with each other. Alex, my dear brother, is overcome by conscience. He feels that he can no longer go on betraying me. This fit of remorse comes upon him after he has made love to you in this room on his brother's bed. He tells you that the affair must be broken off. You argue, even fight – that will explain those bruises on your face. But you make up – and then go downstairs. He takes a sheet of paper from the drawer – there – a sheet of my paper and writes you a farewell letter.' He held up the note. 'It isn't a forgery, he really did write it – to my dictation. He thought it was a ticket to freedom and 100,000 dollars. To catch a jackal it is necessary to bait the trap, you understand. So – to continue – he writes this letter, then he takes your pistol from another

745

drawer, and blows his brains out. Yes, it is your pistol, Kristina – the snake-pistol I bought you two years ago.'

He took it from his pocket and weighed it in his gloved hand.

'Then what happens?' he continued. 'Isn't it obvious? You hear the shot and come running upstairs. You see your dead lover, you read the note. You are overcome, you cannot bear the thought of life without him so you turn the pistol on yourself. Very romantic – like a lovers' suicide pact. And while all this is going on, I am quietly working on my papers in Queensland. I shall come home tomorrow afternoon and discover the tragedy. I shall weep for my dead wife and mourn for my dead brother. End of scenario.'

There was a long silence. Then in a small voice she said: 'Don't you ever frighten yourself? Don't you ever wonder if one day the luck will turn against you?'

'I don't believe in luck,' he said shortly. 'A man makes his own fate. Alex chose his own path, he knew where it must lead.'

'The Cretan code,' she said.

'Yes. A man is nothing without honour.'

'You call this honourable? This act of bloody murder! Oh, no, Marcos. That I will not take. You killed him meanly, for revenge, to satisfy your own vanity. There is no honour in it.'

'If this had happened in Sphakia,' he said coldly, 'you would have been stoned out of the village and left to die. The women would have done it. That is their way with an adulteress. It is not a pleasant thing. I shall be more merciful.'

'I don't think I want your mercy,' she said. 'In any case, it is too late. Think about that, Marcos. If you'd shown a little mercy, a little tenderness at the beginning, even after the beginning, we might have made it. I was prepared to love you, to be a good wife. But it wasn't in you. What happened to your human feelings? Did you leave them behind in the White Mountains?'

'I loved Alex, I cared for him. I loved you and cared for you also.'

'As you love this house, your position, your business. And that isn't enough, Marcos, it really isn't.' She was suddenly weary of it all. 'Give me the gun then. Let me get it over with. That's want you want, isn't it?'

She held out her hand, and at that moment the telephone rang, startling them both. It rang for a long time, shrill and angry.

'Aren't you going to answer it?' she mocked. 'Oh, I forgot, you can't. You are not here, are you?'

He seized her arm and dragged her to the bedside table. He held the gun against her bare breast. 'Answer it!' he shouted. 'Answer it – and watch what you say!'

She picked up the telephone. 'Mrs Coleman speaking. Who is that, please? Police'? She felt him tighten at her side; the gun was pressed hard against her flesh. She listened for a long time, looking up at Marcos, her eyes widening. 'Yes. You're positive? Yes – yes – I understand. Yes – all the evening. Thank you. Yes, I'll be all right. Goodbye.'

She lowered the phone on to its cradle, sat down on the bed and a smile grew on her face like a flower opening; then came laughter, soft at first, but growing louder and crackling with hysteria. The tears ran down her face as he shook her fiercely.

'What did they want? What was that about!'

Her whole body was shaking and she got the words out only with difficulty. 'The Queensland police. Calling from Townsville. You're dead, Marcos.' She laughed again. 'Didn't you know? I thought you knew everything. You took the car out this evening for a drive. You'd had rather a lot to drink. You went off the road, and crashed into a brick wall. The car burned out, with you in it.'

'You're lying!'

She picked up the phone, and held it towards him. 'Want to check? Come to think of it, why don't you call them and say it was all a mistake – just some drunken actor who took your place so that you could do a little murder on the side. Chalk up another death, Marcos.' She crossed herself. 'Poor devil. I shouldn't laugh. God have mercy on his soul.'

Marcos knocked the phone from her hand and it fell on to the crumpled pillow, the dialling tone purring steadily. He lifted the gun and shot Kristina, the bullet entering the forehead between her eyes.

Once before in his life, when he had heard of the death of his mother, Marcos had howled like an animal in pain. The same cry swelled in his lungs now and burst from this throat.

He turned the gun on himself and fired.

Acknowledgments

The publishers wish to thank the following for permission to reprint previously published material. Every effort has been made to locate all persons having any rights in the stories appearing in this book but appropriate acknowledgment has been omitted in some cases through lack of information. Such omissions will be corrected in future printings of the book upon written notification to the publishers.

The New Catacomb (1922). The Estate of Sir Arthur Conan Doyle, Baskerville Investments Ltd and John Murray (Publishers) Ltd/ Jonathan Cape Ltd. From *The Conan Doyle Stories*.

The Hammer of God. The Estate of the late G. K. Chesterton and A. P. Watt & Son. From *The Innocence of Father Brown*, 1929.

The Interruption. The Society of Authors as the literary representative of the Estate of W. W. Jacobs.

The Gioconda Smile by Aldous Huxley. Mrs Laura Huxley and Chatto and Windus Ltd. From *Mortal Coils*.

The Almost Perfect Crime. Henry Holt and John Farquharson Ltd.

The Letter. The Estate of W. Somerset Maugham and William Heinemann Ltd. From *The Complete Short Stories of Somerset Maugham*, 1924.

The Farewell Murder by Dashiell Hammett. A. D. Peters & Co. Ltd. From *The Continental Op*.

They Never Get Caught. Margery Allingham and Chatto and Windus Ltd. From *The Allingham Case-Book*.

The Avenging Chance by Anthony Berkeley. The Society of Authors and Campbell Thomson & McLaughlin Limited. Copyright 1974 The Society of Authors.

The Necklace of Pearls. Dorothy L. Sayers and Victor Gollancz Ltd. From *Hangman's Holiday*, 1935.

The Man Who Knew How (1933). Dorothy L. Sayers and Victor Gollancz Ltd.

The Poetical Policeman. The Estate of the late Edgar Wallace, Hodder &

Stoughton Ltd. and A. P. Watt & Son. From *The Mind of Mr J. G. Reeder*, 1934.

S.O.S. (1925), *Wireless* (1925). The late Agatha Christie and Hughes Massie Limited. Copyright 1925 by Agatha Christie, copyright renewed 1953 by Agatha Christie Mallowan.

The Mallet (1929). James Hilton and John Farquharson Ltd.

Dusk to Dawn. Cornell Woolrich and Victor Gollancz Ltd. From *Nightwebs*.

The Murder by John Steinbeck. Curtis Brown Ltd.

The Homesick Buick. John D. MacDonald and John Farquharson Ltd.

The Enemy. Charlotte Armstrong and A. M. Heath & Company Ltd. From *Ellery Queen's The Golden 13*.

The Conspirators. Michael Gilbert and Curtis Brown Ltd.

Double Image (1954). Roy Vickers and Curtis Brown Ltd.

Lamb to the Slaughter. Roald Dahl and Murray Pollinger. From *Kiss, Kiss*. Copyright 1953 by Roald Dahl.

The Way up to Heaven. Roald Dahl and Penguin Books Ltd and Murray Pollinger. From *Someone Like You*. Copyright 1954 by Roald Dahl.

The Necessity of his Condition. Avram Davidson and A. M. Heath & Company Ltd. From *Ellery Queen's The Golden 13*.

You can't be a little girl all your life. Stanley Ellin, Victor Gollancz Ltd and Mystery Writers of America Inc. From *Killers of the Mind* edited by Lucy Freeman.

Foxer. Brian Cleeve and John Farquharson Ltd.

Special Release (1968) by Eric Parr. Mary Ann Haswell and Faber & Faber.

Scatter his Ashes. Elizabeth Ferrars and David Higham Associates Limited. From *Winter's Crimes II*, 1970.

Jericho and the Two Ways to Die. Hugh Pentecost and A. M. Heath & Company Ltd.

The Niece from Scotland. Christianna Brand and A. M. Heath & Company Ltd.

Carrot for a Chestnut. Dick Francis and John Johnson. Copyright 1972 Dick Francis.

The Perfect Servant. Helen Neilsen and A. M. Heath & Company Ltd. From *Ellery Queen's Mystery Bag*, 1973.

Judgement. Mary Kelly and Richard Scott Simon Ltd.

Fixation by Miles Tripp. A. D. Peters & Co. Ltd.

A Quite Conventional Death. John Garforth and Jonathan Cape Ltd. From *The Times Anthology of Detective Stories*.

The Victim. P. D. James and Elaine Greene Ltd. Copyright 1973 P. D. James.

Suicide or Murder. Jane Aiken Hodge and David Higham Associates Ltd.

Scandal at Sandkop by James McClure. A. D. Peters & Co. Ltd. From *Winter's Crimes 5*.

The Man from the White Mountains. Ted Willis and Elaine Greene Ltd. Copyright 1975 Ted Willis Limited.